P9-EEI-336

JOURNEY to the WEST

CONTENTS

First Edition 1986
Second Printing 1995

TRANSLATOR'S ACKNOWLEDGEMENTS

I am deeply grateful to Li Rongxi for giving generously of his broad, profound and many-sided scholarship in removing errors from this version and resolving problems. I am also greatly indebted to the staff of the Foreign Languages Press, and especially to Huang Jingying for the infinite patience and care with which she has checked and improved typescript and proofs. Responsibility for the many remaining mistakes is mine.

W. J. F.J.

ISBN 7-119-01778-0

Published by Foreign Languages Press
24 Baiwanzhuang Road, Beijing 100037, China

Printed by Beijing Foreign Languages Printing House
19 Chegongzhuang Xilu, Beijing 100044, China

Distributed by China International Book Trading Corporation
35 Chegongzhuang Xilu, Beijing 100044, China
P.O. Box 399, Beijing, China

Printed in the People's Republic of China

JOURNEY to the WEST

by Wu Cheng'en

Translated by W. J. F. Jenner

Volume III

FOREIGN LANGUAGES PRESS BEIJING

CHAPTER SIXTY-SEVEN

The dhyana-nature is stable and Tuoluo Village is saved; The mind of the Way is purified as corruption is removed.

The story tells how Sanzang and his three disciples happily continued along their way after leaving the Lesser Western Heaven. They had been going for over a month, and it was now late spring. The flowers were in bloom and all the woods they could see were full of green shade. After a spell of wind and rain dusk was falling once more. "Disciple," said Sanzang, reining in his horse, "it's getting late. Which way shall we go to look for somewhere to spend the night?" "Don't worry, Master," said Monkey with a smile. "Even if we can't find anywhere to stay we three all have our skills. Tell Pig to cut some grass and Friar Sand to fell some pines. I know a bit of carpentry. We can make ourselves a hut by the road here good enough to stay in for a year. Why the rush?" "But this is no place to stay, brother," said Pig. "The mountain's crawling with wild beasts like tigers, leopards and wolves. Mountain ogres and hobgoblins are all over the place. It's hard enough travelling by daylight. I wouldn't dare spend the night here." "Idiot!" said Monkey. "You're getting more and more hopeless. I'm not just shooting my mouth off. With this cudgel in my hands I could hold up the sky itself if it collapsed."

Master and disciples were in the middle of their conversation when they noticed a hill farm not far away. "Good," said Monkey, "a place for the night." "Where?" the venerable elder asked. "Isn't that a house in the trees over there?" asked Monkey, pointing. "Let's ask if we can put up for the night there. We can be on our way first thing in the morning."

Sanzang was so delighted he urged his horse forward. Dismounting outside the wicker gates he found them firmly fastened. "Open up, open up," he called, knocking on the gates. They were opened from the inside by an old man with a stick who was wearing rush sandals, a black turban and a plain gown. "Who's that shouting?" he asked. Putting his hands together in front of his chest, Sanzang bowed in polite greeting and said, "Venerable patron, I am a monk sent from the east to fetch scriptures from the Western Heaven. As I have reached this distinguished place so late in the day I have come to your residence to ask for a night's lodging. I beg you to be charitable to us." "Monk," the elder said, "you may want to go to the West, but you'll never get there. This is the Lesser Western Heaven, and it's a very long way from here to the Great Western Heaven. This place alone is hard enough to get out of, to say nothing of the difficulties of the rest of the journey." "Why is it hard to get out of?" Sanzang asked. The old man put his hands together and replied, "About a dozen miles west of our village is a Runny Persimmon Lane and a mountain called Seven Perfections." "Why 'Seven Perfections'?" Sanzang asked.

"It's 250 miles across," the old man replied, "and covered with persimmons. There's an old saying that persimmon trees have seven perfections: 1. They prolong life. 2. They are very shady. 3. No birds nest in them. 4. They are free of insects. 5. Their leaves are very beautiful after frost. 6. The fruit is excellent. 7. The branches and leaves are big and fat. That's why it's called Mount Seven Perfections. This is a big, thinly populated area, and nobody has ever been deep into the mountain. Every year over-ripe, rotten persimmons fall on the path, and they fill the rocky lane right up. The rain, dew, snow and frost attack them, and they rot all through the summer until the whole path is a mass of putrefaction. The people round here call it Runny Shit, or Runny Persimmon, Lane. When there's a west wind it smells even worse than a cesspit being emptied. As it's now high spring and there's a strong southeasterly blowing you can't smell it yet." Sanzang felt too depressed to speak.

Monkey could not contain himself. "Silly old fool," he shouted at the top of his voice. "We're here late at night to find somewhere to stay, and you're trying to scare us with all that talk. If your house really is so poky that there's no room for us to sleep indoors we'll spend the night squatting under this tree. So cut the cackle." At the sight of Monkey's hideous face the old man shut his mouth, petrified with fear. Then he plucked up his courage, pointed his stick at Monkey and shouted, "Damn you, you bony-faced, pointy-browed, flat-nosed, sunken-cheeked, hairy-eyed, sickly-looking devil. You've got no sense of respect, sticking your mouth out like that and insulting an old gentleman." "You're not very perceptive, old chap," Monkey replied, putting on a smile. "You don't realize who this sickly-looking devil is. As the manual of physiognomy says, 'A freakish face is like a rock in which fine jade is hidden.' You're completely wrong to judge people on their looks. Ugly I certainly am, but I know a trick or two." "Where are you from?" the old man asked. "What's your name? What powers do you have?" To this Monkey replied with a smile:

"My home is in the Eastern Continent of Superior Body;
My conduct I cultivated on the Mount of Flowers and Fruit.
After studying with the Patriarch of the Spirit-tower Heart Mountain
I learned complete and perfect skill in the martial arts.
I can stir up the oceans, subdue mother dragons,
Carry mountains on my shoulders, and drive the sun along.
At capturing monsters and demons I'm champion;
Ghosts and gods are terrified when I shift the stars.
Great is my fame as sky-thief and earth-turner;
I'm the Handsome Stone Monkey of infinite transformations."

This turned the old man's anger to delight. Bowing to them he said, "Please come into my humble abode and make yourselves comfortable." The four of them then went in together, leading the horse and carrying the load. All that could be seen to either side of the gates were prickly thorns. The inner gates were set in a wall of brick and stone that had more thorns on top of it, and only when they had gone through them did they see a three-roomed tiled house. The old man pulled up chairs for them to sit on while they waited for tea to be brought and gave orders for a meal. Soon a table was brought in and set with wheat gluten, beancurd, sweet potatoes, radishes, mustard greens, turnips, rice and sour-mallow soup. Master and disciples all ate their fill. After the meal Pig pulled Monkey aside and whispered, "'Brother, the old bloke wasn't going to let us stay at first. Now he's given us this slap-up meal. Why?" "It wasn't worth very much, was it?" Brother Monkey replied. "Tomorrow we'll make him give us ten kinds of fruit and ten dishes of food." "You've got a nerve," Pig replied. "You talked him into giving us a meal all right with all that boasting. But we'll be on our way tomorrow. How can he give you things?" "Don't be so impatient," said Monkey, "I've got a way to cope."

Dusk soon started to draw in. The old man brought a lamp, and Monkey asked with a bow, "What is your surname, sir?" "Li," the old man replied. "I suppose this must be Li Village," Monkey continued. "No," said the old man, "this is Tuoluo Village. Over five hundred families live here. Most of them have other surnames. I am the only one called Li." "Benefactor Li," Monkey replied, "with what kind intentions did you give us that ample meal?" "Just now you said that you could capture evil monsters," said the old man. "We have a monster here that we'd like you to capture for us, and we will of course reward you generously." Monkey then chanted a "na-a-aw" of respect and said, "I accept your commission." "Just look at him," said Pig, "asking for trouble. The moment he hears there's a demon to catch he's nicer to him than he would be to his own grandfather. He even chanted a 'na-a-aw' first." "You don't understand, brother," said Monkey. "My 'na-a-aw' clinched the deal. Now he won't hire anyone else."

When Sanzang heard this he said, "You monkey, you always

want to grab things for yourself. If that evil spirit's powers are too great for you to capture him then we monks will be shown up as liars." "Don't be cross with me, Master," Monkey said with a smile. "Let me ask some more questions." "What else?" the old man asked. "This fine village is on an open plain and a lot of people live here," said Monkey. "It's not remote and isolated. What evil spirit would dare come to your door?"

"I will be frank with you," the old man replied. "We had long lived in peace and prosperity here till a sudden, strong wind blew three and a half years ago. Everyone was busy at the time threshing the wheat on the threshing floor or transplanting rice in the paddy fields. We thought it was just a change in the weather. We never imagined that when the wind had blown by an evil spirit would eat the horses and cattle that people had put out to pasture as well as the pigs and the sheep. He swallowed hens and geese whole, and any men or women he found he devoured alive. Since then he's come again each of the last two years to murder us. Venerable sir, if you really do have magic powers to capture the evil spirit and cleanse the place of him, we will most certainly reward you generously and with great respect." "But the monster will be hard to catch," Monkey replied. "Yes," said Pig, "very hard. We're pilgrim monks only here for the night. We'll be on our way tomorrow. We can't catch any monsters." "So you monks just tricked that meal out of me," the old man said. "When we first met you talked very big. You said you could move the stars and capture evil monsters. But now I've told you about this you pretend he can't be caught."

"Old man," said Monkey, "it would be easy to catch the evil spirit, except that you people here don't work together. That's why it's hard." "How can you be so sure that we don't work together?" the old man asked. "If the monster has been harassing you for three years, goodness only knows how many lives he's taken," Monkey replied. "I reckon that if every family put up one ounce of silver the five hundred households could raise five hundred ounces, and with that you could find a priest somewhere who'd exorcise the monster. Why did you cheerfully put up with three years of such cruelty from him?" "You talk of spending money," the old man said. "You're trying to shame us to death. Every family here has spent four or five ounces of silver. The year before last we went to invite a Buddhist monk south of the mountains here to catch the monster, but he failed." "How did the monk try to do it?" Brother Monkey asked. To this the old man replied:

"The monk wore a cassock
And recited the scriptures;
First the Peacock Sutra
And then the Lotus.
He burned incense in a burner,
Held a bell between his hands.
His reading of the scriptures
Alarmed the evil spirit,
Who came straight to the farm
Amid his wind and clouds.
The monk fought with the spirit
And it was a splendid sight:
One of them landed a punch,
The other grabbed at his foe.
The monk had the advantage of
Having a hairless head.
But soon the demon had won,
And gone straight back to his clouds.
When the wound had dried in the sun
We went up close for a look;
The monk's bald head was smashed open
Just like a ripe watermelon."

"In other words," laughed Monkey, "he lost." "He just paid with his life," the old man replied. "We were the ones who lost. We had to buy his coffin, pay for his funeral, and give compensation to his disciple. That silver wasn't enough for the disciple. He's still trying to sue us. He won't call it a day."

"Did you hire anyone else to catch the demon?" Monkey asked, "Last year we invited a Taoist priest to do it," the old man replied. "How did he try?" Monkey asked. "The Taoist," the old man replied,

"Wore a golden crown on his head,
And magic robes on his body,
He sounded his magic wand,
Used charms and water too.
He made gods and generals do his will,
Captured demons and goblins.
A wild wind howled and roared,
While black fog blotted all out.
Demon and Taoist
Were evenly matched;
They fought till nightfall,
When the fiend went back to the clouds.
Heaven and earth were clear
And all of us people were there.
We went out to search for the priest,
Found him drowned in the mountain stream.
When we fished him out to look
He was like a drenched chicken."

"In other words," said Monkey with a smile, "he lost too." "He only paid with his life, but we had to spend a lot of money that wasn't really necessary," the old man replied. "It doesn't matter," Monkey said, "it doesn't matter. Wait till I catch the demon for you." "If you've got the power to catch him I'll ask some of the village elders to write an undertaking to give you as much silver as you want when you've defeated him. You'll not be a penny short. But if you lose don't try to extort money out of us. We must each accept the will of heaven." "Old man," said Monkey, "they've got you terrified of extortion. We're not like that. Send for the elders."

The old man was delighted. He sent his slaves to invite seven or eight old men from among his next-door neighbours, his cousins, his wife's family and his friends. They all came to meet the strangers, and when they had greeted the Tang Priest they cheerfully discussed the capture of the demon. "Which of your distinguished disciples will do it?" they asked. "I will," said Monkey, putting his hands together in front of his chest. "You'll never do, never," said the old man with horror. "The evil spirit's magic powers are enormous, and it's huge too. Venerable sir, you're so tiny and skinny you'd slip through one of the gaps between its teeth." "Old man," said Monkey with a smile, "you're no judge of people. Small I may be, but I'm solid. There's a lot more to me than meets the eye." When the elders heard this they had to take him at his word. "Venerable sir," they said, "how big a reward will you want for capturing the demon?" "Why do you have to talk about a reward?" Monkey asked. "As the saying goes, 'Gold dazzles, silver is white and stupid, and copper coins stink.' We're virtuous monks and we definitely won't take money."

"In that case you must all be lofty monks who obey your vows," the elders said. "But even if you won't accept money we can't let you work for nothing. We all live by agriculture. If you subdue the demon and clean the place up, every family here will give you a third of an acre of good farmland, which will make over 150 acres altogether. Your master and you disciples can build a monastery there and sit in meditation. That would be much better than going on your long journey." "It would be even worse," replied Brother Monkey with a smile. "If we asked for land we'd have to raise horses, do labour service, pay grain taxes and hand over hay. We'll never be able to go to bed at dusk or lie in after the fifth watch. It'd be the death of us." "If you won't accept anything, how are we to express our thanks?" the elders asked. "We're men of religion," said Monkey. "Some tea and a meal will be thanks enough for us." "That's easy," said the elders. "But how are you going to catch the demon?" "Once it comes I'll get it," said Monkey. "But it's enormous," the elders said. "It stretches from the earth to the sky. It comes in wind and goes in mist. How are you ever going to get close to it?" "When it comes to evil spirits who can summon winds and ride on clouds," Monkey replied, "I treat them as mere kids. It makes no difference how big it is — I have ways of beating it."

As they were talking the howl of a great wind made the eight or nine elders start shaking with fear. "Monk, you've asked for trouble and you've got it," they said. "You talked about the monster and here he is." Old Mr. Li opened the door and said to his relations and the Tang Priest, "Come in, come in, the demon's here." This so alarmed Pig and Friar Sand that they wanted to go inside too, but Monkey grabbed each of them with one of his hands and said, "You're a disgrace. You're monks and you ought to know better. Stay where you are, and don't try to run away. Come into the courtyard with me. We're going to see what kind of evil spirit this is." "But brother," said Pig, "they've been through this before. The noise of the wind means that the demon's coming. They've all gone to hide. We're not friends or relations of the demon. We've had no business dealings with him. What do we want to see him for?" Monkey was so strong that with no further argument he hauled them into the courtyard and made them stand there while the wind blew louder and louder. It was a splendid wind that

Uprooted trees and flattened woods, alarming wolves and tigers,
Stirred up the rivers and oceans to the horror of ghosts and gods,
Blowing the triple peaks of the great Mount Hua all upside down,
Shaking the earth and sky through the world's four continents.
Every village family shut fast its gates,
While boys and girls all fled for cover.
Black clouds blotted out the Milky Way;
Lamps lost their brightness and the world went dark.

Pig was shaking with terror. He lay on the ground, rooted into the earth with his snout and buried his head. He looked as if he had been nailed there. Friar Sand covered his face and could not keep his eyes open.

Monkey knew from the sound of the wind that the demon was in it A moment later, when the wind had passed, all that could be vaguely made out in the sky were two lamps. "Brothers," he said, looking down, "the wind's finished. Get up and look." The idiot tugged his snout out, brushed the dirt off himself and looked up into the sky, where he saw the two lamps. "What a laugh," Pig said, laughing aloud, "what a laugh. It's an evil spirit with good manners. Let's make friends with it." "It's a very dark night," said Friar Sand, "and you haven't even seen it, so how can you tell whether it's good or bad?" "As they used to say in the old days," Pig replied, " 'Take a candle when you're out at night, and stay where you are if you haven't one.' You can see that it's got a pair of lanterns to light its way. It must be a good spirit." "You're wrong," Friar Sand said. "That's not a pair of lanterns: they're the demon's eyes." This gave the idiot such a fright that he shrank three inches. "Heavens," he said. "If its eyes are that size goodness knows how big its mouth is." "Don't be scared, brother," said Monkey. "You two guard the master while I go up and see what sort of mood it's in and what kind of evil spirit it is." "Brother," said Pig, "don't tell the monster about us."

Splendid Monkey sprang up into mid-air with a whistle. "Not so fast," he yelled at the top of his voice, brandishing his cudgel, "not so fast. I'm here." When the monster saw him it took a firm stance and began to wield a long spear furiously. Parrying with his cudgel, Monkey asked, "What part do you come from, monster? Where are you an evil spirit?" The monster ignored the questions and continued with its spearplay. Monkey asked again, and again there was no answer as the wild spearplay continued. "So it's deaf and dumb," Monkey smiled to himself. "Don't run away! Take this!" Unperturbed, the monster parried the cudgel with more wild spearplay. The mid-air battle ebbed and flowed until the middle of the night as first one then the other was on top, but still there was no victor. Pig and Friar Sand had a very clear view from the Li family courtyard, and they could see that the demon was only using its spear to defend itself and not making any attacks, while Monkey's cudgel was never far from the demon's head. "Friar Sand," said Pig with a grin, "you keep guard here. I'm going up to join in the fight. I'm not going to let Monkey keep all the credit for beating the monster to himself. He won't be the first to be given a drink."

The splendid idiot leapt up on his cloud and joined in the fight, taking a swing with his rake. The monster fended this off with another spear. The two spears were like flying snakes or flashes of lightning. Pig was full of admiration. "This evil spirit is a real expert with the spears. This isn't 'behind the mountain' spearplay; it's 'tangled thread' spearplay. It's not Ma Family style. It's what's called soft-shaft style." "Don't talk such nonsense, idiot," said Monkey. "There's no such thing as soft-shaft style." "Just look," Pig replied. "He's parrying us with the blades. You can't see the shafts. I don't know where he's hiding them." "All right then," said Monkey, "perhaps there is a soft-shaft style. But this monster can't talk. I suppose it's not yet humanized: it's still got a lot of the negative about it. Tomorrow morning, when the positive is dominant, it's bound to run away. When it does we've got to catch up with it and not let it go." "Yes, yes," said Pig.

When the fight had gone on for a long time the east grew light. The monster didn't dare fight any longer, so it turned and fled, with Monkey and Pig both after it. Suddenly they smelled the putrid and overwhelming stench of Runny Persimmon Lane on Mount Seven Perfections. "Some family must be emptying its cesspit," said Pig. "Phew! What a horrible stink!" Holding his nose, Brother Monkey said, "After the demon, after the demon!" The monster went over the mountain and turned back into himself: a giant red-scaled python. Just look at it:

Eyes shooting stars,
Nostrils gushing clouds,
Teeth like close-set blades of steel,
Curving claws like golden hooks.
On its head a horn of flesh
Like a thousand pieces of agate;
Its body clad in scales of red
Like countless patches of rouge.

When coiled on the ground it might seem a brocade quilt;
When flying it could be mistaken for a rainbow.
From where it sleeps a stench rises to the heavens,
And in movement its body is wreathed in red clouds.
Is it big?
A man could not be seen from one side to the other.
Is it long?
It can span a mountain from north to south.

"So it's a long snake," Pig said. "If it's a man-eater it could gobble up five hundred for a meal and still not be full." "Its soft-shafted spears are its forked tongue," said Monkey. "It's exhausted by the chase. Attack it from behind." Pig leapt up and went for it, hitting it with his rake. The monster dived into a cave, but still left seven or eight feet of tail sticking outside. Pig threw down his rake, grabbed it and shouted, "Hold on, hold on!" He pulled with all his strength, but could not move it an inch. "Idiot," laughed Monkey, "let it go in. We'll find a way of dealing with it. Don't pull so wildly at the snake." When Pig let go the monster contracted itself and burrowed inside. "But we had half of it before I let go," he grumbled. "Now it's shrunk and gone inside we're never going to get it out. We've lost the snake, haven't we?" "The wretched creature is enormous and the cave is very narrow," Monkey replied. "It won't possibly be able to turn round in there. It definitely went straight inside, so the cave must have an exit at the other end for it to get out through. Hurry round and block the back door while I attack at the front."

The idiot shot round to the other side of the mountain, where there was indeed another hole that he blocked with his foot. But he had not steadied himself when Monkey thrust his cudgel in at the front of the cave, hurting the monster so much that it wriggled out through the back. Pig was not ready, and when a flick of the snake's tail knocked him over he could not get back up: he lay on the ground in agony. Seeing that the cave was now empty Monkey rushed round to the other side, cudgel in hand, to catch the monster. Monkey's shouts made Pig feel so ashamed that he pulled himself to his feet despite the pain and started lashing out wildly with his rake. At the sight of this Monkey said with a laugh, "What do you think you're hitting? The monster's got away." "I'm 'beating the grass to flush out the snake'." "Cretin!" said Monkey, "After it!"

The two of them crossed a ravine, where they saw the monster coiled up, its head held high and its enormous mouth gaping wide. It was about to devour Pig, who fled in terror. Monkey, however, went straight on towards it and was swallowed in a single gulp. "Brother," wailed Pig, stamping his feet and beating his chest, "you've been destroyed." "Don't fret, Pig," called Monkey from inside the monster's belly, which he was poking around with his cudgel. "I'll make it into a bridge. Watch!" As he spoke the monster arched its back just like a rainbow-shaped bridge. "It looks like a bridge all right," Pig shouted, "but nobody would ever dare cross it." "Then I'll make it turn into a boat," said Monkey. "Watch!" He pushed out the skin of the monster's belly with his cudgel, and with the skin against the ground and its head uplifted it did look like a river boat. "It may look like a boat," said Pig, "but without a mast or sail it wouldn't sail very well in the wind." "Get out of the way then," said Monkey, "and I'll make it sail for you." He then jabbed his cudgel out as hard as he could through the monster's spine from the inside and made it stand some sixty or seventy feet high, just like a mast. Struggling for its life and in great pain the monster shot forward faster than the wind, going down the mountain and back the way it had come for over seven miles until it collapsed motionless in the dust. It was dead.

When Pig caught up with the monster he raised his rake and struck wildly at it. Monkey made a big hole in the monster's side, crawled out and said, "Idiot! It's dead and that's that. Why go on hitting it?" "Brother," Pig replied, "don't you realize that all my life I've loved killing dead snakes?" Only then did he put his rake away, grab the snake's tail and start pulling it backwards.

Meanwhile back at Tuoluo Village old Mr. Li and the others were saying to the Tang Priest, "Your two disciples have been gone all night, and they're not back yet. They must be dead." "I'm sure that there can be no problem," Sanzang replied. "Let's go and look." A moment later Monkey and Pig appeared, chanting as they dragged an enormous python behind them. Only then did everyone feel happy. All the people in the village, young and old, male and female, knelt down and bowed to Sanzang, saying, "Good sirs, this is the evil spirit that has been doing so much damage. Now that you have used your powers to behead the demon and rid us of this evil we will be able to live in peace again." Everyone was very grateful, and all the families invited them to meals as expressions of their gratitude, keeping master and disciples there for six or seven days, and only letting them go when they implored to be allowed to leave. As they would not accept money or any other gifts the villagers loaded parched grain and fruit on horses and mules hung with red rosettes and caparisoned with flags of many colours to see them on their way. From the five hundred households in the village some seven or eight hundred people set out with them.

On the journey they were all very cheerful, but before they reached Runny Persimmon Lane on Mount Seven Perfections Sanzang smelled the terrible stench and could see that their way was blocked. "Wukong," he said to Monkey, "how are we going to get through?" "It's going to be hard," replied Monkey, covering his nose. When even Monkey said that it was going to be hard Sanzang began to weep. "Don't upset yourself so, my lord," said old Mr. Li and the other elders as they came up to him. "We have all come here with you because we're already decided what to do. As your illustrious disciples have defeated the evil spirit and rid the village of this evil we have all made up our minds to clear a better path for you over the mountain." "That's nonsense, old man," said Monkey with a grin. "You told us before that the mountain is some 250 miles across. You aren't Yu the Great's heavenly soldiers, so how could you possibly make a path across it? If my master is to get across it'll have to be through our efforts. You'll never do it." "But how can we do it through our efforts?" Sanzang asked after dismounting. "It'd certainly be hard to cross the mountain as it is now," Monkey said, still smiling, "and it would be even harder to cut a new path. We'll have to go by the old lane. The only thing that worries me is that there may be nobody to provide the food." "What a thing to say, venerable sir," old Mr. Li said. "We can support you gentlemen for as long as you care to stay here. You can't say that nobody will provide the food." "In that case, go and prepare two hundredweight of parched grain, as well as some steamed cakes and buns," said Monkey. "When our long-snouted monk has eaten his fill he'll turn into a giant boar and clear the old lane with his snout. Then my master will be able to ride his horse over the mountain while we support him. He'll certainly get across."

"Brother," said Pig, "you want to keep all the rest of you clean. Why should I be the only one to stink?" "Wuneng," said Sanzang, "if you can clear the lane with your snout and get me across the mountain that will be a very great good deed to your credit." "Master, benefactors, please don't tease me," said Pig with a smile. "I can do thirty-six transformations. If you ask me to become something that's light or delicate or beautiful or that flies I just can't. But ask me to turn into a mountain, a tree, a rock, a mound of earth, an elephant, a hog, a water buffalo or a camel and I can manage any of them. The only thing is that the bigger I make myself the bigger my belly gets. I can't do things properly unless it's full." "We've got plenty," the people said, "we've got plenty. We've brought parched grain, fruit, griddle cakes and ravioli. We were going to give them to you when we'd made a path across the mountain. They can all be brought out for you to eat now. When you've transformed yourself and started work we'll send some people back to prepare more food to send you on your way with." Pig was beside himself with delight. Taking off his tunic and putting down his nine-pronged rake he said to them all, "Don't laugh at me. Just watch while I win merit doing this filthy job." The splendid idiot made a spell with his hands, shook himself, and turned himself into a giant hog. Indeed,

His snout was long, his bristles short, and half of him was fat;
As a piglet in the mountains he had fed on herbs and simples.
Black was his face and his eyes as round as sun or moon;
The great ears on his head were just like plantain leaves.
His bones he'd made so strong he would live as long as heaven;
His thick skin had been tempered till it was hard as iron.
He grunted with a noise that came from a blocked-up nose;
His gasping breath rasped harshly in his throat.
Each of his four white trotters was a thousand feet high;
Every sword-like bristle was hundreds of yards in length.
Since pigs were first kept and fattened by mankind
Never had such a monster porker been seen as this today.
The Tang Priest and the rest were full of admiration
For Marshal Tian Peng and his magic powers.

Seeing what Pig had turned into, Brother Monkey asked the people who had come to see them off to pile up all the parched grain at once and told Pig to eat it. Not caring whether it was cooked or raw, the idiot downed it all at one gulp, then went forward to clear the way. Monkey told Friar Sand to take his sandals off and carry the luggage carefully and advised his master to sit firm in the carved saddle. Then he took off his own tall boots and told everyone else to go back: "Could you be very kind and send some more food as soon as possible to keep my brother's strength up?"

Of the seven or eight hundred who were seeing the pilgrims off most had come on mules or horses and they rushed back to the village like shooting stars. The three hundred who were on foot stood at the bottom of the mountain to watch the travellers as they went away. Now it was ten miles or more from the village to the mountain, and another journey of over ten miles each way to fetch the food, making over thirty in all, so by the time they were back master and disciples were already far ahead of them. Not wanting to miss the pilgrims, the villagers drove their mules and horses into the lane and carried on after them through the night, only catching them up the next morning. "Pilgrims," they shouted, "wait a moment, wait a moment, sirs. We've brought food for you." When Sanzang heard this he thanked them profusely, said that they were good and faithful people, and told Pig to rest and eat something to build up his strength. The idiot, who was on the second day of clearing the way with his snout, was by now ravenously hungry. The villagers had brought much more than seven or eight hundredweight of food, which he scooped up and devoured all at once, not caring whether it was rice or wheat. When he had eaten his fill he went back to clearing the way, while Sanzang, Monkey and Friar Sand thanked the villagers and took leave of them. Indeed,

The peasants all went back to Tuoluo Village;
Across the mountain Pig had cleared the way.
Sanzang's faith was backed up by great power;
Sun's demon-quelling arts were on display.
A thousand years of filth went in a single morning;
The Seven Perfections Lane was opened up today,
The dirt of six desires all now removed,
Towards the Lotus Throne they go to pray.

If you don't know how much longer their journey was going to be or what evil monsters they would meet listen to the explanation in the next instalment.

CHAPTER SIXTY-EIGHT

In the land of Purpuria the Tang Priest discusses history;
Sun the Pilgrim in his charity offers to be a doctor.

When good is right all causes disappear;
Its fame is spread through all four continents.
In the light of wisdom they climb the other shore;
Soughing dark clouds are blown from the edge of the sky.

All the Buddhas give them help,
Sitting for ever on their thrones of jade.
Smash the illusions of the human world,
Cease!
Cleanse the dirt; provoke no misery.

The story tells how Sanzang and his disciples cleaned the lane of its filth and pressed far ahead along the road. Time passed quickly and the weather was scorching again. Indeed,

The begonias spread their globes of brocade;
Lotus leaves split their own green dishes.
Fledgling swallows hide in the roadside willows;
Travellers wave their silken fans for relief from the heat.

As they carried on their way a walled and moated city appeared before them. Reining in his horse, Sanzang said, "Disciples, can you see where this is?" "You can't read, Master," Monkey exclaimed. "How ever did you get the Tang Emperor to send you on this mission?" "I have been a monk since I was a boy and read classics and scriptures by the thousand," Sanzang replied. "How could you say I can't read?" "Well," Monkey replied, "if you can, why ask where we are instead of reading the big clear writing on the apricot-yellow flag over the city wall?" "Wretched ape," Sanzang shouted, "you're talking nonsense. The flag is flapping much too hard in the wind for anyone to read what, if anything, is on it." "Then how could I read it?" Monkey asked. "Don't rise to his bait, Master," Pig and Friar Sand said. "From this distance we can't even see the walls and moat clearly, never mind words in a banner." "But doesn't it say Purpuria?" Monkey asked. "Purpuria must be a western kingdom," Sanzang said. "We shall have to present our passport." "Goes without saying," Monkey observed.

They were soon outside the city gates, where the master dismounted, crossed the bridge, and went in through the triple gates. It was indeed a splendid metropolis. This is what could be seen.

Lofty gate-towers,
Regular battlements,
Living waters flowing around,
Mountains facing to north and south.
Many are the goods in the streets and markets,
And all the citizens do thriving business.
This is a city fit for a monarch,
A capital endowed by heaven.
To this distant realm come travellers by land and water;
Jade and silk abound in this remoteness.
It is more beautiful than the distant ranges;
The palace rises to the purity of space.
Closely barred are the passes leading here,
When peace and prosperity have lasted for ever.

As master and disciples walked along the highways and through the markets they saw that the people were tall, neatly dressed and well spoken. Indeed, they were not inferior to those of the Great Tang. When the traders who stood on either side of the road saw how ugly Pig was, how tall and dark-featured Friar Sand was, and how hairy and wide-browed Monkey was they all dropped their business and came over to see them. "Don't provoke trouble," Sanzang called to them. "Hold your heads down." Pig obediently tucked his snout into his chest and Friar Sand did not dare look up. Monkey, however, stared all around him as he kept close to the Tang Priest. The more sensible people went away again after taking a look, but the idlers, the curious and the naughty children among the spectators jeered, threw bricks and tiles at the strangers, and mocked Pig. "Whatever you do, don't get into a row," Sanzang said again in great anxiety. The idiot kept his head down.

Before long they turned a corner and saw a gate in a wall over which was written HOSTEL OF MEETING in large letters. "We are going into this government office," Sanzang said. "Why?" Monkey asked. "The Hostel of Meeting is a place where people from all over the world are received, so we can go and disturb them," said Sanzang. "Let's rest there. When I have seen the king and presented our passport we can leave the city and be on our way again." When Pig heard this he brought his snout out, so terrifying the people following behind that dozens of them collapsed. "The master's right," said Pig, stepping forward. "Let's shelter inside there and get away from these damned mockers." They went inside, after which the people began to disperse.

There were two commissioners in the hostel, a senior one and his assistant, and they were in the hall checking over their personnel before going to receive an official when, to their great consternation, the Tang Priest suddenly appeared. "Who are you?" they asked together. "Who are you? Where are you going?" "I have been sent by His Majesty the Tang Emperor to fetch the scriptures from the Western Heaven," the Tang Priest replied, putting his hands together in front of his chest. "Having reached your illustrious country I did not dare to try to sneak through. I would like to submit my passport for inspection so that we may be allowed to continue our way. Meanwhile we would like to rest in your splendid hostel."

When the two commissioners heard this they dismissed their subordinates, put on their full official dress and went down from the main hall to greet the visitors. They instructed that the guest rooms be tidied up for them to sleep in and ordered vegetarian provisions for them. Sanzang thanked them, and the two officials led their staff out of the hall. Some of their attendants invited the visitors to sleep in the guest rooms. Sanzang went with them, but Monkey complained bitterly, "Damned cheek. Why won't they let me stay in the main hall?" "The people here don't come under the jurisdiction of our Great Tang and they have no connections with our country either. Besides, their superiors often come to stay. It is difficult for them to entertain us." "In that case," Monkey replied, "I insist on them entertaining us properly."

As they were talking the manager brought their provisions: a dish each of white rice and wheat flour, two cabbages, four pieces of beancurd, two pieces of wheat gluten, a dish of dried bamboo shoots and a dish of "tree-ear" fungus. Sanzang told his disciples to receive the provisions and thanked the manager. "There's a clean cooking-stove in the western room," the manager said, "and it's easy to light the firewood in it. Would you please cook your own food?"

"May I ask you if the king is in the palace?" Sanzang asked. "His Majesty has not attended court for a long time," the manager replied. "But today is an auspicious one, and he is discussing the issue of a notice with his civil and military officials. You'd better hurry if you want to get there in time to submit your passport to him. Tomorrow will be too late to do it, and goodness knows how long you'll have to wait." "Wukong," said Sanzang, "you three prepare the meal while I hurry there to have our passport inspected. After we have eaten we can be on our way." Pig quickly unpacked the cassock and passport for Sanzang, who dressed himself and set out for the palace, instructing his disciples not to leave the hostel or make trouble.

Before long the Tang Priest was outside the Tower of Five Phoenixes at the outer palace gate. The towering majesty of the halls and the splendour of the tall buildings and terraces beggared description. When he reached the main southern gate he requested the reporting officer to announce to the court his wish to have his passport inspected. The eunuch officer at the gate went to the steps of the throne, where he submitted the following memorial: "There is a monk at the palace gate sent by the Great Tang in the east to worship the Buddha and fetch the scriptures at the Thunder Monastery in the Western Heaven. He wishes to submit his passport for approval. I await Your Majesty's command." When the king heard this he replied happily, "For a long time we have been too ill to sit on our throne. Today we are in the throne room to issue a notice sending for doctors, and now a distinguished monk has arrived in our country." He ordered that the monk be summoned to the steps of the throne. Sanzang abased himself in reverence. The king then summoned him into the throne room, invited him to sit down, and ordered the department of foreign relations to arrange a vegetarian meal. Sanzang thanked the king for his kindness and presented his passport.

When he had read it through the king said with great delight, "Master of the Law, how many dynasties have ruled in your land of Great Tang? How many generations of wise ministers have there been? After what illness did the Tang emperor come back to life, so that he sent you on this long and difficult journey to fetch the scriptures?" On being asked all these questions the venerable elder bowed, put his hands together and said, "In my country,

The Three Emperors ruled,
The Five Rulers established morality.
Yao and Shun took the throne,
Yu and Tang gave the people peace.
Many were the offspring of Chengzhou
Who each established their own states,
Bullying the weak with their own strength,
Dividing the realm and proclaiming themselves rulers.
Eighteen such lords of local states
Divided the territory up to the borders.
Later they became a dozen,
Bringing peace to the cosmic order.

But those who had no chariots of war
Were swallowed up by others.
When the seven great states contended
*Six of them had to surrender to Qin.**
Heaven gave birth to Liu Bang and Xiang Yu,
Each of whom cherished wicked ideas.
The empire then belonged to Han
According to the stipulations agreed between the two.
Power passed from Han to the Sima clan,
Till Jin in its turn fell into chaos.
Twelve states ruled in north and south,
Among them Song, Qi, Liang and Chen.
Emperors ruled in succession to each other
Till the Great Sui restored the true unity.
Then it indulged in evil and wickedness.
*Inflicting misery on the common people.***
Our present rulers, the House of Li,
Have given the name of Tang to the state.
Since the High Ancestor passed on the throne
The reigning monarch has been Li Shimin.
The rivers have run clear and the seas been calm
Thanks to his great virtue and his benevolence.
North of the city of Chang'an
Lived a wicked river dragon
Who gave the timely rain in short measure,
For which he deserved to pay with his death.
One night he came in a dream to the emperor,
Asking the monarch to spare his life.
The emperor promised to grant a pardon
And sent for his wise minister early next day.
He kept him there inside the palace,
Filling his time with a long game of chess.

* This passage outlines the history of China from earliest times till the 3rd century B.C.

** This passage covers the period from the rise of Han at the end of the third century B.C. till the fall of the Sui Dynasty early in the seventh century A.D.

But at high noon the minister
Slept, and in a dream cut off the dragon's head."

On hearing this the king groaned and asked, "Master of the Law, which country did that wise minister come from?" "He was our emperor's prime minister Wei Zheng, astrologer, geographer, master of the Yin and Yang, and one of the great founders and stabilizers of our state," Sanzang explained. "Because he beheaded the Dragon King of the Jing River in his dream, the dragon brought a case in the Underworld against our emperor for having him decapitated after granting a pardon. The emperor became very ill and his condition was critical. Wei Zheng wrote him a letter to take to the Underworld and give to Cui Jue, the judge of Fengdu. Soon after that the emperor died, only to come back to life on the third day. It was thanks to Wei Zheng that Judge Cui was persuaded to alter a document and give His Majesty an extra twenty years of life. He held a great Land and Water Mass and despatched me on this long journey to visit many lands, worship the Buddha and fetch the Three Stores of Mahayana scriptures that will raise all the sufferers from evil up to Heaven."

At this the king groaned and sighed again. "Yours is indeed a heavenly dynasty and a great nation," he said, "with a just ruler and wise ministers. We have long been ill, but not one minister do we have who will save us." On hearing this the venerable elder stole a glance at the king and saw that his face was sallow and emaciated; his appearance was going to pieces and his spirits were very low. The venerable elder was going to ask him some questions when an official of the department of foreign relations came to invite the Tang Priest to eat. The king ordered that his food should be set out with Sanzang's in the Hall of Fragrance so that he could eat with the Master of the Law. Thanking the king for his kindness Sanzang took his meal with him.

Meanwhile, back in the Hostel of Meeting, Brother Monkey told Friar Sand to prepare the tea, the grain and the vegetarian dishes. "There's no problem about the tea and the rice," Friar Sand said, "but the vegetable dishes will be difficult." "Why?" Monkey asked. "There's no oil, salt, soya sauce or vinegar," Friar Sand replied. "I've got a few coins here," Monkey said, "so we can send Pig out to buy them." "I wouldn't dare," said the idiot, who was feeling too lazy to go. "My ugly mug could cause trouble, and then the master would blame me." "If you buy the stuff at a fair price and don't try to get it by asking for alms or theft there couldn't possibly be any trouble," said Brother Monkey. "Didn't you see the commotion just now?" asked Pig. "I only showed my snout outside the gate and about a dozen of them collapsed with fright. Goodness only knows how many I'd scare to death in a busy shopping street." "Well," said Monkey, "as you know so much about the busy shopping streets did you notice what was being sold in them?" "No," said Pig. "The master told me to keep my head down and cause no trouble. Honest, I didn't see anything."

"I won't need to tell you about the bars, grain merchants, mills, silk shops and grocers," said Monkey. "But there are marvellous teahouses and noodle shops selling big sesame buns and steamed bread. You can buy terrific soup, rice, spices and vegetables in the restaurants. Then there are all the exotic cakes, yoghurts, snacks, rolls, fries, and honey sweets. Any number of goodies. Shall I go out and buy you some?"

This description had the idiot drooling; the saliva gurgled in his throat. "Brother," he said, jumping to his feet, "I'll let you pay this time. Next time I'm in the money I'll treat you." "Friar Sand," said Monkey, hiding his amusement, "cook the rice while I go out to buy some other ingredients." Realizing that Monkey was only fooling the idiot, Friar Sand agreed. "Off you go," he said. "Buy plenty and have a good feed." Grabbing a bowl and a dish the idiot went out with Monkey.

"Where are you reverend gentlemen going?" two officials asked him. "To buy some groceries," Monkey replied. "Go west along this street, turn at the drum tower, and you'll be at Zheng's grocery," they said. "You can buy as much oil, salt, soya sauce, vinegar, ginger, pepper and tea as you like there: they've got them all."

The two of them headed west along the road hand in hand. Monkey went past several tea-houses and restaurants but did not buy any of the things on sale or eat any of the food. "Brother," called Pig, "why don't we make do with what we can buy here?" This was the last thing that Monkey, who had only been fooling him, intended to do. "My dear brother," he said, "you don't know how to get a good bargain. If we go a little further you can choose bigger ones." As the two of them were talking a lot of people followed jostling behind them. Before long they reached the drum tower, where a huge and noisy crowd was pushing and shoving and filling the whole road. "I'm not going any further, brother," said Pig when he saw this. "From the way they're shouting they sound as though they're out to catch monks. And we're suspicious-looking strangers. What'll we do if they arrest us?" "Stop talking such nonsense," said Monkey. "We monks haven't broken the law, so monk-catchers would have no reason to arrest us. Let's carry on and buy the ingredients we need at Zheng's." "No," said Pig, "never. I'm not going to ask for trouble. If I try to squeeze through that crowd and my ears get pulled out to their full length they'll collapse with fright. Several of them might get trampled to death, and it would cost me my life." "Very well then," said Monkey. "You stand at the foot of this wall while I go and buy the things. I'll bring you back some wheaten cakes." The idiot handed the bowl and dish to Monkey then stood with his back to the crowd and his snout against the foot of the wall. He would not have moved for anything in the world.

When Monkey reached the drum tower he found that the crowds really were very dense. As he squeezed his way through them he heard people saying that a royal proclamation had been posted at the tower: this was what all the people were struggling to see. Monkey pushed forward till he was close to it, then opened wide his fiery eyes with golden pupils to read it carefully. This is what was written:

We, the King of Purpuria in the Western Continent of

> Cattle-gift, from the beginning of our reign gave peace to the four quarters and tranquillity to the people. Recently the state's misfortunes have confined us to our bed with a chronic illness that has continued for a very long time. Recovery has proved impossible, and the many excellent prescriptions of our country's Royal College of Medicine have not yet effected a cure. We hereby issue an invitation to all experts in medicine and pharmacy among the wise men of the world, whether from the north or the east, from China or from foreign countries, to ascend to the throne hall and heal our sickness. In the event of a recovery we will give half our kingdom. This is no empty promise. All those who can offer cures should come to this notice.

When Monkey had read this he exclaimed with delight, "As they used to say in the old days, 'Make a move and your fortune's one third made.' I was wrong to stay put in the hostel. There's no need to buy groceries, and fetching the scriptures can wait for a day while I go and have a bit of fun as a doctor." The splendid Great Sage bent low, got rid of the bowl and dish, took a pinch of dust, threw it into the air, said the words of a spell and made himself invisible. He then went up to the notice, quietly took it down, and blew towards the southeast with a magic breath.

Immediately a whirlwind arose that scattered all the people there. Monkey then went straight back to where Pig was standing, his nose propped against the foot of the wall as if he were fast asleep. Brother Monkey folded the notice up, slipped it inside the lapel of Pig's tunic without disturbing him turned and went back to the hostel.

As soon as the whirlwind started blowing all the people in the crowd at the foot of the drum tower covered their heads and shut their eyes, never imagining that when the wind fell the royal proclamation would have disappeared. They were horror-struck. That morning twelve palace eunuchs and twelve guards officers had come out to post it, and now it had been blown away after less than six hours. In fear and trembling the people searched all around for it until a piece of paper was spotted sticking out of Pig's lapel. "So you took the proclamation down, did you?" they asked, going up to him.

Looking up with a start the idiot thrust his nose up at them, making the guards officers stagger about and collapse with terror. He turned to flee, only to be grabbed by several bold spirits who blocked his way. "You've taken down the royal proclamation inviting doctors, so you're coming to the palace to cure His Majesty," they said. "Where else d'you think you're going?" "I'm your son if I tore the poster down," said Pig in panic. "I'd be your grandson if I could cure disease." "What's that sticking out of your tunic?" one of the officers asked.

Only then did the idiot look down and see that there really was a piece of paper there. Opening it he ground his teeth and swore, "That macaque is trying to get me killed!" He gave an angry roar and was just about to tear it up when they all stopped him. "You're a dead man," they said. "That's a proclamation His Majesty issued today. How dare you tear it up? As you've put it in your tunic you're no doubt a brilliant doctor. Come with us at once!" "You don't understand," shouted Pig. "It wasn't me that took it down. It was my fellow disciple Sun Wukong. He sneaked it into my tunic then abandoned me. We'll all have to go and find him to get to the bottom of this." "Nonsense," they said. "We've got a bell here — we're not going off to play one that's still being cast. You can say what you like. Drag him off to see His Majesty." Not bothering to get to the truth of the matter they pushed and pulled the idiot, who stood his ground as firmly as if he had taken root there. Over ten of them tried to move him without any success. "You've got no respect," said Pig. "If you go on pulling at me and make me lose my temper I'll go berserk, and don't blame me then."

It had not taken long for this commotion to stir up the whole neighbourhood, and Pig was now surrounded. Two elderly palace eunuchs in the crowd said, "You look very odd and you sound wrong too. Where are you from, you ruffian?" "We're pilgrims sent from the east to fetch the scriptures from the Western Heaven" Pig replied. "My master is the younger brother of the Tang emperor and a Master of the Law. He's just gone to the palace to hand his passport over for inspection. I came here with my brother disciple to buy some groceries, but there were so many people by the tower that I was scared to go any further. He told me to wait here. When he saw the proclamation he made a whirlwind, took it down, sneaked it into my tunic and went away." "We did see a monk with a plump white face going in through the palace gates," one of the eunuchs said. "Perhaps that was your master." "Yes, yes," said Pig. "Where did your fellow disciple go?" the eunuch asked. "There are four of us altogether," said Pig. "When the master went to present his passport the other three of us stayed with our luggage and our horse in the Hostel of Meeting. My brother's played a trick on me and gone back there ahead of me." "Let go of him, officers," the eunuch said. "We'll all go to the hostel together and find out what's really happening."

"You two ladies are very sensible," said Pig. "Monk, you don't know about anything," said the officers. "How can you address gentlemen as ladies?" "You're shameless," laughed Pig. "You've made them change sex. Fancy calling these two old females gentlemen instead of women or ladies!" "That's enough of your insolence," they all said. "Find your fellow disciple at once."

The noisy crowd in the street, which was not to be numbered in mere hundreds, carried him to the hostel gates. "Don't come any further, gentlemen," Pig said. "My brother won't let you make a fool of him the way I do. He's a ferocious and serious character. When you meet him you'll have to bow deeply to him and call him 'Lord Sun', then he'll look after you. If you don't he'll turn nasty and this business will fail." To this the eunuchs and officers replied, "If your brother really has the power to cure our king he'll be given half the country and we will all bow to him."

The idlers were still making a commotion outside the hostel gates as Pig led the eunuchs and officers straight inside, where Monkey could be heard laughing with pleasure as he told Friar Sand about how he had taken the proclamation down. Pig went up to him, grabbed him and yelled, "Why won't you act like a man? You said you'd buy me noodles, buns, and steamed bread to lure me out, but it was only an empty promise. Then you made a whirlwind, took down the royal proclamation, and sneakily put it in my tunic. You made a real idiot of me. What kind of brother are you?" "Idiot," laughed Monkey, "you must have got lost and gone the wrong way. I couldn't find you when I rushed back from buying the groceries the other side of the drum tower, so I came back ahead. Where did I tear any royal proclamations down?" "The officials who were guarding it are here," said Pig.

Before he had finished speaking the eunuchs and officers came up, bowed low and said, "Lord Sun, His Majesty is very fortunate today as Heaven has sent you down to us. We are sure that you will display your great skill and give him the benefit of your outstanding medical knowledge. If you cure our king you will receive half the country and half the state." On hearing this Monkey composed his face, took the proclamation from Pig and said, "I suppose you are the officials who were guarding the notice." "We slaves are eunuchs in the Bureau of Ritual," said the eunuchs, kowtowing, "and these gentlemen are officers in the royal guard." "I did take the royal proclamation down," Monkey said, "and I used my younger brother to bring you here. So your lord is ill. As the saying goes, 'Don't sell medicine carelessly, and don't send for any old doctor when you're ill.' Tell your king to come here and ask me himself to help him. I can get rid of his illness at a touch." This shocked all the eunuchs. "That is very big talk, so you must be a man of great breadth of spirit," the officers said. "Half of us will remain here to press the invitation in silence while the other half go back to the palace to report."

Four of the eunuchs and six of the guards officers went straight into the palace without waiting to be summoned and said at the steps of the throne room, "Congratulations, Your Majesty." When the king, who was in the middle of a cultivated conversation with Sanzang after their meal together, heard this he asked, "What on?" "When we, your slaves, took out Your

Majesty's proclamation sending for doctors this morning and posted it at the foot of the drum tower, a holy monk from Great Tang in the east took it down," they replied. "He is now in the Hostel of Meeting and wants Your Majesty to go in person to ask his help. He can get rid of illness at a touch. That is why we have come to submit this report."

This news delighted the king. "How many distinguished disciples do you have, Master of the Law?" he asked. Putting his hands together in front of his chest Sanzang replied, "I have three stupid followers." "Which of them is a medical expert?" the king asked. "To be frank with Your Majesty," Sanzang replied, "they are all country bumpkins fit only for carrying baggage, leading the horse, finding their way along streams, or leading me over mountains and rivers. In dangerous places they can defeat monsters, capture demons, and subdue tigers and dragons. None of them knows anything about medicines." "Aren't you being too hard on them?" the king asked. "It was very fortunate that you came to court when we entered the throne hall this morning: this was surely destined by Heaven. If your disciple knows nothing about medicine why would he have taken down our proclamation and demanded that we go to greet him in person? He must surely be a great physician." He then called, "Civilian and military officers, we are much too weak to ride in our carriage. You must all leave the palace and go on our behalf to invite the Venerable Sun to treat our disease. When you meet him you must on no account show him any disrespect. You must address him as 'Holy monk, Venerable Sun' and treat him with the deference due to your own sovereign."

Having received these orders the officials went straight to the Hostel of Meeting with the eunuchs and guards officers responsible for the proclamation. There they arranged themselves in their companies to kowtow to Monkey. Pig was so frightened that he hid in the wing, while Friar Sand slipped behind the wall. Just look at the Great Sage sitting solemnly and unmoving in the middle of the room. "That macaque is really asking to have his head cut off," Pig thought resentfully. "All those officials bowing to him, and he's not bowing back or standing up either." Soon afterwards, when the rituals had been performed, the officials addressed Monkey as if he were their monarch: "We report to the holy monk, the Venerable Sun, that we officials of the Kingdom of Purpuria have come at the command of our king to do respectful homage to the holy monk and invite him to the palace to treat our sick king." Only then did Brother Monkey stand up and reply, "Why hasn't your king come?" "His Majesty is too weak to ride in his carriage," the officials all replied, "which is why he ordered us to pay homage to you, holy monk, as if you were our sovereign, kowtow to you and invite you to come." "In that case," said Monkey, "will you gentlemen please lead the way. I'll follow you." The officials then formed themselves into a column in accordance with their ranks and set out. Monkey tidied his clothes and got to his feet. "Brother," said Pig, "whatever you do, don't drag us in." "I won't," Monkey replied, "provided you two accept the medicine for me." "What medicine?" Friar Sand asked. "You must accept all the medicine people send me," Monkey replied. "I'll collect it when I come back." The two of them undertook this commission.

Monkey was soon at the palace with the officials, who went in first to inform the king. He raised high the curtains of pearls, flashed his dragon and phoenix eyes, opened his golden mouth and spoke majestically, "Which gentleman is the holy monk, the Venerable Sun?" Taking a step forward, Monkey shouted at the top of his voice, "I am." The voice was so ugly and the face so hideous that the king fell back on his dragon throne. In their alarm the female officials and the palace eunuchs helped him to the inner quarters. "He's terrified His Majesty to death," they said. "Monk," all the officials said angrily to Monkey, "how could you be so rough and crude? How dared you take the proclamation down?"

When Brother Monkey heard this he replied with a smile, "You shouldn't be angry with me. If you're going to be so rude to me your king won't get better in a thousand years." "But how long does human life last?" the officials asked. "How is it that he won't get better even in a thousand years?" "He's a sick ruler now," said Monkey. "When he dies he'll be a sick ghost, and whenever he's reincarnated he'll be a sick man again. That's why he won't get better even in a thousand years." "You've got no sense of respect at all," the infuriated officials replied. "How dare you talk such nonsense!" "It's not nonsense," Monkey laughed. "Listen and I'll explain:

"Mysterious indeed are the principles of medicine;
Flexibility of mind is a quality required.
Use eyes and ears, ask questions, take the pulses:
Omit but one and the examination's incomplete.
First look for outward signs of the patient's vital energy.
Dried? Smooth? Fat? Thin? Active? Does he sleep well?
Secondly, listen to whether the voice is clear or harsh:
Determine if the words he speaks are true or crazed.
Third, you must ask how long the disease has lasted,
And how the patient eats, drinks and relieves himself.
Fourth, feel the pulses and be clear about the veins:
Are they deep, shallow, external or inside?
Should I not look and listen, ask questions, and take the pulses,
Never in all his days will the king be well again."

In the ranks of the civil and military officials there were some fellows of the Royal College of Medicine who when they heard these words praised Monkey publicly: "The monk is right. Even a god or an immortal would have to look, listen, ask questions and take the pulses before treating a patient successfully with his divine gifts." All the officials agreed with these remarks, then went up to the king and submitted: "The reverend gentleman wishes to look, listen, ask questions and take the pulses before he can prescribe properly." "Send him away," the king said over and over again as he lay on his dragon bed. "We cannot bear to see any strangers." His attendants then came out from the inner quarters and announced, "Monk, His Majesty commands that you go away. He cannot bear to see a stranger."

"If he won't see a stranger," Monkey replied, "I know the art of taking the pulses with hanging threads." "That is something of which we have only heard," exclaimed all the officials, concealing their delight, "but that we have never seen with our own eyes. Please go back in and submit another report." The personal attendants then went back into the inner quarters and reported, "Your Majesty, the Venerable Sun can take your pulses with hanging threads: he does not need to see Your Majesty's face." At this the king reflected, "In the three years we have been ill we have never tried this technique. Send him in." At once the courtiers in attendance announced, "His Majesty has consented to pulse-taking by the hanging threads. Send the Venerable Sun to the inner quarters at once to make his diagnosis."

Monkey then entered the throne hall, where the Tang Priest met him with abuse: "Wretched ape! You will be the death of me!" "My good master," Monkey replied with a smile, "I'm bringing you credit. How can you say I'll be the death of you?" "In all the years you've been with me," Sanzang shouted, "I have never seen you cure a single person. You know nothing about the nature of drugs, and you have never studied medical books. How can you be so reckless and bring this disaster on us?" "You don't realize, Master," said Monkey with a smile, "that I do know the odd herbal remedy and can treat serious illnesses. I guarantee I can cure him. Even if the treatment kills him I'll only be guilty of manslaughter through medical incompetence. That's not a capital offence. What are you afraid of? There's nothing to worry about, nothing. You sit here and see what my pulse diagnosis is like." "How can you talk all this rubbish," Sanzang asked, "when you have never read the *Plain Questions*, the *Classic of Difficulties*, the *Pharmacopoeia* and the *Mysteries of the Pulses*, or studied the commentaries to them? How could you possibly diagnose his pulses by hanging threads?" "I've got golden threads on me that you've never seen," Monkey replied, putting out his hand to pull three hairs from his tail, hold them in a bunch, call, "Change!" and turn them into three golden threads each twenty-four feet long to match the twenty-four periods of the solar year. Holding these in his hand he said to the Tang Priest, "These are golden threads, aren't they?" "Stop talking, reverend gentleman," said the eunuchs in attendance on the king. "Please come inside and make your diagnosis." Taking his leave of the Tang Priest Monkey followed the attendants into the inner quarters to see his patient. Indeed,

The heart has a secret prescription that will save a country;
The hidden and wonderful spell gives eternal life.

If you do not know what illness was diagnosed or what medicines were used and wish to learn the truth listen to the explanation in the next instalment.

CHAPTER SIXTY-NINE

The heart's master prepares medicine in the night; The monarch discusses a demon at the banquet.

The story tells how the Great Sage Sun went with the eunuchs in attendance on the king to the inner quarters of the palace and stood outside the doors of the royal bed-chamber. Handing the three golden threads to the eunuchs to take inside he gave them these instructions: "Tell the queens and consorts of the inner palace or the eunuchs in personal attendance to fasten these threads to His Majesty's left wrist at the inch, the bar and the cubit* then pass them out of the window to me." The eunuchs did as he said, asking the king to sit on his dragon bed while they fastened one end of the golden threads to the inch, the bar and the cubit and passed the other ends outside.

Monkey took these ends and first held the end of one between the thumb and the forefinger of his right hand and felt the pulse at the inch point. He held the next against his middle finger and felt the pulse at the bar, and then pressed his thumb against his third finger and felt the cubit pulse. Next he regulated his own breathing to examine the four functions, the five depressions, the seven exterior and eight interior symptoms, the nine tempers, the deep pulses within the floating ones and the floating ones within the deep ones. He thus determined the insufficiencies and excesses of the functioning of organs, then told the eunuchs to take the threads off the king's left wrist and fasten

* Three points on the wrist over the radial artery that on the left hand are where the pulses of the heart, liver and kidney are felt. The equivalent points on the right wrist are the pulses of the lung, the spleen and the "vital gate".

them to the same points on the right wrist. He felt the threads one by one with the fingers of his left hand.

With a shake he put the golden threads back on his body and shouted at the top of his voice, "Your Majesty, the inch pulse on your left wrist is strong and tense, the bar pulse is sluggish and tardy, and the cubit is hollow and deep. On your right wrist the inch is floating and slippery, the bar is slow and knotted, and the cubit is frequent and firm. The left inch being strong and tense means that you have an internal emptiness and pains in the heart. The left bar being sluggish and tardy shows that you sweat and that your muscles feel numb. The hollowness and depth of the cubit suggest red urine and bloody stools. The floating, slippery inch pulse on the right wrist shows internal accumulations and blocked channels. The bar being slow and knotted is from indigestion and retained drinking. The frequency and wiriness of the cubit shows a chronic opposition of irritable fullness and empty coldness. My diagnosis of Your Majesty's ailment is that you are suffering from alarm and worry. The condition is the one known as the 'pair of birds parted'." When the king heard this inside his chamber he was so delighted that his spirits revived and he shouted in reply, "You have understood my illness through your fingers. That is indeed my trouble. Please go out and fetch some medicine."

Monkey walked slowly out of the inner palace, by when the eunuchs watching him had already given the news to everyone. When Monkey emerged a moment later the Tang Priest asked him how it had gone. "I made a diagnosis from his pulses," Monkey said. "I now have to prepare the medicine for his condition." All the officials then came forward to ask, "Holy monk, reverend sir, what is the 'pair of birds parted' condition of which you spoke just now?" "It's when a cock bird and a hen who were flying together are suddenly separated by a violent storm," replied Monkey with a smile. "The hen misses the cock and the cock misses the hen. Isn't that 'a pair of birds parted'?" At this the officials all cried out over and over again in admiration, "He really is a holy monk! He really is a divine doctor!"

"You have diagnosed the condition," said one of the fellows of the Royal College of Medicine, "but what drugs will you use to treat it?" "There's no need to stick to prescriptions," said Monkey. "I'll choose the drugs when I see them." "According to the medical classic, 'There are 808 varieties of medicine and 404 varieties of sickness,' " said the fellows of the Royal College of Medicine. "How can it be right to use all the medicines when one person does not have all the ailments? You can't just choose your drugs on sight." To this Monkey replied, "The ancients said, 'In preparing medicines do not stick rigidly to the formulae; use them as appropriate.' That's why I've asked for the full range of pharmaceutical materials so that I can make adjustments as I need to." The fellows of the Royal College could say no more to this, but went out through the palace gates and sent those of the college's staff who were on duty to tell all the pharmacies in the city, whether selling raw materials or prepared drugs, to send three pounds of each to Monkey. "This is no place for preparing medicine," said Monkey. "All the medicines and a set of pharmacist's utensils must be sent to the Hostel of Meeting and handed over to my two fellow disciples." The fellows did as they were told. Three pounds of each of the 808 ingredients of medicine together with pharmacist's rollers, hand-mills, sieves, mortars, bowls, pestles and the like were all sent to the hostel, handed over and received.

Monkey went back into the throne hall and asked his master to return to the hostel with him while he prepared the medicine. Sanzang was just getting up to go when the king sent a command from the inner quarters that the Master of the Law was to stay behind and spend the night in the Hall of Literary Splendour; the next morning, after taking the medicine and recovering from his illness, the king would reward them, inspect the passport and send them on their way. Sanzang was horrified. "Disciple," he said, "he means to keep me here as a hostage. If he is cured he will be happy to send us on our way, but if the treatment fails my life is over. You must be very careful and pay full attention when preparing the medicine." "Don't worry, Master,"

Monkey said with a smile, "Enjoy yourself here. I'm a superb doctor."

Taking his leave of Sanzang and of all the officials the splendid Great Sage went straight back to the hostel where Pig welcomed him with a grin. "Brother," he said, "I know what you're up to." "What?" Monkey asked. "If fetching the scriptures doesn't come off you'll be left without any capital to start up a business." Pig replied. "Now you've seen how prosperous this place is you're planning to open a chemist's shop here." "Don't talk nonsense," shouted Monkey. "When I've cured the king I'll use my success to leave the court and be on our way. I'm not going to be running a chemist's." "Well," said Pig, "if you're not opening a shop, why get three pounds of each of 808 different ingredients to treat one man? How much of it will you need? How many years will it take for him to finish the lot?" "He'll never finish that much," Monkey replied. "The fellows of their Royal College of Medicine are a load of idiots. The only reason why I sent for so many ingredients was to baffle them and stop them knowing which ones I'm going to use. Then they won't be able to find out what my miraculous prescription is."

As they were talking two of the hostel staff came in and fell to their knees before them to say, "We beg the holy monks and reverend gentlemen to partake of their evening repast." "This morning you treated us rather differently," said Monkey, "so why go on your knees to invite us now?" "When you first came, my lords," the hostel orderlies replied, "we were too blind to recognize your illustrious faces. Now we have heard how you are using your outstanding medical powers to treat our king. If His Majesty recovers his health he will share the kingdom with you, so we'll all be your subjects. So it's only proper for us to kowtow to you and to invite you politely to eat." On hearing this Monkey cheerfully took the place of honour while Pig and Friar Sand sat to his left and right. As the vegetarian meal was served Friar Sand asked, "Where's our master, brother?" "The king's kept him as a hostage," Monkey replied. "When the king's cured he'll reward us and send us on our way." "Is he being well looked after?" Friar Sand continued. "His host's a king," Monkey replied, "so of course he's in luxury. When I went there he had three senior ministers looking after him and he was invited into the Hall of Literary Splendour." "In that case," said Pig, "the master's still doing much better than us. He's got ministers looking after him, and we've only got a couple of hostel orderlies to serve us. So I'm going to forget about him and eat a good meal." Thus the three of them enjoyed their meal at ease.

It was now late. "Tidy the dishes away," Monkey said to the hostel orderlies, "and fetch me plenty of oil and candles. The best time for us to make up the medicine will be in the quiet of the night." The orderlies brought oil and candles as instructed and were then dismissed. In the still silence of the middle of the night Pig asked, "Brother, what medicines are we going to make? Let's get on with it. I need my shut-eye." "Get an ounce of rhubarb and grind it to a fine powder with a roller," said Brother Monkey. "Rhubarb has a bitter taste and a cold nature and isn't noxious," said Friar Sand. "Its nature is deep, not superficial; it's an active medicine, not a defensive one. It removes stagnations and clears obstructions, settles disorder and brings about peace, and they call it 'the general'. It's a cathartic drug. But perhaps it's wrong for someone in an empty, weakened state after a long illness." "There's something you don't know, brother," Monkey said. "This drug helps phlegm, makes the vital forces travel smoothly, and calms the heat and cold that become congested in the stomach. Just leave me alone and fetch me an ounce of croton seeds. Shell them, peel them, hammer the poisonous oil out of them, then grind them to a fine powder with a roller." "Croton seed is acrid, hot by nature and poisonous," said Pig. "It cuts away hard accumulations, deals with submerged cold in the lungs and bowels, and clears obstructions. It smooths the way for water and grain. It's a warrior for storming passes and gates. You must be very careful how you use it." "Brother," Monkey replied, "what you don't understand is that this is a drug that destroys knots, opens the intestine and can cure swelling of the heart and dropsy. Hurry up and get it ready. And I'll want an adjuvant to back it up."

The two of them started work on grinding the two drugs to a fine powder. "You'll need dozens more, brother," they said, "so which'll they be?" "That's all," Monkey replied. "But you've got three pounds of each of 808 different medicinal ingredients," Pig said. "If all you're going to use is two ounces you've been making a fool of these people." Monkey then produced a patterned porcelain dish and said, "Stop talking, brothers. Take this dish and fill it half full with soot scraped from a cooking pot." "Whatever for?" Pig asked. "I need it for the medicine," Monkey replied. "I never heard of soot from a cooking pot being used in medicine," said Friar Sand. "It's called 'frost on the flowers'," said Monkey, "and it helps treat all kinds of illness. Didn't you know that?" The idiot then scraped off half a dishful and ground it up to a fine powder.

Monkey then handed him another dish and said, "Now fetch me half a dishful of our horse's piss." "What for?" Pig asked. "To make the medicine up into pills with," Monkey replied. "Brother," said Friar Sand with a smile, "this is no joking matter. Horse piss stinks. You can't use it in medicine. I've only seen vinegar paste, old rice paste, refined honey and clean water used for making pills. Who ever heard of horse piss used to make pills? It's got a terrible stink. Anyone with a weak spleen would throw up at the first sniff. If he goes on and takes the rhubarb and croton seeds he'll be vomiting at one end and having the runs at the other. That'll be no joke." "You don't know the inside story," said Monkey. "That horse of ours is no ordinary horse. He used to be a dragon in the Western Ocean. If he'll give us some of his piss it'll cure any illness you could have. My only worry is that he might refuse." When Pig heard this he went and stood beside the horse, who was lying down asleep. The idiot kicked the horse till he got to his feet then pressed himself against the horse's stomach for a very long time but without seeing any sign of piss. He ran back to Monkey to say, "Brother, never mind about treating the king. Hurry up and cure the horse. He's done for: he's dried right up.

There's no way we're going to get a drop of piss out of him." "I'll go with you," smiled Monkey. "I'll come and have a look too," said Friar Sand.

When the three of them reached the horse he started to jump about and shout in human language at the top of his voice, "How can you be so ignorant, brother? I used to be a flying dragon in the Western Ocean. The Bodhisattva Guanyin saved me after I'd offended against the Heavenly Code. She sawed off my horns, removed my scales and turned me into a horse to carry the master to the Western Heaven to fetch the scriptures. This way I'll be able to redeem my crimes. If I pissed into any river I was crossing the fish in the water would drink it and turn into dragons. The grass on any mountain we were going over that got a taste of it would become magic fungus for immortal boys to gather and give themselves eternal life. So of course I can't casually drop it in a vulgar, worldly place like this." "Watch your words, brother," said Monkey. "This is the city of a western king, not some vulgar, worldly place. You wouldn't be casually dropping it here. As the saying goes, many hands make light work. We've got to cure the king. When we do we'll all be covered in glory. If we fail I'm afraid we won't be able to leave this country with any credit."

"Wait a moment," the horse finally said. Look at him as he springs forward then squats back on his haunches, grinds his teeth noisily and only with the greatest strain manages to squeeze out a few drops before standing up again. "What a deadbeat," said Pig. "You could give us a few more even if they were drops of gold." Seeing that the dish was now about a third full Monkey said, "That'll do, that'll do. Take it away." Only then did Friar Sand feel cheerful.

The three of them then returned to the main hall, mixed the piss with the ingredients that had already been prepared, and rolled the mixture into three large round balls. "They're too big, brothers," said Monkey. "They're only walnut-sized," Pig replied. "That wouldn't be enough for a single mouthful if I were taking them." The three disciples then put the pills into a large box and went to bed fully dressed.

It was soon dawn, and despite his sickness the king held court, asking the Tang Priest to come to see him and sending all his officials straight to the Hostel of Meeting to pay their respects to the holy monk, the Venerable Sun, and fetch the medicine.

When the officials reached the hostel they prostrated themselves before Brother Monkey with the words, "His Majesty has sent us to pay our respects and fetch the miraculous medicine." Monkey told Pig to fetch the box, which he opened and handed to the officials. "What is this medicine called?" they asked. "We would like to be able to inform His Majesty when we see him." "It's called Black Gold Elixir," Monkey replied, at which Pig and Friar Sand had to hide their grins as they thought, "of course they're black gold — they were made with soot scraped off cooking pots."

"What should be taken with the pills to guide them on their way?" the officials asked. "There are two kinds of guide that can be taken with them," Monkey replied. "One's easily got hold of. That is a decoction of six ingredients to be taken as a hot potion." "What six ingredients?" the officials asked. "A fart from a flying crow," Monkey replied, "piss from a carp in a fast-flowing stream, some of the face-powder used by the Queen Mother of the West, soot from elixir refined in Lord Lao's furnace, three pieces of a worn-out head cloth of the Jade Emperor's, and five whiskers from a trapped dragon's beard. A decoction of those six ingredients taken with the pills would clear up your king's illness straight away."

When the officials heard this they replied, "Those are things that are not to be found in this world, so please tell us what the other guide is." "The pills should be taken with rootless water," said Monkey. "That's very easily got hold of," smiled the officials. "How can you be so sure?" Monkey asked. "We have a saying here," the officials replied, "that if you need rootless water you take a bowl or a dish to a well or a stream, fill it with water, and hurry back with it. Don't spill a drop, don't look behind you, and give it to the patient to take with the medicine." "But well water and stream water both have roots," Monkey said. "The rootless water I'm talking about has to fall from the sky and be drunk before it touches the ground. Only then can it be called rootless." "That's easily got too," the officials said. "The medicine shouldn't be taken till the next cloudy, wet day."

The officials then kowtowed to thank Monkey and took the medicine back with them to present to the king, who delightedly ordered his attendants to bring it to him. "What are these pills?" he asked when he saw them. "The holy monk says they are Black Gold Elixir and have to be taken with rootless water," the officials replied. The king then sent some of his palace women to fetch rootless water. "The holy monk says that rootless water can't be got from wells or streams," the officials said. "It has to be water that has come down from the sky and not yet touched the ground." The king then ordered his aides to issue a decree inviting magicians to summon rain. The officials then issued a proclamation as the king had ordered.

Back in the hall of the Hostel of Meeting Brother Monkey said to Pig, "He must be given some rain now so he can take his medicine. This is very urgent. How are we going to get some? I reckon he's a very virtuous and worthy king, so why don't we help him get a little rainwater to take his medicine with?" "But how are we going to help him get some rootless water?" Pig asked. "Stand on my left and be my Sustainer Star," Monkey said to him, then told Friar Sand, "stand on my right as my Straightener Star while I help him to get some rootless water."

The splendid Great Sage then paced out a magic pattern and said the words of a spell. Soon a dark cloud appeared to their east that came closer till it was over their heads. "Great Sage," called a voice from it, "Ao Guang, the Dragon King of the Eastern Sea, is here to call on you." "I wouldn't have troubled you if it hadn't been important," Monkey said. "Could I ask you to help by giving the king here some rootless water to take his medicine with?" "When you summoned me, Great Sage," the dragon king replied, "you said nothing about water. I have only come by myself. I haven't brought any rain-making equipment, to say nothing of wind, clouds, thunder and lightning. So how can I make it rain?" "There'll be no call for wind, clouds, thunder or lightning this time," Monkey said, "and we don't need much rain either. We just need enough water for someone to take his medicine with." "In that case I'll do a couple of sneezes and spit out some saliva," the dragon king said. "That ought to be enough for him to take his medicine." "Terrific," said Monkey, delighted. "Don't waste a moment. Do it as soon as you can."

The ancient old dragon gradually brought his dark cloud down till it was just over the palace, though he kept himself entirely concealed. He spat out a mouthful of saliva that turned into timely rain, whereupon all the officials at court exclaimed, "Ten million congratulations, Your Majesty. Heaven is sending down timely rain." The king then ordered, "Take vessels out to hold the rain. All officials, whether inside or outside the palace and irrespective of their rank, must gather this sacred water to save our life." Just watch as all the civil and military officials as well as the consorts, concubines, three thousand beauties, and eight hundred charming ladies-in-waiting of the three harems and the six compounds of the inner palace all stood there holding cups, dishes, bowls and plates to catch the timely rain. Up in the sky the ancient dragon so controlled his saliva that all of it fell within the palace. After about two hours the dragon king took his leave of the Great Sage and went back to the sea. When the officials gathered all the cups, dishes, bowls and plates together they found that some had caught one or two drops of water, some three to five, and some none at all. When it was all put together there were a little over three dishes full of it, and this was all presented to the king. Indeed,

The throne hall was filled with exquisite fragrance;
Fine scents were wafting round the Son of Heaven's court.

The king then dismissed the Master of the Law and had the Black Gold Elixir and the timely rain carried into the inner quarters, where he took the first pill with the first dish of timely rain, then the second pill with the second dish. In three efforts he finished all three pills and all three dishfuls. Soon afterwards there was a noise from his stomach like the endless turning of a windlass. He sent for his chamber pot and evacuated four or five times before taking some rice porridge and collapsing on his dragon bed. When two of his consorts inspected the chamber pot they saw it contained huge amounts of faeces and mucus, and amid it all a ball of glutinous rice. "The root of the disorder has come out," the consorts reported, going over to the royal bed. The king was very pleased to hear this and ate some rice. A little later his chest felt eased and his natural forces and blood were in harmonious balance once more. He was full of vigour and the strength came back to his legs, so he rose from his bed, dressed in his court clothes and went into the throne hall, where he greeted the Tang Priest by prostrating himself. The venerable elder returned this courtesy as quickly as he could When this had been done the king helped Sanzang to his feet with his own hands and told his courtiers, "Write a note at once sending our personal and respectful greetings and have an official go to invite the three illustrious disciples of the Master of the Law to come here. Meanwhile the eastern hall of the palace is to be opened up and the department of foreign relations is to arrange a banquet of thanksgiving." Having been given these commands the officials carried them out. The scribes wrote out the note and the caterers prepared the meal. A state is indeed strong enough to overturn a mountain, and everything was done in an instant.

When Pig saw the officials come to deliver the note he was beside himself with delight. "Brother," he said, "it really must be miracle medicine. From the way they're coming to thank you you must have pulled it off." "You've got it all wrong, brother," said Friar Sand. "As the saying goes, 'One man's good fortune affects his whole household.' We two made up the pills, so we take a share of the credit. So just enjoy yourself and stop talking." Hey! Just look at the three brothers as they all happily go straight to the palace, where all the officials received them and led them to the eastern hall.

Here they saw the Tang Priest with the king and his ministers and the banquet all set out ready. Brother Monkey, Pig and Friar Sand all chanted a "na-a-aw" of respect to their master, after which the officials all came in. In the best place there were set out four tables of vegetarian food. It was the sort of banquet at which there are ten times as many dishes as you can eat. In front of these tables was one of meat dishes, and on this too you could see ten dishes of rare delicacies while you ate one. To either side four or five hundred more single tables were most neatly set out.

As the ancients had it:
"A hundred rare delicacies,
A thousand goblets of fine wine,
Rich cream and yoghurt,
Fat, red meat like brocade."
Precious and many-coloured decorations,
Heavy fragrances of fruit.
Huge sugar dragons coil round sweet lions and immortals:
Ingots of cake draw furnaces escorted by phoenixes.
For meat there was pork and mutton, goose, chicken, duck and fish;
For vegetables, bamboo shoots, beansprouts, fungus and button mushrooms.
Delicious noodles in soup,
Translucent creamy sweets,
Succulent millet,
Fresh wild rice congee,
Pungent, tasty soup with rice noodles,
Dishes in which sweetness vied with beauty.
Monarch and subjects raised their cups as the diners took their seats;
Officials seated by rank slowly passed the jugs.

Holding a cup in his hand the king first seated the Tang Priest, who said, "As a monk I may not drink liquor." "This is alcohol-free wine," the king said. "Could you not drink one cup of this, Master of the Law?" "But wine is the first prohibition for us monks," said Sanzang. The king felt awkward. "If you may not drink, Master of the Law, how can I congratulate you?" "My three badly-behaved disciples will drink on my behalf," Sanzang replied. The king then happily passed the golden goblet to Monkey, who took it, made a courteous gesture to the assembly, and downed a cupful. Seeing how cheerfully he downed it the king offered him another cup. Monkey did not decline it but drank again. "Have a third goblet," said the king with a smile, and Monkey accepted and drank for a third time. The king then ordered that the cup be refilled and said, "Have another to make it four for the four seasons."

Pig, who was standing beside Monkey, had to put up with the saliva gurgling inside him as the wine would not come his way; and now that the king was pressing Monkey so hard to drink he started to shout, "Your Majesty, that medicine you took owes something to me. Those pills include 'orse —" When Monkey heard this he was terrified that the idiot was going to give the game away, so he handed Pig the cup. Pig took the cup, drank and stopped talking. "Holy monk," said the king, "just now you said there was horse in the pills. What sort of horse?" "This brother of mine has a very loose tongue," said Monkey, cutting in. "We've got a really good formula that has been tried and tested, and he wants to give it away. The pills Your Majesty took this morning included not 'orse but Aristolochia." "What class of medicine is Aristolochia?" the king asked. "What conditions can it cure?" One of the fellows of the Royal College of Medicine who was standing beside the king said, "Your Majesty,

> *Aristolochia is bitter, cold and free of poison,*
> *Ends shortness of breath and cures phlegm well,*
> *Circulates the energy, removes blood infections,*
> *Fills emptiness, soothes coughs and eases the heart.*

"It was the right thing to use, the right thing to use," the king said. "The Venerable Pig must have another cup." The idiot said nothing more, but downed three goblets. The king then gave three cupfuls to Friar Sand, who drank them. Everyone then sat down.

When they all had been feasting and drinking for a long time the king raised a large goblet once more and handed it to Monkey. "Please sit down, Your Majesty," Monkey said. "I've been drinking hard in every round. I'd never refuse." "Holy monk," the king said, "we are under a profound debt of gratitude to you that we will never be able to repay. Please drain this great goblet: we have something to say to you." "Say what you will first," Monkey replied, "I'll drink after." "We suffered from that melancholia for years on end," the king said, "and one dose of your miraculous pills cured it." "When I saw Your Majesty yesterday I realized you were suffering from melancholia," Monkey said, "but I don't know what's getting you down."

"There's an old saying that a family doesn't talk about its dirt to strangers," the king replied. "As you are our benefactor, holy monk, we shall tell you, but please don't laugh." "I'd never dare," Monkey said. "Please speak freely." "How many countries did you holy monks come through on your way here from the east?" the king asked. "Five or six," Monkey replied. "What titles do the queens of the other kings have?" the king went on to ask. "They're called the queens of the Main Palace, East Palace and West Palace," Monkey replied. "We don't use titles like that," the king said. "We call the principal queen the Queen of the Sacred Golden Palace, the eastern queen the Queen of the Sacred Jade Palace and the western queen the Queen of the Sacred Silver Palace. But now only the Jade and Silver Queen are here." "Why isn't the Golden Queen in the palace?" Monkey asked. "She has been gone for three whole years," the king replied in tears. "Where did she go?" Monkey asked. "At the Dragon-boat Festival three years ago," the king said, "we were in the Pomegranate Pavilion of the palace gardens with our queens and consorts, unwrapping rice dumplings, putting artemisia out, drinking calamus and realgar wine and watching the dragon boats race when all of a sudden there was a gust of wind. An evil spirit appeared in mid-air. He said he was the Evil Star Matcher who lives in the Horndog Cave on Mount Unicorn and was short of a wife. Seeing how beautiful and charming our Golden Queen is he wanted her for his wife and insisted we should hand her over at once. If we did not do so by the time he had asked three times he was going to eat us up first, then our officials and all the commoners living in the city. We were so concerned over the fate of our country and our people that there was no alternative: the Golden Queen had to be pushed outside the pavilion to be carried noisily off by the evil spirit. All this gave us such a fright that the rice dumpling we were eating turned solid inside us. On top of that we have been unable to sleep for worrying, which is why we were ill for three years. Since taking you holy monks' miraculous pills we have evacuated our bowels three times, and the accumulations from three years ago have all been passed. That is why our body now feels light and strong and our spirit is restored to what it was. Our life has today been given to us by you holy monks; this is a gift more weighty than Mount Tai."

When Brother Monkey heard this he was very happy indeed and he downed the huge goblet of wine in two gulps. "Your Majesty," he said with a smile to the king, "so that's what caused your shock and your depression. Today you've been lucky: you met me and you were cured. But I don't know whether you want the Golden Queen back in the palace." To this the king answered with tears, "We have been longing for her night and day, but nobody has ever been able to catch the evil spirit. Of course we want her back in our country." "What if I go to deal with that evil creature for you?" said Monkey. The king fell to his knees and replied, "If you can rescue our queen we will gladly take our three queens and nine consorts away from the capital and go to live as commoners, leaving the whole kingdom to be yours to reign over, holy monk." When Pig, who was sitting beside them, heard all this being said and such great honours being done he could not help bursting into noisy laughter. "This king's got no sense of what's proper," he chortled. "Fancy giving up his kingdom and going on his knees to a monk for the sake of his old woman."

Monkey hurried forward to help the king back on his feet and ask, "Your Majesty, has the evil spirit been back since he got the Golden Queen?" "In the fifth month of the year before last," the king said, "he carried off the Golden Queen. In the tenth month he came back to demand a couple of ladies in waiting to serve her, and we presented him with a couple. In the third month of last year he came to demand another couple, and two more in the seventh month. Then in the second month of this year it was a fourth pair. We do not know when he will be back again." "If he comes that often you must be terrified of him," Monkey replied. "Because he has come so frequently we are afraid of him and of his murderous intentions," said the king. "In the fourth month last year we ordered the building of a demon shelter, so that whenever we hear the wind and know that he's coming we can shelter there with our two queens and nine consorts." "Would Your Majesty mind taking me to see the shelter?" Monkey asked, and the king led Monkey by his left hand from the table. All the officials rose to their feet. "Brother," protested Pig, "you're very unreasonable. Why leave this royal wine and break up the banquet to go looking at something?" Hearing this and realizing that Pig was worried for his stomach the king told his attendants to have two tables of vegetarian food brought along so that Pig could go on being wined outside the demon shelter. Only then did the idiot stop making a fuss and join in with his master and Friar Sand saying, "Let's break up the banquet."

As a column of civil and military officials led the way the king and Monkey went arm-in-arm through the living quarters of the palace to the back of the royal gardens, but there were no great buildings to be seen. "Where's the demon shelter?" Monkey asked, and before the words were out of his mouth two eunuchs levered open a square flagstone with red lacquered crowbars. "Here it is," said the king. "Twenty feet or more below us a large underground palace hall has been excavated. In it there are four great vats of purified oil in which lights burn night and day. When we hear the wind we take shelter here and the flagstone is put on again from outside." "So the evil spirit doesn't want to kill you," said Monkey with a smile. "If he did this would give you no protection." Just as he was speaking there came the roaring of a wind from due south that made the dust fly. In their alarm all the officials complained, "That monk has the mouth of an oracle. The moment he mentions the evil spirit it turns up." The panic-stricken monarch abandoned Monkey and scuttled into his underground shelter. The Tang Priest went with him, and all the officials fled for cover.

Pig and Friar Sand wanted to hide too, but Monkey grabbed one of them with each hand and said, "Don't be afraid, brothers. You and I are going to identify him and see what sort of evil spirit he is." "Nonsense," said Pig. "What do we want to identify him for? The officials have all hidden and the king's shut himself away. Why don't we clear off? What kind of hero are you trying to be?" But struggle though he might the idiot could not break free. When Monkey had been holding on to him for some time an evil spirit suddenly appeared in mid-air. Just see what it looked like:

A loathsome great body nine feet tall,
Round eyes flashing like lamps of gold.
Two huge ears sticking out as if they were round fans,
Four steel fangs like very long nails.
Red hair curled at his temples; his brows were as flames;
His nose was a hanging trough; his nostrils flared.
His whiskers were strands of cinnabar thread,
And jutting cheekbones shaped his greeny face.
On red-muscled arms were hands of indigo blue,
And ten sharp claws grasped a spear.
A leopardskin kilt was tied round his waist.
Bare feet and tangled hair completed his fiendish looks.

"Friar Sand," asked Monkey when he saw the evil spirit, "can you recognize him?" "I don't know who he is," Friar Sand replied. "I've never seen him before." "Pig," Monkey next asked, "do you know?" "I've never had a cuppa or a drink with him," Pig replied. "He's no friend or neighbour of mine. How could I know?" "He reminds me of the sallow-faced golden-eyed gatekeeper ghost under the Equal of Heaven of the Eastern Peak." "No he isn't, no he isn't," said Pig. "How do you know he isn't?" Monkey asked. "Because ghosts are spirits of the dark and the underworld," Pig replied. "They only come out at night, between five and midnight. It's only ten in the morning, and no ghost would ever dare come out now. And even if it was a devil it'd never ride a cloud. Ghosts that stir up winds make whirlwinds, not gales. Perhaps he's the Evil Star Matcher." "You're not such an idiot after all," said Monkey. "That sounds sensible, so you two look after the master while I go to ask him his name. That'll help me rescue the Golden Queen and bring her back to the palace for the king." "Go if you must," Pig replied, "but don't tell him anything about us." Monkey did not deign to answer, but leapt straight up on his magic light. Goodness!

To settle the nation he started by curing the king;
To preserve the Way love and hatred had to go.

If you don't know who won the battle that followed when Monkey rose up into the sky or how the evil monster was captured and the Golden Queen rescued listen to the explanation in the next chapter.

CHAPTER SEVENTY

The evil monster's treasures emit smoke, sand and fire; Wukong steals the golden bells by trickery.

The story tells how Brother Monkey summoned up his divine prestige and rose up into the air on his magic light, wielding his iron cudgel. "Where are you from, evil monster?" he asked, shouting in the evil spirit's face. "And where are you going to wreak havoc?" "I'm the vanguard warrior under the Great King Evil Star Matcher from Horndog Cave on Mount Unicorn," shouted the demon at the top of his voice, "that's who I am. His Majesty has ordered me to fetch two ladies-in-waiting to serve Her Majesty the Golden Queen. Who are you and how dare you question me?" "I'm Sun Wukong, the Great Sage Equalling Heaven," Monkey replied. "I was passing through this country while escorting the Tang Priest to worship the Buddha in the Western Heaven. Now I know that your gang of monsters was oppressing the king I'm going to use my heroic powers to bring the country back to order and wipe out this evil. And now you've come along to throw your life away just when I didn't know where to find you." When the monster heard this he foolishly thrust his spear at Monkey, who struck back at his face with the iron cudgel. They fought a splendid battle up in mid-air:

> *The cudgel was the sea-settler from the dragon's palace;*
> *The spear was of iron tempered by mankind.*
> *An ordinary weapon was no match for that of an immortal;*
> *In a few clashes its magic powers all drained away.*
> *The Great Sage was an immortal of the Supreme Ultimate;*

The spirit was only an evil monster.
How could a demon approach a True One?
In the face of truth the evil would be destroyed.
One stirred up wind and dust to terrify a king;
The other trod on mist and cloud to blot out sun and moon.
When they dropped their guard to try for victory
Neither of them dared to show off.
The Heaven-equalling Great Sage was the abler fighter:
With a loud clash of his cudgel the spear was broken.

When his spear was quickly broken in two by Monkey's iron cudgel the evil spirit was in fear for his life, so he turned the wind right round and fled westwards.

Instead of chasing him Monkey brought his cloud down to the entrance of the underground demon shelter. "Master," he called, "you and His Majesty can come out now. The monster's run away." Only then did the Tang Priest come out of the underground shelter, supporting the king. The sky was clear, and all traces of the evil spirit had disappeared. The king went over to the table, filled a golden goblet from the wine bottle with his own hands, and presented it to Monkey with the words, "Holy monk, allow us to offer our provisional thanks." Monkey took the cup, but before he could reply an official came in from outside the western gate of the palace to report, "The western gate is on fire."

As soon as he heard this Monkey threw the wine, cup and all, up into the air. The cup fell with a clang. This so alarmed the king that he bowed to Monkey with the words, "Forgive us, holy monk, forgive us. We have treated you shabbily. The proper thing would have been to ask you into the throne hall to bow to you in thanks. We only offered you the wine here because it was to hand. Did you not throw the goblet aside because you were offended, holy monk?" "Nothing of the sort," laughed Monkey, "nothing of the sort." A moment later another official came in to report, "There's been a miraculous fall of rain. No sooner had the western gate caught fire than a heavy rainstorm put it out. The streets are running with water and it all smells of wine." "Your Majesty," said Monkey with another smile, "you thought I'd taken offence when I tossed the cup aside, but you were wrong. When the evil spirit fled westwards I didn't go after him, so he started that fire. I just used the goblet to put out the demon's fire and save the people outside the western gate. It didn't mean anything else."

The king, even more delighted than before, treated Monkey with still greater respect. He invited Sanzang and his three disciples to enter the throne hall with him, clearly intending to abdicate in their favour. "Your Majesty," said Brother Monkey with a smile, "the demon who was here just now said he was a vanguard warrior under the Evil Star Matcher who'd come here to fetch palace girls. Now he's gone back beaten he's bound to report that damned monster, who's certain to come here to fight me. I'm worried that if he comes here at the head of his hordes he'll alarm the common people and terrify Your Majesty. I'd like to go out to meet him, capture him in mid-air and bring back your queen. But I don't know the way. How far is it to his cave from here?" "We once sent some of the horsemen and infantry of our night scouts to find out what was happening," the king replied. "The return journey took them over fifty days. It's over a thousand miles away to the south." "Pig, Friar Sand," said Monkey on learning this, "stay on guard here. I'm off." "Wait another day, holy monk," said the king, grabbing hold of him. "Don't go till we have had some dried provisions prepared for you. We'll give you silver for the journey and a fast horse too." "You're talking as if I'd have to go slogging up mountains and over ridges, Your Majesty," Monkey replied. "I tell you truthfully that I can do the return journey of a thousand miles each way before a cup of wine you've poured out has had time to get cold." "Holy monk," the king replied, "I hope you won't take offence at our saying this, but your distinguished features are very much like those of an ape. How can you have such magical powers of travel?" To this Monkey replied:

"Although my body is the body of an ape,
When young I mastered the paths of life and death.
I visited all the great teachers who taught me their Way
And trained myself by night and day beside the mountain.
I took heaven as my roof and the earth as my furnace
And used both kinds of drug to complete the sun and moon,
Taking from positive and negative, joining fire and water,
Until suddenly I was aware of the Mystic Pass.
I relied entirely on the Dipper for success in my movements,
Shifting my steps by relying on the handle of that constellation.
When the time is right I lower or increase the heat,
Taking out lead and adding mercury, watching them both.
By grouping the Five Elements transformations are made;
Through combining the Four Forms the seasons can be distinguished.
The two vital forces returned to the zodiac;
The three teachings met on the golden elixir road.
When understanding of the laws came to the four limbs
The original somersault was given divine assistance.
With a single bound I could cross the Taihang mountains;
At one go I could fly across the Cloud-touching Ford.
A thousand steep ridges are no bother to me,
Nor hundreds of rivers as great as the Yangtse.
Because my transformations are impossible to stop
I can cover sixty thousand miles in a single leap."

The king was both alarmed and delighted to hear this. He presented a cup of royal wine to Monkey with a chuckle and the words, "Holy monk, you have a long and tiring journey ahead of you. Won't you drink this wine to help you on your way?" All the Great Sage had on his mind was going off to defeat the demon, he was not at all interested in drinking. "Put it down," he said. "I'll drink it when I come back." No sooner had the splendid Monkey said this than he disappeared with a whoosh. We will not describe the amazement of the king and his subjects.

Instead we tell how with a single leap Monkey was soon in sight of a tall mountain locked in mists. He brought his cloud down till he was standing on the summit. When he looked around he saw that it was a fine mountain:

Soaring to the heavens, occupying the earth,
Blocking out the sun and making clouds.
Where it soared to the heavens
The towering peak rose high;
In the earth it occupied
Its ranges spread afar.
What blocked the sun
Was the ridge dark with pines;
Where clouds were made
Was among the boulders glistening underneath the scar.
The dark pines
Were green throughout all seasons;
The glistening boulders
Would never change in many a thousand years.
Apes could often be heard howling in the night,
And evil pythons would often cross the deep ravines.
On the mountains birds sang sweetly
While the wild beasts roared.
Mountain roebuck and deer
Moved around in many a pair.
Mountain magpies and crows
Flew in dense flocks.
There was no end of mountain flowers in sight,
While mountain peaches and other fruit gleamed in season.
Steep it was, and the going impossible,
But this was still a place where evil immortals could live in retirement.

The Great Sage gazed with unbounded delight and was just about to look for the entrance to the cave when flames leapt out from a mountain hollow. In an instant the red fire blazed to the heavens, and from the flames there poured out evil smoke that was even more terrible than the fire. What splendid smoke! This is what could be seen:

The fire glared with a myriad golden lamps;
The flames leapt in a thousand crimson rainbows.
The smoke was not a stove chimney's smoke,
Nor the smoke of grass or wood,
But smoke of many colours,
Blue, red, white, black and yellow.
It blackened the columns outside the Southern Gate of Heaven,
Scorched the roofbeams in the Hall of Miraculous Mist.
It burned so hard that
Wild beasts in their dens were cooked through, skins and all,
And the forest birds lost all their plumage.
At the mere sight of this appalling smoke he wondered
How the demon king could be captured in the mountain.

Just as the Great Sage was transfixed with terror a sandstorm burst out of the mountain. What magnificent sand! It blotted out the sun and the sky. Look:

Swirling masses of it filled the sky,
Dark and turbid as it covered the earth.
The fine grains blinded the people everywhere,
While bigger cinders filled the valleys like rolling sesame seeds.
Immortal boys collecting herbs lost their companions;
Woodmen gathering firewood could not find their way home.
Even if you were holding a bright-shining pearl
It still would have blown too hard for you to see.

Monkey had been so absorbed in enjoying the view that he

did not notice the sand and cinders flying into his nose till it started tickling. Giving two great sneezes he stretched his hand out behind him, felt for two pebbles at the foot of a cliff and blocked his nostrils with them, then shook himself and turned into a fire-grabbing sparrowhawk that flew straight in among the flames and smoke, made a few swoops, and at once stopped the sand and cinders and put out the fires. He quickly turned back into himself, landed, and looked around again. This time he heard a banging and a clanging like a copper gong. "I've come the wrong way," he said to himself. "This is no den of demons. The gong sounds like an official messenger's gong. This must be the main road to some country, and that must be an official messenger on his way to deliver some document. I'll go and question him."

As Monkey went along what looked like a young demon appeared. He was holding a yellow flag, carrying a document on his back and beating a gong as he hurried along so fast he was almost flying. "So this is the so-and-so who was beating that gong," Monkey said. "I wonder what document he's delivering. I'll ask him." The splendid Great Sage shook himself and turned into a grasshopper that lightly flew over and alighted on his document bag. Here Monkey could hear the evil spirit talking garrulously to himself as he beat the gong. "Our king is thoroughly vicious. Three years ago he took the Golden Queen from the Kingdom of Purpuria, but fate's been against him and he hasn't been able to get his hands on her. The poor palace ladies he took had to suffer on her behalf. He killed two of them who came, then the next four. He demanded them the year before last, last year and earlier this year. When he sent for two more this time he found his match. The vanguard warrior who went to demand the palace ladies was beaten by someone called Sun the Novice or whatever. He didn't get his palace girls. It made our king so angry he wants to wage a war on Purpuria. He's sent me with this declaration of war. Their king will be all right if he doesn't fight, but if he does fight it'll be a disaster for him. When our king uses his fire, smoke and sandstorms their king, ministers and common people will all die.

Then we'll take over their city. Our king will be its monarch and we'll be his subjects. But even though we'll get official posts it goes against Heaven."

Monkey was very pleased to hear this. "So there are even some decent evil spirits," he thought. "That last remark — 'it goes against Heaven' — was very good. I wonder what he meant when he said that fate has been against their king and he hasn't been able to get his hands on the Golden Queen. Let me ask him some questions." With a whining buzz he flew away from the evil spirit to a point some miles ahead of him on the road, shook himself and turned into a Taoist boy:

He wore his hair in two bunches
And a robe of a hundred patches.
He beat on a fisherman's drum
As he sang some Taoist snatches.

As Monkey came round the slope towards the little devil he raised his hands in greeting and said, "Where are you going, sir? What official document is that you're delivering?" The devil seemed to recognize him as he stopped beating his gong, returned his greeting and said with a titter, "Our king's sent me to Purpuria with a declaration of war." "Has that woman from Purpuria slept with the king yet?" Monkey asked, pressing on with his questioning. "When he brought her here the other year," the little devil replied, "an immortal gave the Golden Queen a magic robe as her wedding dress. As soon as she put it on she was covered from head to foot with spikes. Our king didn't dare so much as caress her. Even the slightest touch makes his hand hurt. I don't know why it happened. So from that year till this he hasn't had her. When his vanguard fighter was sent this morning to demand two more palace ladies to serve her he was beaten. Our king was so angry he sent me with this declaration of war. He's going to fight him tomorrow." "So is the king in a bad mood?" Monkey asked. "Yes, he's in a bad mood back there," said the little devil. "You ought to go and sing him some Taoist songs to cheer him up."

The splendid Monkey put his arms in his sleeves, ready to

go, while the evil spirit went on his way beating his gong as before. Monkey then turned murderous. He brought out his cudgel, turned round and hit the little devil on the back of his head. The unfortunate demon's head was smashed to a pulp. The blood gushed out as his skin split open and his neck was broken. He was dead. Monkey then put his cudgel away and said to himself with regret, "I was in too much of a hurry. I never asked him his name. Too bad." He took the declaration of war from the body and put it in his sleeve. Then he hid the yellow flag and the gong in the undergrowth by the path and was dragging the body by its ankles to throw it down the ravine when he heard something clinking. An ivory tablet inlaid with gold could be seen at the demon's waist. The writing on it read:

> *This is our trusted subordinate Gocome. He is of short stature and has a spotty and unbearded face. This tablet is to be kept permanently at his waist. Anyone without this tablet is an impostor.*

"So the wretch was called Gocome. But after being hit by this cudgel of mine he's gone and won't be coming back." He then undid the ivory tablet, fastened it at his own waist, and was just about to throw the body down when he remembered the terrible fire and smoke and decided he could not bring himself to look for the cave palace. He raised the cudgel, rammed it into the demon's chest, lifted him up into the air and went straight back to Purpuria to announce his first success. Watch him as he goes whistling back to that country.

Pig was in front of the throne room guarding the king and his master when suddenly he turned round to see Monkey carrying the demon through the air. "Hey," he complained, "that was an easy piece of work. If I'd known you were going to get him I'd have done it and got the credit." Before he had finished speaking Monkey brought the cloud down and threw the demon at the foot of the steps. Pig ran over and struck the body with his rake. "I'll take the credit for that," he said. "You? The credit?" Monkey replied. "Don't try to rob me of it," Pig said

I've got proof. Can't you see the nine holes I made in him with my rake?" "See if he's got a head," said Monkey. "So he doesn't have a head," Pig replied. "Now I know why he never moved when I hit him." "Where's the master?" Monkey asked. "Talking to the king in the throne hall," said Pig. "Go and ask him to come out," said Monkey, and Pig hurried up into the hall. At Pig's nod Sanzang rose to his feet and came out at once to see Monkey, who thrust the declaration of war into his sleeve with the words, "Look after this, Master, and don't let the king see it."

Before the words were all out of his mouth the king too came out of the hall to greet Monkey and say, "You're back, holy monk, venerable sir. How did the capture of the demon go?" "Isn't that a demon at the foot of the steps?" Monkey asked, pointing. "I killed him." "True," said the king, "it is the body of an evil spirit, but it isn't the Evil Star Matcher. We have twice seen the Evil Star Matcher with our own eyes. He is eighteen feet tall and nine feet across the shoulders. His face shines like gold and his voice is like thunder. He's not a miserable little wretch like that." "You Majesty is right," Monkey replied, "this isn't him. It's just a little messenger devil I happened to meet. I killed him and brought him back as a trophy." "Splendid," said the king, who was very pleased indeed, "splendid. This is the first success. We have often sent people out to find out what is happening but they never discover anything. Then you just have to go out, holy monk, to bring one straight back. You really do have divine powers." "Fetch some warm wine," he ordered, "and give it to the reverend gentlemen."

"Never mind about the wine," said Monkey. "I want to ask Your Majesty whether the Golden Queen left any keepsakes when she went. If so, give me some." The word "keepsakes" cut the king to the heart. He could not help sobbing aloud with tears pouring down as he replied:

"When we were enjoying the festival that year
The Evil Star Matcher gave a mighty shout,
He took our wife to be his bandit queen;

To save the land we had to send her out.
We had no time for talk or parting words,
Nor could I see her off along her way.
She left no keepsake and no perfume bag;
We would be lonely here until today."

"Your Majesty is here," Monkey said, "so why upset yourself? If the queen didn't leave any keepsake there must be some things in the palace that she's specially fond of. Give me one of them." "What do you want it for?" the king asked. "That demon king's magic powers are quite something," said Monkey, "and from what I've seen of his fire, smoke and sand he'll be really hard to capture. Even if I do capture him the queen might refuse to come back here with a stranger like me. I must have some favourite thing of hers so that she'll trust me and let me bring her back. That's why I want it." "There is a pair of gold bracelets in her dressing room in the Sunlight Palace that she used to wear," the king replied. "She only took them off that day as it was the Dragonboat Festival and she was going to wear multicoloured threads instead. She was very fond of those bracelets. They have been put away in her dressing table. We have not been able to bear the sight of them since she left us: seeing them is like seeing her lovely face, and it makes us feel even more ill than ever." "Say no more," Monkey replied, "and have the bracelets brought here. If you can bring yourself to part with them, give me both. If you can't I'll take just one." The king ordered the Jade Queen to fetch them, which she did, handing them to the king. At the sight of them he called out, "My beloved and tender-hearted queen," several times, then handed them to Monkey, who took them and put them on his arm.

The splendid Great Sage could not stay to drink the celebratory wine, but whistled back to Mount Unicorn on his somersault cloud. Now he had no interest in the view as he headed straight for the cave palace. While he was walking along he heard noisy shouts so he stopped to take a careful look around. About five hundred of the soldiers of all ranks guarding the entrance to Horndog Cave were

Drawn up in massed array,
In close order.
Drawn up in massed array they held their weapons
Gleaming in the sun.
In close order they unfurled their banners
That fluttered in the breeze.
Tiger and bear generals did transformations;
Leopard and tiger-cat marshals were full of spirit.
Fiercely savage were the wolves;
The elephants were mighty and imposing.
Crafty hares and water-deer swung sword and halberd;
Great snakes and pythons carried cutlass and bow.
Orang-utans that understood human speech
Controlled the formations and gathered intelligence.

When Monkey saw this he ventured no closer but went straight back the way he had come. Do you know why? Not because he was afraid of them. He went back to where he had killed the little devil, recovered the yellow flag and the gong, made a hand spell, thought of what he wanted to become, faced the wind, shook himself and turned into the likeness of Gocome. Then he started hitting the gong as he strode straight back towards Horndog Cave. He was going to look at the layout of the cave when he heard an orang-utan say, "You're back, Gocome." "Yes," Monkey had to reply. "Hurry up," the orang-utan said. "Our king is waiting in the Flaying Pavilion to hear what you have to report." As soon as he heard this Monkey hurried straight in through the main gate beating his gong and looking around. He saw that rooms and halls had been carved out of the beetling crag. On either side bloomed rare and precious flowers, while all around stood ancient cypresses and tall pines. Before he realized it he was through the inner gate, and suddenly looking up he saw a pavilion made light by the eight windows in it. In the pavilion was a splendid chair inlaid with gold on which a demon king was sitting upright. He was a truly terrifying sight. This is what he looked like:

A shimmering red glow rose from the top of his head;
A mighty and murderous air burst from his chest.
Sharp were the fangs that protruded from his mouth;
Red smoke rose from the scorched hair at his temples.
The bristles of his moustache were like embedded arrows;
His body was covered with hair like brushed-up felt.
Eyes bulged like bells to rival the Evil Star:
Hands held an iron mace like Mahadeva.

When Monkey saw the evil spirit he acted towards him in an offhand way, showing no trace of respect, but looking away and keeping on hitting his gong. "So you're back, are you?" said the demon king. Monkey did not reply. "Gocome," the demon king asked again, "you're back, are you?" Still Monkey did not reply. The demon king then went over to him, grabbed him and said, "Why are you still beating your gong now you're back home? And why don't you answer when I ask you a question?"

"What do you mean by your 'Why? Why? Why?' " Monkey replied. "I told you I didn't want to go but you insisted. When I got there I saw huge numbers of foot soldiers and cavalry drawn up in order of battle. As soon as I was spotted they shouted, 'Seize the demon! Seize the demon!' They pushed and shoved and dragged and carried me into the city, where I saw their king. He told them to cut my head off, but luckily his two groups of advisers said that in international conflicts envoys should not be executed, so I was spared. They took the declaration of war, marched me out of the city, gave me thirty strokes in front of their army, and let me come back here to report. Before long they'll be here to fight you." "In other words," the monster said, "you had a bad time. I don't blame you for refusing to answer when I asked you those questions." "It wasn't that," said Monkey. "The reason I didn't answer was because of the pain." "How strong are their forces?" the demon king asked. "I was reeling from shock and too badly frightened by the beating to be able to count them," Monkey replied. "All I could see were masses of weapons drawn up there:

Bows and arrows, spears and sabres, suits of armour,
Dagger-axes, halberds, swords and tasselled banners.
Pikes, partisans, helmets,
Axes, round shields, and iron caltrops.
Long staves,
Short cudgels,
Steel forks, cannons and casques.
They were wearing tall boots, hats and quilted jackets,
And carrying cudgels, small pellet-bows and maces of bronze."

"That's neither here nor there," laughed the demon king when he heard this. "Weapons like that can be finished off in a single blaze. Go and tell the Golden Queen all about it and ask her not to upset herself. Ever since she heard me lose my temper this morning and decide to go to war she's been crying her eyes out. Tell her that their army is so fierce and brave that they're bound to beat us. That'll calm her down for a while."

This delighted Monkey, who thought, "Just what I want." Watch him as he goes the way he knows, through the side door and across the hall. Inside there were tall buildings: it was not like outside. He went straight to the women's quarters at the back, where he saw from a distance a handsome and decorated doorway. That was where the Golden Queen lived. When he went to see her there were two groups of fox and deer spirits dressed like beautiful women to wait on her. The queen sat in the middle with her fragrant cheeks in her hands and tears pouring from both her eyes. Indeed, she had

A beautiful face so soft and charming,
A bewitching countenance so fair.
But her raven-black hair was uncombed
And piled untidily on her head;
She did not want to dress up
And wore no hair ornaments or rings.
Her face was unpowdered,

And she wore no rouge.
Her hair was not oiled
But all in a tangle.
She pouted her cherry lips,
Ground her silver teeth,
Frowned with her brows like moth antennae,
And let her eyes sparkle with tears.
All her heart
Was filled with memories of Purpuria's king;
All the time
She longed to escape from the net that held her.
Truly,
Ill-fated have been many lovely ladies
Left in their wordless grief to face the eastern wind.

Monkey went up to her and greeted her with a "Hello." "You impudent boorish freak," said the queen. "I remember how when I was living in splendour with my king in Purpuria even the king's tutor and the prime minister had to prostrate themselves in the dust when they met me: they would never have dared look me in the face. How dare you say 'Hello' to me, you lout? Where are you from, you coarse beast?" "Please don't be angry, ma'am," the serving women said. "He's one of His Majesty's most trusted lieutenants. His name is Go-come. He was the one who was sent with the declaration of war this morning." At this the queen controlled her temper and asked, "Did you go inside Purpuria when you delivered the declaration?" "I took it straight to the capital and right into the throne hall," said Monkey. "I saw the king himself and got an answer from him." "What did the king say when you saw him?" the queen asked. "I have already told His Majesty here what he said about war and about the dispositions of their forces," Monkey replied. "But there was also a private message from the king, who misses you, ma'am. There's something private I have come to report to you, but with all these attendants around this is no place to talk."

When the queen heard this she dismissed her foxes and deer.

Brother Monkey shut the door of the palace, rubbed his face, and turned back into himself. "Don't be afraid of me," he said to her. "I'm a monk sent by the Great Tang in the east to see the Buddha and fetch the scriptures at the Thunder Monastery in India. My master is Tang Sanzang, the younger brother of the Tang Emperor. I'm Sun Wukong, his senior disciple. When we were in your capital to present our passport for approval I saw a notice calling for doctors that your king and his ministers had posted. Then I used my medical skills to cure the illness he had contracted from missing you. When we were drinking at the banquet he gave to thank me he told me that you had been carried off by the evil spirit. As I can subdue dragons and tigers I was specially invited to capture the demon, rescue you and take you back to your country. I was the one who defeated the vanguard and killed the little devil. When I saw from outside the gates how ferocious the demon king was I turned myself into Gocome's double and came here to bring you a message."

The queen said nothing when she heard this. Then Monkey produced the bracelets and presented them to her with both hands. "If you don't believe me, just look; where did these come from?" he asked. As soon as she saw them the queen burst into tears, came down from where she was sitting, bowed to him in thanks and said, "Reverend sir, if you really can save me and get me back to court I will remember my deep debt of gratitude to you even when I'm old and toothless."

"Let me ask you something," said Monkey. "What treasure does he use to produce that fire, smoke and sand?" "It's no treasure," the queen said, "just three golden bells. As soon as he shakes the first one three thousand feet of burning flames shoot out. When he shakes the second one a three-thousand-foot column of smoke gushes out to kipper people. And when he shakes it the third time a blinding three-thousand-foot sandstorm blows up. The fire and smoke are nothing much, but the sand is lethal. If it gets up your nostrils it can kill you." "It's terrible," Monkey said, "terrible. I've experienced it and I had to sneeze a couple of times. I wonder where he keeps the bells." "He never puts them down," the queen replied. "He keeps them at his waist whether he's going somewhere, staying at home, sitting down or sleeping. They are always with him." "If you still care for Purpuria and want to see your king again you must forget about your distress and grief for the moment," said Monkey. "Make yourself look attractive and happy. Talk to him like a loving wife and get him to give you the bells to look after. When I've stolen them and defeated the monster I'll take you back to be reunited with your royal husband so that you can live in peace together."

The queen did as Monkey said while he turned himself back into the demon king's trusted lieutenant, opened the doors again and called the serving women back in. "Go to the pavilion at the front, Gocome," the queen said, "and ask His Majesty to come here as I've something to say to him." The splendid Monkey assented and went to the Flaying Pavilion, where he said to the evil spirit, "Your Majesty, Her Majesty would like to see you." "All she usually does is curse me, so why is she sending for me now?" the demon king happily asked. "When she asked me about the king of Purpuria I told her, 'He doesn't want you any more: he's got a new queen now.' When she heard that Her Majesty stopped missing him. That's why she sent me out with this invitation." "You're very able," the demon king said, "and when we've destroyed Purpuria I'll make you my high chancellor in personal attendance."

Monkey thanked the demon king for his kindness and hurried to the door of the living quarters at the back, where the queen greeted him with happy smiles and her hands on his arms. The king stepped back with an awkward noise. "Don't," he said, "don't. I'm very grateful for this sign of your affection, ma'am, but I don't dare stand next to you in case it hurts my hand." "Sit down, Your Majesty," the queen said. "I have something to say to you." "There's no objection to you speaking," the demon king replied. "I'm very much obliged to Your Majesty for condescending to love me," she said. "For three years now you have not shared my pillow although we were fated from our earlier lives to be married. I never expected that Your Majesty would treat me as a stranger instead of your wife. I remember that when I was queen of Purpuria the king gave all the valuable tribute from foreign countries to the queen to look after when he had seen it. But you have no treasures here. The servants wear marten hides and feed on blood. I have seen no fine silks, brocades, gold or pearls here. All the covers and blankets are of skins and felt. Or perhaps you do have some treasures that you won't let me see or look after because you regard me as a stranger. They say you have three bells. I think they must be treasures. Why do you always keep them with you, even when you're travelling or sitting down? There's no reason why you shouldn't give them to me to look after. I can give them to you when you need them. That would be one way of being a wife to you and it would show that we trust each other in our hearts. The only reason why you don't do this must because you regard me as an outsider."

At this the demon king burst into loud laughter, then bowed to her and said, "Ma'am, you're justified in your complaint. Here are the treasures, and today I'm giving them to you to look after." He undid his clothing to bring them out. Monkey watched with unwavering eyes as the monster pulled two or three layers of clothing aside to bring out the three bells that he carried next to his skin. Putting cotton-wool in to muffle them he wrapped them up in a piece of leopard skin and handed them to the queen with the words, "They're nothing, but please look after them very carefully. Whatever you do don't shake them." "I understand," the queen replied as she accepted them. "I shall keep them on my dressing table and nobody will move them at all." Then she gave these orders: "My little ones, lay on a banquet. His Majesty and I are going to have a few drinks to celebrate our happy union." At once the serving women brought in fruit, vegetables and the flesh of water deer, raccoon-dogs, deer and hare and poured out coconut toddy that they offered them. The queen made herself so bewitchingly attractive that she swept the evil spirit off his feet.

Monkey meanwhile went to fetch the bells. Feeling and groping, he found his way to the dressing-table, gently took the three bells, crept out through the doors of the inner quarters and left the cave palace. When he reached the Flaying Pavilion there was nobody about, so he opened the leopard-skin wrapper to have a look. One of the bells was as big as a teacup and the other two the size of fists. With reckless folly he tore the cotton-wool apart. There was a loud clang and smoke, fire and sand came gushing out. Desperately Monkey tried to stop them but could do nothing. The pavilion was by now ablaze, sending the evil spirits on the gates all crowding in alarm inside the inner quarters. "Put the fire out," said the demon king, who was badly rattled. As he rushed out to look he saw that Gocome had taken the golden bells, went up to him and shouted, "Dirty slave! Why did you steal my precious golden bells? What sort of nonsense are you up to? Arrest him!" The tiger and bear generals, the leopard and tiger-cat marshals, the elephants, grey wolves, cunning water deer, crafty hares, long snakes, great pythons, orang-utans and all the other troops on the gates rushed him in a crowd.

Monkey was thrown into panic. Dropping the golden bells he turned back into himself, pulled out his gold-banded as-you-will cudgel, went and charged at them, going through his cudgel routines and lashing out wildly. The demon king took his treasures back and ordered, "Shut the main gates." At this some of the demons shut the gates and others went into battle. Unable to get away, Monkey put his cudgel away, shook himself and turned into a silly fly that attached itself to a spot on the stone wall which was not burning. None of the demons could find him. "Your Majesty," they reported, "the thief's got away, the thief's got away." "Did he get out through the gates?" the demon king asked. "The front gates are firmly locked and bolted," the demons replied. "He can't have got out through them." "Make a careful search," said the demon king, and while some of them fetched water to douse the fire the others made a close search but found no trace of him.

"What sort of thief is he?" the demon king asked with fury. "He's got a hell of a nerve, turning himself into Gocome's double, coming in here to report back to me, then staying with me till he found a chance to steal my treasures. It's lucky he didn't take them out, if he'd taken them over the mountain top and there had been a heavenly wind it would have been a disaster." "Your Majesty's good fortune is divine," said the tiger general, stepping forward. "It was because our luck has not yet run out that he was discovered." Then the bear marshal came forward to say, "Your Majesty, the thief was none other than the Sun Wukong who beat our vanguard warrior. I think he must have run into Gocome when he was on his way, killed him, taken his yellow flag, gong and ivory tablet, and turned into his double to come here and deceive Your Majesty." "Yes, yes," the demon king replied, "you're clearly right. Little ones," he ordered, "make another careful search and be on your guard. Whatever you do, don't open the gates and let him out." It is rightly said that

By being too clever one becomes a fool;
What was once a joke can turn out to be real.

If you don't know how Brother Monkey got out through the demons' gates, listen to the explanation in the next instalment.

CHAPTER SEVENTY-ONE

Under a false name Monkey beats the demon hound;
Guanyin appears to subdue the demon king.

Matter has always been empty;
Emptiness said to be matter is only natural.
When one penetrates the dhyana of matter's emptiness
There is no need for cinnabar to be refined into elixir.
Rest not when pursuing perfection of virtue and conduct;
Endure suffering to achieve hard-won skills.
Sometimes one only turns to heaven when one's actions are complete,
To win an unchanging and immortal face.

The story tells how the Evil Star Matcher had the front and back gates tightly closed while Monkey was hunted for. The din went on till dusk, but no sign of him did they find. The demon king sat in the Flaying Pavilion, where he called his demons together and issued orders to the guards on all the gates to carry bells, shout passwords, beat drums and strike clappers. Everyone was to have an arrow on his bowstring or a sword unsheathed as he took his turn to keep watch during the night. Sun Wukong, who had turned into a fly, was sitting by the gates. Seeing how strict the security was at the front gates he spread his wings and flew to the gateway of the living quarters to take a look. He saw the Golden Queen slumped across a low table, the tears flowing down as she wept quietly in her sorrow, so he flew inside and landed lightly on the loose black clouds of her hair to listen to what she was crying about. A moment later she said tearfully, "My lord, you and I,

Burnt in an earlier life the incense of separation,
And now I have encountered an evil demon king.

For three years I have been gone: when will we two be reunited?
Great is the grief of mandarin ducks that are parted.
Just when the priest had brought me your message
Our union has been severed once more and the monkey is dead.
Because he was too curious about the golden bells
I long for you now more desperately than ever."

When he heard this Monkey went behind her ear, where he whispered, "Don't be afraid, Your Majesty. I'm the holy monk, the venerable Sun Wukong, who was sent from your country. I'm still alive. It was all because I was too impatient. I went to your dressing table and stole the golden bells. While you were drinking with the demon king I sneaked out to the pavilion in the front, but I couldn't restrain myself from opening them up to take a look at them. I didn't mean to, but I tore the cotton wool muffling the bells, and the moment they rang flame, smoke and sand came gushing out. I panicked, threw the bells down, turned back into myself, and tried hard to fight my way out with my iron cudgel. When I failed and was scared they'd kill me I turned into a fly, and hid on the door pivot till just now. The demon king has made the security precautions even stricter and he won't open the doors. Will you act like a wife to him and lure him in here to sleep so that I can escape and find some other way of rescuing you?"

When the queen heard this she shivered and shook, and her hair stood on end as if a spirit were pulling it; she was terrified, as if her heart was being pounded by a pestle. "Are you a man or a ghost?" she asked, the tears streaming down. "Neither man nor ghost," he replied. "At the moment I've turned into a fly and I'm here. Don't be afraid. Hurry up and ask the demon king here." The queen still refused to believe him. "Stop appearing in this nightmare," she said in a low voice through her tears. "I'm not in a nightmare," said Monkey. "If you don't believe me put your hand out and open it. I'll jump down into it for you to see." The queen then put out her open hand. Monkey flew down and landed lightly on her jade palm. He was just like

A black bean on a lotus flower,
A bee resting on a peony blossom,
A raisin fallen into a hydrangea,
A black spot on a wild lily stalk.

The queen raised her hand and said, "Holy monk." "I'm the holy monk transformed," Monkey replied. Only then did the queen believe him. "When I invite the demon king here what are you going to do?" she asked. "There's an old saying that there's nothing like liquor for ending a life," Monkey replied, "and another that there's nothing like liquor for solving any problem. Liquor's very useful stuff. The best thing is to give him plenty to drink. Call one of your personal slave-girls in and let me have a look at her so I can make myself look like her and wait on you. Then I'll be able to make my move."

The queen did as he told her. "Spring Beauty, where are you?" she called, and a fox with a beautiful face came in round the screen, knelt down and said, "What orders did Your Majesty call me in to receive?" "Tell them to come in and light the silk lanterns, burn some musk, and help me into the front room," the queen said. "Then I shall ask His Majesty to bed." Spring Beauty went to the front and called seven or eight deer and fox spirits who lined up on either side of her. They carried two pairs of lanterns and one pair of portable incense-burners. By the time the queen bowed to them with her hands together the Great Sage had already flown off. Spreading his wings, the splendid Monkey flew straight to the top of Spring Beauty's head, where he pulled out one of his hairs, blew a magic breath on it, and called, "Change!" It turned into a sleep insect that landed lightly on Spring Beauty's face. Now when sleep insects reach a human face they crawl into the nostrils, and once they are inside the person goes to sleep. Spring Beauty did indeed start feeling sleepy. She could not keep on her feet, but swayed about and felt dozy as she hurried to where she had been resting before, collapsed head first and fell into a deep sleep. Brother

Monkey then jumped down, shook himself, turned into Spring Beauty's exact likeness and went back round the screen to line up with the others.

As the Golden Queen walked into the front part of the palace a little devil saw her and reported to the Evil Star Matcher, "The queen's here, Your Majesty." The demon king hurried out of the Flaying Pavilion to greet her. "Your Majesty," the queen said, "the smoke and fire have been put out and there's no sign of the thief. As it's late now I've come to urge you to come to bed." "How considerate you are, my queen," the monster replied, utterly delighted to see her. "The thief was Sun Wukong who defeated my vanguard warrior then killed my lieutenant and came here disguised as him to fool us. We've searched but can't find a trace of him. It makes me feel uneasy." "The wretch must have got away," the queen replied. "Relax, Your Majesty, stop worrying, and come to bed."

Seeing the queen standing there and inviting him so earnestly the demon king could not refuse too insistently, so he told the other demons to be careful with the fires and lamps and be on their guard against robbers before he went to the living quarters at the back with the queen. Monkey, disguised as Spring Beauty, led their way with the other slave girls. "Bring wine for His Majesty," the queen said. "He's exhausted." "Indeed I am," said the demon king with a smile, "indeed I am. Fetch some at once. It'll calm our nerves." The imitation Spring Beauty and the other servants then laid out fruit and high meat and set a table and chairs. The queen raised a cup and the demon king did likewise; each gave the other a drink from their own. The imitation Spring Beauty, who was standing beside them, said as she held the jug, "As tonight is the first time Your Majesties have given each other a drink from your own cups I hope that you will each drain them dry for double happiness." They did indeed both refill their cups and drain them again. "As this is so happy an occasion for Your Majesties why don't we slave girls sing and dance for you?" the imitation Spring Beauty suggested.

Before the words were all out of her mouth melodious voices could be heard as the singing and dancing began. The two of them drank a lot more before the queen called for the singing and dancing to end. The slave girls divided themselves into their groups and went to line up outside the screen, leaving only the imitation Spring Beauty to hold the jug and serve them wine. The queen and the demon king spoke to each other like husband and wife, and the queen was so full of sensuality that the demon king's bones turned soft and his sinews went numb. The only trouble was that the poor demon was not lucky enough to enjoy her favours. Indeed, it was a case of "happiness over nothing, like a cat biting a piss bubble".

After talking and laughing for a while the queen asked, "Were the treasures damaged, Your Majesty?" "Those are treasures that were cast long, long ago," the demon king said, "so they couldn't possibly be damaged. All that happened was that the thief tore the cotton wool that was muffling the bells and the leopard skin wrapper was burnt." "Where have they been put away?" the queen asked. "No need for that," the demon king replied. "I carry them at my waist." Hearing this, the imitation Spring Beauty pulled out a handful of his hairs, chewed them up into little bits, crept closer to the demon king, put the pieces of hair on the demon's body, blew three magic breaths, said "Change!" very quietly, and turned the pieces of hair into three revolting pests: lice, fleas and bedbugs. They all made for the demon king's body and started biting his skin wildly. Itching unbearably, the demon king put his hands inside his clothing to rub the irritation. He caught a few of the lice between his fingers and took them to a lamp for a closer look.

When the queen saw them she said mockingly, "Your Majesty, your shirt must be filthy. It can't have been washed for ages. I expect that's why they're there." "I've never had insects like these before," he said in embarrassment. "I would have to make a fool of myself tonight." "What do you mean, making a fool of yourself, Your Majesty?" the queen said with a smile. "As the saying goes, even the emperor has three imperial lice. Undress and I'll catch them for you." The demon king really did undo his belt and take his clothes off.

The imitation Spring Beauty was standing beside the demon king looking closely at the fleas leaping around between each layer of clothing, on which were rows of enormous bedbugs. Lice and nits were crowded as closely together as ants coming out of their nest. When the demon king took off the third layer of clothing and revealed his flesh the golden bells were also swarming with countless insects. "Your Majesty," said the imitation Spring Beauty, "hand me the bells so that I can catch the lice on them for you." The demon king was so overcome with shame and alarm that he handed the three bells to Spring Beauty, not noticing that she was an impostor.

The imitation Spring Beauty took the bells and made a long show of catching lice. When she saw the demon king looking down to shake his clothes she hid the golden bells, pulled out a hair and turned it into three more bells just like the originals that she carried to the lamp to examine. She then wriggled, braced herself, put the lice, bedbugs and fleas back on her body and returned the imitation bells to the monster. He took them but was still too befuddled to see that they were copies. Passing them with both his hands to the queen he said, "Put them away now, but be very careful with them, not like before." The queen took the bells, quietly opened the chest, put them inside, and locked them in with a golden lock. Then she drank several more cups of wine with the demon king. "Dust and clean the ivory bed," she ordered the serving women, "and spread the brocade quilt. His Majesty and I are going to bed." The demon king expressed his thanks but said, "I have no such luck. I don't dare go with you. I'll take one of the palace women with me and go to bed in the western part of the palace. I wish you a good night by yourself, ma'am." With that each of them went to bed, and we will say no more of that.

Meanwhile the successful imitation Spring Beauty tucked the treasures into her belt and turned back into Monkey. He shook himself, took back the sleep insect, and headed for the front of the palace, where nightsticks and bells sounded together to mark the third watch. Splendid Monkey made himself invisible by making a spell with his hands and saying the words of it. Going straight to the gates he saw that they were very firmly locked and bolted, so he brought out his gold-banded cudgel, pointed it at the door and made unlocking magic. The gates swung easily open. Hurrying outside he stood by the gates and shouted two or three times at the top of his voice, "Evil Star Matcher, give us back our Golden Queen."

This startled all the devils, who hurried to look and saw that the gates were open. Quickly they fetched lamps to find the locks and fasten the gates once more. Several of them were sent running back inside to report, "Your Majesty, there's someone outside the main gates shouting your title and demanding the Golden Queen." The slave girls hurried out to say very quietly, "Stop yelling. His Majesty's only just gone to sleep." Monkey gave another loud shout at the front gates, but the little devils still dared not disturb their master. This happened three or four times over, but they never went in to report. The Great Sage kept up his din till daybreak, by when his patience was exhausted and he swung his iron cudgel to hit the gates. This so alarmed the demons big and small that while some of them barricaded the gates the others went in to report. As soon as the demon king woke up and heard the cacophonous din he got up, dressed and emerged from his bed-curtains to ask, "What's all the shouting about?" "Sir," said the kneeling slave girls, "someone's been shouting and cursing outside the cave half the night. We don't know who it is. Now he's attacking the gates."

As the demon king went out through the gates of the palace several panic-stricken little devils appeared to kowtow to him and say, "There's someone shouting and cursing outside. He's demanding the Golden Queen, and if we say so much as half a 'no' he goes on and on at us, swearing in a thoroughly horrible way. When Your Majesty still hadn't come out at daybreak he got so desperate he started attacking the gates." "Don't open them," the demon king said. "Go and ask him where he's from and what he's called. Report back as quickly as you can."

The little devils hurried off to ask through the gates, "Who are you, knocking at our gates?" "I'm your grandpa sent by Purpuria to take the Golden Queen back to her own country," Monkey replied. When the little devils heard this they reported it to the demon king, who went back to the living quarters at the back to question the queen about why the attacker had come. The queen had only just arisen and had not yet done her hair or washed when slave girls came in to report, "His Majesty's here." The queen hastily tidied up her clothes and let her black tresses hang loose as she went outside to greet him. He had just sat down and had not yet asked her any questions when little demons were heard again asking, "The Grand Par from over there has smashed the gates down." How many officers are there in your country, ma'am?" The demon king asked with a smile. "Inside the palace there are forty-eight brigades of horse and foot, and a thousand good officers; and there are ever so many marshals and commanders on the frontiers." the queen replied. "Are any called Grand Par?" the demon king asked. "When I was in the palace all I knew about was helping His Majesty in the inner quarters and instructing the consorts and concubines every morning and evening," the queen said. "There were no end of things happening outside. How could I possibly remember the names?" "This one calls himself Grand Par," the demon king replied. "There's no such name I can think of in the book *The Hundred Surnames*. You're a very intelligent and well-born lady, ma'am, and you've lived in a royal palace. You must have read a lot of books. Can you remember coming across that name in any of them?" "There's a passage in the *Thousand Word Classic* that goes, 'received grand instruction'," the queen replied. "I think that must refer to him."

"I'm sure you're right," the demon king said with pleasure, "I'm sure you're right." He then got up, took his leave of the queen, went to the Flaying Pavilion, fastened his armour on neatly, mustered his devil soldiers, had the gates opened, and went straight outside with his flower-scattering battle-axe in his hand. "Who's the Grand Par from Purpuria?" he yelled stridently at the top of his voice. Grasping his gold-banded cudgel in his right hand and pointing with his left Monkey replied, "What are you shouting at me for, nephew?" The sight of him drove the demon king into a fury. "Damn you," he shouted:

"You've a face just like a monkey's;
You resemble a macaque.
A ghost is what you look like;
Don't try to knock me back."

"Impudent devil," laughed Monkey, "trying to bully your superiors and push your master around. You're blind. I remember how when I made havoc in Heaven five hundred years ago all the nine heavenly generals only dared speak to me with the greatest respect. If I make you call me Grandpa I'm letting you off lightly." "Tell me your name immediately," the demon king shouted. "What fighting skills have you got that give you the nerve to come rampaging here?" "You'd have done better not to ask me what I'm called," Monkey replied. "But as you insist on me telling you I'm afraid you'll be in a hopeless mess. Come here and stand still while I tell you:

Heaven and earth were the parents that bore me;
My foetus was formed from the sun and moon's essence.
The magic rock was pregnant for years beyond number;
Strange indeed was the miraculous root's gestation.
When I was born the Three Positives were at their height;
Now I have been converted all is in harmony.
Once I was declared the chief of all the demons,
Who bowed to me by the red cliff as subduer of monsters.
The Jade Emperor issued a decree of summons,
And the Great White Planet came with the edict,
Inviting me to Heaven to take up my office,
But as Protector of the Horses I had no joy.
When I first planned rebellion in my mountain cave
Boldly I led my armies against the Jade Emperor.
The Pagoda-carrying Heavenly King and Prince Nezha
Were utterly helpless when they fought against me.
Then the White Planet made a new suggestion,

And brought another edict urging me to make peace.
I was made Great Sage Equalling Heaven,
And proclaimed as one of the pillars of the state.
Because I disrupted the banquet of peaches
And stole elixir when drunk I met with disaster.
Lord Lao Zi submitted a memorial in person,
And the Queen Mother of the West did homage to the throne.
Knowing that I was running riot with the law,
They mustered heavenly forces and issued movement orders.
A hundred thousand vicious stars and evil planets
Were packed in close array with their swords and their halberds.
Heaven-and-earth nets were spread across the mountain
As all of the soldiers raised their weapons together.
A bout of bitter fighting left neither side the victor,
So Guanyin recommended the warrior Erlang.
The two of us fought together for mastery;
He was helped by the Seven Brothers who come from Plum Hill.
Each of us played the hero and did our transformations:
The three sages at the gates of Heaven opened the clouds.
Then Lord Lao Zi dropped his diamond noose,
And the gods led me as a prisoner to the steps of the throne-hall.
They did not bother with a detailed indictment:
The sentence was death by a thousand cuts.
Axe and hammer could not kill me,
And I was unharmed by sword or sabre.
Fire and thunderbolts were neither here nor there;
They had no way to destroy my immortal body.
I was taken under escort to the Tushita Heaven,
And all was arranged to refine me in the furnace.
Only when full time was up did they open up the vessel,
And I came bounding out from the middle of the crucible.

In my hands I was wielding this as-you-will cudgel
As I somersaulted up to the Jade Emperor's throne.
All the stars and constellations went into hiding,
And I could play the vandal in the palaces of Heaven.
The Miraculous Investigator rushed to invite the Buddha,
Then Sakyamuni and I both displayed our powers.
Turning my somersaults in the palm of his hand
I roamed all over the heavens before my return.
The Buddha then, using both foresight and deception,
Crushed and held me at the ends of the heavens.
After a period of over five hundred years
My body was delivered and I could once more play up.
Guarding the Tang Priest on his journey to the West,
Brother Sun Wukong is very intelligent.
I subdue the demons on the westward road:
Every evil spirit is struck with terror."

When the demon king heard him tell that he was Sun Wukong he said, "So you're the so-and-so who made havoc in Heaven. If you were released to guard the Tang Priest on his journey west then you should be on your way there. Why are you being such a busybody and making trouble for me? You're acting as if you were the slave of Purpuria. By coming here you've thrown your life away." "Thieving damned monster," Monkey shouted back. "You don't know what you're talking about. I was politely invited to help by the king of Purpuria. He addressed me very respectfully and treated me well. I'm a thousand times higher than that king. He treated me as if I were his father and mother or a god. How can you say I'm acting like a slave? I'll get you, you monster, for bullying your superiors and trying to push your master around. Stay there and take this from your grandpa." The monster then moved his hands and feet as fast as he could, dodged the blow from the cudgel and struck back at Brother Monkey's face with his flower-scattering axe. It was a fine battle. Just watch!

The gold-banded as-you-will cudgel,
The flower-scattering axe and its wind-keen blade.

One ground his teeth with terrible ferocity;
The other gnashed his molars and displayed his might.
One was the Great Sage Equalling Heaven descended to earth,
The other an evil demon king come down to the lower world.
Both snorted out clouds and shining mists that lit up the heavenly palace,
Sent stones and sand flying that blotted out the Dipper.
They came and went through many a movement,
Twisting and turning and giving off golden light.
Each used all of his talents to the full;
Both staked the whole of their magical powers.
One wanted to take the queen back to the capital;
The other would happily have stayed with her in the cave.
There was no deep reason for the struggle:
He was ready to give his life for the sake of the king.

When the two of them had fought fifty rounds without result the demon king realized that Monkey was too strong a fighter for him to be able to beat. Blocking the iron cudgel with his axe the demon said, "Stop, Sun the Novice. I haven't had my breakfast yet today. Let me eat, then I'll have it out with you." Monkey was well aware that he wanted to fetch the bells, so he put his cudgel away and said, "A hero doesn't chase an exhausted hare. Off you go. Have a good meal, and get ready to come back and die."

The demon quickly turned and rushed inside, where he said to the queen, "Get me my treasures at once." "What for?" she asked. "The man challenging me to battle this morning was a disciple of the monk who's going to fetch the scriptures," he said. "He's called Sun Wukong, or Sun the Novice, and Grand Par was just a nickname. I've been battling it out with him all this time, but still there's no outcome. Just wait while I take my treasures out and set off smoke and flames to burn that ape." These words made the queen feel very uneasy. If she didn't fetch the bells, she was worried that he might be suspicious, but if she did she feared that Sun the Novice would be killed. As she was hesitating the demon king pressed her again: "Hurry up and fetch them." She had no choice but to undo the lock, bring out the three bells and hand them to the demon king, who took them and went outside the cave again. The queen sat in the inner quarters, her tears pouring down like rain, as she thought that Monkey would not possibly be able to escape with his life. Neither of them realized that the bells were only copies.

Once outside the cave the demon stood upwind and shouted, "Stay where you are, Sun the Novice. Watch while I ring these bells." "You have your bells, but why shouldn't I have mine?" Monkey replied. "You can ring yours, so why shouldn't I ring mine?" "What bells have you got?" the demon king asked. "Show me." Monkey pinched his iron cudgel to make it into an embroidery needle that he tucked into his ear then brought out the three real treasures from at his waist. "Here are my purple gold bells," he said to the demon king. The sight of them came as a shock to the demon. "That's funny," he thought, "very funny. Why are his bells exactly the same as mine? Even if they'd been cast from the same mould they'd not have been properly smoothed: you'd expect some extra marks or missing knobs. How can they be identical with this?" "Where did you get your bells from?" he went on to ask again. "Where are yours from, dear nephew?" Monkey replied. Being honest, the demon king replied, "These bells of mine,

Come from deep in the Way of the Immortal of Great Purity,
Are made of gold long refined in the Eight Trigrams Furnace
Formed into bells renowned as ultimate treasures
Left by Lord Lao Zi left till the present day."

"That's where my bells come from too," Monkey replied with a smile. "How were they made?" the demon king asked. "These bells of mine," said Monkey,

"Were made of gold refined in the furnace

When Lord Lao Zi made elixir in the Tushita Palace.
They are cyclical treasures. The two threes make six:
Mine are the female and yours are the male."

"The bells are golden elixir treasures," the demon king said, "not birds or beasts. They can't be male or female. As long as they yield what's precious when they're rung they're good ones." "Words prove nothing," said Monkey. "Show it by actions. Shake yours first." The demon king then rang his first bell three times. No fire came out. He rang his second three times. No smoke came out. He rang his third three times, and no sand came out either. "Very odd," he said, making wild gestures, "very odd. The world's changed. These bells must be hen-pecked. When the males see the females they don't dare to do their stuff." "Stop, nephew," said Monkey. "Now I'm going to shake mine to show you what happens." The splendid ape then grasped all three bells in one hand and rang them together. Watch as clouds of red flames, black smoke and yellow sand all come gushing out, setting the trees and the mountain ablaze. Monkey then said the words of another spell and shouted "Wind!" towards the southeast; and a wind did indeed spring up that fanned the flames. With the power of the wind behind them the flames and smoke filled the heavens, blazing red and deepest black, and the earth was covered by the yellow sandstorm. The Evil Star Matcher's souls fled from his body in his terror, but he had nowhere to turn: amid that fire there was no way of escaping with his life.

Then a penetrating shout was heard from mid-air: "Sun Wukong, I am here." Monkey quickly looked up and saw that it was the Bodhisattva Guanyin holding her vase of pure water in her left hand and a sprig of willow in her right with which to sprinkle sweet dew and put out the flames. In his alarm Monkey hid the bells at his waist, put the palms of his hands together and prostrated himself in a kowtow. The Bodhisattva flicked a few drops of sweet dew from her willow sprig and in an instant both flames and smoke disappeared, while no sign of the yellow sand remained to be seen. "I did not realize, Most Merciful One, that you were coming down to the mortal world," said Brother Monkey as he kowtowed, "and it was wrong of me to fail to keep out of your way. May I venture to ask where you are going, Bodhisattva?" "I am here especially to find and take this evil monster," the Bodhisattva replied.

"What is the monster's background, and how can he put you to the trouble of capturing him in your illustrious person?" Monkey asked. "He is a golden-haired giant hound on which I used to ride," the Bodhisattva replied. "The boy in charge of it fell asleep and failed to keep proper guard over it, so that the wicked beast bit through its iron chains and escaped to save the king of Purpuria from disaster." When Monkey heard this he hastily bowed and said, "You have it the wrong way round, Bodhisattva. He's been mistreating the king and his queen, and thus damaging public morality. So how can you say that he has saved the king from disaster when in fact he has brought him disaster?" "You would not know," the Bodhisattva replied, "that when the previous king of Purpuria was reigning and the present king was the crown prince and had not yet taken the throne he was a superb archer and huntsman. Once he led his men and horses hunting with falcon and hound. They came to the Fallen Phoenix Slope, where a young peacock and peahen, two children of the Buddha's mother in the West, the Bodhiṣattva Maurya Vidya Rani were resting. When the king shot with his bow he wounded the cock, while the hen died with an arrow still in her. After the Buddha's mother realized to her regret what had happened she ordered that the prince should be separated from his wife for three years and suffer himself the way birds do when they are parted from their mates. At the time I was riding that hound and we both heard her say that. I never imagined that the beast would remember it and come back to mistreat the queen and thus save the king from disaster. That was three years ago, and now that the misdeed has been paid for it was fortunate that you came along to cure the king. I am here to recover the wicked and evil creature." "Bodhisattva," said Monkey, "this may well be so, but he did sully the queen, damage public morality, offend ethics and break the law. You can't let him off a non-capital punishment. Let me give him twenty blows before handing him over for you to take back." "Wukong," said the Bodhisattva, "as you know I am here you really ought to show me the respect I deserve and spare him completely. This still counts as one of your successes in subduing a demon. If you hit him with your cudgel it'll kill him." Monkey dared not disobey, but bowed and said, "If you're taking him back to the ocean with you, Bodhisattva, you mustn't let him escape and come down to the human world again. That would be quite a catastrophe."

Only then did the Bodhisattva shout, "Wicked beast! Turn back into your own form! What are you waiting for?" The monster could be seen doing a roll and turning back into himself. Then he shook his fur for the Bodhisattva to mount on his back. The Bodhisattva looked down at his neck to see that the three golden bells were missing. "Wukong," she said, "give me my bells back." "I don't know where they are," Monkey said. "Thieving ape," the Bodhisattva shouted. "If you hadn't stolen those bells then ten Sun Wukongs, never mind one, would have dared go nowhere near him. Hand them over at once." "I really haven't seen them," Monkey replied with a smile. "In that case I'll have to recite the Band-tightening Spell," said the Bodhisattva. This scared Monkey, who could only plead, "Don't say it, don't say it. The bells are here." This was indeed a case of

Who could untie the bells from neck of the giant hound?
To find that out ask the one who first fastened them on.

The Bodhisattva then placed the bells round the giant hound's neck, and flew up to her high throne. Watch as the

Four-stalked lotus flowers blazed with fire;
Her whole body was thickly clad in cloth of gold.

We will say no more of how the Great Merciful One returned to the Southern Ocean.

The Great Sage Sun Wukong then tidied up his clothing and charged into the Horndog Cave swinging his iron cudgel and killing to his heart's content. He wiped all the demons out till he reached the inner quarters of the palace and asked the Golden Queen to go back to her country. She prostrated herself to him for a long time. Monkey told her all about how the Bodhisattva had subdued the demon and why she had been separated from her husband. Then he gathered some soft grasses that he twisted together into a long straw dragon. "Sit on this, ma'am," he said, "and shut your eyes. Don't be afraid. I'm taking you back to court to see your master." The queen followed his instructions carefully while he used his magic power. There was a sound of the wind whistling in her ears.

An hour later he brought her into the city. Bringing his cloud down he said, "Open your eyes, ma'am." When the queen opened her eyes and looked she recognized the phoenix buildings and dragon towers. She was very happy, and getting off the straw dragon she climbed the steps of the throne hall. When the king saw her he came straight down from his dragon throne to take the queen by her jade hand. He was just going to tell her how much he had missed her when he suddenly collapsed, shouting: "My hand hurts, my hand hurts." "Look at that mug," Pig said, roaring with laughter, "he's out of luck. No joy for him. The moment he meets her again he gets stung." "Idiot," said Monkey, "would you dare grab her?" "What if I did?" Pig asked. "The queen's covered with poisonous spikes," Monkey replied, "and she has poison on her hands. In the three years she was with the Evil Star Matcher in Mount Unicorn the monster never had her. If he had, his whole body would have been in agony. Even touching her with his hand made his hand ache." "Then what is to be done about it?" the officials asked. While all the officials were wondering what to do in the outer palace and the consorts and concubines in the inner palace were full of terror, the Jade and the Silver Queen helped their king to his feet.

Amid the general alarm a voice was heard in the sky shouting, "Great Sage, I'm here." Brother Monkey looked up, and this is what was to be seen:

> *The cry of a crane soaring through the heavens,*
> *Then flying straight down to the palace of the king.*
> *Beams of auspicious light shone about;*
> *Clouds of holy vapours drifted all around.*
> *Mists came from the cloak of coir that covered his body:*
> *Rare were the straw sandals on which he trod.*
> *The fly-whisk in his hand was made of dragon whiskers,*
> *And silken tassels hung around his waist.*
> *He joined human destinies together throughout heaven and earth*
> *As he roamed free and easy all over the world.*
> *He was the Purple Clouds Immortal of the Daluo Heaven,*
> *Come down to earth today to lift an enchantment.*

Monkey went over to him to greet him with, "Where are you going, Zhang Boduan of the Ziyang sect?" The True Man of Ziyang came to the front of the hall, bowed and replied, "Great Sage, the humble immortal Zhang Boduan greets you." "Where have you come from?" Monkey replied. "Three years ago I passed this way when going to a Buddha assembly," the True Man said. "When I saw that the King of Purpuria was suffering the agony of being parted from his wife I was worried that the demon would defile the queen. That would have been an affront to morality and made it hard for the queen to be reunited with the king later on. So I turned an old coir cloak into a new dress of many colours and gave it to the demon king. He made the queen wear it as her wedding dress. As soon as she put it on poisonous barbs grew all over her body. They were the coir cloak. Now that you have been successful, Great Sage, I've come to lift the spell." "In that case," said Monkey, "thank you for coming so far. Please remove the barbs at once." The True Man stepped forward, pointed at the queen, and removed the coir cloak. The queen's body was once more as it had originally been. The True Man shook the cloak, put it over his shoulders, and said to Monkey, "Please forgive me if I leave now, Great Sage." "Don't go yet," said Monkey. "Wait till the king has thanked you." "I won't trouble him," said the True Man with a smile, then raised his hands together in salute, rose up into the sky and went. The king, queen and the officials high and low were so astonished that they all bowed to the sky.

When the bowing was over the king ordered that the eastern hall of the palace be thrown open so that they could give thanks to the four monks. The king led all his officials to go down on their knees and kowtow to them, and husband and wife were reunited. In the middle of the celebratory banquet Monkey said, "Master, bring out that declaration of war." The venerable elder produced it from his sleeve and handed it to Monkey, who passed it in turn to the king. "This was a letter that the demons sent his lieutenant to deliver," Monkey said. "He was the officer I killed and brought here as a trophy. Then I turned myself into the officer and went back to the cave to report. That was how I saw Her Majesty and stole the golden bells. He almost caught me, but I did another change, stole them again, got them out and fought him. It was lucky for him that the Bodhisattva Guanyin came to collect him and tell me why you and Her Majesty were parted." He told the whole story from beginning to end in great detail. Everyone in the country — whether ruler or ministers, whether within the palace or outside — expressed admiration and gratitude. "In the first place," said the Tang Priest, "it was because of Your Majesty's own good fortune, and in the second place it was thanks to my disciple's efforts. We are deeply obliged to you for this sumptuous banquet today, and now we must take our leave of you. Please do not delay us poor monks on our pilgrimage to the West." When the king realized that his efforts to keep them there would be of no avail he inspected and returned the passport and arranged a great procession of royal coaches. The Tang Priest was invited to sit in his own dragon carriage, while the king, his queens and his consorts themselves all pushed it along as they saw them on their way then bade them farewell. Indeed,

He was fated to have his melancholy washed clean away:
The mind finds peace of itself when thought and worrying cease.

If you do not know what of good or ill lay in store for them on the way ahead listen to the explanation in the next instalment.

CHAPTER SEVENTY-TWO

The Seven Emotions confuse the basic in Gossamer Cave; At Filth-cleansing Spring Pig forgets himself.

The story tells how Sanzang took his leave of the king of Purpuria, got everything ready, saddled the horse and headed westwards. They crossed many a mountain and river. Before they realized it autumn and winter were over and spring's brightness and charm were back. Master and disciples were enjoying the scenery as their way led them across the greenery when they suddenly noticed a building amid trees. Sanzang dismounted and stood beside the main track. "Master," Brother Monkey asked, "the road is easy and there is no evil about, so why have you stopped?" "You aren't at all understanding, brother," Pig said. "The master is feeling sleepy after being in the saddle for so long. You ought to let him come down and have a rest." "It's not that," Sanzang said. "I can see a house over there. I was thinking of going there myself to beg for some food."

"What a thing for the master to say," said Monkey with a smile. If you want some food I'll go and beg some for you. As the saying goes, 'Your teacher for a day is your father for the rest of your life.' It would be outrageous for me, your disciple, to sit here idly and let my master go begging." "There's no need to say that," Sanzang replied. "Usually you three have to cross enormous distances as far as the eye can see to beg for our food. Today there's a house so close it's in shouting distance, so let me beg this time." "But, Master, you wouldn't know what to do," said Pig. "As the saying goes, when three people go travelling it's the youngest who does the rough jobs. You're the senior one and we're all only disciples. As the old book says, 'When there is a job to be done the disciple does it.' Let me go." "Disciples,"

said Sanzang, "the weather is good today. It's not at all like the times when you all have to go far away in wind and rain. Let me go to this house. Whether I get any food or not I shall soon be back and we shall be on our way." Friar Sand, who was standing beside them, smiled and said, "Stop arguing so much, brother. As the master has made his mind up you shouldn't disobey him. If you upset him he won't eat any of the food you are able to beg."

Pig accepted this suggestion and brought out the begging bowl and a change of hat and cassock for the master, who went straight to the farm building to look at it. It really was a fine place. He could see:

A high-rising stone bridge,
Ancient trees growing close together.
Where the stone bridge rose high
A babbling brook joined a long stream;
Amid close-growing ancient trees
Hidden birds sang sweetly on the distant hill.
Across the bridge were several thatched houses
As pure and elegant as an immortal's hermitage.
There was also a thatched hut
So pure and white it would put a Taoist temple to shame.
Before the hut could be seen four beauties
All busily embroidering phoenix designs.

As there were no males but only these four girls to be seen the reverend gentleman did not dare go inside, but slipped back under the tall trees and stood stock still. He could see that each of the girls

Were rock-hard in their ladylike propriety,
And happy as the spring in their orchid natures.
Red glows set off their tender cheeks;
Crimson make-up was spread on their lips.
Their moth brows were as fine as a crescent moon,
While their clouds of hair were piled up like cicada wings.

Had any of them stood among the flowers
Wandering bees would have taken them for blossoms.

He stood there for an hour. The silence was complete, unbroken by dog or cock. "If I'm not even capable of begging us a meal my disciples will laught at me," he thought. "If the master can't beg a meal, what hope do his disciples have of ever getting to see the Buddha?"

He did not know what to do, but it seemed wrong to stay there any longer, so he went back towards the bridge, only to notice a pavilion inside the compound of thatched cottages. In the pavilion three more girls were juggling a ball with their feet. Look at them. They were different from the other four:

Their turquoise sleeves are waving
And their embroidered skirts are swaying.
The waving turquoise sleeves
Cover their delicate jade bamboo-shoots of fingers,
The swaying embroidered skirts
Half show their tiny golden lotus feet.
Perfect are their faces and bodies,
Endless the movements of their slippered heels.
As they grab for the head they vary in height;
They pass the ball around most smoothly.
One turns around and kicks an "over-the-wall flower",
Then does a backward somersault called "crossing the sea".
After lightly taking a pass like a lump of clay
A single spear is hard pressed by a pair of sticks.
A shining pearl is put on the Buddha's head
And held between the tips of their fingers.
Skilfully they hold the ball as a narrow brick,
Twisting their feet in the sleeping fish position.
Their backs held level, they squat with bended knee;
Turning their necks they kick their heels in the air.
They can make benches fly around;
Very stylish are the capes upon their shoulders.

Their trouser-legs are bound with tapes to let them move,
While their necklaces swing as they sway.
They kick the ball like the Yellow River flowing backwards,
Or goldfish purchased on the beach.
When you mistake one of them for the leader
Another one turns to carry the ball away.
They all hold their calves so trimly in the air,
Pointing their toes to catch the ball.
They raise their heels to spin straw sandals,
Planting them upside-down and picking them up in a turn.
As they step back their shoulder-capes spread out
Fastened only with a hook.
The pedlar's basket comes down long and low,
Then they grab for the goal.
At the really magnificent footwork
All the beauties shout with admiration.
The silken clothes of all are soaked in sweat;
Feeling tired and relaxed they ended their game.

The description could go on and on. There is another poem that tells more:

Kicking the ball in the April weather,
Beauties blown along by the magical wind.
Sweat stained their powdered faces like dew on a flower;
The dust on their moth eyebrows was mist hiding willows.
Their turquoise sleeves hanging low covered jade fingers;
Trailing embroidered skirts showed golden lotus feet.
After kicking the ball many times they were charmingly tired;
Their hair was dishevelled and their topknots askew.

After watching for a long time Sanzang could only go to the bridge and call loudly, "Bodhisattvas, fate brings me here as a poor monk to beg for the gift of some food." As soon as the women heard him they cheerfully put aside their needlework and balls to come out smiling and giggling through the gates to greet him. "Reverend sir," they said, "we're sorry we didn't welcome you sooner. As you have come to our poor farm we couldn't possibly feed you on the path. Please come inside and sit down." When Sanzang heard this he thought, "Splendid, this is splendid. The West really is Buddha's land. If even these womenfolk are so diligent about feeding monks the men are bound to be pious followers of the Buddha."

Sanzang stepped forward to greet the women and followed them into the thatched cottages. As he passed the pavilion and looked he saw that on the other side of it there were no buildings. All that could be seen were

Towering mountain-tops,
Distant ranges of the earth.
The towering mountain-tops touch the clouds;
The distant ranges of the earth lead to peaks in the ocean.
From the stone bridge by the gates
One looks on a stream that bends nine times;
The peach and plum trees in the orchard
Vie in abundance of blossom.
Creepers and vines hang from three or four trees;
The fragrance of orchids is spread by thousands of flowers.
From afar this retreat rivals Penglai's fairyland;
Seen from close to the mountain beats Tai and Hua.
This is truly a retreat for demon immortals,
An isolated house with no neighbours around.

One woman came forward to push the stone gates open and invite the Tang Priest to come in and sit down. All he could do was go inside. When he looked up he saw that the tables and seats were all of stone, and the atmosphere was oppressively cold. This alarmed the venerable elder, who thought, "This is a thoroughly sinister place. I'm sure it's evil." "Please sit down, venerable elder," the women all said with simpering smiles. He had no choice but to sit down. A little later he found himself shuddering.

"What monastery are you from, reverend sir?" the women asked. "For what purpose are you collecting alms? Are you repairing roads and bridges, founding monasteries, worshipping at pagodas, or having Buddha statues made and sutras printed? Won't you show us your donation book?" "I am not a monk collecting donations," the venerable elder replied. "If you're not here to ask for charity then why are you here?" the women asked. "We have been sent by Great Tang in the east to the Thunder Monastery in the Western Heaven to fetch the scriptures," Sanzang replied. "As our stomachs were empty when we happened to be passing this distinguished place I have come to beg a vegetarian meal from you in your kindness. After that we poor monks will be on our way again." "Splendid, splendid," the women all said. "As the saying goes, monks from afar most love to read the scriptures. Sisters! We must treat them well. Let's give them some vegetarian food as quickly as we can."

While three of the women kept him company, talking about such matters as primary and secondary causation, the other four went into the kitchen, where they tucked up their clothes, rolled up their sleeves, fanned the fire and scrubbed the cooking pots. Do you know what it was they prepared? They were frying in human fat, and what they cooked was human flesh, stewed into black paste as if it were wheat gluten, and human brain cut out to fry like pieces of beancurd. Then they placed the two dishes on a stone table and said to Sanzang, "Do eat. We were too rushed to prepare anything good, so please make do with this. It'll stave off the pangs of hunger. There will be some more dishes to follow."

As soon as Sanzang used his nose and smelled the stench of flesh he would not eat, but bowed with his hands together before his chest and said, "Bodhisattvas, I have been a vegetarian since birth." "But this is vegetarian food, reverend sir," the women all replied with smiles. "Amitabha Buddha!" exclaimed Sanzang. "If as a monk I ate vegetarian food like that I would never have any hope of seeing the Buddha or fetching the sutras." "Reverend sir," the women said, "as a monk you shouldn't be so choosy about what you're given." "I never could be," Sanzang said, "I never could be. I am under the orders of the Great Tang emperor to harm not even the tiniest life, to save all I see suffering, to put all the food-grain I am given into my mouth with my fingers, and to cover my body with the threads of silk that come my way. I would never dare pick and choose among my benefactors' gifts." "Even if you're not picking and choosing," the women replied with smiles, "you do seem to have come here to complain. Please eat some of the food and don't mind if it's a little coarse and flavourless." "It's not that I don't want to eat it," Sanzang said, "it's that I'm afraid I'd be breaking my vows. I hope that you Bodhisattvas will remember that setting living beings free is better than keeping them with you and let me go on my way."

As Sanzang struggled to get out the women blocked the gateway and refused to let him go. "Business bringing itself to our door!" they all said. "You've no more chance of getting away from here than of covering up a fart with your hands. Where do you think you're going?" They were all quite skilled in the martial arts and quick movers too, and after they had grabbed Sanzang they dragged him like a sheep and threw him to the ground. Then they all held him down, tied him up, and suspended him from the rafters. There is a special name for the way they hung him up there: The Immortal Shows the Way. One hand was strung up by a rope so that it pointed forward. The other hand was fastened to his waist by another rope that was also holding him aloft, and his legs were both held up by a third rope behind him. The three ropes had him suspended from a beam with his back on top and his belly pointing down. As Sanzang endured the agony and held back his tears he thought with bitter regret, "How evil my destiny is. I thought I was coming to beg for a vegetarian meal from good people. I never imagined I'd be falling into the fiery pit. Disciples! Rescue me as soon as you can if I am ever to see you again. If you don't get here within four hours I shall be dead."

Despite his misery Sanzang kept a careful eye on the women. When they had him tied up securely and hanging there they started to remove their clothes. This alarmed the venerable elder, who thought, "They must be taking their clothes off because they are going to beat me. Perhaps they are going to eat me too." The women only unbuttoned their gauze blouses, exposing their stomachs. Then each of them produced a silken rope about as thick as a duck egg from her navel. These they made move like bursting jade or flying silver as they fastened the gates of the farm.

We leave them and go back to Monkey, Pig and Friar Sand, who were all still waiting by the main road. While the other two were pasturing the horse and looking after the baggage Monkey was amusing himself by leaping from tree to tree and climbing around the branches as he picked leaves and looked for fruit. Suddenly he turned round and saw a sheet of light. This so alarmed him that he jumped out of the tree with a shout of, "This is terrible! Terrible! The master's luck is out." He pointed as he continued, "Look at the farm. What do you think?" When Pig and Friar Sand both looked they saw a sheet of something like snow but brighter and like silver but shinier. "That's done it," said Pig, "that's done it. The master's run into evil spirits. We'd better go and rescue him straight away." "Stop yelling, brother," said Monkey. "Neither of you can see just what's there. Wait while I go and take a look." "Do be careful, brother," said Friar Sand. "I can cope," Monkey replied.

The splendid Great Sage tightened his tigerskin kilt, pulled out his gold-banded cudgel and took a few strides forward to see that the silken ropes had formed something like a web with thousands of strands. When he felt it with his hands it was somewhat soft and sticky. Not knowing what it was, Monkey raised his cudgel and said, "Never mind thousands of strands. This cudgel could break through tens of thousands of them." He was just about to strike when he stopped to think, "If they were hard I could certainly smash them, but then soft ones would only be knocked flat, and if I alarm the demons and get caught myself that would be a disaster. I'd better make some enquiries before I do any hitting."

Who do you think he asked? He made a spell with his hands, said the words of it and sent for an old local god, who ran round and round in his shrine just as if turning a mill. "Old man," his wife asked, "what are you rushing round and round for? You must be having a fit." "You don't understand," the local god replied. "There's a Great Sage Equalling Heaven here. I didn't go to meet him. But he's sending for me." "Go and see him then," his wife replied, "and that'll be that. Why charge round and round in here?" "But if I go and see him that cudgel of his hits very hard," the local deity said. "He doesn't care what you're like — he just hits you." "He won't possibly hit you when he sees how old you are," his wife replied. "He's been cadging free drinks all his life," the local god said, "and he really loves hitting old people."

After talking for a while with his wife the local god had no choice but to go outside and kneel shivering and shaking by the roadside, calling out, "Great Sage, the local deity kowtows to you." "Get up," Brother Monkey replied, "and stop pretending to be so keen. I'm not going to hit you. I'm just passing through. Tell me where this is." "Which way have you come, Great Sage?" the local deity asked. "I've come from the east and I'm heading west," said Monkey. "Which mountain have you reached on your journey from the east?" the local deity asked. "That ridge there," Monkey replied. "Our baggage and the horse are there, aren't they?" "That is Gossamer Ridge," the local deity replied. "Under the ridge there's a cave called Gossamer Cave where seven evil spirits live." "Male or female ones?" Monkey asked. "She-devils," the local deity replied. "How powerful is their magic?" Monkey asked. "I'm much too weak and insignificant to know that," the local god replied. "All I can tell you is that a mile due south of here there is a natural hot spring called the Filth-cleansing Spring," the local god said, "where the Seven Fairies from on high used to bathe. When the seven evil spirits settled here and took over the Filth-cleansing Spring the good spirits didn't try to fight them for it. They let the spirits have it for nothing. I reckon that if even good spirits from Heaven don't dare offend them the evil spirits must have tremendous powers." "What have they taken the spring over for?" Monkey asked. "Ever since taking the bathing pool over the monsters have been coming to bathe there three times a day," the local god replied. "It's already after eleven. They'll be along at noon." "Go back now, local god," Monkey said when he heard all this, "and wait while I capture them." The old local god kowtowed to him and went back to his shrine all of a tremble.

The Great Sage then gave a solo display of his magical powers, shaking himself, turning into a fly, and landing on the tip of a blade of grass to wait beside the path. A little later he heard a rustling, hissing sound like that of silkworms eating leaves or an ocean tide coming in. In the time it takes to drink half a cup of tea the silken ropes had all gone, and the farm looked just the same as it had before. Then there was a creaking noise as the wicker gate opened and the seven women came out laughing and talking noisily. Monkey watched carefully from where he was hiding and saw them talking and laughing as they held each other by the hand and walked shoulder to shoulder across the bridge. They were real beauties:

Compare them with jade and they were more fragrant;
They were like flowers but able to talk.
Their willowy brows were like distant hills;
Sandalwood-scented mouths were bursting cherries.
Hair ornaments were of jade;
Golden lotus feet darted out under crimson skirts.
They were like the moon goddess come down to earth,
Immortal girls descending to the world.

"No wonder the master wanted to come begging for food," thought Monkey with a laugh, "with all these lovelies here. If these seven beauties have captured him he won't be enough for a single meal for them. They couldn't make him last a couple of days. And if they take it in turns to have their way with him they'll kill him straight off. I'd better go and listen to what they're plotting."

The splendid Great Sage flew over with a high-pitched buzz and landed on the topknot of the woman who was walking in front. When she was over the bridge the women behind her caught up with her and called out, "Sister, let's have a bath before we steam the fat monk and eat him up." "These monsters aren't at all economical," Monkey smiled to himself. "They'd save a lot of firewood if they boiled him. Why steam him instead?" The women walked south, picking flowers and throwing grass at each other, and were soon at the bathing pool, where a very magnificent wall and gateway appeared, with fragrant flowers, among them a bed of orchids, growing all around. One of the women behind him stepped forward and with a whistling sound pushed the double gates open, revealing the pond of naturally hot water inside. As for this water,

When heaven and earth were first separated
There were ten suns in the sky
Till Yi, the fine archer,
Shot nine of the sun-crows down to the earth,
Leaving only one golden crow star,
The true fire of the sun.
The nine hot springs in heaven and earth
Are the other nine crows transformed.
These nine hot springs are
Cool Fragrance Spring,
Mountain-companions Spring,
Warm Spring,
Donghe Spring,
Mount Huang Spring,
Xiao'an Spring,
Guangfen Spring,
Hot Water Spring,
And this Filth-cleansing Spring.

There is a poem about it that goes:

The same vital force runs in all four seasons;

Spring continues throughout the autumn.
The scalding water bubbles like a cauldron;
The snow-white waves are boiling hot.
If the waters are spread they help the crops to grow;
Left where they are they wash worldly dust away.
Little bubbles spread out like pearls
Rolling ones rise like pieces of jade.
It is rich and smooth although not wine,
Clear, calm and naturally warm.
The whole place thrives on its air of good omen:
It brings good fortune and the natural truth.
When the beauties wash their flesh is smooth as ice;
As dirt is soaked away their jade-like bodies are made new.

The bathing pool was about fifty feet across, a hundred feet long and four feet deep. The water was pure and translucent, and from the bottom of it came up bubbles like rolling pearls or floating jade. In the four sides of the pool there were six or seven pipes through which the water flowed out, keeping warm even when it reached fields up to a mile away. Beside the pool was a three-roomed pavilion, next to the back wall of which stood an eight-legged bench. At each end of the pavilion was a clothes stand painted in coloured lacquers. All this secretly delighted Monkey, who flew straight to one of the stands and landed on it.

When the women saw how clear and warm the water was they wanted to bathe in it, so they all took their clothes off and hung them on the stands before going into the pool together. This is what Monkey saw:

They undid the buttons on their clothes,
Loosened the knots in their gauzy sashes.
Silvery white were their creamy breasts,
Snowy their bodies that looked like jade.
Their arms and elbows were cool as ice,
And scented shoulders more lovely than if powdered.
Soft and supple the skin on their stomachs,

Glistening and clean their backs.
Their knees and wrists were rounded and soft;
Only three inches long were their golden lotus feet.
And as for what lay in between,
They showed a glimpse of the cave of pleasure.

The women all jumped into the water and enjoyed themselves as they frolicked in the waves. "If I wanted to hit them," Monkey thought, "I'd only need to stir the water with my cudgel. It would be like pouring boiling water on a nest of mice: I could kill the lot of them. What a pity. If I hit them I'd kill them, but it wouldn't do my reputation any good. As they say, a real man doesn't fight women. It'd be hopeless if a man like me killed these girls. If I'm not going to hit them I'll have to make things difficult for them so that they can't move." The splendid Great Sage made a spell with his hands, said the words of it, shook himself and turned into a hungry eagle.

His feathers were like frost or snow,
His eyes like bright stars.
When evil foxes saw him their souls were scared out of them;
And crafty hares were struck with terror.
His steely claws were sharp as spear-points;
His air was both majestic and ferocious.
He used his talons to seize his food,
And was ready to catch his flying prey himself.
He could fly high and low across the chilly sky,
Swooping through clouds and on his quarry at will.

With a whoosh of his wings he flew towards them, stretched his sharp talons to seize all seven sets of clothes that were hung on the stands and flew straight back to the ridge with them. Here he reverted to his own form to see Pig and Friar Sand.

Just look at the idiot as he comes up to Brother Monkey and says with a grin, "The master must have been taken to a pawnbroker's." "How can you tell?" asked Friar Sand. "Can't you see all those clothes our brother's grabbed?" Pig replied. "These are the evil spirits' clothes," said Monkey, putting them down.

"How on earth did you get so many?" Pig asked. "There are seven outfits," said Monkey. "How did you strip them so easily, and strip them naked at that?" Pig asked. "I didn't have to strip them," said Monkey. "This place is called Gossamer Ridge, and the farm is called Gossamer Cave. The seven she-devils who live there captured the master, hung him up in their cave and all went off to bathe in the Filth-cleansing Spring. It's a natural hot spring. Their plan was to have a bath then steam the master and eat him. I went there with them and watched them undress and get into the water. I wanted to hit them, but I was worried it would contaminate my cudgel and ruin my reputation so I didn't. I just turned myself into a hungry eagle and grabbed their clothes in my talons. Now they're all squatting in the water, too embarrassed to come out. Let's rescue the master and be on our way as quickly as we can."

"Brother," grinned Pig, "you always leave something undone. You could see that they were evil spirits, so why didn't you kill them first then rescue the master? Even if they're too embarrassed to come out now they'll certainly come out after nightfall. They're bound to have enough old clothes at home to be able to put on an outfit each and come after us. Even if they don't come after us they live here permanently and we'll have to come this way back after we've fetched the scriptures. As the saying goes, it's better to get into debt on a journey than to get into a fight. When they stop us and make a row they'll really have it in for us." "So what do you suggest?" Monkey asked. "If you ask me we should kill the demons then rescue the master," said Pig. "That's what's called cutting down weeds and digging them out by the roots." "I'm not going to hit them," Monkey replied. "If you want them hit go and do it yourself."

Pig then summoned up his spirits and in high delight rushed straight there, his rake held aloft. As he suddenly pushed the gates open and looked inside he saw the seven women squatting in the water and wildly cursing the eagle. "Feathery beast," they were saying, "cat-headed monster. What the hell can we do now you've carried our clothes off?" Pig could not help laughing as he said to them, "Bodhisattvas, carry on with your bath. Do you mind if I join you?" "You monk, you're a disgrace," the devils retorted angrily as they saw him. "We're laywomen and you're a man of religion. As the ancient book has it, 'From the age of seven boys and girls do not share the same mat.' You mustn't possibly bathe in the same pool as us." "But the weather's so scorching hot I've got no choice," said Pig. "You'll have to make the best of it and let me take a wash. What do you have to show off all that book-learning about sharing mats for?"

With no further argument the idiot dropped his rake, stripped off his cotton tunic and jumped in with a splash, to the fury of the demons who all rushed at him to hit him. Little did they realize how expert Pig was in the water. Once in the pool he shook himself and turned into a catfish spirit. The demons then tried to grab him but even when they caught him they could not get a firm grip. If they grabbed to the east he suddenly shot westwards, and if they tried to grab him to the west he went east. The funny thing was that he kept wriggling around their crotches. The water was about chest-high, and after swimming around at the surface and then at the bottom of the pool for a while he had covered all of it and was panting and exhausted.

Only then did Pig jump out, turn back into himself, put his tunic back on, pick up his rake and shout, "Who am I then? You thought I was a catfish spirit!" At the sight of him the demons all trembled with fright and said to Pig, "When you came here first you were a monk, then you turned into a catfish in the water and we couldn't catch you. Now you've dressed like that. Where have you come from? You must tell us your name." "Bloody demons, you really don't know who I am," said Pig. "I'm a disciple of the Venerable Tang Priest, who has been sent from Tang in the east to fetch the scriptures. My title is Marshal Tian Peng and I'm called Zhu Wuneng, or Pig. You've hung my master up in your cave and you're planning to steam him and eat him. Is my master just a meal for you to cook? Stretch your heads out at once. I'm going to smash you all with my rake and wipe the lot of you out."

At this the demons were scared out of their wits. They fell to their knees in the water, kowtowed to him and said, "Please be kind, reverend sir. We were blind and we captured your master by mistake. Although we did hang him up we haven't tortured him. We beg you in your compassion to spare our lives. We'll gladly give you some money for the journey and send your master on his way to the Western Heaven." "Cut that talk out," said Pig, waving his hands. "It's quite right what they say: 'Once you've been tricked by a confectioner you won't believe sweet-talkers again.' I'm going to hit you with my rake, then we can all go our separate ways."

The idiot was thoroughly rough and crude and wanted to show off his powers. He was unmoved by their fragrant feminine beauty. Raising his rake he charged them, lashing out wildly without caring what he was doing. The demons acted desperately. Forgetting about their modesty they cared only about saving their lives as covering their private parts with their hands they jumped out of the water and ran into the pavilion. Standing there they used magic to make thick silken ropes come out of their navels, filling the sky with a huge silken canopy under which Pig was caught. When the idiot looked up he could not see the sun in the heavens. He tried to run outside, but he could not lift his feet, which were tangled in silken ropes that covered the ground. When he tried to move his feet he tripped and staggered. He tried going left, but his head crashed to the ground, then tried going right and came a cropper. So he turned round as quickly as he could and kissed the dirt, got himself back on his feet, and collapsed head first once more. Goodness only knows how many times he stumbled and fell till his whole body was numb, his feet sore, his head aching and his eyes blurred. He could no longer even crawl, but lay groaning on the floor. Then the demons tied him up. They neither beat him up nor wounded him, but sprang outside to rush back to their cave, leaving the silken canopy to blot out the daylight.

When they reached the stone bridge they stopped and said the words of a spell. In an instant the silk canopy had been put away, and they all rushed stark naked into the cave, covering their private parts with their hands as they ran giggling past the Tang Priest. Once inside their bedrooms carved out of the rock they put on old clothes and went straight to the back door of the cave, where they stood and called, "Where are you, children?"

Now each she-devil had a child, not one that she had borne, but an adopted child who had taken her as a mother. They were called Bee, Hornet, Cockroach, Spanish-fly, Grasshopper, Wax-insect and Dragonfly, for such they were. The evil spirits had spread their nets across the sky, caught these seven insects and been on the point of eating them. But as the old saying goes, "Birds have bird language and beasts have beast language." The insects had pleaded for their lives and volunteered to take the spirits as their own mothers. Ever since then they had gathered blossoms in the spring and summer flowers for the evil spirits, and as soon as they heard the shouts they appeared and asked, "What orders do you have for us, mothers?" "Sons," the demons replied, "this morning we made a mistake and provoked the monk from Tang. His disciples trapped us in the pool and disgraced us. We were almost killed. You must do your utmost. Go outside and drive them away. When you've beaten them come to your uncle's to meet us." The she-devils then fled for their lives and went to the home of their teacher's senior disciple, where their wicked tongues were to give rise to more disasters, but of that we shall not now speak. Watch while the insects rub their fists in their hands and go out to confront their enemies.

Pig, meanwhile, whose head was spinning after falling over so often, looked up and suddenly saw that the silken canopy and ropes had all disappeared. Groping around he picked himself up, and despite his pain he made his way back the way he had come. As soon as he saw Monkey he grabbed him and said, "Brother, is my head bulging? Is my face all blue?" "What happened to you?" Monkey asked. "Those damned creatures caught me under a silken net and tripped me up goodness knows how many times with silk ropes," Pig replied. "My waist was twisted, my back felt broken and I couldn't move an inch. Then the silk canopy and the ropes all disappeared, so I could escape and come back." "Forget about it," said Friar Sand when he saw him, "forget about it. You asked for trouble. I'm sure the demons have all gone back to the cave to harm the master. We must go and rescue him straight away."

When Monkey heard this he set out at once as fast as he could and rushed back to the farm while Pig led the horse. Here the seven little devils could be seen standing on the bridge, blocking their way and saying, "Not so fast, not so fast. We're here." "What a joke!" said Pig when he saw them. "They're just a bunch of kids. They're only two foot five or six, well under three foot, and they can only weigh eight or nine pounds, not even ten." "Who are you?" he shouted. "We're the sons of the seven immortal ladies," the little devils replied. "You've insulted our mothers, and now you've got the effrontery to attack us, you ignorant fools. Stay where you are, and watch out." The splendid monsters then launched a wild onslaught on Pig, who was in a flaming temper after falling over so often. Seeing how tiny the insects were he lifted his rake to strike furious blows at them.

When the little devils saw how ferocious the idiot was they all reverted to their original forms, flew into the air and shouted, "Change!" In an instant each of them became ten, each ten became a hundred, each hundred became a thousand, and each thousand became ten thousand. Every one became a countless number. This is what could be seen:

The sky was full of wax-flies,
Dragonflies danced all over the land.
Bees and hornets went for the head,
Cockroaches jabbed at the eyes.
Spanish-flies bit before and behind,
While grasshoppers stung above and below.
His face was black and crawling with insects:
Even devils or deities would have been scared by their speed.

"Brother," said Pig in alarm, "you can say what you like about it being easy to fetch the scriptures, but on this road to the west even the insects give you a bad time." "Don't be afraid, brother," said Monkey. "Go for them." "But they're flying into my head and my face and all over my body," replied Pig. "They're at least ten layers deep and all stinging me. How can I go for them?" "No problem," said Monkey, "no problem. I know a trick." "Whatever it is, brother," said Friar Sand, "use it right now. His shaven head has swollen up with those bites in no time at all."

The splendid Great Sage pulled out a handful of hairs, chewed them into little bits and blew them out, telling them to turn to golden eagles, falcons, hawks, white eagles, vultures, ospreys and sparrowhawks." "Brother," said Pig, "what's that jargon about goldens and all that?" "Something you don't know about," Monkey replied. "Golden eagles, falcons, hawks, white eagles, vultures, ospreys and sparrowhawks are the seven birds of prey that my hairs turned into. That's because the she-devils' children are insects." Because the birds were so good at catching insects they got one every time they opened their beaks, grabbed at them with their claws or struck them with their wings. They wiped all the insects out in an instant, leaving no trace of them in the sky. The ground was piled over a foot deep with their bodies.

Only then could the three brothers charge across the bridge and into the cave, where they found their master hanging groaning and sobbing in mid-air. "Master," said Pig, going up to him, "are you hanging around here for fun? I don't know how many times I've had to fall over on your account." "Untie the master before we take this conversation any further," said Friar Sand. Brother Monkey then snapped the ropes and set the master free, asking, "Where did the evil spirits go?" "All seven of them ran stark naked through to the back," the Tang Priest replied. "They were calling for their sons." "After them, brothers!" said Monkey. "Follow me!"

The three of them, each holding his weapon, went searching in the back garden, but no sign of them could be found. They looked for them without success under all the peach and plum trees. "They've gone," said Pig, "they've gone." "We can stop looking for them," said Friar Sand. "I'm going to help the master away from here." The three brothers then went back to the front, where they asked the Tang Priest to mount up. "You two help the master along the way," said Pig. "I'm going to smash these buildings to the ground with my rake. Then they'll have nowhere to live when they come back." "Smashing the place would be too much effort," said Monkey. "The best way to cut off their roots would be to find some firewood." The splendid idiot then gathered some dead pine, broken-off bamboo, dried-out willow and withered creepers that he set alight. The roaring blaze destroyed everything. Only then did master and disciples feel easy enough to be on their way. If you don't know what of good or evil the demons were to do to them, listen to the explanation in the next instalment.

CHAPTER SEVENTY-THREE

The emotions bear a grudge and inflict disaster;
The heart's master smashes the light when he meets the demons.

The story tells how the Great Sage Sun supported the Tang Priest as they hurried along the main road to the west together with Pig and Friar Sand. Within a few hours they were in sight of a compound with many tall towers and imposing buildings. "Disciple," said Sanzang, reining in his horse, "what's that place?" Monkey looked up to gaze at it and this is what he saw:

Tall towers girdled by hills,
Streams winding round pavilions.
Dense grew the wood in front of the gates,
And outside the buildings the scent of flowers hung heavy.
White egrets perched among the willows,
Like flawless jades half hidden in a mist;
Golden orioles sang in the peach-trees,
Flashes of gold in the fiery blossom.
Wild deer in couples
Trod lost to the world across cushions of greenery;
Pairs of mountain birds
Sang as they flew among the red tree-tops.
It was like the Tiantai Cave of Liu and Ruan,
And rivalled the home of the immortals in fairyland.

"Master," Brother Monkey reported, "that's no princely palace or rich man's mansion. It looks like a Taoist temple or Buddhist monastery. We'll know for sure when we get there." On hearing this Sanzang whipped on his horse, and when master and disciples reached the gates to look there was a stone tablet set over the gateway on which was written YELLOW FLOWER

TEMPLE. Sanzang dismounted. "Yellow Flower Temple means it's a Taoist place," said Pig, "so it's all right for us to go in and see them. Although we wear different clothes we cultivate our conduct the same way." "You're right," said Friar Sand. "We can go in and have a look round, and at the same time the horse can have a feed. If it looks suitable we can arrange a meal for the master."

The master accepted their suggestions and the four of them went inside. A couplet was pasted up on either side of the inner gates:

Palace of immortals: yellow shoots and white snow.
Home of men who can fly: rare and wonderful flowers.

"So the Taoist here refines drugs, plays with a furnace and totes a crucible," said Monkey with a grin. "Watch your words," said Sanzang, giving him a pinch, "watch your words. We don't know them and they are no relations of ours. This is only a passing encounter. Never mind what they are like." Before he had finished saying these words he went in through the inner gate, where he found the doors of the main hall shut tight and a Taoist master sitting under a covered walkway making elixir pills. Just look at how he was dressed:

On his head a bright red hat all set with gold,
On his body a jet-black Taoist robe,
On his feet a pair of deep green cloud-treading shoes,
Round his waist a brilliant yellow Lü Dongbin sash.
His face was round like a golden melon,
His eyes like bright stars.
His nose was as big and as high as a Muslim's,
And his lips turned back like a Tartar's.
His heart, set on the Way, was hidden thunder;
He was a true immortal, subduer of tigers and dragons.

As soon as he saw him Sanzang shouted at the top of his voice, "My respectful greetings, venerable Taoist master." The Taoist looked up with a start and was so alarmed by what he saw that he dropped the elixir on which he was working. Then he neatened his hair-pins and clothes, came down the steps and greeted Sanzang: "Venerable sir, excuse me for failing to meet you. Please come inside and sit down." The venerable elder happily went up into the main hall. On pushing the doors open he saw the statues of the Three Pure Ones and an altar on which stood incense burners and incense, so he planted some joss-sticks in the burner and performed a triple set of obeisances to the Pure Ones before bowing to the Taoist master. He then went to the guest seats, where he sat down with his disciples. Immortal boys were told to bring tea at once, whereupon two boys went inside to fetch the tea-tray, wash the teacups, wipe the teaspoons and prepare some refreshments to eat with it. Their rushing about soon disturbed the pilgrims' enemies.

Now the seven devils from Gossamer Cave had been fellow-students of the Taoist master here, and it was here that they had hurried after putting on their old clothes and calling for their sons. They were making themselves new clothes at the back of the temple when they noticed the boys preparing the tea and asked, "What visitors have arrived, boys? What are you in such a rush for?" "Four Buddhist monks have just turned up," the boys replied, "and the master has told us to prepare tea for them." "Is one of the monks pale and fat?" the she-devils asked. "Yes." "Does one of them have a long snout and big ears?" they asked again. "Yes." "Then take the tea in as quickly as you can," the she-devils said, "and tip your master a wink to come in here. We've got something urgent to say to him."

The boys took five cups of tea out to the Taoist master, who tucked back his sleeves and passed a cup with both hands first to Sanzang and then to Pig, Friar Sand and Brother Monkey. After the tea had been drunk the cups were collected and the boys gave their master a look, at which he bowed and said, "Please sit down, gentlemen. Boys, put the tray down and keep them company. I have to go out. I'll be back." Sanzang and his disciples went out of the hall to look around, guided by one boy.

When the Taoist master went back to the abbot's lodgings

the seven women all fell to their knees and said, "Brother, brother, please listen to what we have to say." The Taoist master helped them to their feet and said, "When you came here this morning you wanted to tell me something, but because of the elixir pills I was making I couldn't see any women. That's why I had to refuse. I have visitors out there now, so you can tell me later." "We have to report, elder brother," the she-devils said, "that it's because the strangers are here that we're talking to you. If the strangers go away there'll be no point in telling you." "What are you talking about, sisters?" the Taoist master said. "Why do you have to talk to me just now, when the strangers are here? Have you gone off your heads? I'm a man who lives in peace and quiet cultivating immortality, but even if I were a layman with wife and children and family responsibilities I'd wait till my visitors had left before attending to them. How can you be so ill-behaved and disgrace me? Now let me go." All the she-devils grabbed him and said, "Please don't lose your temper, elder brother. Tell us where the visitors come from." The Taoist master pulled a long face and ignored them. "When the boys came in for the tea just now they told us the visitors are four Buddhist monks," the she-devils said. "They're monks," said the Taoist master angrily, "what of it?" "Does one of the four monks have a pale, fat face," the she-devils asked, "and one of them a long snout and big ears? Did you ask them where they're from?" "Yes," the Taoist said, "there are two like that among them. How did you know? I suppose you've seen them somewhere."

"You don't know the terrible things that have happened, brother," the devils said. "That monk was sent by the Tang court to fetch the scriptures from the Western Heaven. He came to our cave this morning begging for food. We captured him because we'd heard of this Tang Priest." "Why did you capture him?" the Taoist asked. "We've long known that the Tang Priest has a pure body because he has cultivated his conduct for ten successive incarnations," the devils replied. "Anyone who eats a piece of his flesh will live for ever. That's why we captured him. Later the monk with a long snout and big ears kept us in the Filth-cleansing Spring. First he stole our clothes and then he used his magical powers to insist on bathing with us. He jumped into the water and turned himself into a catfish. From the way he kept swimming around between our thighs he obviously had very improper ideas. He was thoroughly disgraceful. Then he jumped out of the water and turned back into himself. As we weren't going to let him have his way he tried to kill us all with his nine-pronged rake. If we hand't known a thing or two he'd have murdered the lot of us. We fled in fear and trembling and sent your nephews into battle. We don't know whether they are alive or dead. We have come here to fling ourselves on your mercy and beg you to avenge your fellow-students from long ago."

On hearing this the Taoist was furious, as could be seen from his changed expression. "What outrageous monks!" he exclaimed. "What hooligans! Don't you worry: I'm going to sort them out." "If you're going to fight them," said the she-devils in gratitude, "you must let us help you." "There'll be no need to fight," said the Taoist, "no need. As the saying goes, you have to lower yourself to fight someone. Come with me."

The women went with him into his room, where he carried a ladder behind the bed, climbed up to the rafters and brought down a little leather box. It was eight inches high, a foot long, four inches wide and locked with a tiny brass lock. From his sleeve he produced a square handkerchief of goose-yellow silk, to the fringes of which a tiny key was tied. Unlocking the box he brought out a packet containing a drug. This drug was:

A thousand pounds of droppings
From all kinds of mountain birds,
Boiled in a copper cauldron,
Reduced on an even fire,
Till the thousand pounds were only a spoonful
That was then reduced to a third.
This was fried even longer,
Refined and smoked once again,

To make the poisonous drug,
More precious than treasures or jewels.
Were you to try out its flavour,
One taste would send yon to Hell.

"Sisters," said the Taoist master, "any mortal who eats one grain of this treasure of mine will be dead when it reaches his stomach. Only three grains would be enough to kill a god or an immortal. As these monks may have mastered something of the Way they'll need three grains. Fetch my balance." One of the women brought a balance at once. "Weigh out twelve grains," he said, "and divide that into four portions." Then he took twelve red jujubes, pinched holes in them, stuffed a grain of the drug in each, and put them into four teacups. These were then placed with a fifth cup containing two black jujubes on a tray. "Let me question them," he said. "If they aren't from Tang that'll be the end of it; but if they are I'll ask for fresh tea and you can give this tea to the boys to bring in. Once they drink it they'll all die and you'll be avenged. That'll cheer you up." The seven women were beside themselves with gratitude.

The Taoist changed into another robe and walked out again with a great show of feigned courtesy. He urged the Tang Priest and the others to sit down in the guest seats again. "Please excuse me, venerable sir," the Taoist said. "The reason why I neglected you just now was because I was at the back telling my disciples to choose some greens and radishes to cook as a vegetarian meal for you." "We Buddhist monks came empty-handed," said Sanzang. "We could not possibly trouble you for a meal." "We are all men of religion," replied the Taoist master with a smile. "Whenever we go to a monastery or temple we are entitled to three pints of rice, so why talk of being empty-handed? May I ask you, reverend sir, what monastery you are from, and why you are here?" "I have been sent by His Majesty the Great Tang emperor to fetch the scriptures from the Great Thunder Monastery in the Western Heaven," Sanzang replied. "As we were passing your Taoist temple we came in to pay our respects." At this news the Taoist's face was full of animation, as he said, "It was only because I did not realize you were so faithful to the most virtuous Buddha that I failed to come out a long way to meet you. Please forgive me. Please forgive me." Then he told the boys to bring fresh tea at once and get a meal ready as soon as possible, at which the boys went straight inside to fetch the tea. "Here's some good tea that's all ready," the women called to them. "Take this in." The boys did indeed take the five cups in, and the Taoist master hurriedly passed a cup of red jujube tea to the Tang Priest. As Pig was so big the Taoist took him for the senior disciple, and he thought Friar Sand was the next senior. Thinking that Monkey was the junior one the Taoist only handed him his cup fourth.

By the time the sharp-eyed Brother Monkey took his cup he had already noticed that there were two black jujubes in the cup left on the tray. "Let's change cups, sir," he said. "To be honest with you," the Taoist replied with a smile, "as a poor Taoist living out here in the wilds I am rather short of tea and food at the moment. I was looking for fruit out at the back just now and I could only find these twelve red jujubes to put into four cups of tea to offer you. As I had to take something with you I made another cup with these inferior jujubes to keep you company. This is just a gesture of respect." "What nonsense," said Monkey with a smile. "As the ancients said, 'You are never poor if you are at home; but poverty on a journey is killing.' You're at home here, so why all this talk about being poor? It's wandering monks like us who are really poor. I'll swop with you. I insist." "Wukong," said Sanzang when he heard this, "this immortal gentleman is being very hospitable. You have yours. There is no need for a swop." Monkey had no choice. Taking the cup with his left hand he covered it with his right and watched them.

Pig, however, who apart from feeling hungry and thirsty had an enormous appetite at the best of times, picked the three red jujubes out of the cup as soon as he saw them and swallowed them noisily. The master ate his too, as did Friar Sand. In that very instant Pig's face changed colour, tears started pouring from Friar Sand's eyes and the Tang Priest began to foam at the mouth. Unable to sit upright, all three of them fainted and fell to the floor.

Realizing that they had been poisoned, the Great Sage raised his teacup in his hands and threw it at the Taoist master's face. The Taoist stopped it with his sleeve and it shattered noisily as it fell to the floor. "You lout, monk," said the Taoist in fury, "how dare you smash my cup?" "Animal," said Monkey abusively, "just look what you've done to those three! What have I ever done to you for you to give my people poisoned tea?" "Beast," said the Taoist master, "you asked for it. Don't you realize that?" "We've only just come here and talked about things like where we should sit and where we're from," said Monkey. "We didn't talk big. How can you say we asked for this trouble?" "Did you beg for food in Gossamer Cave?" the Taoist master asked. "Did you bathe in the Filth-cleansing Spring?" "There were seven she-devils in the Filth-cleansing Spring," Monkey replied. "From what you're saying you must be in cahoots with them. I'm sure you're an evil spirit yourself. Stay where you are and take this!" The splendid Great Sage felt in his ear for his gold-banded cudgel, waved it to make it as thick as a rice-bowl, and struck at the Taoist master's face. The Taoist rapidly turned and dodged the blow, then produced a fine sword with which he fought back.

Their cursing and fighting had by now disturbed the seven she-devils inside, who all rushed out shouting, "Spare yourself the trouble, elder brother. Let us catch him." At the sight of them Monkey became angrier than ever. Whirling his iron cudgel around with both hands he dropped his guard and tumbled in among them, lashing out wildly. The seven women then undid their clothes, revealing their white stomachs, and from their navels they produced by magic thick silken ropes that came reeling out in such abundance that they formed a canopy under which Brother Monkey was confined.

Seeing that things were going badly Monkey got up, said the words of a spell, did a somersault, smashed through the canopy and escaped. Then he stood gloomily in mid-air, controlling his temper and watching as the flashing silken ropes criss-crossed like the warp and weft of cloth on the loom. Within a moment the Yellow Flower Temple's towers and halls were all completely concealed. "Terrible," said Monkey, "they're terrible. I've never been up against anything like that before. No wonder Pig fell over so often. What am I to do now? The master and my brothers have been poisoned. This gang of devils are all hand in glove, and I know nothing about their background. I'll go back and question that local god."

The splendid Great Sage brought his cloud down to land, made a spell with his fingers, said the sacred syllable *Om*, and forced the old local god to come to him again. The old deity knelt beside the path, trembling with fear and kowtowing as he said, "Great Sage, you went to rescue your master. Why are you back again?" "I rescued him this morning," Monkey replied, "and a little way ahead from there we reached a Yellow Flower Temple. When I went in with the master to look around, the head Taoist of the temple greeted us, and in the middle of our conversation he knocked out my master and the other two with poisoned tea. Luckily I didn't drink any, but when I was going to hit him with my cudgel he started talking about begging for food at Gossamer Cave and bathing at the Filth-cleansing Spring, so I knew he was a monster. No sooner had he raised his hand to fight back than the seven women came out and set off their silken ropes. It was a good thing I had the know-how to get away. I reckon that as you're a god who lives round here you're bound to know their background. What sort of evil spirit are they? Tell me the truth if you don't want to be hit." "It's less than ten years since those evil spirits came here," said the local deity, kowtowing. "When I was making an inspection three years ago I saw what they really are: seven spider spirits. The silken ropes that come out of them are spiders' webs." The news thoroughly delighted Monkey, who said, "From what you tell me they're no problem. Very well then. You can go back while I use magic to subdue him." The local god kowtowed and went.

Monkey then went to the outside of the Yellow Flower

Temple, pulled seventy hairs out of his tail, blew on them with magic breath and shouted, "Change!" The hairs turned into seventy little Monkeys. He then blew a magic breath on his gold-banded cudgel, called "Change!" and turned it into seventy two-pronged forks, one of which he gave to each of the little Monkeys. Monkey himself used one of the forks to twist the silken ropes as he stood outside, then they all attacked together to the rhythm of a tune, tearing the ropes to pieces, each of them tearing off over ten pounds of rope. They dragged seven spiders out from inside. Each was about the size of a wicker basket. All of them held their hands and feet together and had ropes round their necks. "Spare us, spare us," they said. The seventy little Monkeys then pressed the seven spiders to the ground, refusing to let them go. "Don't hit them," said Monkey. "All we want is to make them give my master and my brothers back." "Elder Brother," shrieked the demons at the tops of their voices, "give the Tang Priest back and save our lives." The Taoist master rushed outside saying, "Sisters, I'm going to eat the Tang Priest. I can't save you."

This infuriated Brother Monkey. "If you won't give my master back just watch what happens to your sisters." The splendid Great Sage waved his fork, turned it back into an iron cudgel that he lifted with both hands and smashed the seven spider spirits to pulp. Then he shook his tail a couple of times, put the hairs back on it and charged inside alone, swinging his cudgel to fight the Taoist master.

When the Taoist master saw Monkey kill his seven fellow-students it was more than he could bear. Goaded to fury, he raised his sword to fight back. In this battle each of them was seething with anger and giving full play to his divine powers. It was a fine battle:

The evil spirit swung a fine sword;
The Great Sage raised his gold-banded cudgel.
Both were fighting for Sanzang of the Tang,
On whose account the seven women had been killed.
Now they were fighting with all-round skill,

Showing their mighty powers with their weapons.
Powerful was the Great Sage's aura,
And rough the courage of the evil immortal.
Their vigorous moves were as rich as brocade,
And both hands moved as fast as a windlass.
Noisily clanged the sword and cudgel,
And ominously pale were the floating clouds.
Few were the words they spoke
As they used their cunning,
Moving to and fro like brush-strokes in a painting.
The wind and dust they raised scared wolves and tigers;
The stars disappeared as heaven and earth went dark.

When the Taoist master had fought fifty or sixty rounds with the Great Sage he felt his hand weakening and his sinews getting slack, so he undid his belt and with a loud flapping noise took off his black robe. "Well, my lad," said the Great Sage with a laugh, "if you can't beat me you still won't be able to when you strip off." Once the Taoist master had stripped off his clothes he raised both hands to reveal under his ribs a thousand eyes flashing golden light. It was terrible:

Dense yellow smoke,
Brilliant golden light.
The dense yellow smoke
Gushed out as clouds from under his ribs;
The brilliant golden light
Came from a thousand eyes like fire.
To left and right they seemed like golden pails;
To east and west they resembled bells of bronze.
Thus an evil immortal used his magic power,
A Taoist master showed divine ability,
Dazzling the eyes, blotting out sun, moon and sky,
Blanketing people with acrid vapours.
The Great Sage Equalling Heaven
Was caught in the golden light and yellow smoke.

Monkey started lashing out desperately with his hands and feet, but could only spin around inside the golden light, unable to take a step either forwards or backwards. It was as if he were turning round and round in a bucket. It was hopeless. He was unbearably hot. In his anxiety he leapt into the air, smashing against the golden light, and crashing head first to the ground. His head ached where he had hit it, and felt anxiously to find that the top of his scalp was tender. "What lousy luck," he thought, "what lousy luck. This head's useless today. Usually swords and axes can't hurt it, so why has golden light bruised it now? After a while it's bound to go septic, and even if it does get better I might have tetanus." He was still feeling unbearably hot. "I can't move forward or back," he thought, working out a plan, "or to left or right, and I can't smash my way through by going up. Whatever shall I do? I'll bloodly well have to get out by going down."

The splendid Great Sage said the words of a spell, shook himself, and turned into one of those scaly diggers called pangolins. Indeed,

Four sets of iron claws
Dug through the mountain, smashing rocks like powder.
The scales covering his body
Carved through ridges and crags like slicing scallions.
His eyes were as bright
As two gleaming stars;
His mouth was sharper
Than a steel drill or brazen auger.
He was the scaly mountain-borer used in medicine,
The creature known as the pangolin.

Watch him as he burrows into the ground with his head, not coming out again till he has covered over six miles. The golden light could only enclose about three miles. When he emerged and turned back into himself he was exhausted. His muscles ached, his whole body was in pain, and he could not help weeping. Suddenly he burst out with, "Master,

Since leaving the mountain and joining the faith
I've worked very hard on our way to the West.

The waves of the ocean are nothing to fear,
But in this dry gulch I've come out second best."

Just as the Handsome Monkey King was feeling miserable the sound of sobs could suddenly be heard from the other side of the mountain. Leaning forward and drying his tears he turned to look. A woman appeared, dressed in deep mourning and sobbing at every step as she came from the other side of the mountain. She was holding a dish of cold rice gruel in her left hand and several pieces of yellow paper money for burning to the dead in her right. Monkey sighed and nodded as he said to himself, "This is a case of

Weeping eyes meeting weeping eyes,
One broken heart coming across another.

I wonder what this woman is crying about. I'll ask her." Before long the woman was coming along the path towards him. "Lady Bodhisattva," asked Brother Monkey with a bow, "who are you weeping for?" Through her tears the woman replied, "My husband was murdered by the master of the Yellow Flower Temple with poisoned tea because he got into a quarrel with him over the purchase of some bamboo poles. I'm going to burn this paper money as a mark of my love for him." This made Monkey's tears flow. The sight made the woman say angrily, "You ignorant fool. I'm grieving over my husband, but what business do you have to be weeping and looking so miserable? Are you mocking me?"

"Please don't be angry, Bodhisattva," said Monkey with a bow. "I'm Sun Wukong the Novice, the senior disciple of Tang Sanzang, the younger brother of the Great Tang Emperor in the east. When we passed the Yellow Flower Temple on our way to the Western Heaven we stopped to rest, but the Taoist master there is some kind of evil spirit who's the sworn brother of seven spider spirits. When the spider spirits wanted to kill my master in Gossamer Cave I and my brother disciples Pig and Friar Sand managed to save him. The spider spirits fled to the Taoist's place and told him a pack of lies about us bullying them, so the Taoist knocked out my master and brothers. The three of them and the horse are now prisoners in his temple. I was the only one who didn't drink the tea. I smashed the cup and he attacked me. Because of the noise the seven spider spirits rushed outside to give out their silken ropes and catch me in the web they wove. I only got away by magic. After I'd found out who they really were I used my power of giving myself extra bodies to tear the silken ropes to pieces, drag the demons out and beat them to death. The Taoist master wanted revenge, so he went for me with his sword. When we'd gone sixty rounds he fled beaten, took off his clothes, and used the thousand eyes he has under his ribs to give off countless beams of golden light. I was caught under them, unable to move forwards or backwards, so I turned into a pangolin and burrowed my way out underground. It was when I was feeling thoroughly depressed that I heard you weeping, which was why I asked you those questions. When I saw that you had paper money to give your husband I felt wretched and miserable because I've got nothing for my master when he dies. Making fun of you was the last thing on my mind!"

Putting down the gruel and the paper money the woman returned Brother Monkey's bow and said, "Please forgive me. I didn't realize that you were a sufferer too. From what you've just said you don't know who that Taoist is. He's really the Demon King Hundred-eye, who's also known as the Many-eyed Monster. You must have tremendous magical powers to have escaped from the golden light and fought so long, but you couldn't get near him. I'll tell you about a sage you can send for who would be able to smash the golden light and defeat the Taoist."

Monkey's immediate response was to chant a "na-a-aw" of respect and say, "If you know the sage's background, lady Bodhisattva, may I trouble you to tell me about it? If there is such a sage I'll fetch him to rescue my master and avenge your husband." "I'll tell you," the woman said, "and you can fetch the sage, who will subdue the Taoist, but that will only bring revenge. I'm afraid the sage won't be able to rescue your master." "Why not?" Monkey asked. "His poison is truly lethal," the woman replied. "When people are laid low by it the very marrow of their bones rots within three days. I'm afraid that by the time you've been to see the sage and come back again you'll be too late to save him." "I know how to travel," Monkey replied. "However far it is I'll only take half a day." "If you can travel then listen to this," the woman said. "About three hundred miles from here there's a mountain called Mount Purple Clouds, and in the mountain there's a Thousand Flower Cave where there lives a sage called Vairambha who will be able to defeat that demon." "Where's the mountain?" Monkey asked. "Which direction should I take?" "It's due south of here," the woman replied, pointing; and by the time Brother Monkey looked back at her she had disappeared.

Monkey quickly did a kowtow and said, "Which Bodhisattva was that? After all that burrowing your disciple was feeling too stupid to recognize you. I beg you to tell me your name so that I can thank you." At this there came a shout from mid-air, "Great Sage, it's me." Monkey quickly looked up to see that it was the Old Lady of Mount Li. Catching up with her in the sky he thanked her with the words, "Where have you come from to give me these instructions?" "On my way back from Dragon Flower Assembly I noticed that your master was in trouble," the Old Lady replied. "It was to save his life that I pretended to be a woman in mourning for her husband. Hurry up and fetch the sage. But don't tell her I sent you: she is rather difficult."

Thanking her, Monkey took his leave and set off straight away on his somersault cloud. Once at Mount Purple Clouds he brought his cloud down and saw the Thousand Flower Cave. Outside the cave:

Blue pines masked the splendid view,
Turquoise cypresses surrounded the immortal's home.
Green willows were packed close along the mountain paths,
Rare flowers filled the watercourses.
Orchids grew all around stone buildings,

And scented blooms gave colour to the crags.
Flowing water linked ravines with green,
While clouds enclosed the emptiness of trees.
Noisily sang wild birds,
Slowly strolled the deer,
Elegant grew the bamboo,
And all the red plums were open.
Rooks perched in ancient woods,
While spring birds chirped in the tree of heaven.
Summer wheat filled spreading acres,
And autumn millet grew all over the land.
No leaf fell in all four seasons,
And flowers bloomed throughout the year.
Auspicious rosy glows joined with the Milky Way,
And clouds of good omen were linked with the Great Emptiness.

The Great Sage was delighted as he went inside, seeing boundless beauty at every stage. He went straight on, but found it deserted and completely silent. Not even a chicken or a dog could be heard. "I think that this sage must be out," Monkey thought. When he had gone a mile or two further on he saw a Taoist nun sitting on a couch. This is what she looked like:

She wore a five-flowered hat of brocade,
And a robe of golden silk.
Her cloud-treading shoes were patterned with phoenixes
And round her waist was a sash with double tassels.
Her face looked as old as autumn after a frost,
But her voice was as charming as swallows in the spring.
Long had she mastered the Dharma of Three Vehicles,
And she was ever mindful of the Four Truths.
She knew true achievement, that emptiness is empty,
And through her training had acquired great freedom.
She was the Buddha of the Thousand Flower Cave,
The illustrious Vairambha of great fame.

Monkey went straight up to her without stopping and said, "Greetings, Bodhisattva Vairambha." The Bodhisattva then came down from her couch, put her hands together to return his greeting and said, "Great Sage, it was remiss of me not to come out to greet you. Where have you come from?" "How do you know that I'm the Great Sage?" Monkey asked. "When you made havoc in Heaven the other year," Vairambha replied, "your picture was circulated everywhere. That's why everyone can recognize you." "How true it is," Monkey said, "that

While good deeds stay at home
Bad deeds are known far and wide.

Take my conversion to Buddhism, for example. You didn't know about that." "Congratulations," said Vairambha. "When did that happen?" "Not long ago my life was spared to escort my master the Tang Priest on his journey to the Western Heaven to fetch the scriptures," Monkey replied. "My master has been laid low with poisoned tea by the Taoist of the Yellow Flower Temple. When I was fighting with him he caught me in his golden light, and I had to use magic to escape. I have come here to pay you my respects, Bodhisattva, and ask your help because I've heard that you are able to destroy his golden light." "Who told you that?" the Bodhisattva asked. "I have not left here since the Ullambana assembly over three hundred years ago. I've lived in complete secrecy and nobody has heard of me, so how is it that you know of me?" "I'm an underground devil," Monkey replied, "and I can make my own enquiries anywhere at all." "Never mind," Vairambha said, "never mind. I shouldn't really go, but as you have honoured me with a visit, Great Sage, and as the great cause of fetching the scriptures must not be allowed to fail I'll go with you."

Monkey thanked her and said, "It's very ignorant of me to hurry you along in this way. I wonder what weapon you use." "I have an embroidery needle that will put an end to that damned creature," said the Bodhisattva

This was too much for Monkey. "Old Lady, you've been wasting my time," he said. "Had I known it was an embroidery needle I wouldn't have had to trouble you. I could have provided a hundredweight of them." "Your embroidery needles are all made of iron, steel or gold," the Bodhisattva replied. "They're no use. My treasure isn't iron and isn't steel and isn't gold. It was tempered by my son in the Sun." "Who is he?" asked Monkey. "He is the Star Lord of the Mane," Vairambha replied. This came as a shock to Monkey, who gazed at the golden light then turned to Vairambha and said, "The Yellow Flower Temple is where that golden light is coming from." Vairambha then took from the lapel of her gown an embroidery needle about the thickness of an eyebrow hair and half an inch long. Holding it between her fingers she threw it into the air. A few moments later there was a loud noise and the golden light was shattered. "That's wonderful, Bodhisattva, wonderful!" exclaimed a delighted Monkey. "Let's find your needle now." "Isn't this it here?" asked Vairambha, who was holding it in her hand. Brother Monkey brought his cloud down to land with hers and went into the temple, where he found the Taoist with his eyes shut, unable to move. "Stop playing blind, damned demon," he said abusively, taking his cudgel from his ear ready to hit the Taoist with. "Don't hit him, Great Sage," said Vairambha. "Go and see your master."

On going straight to the reception room at the back Monkey found the three of them bringing up mucus and spittle where they lay on the floor. "What am I to do?" wept Monkey. "What am I to do?" "Don't grieve, Great Sage," said Vairambha. "As I've come out today I think I might as well accumulate some merit by giving you three of these pills that are an antidote to the poison." Monkey turned round to bow down and beg her for them, whereupon she produced a torn paper packet from her sleeve containing three red pills that she handed to Monkey, telling him to put one in each of their mouths. This he did, forcing their teeth apart. A few moments later they all started vomiting as the drug reached their stomachs, bringing up the poison and coming back to life. Pig was the first to scramble to his feet. "I feel suffocated," he said. Sanzang and Friar Sand both came round too, saying that they felt very dizzy. "Your tea was poisoned," Brother Monkey explained. "It was the Bodhisattva Vairambha who saved you. Hurry up and bow to her in thanks." Sanzang bowed to her to show his gratitude as he straightened up his clothes.

"Brother," said Pig, "where's that Taoist? I've got some questions to ask him about why he tried to murder me." Monkey then told him all about the spider spirits. "If spider spirits are his sisters that damned creature must be an evil spirit too," said Pig with fury. "He's standing outside the main hall pretending to be blind,"said Monkey, pointing. Pig grabbed his rake and was about to hit the Taoist with it when Vairambha stopped him and said, "Control your temper, Marshal Tian Peng. As the Great Sage knows, I have no servants in my cave. I am going to take him as my doorkeeper." "We are deeply indebted to your great power," Monkey replied, "and we will of course obey. But we would like you to turn him back into his real self so that we can have a look at him." "Easily done," said Vairambha, stepping forward and pointing at the Taoist, who collapsed into the dust and reverted to his real form of a giant centipede spirit seven feet long. Picking him up with her little finger Vairambha rode her auspicious cloud straight back to the Thousand Flower Cave. "That old lady's a real terror," said Pig, looking up. "How did she manage to subdue that evil creature?" "When I asked her what weapon she had to smash the golden light with," Monkey replied, "she told me about a golden embroidery needle of hers that her son had tempered in the sun. When I asked her who her son was she told me he was the Star Lord of the Mane. As I remember, the Mane Star is a cock, so his mother must be a hen. Hens are very good at dealing with centipedes, which is why she could subdue him."

On hearing this Sanzang performed no end of kowtows. "Disciples," he ordered, "go and get things ready." Friar Sand then went inside to find some rice and prepare a vegetarian meal, so that they could all eat their fill. Then they led the horse up, shouldered the carrying-pole, and asked the master to set out. Monkey started a blaze in the kitchen that in an instant burnt the whole temple to ashes. He then set out on his way. Indeed,

The Tang Priest thanked Vairambha for saving his life;
The emotions were eliminated and the Many-eyed Monster removed.

As for what happened on the way ahead, listen to the explanations in the next instalment.

CHAPTER SEVENTY-FOUR

Li Changgeng reports the demons' vicious nature; The Novice displays his powers of transformation.

Emotions and desires are in origin all the same;
Both emotions and desires are completely natural.
Many a gentleman refines himself in the Buddhist faith;
When desire and emotions are forgotten, dhyana comes.
Don't be impatient; be firm of heart;
Be free of dust like the moon in the sky.
Make no mistake in your labours and your progress;
When your efforts are completed you will be an enlightened immortal.

The story tells how Sanzang and his disciples, having broken through the net of desires and escaped from the prison-house of the emotions, let the horse travel west. Before they had been going for very long the summer was over and the new coolness of early autumn was refreshing their bodies. What they saw was:

Driving rains sweeping away the last of the heat,
Alarming the leaf of the parasol tree.
At evening glow-worms flew by the sedgy path
While crickets sang beneath the moon.
The golden mallows opened in the dew;
Red knotweed covered the sandbanks.
Rushes and willows were the first to lose their leaves
As cold cicadas sang in tune.

As Sanzang was travelling along a high mountain appeared in front of him. Its peak thrust up into the azure void, touching the stars and blocking out the sun. In his alarm the venerable elder said to Monkey, "Look at that mountain in front of us. It's very high. I don't know whether the path will take us across." "What a thing to say, Master," said Monkey with a smile. "As the old saying goes,

However high the mountain there will be a way across;
However deep the river there's always a ferryman.

There's no reason why we shouldn't get over it. Stop worrying and carry on." When Sanzang heard this his face broke out in smiles and he whipped his horse forward to climb straight up the high crag.

After a mile or two an old man appeared. His white hair was tangled and flying in the wind while his sparse whiskers were being blown about like silver threads. He wore a string of prayer-beads round his neck and held a dragon-headed walking-stick as he stood far away at the top of the slope shouting, "Venerable gentleman travelling west, stop your worthy steed. Rein in. There is a band of demons on this mountain who have eaten all the people in the continent of Jambu. Go no further!" At this Sanzang turned pale with terror, and because the horse was not standing steadily and he himself was not well seated in the carved saddle he crashed to the ground and lay in the grass, moaning but unable to move.

Monkey went over to help him to his feet with the words, "Don't be afraid, don't be afraid. I'm here." "Did you hear the old man up on the crag telling us that there's a band of demons on this mountain who have eaten everyone in the continent of Jambu?" said Sanzang. "Who'll dare go to ask him what this is really all about?" "Sit there while I go and ask him," Monkey replied. "With your ugly face and coarse language I'm afraid you may shock him," said Sanzang, "so you won't get the truth from him." "I'll make myself a bit better looking before questioning him," laughed Brother Monkey. "Do a change to show me," said Sanzang, and the splendid Great Sage made a spell with his fingers, shook himself, and turned into a very neat little monk, clear-eyed, fine-browed, round-headed and regular of features. He moved in a most refined way and said nothing vulgar when he opened his mouth. Brushing his brocade tunic he stepped forward and said to the Tang Priest, "Master, have I changed for the better?" "Yes," said the delighted Sanzang. "Marvellous," said Pig, "but the rest of us look shabby by comparison. Even if I rolled around for two or three years on end I couldn't make myself look as elegant as that."

The splendid Great Sage left them behind as he went straight up to the old man, bowed to him and said, "Greetings, venerable sir." Seeing how young and cultivated he looked, the old man returned his greeting and stroked his head in an offhand way. "Little monk," the old man said with a smile, "where have you come from?" "We are from the Great Tang in the east," Monkey replied, "going to worship the Buddha and fetch the scriptures. When we came here and heard you tell us that there are demons here my master was terrified. He sent me to ask you about them. What sort of evil spirits would dare go in for that sort of crime? I would trouble you, venerable sir, to tell me all the details so that I can put them in their place and send them on their way." "You're much too young, little monk," said the old man with a smile, "to know what's good for you. Your remarks aren't helpful. Those evil spirits have tremendous magical powers. How can you have the nerve to talk of putting them in their place and sending them on their way?" "From what you are saying," Monkey replied with a smile, "you seem to be trying to protect them. You must be a relation of theirs, or else a neighbour or a friend. Why else would you be promoting their prestige and boosting their morale, and refusing to pour out everything you know about their background?" "You certainly know how to talk, monk," said the old man, nodding and smiling. "I suppose you must have learned some magic arts while travelling with your master. Perhaps you know how to drive away and capture goblins, or have exorcised people's houses for them. But you've never come up against a really vicious monster." "What sort of vicious?" Monkey said. "If those evil spirits send a letter to Vulture Mountain the five hundred arhats all come out to meet them," the old man said. "If they send a note to the Heavenly Palace the Ten Bright Shiners all turn out to pay their respects. The dragons of the Four Oceans were their friends and they often meet the immortals of the Eight Caves. The Ten Kings of the Underworld call them brothers; the local gods and city gods are good friends of theirs.

When the Great Sage heard this he could not help bursting into loud guffaws. "Stop talking," he said, grabbing hold of the old man, "stop talking. Even if that demon is friends with all those young whipper-snappers, my juniors, that's nothing really remarkable. If he knew I was coming he'd clear off the same night." "You're talking nonsense, little monk," the old man said. "How can any of those sages be juniors and young whipper-snappers to you?" "To be truthful with you," Monkey replied with a grin, "my people have lived for many generations in the Water Curtain Cave on the Mountain of Flowers and Fruit in the land of Aolai. My name is Sun Wukong. In the old days I used to be an evil spirit too and did some great things. Once I fell asleep after drinking too much at a feast with the other demons and dreamed that two men came to drag me off to the World of Darkness. I got so angry that I wounded the demon judges with my gold-banded cudgel. The kings of the Underworld were terrified and I practically turned the Senluo Palace upside-down. The judges in charge of the case were so scared that they fetched some paper for the Ten Kings to sign. They promised to treat me as their senior if I let them off a beating." "Amitabha Buddha!" exclaimed the old man when he heard this. "If you talk big like that you won't be able to grow any older." "I'm old enough, fellow," said Monkey. "How old are you then?" the old man asked. "Guess," Monkey replied. "Six or seven," the old man said. "I'm ten thousand times as old as that," laughed Monkey, "I'll show you my old face, then you'll believe me." "How can you have another face?" the old man asked. "This little monk has seventy-two faces," Monkey replied.

Not realizing that Monkey really had these powers the old man went on questioning him till Monkey rubbed his face and turned back into himself, with his protruding teeth, big mouth, red thighs and tigerskin kilt round his waist. As he stood there at the foot of the rocky scar, holding his gold-banded cudgel, he was the living image of a thunder god. The sight of him made the old man turn pale with terror and go so weak at the knees that he could not keep himself upright but collapsed to the ground. When he got to his feet again he lost his balance once more. "Old man," said the Great Sage, going up to him, "don't get yourself so frightened over nothing. I may look evil but I'm good inside. Don't be afraid! You were kind enough just now to tell us that there are demons here. Could I trouble you to let me know how many of them there are? I'll thank you very much if you do." The old man trembled, unable to speak and acting as if deaf. He replied not a word.

Getting no answer from him, Monkey went back down the slope. "So you are back, Wukong," Sanzang said. "What did you find out?" "It's nothing," said Monkey with a smile, "nothing. Even if there are one or two evil spirits on the way to the Western Heaven, the people here only worry so much about them because they're such cowards. No problem! I'm here!" "Did you ask him what mountain this was and what cave," said Sanzang, "how many monsters there are, and which is the way to Thunder Monastery?" "Please excuse me if I speak frankly, Master," put in Pig. "When it comes to transformations, trickery and deception then four or five of us would be no match for Brother Monkey. But a whole parade of Monkeys couldn't touch me for honesty." "That's right," said the Tang Priest, "that's right. You're honest." "Goodness knows why," said Pig, "but he just rushed in without a second thought, asked a couple of questions, and came running back in an awful mess. I'm going to find out the truth." "Do be careful, Wuneng," said the Tang Priest.

The splendid idiot put his rake in his belt, straightened up his tunic, and swaggered straight up the slope to call to the old man, "Respectful greetings, sir." The old man had finally managed to get back on his feet with the help of his stick after seeing that Monkey had gone, and was still shaking and about to depart when Pig suddenly appeared. "Sir," he said, more shocked than ever, "whatever kind of nightmare am I in the middle of? The first monk was ugly enough, but at least he looked a little bit human. But this one's got a snout like a pestle, ears like rush fans, a face like iron plates, and a neck covered in bristles. It doesn't look at all human." "You must be in a very bad mood to run me down like that, old man," laughed Pig. "Is that how you see me? Ugly I may be, but if you can bear to look at me for a while you'll find I get quite handsome."

Only when the old man heard Pig using human speech did he address him by asking, "Where are you from?" "I'm the Tang Priest's second disciple," Pig replied, "and my Buddhist names are Wuneng or Bajie. The one who came and asked you questions just now was Sun Wukong the Novice, the senior disciple. My master has sent me to pay my respects to you because he's angry with Sun Wukong for offending you and not finding out the truth. Could you please tell me, sir, what mountain this is, what caves there are on it, what demons live in them, and which is the main route west?" "Are you honest?" the old man asked. "I've never been false in all my life," Pig replied. "You mustn't talk a whole lot of fancy nonsense like the other monk just now," said the old man. "I'm not like him," Pig replied.

Leaning on his stick, the old man said to Pig, "This is Lion Ridge, and it is 250 miles around. In it there is a Lion Cave where there are three demon chieftains." "You're worrying over nothing, old man," said Pig, spitting. "Why go to all that trouble just to tell us about three demons?" "Aren't you afraid?" the old man said. "To tell you the truth," Pig replied, "my elder brother'll kill one with one swing of his cudgel, I'll kill another with one bash from my rake, and the other disciple will kill the third one with his demon-quelling staff. And with the three of them dead our master will be able to cross the ridge. No problem!" "You don't know the whole story, monk," said the old man with a smile. "Those three demon chiefs have the most tremendous magic powers. As for the little demons under their command, there are five thousand on the southern end of the ridge, five thousand on the northern end, ten thousand on the road east, ten thousand on the road west, four or five thousand patrollers, and another ten thousand on the gates. Then there are any number who work in the kitchen and gather firewood. There must be 47,000 or 48,000 altogether. They all have names and carry passes, and all they do is eat people."

On learning this the idiot ran back, shivering and shaking. As soon as he was near the Tang Priest he put down his rake and started shitting instead of reporting back. "What are you squatting there for instead of making your report?" shouted Monkey when he saw the idiot. "Because I'm shit scared," Pig replied. "No time to talk now. The sooner we all run for our lives the better." "Stupid fool," said Monkey. "I wasn't frightened when I questioned him, so why should you be in such a witless panic?" "What is the situation?" Sanzang asked. "The old man says that this is Lion Mountain," Pig replied, "and that there's a Lion Cave in it. There are three chief demons there, and they have 48,000 little devils under them. All they do is eat people. So if we step on their mountain we'll just be serving ourselves up as a meal to them. Let's forget about it." On hearing this Sanzang shivered, his hairs standing on end. "What are we to do, Wukong?" he asked. "Don't worry, Master," said Monkey. "It can't be anything much. There are bound to be a few evil spirits here. It's just that the people here are such cowards that they exaggerate about how many demons there are and how powerful they are. They get themselves into a funk. I can cope."

"You're talking nonsense, brother," said Pig. "I'm not like you. What I found out was the truth. I wasn't making any of it up. The hills and valleys are all crawling with demons. How are we going to move ahead?" "You're talking like an idiot," said Monkey with a grin. Don't scare yourself over nothing. Even if the hills and valleys were crawling with demons I'd only need half a night to wipe them all out with my cudgel." "You're shameless," said Pig, "quite shameless. Stop talking so big. It would take seven or eight days just to call the roll. How could you wipe them all out?" "Tell me how you'd do it," laughed Monkey. "However you grabbed them, tied them up, or fixed them where they are with fixing magic you'd never be able to do it so fast," said Pig. "I wouldn't need to grab them or tie them up," said Monkey. "I'll give my cudgel a tug at both ends, say 'Grow!', and make it over four hundred feet long. Then I'll wave it, say 'Thicken!', and make it eighty feet around. I'll roll it down the southern slope and that'll kill five thousand of them. I'll roll it down the northern slope and kill another five thousand. Then I'll roll it along the ridge from east to west, and even if there are forty or fifty thousand of them I'll squash them all to a bloody pulp." "Brother," said Pig, "if you kill them that way, like rolling out dough for noodles, you could do it in four hours." "Master," said Friar Sand with a laugh, "as my elder brother has such divine powers we've got nothing to fear. Please mount up so that we can be on our way." Having heard them discussing Monkey's powers Sanzang could not but mount with an easy heart and be on his way.

As they travelled along the old man disappeared. "He must have been an evil spirit himself," said Friar Sand, "deliberately coming to frighten us with cunning and intimidation." "Take it easy," said Monkey. "I'm going to take a look." The splendid Great Sage leapt up to a high peak but saw no trace of the old man when he looked around. Then he suddenly turned back to see a shimmering coloured glow in the sky, shot up on his cloud to look, and saw that it was the Great White Planet. Walking over and grabbing hold of him, Monkey kept addressing him by his personal name: "Li Changgeng! Li Changgeng! You rascal! If you had something to say you should have said it to my face. Why did you pretend to be an old man of the woods and make a fool of me?" The planet hastened to pay him his respects and said, "Great Sage, I beg you to forgive me for being late in reporting to you. Those demon chiefs really have tremendous magical abilities and their powers are colossal. With your skill in transformations and your cunning you may just be able to get over, but if you slight them it will be very hard." "I'm very grateful," Monkey thanked him, "very grateful. If I really can't get across this ridge I hope that you'll go up to Heaven and put in a word with the Jade Emperor so he'll lend me some heavenly soldiers to help me." "Yes, yes, yes," said the

Great White Planet. "Just give the word and you can have a hundred thousand heavenly troops if you want them."

The Great Sage then took his leave of the planet and brought his cloud down to see Sanzang and say, "The old man we saw just now was actually the Great White Planet come to bring us a message." "Disciple," said Sanzang, putting his hands together in front of his chest, "catch up with him quick and ask him where there's another path we could make a detour by." "There's no other way round," Monkey replied. "This mountain is 250 miles across, and goodness knows how much longer it would be to go all the way around it. How ever could we?" At this Sanzang could not restrain himself from weeping. "Disciple," he said, "if it's going to be as hard as this how are we going to worship the Buddha?" "Don't cry," Monkey said, "don't cry. If you cry you're a louse. I'm sure he's exaggerating. All we have to do is be careful. As they say, forewarned is forearmed. Dismount and sit here for now." "What do you want to talk about now?" Pig asked. "Nothing," replied Monkey. "You stay here and look after the master carefully while Friar Sand keeps a close eye on the baggage and the horse. I'm going up the ridge to scout around. I'll find out how many demons there are in the area, capture one, ask him all the details, and get him to write out a list with all of their names. I'll check out every single one of them, old or young, and tell them to shut the gates of the cave and not block our way. Then I can ask the master to cross the mountain peacefully and quietly. That'll show people my powers." "Be careful," said Friar Sand, "do be careful!" "No need to tell me," Brother Monkey replied with a smile. "On this trip I'd force the Eastern Ocean to make way for me, and I'd smash my way in even if it were a mountain of silver cased in iron."

The splendid Great Sage went whistling straight up to the peak by his somersault cloud. Holding on to the vines and creepers, he surveyed the mountain only to find it silent and deserted. "I was wrong," he said involuntarily, "I was wrong. I shouldn't have let that old Great White Planet go. He was just trying to scare me. There aren't any evil spirits here. If there were they'd be out leaping around in the wind, thrusting with their spears and staves, or practising their fighting skills. Why isn't there a single one?" As he was wondering about this there was a ringing of a bell and a banging of clappers. He turned round at once to see a little devil boy with a banner on which was written BY ORDER over his shoulder, a bell at his waist and clappers in his hands that he was sounding. He was coming from the north and heading south. A closer look revealed that he was about twelve feet tall. "He must be a runner," thought Monkey, grinning to himself, "delivering messages and reports. I'll take a listen to what he's talking about."

The splendid Great Sage made a spell with his hands, said the magic words, shook himself and turned into a fly who landed lightly on the devil's hat and tilted his head for a good listen. This is what the little devil was saying to himself as he headed along the main road, sounding his clappers and ringing his bell: "All we mountain patrollers must be careful and be on our guard against Sun the Novice. He can even turn into a fly!" Monkey was quietly amazed to hear this. "That so-and-so must have seen me before. How else could he know my name and know that I can turn into a fly?" Now the little devil had not in fact seen him before. The demon chief had for some reason given him these instructions that he was reciting blindly. Monkey, who did not know this, thought that the devil must have seen him and was on the point of bringing the cudgel out to hit him with when he stopped. "I remember Pig being told," he thought, "when he questioned the planet that there were three demon chieftains and 47,000 or 48,000 junior devils like this one. Even if there were tens of thousands more juniors like this it would be no problem. But I wonder how great the three leaders' powers are. I'll question him first. There'll be time to deal with them later."

Splendid Great Sage! Do you know how he questioned the demon? He jumped off the devil's hat and landed on a tree top, letting the junior devil go several paces ahead. Then Monkey turned round and did a quick transformation into another junior devil, sounding clappers, ringing a bell and carrying a flag over his shoulder just like the real one. He was also dressed identically. The only difference was that he was a few inches taller. He was muttering the same things as the other as he caught him up, shouting, "Hey, you walking ahead, wait for me." Turning round, the junior devil asked, "Where have you come from?" "You're a nice bloke," Monkey said with a smile, "not even recognizing one of your own people." "You're not one of ours," said the demon. "What do you mean?" Monkey asked. "Take a look and see if you can recognize me." "I've never seen you before," the demon said. "I don't know you." "It's not surprising you don't know me," said Monkey. "I work in the kitchens. We've rarely met." "You don't," said the demon, shaking his head, "you don't. None of the brothers who do the cooking has got a pointy face like yours." "I must have made my face too pointy when I did the transformation," thought Monkey, so he rubbed it with his hands and said, "It isn't pointy." Indeed it was not. "But it was pointy just now," the little devil said. "How did you stop it being pointy just by rubbing it? You're a very shady character. I don't have the faintest idea who you are. You're not one of us. I've never met you. Very suspicious. Our kings run the household very strictly. The kitchen staff only work in the kitchen and the mountain patrols keep to patrolling the mountain. How could you possibly be a cook and a patroller?" "There's something you don't know," said Monkey, improvising a clever answer. "I was promoted to patrolling because the kings saw how well I'd worked in the kitchens."

"Very well then," said the little devil. "We patrollers are divided into ten companies of forty each, which makes four hundred in all. We're all known by our ages, appearances, names and descriptions. Because Their Majesties want to keep the organization neat and roll-calls convenient they've given us all passes. Have you got one?" Monkey, who had seen what the devil looked like and heard what he had said, had been able to turn himself into the devil's double. But not having seen the devil's pass he was not carrying one himself. Instead of saying that he did not have one the splendid Great Sage claimed that he had. "Of course I've got one," he said. "But it's a new one that's only just been issued to me. Show me yours."

Not realizing what Monkey was up to, the little devil lifted his clothers to reveal a gold-lacquered pass with a silken cord through it fastened next to his skin that he lifted out to show Monkey. Monkey saw that on the back of it were the words "Demon-suppresser", while on the front was handwritten "Junior Wind-piercer." "Goes without saying," Brother Monkey thought, "all the ones in mountain patrols have 'Wind' at the end of their names. Put your clothes down now," he said, "and come over here while I show you my pass." With that he turned away, put a hand down to pull a little hair from the tip of his tail, rubbed it between his fingers, called "Change!" and turned it into another gold-lacquered pass on a green silken cord on which were handwritten the words "Senior Wind-piercer". With his liking for taking things to extremes and his gift of finding the right thing to say, Monkey remarked, "There's something you don't know. When Their Majesties promoted me to patrolling for doing so well in the kitchen they gave me a new pass as a Senior Patroller and put me in charge of you forty lads in this company." At this the demon at once gave a "na-a-aw" of respect and said, "Sir, I didn't recognize you as you've only just been appointed. Please forgive me if anything I said offended you." "I'm not angry with you," said Monkey, returning his courtesy. "There's just one thing. I want some money from you all to mark our first meeting: five ounces of silver each." "Please be patient, sir," the little devil replied. "When I get back to the southern end of the ridge to meet the rest of our company we'll all give it to you together." "In that case I'm coming with you," said Monkey, and he followed behind as the demon led the way.

After a mile or two a writing-brush peak was seen. Why was it called a writing-brush peak? Because on the top of the mountain there was a pinnacle about forty or fifty feet high that looked just like a writing brush standing upright on a brush stand. Going up to it Monkey lifted his tail, jumped to the top of the pinnacle, sat down and called, "Come here, all of you." The young Wind-piercers all bowed low beneath him and said, "We're at your service, sir." "Do you know why Their Majesties appointed me?" Monkey asked. "No," they replied. "Their Majesties want to eat the Tang Priest," said Monkey, "but they're worried about Sun the Novice's tremendous magic powers. They've heard that he can do transformations and are worried that he might turn himself into a young Wind-piercer and come along the path here to find out what's going on. That's why they've made me senior Wind-piercer to check up on you and find out if there are any impostors among you." "We're all genuine, sir," the junior Wind-piercers all replied at once. "If you're all genuine do you know what powers His Senior Majesty has?" Monkey asked. "Yes," one of the young Wind-piercers said. "In that case," said Monkey, "tell me about them at once. If what you say matches what I know, you're genuine. If it's at all wrong you're impostors, and I'll take you to Their Majesties for punishment."

Seeing him sitting up on high, playing wise and cunning as he shouted at them, the young devils had nothing for it but to tell him the truth. "His Majesty has vast magical abilities and enormous powers," one of the young devils replied. "He once devoured a hundred thousand heavenly warriors in a single mouthful." "You're an impostor," Monkey spat out when he heard this. "Sir, Your Honour," said the young devil in panic, "I'm real. How can you call me an impostor?" "If you're genuine why did you talk such nonsense?" Monkey replied. "No matter how big he is His Majesty couldn't have swallowed a hunderd thousand heavenly soldiers in a single mouthful." "This is something you don't know about, sir," the young devil replied. "His Majesty can do transformations. He can make himself tall enough to hold up the sky or as small as a cabbage seed. Some years ago when the Queen Mother invited all the immortals to a peach banquet she didn't send him an invitation, so His Majesty wanted to fight Heaven. The Jade Emperor sent a hundred thousand heavenly soldiers to subdue His Majesty, gave himself a magical body and opened his mouth that was as big as a city gate. He made as if to swallow hard, which frightened the heavenly soldiers so much that they dared not give battle, and the Southern Gate of Heaven was shut. That's how he could have swallowed a hundred thousand heavenly soldiers at a single mouthful."

Monkey grinned to himself and thought, "Frankly, I've done that too. What powers does His Second Majesty have?" he asked. "His Second Majesty is thirty feet tall with brows like sleeping silkworms, phoenix eyes, a voice like a beautiful woman, tusks like carrying-poles and a nose like a dragon. If he's in a fight he only needs to wrinkle his nose for his enemy to be scared witless even if he's covered in bronze and iron." "Evil spirits who get people with their noses are easy enough to catch," said Monkey, who then asked, "and what powers does His Third Majesty have?" "He's no monster from the mortal world," the young devil replied. "His name is Ten Thousand Miles of Cloud Roc. When he moves he rolls up the wind and shifts the waves, shaking the north as he heads for the south. He carries a treasure about with him called the Male and Female Vital Principles Jar. Anyone who's put in that jar is turned liquid in a few moments."

That news gave Monkey something to worry about. "I'm not scared of the monsters," he thought, "but I'll have to watch out for his jar." Then he said aloud, "Your account of Their Majesties' powers isn't bad — it fits exactly with what I know. But which of them wants to eat the Tang Priest?" "Don't you know, sir?" said the young Wind-piercer. "As if I didn't know better than you!" shouted Monkey. "I was told to come and question you because they're worried that you don't know all the details." "Our Senior King and Second King have long lived in Lion Cave on Lion Mountain," the young devil replied, "but the Third King doesn't live here. He used to live over a hundred miles to the west of here in the capital of a country called Leonia. Five hundred years ago he ate the king of the country, his civil and military officials, and everybody else in the city, young and old, male and female. So he seized their country, and now all the people there are evil monsters. I don't know which year it was in which he heard that the Tang court has sent a priest to the Western Heaven to fetch the scriptures. They say this priest is a good man who has cultivated his conduct for ten incarnations, and anyone who eats a piece of his flesh will live for ever and never grow old. But the Third King is worried about the priest's disciple Sun the Novice who's a real terror, so he's come to swear brotherhood with our two kings. All three are now working together to catch the Tang Priest."

"Damn this thoroughly ill-behaved monster," thought Brother Monkey with great fury. "I'm protecting the Tang Priest while he works for the true achievement. How dare they plot to eat my man?" With a snort of fury he ground his steel teeth and brandished his iron cudgel as he leapt down from the high pinnacle and smashed the poor young devil's head into a lump of meat. When he saw what he had done Monkey felt sorry. "Oh dear," he thought, "he meant well, telling me all about the house. Why did I finish him off all of a sudden like that? Oh well! Oh well! That's that." The splendid Great Sage had been forced to do this because his master's way ahead had been blocked. He took the little devil's pass off him, tied it round his own waist, put the "By order" flag over his shoulder, hung the bell from his waist and sounded the clappers wlth his hand. Then he made a hand-spell into the wind, said a spell, shook himself, turned into the exact likeness of the junior Wind-piercer, and went straight back the way he had come, looking for the cave to find out about the three demon chieftains. Indeed,

The Handsome Monkey King had a thousand transformations
And the true power of magic to make ten thousand changes.

Monkey was rushing deep into the mountains along the way he had come when suddenly he heard shouts and whinnies. As he looked up he saw tens of thousands of little devils drawn up outside the entrance to the Lion Cave with their spears, sabres, swords, halberds, flags and banners. Monkey was delighted. "Li

Changgeng, the planet, was telling the truth," he thought. "He wasn't lying at all." The devils were drawn up in a systematic way, each 250 forming a company, so that from the forty standards in many colours that were dancing in the wind he could tell that there were ten thousand infantry and cavalry there. "If I go into the cave disguised as a junior Wind-piercer and one of the demon chiefs questions me about my mountain patrol," Monkey thought, "I'll have to make up answers on the spur of the moment. The moment I say anything at all wrong he'll realize who I am and I won't be able to get away. That army on the gates would stop me and I'd never get out. If I'm going to catch the demon kings I'll have to get rid of the devils on the gates first." Do you know how he was going to do that? "The old demons have never seen me," he thought, "they've only heard of my reputation. I'll talk big and scare them with my fame and prestige. If it's true that all living beings in the middle land are destined to have the scriptures brought to them, then all I need do is talk like a hero and scare those monsters on the gate away. But if they're not destined to have the scriptures brought to them I'll never get rid of the spirits from the gates of this cave in the west even if I talk till lotus flowers appear." Thus he thought about his plans, his mind questioning his mouth and his mouth questioning his mind, as he sounded the clappers and rang the bell. Before he could rush in through the entrance to Lion Cave he was stopped by the junior devils of the forward camp, who said, "You're back, young Wind-piercer." Monkey said nothing but kept going with his head down.

When he reached the second encampment more young devils grabbed hold of him and said, "You're back, young Wind-piercer." "Yes," Monkey replied. "On your patrol this morning did you meet a Sun the Novice?" they asked. "I did," Monkey replied. "He was polishing his pole." "What's he like?" the terrified devils asked. "What sort of pole was he polishing?" "He was squatting beside a stream," Monkey replied. "He looked like one of those gods that clear the way. If he'd stood up I'm sure he'd have been hundreds of feet tall, and the iron cudgel he was holding was a huge bar as thick as a rice-bowl. He'd put a handful of water on a rocky scar and was polishing the cudgel on it muttering, 'Pole, it's ages since I got you out to show your magic powers: This time you can kill all the demons for me, even if there are a hundred thousand of them. Then I'll kill the three demon chiefs as a sacrificial offering to you.' He's going to polish it till it shines then start by killing the ten thousand of you on the gates."

On hearing this the little devils were all terror-struck and their souls all scattered in panic. "Gentlemen," Monkey continued, "that Tang Priest has only got a few pounds of flesh on him. We won't get a share. So why should we have to carry the can for them? We'd do much better to scatter." "You're right," the demons said. "Let's all run for our lives." If they had been civilized soldiers they would have stayed and fought to the death, but as they were all really wolves, tigers and leopards, running beasts and flying birds, they all disappeared with a great whoosh. Indeed, it wasn't as if the Great Sage Sun had merely talked big: it was like the time when Xiang Yu's army of eight thousand soldiers disappeared, surrounded by foes who were former comrades. "Splendid," said Monkey to himself with self-congratulation, "the old devils are as good as dead now. If this lot run away at the sound of me they'll never dare look me in the face. I'll use the same story when I go in there. If I said anything different and one or two of the young devils had got inside and heard me that would give the game away." Watch him as he carefully approaches the ancient cave and boldly goes deep inside. If you don't know what of good or ill was to come from the demon chieftains listen to the explanation in the next instalment.

CHAPTER SEVENTY-FIVE

The Mind-ape bores a hole in the Male and Female Jar; The demon king returns and the way is preserved.

The story tells how the Great Sage Sun went in through the entrance of the cave and looked to either side. This is what he saw:

Hills of skeletons,
Forests of bones,
Human heads and hair trampled into felt,
Human skin and flesh rotted into mud,
Sinews twisted round trees,
Dried and shining like silver.
Truly there was a mountain of corpses, a sea of blood,
An unbearable stench of corruption.
The little devils to the east
Sliced the living flesh off human victims;
The evil demons to the west
Boiled and fried fresh human meat.
Apart from the heroic Handsome Monkey King
No common mortal would have dared go in.

He was soon inside the second gates, and when he looked around here he saw that things were different from outside. Here was purity, quiet elegance, beauty and calm. To left and right were rare and wonderful plants; all around were tall pines and jade-green bamboo. After another two or three miles he reached the third gates, slipped inside for a peep, and saw the three old demons sitting on high. They looked thoroughly evil. The one in the middle

Had teeth like chisels and saws,
A round head and a square face.
His voice roared like thunder;
His eyes flashed like lightning.
Upturned nostrils faced the sky;
Red eyebrows blazed with fire.
Wherever he walked
The animals were terrified;
If he sat down
The demons all trembled.
He was the king among the beasts,
The Blue-haired Lion Monster.

The one sitting on his left was like this:

Phoenix eyes with golden pupils,
Yellow tusks and powerful thighs.
Silver hair sprouting from a long nose,
Making his head look like a tail.
His brow was rounded and wrinkled,
His body massively heavy.
His voice as delicate as a beautiful woman's,
But his face was as fiendish as an ox-headed demon's.
He treasured his tusks and cultivated his person for many years,
The Ancient Yellow-tusked Elephant.

The one on the right had

Golden wings and a leviathan's head,
Leopard eyes with starry pupils.
He shook the north when he headed south,
Fierce, strong and brave.
When he turned to soaring
Quails laughed but dragons were terrified.
When he beat his phoenix wings the birds all hid their heads,
And the beasts all lost their nerve when he spread his talons.

He could fly thirty thousand miles through the clouds,
The Mighty Roc.

Beneath these two were ranged a hundred and ten commanders high and low, all in full armour and looking most imposing and murderous. The sight delighted Brother Monkey, who strode inside, quite unafraid, put down his clappers and bell, and called, "Your Majesties." The three old demons chuckled and replied, "So you're back, young Wind-piercer." "Yes," Monkey replied. "When you were patrolling what did you find out about where Sun the Novice is?" "Your Majesties," Monkey replied, "I don't dare tell you." "Why not?" the senior demon chief asked. "I was walking along sounding my clappers and ringing my bell following Your Majesties' orders," Monkey said, "when all of a sudden I looked up and saw someone squatting and polishing a pole there. He looked like one of the gods that clear the way. If he'd stood up he'd have been well over a hundred feet tall. He'd scooped up some water in his hand and was polishing his iron bar on the rocky scar. He was saying to himself that his cudgel still hadn't the chance to show its magical powers here and that when he'd shined it up he was coming to attack Your Majesties. That's how I realized he was Sun the Novice and came here to report."

On hearing this the senior demon chief broke into a sweat all over and shivered so that his teeth chattered as he said, "Brothers, I don't think we should start any trouble with the Tang Priest. His disciple has tremendous magical powers and he's polishing his cudgel to attack us. Whatever are we to do?" "Little ones," he shouted, "call everybody, high and low, who's outside the cave to come inside and shut the gates. Let them pass." "Your Majesty," said one of the subordinate officers who knew what had happened, "the little devils outside have all scattered." "Why?" the senior demon asked. "They must have heard about his terrible reputation. Shut the gates at once! At once!" The hosts of demons noisily bolted all the front and back gates firmly.

"Now they've shut the gates they might ask me all sorts of

questions about things in here," Monkey thought with alarm "If I don't know the right answers I'll give the game away and they'll catch me. I'd better give them another scare and get them to open the gates to let me out." "Your Majesty," he said, stepping forward, "there were some other wicked things he said." "What else?" the senior demon chief asked. "He said he was going to skin Your Senior Majesty," replied Brother Monkey, "slice up the bones of His Second Majesty, and rip out His Third Majesty's sinews. If you shut the gates and refuse to go out he can do transformations. He might turn himself into a fly, get in through a crack between the gates and catch us all. Then we'll be done for." "Be very careful, brothers," said the senior demon. "We haven't had a fly here for years, so any fly that gets in will be Sun the Novice." "So I'll change into a fly and frighten them into opening the gates," thought Monkey, smiling to himself. The splendid Great Sage then slipped aside, reached up to pull a hair from the back of his head, blew on it with a magic breath, called "Change!" and turned it into a golden fly that flew straight into the old demon's face. "Brothers," said the old demon in a panic, "this is terrible! He's inside!" All the demons great and small were so alarmed that they rushed forward to swat the fly with their rakes and brooms.

The Great Sage could not help giggling aloud, which was just what he should not have done as it revealed his true face. The third demon chief leapt forward, grabbed him and said, "Brothers, he almost had us fooled." "Who had who fooled?" the senior demon asked. "The young devil who reported just now was no junior Wind-piercer," the third chief replied, "but Sun the Novice himself. He must have run into a junior Wind-piercer and somehow or other murdered him and done this transformation to trick us." "He's rumbled me," thought Monkey with alarm, rubbing his face. "What do you mean, I'm Sun the Novice?" Monkey said to the senior demon chief. "I'm a junior Wind-piercer. His Majesty's mistaken." "Brother," said the senior demon, "he really is a junior Wind-piercer. He's in the roll-call out front three times a day. I know him. Do you have a pass?" he went on to ask Monkey. "Yes," Monkey replied, pulling his clothes apart to produce it. Seeing that it looked genuine the senior demon said, "Brother, don't mistreat him." "Elder brother," the third demon chief replied, "didn't you see him slip aside just now and giggle? I saw him show his face: it's like a thunder god's. When I grabbed hold of him he turned back into what he looks like now. Little ones," he called, "fetch ropes!" The officers then fetched ropes.

The third demon chief knocked Monkey over and tied his hands and feet together. When his clothes were stripped off he was most evidently the Protector of the Horses. Now of the seventy-two transformations that Monkey could perform, when he turned himself into a bird, a beast, a plant, a tree, a vessel or an insect he changed his whole body. When he turned into another person, however, he could only change his head and face but not his body, and indeed he was still covered with brown hair and had red thighs and a tail. "That's Sun the Novice's body," the senior demon chief said when he saw this, "and a junior Wind-piercer's face. It's him! Little ones," he ordered, "bring wine and give His Third Majesty a cup of it to congratulate him. Now that we've captured Sun the Novice the Tang Priest is as good as a meal in our mouths." "We mustn't drink now," said the third demon chief. "Sun the Novice is a slippery customer and is good at escaping by magic. I'm worried he might get away. Tell the juniors to bring the jar out and put him inside. Then we can drink."

"Yes, yes," said the senior demon chief with a smile, who then chose thirty-six little demons to go inside, open the store-rooms, and carry the jar out. Do you know how big the jar was? It was only two feet four inches high. So why were thirty-six people needed to carry it? It was because the jar was a treasure of the two vital forces, male and female, and contained the seven precious things, the eight trigrams and the twenty-four periods of the year that thirty-six carriers were required to match the number of the stars of the Dipper. Before long the precious jar had been carried out, set down outside the third pair of gates, cleaned up and opened. Monkey was untied.

stripped bare and sucked inside the jar with a hiss by magical vapour that came out of it. The lid was then put back on and sealed on with a label, after which the demons went off to drink, saying, "Now that he's in our jar that monkey can forget all about his journey west. The only way he'll be able to pay his respects to the Buddha and fetch the scriptures now will be by pushing the wheel of destiny backwards and being reborn." Watch how all the demons great and small go laughing off to celebrate. But of that no more.

Once inside the jar the Great Sage, who was very cramped, decided to transform himself and squat down in the middle, where he found it very cool. "Those evil spirits don't live up to their reputation," he said to himself, laughing aloud. "Why ever do they tell people that anyone put in this jar will be turned to pus and blood in a few moments. It's so cool that spending seven or eight years here would be no problem."

Alas! The Great Sage did not know about this treasure. Anyone put inside it who said nothing for a year would stay cool for a year; but the moment a voice was heard fires began to burn. Before Monkey had finished speaking the whole jar was full of flame. Luckily he could use the knack of making fire-averting magic with his hands as he sat in the middle of the jar completely unafraid. When he had endured the flames for an hour forty snakes emerged from all around to bite him. Swinging his arms about him Monkey grabbed hold of all of them, twisted with all his strength, and broke them into eighty pieces. A little later three fire dragons appeared to circle above and below Monkey, which was really unbearable. It drove Monkey into a helpless desperation of which he was only too conscious. "The other things were no trouble," he said, "but these three fire dragons are a real problem. If I don't get out soon the fire will attack my heart, and what then? I'll make myself grow," he went on to think, "and push my way out." The splendid Great Sage made a spell with his hands, said the words of a spell and called out, "Grow!" He made himself over a dozen feet tall, but as he grew the jar grew with him, enclosing him tightly. When he made himself smaller, the jar shrank too. "This is terrible," Brother Monkey thought with alarm, "terrible. It grows when I grow and shrinks when I get smaller. Why? What am I to do?" Before he had finished speaking his ankle began to hurt. Putting his hand down at once to feel it he found that it had been burnt so badly it had gone soft. "I don't know what to do," he said with anxiety. "My ankle's been cooked tender. I'm a cripple now." He could not stop the tears from flowing. Indeed,

When suffering at the demons' hands he thought of his master;
In facing deadly peril he worried about the Tang Priest.

"Master," he exclaimed, "since I was converted by the Bodhisattva Guanyin and delivered from my heavenly punishment you and I have toiled over many a mountain. I've beaten and wiped out a lot of monsters, subdued Pig and Friar Sand, and gone through no end of suffering. All this was done in the hope of reaching the west and completing the true achievement together. Never did I expect to meet these vicious demons today. Now I've been stupid enough to get myself killed in here I've left you stuck in the middle of the mountains. What a mess to be in for someone who used to be as famous as I was!" Just when he was feeling thoroughly miserable he suddenly remembered, "Years ago the Bodhisattva gave me three life-saving hairs on the Coiled Snake Mountain. I wonder if I've still got them. I'd better look for them." He felt all over his body and found three very rigid hairs on the back of his head. "All the other hair on my body is soft except for these three that are as hard as spears," he said with delight. "They must be my lifesavers." Gritting his teeth against the pain, he pulled the three hairs out, blew on them with magic breath and called, "Change!" One of them turned into a steel drill, one into a strip of bamboo, and one into a silken cord. He made the bamboo strip into a bow to which he fixed the drill. After a noisy spell of drilling at the bottom of the jar he made a hole through which the light came in. "I'm in luck," he said with glee, "I'm in luck. Now I can get out." No sooner had he transformed himself ready to escape than the jar became cool again. Why was that? It cooled because the hole he had bored in it let the male and female vital forces escape.

The splendid Great Sage put his hairs back, made himself small by turning into the tiniest of insects, a very delicate creature as thin as a whisker and as long as an eyebrow hair, and slipped out through the hole. Instead of making his escape Monkey flew straight to the senior demon chief's head and landed on it. The senior demon, who was drinking, slammed his goblet down and asked, "Third brother, has Sun the Novice been liquefied yet?" "Is the time up?" the third demon chief asked. The senior demon told his messengers to carry the jar in. When the thirty-six young devils picked the jar up they found that it was far lighter. "Your Majesty," they reported with alarm, "the jar's lighter." "Nonsense!" the senior demon shouted. "It has the full powers of the male and female vital forces. It couldn't possibly get lighter." One of the junior demons who liked showing off picked the jar up and said, "Look. It is lighter, isn't it?" When the senior demon took the lid off to look in he saw that it was bright inside. "It's empty," he could not help shouting aloud, "it's leaked." And Monkey, sitting on his head, could not help shouting, "Search, my lads! He's escaped." "He's escaped," all the monsters shouted, "he's escaped!" The order was then given to shut the gates.

With that Monkey shook himself, took back the clothes that had been taken off him, turned back into himself and leapt out of the cave. "Behave yourselves, evil spirits," he flung back insultingly. "I've bored through the jar and you can't keep anyone in it any more. You'll have to take it outside and shit in it." Shouting and yelling with glee he went straight back on his cloud to where the Tang Priest was. Here he found the venerable gentleman making symbolic incense with a pinch of earth and praying to the sky. Monkey stopped his cloud to listen to what he was saying. Sanzang had his hands together in front of his chest and was saying to Heaven,

> *"All you immortals up there in the clouds,*
> *The Dings and the Jias and each god and goddess,*
> *Protect my disciple, whose powers are enormous,*
> *And magic is boundless, the good Sun the Novice."*

When the Great Sage heard this he decided to redouble his efforts. Putting his cloud away he went up to Sanzang and called, "Master, I'm back." Sanzang held him as he said, "Wukong, you have been to great trouble. I was very concerned because you had gone so far into these high mountains and not come back for so long a time. How dangerous is the mountain in fact?" "Master," Monkey replied with a smile, "that trip just now depended in the first place on the good destiny of all the living beings in the east, secondly on your boundless achievement and great virtue, and thirdly on your disciple's magical powers." Then he told the whole story of how he had pretended to be a Wind-piercer, been drawn into the jar and escaped. "Now I've seen your face again, Master, it's like having a second life."

Sanzang expressed endless thanks then asked, "Did you not fight the evil spirits this time?" "No, I didn't," replied Brother Monkey. "Then you won't be able to escort me safely across this mountain," Sanzang said, at which Monkey, who hated to admit he was beaten, shouted, "What do you mean, I won't be able to escort you?" "If you and they have not yet had it out and you can only give me evasive answers I will never dare press ahead," the venerable elder replied. "Master," laughed the Great Sage, "you really don't understand. As the saying goes, you can't spin a thread from a single strand of silk, and you can't clap one-handed. There are three demon chiefs and thousands of the little devils. How could I fight them all single-handed?" "If you are that outnumbered you would indeed find it hard by yourself," Sanzang replied. "Pig and Friar Sand also have their talents. I shall tell them to go with you to help you clean up the path across the mountain and escort me over it." "What you say is completely right, Master," replied Monkey with a smile. "Tell Friar Sand to protect you while Pig comes with me." "Brother," said Pig in alarm, "you're a poor judge.

I'm rough and I can't do anything much. I'd just get in the way as I walked along. What use would I be to you?" "You may not be up to much, brother," Monkey replied, "but you're someone. As the saying goes, even a fart can swell the wind. You'd make me feel a bit braver." "All right," Pig said, "all right. You can take me with you. But don't play any of your tricks on me when the going gets tough." "Don't forget that Friar Sand and I will be waiting here," said Sanzang.

The idiot braced himself and set off a gale with Monkey that carried them by cloud up to the top of the mountain where the entrance to the cave was. They saw at once that the gates were shut tight. There was nobody in sight anywhere around. Monkey went forward, his iron cudgel in his hands, to shout at the top of his voice, "Open up, evil monsters! Come out right now and fight Monkey!" When the young devils in the cave went inside to report the senior demon shook with terror as he commented,

"I've heard tell for years of that monkey's ferocity;
Now I can vouch for the story's veracity."

"What do you mean, elder brother?" the second demon chief asked. "When that Sun the Novice first turned himself into a fly to sneak in here none of us realized who he was except our Third Brother, who put him in the jar. He used his skills to drill a hole in the jar, pick up his clothes and get out. Now he's outside challenging us to battle. Who's brave enough to be the first to take him on?" Nobody replied. The senior demon asked again; again there was no response. Everyone was pretending to be deaf and dumb. "We've got ourselves a lousy reputation in the West already," the senior demon chief said in fury. "Now that Sun the Novice has treated us with such contempt today our reputation will stand even lower if we don't fight him. I'm going out there to chance my old life on three rounds with him. If I can hold out for those three rounds the Tang Priest will still be a meal in our mouths. If I can't then shut the gates and let them pass." He then kitted himself out in his armour, had the gates opened and went out. As Monkey and Pig watched from beside the gates they saw that he was a fine monster:

On iron brow and brazen head a precious helmet
With tassels dancing brightly in the wind.
His eyes both flashed as if with lightning,
And ruddy glowed the hair at his temples.
Pointed and sharp were his silvery claws,
And his saw-like teeth were set close and neat.
His armour was golden, without any seam,
Bound with a dragon sash that could foresee the future.
In his hand flashed a cutlass of steel.
Such martial might is rare in the world.
With a voice that roared like thunder he asked,
"Who is that knocking at my gates?"

"Your grandfather, Lord Sun, the Great Sage Equalling Heaven," said Monkey, turning to face the gate. "Are you Sun the Novice?" asked the demon with a laugh. "You've got a cheek, ape. I never gave you any trouble, so why are you here challenging me to battle?" " 'No waves come without a wind; without the tide the waters are still,' " Monkey replied. "Would I have come looking for you if you hadn't given me trouble? The reason why I'm here to fight is because your gang of foxes and dogs is plotting to eat my master." "From the way you're acting so fierce and shouting at our gates you must want a fight," the old demon replied. "Yes," Monkey said. "Stop all that ranting and raving then," said the demon. "It would be most unfair if I brought out my devil soldiers and drew them up in battle order with flags flying and drums beating to fight you as I'm on my own territory. I'll fight you single-handed with no helpers for either side." When Monkey heard this he shouted, "Keep out of the way, Pig, and let's see how he copes with me." The idiot did indeed get out of the way. "Come over here," the senior demon shouted, "and be a chopping block for me. Let me hack you three times as hard as I can with sword on your bare head. After that I'll let your Tang Priest pass. If you can't take it then hand your Tang Priest over at once. He'll be a tasty morsel to help our rice down." "Bring out a brush and some paper if you have them in your cave and I'll give you a bond. You can hack at me from today till next year, but it'll be nothing to me."

The old demon then summoned up all his might, took up a stance with his feet apart, lifted his sword with both hands and hacked at the top of the Great Sage's head. The Great Sage raised his head, and though there was a mighty crash his scalp did not even go red. "That monkey really does have a hard head," exclaimed the old demon with shock. "You wouldn't know about it," said Monkey with a laugh. "I was

Born with a skull of bronze and iron,
Like nobody else's in all the world.
Hammer and axe will never smash me;
I went in Lord Lao Zi's furnace when I was a boy.
The Star Lords of the Four Dippers helped mould me,
The twenty-eight constellations all used their skill.
I've often been soaked in water but never come to harm,
And all over my body the sinews are knotty.
The Tang Priest, fearing I would not stand firm,
Placed a golden band around my head."

"Cut out that insolence, ape," the senior demon said, "and take these two blows from my sword. I'm most certainly not going to spare your life." "It's nothing," Monkey replied. "Have another cut like that if you like." "You monkey," the old demon said, "you don't know about this sword,

Created in furnaces of metal and fire,
A hundred times tempered by divine craftsmanship.
Its sharp blade follows the Three Strategies,
And it is as strong as described in the Six Plans.
The point is as fine as a housefly's tail,
And supple as the body of a white dragon.
When it goes to the mountains dense clouds arise;
If it plunges into the sea the great waves roll.
It has been burnished times beyond number,
Heated and tempered many hundred times over.
Deep in the mountains it is kept in the caves;

Great is the glory it has won when in battle.
If I use it to strike at your monkish pate
I'll cut it into a pair of gourd ladles."

"You're blind, evil spirit," laughed the Great Sage, "if you think my head is just gourd ladles. I'll let you hack at me if you're silly enough to want to. Have another go and see what happens."

The senior demon raised his sword for another hack, which the Great Sage moved his head forward to meet. With a loud bang his head was split into two, whereupon the Great Sage rolled on the ground and gave himself a second body. The sight so alarmed the demon that he lowered his sword. Watching all this from a distance Pig said with a laugh, "Give him a couple more hacks, old devil, then there'll be four of him." Pointing at Brother Monkey the senior demon said, "I'd heard that you can use self-dividing magic. Why are you showing it off to me now?" "What self-dividing magic?" Monkey asked. "Why was it that the first time I hacked you it made no impact, but this time I cut you in two?" the senior demon asked. "Don't worry, evil spirit," said the Great Sage with a smile. "If you cut me ten thousand times there'll be twenty thousand of me." "You ape," the demon said, "you may be able to divide yourself but you can't put yourself together again. If you can, hit me with your cudgel." "Don't talk nonsense," said the Great Sage. "You asked to take three cuts at me but only took two. Now you've invited me to hit you once I'm not Monkey if I hit you one and a half times." "Very well," said the senior demon.

The splendid Great Sage hugged his two bodies together, rolled, became one body again and struck with his cudgel at the demon's head. The old demon raised his sword to parry the blow. "Damned ape," he said, "you've got a cheek! How dare you come here attacking me with a mourner's staff like that?" "If you ask about this cudgel of mine," shouted the Great Sage, "everybody in heaven and earth has heard of it." "What's it famous for?" the senior demon asked. To this Monkey replied:

"The cudgel is made of nine-cycled wrought iron
Tempered by Lord Lao Zi himself in his furnace.

King Yu called it a divine treasure when he obtained it
To hold the eight rivers and four oceans in place.
In its middle the constellations are secretly set out,
And each end is banded with yellow gold.
Ghosts and gods are amazed at its intricate decorations,
Dragon patterns and phoenix signs.
Known as the Divine Male Cudgel,
It was inaccessibly deep in the bed of the sea.
Its shape can change and it knows how to fly,
Sending clouds of many colours drifting through the air.
Once it was mine I took it back to my mountain,
Where I discovered how its infinite changes.
When I want size it's as thick as a vat,
Or it can be as thin as an iron wire,
Huge as a mountain or small as a needle,
Adapting its length to the wishes of my heart.
Lightly I lift it and coloured clouds spring up,
Or it flies through the sky and flashes like lightning.
The cold air it gives off chills all who feel it,
And ominous mists appear in the sky.
I have carried it with me to beat dragons and tigers,
Travelling to all of the ends of the earth.
Once with this cudgel I made havoc in heaven,
And used its great might to wreck the peach banquet.
The heavenly kings were unable to beat me,
And Nezha was hard pressed to match me in combat.
With this cudgel against them the gods had no safe refuge;
A hundred thousand heavenly troops all scattered and fled.
The gods of thunder guarded the Hall of Miraculous Mist
When the cudgel attacked the Palace of Universal Brightness.
All of the angels at court were flustered
And the Jade Emperor's ministers were thrown into panic.

I raised my cudgel to overturn the Palace of the Dipper,
Then turned back to shake up the South Pole Compound.
Seeing my dread cudgel at his golden gates
The Jade Emperor invited the Buddha to see me.
The soldier takes defeat and victory in his stride;
There is nothing to choose between suffering and disaster.
I stuck it out for full five hundred years
Until I was converted by the Bodhisattva Guanyin.
Then a holy monk appeared in Tang
Who swore a mighty oath to heaven,
To save the souls in the City of the Unjustly Slain
And fetch the sutras at an assembly on Vulture Mountain.
On the journey to the West are many evil monsters
Whose actions would be a great obstacle to him.
So, knowing that my cudgel is matchless in the world,
He begged me to be his companion on the journey.
When it struck down evil spirits they were sent to the Underworld,
Their flesh turned to red dust and their bones all to powder.
Evil spirits everywhere were killed by the cudgel,
In thousands upon thousands too numerous to count.
Up above it wrecked the Dipper and Bull Palace,
And below it ruined the Senluo Court in Hell.
Of the heavenly generals it routed the Nine Bright Shiners,
And it wounded all of the Underworld's judges.
Dropped from mid-air it shakes mountains and rivers;
It is stronger than the sword of an evil star.
With this cudgel alone I protect the Tang Priest
And kill all the evil monsters in the world."

When the monster heard this he trembled, lifted his sword and struck with all his strength. Chuckling, Monkey blocked the blow with his iron cudgel. At first the two of them struggled in front of the cave, but then they both sprang up and fought in mid-air. It was a splendid battle.

The divine rod had once secured the bed of Heaven's River:
The as-you-will cudgel is the finest in the world.
Praise of its powers enraged the demon chief,
Whose mighty cutlass was full of great magic.
When they fought outside the gates they were still open to reason,
But no mercy was shown in their battle in the sky.
One could change his appearance at will;
The other could make himself grow on the spot.
The fight was so intense that the sky filled with clouds,
And all of the plains were enveloped in mist.
One had often determined to devour the monk Sanzang;
The other used his magic to protect the Tang Priest.
All because the Lord Buddha transmitted the scriptures
Evil and good were opposed in harsh conflict.

The senior demon and the Great Sage fought over twenty rounds without either emerging the victor while Pig admired their magnificent battle from down below until, unable to restrain himself, he grabbed his rake and leapt up into the air, riding on the wind to strike at the evil monster's face. The demon panicked, not realizing that Pig had no staying power, but could only rush recklessly in and give people a fright. All the demon could see was that Pig had a long snout, big ears and a vicious way with his rake, so he abandoned the struggle, threw his sword away, turned and fled. "After him," the Great Sage shouted, "after him!" The idiot raised his rake and went down in all his ferocious might straight after the monster. Seeing how close Pig was to him the old demon stood still in front of the mountainside, faced the wind, shook himself, resumed his real appearance and opened his mouth to devour Pig. This so terrified Pig that he fled as fast as he could into the undergrowth, not caring that brambles and thorns were tearing his head. He sat there trembling and listening out for the sound of the cudgel. When Monkey caught up with him the monster opened his jaws to eat Monkey up too. This was just what Monkey intended. Putting his cudgel away he went straight towards the demon, who swallowed him in a single gulp. This gave idiot such a fright as he was hiding in the undergrowth that he grumbled to himself, "You've got no common sense, Protector of the Horses. Why did you go towards the monster when he wanted to eat you up instead of running away? Now he's swallowed you. Today you're still a monk, but tomorrow you'll be a turd." Only when the monster had departed in triumph did Pig emerge from the undergrowth and slip back by the way he had come.

Sanzang and Friar Sand were still waiting for Pig at the foot of the mountain when they saw him come running breathless towards them. "Pig," said Sanzang with horror, "why are you in this terrible state? Why is Wukong not here?" "My brother was swallowed up by the evil spirit in a single gulp," Pig replied amid sobs, at which Sanzang collapsed in terror. A little later he stamped and beat his chest, saying, "Disciple, I thought you were good at subduing demons and were going to take me to see the Buddha in the Western Heaven. Who would have thought that you would die at this demon's hand today? Alas! Alas! All the efforts of my disciples have now turned to dust." The master was thoroughly miserable.

Just look at the idiot. Instead of coming over to comfort his master he calls, "Friar Sand, fetch the luggage. Let's split it between us." "Why, brother?" Friar Sand asked. "Divide it up," Pig replied, "and all of us can go our separate ways. You can go back to the River of Flowing Sand and carry on eating people. I'll go back to Gao Village and see my wife. We can sell the white horse to buy the master a coffin to be buried in." The master was so upset when he heard this that he wept aloud to Heaven.

We shall leave them and return to the senior demon chief. When he had swallowed Monkey he thought he had won, so he went straight back to his cave, where all the other demons came out to ask him how the fight had gone. "I've got one of them," the senior demon said. "Which one is that?" asked the second demon with delight. "Sun the Novice," the senior demon replied. "Where have you got him?" the second demon chief said. "In my stomach," said the senior demon, "I swallowed him." "Elder brother," said the third demon chief with horror, "I forgot to tell you that Sun the Novice wasn't worth eating." "I'm delicious," said the Great Sage from inside the demon's stomach, "and I'll stop you from ever feeling hungry again." This caused the junior devils such a shock that they reported, "This is terrible, Your Senior Majesty. Sun the Novice is talking inside your stomach." "That doesn't frighten me," said the senior demon. "If I'm clever enough to catch him do you think I'm not clever enough to deal with him? Make me some hot salty water at once. I'll pour it into my stomach, vomit him out, and have him fried at my leisure to eat as a snack with some drinks."

The junior devils soon had ready half a bowl of hot salty water that the old demon drained in one, filling his mouth. He then really did vomit, but the Great Sage, who had taken root in his stomach, did not even move. The monster then pressed his throat and vomited again till his head was spinning, his eyes in a daze and his gall-bladder split, but still Monkey would not be shifted. By now the senior demon was gasping for breath. "Sun the Novice," he called, "won't you come out?" "Not yet," Monkey replied. "I don't want to come out now." "Why not?" the old demon asked. "You really don't understand, evil spirit," said Monkey. "Ever since I've been a monk I've had scant food and clothing. Although it's autumn now and getting cool I'm still only wearing a thin tunic. But it's warm in your stomach and there are no draughts down here. I think I'll spend the winter here before coming out."

When the evil spirits heard this they all said, "Your Majesty, Sun the Novice wants to spend the winter in your stomach." "If he wants to spend the winter there I'll take to meditation and use magic to shift him," the senior demon said. "I won't eat anything all winter. The Protector of the Horses will starve to death." "You just don't understand, my boy," the Great Sage said. "I came via Guangzhou when I started escorting the Tang Priest and I've got a folding cooking pan with me that I brought in here to cook myself a mixed grill. I'll take my time enjoying your liver, bowels, stomach and lungs. They'll be enough to keep me going till spring." "Brother," said the second demon chief with shock, "that ape would do it too." "Brother," said the third demon, "perhaps he can eat up some bits and pieces, but I don't know where is he going to set up his pan." "The collar bone is an ideal stand," replied Monkey. "This is terrible," said the third demon. "If he sets up his pan and lights a fire won't the smoke get into your nose and make you sneeze?" "That'll be no problem," said Monkey with a laugh. "I'll use my gold-banded cudgel to push a hole through his skull. That'll be a skylight for me and serve as a chimney too."

The old demon heard this and was most alarmed despite saying that he was not afraid. All he could do was to summon up his courage and call, "Don't be scared, brothers. Bring me some of that drugged wine. When I down a few goblets of that the drugs will kill the monkey." At this Monkey smiled to himself and thought, "When I made havoc in Heaven five hundred years ago I drank the Jade Emperor's wine and ate Lord Lao Zi's elixir, the Queen Mother's peaches, the marrow of phoenix bones and dragon livers. I've eaten everything. What kind of drugged wine could do me any harm?" By then the junior devils had strained two jugfuls of drugged wine, a goblet of which they handed to the senior demon chief, who took it in his hands. Monkey, who could smell it from inside the demon's belly, called out, "Don't give it to him!" The splendid Great Sage then tipped his head back and turned it into the bell of a trumpet that he placed wide open below the demon's throat. The demon gulped the wine down noisily and Monkey noisily received it. The demon swallowed the second cupful and Monkey noisily drank that too. This went on till Monkey had drunk all of the seven or eight cupfuls that the demon downed. "That's enough," the demon said, putting the goblet down. "Normally my stomach feels as if it's on fire after a couple of cups of this wine," he said, "but this time my face hasn't even gone red after seven or eight." Now the Great Sage was not a heavy drinker, so after taking these seven or eight cupfuls he started to act drunk in the demon's stomach, propping himself up, falling flat on his face, kicking about him, swinging on the demon's liver, doing headstands and somersaults, and dancing wildly. This caused the monster such unbearable pain that he collapsed. If you don't know whether he lived or died listen to the explanation in the next instalment.

CHAPTER SEVENTY-SIX

When the heart spirit stays in the home the demons submit;
The Mother of Wood helps bring monsters to the truth.

The story tells how after the Great Sage had struggled in his stomach for a while the senior demon collapsed in the dust. He made no sound and was not breathing either. As he said nothing Monkey thought the demon was dead, so he stopped hitting him. When the demon chief recovered his breath he called out, "Most merciful and most compassionate Bodhisattva, Great Sage Equalling Heaven." "My boy," said Monkey when he heard this, "don't waste your effort. You could save yourself a few words by simply calling me Grandpa Sun." Desperate to save his skin, the evil monster really did call out, "Grandpa! Grandpa! I was wrong. I shouldn't have eaten you, and now you're destroying me. I beg you, Great Sage, in your mercy and compassion to take pity on my antlike greed for life and spare me. If you do I'll escort your master across the mountain."

Although the Great Sage was a tough hero he was most eager to help the Tang Priest in his journey, so on hearing the evil monster's pathetic pleas and flattery he decided once more to be kind. "Evil monster," he shouted, "I'll spare your life. How are you going to escort my master?" "We don't have any gold, silver, pearls, jade, agate, coral, crystal, amber, tortoise-shell or other such treasures here to give him, but my two brothers and I will carry him in a rattan chair across the mountain." "If you could carry him in a chair that would be better than treasure," said Monkey with a smile. "Open your mouth: I'm coming out." The demon then opened his mouth, whereupon the third chief went over to him and whispered in his ear, "Bite him as he comes out, brother. Chew the monkey to bits and swallow him. Then he won't be able to hurt you."

Now Monkey could hear all this from inside, so instead of coming straight out he thrust his gold-banded cudgel out first as a test. The demon did indeed take a bite at it, noisily smashing one of his front teeth in the process. "You're a nice monster, aren't you!" exclaimed Monkey, pulling his cudgel back. "I spare your life and agree to come out, but you try to murder me by biting me. I'm not coming out now. I'm going to kill you. I won't come out! I won't!" "Brother," the senior demon chief complained to the third one, "what you've done is destroy one of your own kind. I'd persuaded him to come out but you would have to tell me to bite him. Now I'm in agony from my broken tooth. What are we to do?"

In the face of the senior demon chief's complaints the third demon chief tried the method of making the enemy lose his temper. "Sun the Novice," he yelled at the top of his voice, "you have a thundering reputation. They tell of how mighty you were outside the Southern Gate of Heaven and at the Hall of Miraculous Mist. I'd heard that you've been capturing demons along your way to the Western Heaven. But now I see that you're only a very small-time ape." "What makes me small-time?" Monkey asked. " 'A hero who only roams three hundred miles around will go three thousand miles to make his fame resound,' the third chief replied. "Come out and fight me if you're a real tough guy. What do you mean by messing about in someone else's stomach? If you're not small-time what are you?" "Yes, yes, yes," thought Monkey when he heard this. "It wouldn't be at all difficult for me to tear this demon's bowels to bits, rip up his liver, and kill him. But I'd destroy my own reputation in the process. I'll have to forget about it. Open your mouth and I'll come out and fight you. The only problem is that this cave of yours is much too cramped for me to use my weapons. We'll have to go somewhere where there's more room." On hearing this the third demon chief mustered all the demons young and old from all around. There were over thirty thousand of them armed with the finest and sharpest weapons who came out of the cave to form a line of battle symbolizing heaven, earth and mankind. They were all waiting for Money to come out of the senior demon's mouth before rushing him. The second demon chief then helped the senior demon out through the entrance of the cave, where he shouted, "Sun the Novice! If you're a tough guy come out. There's a good battlefield here for us to fight on."

The Great Sage could tell that this was an open area from the calls of crows, magpies and cranes that he could hear in the monster's belly. "If I don't come out I'll be breaking faith with them," he thought. "But if I do these demons are beasts at heart behind their human faces. They tried to lure me out and bite me when they promised to carry the master across the ridge. Now they've got their army here. Oh well! I'll let them have it both ways. I'll go out but I'll leave a root in his stomach too." With that he put his hand behind him to pluck a tiny hair from his tail, blew on it with magic breath, called "Change!" and made it into a string as fine as a hair but some four hundred feet long. As the string came outside it grew thicker in the wind. One end Monkey fastened round the evil monster's heart in a slip-knot that he did not tighten — if he had it would have caused great pain. The other end he held in his hand as he said to himself, "If they agree to escort my master across the ridge when I come out this time I'll leave it at that. But if they refuse and go for me with their weapons so hard that I can't cope with them I'll just need to pull this rope. I'll get the same results as if I were still inside." He then made himself tiny and crawled up as far as the throat, from where he could see that the evil spirit had opened his mouth wide. Rows of steel teeth were set above and below like sharp knives. "This is no good," he thought at once, "no good at all. If I take this rope out through his mouth and he can't stand the pain he'll be able to cut through it with a single bite. I'll have to go out where there aren't any teeth." The splendid Great Sage paid out the string as he crawled up the demon's upper palate and into his nostril, which made his nose itch. The demon sneezed with a loud "atishoo", blowing Monkey out.

As he felt the wind blowing him Monkey bowed and grew over thirty feet long, keeping the string in one hand and holding the iron cudgel in the other. The wicked monster raised his steel sword as soon as he saw Monkey appear and hacked at his face. The Great Sage met the blow one-handed with his cudgel. Then the second demon chief with his spear and the third chief with his halberd went for him furiously. The Great Sage relaxed his pull on the rope, put his iron cudgel away and made off at speed by cloud, afraid that he would be unable to fight properly when surrounded by so many young devils. Once he had leapt out of the demons' camp he brought his cloud down on a spacious and empty mountain top and pulled with both hands on the rope as hard as he could. This gave the senior demon a pain in the heart. The demon struggled upwards in agony, whereupon the Great Sage pulled him down again. As they all watched from afar the junior demons all shouted, "Don't provoke him, Your Majesty! Let him go. That ape has no sense of when things ought to be done. He's flying a kite before the beginning of April." When the Great Sage heard this he gave a mighty stamp, at which the senior demon came whistling down out of the sky like a spinning-wheel to crash into the dust, making a crater some two feet deep in the hard earth at the foot of the mountain.

This gave the second and third demon chiefs such a fright that they landed their clouds together and rushed forward to grab hold of the rope and kneel at the foot of the mountain. "Great Sage," they pleaded, "we thought you were an immortal of vast and boundless generosity. We'd never dreamed that you would be as small-minded as a rat or a snail. It's true that we lured you out to give battle, but we never expected that you would tie a rope round our eldest brother's heart." "You're a thorough disgrace, you damned gang of demons," said Monkey with a laugh. "Last time you tried to trick me into coming out so you could bite me and this time you've lured me out to face an army ready for battle. It's obvious that you've got tens of thousands of soldiers here to tackle me when I'm alone. Most unreasonable. I'll pull him away. I'm going to drag him off to see my master." "If in your mercy and compassion you spare our lives, Great Sage," the demons said, all kowtowing together, "we vow to escort your master across this mountain."

"If you want to live all you have to do is cut the rope with your sword," said Monkey with a laugh. "My lord," the senior monster said, "I can cut the rope outside, but it's no good having the length inside that's tied round my heart. It sticks in my throat so uncomfortably that it makes me feel sick." "In that case," said Monkey, "open your mouth and I'll go back inside to undo the rope." This alarmed the senior demon, who said, "If you don't come out when you go in this time I'll be in a mess, a real mess." "I know how to undo the end of the rope that's in you from the outside," Monkey replied. "But when I've undone it will you really escort my master across?" "We will as soon as you've undone it," the senior demon chief replied. "I wouldn't dare lie about this." Now that he had satisfied himself the demon was telling the truth Monkey shook himself and put the hair back on his body, whereupon the monster's heart pains stopped. It was the Great Sage Sun's transforming magic that had tied the hair round his heart in the first place, which was why the pain ended as soon as the hair was put back on Monkey. The three demon chiefs then rose up into the air to thank him with the words, "Please go back now, Great Sage, and pack your luggage. We will carry a chair down to fetch him." The demon horde then all put their weapons down and went back into the cave.

Having put his rope away the Great Sage went straight back to the eastern side of the ridge, and when he was still a long way away he saw the Tang Priest lying on the ground, rolling around and howling. Pig and Friar Sand had opened the bundles of luggage and were dividing it up. "Don't tell me," thought Monkey with a quiet sigh. "No doubt Pig has told the master that I've been eaten up by evil spirits. The master's sobbing his heart out because he can't bear to be without me and the idiot's dividing the things ready for us all to split up. Oh dear! I can't be sure, so I'd better go down and give the master a shout." Bringing his cloud down, Monkey shouted, "Master!" As soon as Friar Sand heard this he started complaining to Pig. "All you want is to see people dead, just like a coffin stand," he said. "Our elder brother wasn't killed but you said he was and started this business here. Of course he's bound to kick up a row." "But I saw him with my own eyes being eaten up by the evil spirit in one mouthful," Pig replied. "I'm sure we're just seeing that ape's spirit because it's an unlucky day." Monkey then went up to Pig and hit him in the face with a slap that sent him staggering. "Cretin!" he said. "Is this my spirit you can see?" Rubbing his face, the idiot replied, "But the monster really did eat you up, brother. How can you, how can you have come back to life?" "Useless gumboil!" said Monkey. "After he ate me I grabbed his bowels, twisted his lungs, tied a rope round his heart and tore at him till he was in horrible agony. Then they all kowtowed and pleaded with me, so I spared his life. Now they're bringing a carrying-chair here to take the master over the mountain." As soon as Sanzang heard this he scrambled to his feet, bowed to Monkey and said, "Disciple, I've put you to enormous trouble. If I had believed what Wuneng said we would have been finished." "Chaff-guzzling idiot," Monkey said abusively, taking a swing at Pig with his fist, "you're thoroughly lazy and barely human. But don't get upset, Master. The monsters are coming to take you across the mountain." Friar Sand too felt deeply ashamed, and quickly trying to cover it up he packed up the luggage and loaded the horse to wait on the road.

The story returns to the three demon chiefs, who led their devilish hosts back into the cave. "Elder brother," said the second demon, "I'd imagined that Sun the Novice had nine heads and eight tails, but he turns out to be nothing but that pipsqueak of a monkey. You shouldn't have swallowed him. You should have fought him. He'd have been no match for us. With our tens of thousands of goblins we could have drowned him in our spit. But by swallowing him you let him use his magic and cause you agony, so that you didn't dare have it out with him. When I said we'd take the Tang Priest across the mountains just now I didn't mean it. It was only a way of luring him out because your life was in danger. I most certainly won't escort the Tang Priest." "Why not, good brother?" the senior demon chief asked. "If you and I draw up three thousand junior devils ready for battle I can capture that ape," the second demon replied. "Never mind about three thousand," the senior demon chief said. "You can have our whole force. If we capture him it'll be a credit to us all."

The second demon chief then mustered three thousand junior demons whom he led to a place beside the main road, where they were put into battle formation. He sent a herald with a blue flag to carry a message. "Sun the Novice," the herald said, "come out at once and fight His Second Majesty." When Pig heard this he said with a laugh, "As the saying goes, brother, liars don't fool the people at home. You lied to us when you came back, you trickster. You said you'd beaten the evil spirits and that they'd be bringing a carrying-chair to take the master across. But here they are challenging you to battle. Why?" "The senior demon did surrender to me," Monkey replied, "and he wouldn't dare show his face. The sound of my name alone is enough to give him a headache. The second demon chief must be challenging me to battle because he can't bring himself to escort us across. I tell you, brother, those three evil spirits are brothers and they have a sense of honour. We're three brothers but we don't. I've beaten the senior demon, so the second demon's come out. There's no reason why you shouldn't fight him."

"I'm not scared of him," Pig said. "I'll go and give him a fight." "If you want to, go ahead," Monkey replied. "Brother," said Pig with a laugh, "I'll go, but lend me that rope." "What do you want it for?" Monkey asked. "You don't know how to get into his belly or tie it to his heart, so what use would it be to you?" "I want it tied round my waist as a lifeline," replied Pig. "You and Friar Sand are to hold on to it and let it out for me to fight him. If you think I'm beating him pay more rope out and I'll capture him, but if he's beating me, pull me back. Don't let him drag me off." At this Monkey smiled to himself and thought, "Another chance to make a fool of the idiot." Monkey then tied the rope round Pig's waist and sent him off into battle.

The idiot lifted his rake and rushed up the steep slope shouting, "Come out, evil spirit! Come and fight your ancestor Pig!" The herald with the blue flag rushed back to report, "Your Majesty, there's a monk with a long snout and big ears here." The second demon chief came out of the encampment, saw Pig, and without a word thrust his spear straight at Pig's face. The idiot raised his rake and went forward to parry the blow. The two of them joined battle in front of the mountainside, and before they had fought seven or eight rounds the idiot began to weaken. He was no longer able to hold the evil spirit off. "Brother," he shouted, turning back in a hurry, "pull in the lifeline, pull in the lifeline!" When the Great Sage heard this from where he stood he loosened his hold on the rope and dropped it. The idiot started to run back now that he was defeated. At first he had not noticed the rope trailing behind him, but after he turned back, relaxing the tension on it, it started to get tangled round his legs. He tripped himself over, climbed to his feet and tripped over again. At first he only staggered, but then he fell face-down into the dust. The evil spirit caught up with him, unwound his trunk that was like a python, wrapped it round Pig and carried him back in triumph to the cave. The devilish host chorused a paean of victory as they swarmed back.

When Sanzang saw all this from the foot of the slope he became angry with Monkey. "Wukong," he said, "no wonder Wuneng wishes you were dead. You brother-disciples don't love each other at all. All you feel is jealousy. He told you to pull in his lifeline, so why didn't you? Why did you drop the rope instead? What are we to do now you have got him killed?" "You're covering up for him again, Master," said Monkey, "and showing favouritism too. I'm fed up. When I was captured it didn't bother you at all. I was dispensable. But when that idiot gets himself caught you blame me for it. Let him suffer. It'll teach him how hard it is to fetch the scriptures." "Disciple," said Sanzang, "was I not worried when you went? I remembered that you could change into other things, so I was sure you would come to no harm. But the idiot was born clumsy and can't transform himself, which makes this a very dangerous business. You must go and rescue him." "Stop complaining, Master," said Brother Monkey. "I'll go and save him."

Monkey rushed up the mountain thinking resentfully, "I'm not going to make life easy for that idiot if he wishes me dead. I'll go and see what the evil spirits are doing with him. Before I rescue him I'll let him suffer a bit." He then made magic with his hands, said the words of a spell, shook himself, turned into the tiniest of insects and flew into the cave, where he landed at the bottom of one of Pig's ears to be taken inside with the evil spirit. The second demon chief had led his three thousand junior devils trumpeting and drumming loudly to the cave, where they stopped. He now took Pig inside and said, "I've got one, elder brother." "Show me," the senior demon replied. Unwinding his trunk the second demon chief flung Pig to the ground and said, "There he is." "That one's useless," said the senior demon. "Your Majesty," put in Pig when he heard this, "if I'm no use let me go and find a more useful one to capture." "He may not be any use," said the third demon chief, "but he is the Tang Priest's disciple Zhu Bajie. Tie him up and put him to soak in the pool at the back. When his bristles have been soaked off we can open his belly up, salt him and dry him in the sun. He'll go down well with some wine on a rainy day." "That's that then," exclaimed Pig in horror. "I've fallen into the clutches of a demon who's a salt-pork pedlar." The demon hordes fell on him, tied his hands and feet together, carried him to the pool at the back, pushed him in and went back.

When the Great Sage flew there to have a look he saw the idiot with his four limbs pointing upwards and his snout downwards as he half floated and was half sinking, grunting through his snout. He really was a ridiculous sight, like a big blackened frost-bitten lotus pod that has shed its seeds in September or October. Seeing his face the Great Sage felt both loathing and pity for him. "What shall I do?" he wondered. "After all, he is another member of the Dragon Flower Assembly. I just wish he wouldn't keep trying to divide up the luggage, split our band, and incite the master to say the Band-tightening Spell. The other day I heard Friar Sand say that he'd stashed some money away for himself. I wonder if it's true. ' I'll give him a scare and find out."

The splendid Great Sage flew down to his ear and called in a disguised voice, "Zhu Wuneng, Zhu Wuneng." "This is terrible," thought Pig in alarm. "Wuneng is the name the Bodhisattva Guanyin gave me. I've been called Zhu Bajie all the time I've been with the Tang Priest. How can there be anyone here who knows my name is Wuneng?" So he could not restrain himself from asking, "Who's that calling my Buddhist name?" "Me," said Monkey. "Who are you?" the idiot asked. "I'm a catcher," Monkey replied. "Where from, sir?" asked Pig in terror. "From the Fifth King of the Underworld, and he's sent me to fetch you," said Monkey. "Then please go back and ask the Fifth King as he's such a good friend of my senior fellow-disciple Sun Wukong to give me a day's grace. You can come for me tomorrow." "You're talking nonsense," Monkey replied. "If King Yama of Hell decides you're to die in the third watch nobody will keep you till the fourth. Come with me at once if you don't want me to put a rope round your neck and drag you off."

"Do me a favour," said the idiot. Even with a face like mine still want to go on living. I'll certainly die if I have to, but give me a day till these evil spirits have captured my master and the rest of us, so I can see them again before we're all done for." "Very well then," said Monkey, grinning to himself. "I've got about thirty people to capture around here in this batch. When I've caught them I'll come back for you. That'll give you a day's grace. Give me some money. I'm sure you've got some." "Oh dear," said Pig, "we monks don't have money." "If you haven't then I'm dragging you off," said Brother Monkey. "Come with me." "Don't be so impatient, sir," said the idiot, panicking. "I know that rope of yours is what they call the life-taking rope. Once it's round you you're dead. Yes, I have got some money. I've got a bit, but not much." "Where is it?" Monkey demanded. "Give it me at once." "Oh dear, what a pity!" said Pig. "From when I became a monk right up till now the kind people who feed monks have given me a bit more alms than the others because my belly's so big. I saved all the little bits of silver till I had about half an ounce. They were awkward to keep, so when we were in a city some time ago I asked a silversmith to melt them all together. The wicked man stole a few grains of it, so the ingot he made only weighed forty-six hundredths of an ounce. Take it." "The idiot hasn't even got his trousers on," grinned Monkey to himself, "so where can he have hidden it? Hey, where's your silver?" "It's stuffed inside my left ear," Pig replied. "I can't get it myself because I'm tied up, so take it out yourself."

When Monkey heard this he put his hand out and took the silver from inside Pig's ear. It was indeed an ingot shaped like a saddle that weighed only forty-five or forty-six hundredths of an ounce. As he held it in his hands Monkey could not help roaring with laughter. Recognizing Monkey's voice the idiot started cursing him wildly from the water: "Damn and blast you, Protector of the Horses, for coming to extort money from me when I'm in such misery." "I've got you now, you dreg-guzzler!" said Monkey. "Goodness only knows what I've had to suffer for the sake of protecting the master, while you've been making your fortune." "Nonsense!" Pig retorted. "Call this a fortune? It's just what I've scraped off my teeth. I resisted spending it on my stomach, so I saved it to buy myself some cloth to get a tunic made. You've got it out of me by intimidation. You ought to share it with me." "You won't get a cent of it," Monkey replied. "I've paid you to spare my life," said Pig, "so now you damn well ought to rescue me." "Don't be so impatient," said Monkey. "I'll rescue you all in good time." Putting the silver away he turned back into himself and used his cudgel to bring Pig close enough to grab him by his feet, drag him ashore and untie him. Pig then sprang up, took off his clothes, wrung them out, shook them, and draped them still dripping wet over his shoulders. "Brother," he said, "open the back gates. Let's go." "There's no glory in sneaking out the back way," replied Monkey. "We'll leave by the front gates." "My feet are still numb after being tied up." said Pig. "I can't run." "Buck up and come with me," said Monkey.

The splendid Great Sage charged out, clearing his way by swinging his cudgel. The idiot had no choice but to endure the pain and keep close to him. When he saw the rake propped up by the second pair of gates he went over to it, pushed the junior devils aside, retrieved it and rushed forward, lashing out wildly. He and Brother Monkey charged through three or four pairs of gates, and goodness only knows how many junior devils they killed. When the senior demon chief heard all this he said to the second chief, "You captured a fine one! A fine one indeed! Look! Sun the Novice has rescued Pig and they've wounded or killed the juniors on the gates." The second demon at once sprang to his feet and rushed out through the gates brandishing his spear. "Damned macaque," he shouted at the top of his voice. "What a bloody cheek! How dare you treat us with such contempt!" As soon as the Great Sage heard this he stopped still. The monster thrust his spear straight at him without allowing any argument. With the unhurried skill of the expert Monkey raised his iron cudgel to hit back at the demon's face. The two of them fought a splendid battle outside the entrance to the cave:

The yellow-tusked elephant in human form
Had sworn brotherhood with the Lion King.
Persuaded by the senior monster
They plotted together to eat the Tang Priest.
Huge were the powers of the Great Sage, Heaven's equal,
Who helped the good against the bad and killed off demons,
The incompetent Pig had met with disaster,
So Monkey saved him and led him outside.
When the demon king pursued them with great ferocity
The spear and the cudgel each showed off its powers.

The spear moved like a snake in the woods;
The cudgel arose like a dragon from the sea.
Where the dragon emerged the clouds were thick;
Dense hung the mist where the snake went through the woods.
It was all for the sake of the Tang Priest
That they fought each other with ferocity and hatred.

When he saw the Great Sage start fighting the evil spirit, Pig stood on the spur, his rake upright. Instead of joining in to help, he watched with stupefied amazement. Monkey's cudgel was so powerful and his martial skills so faultless the evil spirit used his spear to parry Monkey's blows while unrolling his trunk to wrap round him. As Monkey knew about this trick he held his gold-banded cudgel out horizontally in both hands and raised them. The evil spirit's trunk caught Monkey round the waist but missed his hands. Just watch how Monkey belabours the evil spirit's trunk with his cudgel.

When Pig saw this he beat his chest and said, "Oh dear! That monster's got lousy luck. When he caught me he got my arms too because I'm so clumsy, but he didn't when he caught that slippery character. He's got his cudgel in both hands, and all he needs to do is shove it up the monster's trunk to give him such a pain in the nostrils that it'll make the snot run. The monster'll never be able to hold him." Monkey had not thought of this before Pig gave him the idea, but now he waved his cudgel to make it as thick as a hen's egg and over ten feet long and actually did shove it hard up the monster's trunk. This gave the evil spirit such a shock that he unravelled his trunk with a swishing noise. Monkey brought his hand round to grab the trunk and drag it forcefully towards him. To spare himself any more agony the monster stepped out and moved with Monkey's hand. Only then did Pig dare approach, raising his rake to hit wildly at the monster's flanks. "No," said Brother Monkey, "that's no good. The prongs of your rake are so sharp they might break his skin. If he starts bleeding heavily and the master sees it he'll say we've been killing again. You'd better turn it round and hit him with the handle."

The idiot then raised the handle of his rake and struck the monster at every step while Monkey dragged him by the trunk. They looked like a pair of elephant boys as they led him down to the foot of the mountain, where Sanzang could be seen gazing with concentration at the two of them coming noisily towards him. "Wujing," he said to Friar Sand, "what is it Wukong is leading?" "Master," replied Friar Sand when he saw them, "big brother is dragging an evil spirit here by the nose. He really enjoys slaughter." "Splendid, splendid," said Sanzang. "What a big evil spirit, and what a long nose! Go and ask him if he's happy and willing to escort us over the mountain. If he is he must be spared and not be killed." Friar Sand at once rushed straight towards them shouting, "The master says you mustn't kill the monster if he's really willing to escort him across the mountain." As soon as he heard this the demon fell to his knees and promised to do so in a very nasal voice. His voice was like this because Monkey was pinching his nostrils shut, making it sound as though he had a heavy cold. "Lord Tang," he said, "I'll carry you across by chair if you spare my life." "My master and we disciples are good people," Monkey replied. "As you've said this we'll spare your life. Fetch the chair at once. If you break your word again we most certainly won't spare your life when we catch you next time." The freed monster kowtowed and left. Monkey and Pig went to report to the Tang Priest on everything that had happened to them. Pig was overcome with shame as he spread his clothes out to dry in the sun while they waited.

The second demon chief returned trembling and shaking to the cave. Even before his return some junior devils had reported to the senior and the third demon chiefs that Monkey had dragged him off by the trunk. In his anxiety the senior demon had led his hosts out with the third demon when they saw the second chief coming back alone. As they brought him inside and asked him why he had been released the second chief told them all about Sanzang's words of mercy and goodness. They looked at each other, at a loss for words. "Elder brother," said the second demon chief, "shall we take Sanzang across?" "What a thing to say, brother," replied the senior chief. "Sun the Novice is a monkey who shows the greatest benevolence and sense of justice. If he had wanted to kill me when he was in my stomach he could most certainly have done so. He only grabbed your trunk. He might have dragged you off and not let you go. All he did was to pinch your trunk and break its skin, and that's given you a scare. Get ready at once to take them across." The third demon chief smiled and said, "Yes, yes, yes!" "From the way you're talking, my good brother," said the senior demon, "it sounds as though you're reluctant to let the Tang Priest go. If you don't, we'll take him across."

The third demon chief smiled again and said, "Elder brothers, it would have been luckier for those monks if they hadn't asked us to escort them but had slipped quietly across instead. By asking us to escort them they've fallen in with our plan to lure the tiger down from the mountain." "What do you mean by 'luring the tiger from the mountain'?" the senior demon asked. "Summon all the demons in our cave," the third demon chief continued. "Choose one thousand from the ten thousand of them, then a hundred from the thousand, then sixteen and thirty from the hundred." "Why do you want sixteen and thirty?" the senior demon asked. "The thirty must be good cooks," the third demon chief replied. "Give them the best rice and flour, bamboo shoots, tea, gill fungus, button mushrooms, beancurd and wheat gluten. Send them to put up a shelter seven to ten miles along the way and lay on a meal for the Tang Priest." "And what do you want the sixteen for?" the senior demon asked. "Eight to carry the chair and eight to shout and clear the way," the third demon replied. "We brothers will accompany them for a stage of their journey. About 150 miles west of here is my city, and I've plenty of troops there to greet them. When they get to the city we'll do such and such and so on. . . . The Tang Priest and his disciples won't be able to see what's happening to them. Whether we catch the Tang Priest or not depends completely on those sixteen demons."

The senior demon was beside himself with delight on hearing this. It was as if he had recovered from a drunken stupor or woken up from a dream. "Excellent, excellent," he said, whereupon he mustered the demons, chose thirty to whom he gave the food and another sixteen to carry a rattan chair. As they set out the senior demon gave the following instructions to the rest of the demons: "None of you are to go out on the mountain. Sun the Novice is a very cautious ape, and if he sees any of you around he'll be suspicious and see through our plan."

The senior demon then led his underlings to a place beside the main road, where he called aloud, "Lord Tang, today's not an unlucky one, so please come across the mountain straight away." "Who is that calling me, Wukong?" Sanzang asked when he heard this. "It's the demons I beat," Monkey replied. "They're bringing a chair to carry you." Putting his hands together in front of his chest Sanzang looked up to the sky and said, "Splendid, splendid! But for my worthy disciple's great abilities I could not proceed on my journey." He then walked forward to greet the demons with the words, "I am most grateful for the consideration you gentlemen are showing. When my disciples and I return to Chang'an we will praise your admirable achievements." "Please get into the carrying-chair, my lord," the demons said, kowtowing. Having mortal eyes and body Sanzang did not realize that this was a trick. The Great Sage Sun, a golden immortal of the Supreme Monad with a loyal nature, thought that because he had captured and released the demons they were now won over. He never imagined that they had other plots in mind, so he did not investigate closely but went along with his master's ideas. He told Pig to tie the luggage on the horse and keep close to the master with Friar Sand while he cleared the way with his iron cudgel, watching out to see if all was well. While eight devils carried the chair and eight shouted in turn to clear the way the three demon chiefs steadied the poles of the chair. The master was delighted to sit upright in it and go up the high mountain by the main track, little realizing that

> *Great grief would return in the midst of rejoicing;*
> *"Extremes," says the classic, "create their negation."*
> *Fated they were to meet with disaster,*
> *A star of ill-omen to mark desolation.*

The band of demons worked with one mind to escort them and serve them diligently at all times. After ten miles there was a vegetarian meal and after fifteen more miles another one. They were invited to rest before it grew late, and everything along their way was neat and tidy. Each day they had three most satisfactory and delightful meals and spent a comfortable night where they were able to sleep well.

When they had travelled about 150 miles west they found themselves near a walled city. Raising his iron cudgel the Great Sage, who was only a third of a mile ahead of the carrying-chair, was so alarmed by the sight of the city that he fell over and was unable to rise to his feet. Do you know why someone of his great courage was so frightened by what he saw? It was because he saw a very evil atmosphere hanging over the town.

> *Crowds of evil demons and monsters,*
> *Wolf spirits at all four gates.*
> *Striped tigers are the commanders;*
> *White-faced tiger-cats are senior officers.*
> *Antlered stags carry documents around;*
> *Cunning foxes walk along the streets.*
> *Thousand-foot pythons slither round the walls;*
> *Twenty-mile serpents occupy the roads.*
> *At the base of high towers grey wolves shout commands;*
> *Leopards speak in human voices by pavilions.*
> *Standard-bearers and drummers — all are monsters;*
> *Mountain spirits patrol and stand sentry.*
> *Crafty hares open shops to trade;*
> *Wild boars carry their loads to do business.*
> *What used to be the capital of a heavenly dynasty*
> *Has now become a city of wolves and tigers.*

Just as he was being overcome by terror the Great Sage heard a wind from behind him and turned quickly to see the third demon chief raising a heaven-square halberd with a patterned handle to strike at his head. Springing to his feet, the Great Sage struck back at the monster's face with his gold-banded cudgel. Both of them were snorting with rage and fury as they ground their teeth and fought a wordless struggle. Monkey then saw the senior demon chief giving out orders as he lifted his steel sabre to hack at Pig. Pig was in such a rush that he had to let the horse go as he swung his rake around to hit wildly back. Meanwhile the second demon chief was thrusting with his spear at Friar Sand, who parried with his demon-quelling staff.

The three demon chiefs and the three monks were now all fighting in single combat, ready to throw away their lives. The sixteen junior devils obeyed their orders, each giving play to his talents as they grabbed hold of the white horse and the luggage and crowded round Sanzang, lifting up his chair and carrying him straight to the city. "Your Senior Majesty, please decide what to do now we've captured the Tang Priest," they shouted. All the demons of every rank on the city walls came rushing down to throw the city gates wide open. Every battalion was ordered to furl its flag, silence its drums, and on no account shout war-cries or strike gongs. "His Senior Majesty has given orders that the Tang Priest is not to be frightened. He can't endure being scared. If he is, his flesh will turn sour and be inedible." The demons were all delighted to welcome Sanzang, bownig and carrying him into the throne hall of the palace, where he was invited to sit in the place of honour. They offered him tea and food as they bustled around him in attendance. The venerable elder felt dizzy and confused as he looked about and saw no familiar faces. If you don't know whether he was to escape with his life listen to the explanation in the next instalment.

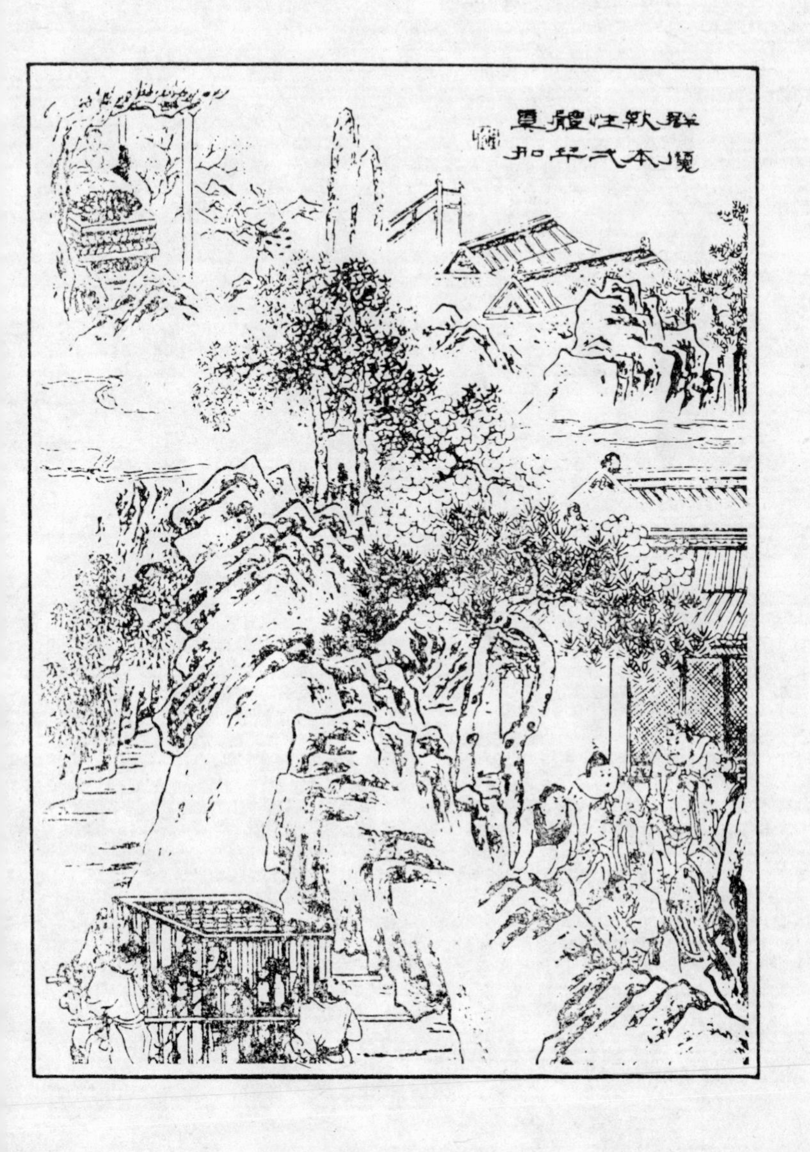

CHAPTER SEVENTY-SEVEN

The demon host mistreats the fundamental nature;
The one body pays his respects to the Buddha.

We will tell now not of the sufferings of the venerable Tang Elder but of the three demon chiefs in strenuous combat with the Great Sage and his two brother disciples in the low hills to the east outside the city. It was indeed a good hard battle, like an iron brush against a copper pan:

Six types of body, six types of weapon,
Six physical forms, six feelings.
The six evils arise from the six sense organs and the six desires;
The six gates to nirvana and the six ways of rebirth are struggling for victory.
In the thirty-six divine palaces spring comes of itself;
The six times six forms do not want to be named.
This one holding a gold-banded cudgel
Performs a thousand movements;
That one wielding a heaven-square halberd
Is exceptional in every way.
Pig is even more ferocious with his rake;
The second demon's spear-play is superb and effective.
There is nothing commonplace about young Friar Sand's staff
As he tries to inflict a blow that is fatal;
Sharp is the senior demon's sabre
Which he raises without mercy.
These three are the true priest's invincible escorts;
The other three are evil and rebellious spirits.
At first the fight is not so bad,
But later it becomes more murderous.

All six weapons rise up by magic
To twist and turn in the clouds above.
They belch out in an instant clouds that darken the sky,
And the only sounds to be heard are roars and bellows.

After the six of them had been fighting for a long time evening was drawing in, and as the wind was also bringing cloud it became dark very quickly. Pig was finding it harder and harder to see as his big ears were covering his eyelids. His hands and feet were besides too slow for him to be able to hold off his opponent, so he fled from the fight, dragging his rake behind him. The senior demon chief took a swing at him with his sword that almost killed him. Luckily Pig moved his head out of the way, so that the blade only cut off a few of his bristles. The monster then caught up with Pig, opened his jaws, picked Pig up by the collar, carried him into the city and threw him to the junior demons to tie up and take to the throne hall. The senior demon chief then rose back into the air by cloud to help the other two.

Seeing that things were going badly Friar Sand feinted with his staff and turned to flee only to be caught, hands and all, when the second demon unravelled his trunk and noisily wrapped it round him. The demon took him too into the city, ordering the junior demons to tie him up in the palace before rising up into the sky again to tell the others how to catch Monkey. Seeing that both his brother disciples had been captured Monkey realized that it was going to be impossible for him to hold out single-handed. Indeed,

A couple of fists can defeat a good hand,
But cannot a competent foursome withstand.

With a shout Brother Monkey pushed the three demons' weapons aside, set off his somersault cloud and fled. When the third demon chief saw Monkey ride off by somersault he shook himself, resumed his real form, spread his wings and caught up with the Great Sage. You may well ask how the demon could possibly catch up with him. When Monkey made havoc in heaven all that time ago a hundred thousand heavenly soldiers had failed to capture him. Because he could cover 36,000 miles in a single somersault of his cloud, none of the gods had been able to catch up with him. But this evil spirit could cover 30,000 miles with one beat of his wings, so that with two beats he caught up with Monkey and seized him. Monkey could not get out of the demon's talons no matter how hard he struggled or how desperately he longed to escape. Even when he used his transformation magic he still could not move. If he made himself grow the demon opened his grip but still held firmly to him; and if he shrank the demon tightened his clutch. The demon took him back inside the city, released his talons, dropped him into the dust, and told the fiendish hordes to tie him up and put him with Pig and Friar Sand. The senior and the second demon chiefs both came out to greet the third chief, who went back up into the throne hall with them. Alas! This time they were not tying Monkey up but sending him on his way.

It was now the second watch of the night, and after all the demons had exchanged greetings the Tang Priest was pushed out of the throne hall. When he suddenly caught sight in the lamplight of his three disciples all lying tied up on the ground the venerable master leaned down beside Brother Monkey and said through his tears, "Disciple, when we meet with trouble you normally go off and use your magic powers to subdue the monsters causing it. Now that you too have been captured can I survive, poor monk that I am?" As soon as Pig and Friar Sand heard their master's distress they too began to howl together. "Don't worry, Master," said Monkey with a hint of a smile, "and don't cry, brothers. No matter what they do they won't be able to hurt us. When the demon chiefs have settled and are asleep we can be on our way." "You're just making trouble again, brother," replied Pig. "We're trussed up with hempen ropes. If we do manage to work them a bit loose they spurt water on them to shrink them again. You might be too skinny to notice, but fat old me's having a terrible time. If you don't believe me take a look at my arms. The rope's cut two inches deep into them. I'd never get away." "Never mind hempen ropes," said Monkey with a laugh, "even if they were coir cables as thick as a rice-bowl they'd be no more than an autumn breeze to me. What's there to make a fuss about?"

As master and disciples were talking the senior demon could be heard saying, "Third brother, you really are strong and wise. Your plan to capture the Tang Priest was brilliant and it worked." "Little ones," he called, "five of you carry water, seven scrub the pans, ten get the fire burning and twenty fetch the iron steamer. When we've steamed the four monks tender for my brothers and me to enjoy we'll give you juniors a piece so that you can all live for ever." "Brother," said Pig, trembling, when he heard this, "listen. That evil spirit's planning to steam and eat us." "Don't be afraid," said Monkey. "I'm going to find out whether he's an evil spirit still wet behind the ears or an old hand."

"Brother," said Friar Sand, sobbing, "don't talk so big. We're next door to the king of Hell. How can you talk about whether he's wet behind the ears or an old hand at a time like this?" The words were not all out of his mouth before the second demon chief was heard to say, "Pig won't steam well." "Amitabha Buddha!" said Pig with delight. "I wonder who's building up good karma by saying I won't steam well." "If he won't steam well," the third chief said, "skin him before steaming him." This panicked Pig, who screamed at the top of his voice, "Don't skin me. I may be coarse but I'll go tender if you boil me." "If he won't steam well," the senior demon chief said, "put him on the bottom tray of the steamer." "Don't worry, Pig," said Monkey with a laugh, "he's wet behind the ears. He's no old hand." "How can you tell?" Friar Sand asked. "Generally speaking you should start from the top when steaming," Monkey replied. "Whatever's hardest to steam should be put on the top tray. Add a bit of extra fuel to the fire, get up a good steam and it'll be done. But put it at the bottom and lower the steam and you won't get the steam up even if you cook it for six months. He must be wet behind the ears if he says that Pig should be put on the bottom tray because he's hard to cook." "Brother," Pig replied, "if he followed your advice I'd be slaughtered alive. When he can't see the steam rising he'll take the lid off, turn me over and make the fire burn hotter. I'll be cooked on both sides and half done in the middle."

As they were talking a junior devil came in to report that the water was boiling. The senior chief ordered that the monks be carried in, and all the demons acted together to carry Pig to the lowest shelf of the steamer and Friar Sand to the second shelf. Guessing that they would be coming for him next Brother Monkey freed himself and said, "This lamplight is just right for some action." He then pulled out a hair, blew on it with magic breath, called, "Change!" and turned it into another Monkey he tied up with the hempen rope while extracting his real self in spirit form to spring up into mid-air, look down and watch. Not realizing that he was an imitation the crowd of demons picked up the false Monkey they saw and carried him to the third tray of the steamer, near the top. Only then did they drag the Tang Priest to the ground, tie him up, and put him into the fourth tray. As the dry firewood was stacked up a fierce fire blazed. "My Pig and Friar Sand can stand a couple of boilings," sighed the Great Sage up in the clouds, "but that master of mine will be cooked tender as soon as the water boils. If I can't save him by magic he'll be dead in next to no time."

The splendid Great Sage made a hand-spell in mid-air, said the magic words "*Om* the blue pure dharma world; true is the eternal beneficence of Heaven", and summoned the Dragon King of the Northern Ocean to him. A black cloud appeared among the other clouds, and from it there came at once an answering shout, "Ao Shun, the humble dragon of the Northern Ocean, kowtows in homage." "Arise, arise," said Monkey. "I would not have ventured to trouble you for nothing. I've now got this far with my master the Tang Priest. He's been captured by vicious monsters and put into an iron steamer to be cooked. Go and protect him for me and don't let the steam harm him." The dragon king at once turned himself into a cold wind that blew underneath the cooking pot and coiled around to shield it from all the heat of the fire. Thus were the three of them saved from death.

As the third watch was drawing to an end the senior demon

chief announced a decision. "My men," he said, "we have worn out brains and brawn to capture the Tang Priest and his three disciples. Because of the trouble we went to in escorting them we have not slept for four days and nights. I don't think that they'll be able to escape now that they're tied up and being steamed. You are all to guard them carefully. Ten of your junior devils are to take it in turns to keep the fires burning while we withdraw to our living quarters for a little rest. By the fifth watch, when it's about to get light, they're bound to be cooked tender. Have some garlic paste, salt and vinegar ready and wake us up; then we'll be able to eat them with a good appetite." The devils did as they had been ordered while the three demon chiefs returned to their sleeping chambers.

Up in the clouds Brother Monkey clearly heard these instructions being given, so he brought his cloud down. As there was no sound of voices from inside the steamer he thought, "The fire is blazing away and they must be feeling hot. Why aren't they afraid? Why aren't they saying anything? Hmm . . . Could they have been steamed to death? Let me go closer and listen." The splendid Great Sage shook himself as he stood on his cloud and turned into a black fly. As he alighted on the outside of the iron steamer's trays to listen he heard Pig saying inside, "What lousy luck! What lousy luck! I wonder whether we're being closed-steamed or open-steamed." "What do you mean by 'closed' and 'open', brother?" Friar Sand asked. "Closed steaming is when they cover the steamer and open steaming is when they don't," Pig replied. "Disciples," said Sanzang from the top tray, "the cover is off." "We're in luck!" said Pig. "We won't be killed tonight. We're being open-steamed." Having heard all three of them talking Monkey realized that they were still alive, so he flew away, fetched the iron steamer lid and placed it lightly on the steamer. "Disciples," exclaimed Sanzang in alarm, "they've covered us up." "That's done it," said Pig. "That means closed steaming. We're bound to die tonight." Friar Sand and the venerable elder started to sob. "Don't cry," said Pig. "A new shift of cooks has come on duty." "How can you tell?" Friar Sand asked. "I was delighted at first when they carried me here," Pig replied. "I've got a bit of a feverish chill and I wanted warming up. But all we're getting at the moment is cold air. Hey! Mr. Cook, sir! What are you making such a fuss about putting more firewood on for? Am I asking for what's yours?"

When Monkey heard this he could not help laughing to himself. "Stupid clod," he thought. "Being cold is bearable. If it got hot you'd be dead. The secret will get out if he goes on talking. I'd better rescue him. . . . No! I'd have to turn back into myself to rescue them, and if I did that the ten cooks would see me and start shouting. That would disturb the old monsters and I'd be put to a lot more trouble. I'll have to use some magic on the cooks first." Then a memory came back to him. "When I was the Great Sage in the old days I once played a guessing game with the Heavenly King Lokapala at the Northern Gate of Heaven and won some of his sleep insects off him. I've got a few left I can use on them." He felt around his waist inside his belt and found that he had twelve of them left. "I'll give them ten and keep two to breed from," Monkey thought. Then he threw the insects into the ten junior devils' faces, where the insects went up their nostrils, so that they all started feeling drowsy, lay down and went to sleep. One of them, however, who was holding a fire-fork slept very fitfully, kept rubbnig his head and face, pinching his nose and continuously sneezing. "That so-and-so knows a trick or two," thought Monkey. "I'll have to give him a double dose." He threw one of his remaining insects into the demon's face. "With two insects the left one can go in when the right one comes out and vice versa," Monkey thought. "That should keep him quiet." With that the junior demon gave two or three big yawns, stretched himself, dropped the fork and slumped down, fast asleep. He did not get up again.

"What marvellous magic; it really works," said Monkey, turning back into himself. Then he went close to the steamer and called, "Master." "Rescue me, Wukong," said the Tang Priest when he heard him. "Is that you calling to us from outside?" Friar Sand asked. "If I weren't out here would you prefer me to be suffering in there with you?" Monkey replied.

"Brother," said Pig, "you sloped off and left us to carry the can. We're being closed-steamed in here." "Stop yelling, idiot," said Monkey with a laugh. "I'm here to rescue you." "Brother," said Pig, "if you're going to rescue us do it properly. Don't get us put back in here for another steaming." Monkey then took the lid off, freed the master, shook the hair of his that he had turned into an imitation Monkey and put it back on his body, then released Friar Sand and Pig, taking one tray at a time. As soon as he was untied, the idiot wanted to run away. "Don't be in such a hurry!" said Monkey, who recited the words of a spell that released the dragon before going on to say to Pig, "We've still got high mountains and steep ridges ahead of us on our way to the Western Heaven. The going's too heavy for the master — he isn't a strong walker. Wait till I've fetched the horse."

Watch him as with light step he goes to the throne hall, where he saw that all the demons young and old were asleep. He undid the rope attached to the horse's reins, being even more careful not to alarm him. Now the horse was a dragon horse, so had Monkey been a stranger he would have given him a couple of flying kicks and whinnied. But Monkey had kept horses and held the office of Protector of the Horses, and this horse was besides their own. That was why the animal neither reared nor whinnied. Monkey led the horse very quietly over, tightened the girth and got everything ready before inviting his master to mount. Trembling and shaking, the Tang Priest did so. He too wanted to go. "Don't you be in such a hurry either," Monkey said. "There'll be plenty more kings along our journey west and we'll need our passport if we're to get there. What other identity papers do we have? I'm going back to find the luggage." "I remember that when we came in the monsters put the luggage to the left of the throne hall," said the Tang Priest. "The loads must still be there."

"Understood," said Monkey, who sprang off at once to search for it by the throne hall. When he suddenly saw shimmering lights of many colours Brother Monkey knew that they came from the luggage. How did he know? Because the light came from the night-shining pearl on the Tang Priest's cassock. He rushed towards it and found that their load was unopened, so he took it out and gave it to Friar Sand to carry, while Pig led the horse and he took the lead.

They were hurrying to go straight out through the main southern gate when they heard the noise of watchmen's clappers and bells. They found the gates locked and paper seals over the locks. "How are we going to get out if the place is so closely guarded?" Monkey wondered. "Let's get out the back door," said Pig. With Monkey leading the way they rushed straight to the back gates. "I can hear clappers and bells outside the back gates as well, and they're sealed too," Monkey said. "What are we to do? If it weren't for the Tang Priest's mortal body it wouldn't bother us three: we could get away by cloud and wind. But the Tang Priest hasn't escaped from the Three Worlds* and is still confined within the Five Elements. All his bones are the unclean ones he got from his mother and father. He can't lift himself into the air and he'll never get away." "No time for talking now, brother," said Pig. "Let's go somewhere where there aren't any bells, clappers or guards, lift the master up and climb over the wall." "That won't do," said Monkey. "We could lift him over now because we've got to, but you've got such a big mouth you'd tell people everywhere when we're taking the the scriptures back that we're the sort of monks who sneak over people's walls." "But we can't bother about behaving properly now," replied Pig. "We've got to save our skins." Monkey had no choice but to do as he suggested, so they went up to wall and worked out how to climb over.

Oh dear! Things would have to work out this way: Sanzang was not yet free of his unlucky star. The three demon chiefs who had been fast asleep in their living quarters suddenly awoke and heard that the Tang Priest had escaped, got up, threw on their clothes and hurried to the throne hall of the palace. "How many times has the Tang Priest been steamed?" they asked. The

* In Buddhist teaching, the worlds of desire, of form and of pure spirit. Monkey appears to be using the term loosely to refer to the mortal world.

junior devils who were looking after the fires were all so soundly asleep because the sleep insects were in them that not even blows could wake them up. The chiefs woke up some others who were not on duty, who answered rashly, "Ss . . . ss . . . seven times." Then they rushed over to the steamer to see the steamer trays lying scattered on the floor and the cooks still asleep. In their alarm they rushed back to report, "Your Majesties, th . . . th . . . they've escaped."

The three demon chiefs came out of the throne hall to take a close look around the cauldron. They saw that the steamer trays were indeed scattered on the floor, the water was stone-cold and the fire completely out. The cooks supposed to be tending the fire were still so fast asleep that they were snoring noisily. The fiends were all so shocked that they all shouted, "Catch the Tang Priest! At once! Catch the Tang Priest!" Their yells woke up the demons senior and junior all around. They rushed in a crowd to the main front gates carrying their swords and spears. Seeing that the sealed locks had not been touched and that the night watchmen were still sounding their clappers and bells they asked the watchman, "Which way did the Tang Priest go?" "Nobody's come out," the watchmen all replied. They hurried to the back gates of the palace, only to find that the seals, locks, clappers and bells were the same as at the front. With a great commotion they grabbed lanterns and torches, making the sky red and the place as bright as day. The four of them were clearly lit up as they climbed over the wall. "Where do you think you're going?" the senior demon chief shouted, running towards them and so terrifying the reverend gentleman that the muscles in his legs turned soft and numb and he fell off the wall to be captured by the senior demon. The second demon chief seized Friar Sand and the third knocked Pig over and captured him. The other demons took the luggage and the white horse. Only Monkey escaped. "May Heaven kill him," Pig grumbled under his breath about Monkey. "I said that if he was going to rescue us he ought to do a thorough job of it. As it is we're going to be put back in the steamer for another steaming."

The monsters took the Tang Priest into the throne hall but did not steam him again. The second demon chief ordered that Pig was to be tied to one of the columns supporting the eaves in front of the hall and the third chief had Friar Sand tied to one of the columns holding up the eaves at the back. The senior chief clung to the Tang Priest and would not let go of him. "What are you holding him for, elder brother?" the third demon asked. "Surely you're not going to eat him alive. That wouldn't be at all interesting. He's no ordinary idiot to be gobbled up just to fill your stomach. He's a rare delicacy from a superior country. We should keep him till we have some free time one rainy day, then bring him out to be carefully cooked and enjoyed with drinking games and fine music." "A very good suggestion, brother," replied the senior demon with a smile, "but Sun the Novice would come and steal him again." "In our palace we have a Brocade Fragrance Pavilion," said the third demon, "and in the pavilion is an iron chest. I think we should put the Tang Priest into the chest, shut up the pavilion, put out a rumour that we have already eaten him half raw, and get all the junior devils in the city talking about it. That Sun the Novice is bound to come back to find out what's happening, and when he hears this he'll be so miserably disappointed that he'll go away. If he doesn't come to make trouble for another four or five days we can bring the Tang Priest out to enjoy at our leisure. What do you think?" The senior and second demon chiefs were both delighted. "Yes, yes, you're right, brother," they said. That very night the poor Tang Priest was taken inside the palace, put into the chest and locked up in the pavilion. We will not tell how the rumour was spread and became the talk of the town.

Instead the story tells how Monkey escaped that night by cloud, unable to look after the Tang Priest. He went straight to Lion Cave where he wiped out all the tens of thousands of junior demons with his cudgel to his complete satisfaction. By the time he had hurried back to the city the sun was rising in the east. He did not dare challenge the demons to battle because

No thread can be spun from a single strand;
Nobody can clap with a single hand.

So he brought his cloud down, shook himself, turned himself into a junior demon and slipped in through the gates to collect news in the streets and back alleys. "The Tang Priest was eaten raw by the senior king during the night," was what all the people in the city were saying wherever he went. This made Brother Monkey really anxious. When he went to look at the throne hall in the palace he saw that there were many spirits constantly coming and going. They were wearing leather and metal helmets and yellow cotton tunics. In their hands they held red lacquered staves, and ivory passes hung at their waists. "These must be evil spirits who are allowed in the inner quarters of the palace," thought Monkey. "I'll turn myself into one, go in and see what I can find out."

The splendid Great Sage then made himself identical to the demons and slipped in through the inner gates of the palace. As he was walking along he saw Pig tied to one of the columns of the throne hall, groaning. "Wuneng," Monkey said, going up to him. "Is that you, brother?" asked the idiot, recognizing his voice. "Save me!" "I'll save you," said Monkey. "Do you know where the master is?" "He's done for," Pig replied. "The evil spirits ate him raw last night." At this Monkey burst into sobs and the tears gushed out like water from a spring. "Don't cry, brother," said Pig. "I've only heard the junior devils gossiping. I didn't see it with my own eyes. Don't waste any more time. Go on and find out more." Only then did Monkey dry his tears and go to search in the inner part of the palace. Noticing Friar Sand tied to a column at the back of the palace he went up to him, felt his chest and said, "Wujing." Friar Sand also recognized his voice and said, "Brother, is that you here in disguise? Save me! Save me!" "Saving you will be easy," said Monkey, "but do you know where the master is?" "Brother!" said Friar Sand in tears. "The evil spirits couldn't even wait to steam the master. They've eaten him raw."

Now that both of them had told him the same story the

Great Sage was cut to the heart. Instead of rescuing Pig and Friar Sand he sprang straight up into the sky and went to the mountain east of the city, where he landed his cloud and let himself weep aloud. "Poor Master," he said:

"I fought against heaven, was caught in its net,
Till you came along and delivered me, Master.
It became my ambition to worship the Buddha;
I strove to eliminate fiendish disaster.

"I never imagined that now you'd be murdered
And I would have failed on your journey to keep you.
The lands of the West were too good for your fate.
Your life's at an end: in what way can I help you?"

Deep in misery, Monkey said to himself, "It's all the fault of our Buddha, the Tathagata, who had nothing better to do in his paradise than make the three stores of scriptures. If he really wanted to convert people to be good he ought to have sent them to the east himself. Then they would have been passed on for ever. But he couldn't bring himself to part with them. He had to make us go to fetch them. Who'd ever have thought that after all the trouble of crossing a thousand mountains the master would lose his life here today? Oh well! I'll ride my somersault cloud to see the Tathagata Buddha and tell him what's happened. If he's willing to give me the scriptures to deliver to the east then the good achievement will be propagated and we'll be able to fulfil our vow. If he won't give me them I'll get him to recite the Band-loosening Spell. Then I can take the band off, return it to him and go back to my own cave to play the king and enjoy myself again."

The splendid Great Sage jumped to his feet and went straight to India on his somersault cloud. In less than a couple of hours he could see the Vulture Peak in the near distance, and an instant later he had landed his cloud and was heading straight for the foot of the peak. He looked up and saw the four vajrapanis blocking his way and asking him where he was going. "There's something I want to see the Tathagata about," Monkey replied with a bow. Next he was faced by the Vajrapani Yongzhu, the indestructible king of Golden Glow Ridge on Mount Kunlun, who shouted, "Macaque, you're an outrage! When the Bull Demon King was giving you such terrible trouble we all helped you, but now you've come to see us today you're showing no manners at all. If you're here on business you should submit a memorial first and wait till you're summoned before going any further. This isn't like the Southern Gate of Heaven, where you can come and go as you please. Clear off! Out of the way!" Being told off like this when he was feeling so depressed drove Monkey into thundering roars of fury, and his uncontrollable shouts and yells soon disturbed the Tathagata.

The Tathagata Buddha was sitting on his nine-level lotus throne expounding the sutras to his eighteen arhats when he said, "Sun Wukong is here. You must all go out to receive him." In obedience to the Buddha's command the arhats went out in two columns with their banners and canopies. "Great Sage Sun," they said in greeting, "the Tathagata has commanded us to summon you to his presence." Only then did the four vajrapanis at the monastery gates step aside to let Monkey enter. The arhats led him to the foot of the lotus throne, where he went down to kowtow on seeing the Tathagata. He was sobbing and weeping. "Wukong," said the Buddha, "what makes you weep so miserably?"

"Your disciple has often received the grace of your instruction," Brother Monkey replied, "and has committed himself to the school of Lord Buddha. Since being converted to the true achievement I have taken the Tang Priest as my master and been protecting him on our journey. No words could describe what we have suffered. We have now reached the city of Leonia near Lion Cave on Lion Mountain where three vicious monsters, the Lion King, the Elephant King and the Great Roc, seized my master. All of us disciples of his were in a very bad way too, tied up and put in a steamer to suffer the agony of fire and boiling water. Fortunately I was able to get away and summon a dragon king to save the others. But we could not escape our evil star: the master and the others were recaptured when I was trying to sneak them out last night. When I went back into the city this morning to find out what had happened I learned that those utterly evil and ferocious monsters ate my master raw during the night. Nothing is left of his flesh and bones. On top of that my fellow-disciples Wuneng and Wujing are tied up there and will soon be dead too. I'm desperate. That's why your disciple has come to visit the Tathagata. I beg you in your great compassion to recite the Band-loosening Spell so that I can take the band off my head and give it back to you. Let your disciple go back to the Mountain of Flowers and Fruit and enjoy himself." Before he had finished saying this the tears welled up again. There was no end to his howls of misery.

"Don't upset yourself so, Wukong," said the Tathagata with a smile. "You can't beat those evil spirits. Their magical powers are more than you can handle. That is why you are so unhappy." Monkey knelt below the Buddha and beat his breast as he replied, "Truly, Tathagata, I made havoc in Heaven all those years ago and was called Great Sage. Never in all my life had I been beaten before I met these vicious monsters."

"Stop being so sorry for yourself," said the Tathagata. "I know those evil spirits." "Tathagata!" Monkey suddenly blurted out. "They say those evil spirits are relations of yours." "Wicked macaque!" said the Tathagata. "How could an evil spirit be any relation of mine?" "If they're not relations of yours how come you know them?" retorted Monkey with a grin. "I know them because I see them with my all-seeing eyes," the Buddha replied. "The senior demon and the second demon have masters. Ananda, Kasyapa, come here. One of you is to take a cloud to Mount Wutai and the other to Mount Emei. Summon Manjusri and Samantabhadra to come and see me." The two arhats left at once as they had been commanded. "They are the masters of the senior and the second demon chiefs. But the third demon does have some connection with me." "On his mother's or his father's side?" Monkey asked. "When the primal chaos was first separated the heavens opened up in the hour of the rat and the earth at the hour of the ox," the Buddha replied. "Mankind was born at the tiger hour. Then heaven and earth came together again and all living creatures were born, including beasts that walk and birds that fly. The unicorn is the most senior of the beasts that walk and the phoenix is the most senior of the birds that fly. When the phoenixes combined their essential spirit they gave birth to the peafowl and the Great Roc. When the peafowl came into the world she was the most evil of creatures and a man-eater. She could devour all the people for fifteen miles around in a single mouthful. When I was cultivating my sixteen-foot golden body on the peak of the snowy mountain she swallowed me as well. I went down into her belly. I wanted to escape through her backside, but for fear of soiling my body I cut my way out through her backbone and climbed Vulture Peak. I would have killed her, but all the Buddha host dissuaded me: to kill the peahen would have been like killing my own mother. So I kept her at my assembly on Vulture Peak and appointed her as the Buddha-mother, the Great Illustrious Peahen Queen Bodhisattva. The Great Roc was born of the same mother as she was. That is why we are relations of a kind." When Monkey heard this he said with a smile, "By that line of argument, Tathagata, you re the evil spirit's nephew." "I shall have to go and subdue that demon in person," the Tathagata said. Monkey kowtowed as he respectfully replied, "I beg you to condescend to grant us your illustrious presence."

The Tathagata then came down from his lotus throne and went out through the monastery gates with all the Buddha host just as Ananda and Kasyapa arrived bringing Manjusri and Samantabhadra. These two Bodhisattvas bowed to the Tathagata, who asked them, "How long have your animals been away from your mountains, Bodhisattvas?" "Seven days," said Manjusri. "A mere seven days on your mountains is several thousand years in the mortal world," the Tathagata replied. "Goodness knows how many living beings they have destroyed there. Come with me to recapture them at once." The two Bodhisattvas travelled at the Buddha's left and right hand as they flew through the air with the host. This is what could be seen:

The shimmering clouds of blessing parted for Lord Buddha
As in his great compassion he came down from his shrine.
He taught the truth about all beings since creation,
Explaining how everything had been transformed in time.
Before him went five hundred holy arhats;
Behind him were three thousand guardians of the faith.
Ananda and Kasyapa were both in close attendance;
Samantabhadra and Manjusri came to conquer monsters.

The Great Sage had been granted this favour and succeeded in bringing the Lord Buddha and his host with him. It was not long before the city was in sight. "Tathagata," said Monkey, "that's Leonia, where the black vapours are coming from." "You go down into the city first," said the Tathagata, "and start a fight with the evil spirits. Do not win. You must lose and come back up. Leave it to us to recapture them."

The Great Sage then brought his cloud straight down to land on the city wall, where he stood on the battlements and shouted abusively, "Evil beasts! Come out and fight me at once!" This caused such consternation among the junior demons in the towers on the wall that they jumped straight down into the city to report, "Your Majesties, Sun the Novice is on the wall, challenging us to battle." "That ape hasn't been here for two or three days," the senior demon replied. "Now he's back challenging us to battle. Can he have fetched some reinforcements?" "He's nothing to be scared of," said the third demon chief. "Let's all go and have a look." The three chieftains, all carrying their weapons, hurried up on the wall where they saw Monkey. Without a word they raised their weapons and thrust at him. Monkey held them off by swinging his iron cudgel. When they had fought seven or eight rounds Monkey feigned defeat and fled. "Where do you think you're going?" the demon king asked with a mighty shout, and with a somersault Monkey sprang up into mid-air. The three spirits went after him on clouds, but Monkey slipped aside and disappeared completely in the Lord Buddha's golden aura.

All that could be seen were the images of the Three Buddhas of Past, Future and Present, the five hundred arhats and the three thousand Protectors of the Faith who spread all around, encircling the three demon kings so closely that not even a drop of water could leak through. "This is terrible, my brother," said the senior demon chief, lashing out wildly, "that ape is a really sharp operator. How did he manage to bring my master here?" "Don't be afraid, elder brother," said the third demon. "If we all charge together we can cut down the Tathagata with our swords and spears and seize his Thunder Monastery." The demons, who had no sense of proper behaviour, really did raise their swords to charge forward, hacking wildly. Manjusri and Samantabhadra recited the words of a spell and shouted, "Won't you repent now, evil beasts? What else do you hope for?" The senior and the second demon chiefs gave up the struggle, threw down their weapons, rolled and reverted to their true images. The two Bodhisattvas threw their lotus thrones on the demons' backs and flew over to sit on them. The two demons then gave up and submitted.

Now that the blue lion and the white elephant had been captured only the third evil monster was still unsubdued. Spreading its wings it dropped its heaven-square halberd and rose straight up to try to catch the Monkey King with a swing of its sharp talons, but as the Great Sage was hiding in the golden aura the demon dared get nowhere near him. When the Tathagata realized what it was trying to do he made his golden aura flash and shook his head that was the supreme meditator in the wind to turn it into a bright red lump of bloody meat. The evil spirit seized it with a flourish of its sharp talons, whereupon the Lord Buddha pointed upwards with his hand, destroying the muscles in the monster's wings. It could not fly or get away from the top of the Buddha's head, and it reverted to its true appearance as a golden-winged vulture. Opening its beak it said to the Buddha, "Tathagata, why did you use your great dharma powers to catch me like this?" "You have been doing much evil here," the Tathagata replied. "Come with me and you will win credit for a good deed." "You eat vegetarian food in great poverty and suffering at your place," the evil spirit replied, "but here I can eat human flesh and live in no end of luxury. If you kill me by starvation you'll be guilty of a sin." "In the four continents I control countless living beings who worship me," the Buddha replied, "and whenever they are going to perform a service to me I shall tell them to make a sacrifice to you first." The Great Roc would have escaped and got away if it could. As it was he had no choice but to accept conversion.

Only then did Monkey emerge to kowtow to the Tathagata and say, "Lord Buddha, today you have captured the evil spirits and removed a great bane, but my master is dead." At this the Great Roc said bitterly as it ground its teeth, "Damned ape! Why did you have to bring these ferocious men here to persecute me? I never ate that old monk of yours. He's in the Brocade Fragrance Pavilion now, isn't he?" When Monkey heard this he quickly kowtowed to thank the Lord Buddha. Not daring to release the Great Roc, the Buddha made him into a guardian of the dharma in his brilliant halo then led his host back to his monastery on their clouds.

Monkey landed his cloud and went straight into the city, where there was not a single junior demon left. Indeed,

A snake cannot move without its head;
A bird cannot fly without its wings.

They had all fled for their lives when they saw the Buddha capturing their evil kings. Monkey then freed Pig and Friar Sand, found the luggage and the horse, and said to his fellow-disciples, "The master hasn't been eaten. Come with me." He took the two of them straight into the inner compound where they found the Brocade Fragrance Pavilion. Opening the door and looking inside they saw an iron trunk from which could be heard the sound of Sanzang weeping. Friar Sand used his demon-quelling staff to open the iron cage over the chest and raise its lid. "Master," he called. At the sight of them Sanzang wept aloud and said, "Disciples, how were the demons beaten? How did you manage to find me here?" Monkey told him all the details of what had happened from beginning to end and Sanzang expressed boundless gratitude. Then master and disciples found some rice in the palace and ate their fill of it before packing their things and leaving the city along the main road west. Indeed,

Only a true man can find the true scriptures;
The will's shouts and the heart's labours are in vain.

If you don't know when on this journey they were to see the Tathagata listen to the explanation in the next instalment.

CHAPTER SEVENTY-EIGHT

In Bhiksuland the hidden gods are sent on an errand of mercy;
In the palace the monster is revealed and the Way discussed.

A single thought at once disturbs a hundred monsters;
The hardest efforts are all to no avail.
One can only wash away each speck of dust,
Tidy everything and polish well.
Sweep all causation away and come to nirvana;
Waste no time and destroy the thousand demons.
You surely will be free from obstructions,
And rise to the Daluo Heaven when your deeds are done.

The story tells how the Great Sage Sun used all his ingenuity to fetch the Tathagata to subdue the demons and rescue Sanzang and the other two disciples, after which they left the city of Leonia and headed west. When they had been travelling for several more months it was winter, and this is what could be seen:

The plum on the ridge was like broken jade
As the water in the pond slowly turned to ice.
All the red autumn leaves had fallen;
And the green of the pine looked fresher than ever
The pale and scudding clouds were on the point of snowing;
Flat lay the withered grass upon the hills.
As far as the eye could see was chilly brightness
As the unseen cold went right into the bone.

Master and disciples braved the cold, sleeping out in the rain and dining off the wind, until as they were walking along another walled and moated city came into sight. "What sort of place is that over there, Wukong?" Sanzang asked Monkey, who replied, "We'll know when we get there. If it's the capital of a western kingdom we'll have to present our passport to be inspected and returned. If it's a prefecture or county town we'll go straight through." Before master and disciples could finish their conversation they had arrived at the city gates.

Sanzang dismounted and the four of them went in through the curtain wall outside the gates. Noticing an old soldier sleeping shielded from the wind under the south-facing wall, Brother Monkey went up to him, shook him and said, "Sir!" When the old soldier awoke with a start to open his bleary eyes and see Monkey he fell to his knees to kowtow and say, "My Lord!" "There's no need for such alarm," said Monkey. "I'm no evil god, so why call me your lord?" "Aren't you Lord Thunder God?" the old soldier asked, kowtowing again. "What a thing to say," Monkey replied. "We're monks from the east on our way to fetch the scriptures from the Western Heaven. We've just arrived here. Could I ask what this place is called?" This answer finally eased the old soldier's mind. With a yawn he got back on his feet, stretched and said, "Please forgive me, reverend gentlemen. This country used to be called Bhiksuland but its name has been changed to Boytown". "Do you have a king?" Monkey asked. "Yes, yes," the old soldier replied. Monkey then turned to report to the Tang Priest, "This country used to be called Bhiksuland but the name's been altered to Boytown, though I don't know what the change signifies." "If it was Bhiksuland before why is it Boytown now?" the Tang Priest wondered. "I expect there was a King Bhiksu who died," said Pig, "and they changed the name to Boytown when a boy succeeded him." "Impossible," said the Tang Priest, "impossible. Let's go in and make some enquiries in the street." "That's right," said Friar Sand. "The old soldier wouldn't have known anyhow, and on top of that elder brother gave him such a fright that he talked nonsense. We'll ask some more questions in the city."

When they had gone through the third pair of gates they came to a great market on a main street. The people were well-dressed and their bearing distinguished.

A hubbub of voices came from bar and music hall;
High hung the curtains outside splendid shop and teahouse.
Business was good in firms by the thousand;
Wealth flowed free in shopping street and market.
The dealers in metal and silk were swarming like ants,
Caring only for money while struggling for fame and wealth.
With these noble manners, magnificent scenery
And peaceful waters it was a time of prosperity.

The master and his three disciples, who were leading the horse and carrying the baggage, spent some time walking around the streets as they admired the general air of prosperity. In the entrance to every house there was a basketwork coop of the sort geese are kept in. "Disciples," said Sanzang, "why do all the people here put coops in their gateways?" Pig's response to this was to look around and see that there were indeed lines of coops hung with satin curtains of many colours. "Master," said the idiot with a smile, "today must be a lucky one for weddings and celebrations. Everybody's having a wedding." "Nonsense," said Monkey. "How could every single family possibly be having a wedding? There must be some other reason for this. I'm going over to take a look". "You're not to go," said Sanzang, grabbing hold of him. "You look so ugly that people might take offence." "I'll go as something else," Brother Monkey replied.

Making a spell with his hands the splendid Great Sage said the words of a spell, shook himself, turned into a bee, spread his wings, flew to one of the coops and slipped in through the curtains to take a look. A little boy was sitting inside. Monkey looked inside another family's coop and there was a child in that too. He inspected eight or nine households and all of them had a child. All were boys: there was not a single girl. Some were sitting up in their coops and playing and some were crying;

some were eating fruit and some were snoozing. His inspection over, Monkey turned back into his normal self and reported to the Tang Priest, "There are little boys in the coops. The oldest is under six and the youngest only four. I don't know why they're here." Sanzang wondered what the explanation could be.

Turning a corner they saw the gateway to an official building. It was a government hostel with golden pavilions. The venerable elder was delighted. "Disciples," he said, "we will go into this hostel. We can find out where we are, give the horse a rest and put up for the night." "Yes, that's right," said Friar Sand. "Let's go straight in." This the four of them happily did, a fact that the officials there reported to the hostel's superintendent. When the superintendent had led them inside greetings had been exchanged and they had all sat down, the superintendent asked, "Where have you come from, reverend sir?" "I am a monk sent by the Great Tang in the east to fetch the scriptures from the Western Heaven," Sanzang replied. "Now that we have arrived at this excellent establishment I will of course present my passport for inspection. Could we, I wonder, impose on your hospitality for the night?" The superintendent ordered tea, and when it had been drunk he saw to their entertainment and told the staff who were on duty to look after the pilgrims. After thanking him for this Sanzang went on to ask, "Could we go to the palace today to see His Majesty and have our passport inspected?" "That will not be possible this evening," the superintendent replied. "It will have to wait until tomorrow morning. I hope that you will spend a comfortable night in this humble hostel."

A little later, when all had been prepared, the superintendent of the hostel invited the four travellers to take a vegetarian meal with him. He also told his staff to sweep out the guest rooms for them to spend the night in. Sanzang expressed endless gratitude. When they were all seated the venerable elder said, "I wonder if I could trouble you for information on something that I cannot understand. How do you raise children in your country?" "People are the same the whole world over, just as there are never two suns in the sky," the superintendent replied. "Children are born when their time comes after the father's seed has joined with the mother's blood and they have been in the womb for ten lunar months. After they are born they are suckled for three years and their bodies gradually grow. Everybody knows that." "What you tell me is no different from how they grow in my humble country," Sanzang replied. "But when we came into the city we saw a goose coop with a little boy inside in front of every house in the street. This is something I cannot understand, which is why I ventured to raise the question."

"Ignore that, reverend sir," whispered the hostel superintendent into Sanzang's ear. "Don't ask about it. Put it out of your mind. Don't even mention it. Would you like to settle down for the night before starting your journey again tomorrow morning?" Sanzang's response was to seize hold of the superintendent and demand an explanation. "Watch your words," the superintendent replied, shaking his head and wagging his finger, but Sanzang was not going to drop the matter. He insisted on being told all the details. The superintendent had no choice but to dismiss all the staff on duty. When they were alone under the lamplight he whispered to Sanzang, "The goose coops you asked about are there because our king is a bad ruler. Why ever do you have to keep asking about it?" "How is he a bad ruler?" Sanzang asked. "I will not be able to set my mind at ease until you give me an explanation." "This country is really called Bhiksuland," the superintendent replied. "Boytown is only what the people have started calling it. Three years ago an old man dressed as a Taoist came here with a girl just fifteen years old. She was a ravishing beauty, just like a Bodhisattva Guanyin. He presented her to our present king, who was so smitten by her charms that she became the favourite of all his women. She was given the title Queen Beauty. For some time now he's had no eyes for any of his other queens or consorts. He's so insatiable that he's been at it day and night. The result is nervous exhaustion and physical collapse. He's eating and drinking next to nothing. He might die at any moment. The Royal College of Physicians has tried every possible medicine without any success. The Taoist who presented the girl to the king was rewarded with the title of Elder of the Nation. He has a secret foreign formula for making people live a great deal longer. He's been to ten continents and the three magic islands to collect the ingredients. Everything is ready. The only problem is that it needs a terrible adjuvant to help it — a potion made from the hearts of 1,111 little boys. When he's taken it he'll have a thousand years of vigorous life ahead of him. All the little boys being kept in the coops are the ones that have been chosen. Their parents are so afraid of the king that none of them dares weep. That's why they've put out the story that this place is now called Boytown. When you go to the palace tomorrow morning, reverend sir, you must only present your passport to be inspected and returned. Say nothing about any of this." When he had said all this he left them.

Sanzang was so horrified by what he had heard that his bones turned soft and his muscles went numb. He could not help the tears that streamed down his face as he started sobbing aloud. "Foolish king," he exclaimed, "foolish king. Your lechery has ruined your health, and now you are planning to destroy all those young lives. How could you? What misery! The pain of it all is killing me." There is a poem about it that goes:

The wicked monarch's folly makes him forget the truth;
His health is ruined by his unbridled lusts.
Pursuing eternal life by killing little children,
He slaughters his subjects to avoid Heaven's punishment.
This is all more than the merciful monk can bear:
He cannot accept the official's worldly wisdom.
Long are his sighs as he weeps in the lamplight;
Stricken with grief is the Buddha worshipper.

"Master," said Pig, going up to him, "what's the matter with you? What you're doing is like taking a stranger's coffin to your own home and weeping over it. Don't upset yourself like that. As the rhyme goes,

When a monarch insists that his subjects will die
None that are loyal to live will aspire;

When a father commands his own offspring to perish
Any dutiful son will most surely expire.

The people he's going to kill are his own subjects. What are they to you? Take off your clothes, get some sleep and 'don't worry about the ancients.' " "Disciple," said Sanzang, his tears still flowing, "you haven't a shred of compassion. The most important thing for us monks as we accumulate good deeds is to help others. How could this deluded king be so set in his wickedness? Never have I ever heard that eating human hearts could prolong life. How could something so terrible not grieve me?" "Don't grieve so, Master," said Friar Sand. "When you present our passport tomorrow and see the king you can talk to him about it. Even if he doesn't accept your advice you'll be able to see what the Elder of the Nation looks like. Probably he's an evil spirit who's thought all this up because he wants to eat human hearts."

"Wujing is right," said Brother Monkey. "Go to bed now, Master, and tomorrow morning I'll go to court with you to see what this Elder of the Nation is like. If he's human he's probably a heretic who doesn't follow orthodox ways but believes in drugs, and I'll convert him with the essential teachings of intrinsic nature. If he's an evil spirit I'll catch him, show the king what he is, and urge the king to control his desires and build up his strength. Whatever happens I won't let him kill those children." As soon as he heard this Sanzang bowed to Monkey with great courtesy and said, "What an excellent suggestion! But when we see the deluded king we must say nothing about this in case he thinks we are guilty of not knowing our place and spreading slander. What could we do if that happened?"

"I've got my magic powers," Monkey replied. "First of all I'm going to get the little boys in the coops away from the city so that he'll have nobody to take the hearts out of tomorrow. The local officials will of course report this and the king will be bound either to order a discussion with the Elder of the Nation or else to demand more information. This will give us a chance to submit our memorial without getting ourselves into trouble."

Sanzang was very pleased. "How are you going to get the children out of the town now?" he asked. "If you really can rescue them you will be doing the greatest of good deeds, worthy disciple. But do it quick, because if you lose any time you may be too late." Summoning up his might Monkey stood up and gave Pig and Friar Sand their parting instructions: "Sit here with the master while I do my stuff. If you notice a magical wind blowing that'll be the boys leaving the city." Sanzang and the other two disciples said, "We invoke the Saviour Bhaisajya-guru Buddha. We invoke the Saviour Bhaisajya-guru Buddha."

Once outside the doors the Great Sage whistled, rose into mid-air, made a spell with his hands and said the magic words, called out "*Om* pure dharma world," and summoned the city god, the local deities, the officiating immortals, the Protectors of the Faith of the four quarters and the centre, the Four Duty Gods, the Six Dings and the Six Jias and the Guardians of the Teaching. They all came to him where he was in mid-air, bowed to him and said, "Great Sage, what is the urgent business on which you have summoned us in the middle of the night?" "My journey has brought me to Bhiksuland," Monkey replied, "where the king is a bad one who believes in evil doctrines. He wants to take the hearts out of little boys to make the adjuvant to a medicine that he hopes will make him live for ever. My master finds this utterly horrible and has asked me to rescue the boys and destroy the demon. That is why I've asked all you gentlemen here. I want you to use your magical powers to lift all the little boys, coops and all, over the city wall into a mountain hollow or somewhere deep in a forest. Keep them there for a day or two. Give them fruit to eat and don't let them go hungry. Keep watch over them in secret and don't frighten them or make them cry. When I've eliminated the evil, brought the country back to good government and persuaded the king to mend his ways and am about to leave, you must bring them back to me." The gods all listened to their orders then brought their clouds down to land so that they could use their magical powers. The city was filled with a blustering negative wind that brought with it an all-pervasive and sinister fog.

All the stars in the sky were obscured by the negative wind;
The moon was blacked out by the magical fog for many a mile.
At first the wind was gusty,
And then it blew like a hurricane.
When it was gusting
All ran to the gateways to rescue their children;
Then in the hurricane
They wanted to save their own flesh and blood in the coops.
The air turned so chilly that none dared show their heads;
The cold was so piercing that clothes froze like iron.
Vainly did parents look all around;
The families all were stricken with grief.
The sinister wind blew right across the land
As the boys in their baskets were carried off by the gods.
Although that was a night of bereavement and grief
Joy was coming to all the next day.

There is another poem about it that goes:

Compassion has always been strong in the Sakyamuni faith;
The achievement of goodness explains the Great Vehicle.
A multitude of holy ones all accumulate goodness;
For the Three Refuges and Five Precepts** harmony is needed.*
The land of Bhiksu was not to be ruined by its monarch
When a thousand little boys were to forfeit their lives.
Monkey and his master had brought them to safety,
Which conferred more merit than the Great Wisdom.

By the third watch of the night the gods had carried all the

* Buddha, Dharma, Sangha.
** Abstention from killing, stealing, adultery, lying and alcohol.

coops off and hidden them in all the safe places. Monkey then landed his auspicious light and went straight back to the government hostel, where to his secret delight he could hear the other three still chanting, "We invoke the Saviour Bhaisajya-guru Buddha." "Master," he said, going up to them, "I'm back. What was the negative wind like?" "Terrific," said Pig. "How did the rescue of the children go?" Sanzang asked. "Every single one of them has been saved," Monkey replied. "They'll all be brought back when we set out again." The master thanked him over and over again before finally going to sleep.

When Sanzang awoke at dawn he dressed himself in his best vestments and said, "Wukong, I am going to the early audience to present our passport." "If you go by yourself, Master," Monkey replied, "I'm afraid that you won't be able to manage. Let me go with you. Then I'll be able to find out about the evil in this country." "If you go you will refuse to pay homage," said Sanzang, "and the king may well take it amiss." "I won't be seen," said Monkey. "I'll go with you in secret and protect you." This pleased Sanzang very much. He had told Pig and Friar Sand to look after the luggage and horse and was just about to set out when the superintendent of the hostel came in to see him. The superintendent was struck by the difference between vestments he wore this day compared with what he had been wearing the day before.

His cassock was of brocade, set with exotic gems;
On his head he wore a gold-topped Vairocana mitre.
He held a nine-ringed monastic staff
And hid a divine radiance in his breast.
The passport was fastened tightly to his body,
Wrapped in brocade inside another cloth.
He moved like an arhat come down to earth;
His face was truly that of a living Buddha.

When the superintendent had greeted Sanzang courteously he murmured into his ear advice against meddling in matters that were none of his business. Sanzang nodded and assented. The Great Sage stole to a place by the gate, said the words of a spell, shook himself and turned into the tiniest of insects that flew with a high-pitched hum to Sanzang's mitre. Sanzang left the government hostel and headed straight for the palace.

Arriving at the palace gates Sanzang saw a eunuch officer to whom he bowed and said, "This humble monk has been sent by the Great Tang in the east to fetch the scriptures from the Western Heaven. Now that I have reached your distinguished country I must present my passport to be inspected and returned. I beg Your Excellency to report this to His Majesty." This the eunuch duly did. The king was very pleased. "A monk from afar must be a holy man," he said, ordering that Sanzang be asked in. When the venerable elder had paid his respects at the foot of the steps of the throne hall he was invited to enter the hall and take a seat. Sanzang thanked the king and sat down. The king looked weak and enervated. When he raised his hands to make a polite salutation he could not do so properly, and he was incapable of continuous speech. His sight was so blurred that he had to make several attempts to read the document that Sanzang handed to him before he could sign, seal and return it to the Tang Priest, who put it away again.

The king was just about to ask why they were fetching the scriptures when one of his aides reported, "His Excellency the Elder of the Nation is here." Leaning on one of his young eunuch attendants the king struggled down from his throne to greet the Elder. Sanzang hastily got to his feet, stood to one side and looked round to see that the Elder of the Nation was an aged Taoist who advanced with a swagger towards the steps of the throne.

On his head he wore a goose-yellow silken cap,
Round his body a scented cloak of silk and crane feathers,
And at his waist a triple sash of blue velvet.
On his feet were sandals of hemp and grasscloth;
At the top of his rattan stick coiled a dragon.

The pouch at his chest was embroidered with dragon, phoenix and flowers.
His jadelike face radiated well-being;
A grey beard blew about his chin.
Flames shot from golden pupils
In eyes even longer than his eyebrows.
Clouds followed his steps
As he wandered through incense-laden mists.
The officials below the steps received him with obeisances,
Announcing the presence of the Elder of the Nation.

When he reached the throne hall the Elder of the Nation performed no obeisance but arrogantly strode straight in. The king leaned forward in a bow and said. "We are most fortunate that you have condescended to make your immortal way here, Elder of the Nation." He ordered that an embroidered stool be set on his left for the Elder to sit on. Taking a step forward Sanzang bowed and said, "Greetings, Elder of the Nation." The Elder sat majestically on his seat, but instead of returning Sanzang's courtesy he turned to the king and asked, "Where's this monk from?" "He has been sent by the Tang court in the east to fetch the scriptures from the Western Heaven," the king replied, "and is here to present his passport for inspection." "The road west is dark and dismal," said the Elder of the Nation with a smile. "There's nothing good about it." "The West has always been a land of bliss," Sanzang replied. "How could it not be good?" "There is an old saying we once heard that monks are disciples of the Buddha," said the king. "I wonder whether it is true that by being a monk and turning to the Buddha one can live for ever." When Sanzang heard this he put his hands together and replied:

"One who becomes a monk gets away from all kinds of causation. By understanding nature he learns that all dharmas are empty. Great wisdom is casual and drifts in non-living. The true secret is hidden; it wanders in extinction. When the three worlds* are empty all origins are ordered; when the six sense-organs** are purified all troubles are finished. To be resolute, single-minded and enlightened one must understand the heart. When the heart is purified it can shine alone; when the heart is sincere all regions are inbued with it. The true appearance has neither deficiency nor excess and can be seen in life. The images of illusion always decay. Why seek what is beyond one's lot? The way to enter meditation is through meritorious deeds and by sitting in silence; the root of cultivating one's conduct truly is charity and kindness. Great skill appears as clumsiness and knows that all deeds are achieved through inaction. The finest plans involve no calculation; everything must be left alone. It only needs one heart not to move for every action to be perfect. It is truly absurd to try to strengthen the male by drawing on the female and nonsensical to try to extend one's years by taking elixirs.*** The only essential is that all the causation of every speck of dust must be discarded and that every type of matter should be empty. Live plain and pure; let your desires be few. Then naturally you will enjoy life without end for ever."

When the Elder of the Nation heard this he laughed at it. "Phooey," he said, pointing at the Tang Priest, "phooey! You're talking a load of rubbish, monk. Fancy you talking about understanding nature, and you a member of the faith that preaches nirvana. You don't have any idea of where nature comes from. Sitting still like a dead tree to enter dhyana is wasted effort as far as self-cultivation and tempering are concerned. In the words of the saying,

Sit, sit, sit;
Your backside's split.
The fire's too hot;
Good that's not.

What you don't realize at all is this:

"One who cultivates immortality has strong bones; one who

* Of desire, of matter and of non-matter

** The five senses and the mind.

*** References to Taoist practices aimed at lengthening life.

attains the Way has the most magical spirit. Carrying his bowl and ladle he goes into the mountains to visit his friends; he picks every kind of herb to succour humanity. He makes a rainhat from immortal flowers, plucks the fragrant orchid to make his bed. He sings, claps and dances, then goes to sleep. When expounding the Way he teaches the doctrines of the Supreme One; he eliminates the evil of the human world with holy water. He takes the finest breath of heaven and earth, gathers the essence of the sun and moon. By controlling the negative and positive forces he creates the elixir; through the mastery of fire and water the foetus is formed. On the sixteenth day of the month the negative is eliminated, hazily and obscurely. In the twenty-seventh day of winter the positive begins to grow, darkly and mysteriously. He gathers the herbs of each of the four seasons, refining his elixir to nourish the nine transformations. Astride his blue phoenix he ascends to the purple palace; riding his white crane he goes to the jasper capital. He visits all the splendours of Heaven, showing the efficacy of the wonderful Way. Just compare it with the dhyana teachings of your Sakyamuni, your elimination of atman and your nirvana that enables you to shuffle off your stinking husk. None of this lifts you out of the worldly dust. Among the Three Teachings it is supreme; the Way alone has always been esteemed."

The king was delighted to hear this exposition, and all the court officials exclaimed with admiration, "That's splendid, 'the Way alone has always been esteemed.' " Sanzang was overcome by humiliation at all this praise going to his rival. The king then told his department of foreign relations to lay on a banquet of vegetarian food for the monks from a far country when they left the city to travel west.

Sanzang thanked the king for his kindness and withdrew. As he was leaving the throne hall and going out of the palace Monkey flew down from the top of his mitre to say into his ear, "Master, the Elder of the Nation is an evil spirit, and the king has been bewitched. Go back to the hostel and wait for your meal while I get some information here." Sanzang understood this and left through the main gates of the palace.

Of him we will say no more. Watch Monkey as he flies straight to a jade screen in the throne hall and lands on it. From the ranks of officials the military commanders of the capital stepped forward to report, "Your Majesty, last night a cold wind carried away the little boys in their goose coops from every house in every ward of the city. They have vanished without a trace, coops and all." This report both alarmed and angered the king, who said to the Elder of the Nation, "Heaven must be destroying us. We had the good fortune to be given the formula for your elixir after months of serious illness that the royal physicians have been unable to cure. We were preparing to have the boys cut open at noon today and their hearts taken out to be made into the adjuvant for the elixir. Never did we imagine that a cold wind would blow them all away. If this is not Heaven destroying us what is it?" "Don't upset yourself," the Elder of the Nation replied with a smile. "By blowing them away Heaven is giving Your Majesty eternal life." "How can you maintain that Heaven is giving me eternal life when they have just been blown away?" the king asked. "When I was coming to court this morning," the Elder of the Nation replied, "I saw a uniquely marvellous adjuvant that will be far superior to 1,111 little boys' hearts. They would only lengthen Your Majesty's life by a thousand years, but if you take my elixir with this other adjuvant you can live for a hundred million years." The king was mystified about what this adjuvant could be, but only after repeated questions did the Elder of the Nation reply, "The monk from the east who is being sent to fetch the scriptures has pure organs and regular features. His is the body of one who has cultivated his conduct for ten lifetimes. He has been a monk since childhood and has preserved his masculine purity, which all makes him ten thousand times better than those little boys. If you can make a decoction from his heart with which to take my elixir I can guarantee you an extremely long life." When the deluded king heard this he believed it completely. "Why didn't you tell us before?" he said to the Elder of the Nation. "If it's as good as you say we should have kept him when he was here just now and not let him go." "This will present no problem," the Elder of the Nation said. "You have already told the department of foreign relations to give him a vegetarian banquet. He won't possibly leave the city before eating the meal. Urgent orders must be issued to have the gates firmly closed. Send troops to surround the government hostel and bring that monk here. First we will try to win his heart by treating him with courtesy. If he agrees we will cut it out and give him a royal burial, build him a temple and make offerings to him. If he will not agree we'll use rough methods. We can tie him up and cut it out. There will be no problem." The deluded ruler accepted this suggestion and ordered that all the gates be closed. He then sent the officers and men of the royal guard to surround the hostel.

Having found all this out Monkey flew straight to the hostel, turned back into himself and said to the Tang Priest, "Something terrible's happened, Master, something terrible." Sanzang had just begun to eat the king's vegetarian banquet with Pig and Friar Sand when this sudden announcement scattered his three bodily spirits and made smoke come out of his seven orifices. He collapsed in the dust, pouring with sweat, and unable to see clearly or speak. Friar Sand was so alarmed he came forward to help him back to his feet, calling, "Wake up, Master, wake up." "What's so terrible?" Pig asked. "What's so terrible? You should have broken the news gently instead of giving the master such a scare." "When the master left the palace I went back to keep an eye on things," Monkey replied. "That Elder of the Nation is an evil spirit. A moment later the city garrison came to report about the cold wind carrying the little boys away. This upset the king, but the Elder of the Nation cheered him up by saying that this was Heaven giving him eternal life. He wants to use your heart as an adjuvant for the elixir of immortality, Master. The deluded king has accepted this wicked suggestion and ordered his best troops to surround this hostel. He's also sent an aide to ask you for your heart, Master." "What a merciful and compassionate chap you are," said Pig with a laugh. "You saved the boys and made the wind blow all right, but now you've got us in this disastrous mess."

Trembling and shaking, Sanzang dragged himself to his feet, seized hold of Monkey and said imploringly, "Good disciple, how are we to get out of this?" "If you want to get out of this," said Monkey, "there'll have to be a switch." "What do you mean by a switch?" Friar Sand asked. "If you want to survive," Monkey replied, "the disciple will have to become the master and the master the disciple. Do that and we'll be safe." "Save my life," said Sanzang, "and I will gladly become your disciple or even your disciple's disciple." "In that case there must be no hesitation," Monkey replied, continuing, "Pig, mix up some mud at once." The idiot loosened some earth with his rake then, not daring to go outside for water, lifted his tunic to make some water himself. With this he mixed up a lump of foul-smelling mud that he handed to Monkey. Monkey had no option but to beat it out flat and press it against his face so that it looked like a monkey's face. Then he told his master to stand up and neither move nor say anything while he placed the mask on his face, said the words of a spell, blew a magic breath and said, "Change!" The venerable elder now looked just like Monkey. He took off his own clothes and put on Monkey's while Monkey dressed in his master's clothes, made a spell with his hands, said the magic words, shook himself and made himself look just like the Tang Priest. Even Pig and Friar Sand could not tell that he really was not.

Just when they had completed the disguises together there came the sound of gongs and drums as a dense forest of spears and swords appeared. The commanders of the royal guard had surrounded the hostel with their three thousand men. A royal aide came into the main hall of the hostel to ask, "Where is the reverend gentleman from the Tang court in the east?" The superintendent of the hostel anxiously fell to his knees and said, pointing, "In the guest room over there." The aide then went into the room and said, "Venerable elder from Tang, His Majesty has sent for you." Pig and Friar Sand stood on either side of the imitation Monkey to guard him while the imitation Tang Priest went out through the door, bowed and said, "Your Excellency, what does His Majesty wish to say to me? Why has he sent for me?" The aide stepped forward to grab hold of him and say. "You and I are going to the palace. His Majesty must have some use for you." Alas!

> *Wickedness was stronger than goodness and mercy;*
> *Goodness and mercy only led to catastrophe.*

If you don't know whether they were to survive this departure listen to the explanation in the next instalment.

CHAPTER SEVENTY-NINE

Searching the cave to capture the fiend they meet Longevity; The reigning monarch saves the little boys.

The story tells how the royal aide dragged the imitation Tang Priest out of the government hostel and marched him, heavily surrounded by royal guardsmen, straight to the gates of the palace, where he said to the eunuch gate officer, "Please be so good as to report to His Majesty that we have brought the Tang Priest." The eunuch officer hurried into the palace to pass this on to the deluded king, who ordered that they be brought in.

All the officials knelt at the foot of the steps to the throne hall, leaving the imitation Tang Priest standing alone in the middle of them. "King of Bhiksuland," he shouted, "what have you summoned me here to say to me?" "We are sick with a chronic illness that has dragged on for many a day without any improvement," the king replied. "Now the Elder of the Nation has to our good fortune presented us with a prescription that has been made up. All that is needed now is an adjuvant. The reason we have sent for you, reverend sir, is to ask you for the adjuvant. If we recover we will build a temple to you in which offerings will be made in all four seasons and incense will be burnt to you in perpetuity by our country." "I am a man of religion," the imitation Tang Priest replied, "and have brought nothing with me. I do not know what adjuvant the Elder of the Nation has told Your Majesty you need." "Your heart, reverend sir," the deluded monarch replied. "I will be frank with Your Majesty," the imitation Tang Priest said. "I have a number of hearts. I don't know which you want." "Monk," pronounced the Elder of the Nation, who was standing beside the king. "I want your black heart." "Very well then," the imitation Tang Priest replied. "Produce your knife at once and open up my chest. If there is a black heart there I shall offer it to you obediently."

The deluded monarch thanked him delightedly and ordered an official in attendance to bring a small knife with a blade shaped like a cow's ear that was handed to the imitation Tang Priest. Taking the knife, the imitation Tang Priest undid his clothes, thrust out his chest, pressed his left hand against his abdomen and cut the skin of his stomach open with the knife in his right hand. There was a whoosh, and out rolled a whole pile of hearts. The civilian officials all turned pale with fright; the military officers were numbed. When the Elder of the Nation saw this from inside the throne hall he said, "This monk is a suspicious-minded character. He has too many hearts."

The imitation Tang Priest then held up the hearts one by one, each dripping with blood, for all to see. They included a loyal red heart, a pure white heart, a yellow heart, an avaricious heart, a fame-hungry heart, a jealous heart, a calculating heart, an overcompetitive heart, an ambitious heart, an overbearing heart, a murderous heart, a vicious heart, a frightened heart, a cautious heart, a heretical heart and a heart full of indefinable gloom. There was every kind of evil heart except a black one. The deluded ruler was horror-struck, unable to speak until he said in trembling tones, "Put them away! Put them away!" The imitation Tang Priest had taken as much as he could, so he put his magic away and turned back into himself to say to the deluded monarch, "Your Majesty, you're not at all perceptive. We monks all have good hearts. It's only this Elder of the Nation of yours who has a black heart. His would make a good adjuvant for the medicine. If you don't believe me I'll take his out to show you."

When the Elder of the Nation heard this he opened his eyes wide to take a careful look. He saw that the monk's face had changed to something quite different. Heavens! Recognizing him as the Great Sage Monkey who had been so famous five hundred years ago he made a getaway by cloud. Monkey did a somersault and sprang up into mid-air to shout, "Where do you think you're going? Take this from me!" The Elder used his stick with a dragon on its head to meet the blow from Monkey's cudgel. The two of them fought a fine battle up in the sky:

The as-you-will cudgel
And the dragon stick
Making clouds up in the sky.
The Elder of the Nation was really an evil spirit,
Using his fiendish daughter's seductive charms.
The king had made himself ill through his lust;
The monster wanted to butcher the boys.
There was no escape from the Great Sage's divine powers
To catch demons and to rescue their victims.
The cudgel's blows to the head were really vicious;
Splendid was the way in which the stick met them.
They fought so hard that the sky was full of mist,
Casting city and people into darkness and fear.
The souls of civil and military officials went flying;
The faces of the queens and concubines turned pale.
The deluded king tried desperately to hide,
Trembling and shaking, unable to do anything.
The cudgel was as fierce as a tiger from the mountains;
The staff whirled round like a dragon leaving the sea.
Now they made havoc in Bhiksuland
As good and evil were clearly set apart.

When the evil spirit had fought over twenty hard rounds with Monkey his dragon staff was no longer a match for the gold-banded cudgel. Feinting with his staff, the spirit turned himself into a beam of cold light and dropped into the inner quarters of the palace to take the demon queen he had presented to the king out through the palace gates with him. She too turned into cold light and disappeared.

Bringing his cloud down, the Great Sage landed in the palace and said to the officials, "That's a fine Elder of the Nation you have!" The officials all bowed to him, thanking the holy monk. "No need for that," said Monkey. "Go and see where your deluded king is." "When our monarch saw the fighting he hid in terror," the officials replied. "We do not know which of the palaces he is in." "Find him at once," Monkey ordered them. "Perhaps Queen Beauty has carried him off." As soon as the officials heard this they rushed with Monkey straight to the rooms of Queen Beauty, ignoring the fact that these were the inner quarters. They were deserted and there was no sign of the king. Queen Beauty was nowhere to be seen either. The queens of the main, the eastern and the western palaces and the consorts of the six compounds all came to kowtow in thanks to the Great Sage. "Please get up," Monkey said. "It's too early for thanks now. Go and find your sovereign lord."

A little later four or five eunuchs appeared from behind the Hall of Caution supporting the deluded king. All the ministers prostrated themselves on the ground and called out in union, "Sovereign lord! Sovereign lord! We are grateful that this holy monk came here to uncover the impostor. The Elder of the Nation was an evil spirit and Queen Beauty has vanished too." When the king heard this he invited Monkey to come from the inner quarters of the palace to the throne hall, where he kowtowed in thanks to Monkey. "Venerable sir," he said, "when you came to court this morning you were so handsome. Why have you made yourself look different now?" "I can tell you for a fact, Your Majesty," replied Monkey with a grin, "that the one who came this morning was my master Sanzang, the younger brother of the Tang Emperor. I'm his disciple Sun Wukong. There are two more of us disciples, Zhu Wuneng, or Pig, and Sha Wujing, or Friar Sand, who are both now in the government hostel. I turned myself into my master's double and came here to defeat the monster because I knew that you had been deluded by his evil suggestions and were going to take my master's heart to use as an adjuvant for your elixir." When the king heard this he ordered his ministers in attendance to go straight to the hostel to fetch Monkey's master and fellow-disciples.

The news that Brother Monkey had turned back into himself and had fought the evil spirit in mid-air gave Sanzang such a fright that his souls scattered. It was lucky that Pig and

Friar Sand were able to hold him up. His face was still plastered with stinking mud and he was feeling thoroughly depressed and miserable when he heard someone call, "Master of the Law, we are ministers in attendance sent by the king of Bhiksuland to invite you to court to receive His Majesty's thanks." "Don't be afraid, master," said Pig, "don't be afraid. This time he's not sending for you to take your heart out. I'm sure that elder brother has succeeded and they're inviting you there to thank you." "Even if they have come to invite me there because he has succeeded I could not face anyone with this stinking mask on," Sanzang replied. "We've got no option," said Pig. "We'll just have to go to see my elder brother. He's bound to have a solution." The venerable elder really did have no choice but to go to the main hall of the hostel with Pig and Friar Sand carrying the luggage and leading the horse. When the ministers saw him they were all terrified. "My lord," they said, "they both have heads like monsters." "Please don't take offence at our ugliness," Friar Sand replied. "Both of us have the bodies that were left after an earlier life. If my master could see my elder brother he'd become handsome straight away."

When the three of them reached the palace they went straight to the throne hall without waiting to be summoned. As soon as Monkey saw them he turned round and came down from the hall to meet them. Pulling the mud mask off his master's face he blew on him with magic breath, called "Change!" and turned the Tang Priest back into himself. Sanzang was now in better spirits. The king came down from the throne hall to greet him as "Master of the Law" and "ancient Buddha". Master and disciples then tethered the horse and went into the throne hall to be presented.

"Does Your Majesty know where the monsters came from?" Monkey asked. "Let me go and catch them both for you. Then we will have eliminated future catastrophe." When all the queens, consorts and concubines of the three palaces and six compounds, who were behind the screen of bright green jade, heard Monkey saying that he was going to eliminate future catastrophe they cast aside all their inhibitions about appearing in front of an outsider, and a male one at that, as they came out to bow to him and say, "We beg you, holy monk and venerable Buddha, to destroy them completely, root and branch, with your dharma powers. That would be an act of the greatest kindness, and we would of course reward you richly." Quickly responding to their bows Monkey insisted that the king tell him where the monsters lived.

"We asked him when he came here three years ago," the king replied shamefacedly, "and he told us that it was only some twenty miles to the south of the city, in Pure Splendour Grange on Willow Slope. The Elder of the Nation was old and had no son, only the daughter that his second wife had given him. She was just fifteen and unmarried. He offered to present her to us, and because we fancied the girl we accepted her. She was the favourite among all the palace women. We never expected that we would fall so ill that all the prescriptions of the Royal College of Physicians would be of no avail. Then he told us that he had a formula for an elixir for which a decoction of boiled little boys' hearts was needed as the adjuvant. In our folly we believed him and chose some boys from among the common people. At noon today we were going to operate and take out their hearts. We never expected that you would come down to us, holy monk, and that at that very moment all the boys would disappear in their coops. Then he said that as you were a holy monk who had cultivated the truth for ten lifetimes and not yet dissipated your primal masculinity your heart would be ten thousand times more effective than the little boys' ones. In our temporary delusion we did not realize that you would see through the evil monster, holy monk. We hope that you will make full use of your great dharma to eliminate any future catastrophe. All the wealth of the nation will be given to you as your reward." "I will tell you the truth," Monkey replied. "Because my master took pity on the little boys in the coops he told me to hide them. Don't say anything about giving us wealth. When I capture the evil monsters that will be a good deed to my credit. Come with me, Pig." "Whatever you say, elder brother," Pig replied. "The only thing is that I've got an empty belly: I'll be rather weak." The king then ordered the department of foreign affairs to prepare a vegetarian meal at once. Before long the food arrived.

Having eaten his fill, Pig braced his spirits and rose by cloud with Monkey. The king, queens, consorts and civil and military officials were all so astonished that they all kowtowed to the sky, exclaiming, "They really are immortals and Buddhas come down to earth." The Great Sage led Pig twenty miles due south, stopped their wind and cloud and started searching for the demons' home. All he could see was a clear stream running between banks on which grew thousands of willows: he had no idea where the Pure Splendour Grange might be. Indeed,

Endless expanses stretched out in his gaze;
The embankment had vanished amid willows and haze.

When he could not find the grange the Great Sage Sun made a spell with his hands, said the magic word "*Om*" and summoned the local deity, who approached shivering and shaking, fell to his knees and called out, "Great Sage, the local god of Willow Bank kowtows to you." "Don't be afraid," Monkey said, "I'm not going to hit you. Tell me this: is there a Pure Splendour Grange on Willow Hill? And where is it?" "There is a Pure Splendour Cave," the local deity replied, "but there has never been a Pure Splendour Grange. I suppose you have come from Bhiksuland, Great Sage." "Yes, yes," Monkey replied. "The king of Bhiksuland was hoodwinked by an evil spirit till I turned up, saw through the monster, defeated him and drove him away. He turned into a beam of cold light and I don't know where he went. When I asked the king of Bhiksuland about it he told me that when the demon first presented him with the girl three years ago he asked the spirit about his background. The demon said that he lived in Pure Splendour Grange on Willow Hill twenty miles south of the city. I've found this place with its wooded hill but can't see any Pure Splendour Grange. That's why I asked you about it."

"I beg your forgiveness, Great Sage," said the local god, kowtowing. "This is part of the domain of the king of Bhiksuland, and I should have kept a closer watch on things. But the evil spirit had such terrible magical powers. If I had given away what he was doing he would have come and given me a bad time. That is why he has never been caught. Now that you are here, Great Sage, you need only go to the foot of the nine-forked willow on the southern bank, walk round it three times to the left and three times to the right, hit the tree with both hands and shout 'Open up' three times. The Pure Splendour Cave Palace will then appear."

On learning this the Great Sage sent the local god away again, jumped over the stream with Pig and went to look for that willow tree. There was indeed a tree with nine forks on a single trunk. "Stand well back," Monkey ordered Pig, "while I make the gates open. When I've found the demon and chased him out you're to help." In response to this order Pig took up his stand about three hundred yards from the tree while the Great Sage followed the local god's advice and went round the tree three times to the left and three times to the right then hit it with both hands, shouting, "Open up! Open up!" An instant later a pair of double doors opened with a noisy whoosh and the tree was nowhere to be seen. Inside the doors was bright light of many colours but no sign of human life. Confident in his divine might, Monkey charged in. He could see that it was a fine place:

Shimmering clouds, from which
Sun and moon stole their brightness.
White clouds billowing from the caves,
Bright green lichens running wild in the courtyard.
Along the path rare flowers competed in beauty,
While plants on the steps vied in fragrant blossom.
Warm was the air
Where it was ever spring.
This was just like a fairyland,
Or Penglai, the paradise of immortals.
Creepers grew all over the benches;
Vines ran wild across the bridge.

Bees flew into the cave carrying flowers;
Butterflies flirted with orchids as they passed the screen of stone.

Hurrying forward for a closer look Monkey saw that on the stone screen was carved IMMORTAL PALACE OF PURE SPLENDOUR. Unable to restrain himself, he jumped over the stone screen to see the old monster embracing a beautiful woman and telling her breathlessly what had happened in Bhiksuland. "That was our chance," they said together. "Three years' efforts should have paid off today, but that ape's ruined everything."

Monkey charged up to them, brandishing his cudgel and shouting, "I'll get you, you fools. What do you mean, that was your chance? Take that!" Pushing the woman aside, the old monster swung his dragon-headed stick to block the cudgel. It was a fine battle that the two of them fought in front of the cave, and quite unlike the previous one:

The upraised cudgel spat out golden light;
Vicious vapours came from the swinging staff.
The monster said,
"How dare you in your ignorance come to my home?"
Monkey replied,
"I intend to subdue evil monsters."
Said the monster,
"My love for the king was no business of yours,
So why did you come to bully and interfere?"
Answered Monkey,
"A compassionate monk should bring misrule to an end:
We could not endure the slaughter of children."
As they flung words at each other hostility grew:
Staff parried cudgel as blows struck at the heart.
Precious flowers were destroyed as they fought for their lives;
Green moss became slippery when trampled underfoot.
Pale grew the light in the cave as they struggled:
Crushed were the fragrant blooms on the crags.

At the clash of their weapons the birds dared not fly;
Their shouts sent the beauties all running in terror.
Only the monster and Monkey were left
To stir up a hurricane that roared over the earth.
Slowly their battle took them out of the cave
Where Wuneng gave play to his mindless wrath.

The sound of the commotion they were making inside so ex cited Pig where he was waiting outside that his heart itched. A he could get no relief from scratching he raised his rake, smashe the nine-forked willow to the ground, then hit it several time so hard that blood gushed straight out with a barely audibl sound. "This tree's become a spirit," he said, "this tree's spirit." Pig had just raised his rake for another blow when h saw Monkey drawing the monster after him. Without anothe word the idiot rushed forward, raised his rake and struck. Th old monster was already finding Monkey too much to cope with so that Pig's rake made him more desperate than ever. Abandon ing the fight he shook himself, turned back into a beam of col light, and headed east again. The two of them would not le the demon go but headed eastwards in pursuit.

Above the shouts of battle they heard the calls of the phoeni and the crane and looked up to see that it was the Star of Lon gevity from the southern pole of the heavens. Placing a cove over the cold light the old man called out, "Don't be in such hurry, Great Sage; stop chasing him now, Marshal Tian Peng This old Taoist offers his greetings." Monkey returned hi courtesy and asked, "Where have you come from, Longevity m brother?" "You've capped the cold light, so you must hav caught the monster, old fat chops," said Pig with a grin. "Her he is, here he is," said the Star of Longevity, smiling back. " trust you two gentlemen will spare his life." "The old devil' nothing to do with you, brother," said Monkey, "so why hav you come to plead for him?" "He's a messenger of mine," replie the star with a smile. "I carelessly let him escape to become monster here." "Since he's yours make him turn back into wha he really looks like for us to see," said Monkey. The Star o

Longevity then let the cold light out and shouted, "Evil beast! Turn back into yourself at once if you want to be spared the death penalty." The demon turned himself round and revealed that he was really a white deer. Picking the staff up the Star of Longevity said, "You've even stolen my staff, evil beast." The deer lay down in submission, unable to speak, but only kowtowing and weeping. Look at him:

Brindled like a tablet of jade,
And carrying a pair of seven-branched antlers.
When hungry he used to find the herb garden;
On mornings when thirsty he drank from the misty stream.
In his lengthening years he had taught himself to fly
And through many a day had mastered transformation.
Now that he heard the call of his master
He resumed his own form and lay down in the dust.

Thanking Monkey, the Star of Longevity mounted his deer and was just leaving when Monkey grabbed hold of him and said, "Not so fast, brother. There are a couple more jobs still to be done." "What jobs?" the star asked. "The girl hasn't been caught yet and I don't know what sort of monster she is," Monkey replied. "We've also got to go back to Bhiksuland together to see the deluded ruler and show him what they really are." "In that case I'll be patient," the star replied. "You and Marshal Tian Peng can go down into the cave to capture the girl and take her back to show the king what she really is." "Just wait a little while," said Monkey. "We'll soon be back."

Pig then summoned up his spirits and went straight into the Immortal Palace of Pure Splendour with Monkey. "Catch the evil spirit," he shouted, "catch the evil spirit." Hearing this great roar the beauty, who was trembling with fear and unable to escape, rushed behind the stone screen, but there was no rear exit. "Where do you think you're going?" Pig shouted. "I'll get you, you man-trap, you whore spirit. Try my rake!" As the beauty was unarmed she could not fight back, so she dodged the blow and turned herself into a beam of cold light and fled only to be stopped by the Great Sage, who with two thumping blows of his cudgel knocked her off her feet and laid her low in the dust. She turned back into her real form as a white-faced vixen. Unable to restrain himself, the idiot lifted his rake and struck her a blow on the head. The great beauty of so many smiles was now a hairy fox.

"Don't smash her to pulp," Monkey said. "Keep her in that shape to show her to the deluded king." The idiot grabbed her by the tail, not minding the filth, and dragged her out through the cave entrance with Monkey. Here he saw the Star of Longevity stroking the deer's head and giving him a dressing down. "Evil beast," he was saying, "why did you run away from me and come here to turn yourself into a spirit? If I hadn't turned up the Great Sage Sun would certainly have killed you." "What's that you're saying, brother?" asked Monkey springing out of the cave. "I was telling the deer off," the star explained, "telling the deer off." Throwing the body of the dead fox in front of the deer, Pig said, "Your daughter, I suppose." The deer nodded then stretched its head out to sniff the body and whimpered as if with grief at its bereavement until the Star of Longevity cuffed its head and said, "Evil beast. You're lucky to have got away with your life. What are you sniffing her for?" He then took off the belt he wore round his gown, fastened it round the deer's neck, and led it off with the words, "Great Sage, let's go to Bhiksuland." "Wait a moment," said Monkey, "I feel like cleaning the whole place up so that no other evil creatures can ever live here again."

When Pig heard this he raised his rake and started to smash the willow down wildly. Monkey then said the magic word "*Om*" and summoned the local deity once more. "Gather some dried firewood," Monkey ordered him, "and start a roaring fire that will rid this place of yours of evil. Then you won't be bullied any more." The local deity then turned around and with a roaring negative wind led his spirit soldiers to gather all sorts of withered vegetation that had dried out since the previous year: frostbitten grass, autumn grass, knotweed grass, mountain grass, dragonbone grass, rushes and reeds. Once set alight they would burn like oil or grease. "There's no need to go knocking trees over, Pig," said Monkey. "Fill the mouth of the cave with all this and set it alight: that'll burn the place clean out." And indeed once they were lit they turned the evil demons' Pure Splendour home into a fiery furnace.

Only then did Monkey dismiss the local god and go with the Star of Longevity as they dragged the fox to the steps of the throne hall where he said to the king, "Here's your Queen Beauty. Do you want to fool around with her now?" This caused the king a terrible shock. At the sight of the Great Sage Monkey bringing the Star of Longevity with the white deer before the throne hall, monarch, ministers, consorts and queens all dropped to the ground to kowtow. Monkey went up to the king and held him up. "Don't kowtow to me," he said with a smile. "This deer is the Elder of the Nation. It's him you should be kowtowing to." The king was now so overcome with shame that he could only say, "Thank you, holy monk, for saving the boys in my kingdom. It truly was an act of heavenly kindness." He then ordered the department of foreign relations to prepare a vegetarian feast, had the eastern hall of the palace opened up and invited the star, the Ancient of the Southern Pole, to take part in a thanksgiving feast with the Tang Priest and his three disciples. Sanzang bowed in greeting to the Star of Longevity, as did Friar Sand. "If the white deer is one of your creatures, Star of Longevity," they both asked, "how did he get here to become such a nuisance?"

"Some time ago the Lord of Eastern Splendour came to my mountain," the Star of Longevity replied with a smile, "and I persuaded him to sit down for some chess. The wicked creature escaped before our first game was over. It was only when I couldn't find him after my visitor had gone that I worked out by calculating on my fingers that he must have come here. I had just reached here in my search for him when I met the Great Sage Sun using his mighty powers. If I had been any later this beast would be dead." Before he could finish his remarks it was announced that the banquet was ready. It was a splendid vegetarian feast:

The room was overflowing with colour;
Exotic fragrances filled the hall.
Embroidered hangings made the tables magnificent;
Red carpets on the floor shimmered like the glow of dawn.
From duck-shaped censers
Curled the scented smoke of eaglewood;
Before the king's place
Were fragrant vegetables.
See how high the towers of fruit were piled;
Sugar dragons and prowling animals.
Moulded mandarin ducks,
Lion confections,
Looking quite lifelike.
Parrot goblets,
Cormorant ladles,
Shaped like the real thing.
Every kind of fruit in abundance,
Each exquisite dish a delicacy.
Giant longans and tender bamboo-shoots,
Fresh lichees and peaches.
Sweet smelled the jujubes and persimmon cakes;
More fragrant than wine were the pine-nuts and grapes.
Many a sweet dish made with honey,
Steamed pastries of various kinds,
Sugar-drenched doughnuts
Piled up like bouquets of flowers,
Mountains of rolls on golden dishes,
Fragrant rice heaped high in silver bowls,
Long bean noodles in hot chilli soup,
Tasty dishes came in succession.
There was no end of button mushrooms,
"Tree-ear" fungus,

Tender bamboo shoots,
Sealwort,
Vegetables of many flavours,
A hundred kinds of rare delights.
They came and went in endless succession,
All the abundant dishes offered at the feast.

The seating was arranged on the spot, the seat of honour going to the Star of Longevity and the next best place to the Tang Priest. The king sat between them while Brother Monkey, Pig and Friar Sand sat at the side places. There were also three senior ministers present to keep them company, and the musicians and singers of the court theatre were ordered to perform. Holding his purple cloud goblet, the king, toasted them one by one. The only person who would not drink was the Tang Priest. "Brother," said Pig to Monkey, "I'll leave the fruit for you, but you must let me have a good feed of the soup, bread and rice." With no further thought the idiot ate everything all at once. He devoured everything that was brought in and left nothing behind.

When the banquet was coming to an end the Star of Longevity took his leave of them. The king went up to him, knelt, kowtowed and begged the star to tell him the secret of eliminating disease and prolonging life. "I didn't bring any elixir as I was here to search for my deer," the Star of Longevity replied. "I would like to teach you the techniques of self-cultivation, but you are so weak in body and ruined in spirit that you would not be able to convert the elixir. All I have in my sleeve is these three jujubes that I was intending to offer to the Lord of Eastern Splendour to take with tea. As they haven't been eaten I can offer them to you now." The king swallowed them, and he gradually began to feel lighter in body as the illness was cured. This was the origin of his later success in achieving immortality. As soon as Pig saw this he called, "Longevity, old pal, if you've got any fire jujubes give me some." "I didn't bring any," the star replied, "but I'll give you several pounds of them next time." The Star of Longevity then went out of the eastern pavilion, expressed his thanks, called to the white deer, sprang on his back and departed by cloud. We will not relate how the king, queens and consorts in the palace and the common people in the city all burnt incense and kowtowed.

"Disciples," said Sanzang, "let us pack up and take our leave of His Majesty." The king pleaded with them to stay and instruct him. "Your Majesty," said Monkey, "from now on you should be less greedy for your sexual pleasures and accumulate more hidden merit. In whatever you do you should use your strong points to make up for your weaknesses. This is the way to get rid of your illness and prolong your life. That's what we'd tell you." Two dishes full of small pieces of gold and silver were then offered to the pilgrims to help with the expenses of their journey, but the Tang Priest refused to accept a single penny. The king then had no choice but to order the royal carriage and invite the Tang Priest to sit in the dragon and phoenix coach while he, his queens and his consorts pushed the wheels. Thus they escorted him out of the palace. In the streets and markets the common people also came with bowls of pure water and incense-burners to see them on their way from the city.

Suddenly there was the sound of a wind in the sky and 1,111 goose coops landed on both sides of the road. The little boys in them were crying. Unseen in the sky were the deities who had been looking after them: the city and the local gods, the deities of the altars, the True Officials, the Guardians of the Four Quarters and the Centre, the Four Duty Gods, the Six Dings and Six Jias, the Protectors of the Faith and the rest of them, who all responded with a loud shout of, "Great Sage, on your earlier instructions we carried the boys away in the goose coops. Now that we have learned of your success in your task and your departure we have brought every one of them back again." The king, his queens and consorts and all his ministers and subjects fell to their knees to kowtow. "Thank you for your efforts, gentlemen," Monkey shouted to the sky. "Please all return to your shrines now. I'll get the people to make thanksgiving offerings to you." With a soughing noise the magic wind then arose again and departed.

Monkey then told the people of the city to come and collect their children. The news was spread at once, and the people all came to claim the boys in the baskets. They were very happy indeed. Holding the boys in their arms they called them dear ones and darlings. Dancing and laughing they told their children to take hold of the lords from Tang and bring them home so that they could express their thanks for the boys' rescue. Nobody, young or old, male or female, was frightened by the disciples' ugly faces as they all carried Pig, Friar Sand, Monkey and the Tang Priest back to the city in the middle of a crowd that also brought their luggage and led the horse. The king could not stop them. Family after family laid on a banquet or a feast, and those who could not offer hospitality made monkish hats, shoes, tunics, cotton socks, and other inner and outer garments in different sizes that they presented to the pilgrims. Only when they had been entertained in this way for nearly a month were the travellers able to leave the city. Portraits of them were painted and tablets bearing their names set up; to these the people could kowtow, burn incense and make offerings. Indeed,

Great was the gratitude for their enormous kindness,
In saving the lives of infants by the thousand.

If you don't know what happened later listen to the explanation in the next instalment.

CHAPTER EIGHTY

The young girl seeks a mate to build up the male; Protecting his master the Mind-ape sees through a demon.

The story tells how the king, ministers and common people of Bhiksuland escorted the Tang Priest and his three disciples out of the city. Seven miles later they were still unwilling to part from the pilgrims, but Sanzang insisted on getting out of the coach, mounting the horse and taking his leave of them. The people who had been seeing him off did not return to the city until the travellers had vanished from view.

When the four had been travelling for a long time the winter and the spring too were over. There was no end of wild flowers and mountain trees to be seen; fragrant blossoms filled the view. To Sanzang's alarm another towering mountain appeared in front of them. "Disciples," he asked, "is there a way across the high mountain before us? We must be careful." "Master," laughed Brother Monkey, "that's not what a seasoned traveller should be saying. You sound much more like some pampered prince trying to look at the whole sky from the bottom of a well. As the old saying goes, a mountain can't stop the road: it can find its own way across. So why ask whether there's a way?" "Even if this mountain cannot block the road," Sanzang replied, "I am afraid that there may be monsters on the mountain precipices and evil spirits that will emerge from its deep recesses."

"Don't worry," said Pig, "don't worry. We're not far from Paradise here. I guarantee it'll all be nice and peaceful — there won't be any trouble." As they were talking master and disciples reached the foot of the mountain without even noticing. Taking out his gold-banded cudgel Monkey climbed the rock-ace. "Master," he called, "there's a path that goes round the nountain. The going's very easy. Hurry up!" The Tang Priest now put his worries aside and whipped the horse forward. 'Carry the luggage for a while, brother," said Friar Sand to Pig, who did so while Friar Sand held the horse's reins and the naster sat in the carved saddle. They hurried along the main path up the steep slope after Monkey. This was what the mountain looked like:

The peak was wrapped in clouds;
Torrents rushed down ravines.
The paths were heavy with the scent of flowers,
And dense grew the countless trees.
Blue were the gages, white the plums,
Green the willows and red the peaches.
Spring was all but over where the cuckoo sang;
When fledgling swallows chirped the festival was finished.
Craggy boulders,
Blue-green pines shaped like parasols.
The track leading across the ridge
Climbed high over a tracery of rocks;
The beetling precipice
Was overgrown with creepers, grass and trees.
Peaks like a row of halberds vied in elegance;
Far from the ocean wave streams competed in gullies.

As the master was taking an unhurried look at the mountain scenery he was moved to homesickness by the sound of a bird singing. "Disciples," he said,

"After receiving His Majesty's command
I was given my passport in front of the brocade screen.
Watching lanterns on the fifteenth night I left the eastern land,
And then was parted from the emperor of Tang.
Just when the dragon and tiger winds both met
I and my disciples had to struggle with the horse.

Twelve may be the peaks of Mount Wu;
*But when shall I face and see you again?"**

"Master," said Monkey, "you're always suffering from homesickness. You're not like a monk at all. Stop worrying and keep going: don't upset yourself so. As the old saying goes, you've got to work hard if you want to be rich and successful." "What you say is quite right, disciple," said Sanzang, "but I do not know where the road to the west runs." "Master," said Pig, "it's all because our Tathagata Buddha can't bring himself to give those scriptures away. He must have removed the path because he knows we're coming to fetch them. Why else can't we get to the end of the journey?" "Don't talk such nonsense," said Friar Sand. "Just keep going with big brother. As long as we stick with him we're bound to get there in the end."

As they were talking master and disciples came in sight of a great expanse of dark pine forest. In his fear the Tang Priest called out, "Wukong, no sooner have we taken that precipitous track over the mountain than we come to this deep, dark pine forest. Why? We must be careful." "There's nothing to be scared of," said Monkey. "Nonsense," said Sanzang. "Never trust what appears to be absolutely upright, and be on your guard against evil masquerading as goodness. I have been through quite a few pine woods with you, but never one as vast and deep as this. Just look at the trees:

Dense-packed to east and west,
In lines to north and south.
Dense-packed to east and west they reach the end of the clouds;
In lines to north and south they touch the azure firmament.
Thorns and brambles grow close-tangled all about;
Knotweed wraps itself around the branches.
Liana coils round kudzu vine,
Kudzu coils around liana.

---

* The original of these eight lines is made up largely of terms from Chinese dominoes, word-play that is lost in translation.

Where liana coils around kudzu
Travellers cannot move between east and west;
Where kudzu coils round liana
Merchants may not ply between north and south.
In this forest
You could spend half a year,
Not knowing whether sun or moon was out,
Or travel for miles
And never see the stars.
Where the outlook is to the north the view is unbounded;
On southern slopes the bushes are in flower.
There are thousand-year-old locust trees,
Ten-thousand-year-old junipers,
Pines that endure the winter cold,
Mountain peaches that bear fruit,
Wild peonies,
And hibiscus,
All growing in a close-packed profusion,
So wild that not even a god could paint it.
Bird-song could be heard:
Parrots shrieking,
Cuckoos calling,
Magpies in the branches,
Crows feeding their mothers,
Orioles with their aerial dance,
As the mynas adjust their voices.
Quails singing,
Swallows chirping,
Mynahs imitating people,
And thrushes that could recite sutras.
Then there were:
Great beasts swishing their tails,
Tigers gnashing their teeth,
Aged foxes and racoon-dogs disguised as ladies,
Ancient grey wolves at whose baying the forest shook.
Had the Pagoda-carrying Heavenly King come here

His power to suppress demons would have been of no
avail.

The Great Sage Sun was unafraid. Clearing the way ahead with his cudgel, he led the Tang Priest into the depths of the forest. They had been travelling in this carefree style for many hours without seeing any sign of a way out of the forest when the Tang Priest called out, "Disciples, we have been through no end of steep and dangerous mountain woods on our journey west. Thank goodness we have found this purity and elegance and a smooth path. The rare and unusual flowers here are truly delightful. I intend to sit here for a moment to let the horse have a rest. I am, besides, famished. Go and beg me some meat-free food from somewhere."

"Master," said Monkey, "please dismount while I go begging." This the venerable elder did. While Pig tied the horse to a tree Friar Sand put the luggage down, brought out the begging-bowl and handed it to Monkey. "Sit still here, Master," Monkey said, "and don't even say the word 'fear'. I'll be back in a moment." While Sanzang sat upright in the shade of the pines Pig and Friar Sand amused themselves looking for flowers and fruit.

Let us tell of the Great Sage, who somersaulted into mid air, brought his cloud to a hall and looked back. All he could see coming from the pine forest were auspicious clouds and auras that coiled and spread all around. "Good, good," he found himself saying. Do you know why? He was expressing his admiration for the Tang Priest, the reincarnation of the Venerable Golden Cicada and a holy man who had cultivated his conduct for ten successive lifetimes, which explained there was such an aura of good omen above his head.

"Five hundred years ago, when I made havoc in heaven," Monkey thought, "I wandered to the very corners of the oceans and ran wild at the end of the sky. I led a host of spirits and called myself the Great Sage Equalling Heaven. We subdued dragons and tigers, and I took us off the registers of death. I used to wear a triple golden crown and a coat of golden mail, and with my gold-banded cudgel in my hands and my cloud-treading shoes on my feet I had 47,000 demons under me. They all used to call me Lord Great Sage. I really was someone in those days. But ever since being rescued from Heaven's punishment I've been a small-time nobody as his disciple. I reckon that as the master has such an aura of auspicious clouds over his head things are sure to turn out well for us on our way back to the east and I'm bound to win the true achievement."

As Brother Monkey was congratulating himself along these lines he saw a column of black vapour rising from the south of the forest. "That black vapour means evil for sure," he thought with alarm. "No black vapours could come from our Pig or Friar Sand."

While the Great Sage was still trying to make out exactly what the vapours were coming from, Sanzang was sitting in the forest clarifying his mind and contemplating the Buddha-nature as he recited the *Mahaprajnaparamita Heart Sutra* when suddenly he heard a high-pitched cry of "Help!" "This is all very well," said Sanzang with astonishment, "but who could that be calling so deep in the forest?" It must be someone terrified by a wolf, a tiger, a leopard or some other wild beast. I shall go to take a look." The venerable elder rose to his feet and walked through the thousand-year-old cypresses and even more ancient pines, holding on to vines and creepers, as he went close enough to see a woman tied to a big tree. The top half of her body was bound to the trunk with creepers and her lower half buried in the ground. Sanzang stopped to ask, "Why are you tied up here, lady Bodhisattva?" It was quite obvious that the wretched creature was an evil monster, but with his mortal eyes in a worldling's body Sanzang was unable to perceive this. The monster's response to the question was to weep copiously. Just look at the tears rolling down her peachy cheeks. She was so lovely that fish would have sunk and wild geese fallen out of the sky at the sight of her; the beauty of her sorrowing and sparkling eyes would have made the moon hide away and put the flowers to shame. Sanzang did not dare go any closer to her as he opened his mouth to ask, "What crime have you committed, lady Bodhisattva? Tell me so that I can rescue you."

The evil spirit then quickly put together a pack of lies as she replied, "Master, my home is in the country of Pinpo, which is some seventy miles from here. Both my parents are at home, and they are very great lovers of goodness. All their lives they have been on good terms with their relations and devoted to their friends. At the Clear and Bright Festival they invited all their relations and members of their own family to pay their respects at and sweep the ancestral graves. A whole procession of carrying-chairs and horses all went to the graves in the wilds outside the city. Here we set out our offerings and had just burnt the paper models of horses when a band of brigands sprang upon us with the sound of gongs and drums. They charged us shouting 'kill!' My parents and relations all got hold of horses and carrying-chairs and fled for their lives. Because I am so young I was too frightened to run: I just collapsed and was carried back to the mountains by the brigands. The top chieftain wanted me for his lady, the number two chieftain wanted me for his woman, and the third and fourth ones both fancied me for my looks. There were seventy or eighty of them all quarrelling over me and none of them would give way. So they tied me up here in the forest and broke up the band. I've been here for five days and five nights now and I'm only just alive now. I'll soon be dead. Goodness only knows which ancestor however many generations back accumulated the virtue that brought you here to me today, reverend sir. I beg you in your great mercy to save my life. I won't forget your goodness to me even when I lie dead under the nine springs of the underworld." When she had finished speaking her tears flowed like rain.

As Sanzang really did have a merciful heart he could not help weeping and sobbing himself. "Disciples," he shouted. Pig and Friar Sand were still looking for flowers and fruit in the forest when suddenly they heard their master's anguished cry. "Friar Sand," said the idiot, "the master's found a relation here." "What nonsense, brother," said Friar Sand with a smile. "In all the time we've been going we haven't met a single good person, so where could any relation of his have come from?" "If it's not a relation why's the master crying for them?" Pig asked, adding, "You and I had better go to take a look." Friar Sand did indeed go back to where they had been before. Leading the horse and carrying the luggage they went up to the master and asked, "What's up, Master?" The Tang Priest pointed at the tree as he replied, "Pig, untie this lady Bodhisattva and save her life." Without caring whether this was the right or the wrong thing to do, the idiot set to.

The Great Sage meanwhile saw from up in the air the dense black vapours completely obscuring the auspicious glow. "This is bad," he said, "this is bad. If the black vapours are covering the auspicious glow that means something evil is threatening my master. Never mind about begging for food — I'm going back to see the master." He turned his cloud back and landed in the forest, where he saw Pig recklessly untying the ropes. Going up to him Monkey grabbed an ear and threw him to the ground. "The master told me to rescue her," the idiot protested, looking up to see Monkey as he scrambled back to his feet, "so why did you push me over like that? You're just throwing your weight about." "Brother," replied Monkey with a smile, "don't untie her. She's an evil spirit who's been putting on an act to fool us."

"Wretched ape," shouted Sanzang, "talking nonsense again. How can you possibly take a girl like this for an evil spirit?" "There's something you don't know, Master." Monkey replied. "In the old days I tried all these tricks myself when I wanted some human flesh. You couldn't possibly tell what she is." "Master," said Pig, pouting sulkily, "don't let that Protector of the Horses take you in. She's a local girl. We've never had dealings with her before on our long journey from the east and she's no relation or in-law of ours, so how can you say she's an evil spirit? He's trying to get rid of us by making us go ahead so he can turn a somersault and get back here by magic. Then he's going to have a bit of fun with her and ruin our reputation."

"You cretin," shouted Brother Monkey, "stop talking such rubbish. I've never done any such outrageous thing on all our journey to the West. I reckon it must have been some reckless womanizer like yourself who forgot his principles when he saw a good chance. I expect you tricked some family into taking you as their son-in-law and tied her up here." "That's enough of that," said Sanzang, "that's enough. Now then, Bajie. Your elder brother usually sees things very clearly. Ignore what he is saying. Let us be on our way." "Splendid," said Monkey with great delight, "you have a good destiny, Master. Please mount. Once we're out of the pine forest there will be a house where we can beg for some food for you." The four of them then pressed on together, leaving the monster behind.

The story tells how the monster gnashed her teeth with fury as she was left tied there to the tree. "I've heard tell of Sun Wukong's tremendous magic powers for years," she said, "and now that I've seen him today I know that his reputation's well-founded. As that Tang Priest has been cultivating his conduct ever since he was a boy he has never lost a drop of his primal masculinity. I was longing to mate with him so that I could become a golden immortal of the Supreme Ultimate. I never expected that monkey to see through my magic and save him. If I'd been untied and released I could have carried him off whenever I chose and he'd have been mine. Now that Sun Wukong has made those damaging remarks and taken the Tang Priest away my efforts have all been for nothing. Let's see what happens when I give him another couple of shouts." Not shifting her ropes, the evil spirit made the most of the wind being in the right direction to carry some high-pitched words of morality into the Tang Priest's ear. Do you know what she was shouting? "Master," she called, "if you forget your conscience and refuse to save a living being's life what's the use of your fetching the scriptures from the Buddha?"

When the Tang Priest heard this call he reined the horse in and said, "Wukong, go and rescue that girl." "You've started on your way, Master," Monkey replied. "What made you think of her again?" "She is shouting again there," the Tang Priest said. "Did you hear, Pig?" Monkey asked. "My big lugs cover my ear-holes," Pig replied, "and I didn't hear anything." "Did you hear, Friar Sand?" "I was walking ahead, carrying the pole with the luggage," Friar Sand replied. "I wasn't paying attention and I didn't hear anything either." "Neither did I," said Monkey. "What did she say, Master? You were the only one who heard." "What she called was quite right," the Tang Priest called. "She asked what was the use of fetching scriptures when I went to visit the Buddha if I forgot my conscience and refused to save a living being's life. To save a human life is better than building a seven-storeyed pagoda. Rescuing her straight away would be even better than worshipping the Buddha and fetching the scriptures."

"If you're wanting to be charitable, Master," Monkey replied, "you're incurable. Just think of all the demons you've met in all the mountains you've crossed on your journey west since leaving the east. They've often taken you into their caves and I've had to rescue you. I've killed tens of thousands of them with this iron cudgel of mine. So why can't you bring yourself to let a single devil die today? Why do you have to rescue her?" "Disciple," the Tang Priest replied, "there's an old saying, 'Do not fail to do a good deed because it is small; do not commit a bad deed because it is small.' You're still to go and save her." "If that's the way you're going to be, Master, I can't accept that responsibility," Monkey replied. "You insist on rescuing her and I dare not try too hard to dissuade you. When I did make a little attempt to do so you lost your temper again. You can go and rescue her if you want to." "Watch your tongue, ape," Sanzang retorted. "Sit here while Bajie and I go to rescue her."

The Tang Priest went back into the forest and told Pig to undo the ropes around the top half of her body and dig the lower half out with his rake. The demon stamped her feet, fastened her skirt and happily followed the Tang Priest out of the pine forest. When she met Monkey all he did was to wear a mocking smile. "Impudent ape," said the Tang Priest abusively, "what are you smiling at?" "I'm laughing at you," Monkey replied:

"You meet up with good friends when your luck is going well;
And when it's going badly you find yourself a belle."

"Impudent macaque!" said Sanzang, being abusive again. "What nonsense! I have been a monk ever since I came out of my mother's womb. I am now making this journey west at His Majesty's command with the devout intention of worshipping the Buddha and fetching the scriptures. I am not the sort of person to care about wealth and office, so what do you mean by my luck going badly?" "Master," replied Monkey with a grin, "you may have been a monk since you were a child, and you may be good at reading sutras and invoking the Buddha, but you have never studied the text of royal laws. This girl is young and beautiful. If monks like us travel with her we may well meet with evil people who arrest us and turn us in to the authorities. They won't care about worshipping Buddhas or fetching scriptures. They'll treat it as a case of illicit sex, and even if that isn't proved we'll still be convicted of abduction. You will lose your ordination licence, Master, and be beaten half to death. Pig will be sent into exile and Friar Sand sentenced to penal servitude. Even I won't get off scot-free. No matter how I try to talk my way out of it I'll still be found guilty of wrongdoing." "Don't talk such rubbish," Sanzang shouted. "After all, I did save her life. There will be no trouble. We are taking her with us. I will be responsible for whatever happens."

"You may say you'll be responsible, Master," Monkey replied, "but what you don't realize is that so far from rescuing her you're destroying her." "I saved her life by rescuing her from the forest," said Sanzang, "so how can I be destroying her?" "If she had stayed tied up in the forest without any food for three to five days, ten days or even half a month and starved to death," said Monkey, "she would at least have gone to the Underworld with her body in one piece. But now you've taken her away from there. You're on a fast horse and travelling like the wind. The rest of us have to follow you. How will she be able to keep up on her tiny feet? She can barely walk. If she gets left behind and a wolf, a tiger or a leopard eats her up you'll have killed her."

"You are right," Sanzang said. "Thank you for thinking of it. What are we to do about it?" "Lift her up and let her ride on the horse with you," replied Monkey with a grin. "I could not possibly ride on the same horse as her," moaned Sanzang. "Then how is she to travel?" Monkey asked. "Bajie can carry her on his back," Sanzang replied. "You're in luck, idiot," said Monkey. "There's no such thing as a light load on a long journey," Pig replied. "Having to carry her isn't luck." "With your long snout you'll be able to turn it round and chat her up on the quiet while you're carrying her," Monkey replied, "which will be very convenient for you."

Pig's reaction to hearing this was to beat his chest and jump about in fury. "That's terrible," he said, "that's terrible. I'd sooner put up with the pain of a flogging from the master. If I carry her I won't possibly come out of it clean. You've always been a slanderer. I'm not carrying her." "Very well then," Sanzang said, "very well then. I can walk a little further. I shall come down and walk slowly with you. Bajie can lead the horse with nobody riding it." "You've got yourself a good bargain there, idiot," said Monkey, roaring with laughter. "The master's done you a favour by letting you lead the horse." "You are talking nonsense again, ape," said Sanzang. "As the ancients said, 'When a horse is to travel three hundred miles it cannot get there by itself.' If I walk slowly are you going to leave me behind? When I go slowly you will have to go slowly too. We shall all take the lady Bodhisattva down the mountain together. We can leave her in some convent, temple, monastery or house that we come to. Then we will still have rescued her." "You're right, Master," Monkey replied. "Let's press on quickly."

Sanzang took the lead while Friar Sand carried the luggage, Pig led the riderless horse and the girl, and Monkey carried his iron cudgel as they carried on together. Within seven to ten miles the evening was drawing in and a tall building came into sight. "Disciple," said Sanzang, "that must be a temple of some sort. We shall ask to spend the night here and be on our way first thing tomorrow." "What you say is right, Master," said Monkey. "Let's all get a move on." They were soon at the gates, where Sanzang told them, "Keep well out of the way while I go in first to ask if we can stay for the night. If it looks suitable I shall send someone to call to you." So they all stood in the shadows of the poplars while Monkey kept an eye on the girl, his iron cudgel in his hand.

The venerable elder walked forward to see that the gates were hanging crooked and falling to pieces. What he saw when he pushed the gates open chilled him to the heart:

The cloisters were deserted,
The ancient shrine left desolate.
The courtyard was overgrown with moss;
Sagebrush and brambles choked the paths.
The only lanterns came from the fireflies
While the croaking of frogs had replaced the water-clock.
The venerable elder started crying. Indeed,
The desolate halls were falling down,
The lonely cloisters collapsing.
Broken bricks and tiles lay in a dozen heaps,
And all the pillars and beams were askew.
Grass was growing all around;
The kitchens were crumbling and buried in dust.
In derelict towers the drums had lost their skins;
Broken was the glass lamp.
The colour had gone from the Buddha's golden statue;
The figures of arhats lay strewn upon the floor.
Guanyin had turned to mud in the soaking rain,
Her pure vase with a willow spray fallen to the ground.
No monk was to be seen there by day,
And only foxes slept there at night.
As the wind roared with the sound of thunder
This was a place for tiger and leopard to shelter.
The walls around had collapsed
And no gates could be closed to guard it.

There is a poem about this that goes

For many a year had the temple been unrepaired;
In its derelict state it had gone from bad to worse.
The gales had destroyed the faces of the temple guardians,
And rainstorms had washed the heads off the Buddha statues.
The vajrapani had collapsed and been soaked through.
The local god had lost his shrine and stayed outside at night.
Two other things were even more depressing:
Bell and drums lay on the ground instead of hanging in their towers.

Summoning up his courage, Sanzang went in through the inner gates where he saw that the bell-tower and drum-tower had both collapsed, leaving only a single bronze bell planted in the ground, its bottom half the colour of indigo. With the passage of the years the top half of the bell had been bleached in the rain while the earth's vapours had greened the lower part. "Bell," Sanzang called aloud as he touched it,

"Once you roared from high in the tower,
Calling afar from the painted beam where you hung.
At cockcrow you used to ring in the dawn,
And at evening you announced the dusk.
Where now are the lay brothers who begged for the copper,
Or the craftsman who cast it to form you?
Both, I imagine, are now in the Underworld;
They have gone without trace and you are left silent."

The venerable elder's loud sighs had by now disturbed someone in the monastery. A lay brother who was offering incense heard the voice, climbed to his feet, picked up a broken brick and threw it at the bell. The bell's clang gave the venerable elder such a fright that he fell over then scrambled up again to flee, only to trip over the root of a tree and go flying again. As he lay on the ground Sanzang raised his head and said, "Bell,

I was just lamenting your fate
When suddenly you clanged.
On this deserted route to the West
Over the years you have turned into a spirit."

The lay brother came over to Sanzang and steadied him as he said, "Please get up, reverend sir. The bell hasn't become a spirit. It was I who struck it just now." Looking up and seeing how dark and ugly the other was Sanzang said, "I suppose you are a goblin or some other evil creature. I am no ordinary man. I come from Great Tang and I have disciples who can subdue dragons and tigers. If you run into them your life will be lost." "Don't be afraid, my lord," replied the lay brother, falling to his knees. "I'm no evil being. I'm a lay brother who looks after the incense here. When I heard those fine things you were saying just now I wanted to come out and welcome you but I was afraid that it might be some demon knocking at the gates. That was why I didn't dare come out until I'd thrown a piece of brick at the bell to calm my fears. Please rise, my lord." Only then did Sanzang calm himself sufficiently to reply, "Lay brother, that fright was almost the death of me. Take me inside."

The lay brother led Sanzang straight in through the third pair of gates. What the Tang Priest saw here was quite different from outside:

A cloud-patterned wall built of blue bricks,
Halls roofed with green glazed tiles.
The holy statues were sheathed in gold,
The steps made of pure white jade.
Blue light danced in the Buddha hall;
Fine vapours rose from the Vairocana chapel.
Above the Manjusri hall
Were decorations of flying clouds;
In the Library of Scriptures
Were patterns of flowers and green leaves.
On the roof above the triple eaves stood a precious jar;

In the Tower of Five Blessings embroidered covers were spread.
A thousand bright bamboos waved over the dhyana seat;
Ten thousand bluish pines threw their light on the gates.
Jade-coloured clouds reflected gold on this palace;
Auspicious clouds drifted round the woods full of purple mist.
Each morning the fragrant breezes could be smelled all around;
In the evening painted drums were heard on the high hills.
There should be morning sunshine to patch torn robes;
How can the sutra be finished by the light of the moon?
The courtyard at the back is lit by half a wall of lamps;
A column of fragrant smoke shines in the hall.

Sanzang saw this but did not dare go inside. "Lay brother," he called, "why is the front of the monastery so dilapidated but the back so neat and tidy?" "My lord," said the lay brother with a smile, "these mountains are full of evil creatures and brigands. On clear days they roam the mountains to rob and on dull ones they shelter in the monastery. They knock the Buddha statues down to use as seats and burn the wooden pillars for firewood. The monks here are too feeble to argue with them, which is why they have abandoned the wrecked buildings at the front for the brigands to stay in. They have found some new benefactors to build the new monastery for them. Now there is one for the pure and one for the impure. This is how we do things in the West." "So that is the way things are," said Sanzang.

As he walked further Sanzang saw written over the gate in large letters SEA-GUARDING MONASTERY OF MEDITATION. Only then did he stride in through the gates, where a monk appeared coming towards him. Just see what the monk looked like:

His hat of velvet and brocade was held with a pin,
And a pair of bronze rings hung from his ears.
His tunic was made of woollen stuff,

And his eyes were white and bright as silver.
He held in his hand a self-beating drum
As he recited scriptures in an unknown tongue.
Sanzang did not know before
That he was a lama on the road to the West.

As the lama came out he saw how very handsome and elegant Sanzang was: clear-browed and fine-eyed with a broad forehead and level top to his skull, ears hanging to his shoulders and arms so long they came below his knees. He looked like an arhat come down to earth. The lama, his face wreathed in smiles, went up to Sanzang chuckling with delight to grab hold of him, feel his hands and feet, rub his nose and tug at his ears as ways of showing his friendliness. After leading Sanzang into the abbot's lodgings and going through the rituals of greeting the lama asked him, "Where have you come from, venerable Father?" "I have been sent by His Majesty the Emperor of Great Tang in the East to worship the Buddha and fetch the scriptures from Thunder Monastery in India in the West," Sanzang replied. "As we were passing this way when it was becoming dark I have come to your distinguished monastery to put up here for the night before leaving early tomorrow morning. I beg you to grant me this expeditious help."

"You shouldn't say that," replied the lama with a smile, "you shouldn't say that. We didn't really want to become monks. We were all given life by our mothers and fathers and only cut our ties with them because we had unlucky destinies and our families could not afford to keep us. Even though we are now disciples of the Buddhist faith you must not talk empty words." "I spoke in all sincerity," Sanzang replied. "However far is the journey from the east to the Western Heaven?" the monk said. "Along the way there are mountains, there are caves in the mountains and there are spirits in the caves. I don't think that a lone traveller looking as delicate as you could possibly be a pilgrim going to fetch the scriptures." "You are quite right, abbot," Sanzang replied. "I could never have got here alone. I have three disciples who clear my way across the mountains and build me bridges over rivers. It is only because they have protected me that I have been able to reach your monastery." "Where are your three distinguished disciples?" the lama asked. "Waiting outside the gates of the monastery," Sanzang replied. "Father," said the lama with alarm, "you don't realize that there are dangerous tigers, wolves, evil bandits, ghosts and demons here. We don't dare roam far even by day and we shut the gates before nightfall. How can you leave people outside this late?" He then told his disciples to ask them in at once.

Two young lamas hurried outside. At the sight of Monkey they fell over, and then fell over again when they saw Pig. Scrambling to their feet they ran back in as fast as they could and said, "My lord, your luck is out. Your disciples have disappeared. There are only three or four evil monsters standing outside the gates." "What do they look like?" Sanzang asked. "One has a face like a thunder god," the young lamas replied, "one has a face like a tilt-hammer, and one has a green face and terrible fangs. There is a girl with them too — she has oiled hair and a powdered face." "You would not know who they are," replied Sanzang with a smile. "The three ugly ones are my disciples and the girl is someone I rescued in the pine forest." "My lord," the lama said, "how can a master as handsome as you have found yourself such ugly disciples?" "Ugly they may be," Sanzang replied, "but they are all useful. Ask them in straight away. If you take any longer the one who looks like a thunder god is a bit of a trouble-maker. He was not born to a mother and father and he will fight his way in."

The young lamas then hurried outside again and fell to their knees, shivering and shaking, as they said, "My lords, Lord Tang invites you in." "Brother," said Pig, "if he's invited us, that's that. Why are they shivering and shaking?" "They're scared because we're so ugly," Monkey replied. "Rubbish," said Pig. "We were born that way. None of us is ugly from choice." "Make yourself look a bit less ugly," said Monkey, and the idiot really did tuck his snout into his tunic and keep his head down as he led the horse while Friar Sand carried the pole and Brother Monkey brought up the rear, holding his cudgel in his hand and dragging the girl along. They went past the ruined buildings and cloisters and in through the third pair of gates. When they had tethered the horse they went into the abbot's lodgings to meet the lama and take their seats in order of precedence. The lama then went inside to lead seventy or eighty young lamas to greet them, tidy their rooms, give them a vegetarian meal and look after them. Indeed,

In storing up achievement be mindful of mercy;
When the Buddha's Dharma flourishes monks admire each other.

If you do not know how they left the monastery, listen to the explanation in the next instalment.

CHAPTER EIGHTY-ONE

The Mind-ape recognizes a monster in the monastery; The three search for their master in Black Pine Forest.

The story tells how Sanzang and his disciples came to the Meditation Monastery where they met the lamas and were given a vegetarian meal. When the four of them had eaten the girl was also fed. By now night was gradually falling and the lamp was lit in the abbot's lodgings. The lamas, who wanted to ask the Tang Priest about why he was going to fetch the scriptures and were also eager for a look at the girl, stood packed together in rows under the lamp. "Abbot," said Sanzang to the lama he had first met, "when we leave your monastery tomorrow what will the road west be like?" Before answering, the lama fell to his knees. Sanzang quickly helped him up and said, "Stand up, please. Why do you greet me in this way when I ask about the road?" "When you travel west tomorrow, reverend sir, you will find that the road is level," the lama replied. "There is no need to worry. There is just one thing at present that is rather awkward. I wanted to tell you about it as soon as you came in, but I was afraid that it would offend your distinguished self. I only venture to tell you now that the meal is over that you will be most welcome to spend the night in the young lamas' room after your long, hard journey from the east. But it would not be right for the lady Bodhisattva to do so. I don't know where I should invite her to sleep." "Your suspicions are not called for, abbot," Sanzang replied, "and you should not suppose that my disciples and I have wicked ideas. When we were coming through Black Pine Forest this morning we found this girl tied to a tree. My disciple Sun Wukong refused to save her, but out of my enlightened heart I rescued her and have brought her here for you to put up, abbot." "As you have been so generous, reverend Father," the abbot replied, "we can set out a straw mattress behind the devarajas in the Devaraja Hall for her to sleep on." "That's splendid," Sanzang said, "splendid." After this the young lamas took the girl to sleep in the back of the hall while in the abbot's lodgings Sanzang urged the officials of the monastery to put themselves at their ease, whereupon they all dispersed. "We have had a hard day," Sanzang said to Brother Monkey. "We must go to bed early and be up early in the morning." They all slept in the same room, guarding the master and not daring to leave him. Later that night

The moon rose high and all was peaceful;
The Street of Heaven was quiet and nobody moved.
Bright was the Silver River; the stars shone clearly;*
The drum in the tower hastened the changing watch.

We will say nothing more of the night. When Monkey rose at first light he told Pig and Friar Sand to get the luggage and the horse ready then urged the master to start out. But Sanzang wanted to sleep longer and would not wake up, so Monkey went up to him to call, "Master." The master raised his head but still could make no reply. "What will you say, Master?" Monkey asked. "Why is my head spinning," Sanzang replied, "why are my eyes swollen, and why am I aching all over from my skin to my bones?" When Pig heard this he stretched out his hand to feel the master's body. It was feverish. "Now I understand," said the idiot with a grin. "He had several bowls too many of last night's free rice and went to sleep head-down. It's indigestion." "Nonsense," shouted Monkey. "Let me ask the master what's really the matter." "When I got up in the middle of the night to relieve myself," Sanzang replied, "I did not put my hat on. I think I must have caught a chill in the wind." "I'm sure you're right," said Monkey. "Can you travel now?" "I cannot even sit up," Sanzang replied, "let alone mount the horse. The

* The Milky Way

journey will have to wait." "What a thing to say, Master," said Monkey. "As the saying goes, 'A teacher for a day is one's father for life.' As your disciples we are like your sons. There's another saying that

A son does not have to shit silver or gold;
As long as he can do what's needed he'll be fine.

If you're not feeling well you shouldn't be worrying about the journey being delayed. There'll be no problem about waiting for a few days." The three brother-disciples all looked after their master. The morning was followed by midday and dusk, and after a good night dawn returned.

Time fled, and three days had soon passed. The morning after that Sanzang tried to sit up, calling, "Wukong, as I have been very ill these last couple of days I have not asked you before: have people been giving food to the lady Bodhisattva we rescued?" "What are you bothering about her for?" laughed Monkey. "What you should be concerned with is your own illness." "Yes, yes," said Sanzang. "Help me up and fetch me paper, brush and ink. Borrow an inkstone here in the monastery." "What do you want them for?" Monkey asked. "I want to write a letter," Sanzang replied. "I shall seal it up with our passport and ask you to deliver it for me to His Majesty Emperor Taizong in Chang'an." "Easy," said Monkey. "I may not be much good at anything else, but when it comes to delivering letters I'm the champion of the whole world. So wrap the letter up and give it to me. I'll take it to Chang'an in a single somersault, give it to the Tang Emperor, and come back with another somersault before your brush and inkstone have dried up. But why do you want to write a letter? Tell me what you want to say in the letter — you can write it down later." "This is what I will write," said Sanzang, weeping:

"Your subject beats his head three times upon the ground,
With a triple shout of 'Long live Your Majesty' as I bow to my lord.

The civil and military officials are all present,
And four hundred courtiers all listen to what is said.

Years ago I left the East on your command,
Hoping to see the Buddha on the Vulture Peak.
But on my journey I have met with obstructions;
And been delayed by unexpected disaster along the way.

My illness is grave; I cannot move one step;
The gate to Buddha is as distant as the gate to heaven.
I will not live to bring back the scriptures;
I submit with respect that a new envoy should be sent."

When Monkey heard this he could not help bursting out into uproarious laughter. "You're hopeless, Master," he said, "thinking that sort of thing after just a touch of illness. If you were seriously ill you'd only have to ask me to find out whether you were going to live or die. I have my own special way of dealing with it. I'd ask, 'Which king of the Underworld dared think of this? Which of the judges issued the warrant? Which demon messenger is coming to fetch him?' If they make me angry I'll lose my temper the way I did when I made havoc in Heaven, smash my way into the Underworld with my cudgel, capture the ten kings and rip the sinews out of every one of them. I'll show them no mercy." "Stop that boasting, disciple," Sanzang replied. "I am very ill."

"Brother," said Pig, going up to him, "it's very awkward to have the master saying he's in a bad way and you insisting he isn't. Let's settle things as quickly as we can, sell the horse, pawn the luggage, buy a coffin to bury the master in and split up." "You're talking out of turn again, you idiot," Monkey replied. "What you don't realize is that the master used to be our Tathagata Buddha's second disciple. His original name was the Venerable Golden Cicada. This is a great hardship he has to endure because he once slighted the Buddha's Dharma." "But, brother," Pig replied, "even if the master did slight the Buddha's Dharma he was exiled to the East and born into another body amid the sea of right and wrong and the battlefield of tongues.

He swore an oath to go to the Western Heaven, worship the Buddha and fetch the scriptures. Every time he's met an evil spirit he's been tied up; and every time he's come across a monster he's been hung up. He's had to put up with every kind of agony. That should be enough. Why has he had to be ill as well?" "This is something you wouldn't know about," Monkey replied. "The master once dropped off to sleep instead of listening to the Buddha teaching the Dharma, and as he drowsed he trod on a grain of rice with his left foot. That is why he has to be ill for three days in the lower world." "So goodness only knows how many years someone who eats as messily as I do will have to be ill," replied a shocked Pig. "Brother," Monkey replied, "the Buddha will spare ordinary creatures such as you. There's something else you don't know. As the poet said,

Hoeing millet in the noonday sun:
Sweat drops on the ground beneath the millet.
Who understands that of the food that's in the bowl,
Every single grain was won through bitter toil?

The master will only be ill today. Tomorrow he'll be better." "I am feeling different today from how I did yesterday," said Sanzang. "My throat is absolutely parched. Go and find some cold water somewhere for me to drink." "Fine," Monkey replied. "If water's what you want, Master, that means you're better. I'll go and fetch some."

Monkey at once took the begging bowl and went to the kitchen at the back of the monastery, where he came across all the monks red-eyed and sobbing with grief. The only thing was that they dared not cry aloud. "Don't be so petty, little monks," said Brother Monkey. "Before we leave we'll thank you for the days we've spent here, and we'll pay for our cooking fuel and lighting by the day. You really shouldn't be such pustules." "We wouldn't dare accept it," the lamas said at once, falling to their knees, "we wouldn't dare." "What do you mean, you wouldn't dare?" said Monkey. "It must be that long-snouted monk of ours who has an enormous appetite. He'd eat you out of house and home." "My lord," the lamas replied, "there are over a hundred senior and junior lamas in this monastery. If each of us kept you for a single day we could afford to support you for over a hundred days. We're not the sort of skinflints who'd calculate what you will cost us in food."

"If you're not working out the cost then why are you sobbing?" Monkey asked. "Lord," the lamas replied, "there's an evil monster in the monastery. We don't know which mountain it's from. Last night we sent two junior lamas to strike the bell and beat the drum. We heard the sound of the bell and the drum but the lamas never came back. When we looked for them the next day all we found were their monk's hats and shoes lying in the courtyard at the back and their skeletons. They had been eaten. In the three days you have been here six lamas have disappeared from the monastery. That's why we can't help being frightened and grieved. When we realized that your venerable master was ill we couldn't stop these tears stealing out even though we kept the news to ourselves."

"Say no more," said Brother Monkey, who was both shocked and delighted by what he heard. "It must be an evil monster who's killing people here. I'll wipe it out for you." "My lord," the lamas replied, "any evil spirit worthy of the name has magical powers. It's bound to be able to ride clouds, come out of the underworld and disappear again. As the ancients put it so well, 'Trust not the straightest of the straight; beware of the inhuman human.' Please don't take offence, my lord, when we say that if you can rid our monastery of this scourge that would be a great happiness for us. But if you can't catch it things will be pretty difficult." "What do you mean by things being pretty difficult?" Monkey asked. "We will be honest with you, my lord," the lamas replied. "Although there are only a hundred or so of us lamas in this monastery we all became monks as children:

When our hair grows we have it shaved off;
Our clothes are patched with rags.
We rise in the morning to wash our faces,
Then bow with hands together

In submission to the Great Way.
At night we tidy up, burn incense,
And piously pray,
Chanting the name of Amitabha.
When we look up we see the Buddha
On his ninefold lotus throne
Well-versed in the Three Vehicles,
Riding in his mercy on clouds of dharma,
And we long to see the Sakyamuni in the Jeta Park.
Looking down we see into our hearts,
Accept the Five Prohibitions,
Pass through a thousand aeons,
And live each life amid the countless dharmas,
Hoping to understand emptiness and the impermanence of matter.
When the benefactors come,
Old, young, tall, short, fat, thin,
We each beat wooden fish,
Strike bronze chimes,
Slowly and deliberately,
With the two rolls of the Lotus Sutra
And the short Litany of the Emperor of Liang.
When the benefactors do not come,
New, old, strange, familiar, rustic, smart,
We put our hands together,
Eyes shut,
Silent,
Entering meditation on the rush mats,
Firmly closing the gates under the moon.
Let the orioles sing and other birds chirp in idle strife:
They cannot mount our expeditious and compassionate chariot of dharma.
This is why we cannot subdue tigers and dragons,
Or recognize monsters and spirits.
If, my lord, you provoked the evil monster,
To which we hundred and more lamas would be but a single meal,

All of us living creatures would fall to the wheel of rebirth,
This ancient monastery of meditation would be destroyed,
And finally there would be no light at the Tathagata's assembly.
This would cause great troubles."

When Brother Monkey heard the lamas say this anger surged up from his heart and hatred from his gall. "What a stupid lot you lamas are!" he shouted at the top of his voice. "Are you only aware of those evil spirits? Do you know nothing of what I've done?" "Really we don't," the lamas replied in very quiet voices. "Then I'll tell you briefly about it", Monkey said.

"I used to subdue tigers and dragons on the Mountain of Flowers and Fruit;
I once went up to Heaven and made great havoc in its palace.
When I was hungry I nibbled just two or three
Of Lord Lao Zi's elixir tablets;
When I was thirsty I sipped six or seven cups
Of the Jade Emperor's own wine.
When I glare with my golden eyes that are neither black nor white,
The sky turns deathly pale
While the moon is hidden in cloud.
When I wield my gold-banded cudgel that's the right length,
It strikes unseen
And leaves no trace behind.
What do I care about big or little monsters,
However rough or vicious they may be?
Once I go for them
They may run away, tumble about, hide or panic.
Whenever I grab one
They'll be filed down, cooked, ground to bits or pulverized in a mortar.

I'm like one of the eight immortals crossing the sea,
Each of whom gives a unique display of his magical powers.
Lamas, I'll catch that evil spirit and show it to you:
Then you'll know what sort of person this Monkey is."

When the lamas heard this they nodded and said quietly, "From the way this damned baldy is shooting his mouth off and talking big there must be something behind it all." They all made polite noises of respectful assent except for the older lama who said, "Wait. Your master is ill, and catching the evil spirit is not as important as that. As the saying goes,

When a young gentleman goes to a feast
He either gets drunk or eats till he's filled.
When a strong warrior goes into battle
He either is wounded or gets himself killed.

If you two fight it out here you may well get your master into trouble too. It's not a sound idea."

"You're right," said Monkey, "you're right. I'll take my master a drink of cold water and be right back." Picking up the begging bowl he filled it with cold water, went out of the monastery kitchen and back to the abbot's lodgings and called, "Master, cold water for you." Sanzang, who was just then suffering torments of thirst, raised his head, held the bowl with both hands, and took only one sip of the water. It really was a case of

A drop when you're thirsty is just like sweet dew;
Get the right medicine and you'll feel good as new.

Seeing the venerable elder gradually recovering his spirits and looking less worried Monkey asked, "Could you manage some soup and other food, Master?" "That cold water was a magical cure," Sanzang replied. "I have already half recovered from my illness. I would like some food if there is any." "The master's better," Monkey shouted repeatedly at the top of his voice. "He wants some soup and other food." He told the lamas to arrange some at once. They washed and boiled rice, made noodles, cooked pancakes, steamed breadrolls, and prepared vermicelli soup. Four or five tables of food were carried in, but the Tang Priest ate only half a bowl of rice gruel, while Monkey and Friar Sand managed only a tableful between them. Pig gobbled up the rest. The dishes were then taken out, the lamp was lit, and the lamas dispersed.

"How long have we been here now?" Sanzang asked. "Three whole days," Monkey replied. "By tomorrow evening it will be four days." "We could have covered a lot of distance in three days," Sanzang replied. "Never mind about the distance, Master," said Monkey. "We'll be on our way tomorrow." "Yes," said Sanzang, "even if I am still a little poorly there is nothing that can be done." "If we're setting out tomorrow let me catch the evil spirit tonight," said Monkey. "What evil spirit?" Sanzang asked in astonishment. "There's an evil spirit in this monastery that I'm going to catch for them," Monkey replied. "But how can you be having ideas like that before I have even recovered from my illness?" Sanzang asked. "If that monster has magical powers and you fail to catch it, then it will kill me, won't it?"

"You're always running people down," Monkey replied. "Wherever we go I subdue evil creatures. Have you ever seen me come off second best? That could only happen if I did nothing. If I act I'm bound to win." "Disciple," said Sanzang, clutching him, "the saying is quite right that goes:

Do people a good turn whenever you can;
If it is possible treat them with mercy.
Worrying cannot compare with true kindness;
Better be patient than strive for supremacy."

In the face of his master's impassioned pleas and refusal to allow him to subdue the monster, Monkey could only speak frankly. "I'll be honest with you, Master," he said. "The evil spirit has been eating people here." "Who has it eaten?" Sanzang asked with shock. "In the three days we've been here it's eaten six of this monastery's young lamas," Monkey said, to which Sanzang replied:

"Foxes will grieve at the death of the hare;
Creatures will all for their own kind show care.

As it has eaten monks from this monastery and I am a monk too I will let you go, but do be careful." "No need to tell me," said Monkey. "I'll wipe it out the moment I get my hands on it."

Watch him as he tells Pig and Friar Sand in the lamplight to guard the master. When he leapt happily out of the abbot's lodgings and went back to the Buddha Hall he looked and saw that though there were stars in the sky the moon had not yet risen and it was dark inside the hall. He breathed out some of his magic fire to light the glazed lamp then beat the drum that stood to the east and struck the bell to the west. That done, he shook himself and turned himself into a young lama of only eleven or twelve who was wearing a yellow silk shirt and a white cotton tunic, striking a wooden fish with his hand as he recited a sutra. He waited till the first watch without seeing anything happen. The waning moon rose only in the second watch. Then a roaring wind could be heard. It was a splendid wind:

Black mists cast the sky into darkness;
Gloomy clouds cover the earth with murk.
Inky black in every quarter,
All enveloped in indigo.
At first the wind raises dust and dirt;
Then it blows down trees and ravages woods.
Amid the dust and dirt the stars still shine;
When trees go down and woods are ravaged the moonlight is obscured.
It blows so hard the Moon Goddess holds tight to the sala tree
And the Jade Hare hunts all around for the medicine dish.
The Nine Bright Shiner star lords shut their gates;
The dragon kings of the four seas close their doors.
The city god in his temple looks for the little devils;
Immortals in the sky cannot ride their clouds.

The kings of the Underworld search for their horse-faced demons
While the panicking judges get their turbans in a tangle.
The wind blows so hard it moves Mount Kunlun's rocks,
And churns up the waves on rivers and lakes.

As soon as the wind had passed by there was a fragrance of musk and incense and the tinkling of pendants. When Monkey looked up he saw that a woman of great beauty was going towards the Buddha Hall. Monkey mumbled the words of a sutra for all he was worth. The woman went up to him, put her arms around him and asked, "What's that sutra you're reciting?" "One I vowed to," said Monkey. "But why are you still reciting it when the others are all asleep?" she insisted. "I vowed to, so why shouldn't I?" Monkey replied. Keeping a tight hold on him, the woman kissed his lips and said, "Let's go round the back for a bit of fun." Monkey deliberately turned his head aside as he replied, "Stop being so naughty." "Do you know how to tell people's fortunes from their faces?" the woman asked. "I know a bit about it," Monkey replied. "What can you tell about me?" she continued. "You look to me rather like someone who's been driven out by her parents-in-law for carrying on with strangers." "You're wrong," she replied, "you're wrong.

I have not been driven out by my parents-in-law,
Nor have I carried on with strangers.
Because of my ill fate in an earlier life
I was married to a husband who is much too young
And can't do his stuff in the candlelit bedroom:
That is the reason why I have left my husband.

As the stars and moon are so bright tonight and we are fated to come hundreds of miles to meet each other, let's go round to the garden at the back to make love." When Brother Monkey heard this he nodded to himself and thought, "So those stupid lamas all died because they were led astray by lust. Now she's trying to lure me. Lady," he said in reply, "I'm a monk and still very young. I don't know anything about love-making." "Come with me and I'll teach you," the woman replied. "All right then," Monkey thought with an inward smile, "I'll go with her and see how she fixes things."

Shoulder nestling against shoulder and hand in hand the two of them left the Buddha Hall and went straight to the garden at the back. Here the monster tripped Monkey over and sent him to the ground. With wild calls of "My darling" she made a grab for his tool. "So you really want to eat me up, my girl," he said, seizing her hand and throwing her off balance so that she somersaulted to the ground. "So you can throw your sweetie to the ground, can you, my darling?" she said. "If I don't take this chance to finish her off what am I waiting for?" he thought. "As they say, hit first and win, strike second and lose." He leaned forward with his hands on his hips, sprang to his feet and reverted to his own form. With a swing of his gold-banded iron cudgel he struck at the monster's head. In her astonishment she thought, "What a terror this young monk is." When she opened her eyes wide for a better look she realized that he was the Tang Priest's disciple Monkey, but she was not afraid of him. What sort of evil spirit was she, you may wonder.

A golden nose,
Snowy white fur.
She makes her home in a tunnel,
Where she is thoroughly safe.
Three hundred years ago, after training her vital forces,
She paid several visits to the Vulture Peak,
Carrying a full load of flowers and wax candles.
Tathagata sent her down from Heaven.
She was a beloved daughter to the Pagoda-carrying Heavenly King;
Prince Nezha treated her as his own sister.
She was no bird that fills up the sea,
Nor was she a tortoise carrying mountains on its back.

*She did not fear Lei Huan's swords**
*Nor was she afraid of Lü Qian's blade.***
She came and went
Flowing like the mighty Han and Yangtse;
Moved up and down,
Even up a peak as high as Mounts Taishan and Heng.
Seeing the charming beauty of her face
You would never know she was a mouse-spirit with great powers.

In her pride in her enormous magic powers she held up a pair of swords that rang out as she parried to left and right, moving east and west. Although Monkey was rather stronger he could not overpower her. Then magic winds arose on all sides, dimming the waning moon. It was fine battle they fought in the garden at the back:

Evil winds blew from the ground;
Dim was the light of the waning moon.
Deserted was the hall of the Brahma Kings,
And the devils' cloister could not be clearly seen.
The back garden saw a battle
Between the warrior Sun,
A sage in Heaven,
And the furry girl,
A queen among women,
Both competing in magical powers and refusing to submit.
One turned her heart in anger from the dark-skinned baldy;
The other glared with his all-seeing eyes at the finely dressed woman.
With swords in her hands,
She is no female Bodhisattva.

---

* Lei Huan was said to have found a pair of magical swords in Western Jin times.

** At about the same time Lü Qian had a sword that he was told only a very senior official could wear, so he gave it away.

The blows of the cudgel
Were as fierce as a living vajrapani's.
The resounding golden band flashed like lightning;
For an instant the iron shone white as a star.
In fine buildings they grabbed at the precious jade;
In golden halls the mandarin duck figurines were smashed.
As the apes howled the moon seemed small;
Vast was the sky as wild geese called.
The eighteen arhats
Applauded in secret;
Each of the thirty-two devas
Was struck with panic.

The Great Sage Monkey was in such high spirits that his cudgel never missed. Realizing that she was no match for him, the evil spirit frowned suddenly and thought of a plan as she extricated herself and made off. "Where do you think you're going, you baggage?" Monkey shouted. "Surrender at once". The evil spirit paid no attention and fled. When she was hard-pressed by Monkey's pursuit she took the embroidered shoe off her left foot, blew on it with a magic breath, said the words of a spell, called out, "Change!" and turned it into a likeness of herself that came back at him waving a pair of swords. Meanwhile she turned her real body with a shake into a pure breeze and went. This was Sanzang's star of disaster. She headed straight for the abbot's quarters, lifted Sanzang up into a cloud, and, on the instant, before anyone could see anything, she was back at Mount Pitfall and inside the Bottomless Cave, where she told her underlings to prepare a vegetarian marriage feast.

The story switches back to Brother Monkey, who fought with desperate anxiety until he was able to seize an opening and smash the evil spirit to the ground with a single blow, only to find that she was in fact an embroidered shoe. Realizing that he had fallen for a trick he went straight back to see the master. But was the master there? There were only the idiot and Friar Sand muttering together. His chest bursting with fury, Monkey put all thought of what he ought to do out of his head and raised his cudgel to lay about him. "I'll kill the pair of you," he shouted, "I'll kill the pair of you."

The idiot was desperate, but there was no way for him to escape. Friar Sand, however, as a general from the magic mountain who had seen a great deal adopted a very mild and conciliatory approach as he stepped forward, knelt down and said, "Elder brother, I understand. I'm sure that after you've killed us two you intend to go straight back home instead of rescuing the master." "When I've killed you two I'm going to rescue him myself," Monkey retorted. "How can you say that?" replied Friar Sand with a smile. "Without us two it would be a case of

You can't spin a thread from only one strand
Or clap with the palm of a single hand.

Who'd look after the luggage or the horse for you? We'd do much better to forget our differences and fight side by side like Guan Zhong and Bao Shuya than to have a battle of wits like Sun Bin and Pang Juan. As the old saying goes,

To kill a tiger you need your brothers' help;
Have fathers and sons fight together in battle.

I hope you will spare us, brother, so that tomorrow morning we can all work together with a single mind in our search for the master." Although his magical powers were tremendous Monkey knew what was right and needed at the time, so that Friar Sand's entreaties made him change his mind. "Get up, Pig and Friar Sand," he said. "But when we hunt for the master tomorrow you'll have to make a real effort." The idiot was so grateful at being let off that he would gladly have promised Monkey half the sky. "Brother," he said, "leave it all to me." The three brother disciples were so anxious that none of them could sleep. They wished they could make the sun rise in the east with a nod of the head and blow all the stars out of the sky with a single breath.

After sitting there till dawn the three of them packed up and were about to get out, only to find the gateway barred by one of the lamas, who asked, "Where are you going, gentlemen?" "This is most embarrassing," Monkey replied with a smile. "Yesterday I boasted to all the monks that I'd capture the evil spirit for them. So far from me capturing her she's made my master disappear. We're off to look for him." "My lord," said the lamas with horror, "our trivial problem has got your master involved. Where will you look for him?" "I know where I'll look," Monkey replied. "Even though you're going please don't be in such a hurry," said the lamas. "Have some breakfast first." Two or three bowls of hot gruel were brought in that Pig cleaned up with great gusto. "What fine monks," he said. "When we've found the master we'll come back here to see you again." "What you mean is come back to eat their food," said Monkey. "Go and see if the girl is still in the devarajas' hall." "She's gone, my lord," the lamas said, "she's gone. She has spent only one night there and is gone the next morning."

Monkey cheerfully took his leave of the lamas and made Pig and Friar Sand lead the horse and carry the luggage as they headed back east. "Brother," said Pig, "you're wrong. Why are we going east?" "You wouldn't know," said Monkey. "That girl who was tied up in the Black Pine Forest the other day — I saw through her with my fiery eyes and golden pupils, but you all thought she was a good person. And now it's her who's eaten the monks and her who's carried the master off. You all did a fine thing rescuing that 'lady Bodhisattva'. As she's carried the master off we're going back the way we came to look for her." "Good, good," sighed the other two with admiration. "You're much cleverer than you look. Let's go."

The three of them hurried back into the forest, where this was what could be seen:

> *Piles of cloud,*
> *Heavy mists,*
> *Many a layer of rock,*
> *A twisting path.*
> *The tracks of foxes and hares cross each other;*

Tiger, leopard, jackal and wolf move in and out of the undergrowth.
With no sign of a monster to be seen in the wood
They do not know where Sanzang might be found.

In his anxiety Monkey pulled out his cudgel, shook himself and made himself look as he had when he made great havoc in Heaven, with three heads, six arms and six hands wielding three cudgels. With these he lashed out furiously and noisily among the trees. "Friar Sand," said Pig when he saw this, "not finding the master has made him go off his head." In fact Monkey had beat a way through the trees and flushed out two old men — the mountain god and the local deity — who went up to him, knelt down and said, "Great Sage, the god of this mountain and the local deity pay their respects." "That rod certainly gets results," said Pig. "He clears a path with it and flushes out the mountain god and the local deity. If he cleared another path he'd even flush out an evil star."

"Mountain god, local deity," said Monkey, "you're a disgrace. You're hand in glove with the bandits here. When they make a good haul they buy pigs and sheep to sacrifice to you. On top of that you're accomplices of the evil spirit. You helped her kidnap my master and bring him here. Where's he being hidden? If you want to be spared a beating tell me the truth right now."

"Great Sage," the two gods said with alarm, "you are misjudging us. The evil spirit doesn't live on our mountain or come within our jurisdiction. But when the wind blows at night we have heard a thing or two about her." "Tell me everything you know," said Monkey. "The evil spirit carried your master off to a place over three hundred miles due south of here," the local deity replied. "There's a mountain there called Mount Pitfall with a cave in it called the Bottomless Cave. He was taken there by a disguised evil spirit from that cave." This news gave Monkey a shock that he did not reveal. Shouting at the mountain god and the local deity to dismiss them he put his magical appearance away, turned back into himself and said to Pig and

Friar Sand, "The master's a long way from here." "If it's a long way let's go there by cloud," Pig replied.

The splendid idiot went ahead on a wild wind followed by Friar Sand on a cloud. As the white horse had originally been a dragon's son he too came by wind and mist as he carried the luggage on his back. The Great Sage set off by somersault as he headed due south, and before long a high mountain came into view that was blocking the way for the clouds. The three of them took hold of the horse and stopped their clouds. This is what the mountain looked like:

The summit touched the azure sky,
Its peaks joined with the blue of the heavens.
Trees by the million grew on every side,
While flying birds sung noisily all around.
Tigers and leopards moved in packs,
Water deer and roebuck walked through the bushes.
On the southern slopes rare flowers bloomed fragrant;
On the northern side the snow never melted.
Steep and craggy were its ridges,
Sheer were its overhangs and rockfaces.
Pinnacles shot straight up
And deep ravines curved all around.
It was dark green among the pines,
And the rocks were jagged.
It struck fear into the travellers' heart.
No sign could be seen of woodcutters,
And the immortal boys picking herbs had vanished.
The tigers and leopards here could make mists,
And all the foxes set winds roaring.

"Brother," said Pig, "this mountain's so high and sheer there must be evil on it." "Goes without saying," Monkey replied. "High mountains all have monsters; there's never a steep ridge without spirits. Friar Sand," he called, "you and I are going to stay here while we send Pig into the mountain hollows to look around and find out the best way for us to take. If there really is a cave palace he must discover where the entrance is. Find everything out so that we can go in together to find the master and rescue him." "Just my lousy luck," said Pig, "having to go first and take the brunt." "Last night you said we could leave it all to you," Monkey replied, "so why are you trying to get out of it now?" "Stop shouting at me," Pig said. "I'm going." The idiot put down his rake, tugged at his clothes and leapt empty-handed down from the mountain to find the path. If you don't know whether this departure was to be for good or ill listen to the explanation in the next instalment.

CHAPTER EIGHTY-TWO

The girl seeks the male;
The primal deity guards the Way.

The story tells how Pig leapt down the mountainside and found a narrow path. After following it for nearly two miles he came across two she-monsters drawing water from a well. How did he know that they both were monsters? Each of them had on her head an extremely unfashionable hair-style held up by bamboo slivers that stood one foot two or three inches high. "Evil monsters," Pig called, going up to them. The two of them looked at each other and said, "What an outrageous monk. We don't know him and we've never had words with him. So why did he call us evil monsters?" In their fury the monsters raised the pole with which they were going to carry the water and struck at Pig's head.

After a few blows that he could not ward off as he was unarmed the idiot rushed back up the mountain with his head covered by both hands shouting, "Brother! Go back! The monsters are vicious." "What's so vicious about them?" Monkey asked. "There were two evil spirits drawing water from the well in the hollow," said Pig, "and they hit me three or four times with their carrying-pole just because I spoke to them." "What did you call them?" Monkey asked. "Evil monsters," Pig replied. "You got off lightly then," laughed Monkey. "I'm most obliged for your concern," replied Pig. "My head has swollen up where they hit it, and you tell me I've got off lightly." "Soft words will get you anywhere on earth; act rough and you won't move a single step," replied Monkey. "As they're local fiends from round here and we're monks from far away you'd have had to be a bit polite even if you'd had fists growing all over your body. Do you think they should have hit me instead of you? You were the one who called them evil monsters. Courtesy first!" "I never realized," said Pig. "Living on human flesh in the mountains since childhood as you have," said Monkey, "can you recognize two kinds of tree?" "I don't know," Pig said. "Which two trees?" "The willow and the sandalwood," Monkey replied. "The willow has a very soft nature, so that craftsmen can carve it into holy images or make statues of the Tathagata out of it. It's gilded, painted, set with jewels, decorated with flowers, and many worshippers burn incense to it. It receives unbounded blessings. But the sandalwood is so hard that it's used as the pressing-beam in the oil-press with iron hoops round its head, and it's hit with iron hammers too. The only reason it suffers like this is because it's so hard." "You should have told me all this before," said Pig, "then I wouldn't have been beaten."

"Now go back and find out the truth," said Brother Monkey. "But if I go there again they'll recognize me," Pig replied. "Then turn into something else," said Monkey. "But even if I do turn into something else, brother, how am I to question them?" asked Pig. "When you look different go up to them and bow to them," Monkey replied. "See how old they are. If they're about the same age as us call them 'Miss', and if they're a lot older call them 'Lady'." "What a terrible climb-down: why should we be treating them as our relations when they're strangers from this far away?" said Pig. "That's not treating them as relations," replied Monkey. "It's just a way of getting the truth out of them. If they're the ones who've got our master we'll be able to act; and if it isn't them we won't lose any time before going to fight elsewhere." "You're right," said Pig. "I'm going back."

The splendid idiot tucked his rake in his belt, went down into the hollow, shook himself and turned into a fat, dark-skinned monk. He swaggered as he went up to the monsters, chanted a loud "na-a-aw" of respect and said, "Respectful greetings, ladies." "This monk's much better," the two monsters said with delight. "He expresses his respects and knows how to address us properly." Then they asked him, "Where are you from, venerable elder?" "From somewhere," Pig replied. "And where are you going?" they asked. "Somewhere," Pig replied. "What's your name?" they asked. "What it is," Pig replied again. "Better he may be," the monsters said with a laugh, "but he won't tell us about himself. He just echoes our questions." "Ladies," Pig asked, "why are you fetching water?" "You wouldn't know, monk," the demons replied with smiles. "Our lady brought a Tang Priest back to the cave last night and she wants to look after him well. As the water in our cave is none too clean she's sent us two to fetch some of this good water produced by the mating of the Yin and the Yang. She's laid on a vegetarian banquet as well for the Tang Priest: she's going to marry him this evening."

As soon as he heard this the idiot rushed straight back up the mountain shouting, "Friar Sand, bring the luggage here at once. We're dividing it up." "Why, brother?" Friar Sand asked. "When we've divided it up you can go back to man-eating in the Flowing Sands River," Pig replied, "I'll return to Gao Village to see my wife, Big Brother can play the sage on the Mountain of Flowers and Fruit, and the white dragon can be a dragon in the ocean again. The master's getting married in this evil spirits' cave. Let's all go and settle down." "You're talking nonsense again, you idiot," replied Brother Monkey. "I bloody well am not," Pig retorted. "Those two evil spirits who were carrying water said a moment ago that a vegetarian wedding feast is being laid on for the master." "How can you say things like that when the evil spirits are holding the master prisoner in the cave and he's longing for us to go in and rescue him?" said Monkey. "How can we rescue him?" Pig asked. "You two bring the horse and the luggage, while we go with the two she-monsters as our guides," Monkey replied. "When we reach the entrance we can act together."

The idiot could only go with Monkey as he followed the two monsters for five or six miles deep into the mountains before suddenly disappearing. "So the master was captured by a devil in broad daylight," exclaimed Pig with surprise. "You've got good eyesight," said Monkey. "How can you possibly tell what they really were?" "Those two monsters were carrying the water along when suddenly they disappeared. They must be daytime devils." "I think they went into a cave," said Monkey. "Wait while I go to have a look."

The splendid Great Sage opened his fiery eyes with their golden pupils and scanned the whole mountain. He saw no movement, but did spot a ceremonial archway most intricately made with many flowers and colours, triple eaves and fourfold decorations in front of the cliff. Going closer with Pig and Friar Sand he saw four large words written on it:

PITFALL MOUNTAIN: BOTTOMLESS CAVE

"Brothers," said Monkey, "here's the evil spirits' archway, but I still don't know where the entrance is." "Can't be far," said Friar Sand, "can't be far. Let's have a good look for it." When they turned round to look they saw a great rock over three miles around at the foot of the mountain beneath the archway. In the middle of it was a hole the size of a water-vat, which had become very slippery by repeated climbing. "Brother," said Pig, "that's where the evil spirits go in and out of their cave." "That's very strange," said Monkey. "To be frank with the two of you, I've captured quite a few evil spirits since I started escorting the Tang Priest, but I've never seen a cave palace like this one before. Pig, you go down first and find out how deep it is. Then I'll be able to go in and rescue the master." "It'll be hard," said Pig with a shake of his head, "very hard. I'm very clumsy. If I tripped and fell in it might take me two or three years to reach the bottom." "How deep is it then?" Monkey asked. "Look," Pig replied, and as the Great Sage leant over the edge of the hole to take a careful look he saw to his astonishment that it was very deep indeed and must have measured over a hundred miles around. "It's very, very deep, brother," he turned round to say. "Go back then," Pig replied. "The master's beyond saving." "What a thing to say!" Monkey retorted. " 'Have no thoughts of being lazy; put idleness out of your mind.' Put the luggage down, and tether the horse to one of the legs of the archway. You and Friar Sand must block the entrance with your rake and staff while I go inside to explore. If the master really is inside I'll drive the evil spirits out with my iron cudgel, and when they reach the entrance you mustn't let them out. We'll only be able to kill the evil spirits and rescue the master if we work together." The other two accepted their orders.

Monkey sprang into the hole, and under his feet ten thousand coloured clouds appeared, while a thousand layers of auspicious mist shielded him. He was soon at the bottom, which was a very long way down. Inside all was bright; there was the same sunshine, winds, flowers, fruit and trees as in the world above. "What a splendid place," Monkey thought. "It reminds me of the Water Curtain Cave that Heaven gave me in the place where I was born. This is another cave paradise." As he looked around he saw a gate-tower with double eaves around which grew many clumps of pine and bamboo. Inside were many buildings. "This must be where the evil spirit lives," he thought. "I'll go in and find out what's up. No, wait. If I go in like this she'll recognize me. I'd better transform myself." With a shake and a hand-spell he turned himself into a fly and flew lightly up to land on the gate-tower and listen in. From here he saw the monster sitting at her ease in a thatched pavilion. She was dressed far more beautifully than she had been when they rescued her in the pine forest or when she had tried to catch Monkey in the monastery:

Her hair was piled in a crow-black coiffure;
She wore a green velvet waistcoat.
Her feet were a pair of curving golden lotuses;
Her fingers were as delicate as bamboo shoots in spring.
Her powdered face was like a silver dish,
And her red lips were as glossy as a cherry.
She was a regular beauty,
Even more lovely than the lady on the moon.
After capturing the pilgrim monk that morning
She was going to know the pleasure of sharing his bed.

Monkey said nothing as he listened out for what she might say. Before long the cherry of her lips parted as she said with great pleasure, "Lay on a vegetarian feast, my little ones, and quick.

My darling Tang Priest and I are going to be man and wife afterwards." "So it's true," thought Brother Monkey, grinning to himself. "I thought Pig was just joking. I'd better fly in and find the master. I wonder what state of mind he's in. If he's been led astray I'm leaving him here." When he spread his wings and flew inside to look he saw the Tang Priest sitting in a corridor behind a trellis covered with opaque red paper below and left clear above.

Butting a hole through the trellis paper Monkey landed on the Tang Priest's bald head and called, "Master." "Save me, disciple," replied Sanzang, who recognized Monkey's voice. "You're useless, Master," said Monkey. "The evil spirit is laying on a feast, and when you've eaten it you two are getting married. I expect you'll have a son or a daughter to start another generation of monks and nuns. What have you got to be so upset about?" When the venerable elder heard this he gnashed his teeth and said, "Disciple, in all the time since I left Chang'an, accepted you as my follower at the Double Boundary Mountain and started my journey west, when have I ever eaten meat or had any wicked ideas? Now the evil spirit has captured me she is insisting that I mate with her. If I lose my true masculine essence may I fall from the wheel of reincarnation and be fixed for ever behind the Dark Mountains, never to rise again."

"No need to swear any oaths," said Monkey with a grin. "If you really want to fetch the scriptures from the Western Heaven I'll take you there." "I can't remember the way I came in," Sanzang replied. "Never mind about forgetting," said Monkey. "You won't get out of here as easily as you came in, which was from the top downwards. If I save you now you'll have to go from the bottom upwards. If you're very lucky you'll squeeze out through the entrance and get away. But if your luck's out you won't be able to squeeze through and sooner or later you'll die of suffocation." "This is terrible," said Sanzang, the tears pouring from his eyes. "What are we to do?" "No problem," said Monkey, "no problem. The evil spirit's getting some wine prepared for you. You'll have to drink a goblet of it whether you want to or not. But you must pour it out quickly so that it makes a lot of froth. Then I can turn myself into a tiny insect and fly under the bubbles. When she gulps me down into her belly I'll tear her heart and liver to shreds and rip her guts apart. Once I've killed her you'll be able to escape." "But that would be an inhuman thing to do, disciple," said Sanzang. "If all you're interested in is being kind you're done for," Monkey replied. "The evil spirit's a murderess. What do you care so much about her for?" "Oh well," said Sanzang, "never mind. But you will have to stay with me." Indeed,

The Great Sage Sun guarded Tang Sanzang well;
The pilgrim priest depended on the Handsome Monkey King.

Master and disciple had not even finished their discussion when the evil spirit, who had arranged everything, came in along the corridor, unlocked the doors and called, "Reverend sir." The Tang Priest dared not reply. She addressed him again, and again he dared not reply. Why was that? He was thinking that

Divine energy is dispersed by an open mouth;
Trouble starts when the tongue begins to move.

He was thinking with all his heart that if he obstinately refused to open his mouth she might turn vicious and murder him in an instant. Just when he was feeling confused, wondering which difficult alternative to choose and asking himself what to do, the evil spirit addressed him as "Reverend sir" for the third time. The Tang Priest had no choice but to answer, "Here I am, madam." For him to give this reply was to make all the flesh fall off him. Now everybody says that the Tang Priest is a sincere monk, so how could he reply to the she-devil when he was on his way to worship the Buddha and fetch the scriptures from the Western Heaven? What you would not realize is that this was a crisis in which his very survival was at stake, so that he had absolutely no alternative; and although he went through the form of replying he was free of desire inside. But when the evil spirit heard his reply she pushed the door open, helped the Tang Priest to his feet, held his hand, stood with her side pressed against his and whispered in his ear. Just look at her as she lays on the charm and makes herself alluring in every possible way. She did not realize that Sanzang was full of revulsion. "From the way she's making herself so seductive," Monkey thought with a wry grin to himself, "I'm worried that she might get the master interested." Indeed,

The monk in demon trouble met a pretty girl;
The she-devil's beauty was truly superb.
Her slender jade eyebrows were like two willow leaves;
Her round face was set off with peach blossom.
Embroidered shoes gave a sight of a pair of phoenixes;
Her crow-black hair was piled high at the temples.
As smiling she led the master by his hand
His cassock was tinged with orchid and musk.

Her arms around him. the she-devil took the master to a thatched pavilion and said, "Reverend sir, I've had a drink brought here to have with you." "Lady," said the Tang Priest, "as a monk I can take no impure food." "I know," the evil spirit replied. "As the water in the cave isn't clean I've sent for some of the pure water from the mating of the Yin and the Yang up on the mountain, and had a banquet of fruit and vegetables prepared. After that you and I are going to have some fun." When the Tang Priest went into the pavilion with her this is what could be seen:

All within the gates
Was decked in silks and embroideries;
Throughout the hall
Incense rose from golden lion censers.
Black-painted inlaid tables were set in rows,
On which stood dark-lacquered bamboo dishes.
On the inlaid tables
Were all kinds of delicacies;
In the bamboo dishes
Were vegetarian delights:
Crab apples, olives, lotus seeds, grapes, torreya-nuts,

hazelnuts, pine-nuts, lichees, longans, chestnuts, water caltrops, jujubes, persimmons, walnuts, gingko nuts, kumquats and oranges.
There was the fruit that grows on every hill,
The fresh vegetables of each season:
Beancurd, wheat gluten, tree-ear fungus, fresh bamboo shoots, button mushrooms, gill fungus, yams, sealwort, agar, day lily fried in vegetable oil,
Hyacinth beans, cowpeas prepared with mature sauces.
Cucumbers, gourds, gingko, turnip greens.
Peeled aubergines were cooked like quails;
Seeded wax gourds
Taro stewed tender and sprinkled with sugar,
Turnips boiled in vinegar.
Pungent chilli and ginger made it all delicious;
All the dishes were a balance of bland and salty.

Revealing the tips of her jade fingers she raized a dazzling golden goblet that she filled with fine wine. "Dearest reverend gentleman," she said, handing it to him, "my darling, have a drink to celebrate our happy union." Sanzang was covered with embarrassment as he took the wine. He poured a libation into the air as he prayed silently, "Devas who guard the Dharma, Guardians of the Four Quarters and the Centre, Four Duty Gods: your disciple Chen Xuanzang has benefited from the secret protection of all you deities sent by the Bodhisattva Guanyin on my journey to pay my respects at the Thunder Monastery, see the Buddha and seek the scriptures. I have now been captured by an evil spirit on my way. She is forcing me to marry her and has now handed me this cup of wine to drink. If this really is pure wine I can force myself to drink it and still be able to succeed and see the Buddha. But if it is impure wine I will be breaking my vows and fall for ever into the bitterness of the wheel of rebirth."

The Great Sage Sun made himself tiny and was like a secret informant behind his master's ear. When he spoke Sanzang was the only one who could hear him. Knowing that his master was normally fond of the pure wine of grapes he told him to drain the goblet. Sanzang had no choice but to do so, quickly refill the goblet and hand it back to the evil spirit. As he filled it bubbles of happiness formed on the surface of the wine. Brother Monkey turned himself into the tiniest of insects and flew lightly under the bubbles. But when the spirit took the goblet she put it down instead of drinking from it, bowed twice to the Tang Priest and spoke loving words to him with charming bashfulness. By the time she lifted the cup the bubbles had burst and the insect was revealed. Not realizing that it was Monkey transformed the evil spirit took it for a real insect, lifted it out with her little finger and flicked it away.

Seeing that as things were not going as he intended he would be unable to get into her belly Monkey turned himself into a hungry eagle. Indeed,

Jade claws, gold eyes and iron wings:
In terrible might he rose above the clouds.
Cunning hares and foxes felt faint at just the sight,
And hid among mountains and rivers for hundred of miles around.
When hungry it chased small birds into the wind,
And rose to the gate of heaven when replete.
Murderous were its talons of steel;
In times of triumph it stayed aloof in the clouds.

Monkey flew up, swung his jade claws, and noisily overturned the tables, smashing all the fruit, vegetables and crockery, and leaving the Tang Priest alone there as he flew off. This was so terrifying that the she-devil's heart and gall were split open, and the Tang Priest's flesh and bones all turned crisp. Shivering and shaking, the evil spirit threw her arms round the Tang Priest and said, "Dearest reverend gentleman, wherever did that come from?" "I don't know," Sanzang replied. "I went to a great deal of trouble to arrange this vegetarian feast for you," the she-devil said. "Goodness only knows where that feathered brute flew in from and smashed our crockery." "Smashing the crockery doesn't really matter," the junior demons said, "but all the food has been spilt on the floor. It's too dirty to eat now." Sanzang by now realized that this was all the result of Monkey's magic, but he dared not say so. "Little ones," said the she-devil, "I realize now. It must be heaven and earth that sent that thing down here because they can't tolerate my holding the Tang Priest prisoner. Clear all the broken dishes up and lay on another banquet. Never mind whether it's vegetarian or not. Heaven can be our matchmaker and the earth our guarantor. After that the Tang Priest and I will become man and wife." We will say no more of her as she took the Tang Priest to sit in the east corridor.

Instead the story tells of how Monkey flew out, turned back into himself, reached the entrance to the cave and shouted, "Open up!" "Friar Sand," Pig shouted, "our big brother's here." As the two of them drew their weapons away Monkey sprang out. "Is there an evil spirit in there?" Pig asked, grabbing hold of him. "Is the master in there?" "Yes, yes," said Monkey. "The master must be having a hard time in there," said Pig. "Are his arms tied behind his back? Or is he all roped up? Is she going to steam him or boil him?" "None of them," Monkey replied. "She'd just had a vegetarian feast served and was going to do it with him." "So you've been lucky then," said Pig. "You must have drunk a wedding toast." "Idiot!" retorted Monkey. "Never mind about having a wedding drink. I can hardly keep him alive." "Then why are you here?" Pig asked. Monkey told how he had seen the master and done his transformations, ending, "Don't let your fears run away with you, brothers. The master's here, and when I go back in this time I'll definitely rescue him."

Going back inside, Monkey turned into a fly and landed on the gate-tower to listen. He could hear the she-devil snorting with fury as she gave instructions within the pavilion. "Little ones, bring whatever there is, vegetarian or not, and burn paper as offerings to the deities. I'll ask heaven and earth to be the matchmakers. I'm definitely going to marry him." When Monkey heard this he smiled to himself and thought, "That she-devil's completely shameless. She's locked a monk up in her home and now she's going to mess around with him in broad daylight. But don't be in too much of a hurry. Give me time to go in and have a look round." With a buzz he flew along the corridor to see the master sitting inside, tears streaming down his face. Monkey squeezed in, landed on Sanzang's head and called, "Master." Recognizing the voice, Sanzang sprang to his feet and said with tooth-gnashing fury, "Macaque! Other people get their courage from a big gall, but they have to wrap their bodies around it. Your gall is so big that you wrap it round your body. You used your magical powers of transformation to smash the crockery, but what use is that? By fighting that she-devil you've only made her more sex-crazed than ever. She is arranging a banquet with vegetarian and impure food all mixed up and is determined to mate with me. Where will this all end?"

Smiling to himself again, Monkey replied, "Don't be angry with me, Master. I've got a way to save you." "How will you save me?" the Tang Priest asked. "When I flew up just now," said Monkey, "I saw that she has a garden behind here. You must lure her into the garden to fool around and I'll rescue you from there." "How will you rescue me from the garden?" the Tang Priest asked. "Go to the peach trees in the garden with her and stay there. Wait till I've flown to a branch of the peach tree and turned into a red peach. When you want to eat a peach pick the red one first — that will be me. She'll be bound to pick one too. You must insist on giving her the red one. Once she's swallowed it I'll be in her stomach. When I tear her stomach to pieces and rip her guts to shreds she'll be dead and you'll be freed." "With your powers you ought to fight her," said Sanzang. "Why do you want to get into her stomach?" "You don't understand, Master," Monkey replied. "If it were easy to get in and out of this cave of hers I would be able to fight her. But this place is very hard to get into or out of: the way out is complicated and difficult. If I started a fight with her all the fiends in her den, young and old, would overpower me. Then how would it end? We must act carefully if we're all to make a clean getaway." Sanzang nodded, believing all that Monkey said, adding only, "You must stay with me." "I know," said Monkey, "I know. I'll be on your head."

When master and disciple had settled their plan Sanzang leaned forward, took hold of the bars in the corridor's gates and called out, "Lady, lady." As soon as she heard this the evil spirit came rushing over, a simpering smile on her face, to ask, "What do you have to say to me, my wonderful darling?" "Lady," replied Sanzang, "ever since leaving Chang'an and starting on my journey to the west I have had to cross mountains and rivers every single day. When I was staying in the Zhenhai Monastery last night I caught a bad chill and I have been in a sweat today. I was just beginning to feel a little better today when in your kindness, good lady, you brought me into your immortals' palace. As I have been sitting here all day I am now feeling in rather low spirits again. Could you take me somewhere to cheer myself up and have a little fun?" The evil spirit was utterly delighted. "So you're feeling a bit interested, are you, my wonderful darling?" she said. "You and I will go into the garden for some fun. Little ones," she called, "fetch the key, open the garden gates, and sweep the paths in the garden." The demons all hurried off to open the gates and tidy the place up.

Meanwhile the evil spirit was opening the screen and helping the Tang Priest out. Just watch the many young demons — all willowy beauties with oiled hair and powdered faces — crowding around the Tang Priest as they head for the garden. What a splendid monk he was, walking amid these beauties in their gauze and brocade for no other purpose than to be deaf and dumb. If instead of having an iron heart set on the Buddha he had been any ordinary man susceptible to wine and women he would never have succeeded in fetching the scriptures. When they reached the entrance to the garden the evil spirit whispered seductively, "My wonderful darling, let's have some fun here — it'll cheer you up." They went into the garden hand in hand, and when he looked up he saw that it was indeed a splendid place. This is what could be seen:

All over the winding paths
Bluish lichens grow.
Secluded gauze windows
Kept dark by embroidered curtains.
When the breeze arises
Silks and brocades float in the air.
When the gentle rain stops falling
The smooth white skin and jade-like flesh are revealed.
The sun-scorched apricot
Is red as an immortal's rainbow clothes spread out to dry;
The plantain in the moonlight
Is bluer than Lady Taizhen waving her feather fan.
Whitewashed walls enclose
The golden orioles that sing in ten thousand willows.
Within the empty halls
Butterflies flit among begonias in the courtyard.
Look at the Hall of Crystallized Perfumes,
The Green Moth Hall,
The Hall to Recover from Drunkenness,
The Hall of Longing,
Rolling up the brilliance, one behind the other.
On the red curtains
Hooks hold tassels like prawn whiskers.
Now look at the Pavilion to Ease Pain
The Pavilion of Simplicity,
The Pavilion of Thrushes,
The Four Rains Pavilion,
All towering and lofty,
And bearing on decorated tablets
Their names in archaic script.
Look too at the Pool Where Cranes Bathe,
The Goblet-washing Pool,
The Pool of Delight in the Moon,
The Pool for Cleansing Tassels,
Where amid duckweed and algae the gold scales shine.
Then there is the Kiosk of Ink Flowers,

The Kiosk of Strange Boxes,
The Interesting Kiosk,
The Kiosk for Admiring the Clouds
Where bubbles like green ants float on the wine in jade ladles and goblets.
Around the pools and pavilions
Stand rocks from Lake Taihu,
Rocks of purple crystal,
Yingluo rocks,
Jin River rocks,
Greenish and overgrown with tiger-whisker rushes.
East and west of the kiosks and halls are found
A Wooden Mountain,
A Turquoise Screen Mountain,
A Howling Wind Mountain,
A Jade Mushroom Mountain,
All covered in phoenix-tail bamboo.
Trellises of briar roses,
And garden roses,
Growing by a swing,
As a curtain of silk and brocade.
A Pine Pavilion,
A Magnolia Pavilion,
Opposite a Saussurea Pavilion,
Forming a wall of jade with embroidered hangings.
Herbaceous and tree peonies are rivals in luxuriance;
The night-closing magnolias and the jasmine
Are charming every year.
Moist with dewdrops are the purple buds:
They ought to be painted or drawn.
The red hibiscus fills the sky with flaming splendour.
A marvellous subject for poetry.
When it comes to fine scenery
This makes Lang Garden or Penglai not worth a mention;
And as for the flowers,

The finest peonies of Luoyang count for nothing beside them.
In the battle of the blossoms late in the spring
The garden lacks only the flowers of jade.

The venerable elder led the she-devil by the hand as they strolled in the garden, admiring the endless displays of rare and exotic blooms. As they went through many a hall and pavilion he really did seem to be going into an exquisite place. Looking up, he realized that he was by the peach grove. Monkey pinched his master's head to remind him.

Flying to a branch of a peach tree Brother Monkey shook himself and turned into a red peach, and a most fetchingly red one at that. "Lady," the venerable elder said to the evil spirit, "what beautifully scented flowers and ripe fruit you have in this garden.

The blooms are so fragrant bees vie for their nectar;
The birds all compete for the fruit on the branches.

Why are some of the peaches on the trees red and some green?" "If there were no Yin and Yang in the heavens the sun and moon would not be bright," the evil spirit replied with a smile. "If there were no Yin and Yang in the earth the plants and trees would not grow. And if there were no Yin and Yang among people there would be no sexual difference. The peaches on the southern Yang side of these trees are red because they ripen first in the sun's heat. The peaches on the northern Yin side are green because they get no sun and are still unripe. It's all because of the Yin and the Yang." "Thank you, lady, for your explanation," Sanzang replied. "I did not know that." He then reached out and picked a red peach, while the evil spirit also picked a green one. Sanzang bowed as he handed the red one respectfully to the evil spirit with the words, "Lady, you love what is attractive, so won't you take this red peach and give me the green one?"

The she-devil made the exchange, thinking with concealed delight, "What a nice monk. He really is a good man. He is being so loving to me even before we're man and wife." With great pleasure she paid him her affectionate respects. As the Tang Priest started to eat the green peach at once the evil spirit was delighted to do likewise, opening her mouth to bite into the red one. When she parted her red lips and revealed her silver teeth the impatient Monkey did not give her time to bite him but rolled straight down her throat into her stomach. "Reverend gentleman," the terrified evil spirit said, "that peach is a terror. Why did it roll straight down and not let me bite it?" "Lady," Sanzang replied, "the first ripe fruits of a garden are very delicious. That is why it went down so fast." "But it shot straight down before I'd had time to spit the stone out," the evil spirit replied. "Because you are such a lover of what is fine and beautiful and enjoyed it so much," said Sanzang, "you swallowed it before you could bring the stone out."

Once inside her stomach Monkey turned back into himself. "Master," he called, "no need to argue with her now. I've succeeded." "Don't be too hard on her, disciple," Sanzang replied. "Who are you talking to?" the evil spirit asked when she heard this. "I am talking to my disciple Sun Wukong," Sanzang replied. "Where is he?" the evil spirit asked. "In your stomach," Sanzang replied. "He was the red peach you have just eaten." "That's the end of me," exclaimed the evil spirit in horror. "If that ape's got into my stomach I'm dead. Sun the Novice, why did you go to such lengths to get into my stomach?" "No particular reason," replied Monkey from inside her. "I just wanted to eat the six leaves of your liver and your lungs, and your heart with its three hairs and seven apertures. I'm going to clean your insides right out and leave you a skeleton spirit." This sent the evil spirit's souls scattering in terror and shivering and shaking she clung tightly to the Tang Priest and said, "Reverend gentleman, I had thought that

Our destinies were from former lives joined by a red thread;
Our love was as close as the water and the fish.
I never imagined that we lovebirds would be parted

Or that the phoenixes would fly to east and west.
When the waters rose under Lan Bridge the rendezvou
failed;
The meeting came to nothing in the misty temple.
After brief joy we are parted once more;
In whatever year will I meet you again?"

When Monkey heard all this from inside her stomach he wa afraid that the venerable elder would have another attack o benevolence and let her talk her way out of the problem. There upon he started to wield fist and foot, striking out in martia postures and levelling everything around him. He puched he stomach almost to ribbons. Unable to bear the pain, the evil spir collapsed in the dust, not daring to utter a single word for som time. As she was not speaking Monkey imagined that she mus be dead and eased off. She then recovered her breath to som extent and called out, "Where are you, little ones?" Now onc in the garden, they had all had the understanding to go off pick ing flowers, playing in the grass and amusing themselves, leavin the she-devil alone with the Tang Priest for a romantic convers tion. As soon as they heard her calling they rushed over to se the evil spirit lying on the ground, her face a terrible colour a she groaned, unable to move. They hurriedly helped her u crowding round and asking, "What's wrong, madam? Have yo had a heart attack?" "No, no," the evil spirit replied. "Don ask any questions. I've got someone inside me. Take th monk outside if you want to save my life." The junior devi actually did start to carry the Tang Priest, at which Monke yelled from inside her belly, "Don't any of you dare carry hi You must take my master out yourself. I'll only spare your li when you've carried him outside." This left the evil spirit wi no choice as all she cared about was saving her skin. At once sh struggled to her feet, lifted the Tang Priest on her back ar headed for the outside, followed by the junior devils askin "Where are you going, Madam?" To this the evil spirit replie

"'As long as the lakes and the bright moon remain
I'll surely find somewhere to put my golden book.'

Once I've taken this wretch outside I'll find myself another man."

The splendid evil spirit went straight by cloud to the mouth of the cave, where the clang of weapons and wild shouts could be heard. "Disciple," said Sanzang, "why can I hear weapons outside?" "It's Pig rubbing his rake," replied Monkey. "Give him a shout." "Bajie," Sanzang shouted. "Friar Sand," said Pig when he heard this, "the master's out." The two of them drew back their rake and staff, letting the evil spirit carry the Tang Priest out. Indeed,

The Mind Ape had subdued a monster from the inside;
The Earth and Wood door guards welcomed the holy monk.

If you don't know whether the evil spirit's life was spared listen to the explanation in the next instalment.

CHAPTER EIGHTY-THREE

The Mind-ape recognizes the refiner of cinnabar; The girl reverts to her true nature.

The story tells how after Sanzang had been carried out of th cave by the evil spirit Friar Sand went up to him and asked "Where is my oldest brother now that you have come out Master?" "He must know what he's doing," said Pig. "I expec he's exchanged himself for the master to get him out." "You brother is in her stomach," Sanzang replied, pointing at the evi spirit. "It is terribly filthy," Pig said. "Whatever are you doin in there? Come out." "Open your mouth," said Monkey fron inside, "I'm coming out." The she-devil did indeed open he mouth wide. Monkey made himself very small, sprang up int her throat, and was just about to emerge when he became wor ried that she might cheat and bite him. He then pulled out hi iron cudgel, blew on it with magic breath, called "Change!" an turned it into a jujube stone with which he wedged her jaw open With one bound he then leapt outside, taking the iron cudge with him, bowed to resume his own form and raised his cudge to strike her. At once she drew a pair of fine swords, parryin his blow with a loud clang. They fought a splendid battle o the mountain top.

A pair of dancing, flying swords defended her face;
The gold-banded cudgel struck at her head.
One was a heaven-born monkey, the Mind-ape;
The other had the bones of an earth-born girl turne spirit;
The two of them both had been smitten by anger:
Hatred arose at the celebration; the party was ended.
One longed to mate with the primal masculinity,
The other wanted to defeat the incarnation of the femal

When the cudgel was raised to the sky cold mists spread out;
The swords shook up the earth's black dirt like a sieve.
Because the elder would visit the Buddha
They were locked in fierce combat, each showing great prowess.
When water conflicts with fire motherhood is out;
When Yin and Yang cannot combine each goes its own way.
After the two had been fighting for a very long time
The earth moved, the mountains shook and the trees were destroyed.

The sight of their struggle made Pig grumble resentfully about Monkey. "Brother," he said, turning to Friar Sand, "our elder brother is messing around. When he was in her stomach just now he could have used his fists to make her belly red with blood, rip it open and come out. That would have settled her score. Why did he have to come out through her mouth and fight her? Why did he let her run wild?" "You're right," Friar Sand replied, "but it was thanks to him that the master was rescued from the depths of the cave, even if he is in a fight with her now. Let's ask the master to sit here by himself while we two use our weapons to help our brother beat the evil spirit." "No, no," said Pig with a wave of his hand. "He's got his magic powers. We'd be useless." "What a thing to say," retorted Friar Sand. "This is in all of our interests. We may not be much use, but even a fart can strengthen a breeze."

Now that the idiot's dander was up he brandished his rake and shouted, "Come on!" Ignoring the master, they rode the wind and went for the evil spirit, striking wildly at her with their rake and staff. The evil spirit, who was already finding Brother Monkey too much to handle, realized that she would be unable to hold out against two more of them. At once she turned and fled. "After her, brothers," Monkey shouted. Seeing that they were so hot on her heels the evil spirit took the embroidered shoe off her right foot, blew on it with a magic breath said a spell, called "Change!" and turned it into her own double swinging a pair of swords. Then she shook herself, turned into a puff of wind and went straight back. There she was, fleeing for her life because she was no match for them. What happened next was quite unexpected: Sanzang's evil star had still not gone away. As the evil spirit reached the archway in front of the entrance to the cave she saw the Tang Priest sitting there by him-self, so she went up to him, threw her arm round him, grabbed the luggage, bit through the bridle, and carried him back inside horse and all.

The story tells not of her but of Pig, who exploited an open-ing to fell the evil spirit with one blow of his rake, only to find that she was really an embroidered shoe. "You pair of idiots," said Monkey when he saw it. "You should have been looking after the master. Nobody asked you to help." "What about that then, Friar Sand?" said Pig. "I said we shouldn't come here. That ape has had a brainstorm. We beat the monster for him and he gets angry with us." "Beaten the monster indeed!" Mon-key said. "The monster fooled me yesterday by leaving a shoe behind when I was fighting her. Goodness knows how the master is now that you've left him. Let's go straight back and see."

The three of them hurried back to find that the master had disappeared: there was no sign at all of him, the luggage or the white horse. Pig started rushing all over the place in a panic with Friar Sand searching alongside him. The Great Sage Sun was also most anxious. As he searched he noticed half of the bridle rope lying askew beside the path. Picking it up, he could not hold back his tears as he called in a loud voice, "Master! When I went I took my leave of you three and the horse, and all I find on my return is this rope." It was indeed a case of

Being reminded of the steed by seeing the saddle,
Missing the beloved amid one's tears.

The sight of Monkey's tears gave Pig an uncontrollable urge to throw back his head and laugh out loud. "Blockhead," said Monkey abusively. "Do you want us to break up again?" "That's not what I mean," said Pig, still laughing. "The master's been carried back into the cave. As the saying goes, 'third time lucky'. You've already been into the cave twice, so if you go in again you're sure to rescue the master." "Very well then," said Monkey, wiping away his tears, "as this is the way things are I have no choice. I'll have to go back in. You two don't have to worry about the luggage or the horse any more, so guard the cave-mouth properly."

The splendid Great Sage turned round and sprang into the cave. This time he did no transformations but appeared in his own dharma form. This is what he was like:

His cheeks looked strange but his heart was strong;
As a monster since childhood his magic was mighty
A misshapen face that looked like a saddle;
Eyes fiery bright with golden light.
His hairs were harder than needles of steel,
And striking was the pattern of his tigerskin kilt.
In the sky he could scatter a myriad clouds;
In the sea he could stir up thousandfold waves.
Once with his strength he fought heavenly kings,
Putting a hundred and eight thousand warriors to flight.
His title was Great Sage Equalling Heaven;
He was an expert with the gold-banded cudgel.
Today in the West he was using his powers
To return to the cave and rescue Sanzang.

Watch Monkey as he stops his cloud and heads straight for the evil spirit's residence, where he found the gates under the gate towers shut. Not caring whether or not it was the right thing to do, he smashed them open with one swing of his cudgel and charged inside. It was completely quiet and deserted, and the Tang Priest was nowhere to be seen in the corridor. The tables and chairs in the pavilion and all the utensils had completely disappeared. As the cave measured over a hundred miles around, the evil spirit had very many hiding places in it. This was where

she had brought the Tang Priest the previous time, only to b
found by Monkey, so after catching him this time she had move
him elsewhere in case Monkey came looking for him again.

Not knowing where they had gone, Monkey stamped his foo
and beat his chest with fury, letting himself call out at the top o
his voice, "Master! You are a Tang Sanzang formed in misfor-
tune, a pilgrim monk moulded from disaster. Hmm. I knov
the way well enough. Why isn't he here? Where should I loo
for him?" Just when he was howling with impatience and anxiety
his nose was struck by a whiff of incense, which brought hin
back to himself. "This incense smoke is coming from the back,"
he thought, "so I suppose they must be there." He strode in a
the back, his cudgel in his hand, but still saw no sign of life
What he did see were three side rooms. Near the back wall was
lacquered offertory table carved with dragons on which stood
gilt incense-burner. From this came heavily scented incens
smoke. On the table was a tablet inscribed with letters of gol
to which the offerings were being made. The letters read
"Honoured Father, Heavenly King Li". In a slightly inferio
position was written, "Honoured Elder Brother, Third Princ
Nezha". The sight filled Monkey with delight. He stoppe
searching for the monster and the Tang Priest, rubbed his cudge
between his fingers to make it as small as an embroidery needle
tucked it inside his ear, gathered up the tablet and the incense
burner with a sweep of his arms and went straight back ou
through the gates on his clouds. He was still chortling with gle
when he reached the mouth of the cave.

When Pig and Friar Sand heard him they unblocked the entrance to the cave and greeted him with, "You look so happy
you must have saved the master, elder brother." "No need fo
us to save him," Monkey replied with a smile. "We can ask
this tablet for him." "But that tablet isn't an evil spirit and i
can't talk," said Pig, "so how can you ask it for him?" "Look
at it," said Monkey, putting the tablet on the ground. Whe
Friar Sand went up to look he saw "Honoured Father, Heavenly
King Li" and "Honoured Elder Brother, Third Prince Nezha"
written on it. "What does this mean?" Friar Sand asked

The evil spirit makes offerings to it," Monkey replied. "When I harged into her place there was nobody about, only this tablet. think she must be a daughter of Heavenly King Li and the ounger sister of Prince Nezha who so longed for the lower vorld that she pretended to be an evil spirit and carried our naster off. So who better to demand the master from? You wo keep guard here while I take this tablet up to Heaven to odge a complaint with the Jade Emperor and force those heaveny kings to give our master back."

"Brother," said Pig, "there's a saying that goes, 'Bring a apital charge and pay for it with your own head.' You can nly do a thing like that if you're in the right. Besides, a case n the celestial court isn't something to be started lightly. You'd etter tell me what sort of case you're going to bring." "I know vhat I'm going to do," Monkey replied. "I'm going to produce his tablet and incense-burner as evidence and submit a written leposition too." "What will you write in your deposition?" Pig asked him. "Will you tell me?" To this Brother Monkey eplied, "The complainant Sun Wukong, whose age is stated in his document, is the disciple of the monk Tang Sanzang who is oing from the Tang court in the east to fetch the scriptures from he Western Heaven. He submits a complaint that an imitation vil spirit has committed a kidnap. Li Jing, the Pagoda-carrying Heavenly King, and his son Prince Nezha have been slack in conrolling their women's quarters. He has allowed his daughter o run away and turn into an evil spirit in the Bottomless Cave n Mount Pitfall, where she has lured countless deluded people o their deaths. She has now carried my master into a remote orner where he cannot be found. If I had not submitted this omplaint I would have been deeply worried that the heavenly ing and his son in their wickedness had deliberately incited his laughter to become a spirit and cause general disaster. I beg Your Majesty in your mercy to summon the heavenly king to atend a hearing, bring the demon under control and deliver my naster. I would be deeply grateful if Your Majesty would deermine the correct penalty for this offence. This is my respectul submission." When Pig and Friar Sand heard this they said with delight, "Brother, you're bound to win if you submit so reasonable a complaint. Be as quick as you can. If you lose any time you may be too late to stop the evil spirit killing our master." "I'll hurry," said Brother Monkey, "I'll hurry. I'll be back in the time it takes to cook rice at the longest or to make a cup of tea if I'm quick."

With one bound the splendid Great Sage carried the tablet and the incense-burner straight up by auspicious cloud to the outside of the Southern Gate of Heaven, where the Heavenly Kings Powerful and Protector of the Nation greeted him with bows, letting him in and not daring to block his way. He went straight to the Hall of Universal Radiance, where the four heavenly teachers Zhang, Ge, Xu, and Qiu showed him great courtesy and asked, "Why are you here, Great Sage?" "I've got a complaint here," Monkey replied. "There are a couple of people I want to lodge a complaint against." "The scoundrel," thought the appalled heavenly teachers, "who can he be wanting to sue?" They had no choice but to lead him to the Hall of Miraculous Mist and submit their report to the Jade Emperor, who ordered that Monkey be summoned in. Monkey then put down the tablet and the incense-burner, bowed to the emperor, and presented his complaint. This was taken by the Ancient Immortal Ge, who spread it out on the emperor's table. When the emperor had read it through from the beginning and learned what had happened he approved the deposition, wrote an imperial rescript on it, and sent the Great White Planet, the Metal Planet Changgeng, to the Cloud Tower Palace to summon the Pagoda-carrying Heavenly King Li to the imperial presence. Monkey then stepped forward and submitted this memorial: "I beg that the Heavenly Sovereign will punish him effectively as otherwise there will be further trouble." "Let the complainant go too," the Jade Emperor ordered. "What, me?" said Monkey. "His Majesty has issued his decree," said the Four Heavenly Teachers, "so you go with the Metal Planet."

Monkey then went with the planet by cloud. They were soon at the Cloud Tower Palace, the residence of the heavenly king. The Metal Star saw a page standing at the palace gates. Recognizing the planet, the boy went inside to report, "The Great White Planet is here." The heavenly king then came out to welcome the planet. Seeing that the planet was carrying a decree from the Jade Emperor, the heavenly king ordered incense to be burned before turning round and seeing to his fury that Monkey had come too. Why do you think he was furious? When Monkey had made great havoc in heaven all those years earlier the Jade Emperor had appointed the heavenly king as Demon-quelling High Marshal and Prince Nezha as Great God of the Three Altars of the Seas to lead the heavenly troops and subdue Monkey. They had been repeatedly worsted in battle. It was resentment at this defeat five hundred years earlier that goaded him to fury. "Old Changgeng," he said to the planet, showing his irritation, "what kind of decree have you brought here?" "It is a case that the Great Sage Sun has brought against you," the planet replied. The heavenly king had been in a bad enough temper before this, but the word "case" provoked a thunderous outburst of fury: "What case has he got against me?" "He accuses you of masquerading as an evil spirit and kidnapping," the planet said. "Will you please burn incense and read it for yourself."

Seething with anger, the heavenly king had an incense table set up, looked into the sky as he thanked the emperor for his grace, made his obeisances, opened out the decree and read it through. When he saw what it contained he thumped the incense table and exclaimed, "That ape has trumped up a pack of lies." "Please keep your temper," the planet replied. "A tablet and an incense-burner have been submitted to His Majesty as evidence. He says it was your daughter who did it." "All I have are my three sons and a single daughter," said the heavenly king. "My elder son Jinzha serves the Tathagata Buddha as a Vanguard Guardian of the Law Dharma. My second son Moksa is a disciple of Guanyin in the Southern Ocean. My third son Nezha stays with me as my escort at all times. My daughter Zhenying is only six and an innocent child. She could not possibly have become an evil spirit. If you don't believe me I'll carry her out to show you. This ape is really a disgrace. Never mind that I'm one of the most distinguished elder statesmen in heaven and been given the authority to cut heads off before reporting to the throne: not even an ordinary commoner in the lower world should be falsely accused. As the Legal Code says, 'the penalty for false accusation is three grades higher than the crime alleged.' " He then ordered his underlings to fetch demon-binding rope and tie Monkey up. The Mighty Miracle God, General Fishbelly and General Yaksha who were drawn up outside the court rushed on Monkey and tied him up. "Heavenly King Li," the Metal planet pleaded, "please don't invite disaster. I have come here with him from the imperial presence under orders from His Majesty to summon you. That rope of yours is heavy, and it could very quickly hurt him badly or strangle him." "Metal Star," the heavenly king replied, "there's no way I'm going to stand for his false, trumped-up charge. Won't you take a seat while I fetch my demon-hacking sword to kill this ape with? I'll report to His Majesty with you after I've done that." At the sight of the heavenly king fetching the sword the planet trembled with terror. "You've made a terrible mistake," he said to Monkey. "A case before the emperor isn't to be lightly started. You've brought this disaster on yourself by not finding the facts out properly and you'll die for it. This is terrible." Monkey was completely unafraid. "Don't worry, old man," he said with a chuckle, "this is nothing. This has always been my way of doing business: I lose out at first and win in the end."

Before the words were all out of his mouth the heavenly king's sword swung down towards Monkey's head. But Prince Nezha was already in front of Monkey, parrying the blow with his great sword used for cutting men in half at the waist and calling, "Please calm your temper, father." This greatly shocked the heavenly king. Very strange! If a son uses his broadsword to block his father's cutlass he ought to be bawled out, so why did Nezha's father turn pale with shock?

Now when this son had been born to the heavenly king the word *Ne* was written on the palm of his left hand and *Zha* on his right one, which was why he was called Nezha. When only three days old the young prince had caused great trouble by plunging into the sea to clean himself. He had kicked the water crystal palace down, captured a dragon and insisted on pulling its sinews out to make a belt. On learning about this, the heavenly king had been so worried about the disastrous consequences that he had decided to kill the boy. This had made Nezha so indignant that he had seized a sword, cut off his flesh and returned it to his mother, then picked his bones clean and given them back to his father. Having returned his father's seed and his mother's blood he had taken his soul straight off to the Western Paradise to appeal to the Buddha. When the Buddha, who was expounding the sutras to all the Bodhisattvas, heard a call of "Help!" from within his curtained and jewelled canopy he had looked with his wise eyes and seen that it was Nezha's soul. He had made Nezha bones out of green lotus root and clothes from lotus leaves, then recited the spell to revive the dead. Thus it was that Nezha had come back to life. He had used his divine ability and great magical powers to subdue ninety-six caves of demons through dharma. After this Nezha had wanted to kill his father in revenge for having had to pick the flesh off his own bones, leaving the heavenly king with no choice but to beg the help of the Tathagata Buddha. For the sake of harmony the Buddha had given the heavenly king an intricately-made golden as-you-will reliquary pagoda, in each storey of which were Buddhas radiant with splendour. The Buddha called on Nezha to regard these Buddhas as his father, thereby ending the hatred between them. This is why Heavenly King Li is called the Pagoda-bearer. As the heavenly king was at home off duty that day and not carrying the pagoda he was afraid that Nezha was set on revenge. This was why he turned pale with terror.

So he turned his hand back to take the golden pagoda from its stand and hold it as he asked Nezha, "What do you want to say to me, son? Why have you parried my sword with your broadsword?" Throwing his broadsword down, Nezha kowtowed to his father as he replied, "Father, Your Majesty, there is a daughter of our family in the lower world." "My boy," the heavenly king replied, "I have only had you four children. Where could I have got another daughter from?" "You have forgotten, Your Majesty," Nezha replied. "The girl was once an evil spirit. Three hundred years ago she became a monster. She stole and ate some of the Tathagata's incense, flowers and candles on Vulture Peak, and the Tathagata sent us to capture her with heavenly soldiers. When she was caught she should have been beaten to death, but the Tathagata said,

'Raise fish in deep water but never catch them;
Feed deer in the depths of the mountains in the hope of eternal life.'

So we spared her life. In her gratitude she bowed to you as her adoptive father, Your Majesty, and to me as her elder brother. She set up a tablet to us in the lower world to burn incense. I never imagined she'd become an evil spirit again and try to ruin the Tang Priest. Now Sun the Novice has trailed her to her den and brought the tablet up here to use in a case against us before the Jade Emperor. She is your adopted daughter, not my real sister."

This came as a terrible shock to the heavenly king. "Son," he said, "I really had forgotten. What's she called?" "She has three names," the prince replied. Where she originally came from she was called Gold-nosed White-haired Mouse Spirit. Then she was called Half-Bodhisattva-Guanyin because she had stolen the incense, flowers and candles. When she was forgiven and sent down to the lower world she changed her name again and became Lady Earth-gusher." Only then did the heavenly king come to his senses. He put his pagoda down and started to untie Monkey himself. At this Monkey started playing up. "Don't you dare try to untie me!" he said. "If you want to do something you can carry me roped up as I am to see the emperor. Then I'll win my case." The heavenly king felt weak from terror and the prince could say nothing. Everybody fell back.

The Great Sage meanwhile was rolling about and playing up, insisting that the heavenly king take him to the emperor. The heavenly king could do nothing except beg the Metal Planet to put in a good word for him. "There is an old saying," the planet replied, "that one should always be lenient. You went too far: you tied him up and were going to kill him. The monkey is a notorious trouble-maker. How do you expect me to deal with him? From what your worthy son has said, she is your daughter, even though adopted rather than your own, and a child by adoption is especially dear. However one argues it you are guilty." "Surely you can find some way of putting in a good word for me and get me off, venerable planet," said the heavenly king. "I would like to end the quarrel between you," the planet replied, "but I have never done him a good turn that I can remind him of." "Tell him how it was you who proposed that he should be amnestied and given an official post," said the heavenly king.

The Metal Planet did then step forward, stroke Brother Monkey and say, "Great Sage, won't you let us take the rope off before going to see the emperor, just for my sake?" "No need to bother, old man," Monkey replied. "I'm a good roller and I can roll all the way there." "You've got no decent feelings, you monkey," said the planet with a smile. "I did you some good turns in the old days, but you won't do this little thing for me." "What good turn did you ever do me?" Monkey asked. "When you were a monster on the Mountain of Flowers and Fruit you subdued tigers and dragons, forcibly removed yourself from the register of death and assembled hordes of fiends to run wild and wreak havoc. Heaven wanted to have you arrested. It was only because I made strong representations that an edict of amnesty and recruitment was issued and you were summoned to Heaven to be appointed Protector of the Horses. You drank some of the Jade Emperor's wine of immortality, and it was only because I made strong representations again that you were given the title of Great Sage Equalling Heaven. But you refused to know your place. You stole the peaches and the wine and robbed Lord Lao Zi of his elixir, and so it went on till you ended up in a state of no death and no birth. If it hadn't been for me you'd never have got where you are today." "As the ancients put it," Monkey replied, " 'Don't even share a grave with an old man when you're dead: all he'll do is complain.' I was just a Protector of the Horses who made havoc in the heavenly palace: there was nothing much apart from that. Oh well, never mind. I'll show you a bit of consideration as you're such an old man. He can untie me himself." Only then did the heavenly king dare step forward, untie the rope, and ask Brother Monkey to dress and take the seat of honour while they all took it in turn to pay their respects to him.

"Old man," Monkey said to the Metal Planet, "what about it then? I told you I lose first and win later. That's my way of doing business. Make him hurry and see the emperor: delay could be disastrous for my master." "Don't be impatient," the Metal Planet said. "After everything that's happened we should take a cup of tea." "If you drink his tea, accept favours from him, take a bribe to let a criminal escape, and treat imperial edicts with disrespect I wonder what you'll be charged with," Monkey replied. "I won't stop for tea," the Metal Planet replied, "I won't stop for tea. You're even trying to frame me. Hurry up, Heavenly King Li, we must be on our way." The heavenly king dared not go for fear that Monkey would concoct some unfounded story and start playing up: if Monkey started talking wildly he would be unable to argue against him. So once again the heavenly king pleaded with the Metal Planet to put in a good word for him. "I have a suggestion to make," the planet said to Monkey. "Will you follow it?" "I've already agreed about being tied up and hacked at," Monkey replied. "What else have you to say? Tell me! Tell me! If it's a good idea I'll follow it; and if it isn't, don't blame me."

" 'Fight a lawsuit for one day and it'll go on for ten'," said the Metal Planet. "You brought a case before the emperor saying that the evil spirit is the heavenly king's daughter and the heavenly king says she isn't. You two will argue endlessly in front of His Majesty, but I tell you that a day in heaven is a year in the lower world. In that year the evil spirit will have your master under her control in the cave, and she won't just have married him. By then there may have been a happy event and she may have had a little baby monk. Then your great enterprise will be ruined." "Yes," thought Monkey, his head bowed, "when I left Pig and Friar Sand I said I'd be back in the time it takes to cook a meal at longest and at quickest before they could make a cup of tea. I've been ages already and it might be too late. Old man," he said aloud, "I'll take your advice. How do we obey this imperial decree?" "Have Heavenly King Li muster his troops and go down with you to subdue the demon," the Metal Planet replied, "while I report back to the emperor." "What will you say?" Monkey asked. "I'll report that the plaintiff has absconded and that the defendant is therefore excused," the planet replied. "That's very fine," said Monkey with a grin. "I show you consideration and you accuse me of absconding. Tell him to muster his troops and wait for me outside the Southern Gate of Heaven while you and I report back on our mission." "If he says anything when he's there I'll be accused of treason," exclaimed the heavenly king with terror. "What do you take me for?" asked Monkey. "I'm a real man. Once I've given my word a team of horses couldn't take it back. I'd never slander you."

The heavenly king thanked Monkey, who went with the Metal Planet to report back on their mission, while the heavenly king mustered his heavenly troops and went straight to the outside of the Southern Gate of Heaven. When the Metal Planet and Monkey had their audience with the Jade Emperor they said, "The person who has trapped the Tang Priest is the Golden-nosed White-haired Mouse turned spirit. She has fraudulently set up a tablet to the heavenly king and his son. As soon as he found out, the heavenly king mustered his troops to go and subdue the demon. We beg your Celestial Majesty to forgive him." Once the Jade Emperor knew what had happened he dropped the prosecution in his heavenly mercy. Monkey then went back on his cloud to the outside of the Southern Gate of Heaven, where he found the heavenly king and the prince waiting for him with their heavenly soldiers draw up on parade. The heavenly commanders met the Great Sage amid blustering winds and seething mists, then they all took their clouds straight down to Mount Pitfall.

Pig and Friar Sand were wide-eyed at the sight of the heavenly hosts coming down with Brother Monkey. Greeting the heavenly king with due courtesy, the idiot said, "We have put you to great trouble in coming here." "You don't realize, Marshal Tian Peng," the heavenly king replied, "that it was because my son and I accepted a joss-stick from her that the evil spirit in her wickedness captured your master. Please don't be angry with us for being so long. Is this Mount Pitfall? Where is the entrance to the cave?" "I know the way very well by now," said Monkey. "This cave is called the Bottomless Cave and it measures over a hundred miles around. The evil spirit has a great many holes in it. Last time my master was held in the gate tower with double eaves, but it's deadly quiet now. There's not even the shadow of a demon. I don't know where she's taken him to now."

To this the heavenly king replied,

" 'No matter how many the tricks she may try
She'll never escape from the nets of the sky.'

We'll think of something else when we get to the cave entrance."

They all then started out, and after they had gone three or four miles they reached the great rock. "This is it," Monkey said pointing at the entrance that was no larger than the mouth of a large jar. "You'll never capture the tiger's cub unless you go into the tiger's lair," observed the heavenly king. "Who dares go in first?" "I'll go," said Monkey. "No, I'll go first," objected Prince Nezha. "I was the one the emperor ordered to capture the demon." The idiot then started acting up rough, shouting, "It ought to be me first." "Stop that din," said the heavenly king. "I'll decide. The Great Sage Sun and the prince will go down with the soldiers while we three hold the entrance. Then we'll have a co-ordinated action inside and outside, which will make it impossible for her to find her way up to heaven or go further underground. That will show her a bit of our powers." "Yes, sir," they all said in assent.

Watch as Monkey and Prince Nezha slip into the cave at

the head of their troops. As they rode their clouds they looked around and saw that it really was a fine cave:

The pair of sun and moon as before;
A vista of rivers and hills like the other world.
Warm mists spread over pools and wells of pearl;
Much more there is to admire down here.
Crimson houses, painted halls,
Red cliffs, green fields,
Willows in the spring and lotus in the autumn:
A rare and splendid cave heaven.

An instant later they brought their clouds to a halt and went straight to the mansion where the evil spirit had lived before. They went from gateway to gateway in their search, yelling and shouting as they went deeper and deeper inside, trying one place after the next. All the grass for a hundred miles was trampled away. But where was the evil spirit? Where was Sanzang? "The wicked beast," everyone was saying, "she must have got out of this cave ages ago. She'll be far away by now." What they did not know was that down underneath a dark corner in the southeast of the cave there was another, smaller cave, where behind a pair of tiny gates there was a tiny cottage with flowers growing in pots and a few canes of bamboo beside the eaves. The atmosphere was dark and heavy with fragrance. This was where the evil spirit had carried Sanzang and was going to force him to marry her. She was sure that Monkey would never find them; none of them realized that her union was fated to be thwarted. The junior devils were jabbering away in a great crush when a bolder one among them stretched outside the cave for a look around only for her head to butt into a heavenly soldier, who shouted, "They're here!" At this Monkey flew into a rage, grasped the gold-banded cudgel and charged straight down in. The cave was tiny and all the demons from the big cave were in there, so that when Prince Nezha sent his heavenly soldiers crowding into the attack, not a single one of the demons could hide.

Monkey found the Tang Priest, the dragon horse and the

baggage. The senior demon was at her wit's end. All she could do was to kowtow to Prince Nezha, begging him to spare her life. "We are here to arrest you at the Jade Emperor's command," Prince Nezha replied, "which is not something to be treated lightly. My father and I were nearly in terrible trouble because of you." He then shouted at the top of his voice, "Heavenly soldiers, fetch demon-binding rope. Tie all those evil spirits up." The senior demon too had to suffer for a while. They all went back out of the cave together by cloud.

Monkey was chuckling with delight when the heavenly king withdrew his guard from the mouth of the cave and greeted Monkey with the words, "Now I can meet your master." "Many thanks," said Monkey, "many thanks," and he led Sanzang to bow in gratitude to the heavenly king and the prince. Friar Sand and Pig were all for chopping the senior devil into tiny pieces, but the heavenly king said, "She was arrested at the Jade Emperor's command, and must not be mistreated. We must go to report back on our mission."

The heavenly king and Prince Nezha at the head of their heavenly troops and divine officers escorted the evil spirit as a prisoner to report to the heavenly court and receive the emperor's verdict on her. Meanwhile Brother Monkey guarded the Tang Priest while Friar Sand collected the luggage and Pig went over to the horse and invited the master to ride. Then they all set out along their way again. Indeed,

The silken net had been cut, the golden sea dried up,
The precious lock undone, and troubles left behind.

If you do not know what lay in store for them on their way ahead listen to the explanation in the next instalment.

CHAPTER EIGHTY-FOUR

The indestructible protégés of the Buddha complete enlightenment;
The Dharma king comes to the truth through his own nature.

The story tells how Tang Sanzang kept his masculine essence intact and escaped from the terrible snare of mist and flowers. As he headed westwards with Brother Monkey he did not notice that it was already summer: warm breezes were beginning to blow, and the early summer rain was falling. It was a beautiful sight:

Dark is the shade under tender green;
In the gentle breeze the swallows lead their young.
New lotus leaves are opening on the ponds;
Elegant bamboo is gradually reviving.
The fragrant plants join their blue to the sky;
Mountain flowers carpet all the ground.
Beside the stream the rushes are like swords;
The fiery pomegranate blossom makes the picture even more magnificent.

As the master and his three disciples travelled along enduring the heat they suddenly noticed two rows of tall willows, from under the shade of which an old woman emerged, leaning on a small boy. "Don't go any further, monk," she called out. "Stop your horse and go back east as soon as you can. The road west leads nowhere." This gave Sanzang so bad a fright that he sprang off the horse, made a gesture of greeting and said, "Venerable Bodhisattva, in the words of the ancients,

'The sea's breadth allows the fish to leap;
The sky's emptiness lets birds fly.

How could there possibly be no way to the west?" To this the old woman replied, pointing westwards, "If you go that way you will come to the capital of Dharmadestructia in a couple of miles. The king formed a hatred of Buddhism in an earlier existence, and in his present life he is punishing it without just cause. Two years ago he made a monstrous vow to kill ten thousand Buddhist monks. In that time he's killed 9,996 unknown monks in succession. He's just waiting for four famous monks to make up his ten thousand so that he will fulfil the vow. If you go into the city you will be throwing away your lives for nothing." At the sound of this Sanzang was so terrified that he shivered and shook as he replied, "Venerable Bodhisattva, I am deeply moved by your great kindness and infinitely grateful too. But, tell me, is there a suitable way I could take that does not go into the city?" "There's no way round," the old woman replied with a laugh, "no way round. The only way you'll get past it is if you can fly." At this Pig started shooting his mouth off from where he stood beside them: "Don't try to put us off. We can all fly."

Monkey's fiery eyes with their golden pupils really could distinguish good from evil, and he saw that the old woman and the little boy on whom she was leaning were in fact the Bodhisattva Guanyin and the page Sudhana. He hastily flung himself to the ground and began to kowtow, calling out, "Bodhisattva, your disciple failed to welcome you. I'm sorry." The Bodhisattva then rose slowly on her multicoloured cloud, so startling the venerable elder that his legs gave way under him and he kowtowed as he knelt there for all he was worth. Pig and Friar Sand also fell to their knees in alarm and kowtowed to heaven. A moment later she was heading straight back to the Southern Sea amid auspicious clouds.

Monkey then got up and supported his master as he said, "Get up please. The Bodhisattva's already gone back to her island." "Wukong," Sanzang said, "if you knew she was the Bodhisattva why did you not say so before?" "You ask too many questions," Monkey replied with a grin. "When I started kowtowing wasn't that early enough?" "It was lucky the Bodhisattva told us that Dharmadestructia, where they kill monks, is ahead of us," Pig and Friar Sand said to Monkey. "Whatever are we to do?" "Don't be afraid, idiot," Monkey replied. "We've come to no harm from any of the vicious demons and evil monsters we've met already or in the tigers' dens and dragons' pools we've been in. This is just a country of ordinary people. What's there to be so scared of? The only thing is that we can't stay here. It's getting late in the day and some of the villagers are coming back from market in the town. It will be no good if they see we're monks and raise a hue and cry. We'd better take the master away from the main road to some quiet and secluded spot where we can discuss things." Sanzang accepted Monkey's suggestion and they slipped away from the main road to a hollow in the ground where they sat down. "Brother," said Monkey, "you two look after the master while I turn myself into something and go into town to take a look around. I'll find a side road that we can get away along tonight." "Disciple," said Sanzang, "don't take this lightly. The royal law is implacable. You must be careful." "Don't worry," said Monkey with a smile, "don't worry. I can cope."

This said, the Great Sage leapt whistling up into the air. It was very strange:

No rope to hold on to above,
No pole to support him below.
Others are all like their parents,
But the weight of his bones was low.

As he stood in the clouds looking down he saw that the city was full of the most happy and auspicious atmosphere. "What a splendid place," Monkey said. "Why are they trying to destroy the Dharma here?" He looked around for a while, and in the gathering dusk he saw

Bright lights at the crossroads,
Incense and bells in the ninefold hall.
The seven brightest stars shone in the blue heavens,
And the travellers stopped moving in all eight directions.

From the army barracks
The painted bugle could just be heard;
In the drum tower
The copper water-clock began to drip.
All around the evening mists were dense;
Cold fog was thick in the markets.
Two by two the couples went to their beds
As the bright moon's disk was rising in the east.

"If I went down into the streets to look for our way with a face like this," he thought, "anyone I saw would be sure I was a monk. I'd better change." He made a spell with his hands, said the magic words, shook himself and turned into a moth, the sort that flies into the lantern:

A tiny body, a pair of delicate wings,
Who puts out the lamp and flies into the candle when seeking the light.
Formed by changing its own original body,
It makes its magic response in grass that's decaying.
Loving the burning light of the candle's flame,
Endlessly flying around it with never a pause,
The purple-clad moth with its scented wings drives off the fireflies;
What it likes best is the windless calm of the night.

Watch him as he flutters and flies straight to the main streets and the markets, keeping close to the eaves and the corners of the buildings he passes. As he was flying along he noticed an angled row of houses on a corner with a lantern hanging above each doorway. "They must be celebrating the Lantern Festival* here," he thought. "Why else is that line of lighted lanterns there?" Stiffening his wings and flying up for a closer look, he saw that on a square lantern outside the middle house was written, "Accommodation for Commercial Travellers", with "Wang the Second's Inn" beneath it. Only then did Monkey realize that this was an inn. Stretching his head forward for a closer look

* Held on the full moon night of the first month of the lunar calendar.

he saw eight or nine men inside who had all eaten their supper, taken off their clothes and hats, washed their hands and feet and gone to bed. "The master will get through," Monkey thought with secret delight. How did he know that? Because he was having a wicked idea: he would wait till they were all asleep then steal their clothes and hats so that he and his companions could go into the city dressed as laymen.

Oh dear! This was one of those things that don't turn out as you want them to. While Monkey was still thinking about his plan Wang the Second went up to the merchants and said, "Please be vigilant, gentlemen. We have villains here as well as decent people. You must all be careful about your clothes and luggage." As you can imagine, the travelling merchants were all very vigilant, and the innkeeper's advice made them more cautious than ever. So they all got out of bed and said, "You're quite right, host. We travellers have a hard time. We're always worried that if there's some emergency when we're asleep we may not wake up; and if things go wrong we're in a mess. You'd better take all our clothes, hats and bags and look after them for us inside. Tomorrow morning you can give them back to us when we get up." Wang the Second then took all the clothes he could find into his own room. Monkey anxiously spread his wings, flew in there and landed on the hat stand, from where he saw Wang the Second take the lantern down from the door, lower the blinds, and shut the door and window. Only then did he go into his bedroom, undress and lie down.

Now Wang the Second had a wife and two children who were crying and making a noise, in no hurry to sleep. Wang's wife then started mending a torn piece of clothing, so that she too was still awake. "If I have to wait till that woman stops working and goes to sleep," thought Monkey, "I'll be keeping the master waiting too." He then started worrying that if he left it till much later the city gates would be shut, so he lost patience and flew down into the flame of the lamp. It was indeed a case of

He was ready to die when he dived at the blaze,

And with brows scarred by fire to live out his days.

Having extinguished the lamp he shook himself and turned into a rat who gave a couple of squeaks, jumped down, grabbed hat and clothes and went outside. "Old man," the woman said with alarm, "this is terrible. A rat's turned into a spirit."

When Monkey heard this he used another trick, blocking the doorway and yelling at the top of his voice, "That woman's talking nonsense, Wang the Second. Ignore her. I'm not a rat turned spirit. As a decent man I don't do underhand things. I'm the Great Sage Equalling Heaven come down to earth to protect the Tang Priest while he goes to fetch the scriptures from the Western Heaven. I've come to borrow these clothes as a disguise for my master because your king is so wicked. I'll bring them back soon when we're out of the city." Once Wang the Second heard this he scrambled out of bed and started groping around the floor in the dark. He was in such a rush that when he got hold of his trousers he thought they were his shirt: there was no way he could put them on no matter how he tried.

By now the Great Sage had used lifting magic to escape on his cloud, which he turned round to go straight back to the hollow by the road. Sanzang was looking out for him fixedly by the bright light of the moon and the stars, and as soon as he saw Monkey approaching he called out, "Can we get through the capital of Dharmadestructia, disciple?" Coming up and laying the clothes down in front of him, Monkey replied, "Master, you won't get through Dharmadestructia as a monk." "Brother," said Pig, "who do you think you're making things hard for? It's easy to stop being a monk. All you have to do is stop shaving your head for six months and let your hair grow." "We can't wait six months," Monkey replied. "We're going to turn into laymen right now." "But that's a completely ridiculous thing to say," said a shocked Pig. "We're all monks now, and if we turned into laymen straight away we wouldn't be able to wear hats. Even if we could pull them tight enough at the edges we've got no hair to tie the string at the top to." "Stop fooling about,"

Sanzang shouted, "and be serious. What do you really have in mind?"

"I've had a good look at this city, Master," Monkey replied, "and although the king is a wicked one who kills monks he is a true son of heaven. There is an auspicious glow and a happy atmosphere above the city. I know my way round the streets now, and I can understand and talk the local language. I've just borrowed these hats and clothes from an inn for us to dress ourselves up as laymen in. We'll go into the city, put up for the night, get up at the fourth watch and ask the innkeeper to fix us some vegetarian food. At the fifth watch we'll go out through the gate and head west along the main road. If we meet anyone who tries to stop us we can talk our way out of it. I'll tell him we were sent by the ruler of their suzerain state. The king of Dharmadestructia won't dare hold us up. He'll let us go on our way." "Our big brother has arranged things very well," said Friar Sand. "Let's do as he suggests."

The venerable elder did indeed have no option but to take off his monastic tunic and hat and put on a layman's clothing and headwear. Friar Sand changed too, but Pig's head was too big for him to be able to wear a hat. Monkey fetched needle and thread, tore two hats open and sewed them into a single one. Then he put the hat on Pig's head and found a garment big enough for him to wear. Finally he dressed himself and said, "Gentlemen, we must ban the words 'master' and 'disciples' on this journey." "What else can we call each other?" Pig asked. "We must talk like people who address each other as brothers," Monkey replied. "The master can call himself Tang the Eldest. You can be Hogg the Third, and Friar Sand can be Sand the Fourth. I'll be Sun the Second. But when we are in the inn none of you must say anything. Leave all the talking to me. When they ask what line of business we're in I'll say we're horse dealers. I'll pretend that the white horse is a sample and that there are ten of us altogether, of whom we four have come ahead to book rooms at an inn and sell this horse. The innkeeper will be bound to treat us well then. We'll be properly looked after, and before we leave I'll find a piece of broken tile and turn it into silver to pay him with. Then we'll be able to go on our way." Although he was not happy about it the Tang Priest had to go along with this.

The four of them hurried to the city, leading the horse and carrying the luggage. As this was a very peaceful place the city gates were still open although it was already night. They went straight into the city, and as they passed the gateway of Wang the Second's inn they could hear shouting inside. People were yelling, "My hat's disappeared!" and "My clothes have gone!" Pretending he did not know what this was all about, Monkey took them to an inn further along on the other side of the road. This inn was still showing its lantern, so Monkey went up to the gateway and called, "Do you have a vacant room for us innkeeper?" "Yes, yes," a woman answered from inside. "Please come upstairs, gentlemen." Before she had finished speaking a man came out to take the horse. Monkey handed him the horse to take inside. He then led the master into the building in the shadow of the lamp. Upstairs there were tables and chairs conveniently arranged, and when the window was opened they all sat down in the clear moonlight. When someone came with a lighted lamp Monkey blocked the doorway, blew it out and said, "No need for a lamp on a bright night like this."

No sonner had the man with the lamp gone down than a maid came up with four bowls of tea. Monkey took the bowls from her, only for her to be followed by a woman who looked to be about fifty-six or fifty-seven coming up the stairs. Standing beside Monkey she asked, "Where are you gentlemen from? What fine goods do you have?" "We're from the north," Monkey replied, "and we've got a few poor horses to sell." "You're very young to be a horse dealer," the woman said. "This gentleman is Tang the Eldest," Monkey explained, "this is Hogg the Third, and this is Sand the fourth. I'm Sun the Second, an apprentice." "But your surnames are all different," said the woman with a smile. "Yes," Monkey replied, "our surnames are different but we all live together. There are ten of us brothers altogether, and we four have come ahead to fix our board and lodging. The other six have found a place outside the ity to stay tonight. It would have been awkward for them to ome into the city as they've got a herd of horses. They'll come tomorrow morning when we've fixed some accommodation. Ve won't go home till we've sold the horses." "How many orses are there in your herd?" the woman asked. "Over a hunred of all ages," Monkey replied. "They're all like that one f ours, except that they come in different colours."

"Mr. Sun," the woman said with a laugh, "you really know ow to travel. You should have come straight here: no other n would be able to put you up. We have a big courtyard well upplied with troughs and tethering posts and plenty of fodder o. We could feed several hundred horses here. There's just ne thing I should mention. I've been keeping this inn for many ears and it's quite well known. My late husband was called hao, but I'm afraid he died long ago, so this is now called Vidow Zhao's Inn. We have three classes of entertainment for ur guests. Let's get sordid money matters out of the way, then e can be more civilized later. The first thing is to discuss the riffs and agree on one so that we know where we stand when 's time to settle the accounts." "Quite right," Monkey replied. What are your three classes of entertainment? As the saying oes,

Your tariffs may be low, your tariffs may be dear,
But treat us all the same, who come from far or near.

Vhat do your tariffs involve? Could you explain them to me?"

"We have first, second and third-class tariffs," the old oman replied. "The first class is a banquet with five kinds of ruit and five different dishes. The tables are set with confecionery lions and immortals fighting. Two gentlemen share a able, and there are young ladies to sing to them and sleep with hem. It costs half an ounce of silver per head, the price of the oom included." "I'd agree to that," Monkey replied. "Where e come from half an ounce wouldn't even pay for a girl." "For e second-class tariff," the woman continued, "you all eat from he same dishes of food and we provide fruit and warm wine that you help yourselves to in your drinking games. No youn, ladies are provided and it costs one fifth of an ounce of silve each." "I'd agree to that too," Monkey replied. "What abou the third class?" "I wouldn't like to discuss it with such distin guished gentlemen as yourselves," she replied. "No harm in tell ing us about it," Monkey replied, "so that we can choose wha suits us best." "Nobody waits on you in the third class," sh said, "and we provide a big pot of rice for you to eat from a you will. When you're full there's straw for you to spread ou on the ground and sleep on where it suits you. At dawn yo give us a few coppers for the rice and I can assure you we won' argue about how much." "We're in luck," said Pig, "we're i luck. That's the sort of deal I like. I'll eat my fill from the caul dron then have a bloody good sleep in front of the stove." "Wha nonsense, brother," said Monkey. "We've earned an ounce o two of silver on our travels. Give us the first-class treatment."

"Make some good tea," the woman said with great deligh "and tell the kitchen to get the food ready quickly." She the went downstairs calling out, "Kill chickens and geese and boi up some pickled meat for them to have with their rice." The she shouted, "Kill a pig and a sheep. What can't be eaten toda can be served tomorrow. Get some good wine. Use the bes white rice, and make some pancakes with white flour." Whe Sanzang heard all this from upstairs he said, "Whatever shal we do, Sun the Second? They're going to slaughter chicken geese, a pig and a sheep. If they bring us all these we won't b able to eat them as we're all vegetarians." "I've got an idea," said Monkey, and he stamped in the doorway and called ou "Mrs. Zhao, come up here." "What instructions do you have fo me, sir," she asked. "Don't kill any living creatures today. We'r eating vegetarian food today," Monkey replied. "Are you gen tlemen permanent vegetarians, or just vegetarians for thi month?" asked the woman in surprise. "Neither," replied Mon key. "We're vegetarians on *gengshen* days.* Today's one, s

---

* A *gengshen* day, like the *xinyou* day that follows it, occurs once i every cycle of sixty days.

we have to eat meatless food. But after the third watch tonight t'll be a *xinyou* day and the restrictions won't apply. Kill them omorrow. Lay on some vegetarian food today, and make it irst-class."

This made the woman happier than ever. "Don't slaughter anything," she said, hurrying downstairs, "don't slaughter any- hing. Fetch some tree-ear fungus, Fujian bamboo shoots, bean- curd and wheat gluten. Pick some green vegetables in the gar- den, make vermicelli soup, steam some bread rolls, boil more white rice and make some scented tea." Now the cooks were experts because they cooked every day, so that everything was ready in an instant to be set out upstairs. They also had some confectioneries of lions and immortals that were already made for the four travellers to eat their fill of. When the question was asked, "Would you like some mild wine?" Brother Monkey replied, "Eldest Brother Tang won't have any, but the rest of us will have a few cups." The widow then fetched a jug of warm wine.

When drinks had been poured out for the three of them hey heard the sound of banging against wooden boards. "Has some furniture fallen over downstairs, missus?" Monkey asked. "No," the woman replied, "it's some retainers from my farm who arrived late this evening with rent rice. We let them sleep downstairs. As we were short-staffed when you gentlemen arrived I told them to take the sedan-chairs to the brothel to fetch some young ladies to keep you company. They must have hit the underneath of the floorboards with the chair-poles." "You mentioned that before," Monkey said. "But don't send for them now. Today's a fast day, and besides, our brothers aren't here yet. They'll be here tomorrow for sure. Then we can all send for some call-girls and have a good time in your excellent establishment before we sell our horses and go." "What good men," the woman said, "what good men. That way you'll all stay friends and you won't waste your energy." Then she ordered that the sedan-chairs be brought back in as the whores were not to be fetched. The four of them finished their wine and food, the utensils were cleared away, and the meal was over.

"Where are we going to sleep?" Sanzang whispered in Monkey's ear. "Upstairs," Monkey replied. "Too dangerous," Sanzang replied. "We have all had so hard a journey that we may well fall fast asleep. If any of the inn people come in to tidy up and our hats have rolled off they will see our bald heads, realize that we are monks, and raise a hue and cry. That would be a disaster." "You're right," said Monkey, going out to stamp his foot again. "What instructions do you have this time, Mr. Sun?" the woman asked, coming upstairs once more. "Where are we to sleep?" Monkey asked. "Upstairs is best," she replied. "There are no mosquitoes and there's a south wind. Open the windows wide and you'll sleep beautifully." "We won't be able to," said Monkey. "Our Mr. Hogg the Third has a touch of gout, Mr. Sand the Fourth has some rheumatism in his shoulder, Brother Tang can only sleep in the dark, and I don't like the light myself. So this is no place for us to sleep."

As the woman went downstairs, leaning on the banisters and sighing, her daughter, who was carrying a child in her arms, came up to her and said, "Mother, as the saying goes, 'Be stuck on a sandbank for ten days, then said past nine sandbanks in one.' It's too hot now to be doing much business, but once autumn begins we'll have more than we can handle. What are you sighing like that for?" "It's not because business is slack, daughter," the older woman replied. "I was just going to close the inn up this evening when four horse dealers came and took a room. They wanted the first-class tariff. I was hoping to make a little silver out of them, and I'm sighing because we won't earn much: they're fasting." "As they've already eaten they can't very well go to another inn," the daughter replied. "And we'll be able to make money out of them when we serve them meat and wine tomorrow." "They're all poorly," the older woman replied, "and want somewhere dark to sleep because they don't like draughts or light. All the rooms in the inn have got missing tiles, so where am I going to find somewhere dark for them? It'd be best to write off the cost of the meal and tell them to stay somewhere else."

"But we do have somewhere dark in the house, mother," her daughter replied, "where there's no draught and no light. It'll do splendidly." "Where?" the older woman asked. "The big trunk that father had made when he was still alive," the daughter replied. "It's four feet wide, seven feet long and three feet high, and big enough for seven people to sleep in. Tell them to sleep in the trunk." "I don't know whether it'll do," said the older woman. "I'll ask them. Mr Sun, if you won't have our poky little room there's nowhere darker here than our big trunk. It'll keep out light and draughts. So why don't you sleep in the trunk?" "Splendid," Monkey replied. She then told several of the retainers to carry the trunk out and open the lid, while inviting her guests to come downstairs. Monkey led the master and Friar Sand carried the luggage as they went to the trunk, following in the lantern's shadow. The reckless Pig was the first to climb inside. Friar Sand lifted the luggage in then helped the Tang Priest in before getting in himself. "Where's our horse?" Monkey asked. "Tied up eating hay in the stables at the back," replied the servant who was attending them. "Bring it here," said Monkey, "and bring the trough too. Tether the animal next to the trunk." Only then did he get inside himself and call out, "Shut the lid, Mrs. Zhao, fasten the hasp and padlock it. And look it over for us. Glue paper wherever it lets in the light. Open it again early tomorrow morning." "You're very particular," the widow said. After that the doors were fastened and everyone went to bed.

The story switches to the four of them in the chest. Poor things! They were wearing hats, the weather was very hot and it was airless and stuffy. They took off their hats and clothes, and fanned themselves with their monastic hats for lack of fans. They were all crowded in next to each other and did not fall asleep till the second watch. Monkey, however, wanted to make trouble, so he stayed awake. He put his hand out and gave Pig a pinch on the leg. The idiot pulled his leg in and mumbled,

"Go to sleep. We've had a hard day. What do you want to fool around pinching people's hands and feet for?" "We started by laying out five thousand ounces of silver," said Monkey aloud, deliberately making mischief, "and we sold those horses the other day for three thousand. We've got four thousand in the two bags, and we'll sell this herd of horses for another three thousand. That means we'll have doubled our capital. That's not bad." Pig, who was sleepy, did not bother to reply.

Now the floor staff, the water-carriers and the kitchen porters were in league with bandits. After hearing Brother Monkey talking about all the money they had, several of them slipped off to fetch twenty or more armed bandits to come with torches to rob the four horse traders. As they charged in through the gates they gave Widow Zhao and her daughter such a fright that shivering and shaking they fastened the doors of their room and let the robbers take whatever they wanted outside. Now the bandits were not after the inn's property but were looking for the guests. When they went upstairs and found no sign of them there, they lit their torches and held them out while they looked all around. All they could see was a large trunk in the courtyard, to the bottom of which was tethered a white horse. The lid was tightly locked and could not be prized open. "Travelling merchants all know what they're about," the bandits said. "This trunk looks so strong that it's bound to be full of purses, valuables and silk. Let's steal the horse, take the trunk out of town, open it up and share out what's inside. That would be the best thing, wouldn't it?" The bandits then found some rope with which they lifted the box and carried it off, swinging and swaying. "Brother," said Pig, woken up by this, "go to sleep. Why are you rocking us?" "Shut up," Monkey replied. "Nobody's rocking us." Sanzang and Friar Sand had been abruptly awoken too, and they asked, "Who's carrying us?" "Keep quiet," said Monkey, "keep quiet. Let them carry us. If they carry us to the Western Heaven we'll be saved the trouble of walking."

But the successful bandits were not heading west. Instead they headed towards the east of the city, killing the soldiers on the city gate, opening it and letting themselves out. This caused sensation in the streets and the markets, where the watchmen f all the shops reported it to the commander-in-chief of the city arrison and the east city commissioner. As this was their esponsibility the commander-in-chief and the east city commis- ioner mustered a force of infantry, cavalry and bowmen that eft the city in pursuit of the bandits. Seeing that resistance to o powerful a government force would have been pointless, the andits abandoned the trunk and the white horse, scattered into he undergrowth and disappeared. The government troops did ot catch even half a robber: all they captured was the trunk nd the white horse, with which they returned in triumph. The ommander-in-chief examined the horse in the light of the lamps nd saw that it was a fine one:

Threads of silver grew in his mane;
In his tail hung strands of jade.
Forget about Eight Chargers and dragon steeds;*
*This was steadier than the great Sushuang;***
Its bones alone would have sold for a thousand ounces of silver;
It could gallop after the wind for three thousand miles.
When it climbed a mountain it merged into the clouds;
As it neighed at the moon it was as white as snow.
It was truly a dragon from an ocean island,
A unicorn of jade in the human world.

The commander-in-chief rode the white horse instead of his own teed as he led his men back into the city. The trunk was car- ied to his headquarters, where he and the east city commissioner ealed it with strips of paper on which they wrote and set a guard ver it till morning, when they would submit a memorial to the ing and request a decision on what to do with it. After that he other troops were dismissed.

The story now tells how the venerable Tang Priest was

---

* Legendary horses of King Mu of Zhou.

** Another swift horse.

grumbling at Monkey inside the chest. "Ape," he said, "you've killed me this time. If I had been arrested outside and taken to the king of Dharmadestructia I might well have been able to put up a good argument in my defence. But now I am here locked in this trunk. I have been carried off by bandits and recaptured by the army. When we are shown to the king tomorrow we will be all ready for him to put to the sword and make up his ten thousand." "There are people outside!" exclaimed Monkey. "If they open the trunk and take you out you'll either be tied up or hung up. If you don't want to be tied or strung up you'd better show a little patience. When we're taken to see this deluded king tomorrow I'll definitely be able to talk my way out of things. I guarantee that not one hair of yours will be harmed. So stop worrying and go back to sleep."

In the third watch Monkey used one of his magic powers. Slipping his cudgel out he blew on it with a magic breath, called "Change!" and turned it into a triple auger with which he drilled two or three holes near the bottom of the chest, forming a single larger hole. He put the auger away, shook himself, turned into an ant and crawled out. Then he turned back into himself and rode his cloud straight to the palace gates. The king was fast asleep at the time, so Monkey used his Great All-powerful Body-dividing Magic. Plucking all the hairs out of his left arm he blew on them with a magic breath, called "Change!" and turned them into little Monkeys. Then he pulled all the hairs out from his right arm, blew on them with a magic breath, called "Change!" and turned them into sleep-insects. Next he recited the magic word *Om* and told the local deity of the place to take the little Monkeys to distribute them throughout the palace to all the officials in every office and department of government. Each holder of official rank was given a sleep-insect to ensure that he or she would sleep soundly and not get up. Monkey then took his gold-banded cudgel in his hands, squeezed it, waved it, called, "Change, treasure!" and turned it into over a thousand razors of the sort used for shaving the head. Taking one himself, he told all the little monkeys to take one each and shave the heads of everyone in the inner quarters of the palace and in all the government departments and offices. This was indeed a case of:

When the Dharma king would destroy it the Dharma is infinite;
The Dharma runs through heaven and earth, opening the Great Way.
The origins of ten thousand Dharmas all come down to one;
The features of the Three Vehicles are basically the same.
He bored through the trunk to find out the news,
Distributed his golden hairs to smash delusion,
Determined to bring the Dharma king to the true achievement,
To the eternal emptiness of what is not born and dies not.

That night the head-shaving was completed, so Monkey said another spell to dismiss the local deity, shook himself to bring all the hairs back to his arms, then touched all the razors to turn them back into their true form as the gold-banded cudgel, which he made much smaller and hid in his ear again. Finally he reverted to being an ant, crawled back into the trunk, and went on guarding the Tang Priest in his time of danger.

When the palace ladies in the inner quarters got up to wash and do their hair before dawn the next morning they all found that their hair had gone. The same had happened to all the eunuchs, senior and junior, who moved around the palace. They all crowded to the outside of the royal bedchamber, where they played music to wake the king up, all holding back their tears but not daring to speak. Before long the queen in the palace woke up to find her hair gone too. When she hurried with lanterns to the dragon bed she found a monk sleeping in the brocade quilt, at which she could restrain her tongue no longer, thus awakening the king. When the king suddenly opened his eyes wide and saw the queen's bald head he got straight out of bed and said, "Why are you like that, my queen?" "You're the same, Your Majesty," she replied. The king then rubbed his head, which gave him such a fright that the three souls in his body groaned, and his seven spirits flew off into the air. "What has happened to me?" he exclaimed. Just when he was in this panicky state the royal consorts, the palace ladies and the eunuchs young and old all fell to their knees, their heads shaved bald, and said, "Lord, we have all been turned into monks." At the sight of them the king wept. "We think this must be because of all the monks we have killed," he said. He then gave these orders: "None of you are to say anything about the loss of our hair as, if you do, the civil and military officials may slander our country and say that it has been badly governed. Let us now hold court in the throne hall."

Now all the officials high and low in all the departments and offices of government went to court to pay their respects before dawn. As it turned out, all these men had lost their hair in the night too, and they all submitted memorials reporting the fact. All that could be heard was:

The whip of silence sounding three times at the royal audience;
As all report that their heads have now been shaved.

If you do not know what happened to the booty in the trunk that the commander-in-chief had recaptured and whether the Tang Priest and his three disciples were to live or die, listen to the explanation in the next instalment.

CHAPTER EIGHTY-FIVE

The Mind-ape is jealous of the Mother of Wood; The demon chief plots to devour the Master of Dhyana.

The story tells how when the king held his dawn audience the civil and military officials all carried memorials. "Sovereign Lord," they reported, "we beg you to forgive your servants for their lack of decorum." "Gentlemen," the king replied, "you are all as courteous as ever. What lack of decorum are you showing?" "Sovereign Lord," they said, "we do not know why, but all of your servants lost their hair last night." Holding in his hand these memorials about the lost hair, the king descended from his dragon throne to say to the officials, "Indeed, we do not know why either, but everyone in the palace, young and old, lost their hair last night." King and ministers alike all wept as they said, "From now on we will not dare kill any more monks." The king then returned to his throne and the officials took their places in their proper ranks. The king then said, "Let those with business here come forward from their ranks to report. If there is no other business the curtain may be rolled up and the audience ended." The commander-in-chief of the capital's garrison then moved forward from the ranks of military officials and the east city commissioner moved forward from the ranks of the civil officials to kowtow at the steps of the throne and report, "We were patrolling the city on Your Majesty's orders last night when we recaptured a trunk of bandits' booty and a white horse. As we do not dare take unauthorized action over these we beg Your Majesty to issue an edict." The king was delighted. "Bring it here, trunk and all," he ordered.

The two officials then returned to their own offices, mustered a full complement of soldiers and had the trunk carried out.

Sanzang, who was inside, felt his soul leaving his body. "Disciples," he said, "what shall we say in our defence when we reach the king?" "Shut up," said Monkey with a grin. "I've fixed everything. When the trunk's opened the king will bow to us as his teachers. The only thing is that Pig mustn't quarrel about precedence." "If they don't kill me that'll be heaven," Pig replied. "What would I want to quarrel about?" Before these words were all out of his mouth they had been carried to the palace entrance and in through the Tower of Five Phoenixes to be set at the foot of the steps to the throne.

On being invited by the two officials to have the trunk opened and look inside the king ordered that this be done. No sooner was the lid lifted than Pig, who could restrain himself no longer, sprang outside, giving all the officials such a fright that they shivered, unable to speak. Next Brother Monkey could be seen helping the Tang Priest out, while Friar Sand lifted the luggage out. Seeing that the commander-in-chief was holding the white horse, Pig went up to him, made an angry noise and said, "That's my horse. Hand it over!" This so terrified the official that he collapsed head over heels. The four pilgrims all stood upright in the middle of the steps, and when the king saw that they were monks he came down at once from his dragon throne, sent for his queen and consorts from the inner quarters, descended the steps of the throne hall, bowed to them along with all his officials and asked, "What brings you venerable gentlemen here?" "I have been sent by His Majesty the Great Tang Emperor to go to the Great Thunder Monastery in India in the West to worship the living Buddha and fetch the true scriptures," Sanzang replied. "Venerable Master," the king said, "you have come from far away. But why did you sleep in this trunk last night?" "I knew that Your Majesty had sworn a vow to kill Buddhist monks," Sanzang replied, "which is why I did not dare to visit your illustrious country openly, but disguised myself as a layman to arrive late at night to find lodging in one of your inns. We slept in the trunk because we were afraid that our real identity would be discovered. Unfortunately the trunk was stolen by bandits, then brought back here by the commander-in-chief. Now hat I have been able to see Your Majesty's dragon countenance, he clouds have cleared away and the sun has come out. I hope hat Your Majesty will pardon and release me, ascetic monk that am: my gratitude will be as deep as the ocean."

"Venerable Master," the king replied, "you are a distin-;uished monk from our suzerain heavenly dynasty. It was wrong of us not to go out to welcome you. For years we have been ulfilling a vow to kill monks because a monk once maligned us. The vow we made to heaven was to kill ten thousand monks to nake up a round number. We never imagined that today we vould return to the truth and that we would all be turned into nonks. Now all of us, king, officials, queen and consorts, have ad our hair shaved off. I beg, Venerable Master, that you will ot be grudging with your lofty virtue and will take us as your lisciples." When Pig heard this he started roaring with laughter: "If you're going to be our disciples what introductory presents ave you got for us?" "If you will accept us as your follower, Master," the king replied, "we will present you with all the vealth in our kingdom." "Don't talk about wealth to us," said Brother Monkey, "as we're proper monks. As long as you inspect nd return our passport and escort us out of the city I can guaran-ee that your monarchy will last for ever and that you will enjoy long and happy life." On hearing this the king ordered his of-ice of foreign relations to arrange a great feast at which monarch nd officials together returned to the one truth. The passport was mmediately inspected and returned, after which Sanzang was sked to change the name of the country. " 'Dharma' in the name of Your Majesty's country is excellent," Monkey said, "but the destructia' part is nonsense. Now that we've come here you hould change the name to 'Dharmarespectia'. This would uarantee

Clear waters and victory for a thousand generations;
Timely winds and rain with universal peace."

The king thanked them for their gracious kindness, had the royal arriage prepared and escorted the Tang Priest and his three lisciples westwards out of the city.

We will say no more of how monarch and subjects now held to the true faith, but tell how after leaving the king of Dharmarespectia the venerable elder said happily from on his horse, "What excellent magic you used, Wukong. It worked very well." "Elder brother," said Friar Sand, "where did you find so many barbers to shave all those heads in one night?" Monkey then told them all about how he had used his miraculous powers, at which they all laughed so much they could not stop.

Just as they were feeling so cheerful a great mountain came into view, blocking their way. Reining in the horse, the Tang Priest said, "Disciples, see how high that mountain is. You must be very careful." "Don't worry," said Monkey with a grin, "don't worry. I promise you nothing will go wrong." "Don't say that," Sanzang replied. "I can see those jutting peaks, and even from a distance it looks rather sinister. Storm clouds are streaming from it, and I am beginning to feel frightened. My whole body is turning numb and my spirits are disturbed." "You have already forgotten the *Heart Sutra* that the Rook's Nest Hermit taught you," said Brother Monkey. "I can still remember it," Sanzang said. "Even if you can still remember that," said Monkey, "there is a quatrain that you've forgotten." "What quatrain?" Sanzang asked, to which Monkey replied,

> *"Do not go far to seek the Buddha on Vulture Peak;*
> *Vulture Peak is in your heart.*
> *Everybody has a Vulture Peak stupa*
> *Under which to cultivate conduct."*

"Of course I know it, disciple," said Sanzang. "According to that quatrain the thousands of scriptures all come down to cultivating the heart." "Goes without saying," Monkey replied.

> *"When the heart is purified it can shine alone;*
> *When the heart is preserved all perceptions are pure.*
> *If there is any mistake then laziness follows,*
> *And success will not come in a myriad years.*
> *As long as your will is sincere*
> *Thunder Peak is before your eyes.*

But if you're as scared, frightened and disturbed as this the Great Way is distant, and Thunder Peak is far, far away. Forget those wild fears and come with me." When the venerable elder heard this his spirits were revived and his worries disappeared.

The four of them had only gone a few more steps when they reached the mountain. When they raised their eyes this was what they saw:

A fine mountain,
Dappled with many colours.
White clouds drifted around the peak,
And cool were the shadows of the trees in front of the cliff.
The birds rustled in the leaves,
The beasts were ferocious.
Among the woods were a thousand pines,
On the ridge a few bamboos.
Howls came from grey wolves seizing their prey,
And roars from hungry tigers fighting over food.
Long screamed the wild apes searching for fruit;
The David's-deer climbed through blossoms into mists of green.
The wind was blowing,
The waters babbled,
And hidden birds sang in the deserted pass.
Here and there wisteria was climbing
While rare flowers bloomed by the stream amid orchids.
Intricately shaped and strange were the rocks,
And sheer rose the crags.
Foxes and racoon-dogs ran in packs;
Badgers and apes were playing in groups.
The travellers were worried by so high and steep a mountain:
Why was the ancient track so twisted?

While master and disciples were moving timidly ahead they heard the howling of a wind. "There's a wind," said Sanzang in fear. "In the spring there are mild winds," Monkey replied, "in the summer hot ones, in the autumn golden ones and in the winter north winds. There are winds in all four seasons. What's so frightening about a wind?" "This wind is blowing very hard," Sanzang replied. "It is definitely not a wind from heaven." "But winds always come from the earth and clouds from mountains," Monkey replied, "so how could there be a wind from heaven?" Before he had finished speaking a mist arose. That mist really was

Darkness joining up with the sky,
Obscurity making the whole earth dim.
The sun had completely vanished from sight
And no bird sang.
All was as indistinct as primal chaos,
And the air seemed filled with flying dust.
The trees on the mountain could not be seen
Where had the herb-gatherers gone?

"Wukong," said Sanzang in fright, "why is there this mist when the wind is still blowing?" "Don't get upset," Monkey replied. "Get off your horse, Master. I'll go and see whether or not it's sinister while you two keep guard, brothers."

The splendid Great Sage needed only to bow in order to be in mid-air. Holding his hand to his brow for shade, he opened his fiery eyes wide and looked down to see an evil spirit sitting at the foot of a beetling scar. Just look and see what he was like:

A mighty body full of charm,
A heroic manner of great vigour.
The fangs protruding from his mouth were drills of steel;
His nose hung like a jade hook in the middle.
His golden eyes with pupils round gave animals a fright;
Demons and gods were scared of his bristling silver whiskers.
He sat upright by the cliff in terrible might,
Making the mist and wind as he hatched his plot.

On either side of him some thirty or forty junior demons could be seen, all drawn up in line and blowing out mist and wind for all they were worth. Monkey grinned at this and thought, "So my master is clairvoyant. He said it wasn't a heavenly wind, and it was in fact caused by this evil spirit trying to fool us. Now if I went straight down and hit him with what they call a 'garlic-smasher' that'd kill him sure enough, but it would ruin my reputation." Monkey had been a true hero all his life and was quite incapable of playing a dirty trick like that. "I'd better go back and give Pig some attention. I'll ask him to hit the evil spirit first. If Pig's good enough to kill the evil spirit we'll be in luck. If he isn't and the evil spirit captures him I can come back to rescue him and win myself a bit of fame. He's always putting on such an act and being so lazy — he won't make an effort. Still, he is very greedy and partial to a good feed. I think I'll try a trick on him and see how that works."

At once he brought his cloud down to land in front of Sanzang, who asked, "Are the wind and the mist sinister or not?" "It's clear now," Monkey replied. "They've gone." "Yes," said Sanzang, "they have eased off a little." "Master," said Monkey with a smile, "my eyesight is very good usually, but this time I was wrong. I thought there'd probably be a monster behind that wind and mist but there wasn't." "What caused them then?" Sanzang asked. "There's a village not far ahead," Monkey replied, "where the people are so pious that they're steaming white rice and white breadrolls to feed monks with. I think that the mist must have been steam escaping from their steamers. It was the result of their goodness." When Pig heard this he thought Monkey was telling the truth, so he grabbed hold of him and whispered, "Did you eat their food before you came back?" "Only a bit," Monkey replied. "The vegetable dishes were too salty — I didn't want to eat too much." "Blow that," said Pig. "I'd eat my fill of it however salty it was. If it made me really thirsty I'd come back for a drink of water." "Would you like some?" Monkey asked. "Sure thing," Pig replied. "I'm hungry and I'd like some now. What do you think?" "You mustn't even talk about it," said Monkey. "As the ancient book says, 'When the father is present the son must do nothing on his own account.'

Our master, who's as good as a father to you, is here, so none of us should dare go ahead." "If you'll say nothing about it, I'm going," replied Pig with a grin. "Let's see how you do it," Monkey replied. "I'll say nothing." When it came to eating the idiot knew a thing or two. He went up to his master, made a loud "na-a-aw" of respect, and said, "Master, elder brother has just told me that there are people in a village ahead of us who feed monks. Just look at that horse. It looks as though it's going to start playing up. We'll be causing a lot of trouble if we have to ask for grass and other fodder for it. Luckily the wind and the clouds have gone now, so why don't you all sit here for a while while I fetch some tender grass? We can go and beg for food from that house when we've fed the horse." "Splendid," said the Tang Priest with delight. "I wonder why you've become so hard-working today. Be as quick as you can."

Smiling secretly to himself the idiot started out. "Brother," said Monkey, catching up and grabbing hold of him, "they feed monks all right, but only good-looking ones." "In that case I'll have to change again," said Pig. "Yes," said Brother Monkey, "you change." The splendid idiot, who could perform thirty-six transformations, went into a hollow on the mountainside, made a spell with his hands, said the magic words, shook himself and turned himself into a short, skinny monk, beating a wooden fish-shaped drum with his hand and mumbling, "Oh great one, oh great one," because he knew no scriptures to recite.

After putting away the wind and the mist the evil spirit ordered all his devils to form a circle round the main road, ready for any travellers. The idiot's luck was out, and he was soon inside the trap and surrounded by the devils, who grabbed at his clothes and his silken sash as they all crowded in on him together. "Don't pull," Pig said. "You can let me eat in all your houses in turn." "What do you want to eat, monk?" the devils asked. "You feed monks here," Pig replied, "and I've come to be fed." "So you're hoping to be fed, are you, monk?" said the demons. "You don't seem to realize that what we like doing best here is eating monks. We're all evil immortals who've found the Way here in the mountains, and the only thing we want to do is to catch you monks, take you home with us, pop you in the steamer till you're tender and eat you. And you're still hoping for a vegetarian meal!" At this Pig's heart was filled with terror, and he started complaining about Monkey. "That Protector of the Horses is a crook. He lied to me about them feeding monks in this village. There aren't any villagers here and there's nobody who feeds monks. They're all evil spirits." The idiot was being tugged at so hard that he turned back into himself, pulled the rake out from his belt and struck out wildly, driving all the junior devils back.

They rushed back to report to the senior demon, "Disaster, Your Majesty." "What disaster?" the senior demon asked. "A neat-looking monk came along in front of the mountain," they replied, "so we decided to catch him and steam him. We were going to keep what we couldn't eat now for a bad day. Then to our astonishment he transformed himself." "What did he turn himself into?" the senior demon asked. "Not into anything human," they replied. "He's got a long snout, big ears, and a bristly mane on his back. He lashed out furiously at us with a rake that he used two-handed. He gave us such a terrible fright that we've run straight back to report to Your Majesty." "Don't be afraid," the senior demon said. "Let me go and have a look." Swinging his iron mace he went up for a closer look and saw that the idiot really was hideous. This is what he looked like:

A snout like a husking hammer over three feet long;
Tusks like silver nails protruding from his mouth.
Two round eyes that flashed like lightning;
A pair of ears that made a howling wind when they flapped.
The bristles behind his head were rows of iron arrows;
All of his hide was rough and green and scabby.
In his hands he held an amazing object:
A nine-toothed rake of which everyone was afraid.

Summoning up his courage, the evil spirit shouted, "Where are you from? What's your name? Tell me at once and I'll spare your life." To this Pig replied with a laugh, "So you can't recognize your own ancestor Pig either, my boy. Come closer and I'll tell you:

For my huge mouth and tusks and mighty powers
I was made Marshal Tian Peng by the Jade Emperor,
Commanding eighty thousand marines on the River of Heaven,
And happy amid all the joys of the heavenly palace.
Because when drunk I flirted with a palace lady
I decided to play the hero for a while.
One butt from my snout destroyed the Dipper and Bull Palace;
I ate the magic mushrooms of the Queen Mother of the West.
The Jade Emperor himself gave me two thousand hammer-blows,
Made me an exile from the world of Heaven.
This made me determined to nourish my spirit,
And become an evil monster in the lower world.
Just when I had made a good marriage in Gao Village
Fate brought me up against my brother Monkey.
He subdued me with his gold-banded cudgel;
I was forced to bow my head and enter the Buddhist faith.
I do the heavy work, saddle the horse and carry luggage:
I must have been the Tang Priest's debtor in an earlier life.
As the iron-footed Marshal Tian Peng my surname was Zhu;
My name as a Buddhist is Zhu Bajie."

When the evil spirit heard this he shouted, "So you're the Tang Priest's disciple. I've long heard that his flesh is very tasty. You're one of the people I most want to catch. I'm not going to spare you now you've fallen into my clutches. Stay where you are, and take this from my mace." "Evil beast," Pig replied. "You must have been a dyer before." "What do you mean, I must have been a dyer?" the evil spirit asked. "If you weren't a dyer, how come you know how to use a pestle?" Pig retorted, and with no further argument the monster was upon him, striking furiously. They fought a fine battle in the mountain hollow:

A nine-toothed rake,
An iron mace.
As the rake went through its movements they were like a howling gale;
The mace's skilful blows came as thick and fast as rain.
One was an unknown ogre blocking the mountain road;
The other was the offending Tian Peng now guarding his true nature's master.
When one's nature is right monsters cause no fear;
When the mountain is high earth cannot come from metal.
One fought with his mace like a python from a pool;
The other's rake was like a dragon from the waters.
Their angry shouts shook mountains and rivers;
Their mighty roars caused terror down in hell.
Each of the heroes displayed his prowess,
Staking his life on his magical powers.

We will say no more of how Pig set a mighty wind blowing as he fought the evil spirit, who ordered his junior devils to keep Pig surrounded. Instead the story tells how Brother Monkey suddenly gave a bitter laugh behind the Tang Priest's back. "Why are you laughing like that, elder brother?" Friar Sand asked. "Pig really is an idiot," Monkey replied. "As soon as he heard that they feed monks there he fell for my trick. He's been away a long time now. If he'd beaten the evil spirit with a single blow of his rake you'd have seen him coming back in triumph by now, loudly insisting on his great victory. But if the demon's been too much for him and captured him my luck's out. Goodness only knows how often he'll have cursed the Protector of the Horses behind my back. Say nothing while I go to take a look around, Wujing." With that the splendid Great Sage, who did not want the venerable elder to know what was happening, quietly pulled a hair out of the back of his head, blew on it with magic breath, said "Change!" and turned it into his own double to stay with the master together with Friar Sand. Then his real self disappeared as he leapt up into the air to look around. He saw the idiot lashing out wildly with his rake at the devils who were surrounding him and gradually getting the better of him.

This was more than Monkey could bear. Bringing his cloud down to land, he shouted at the top of his voice, "Take it easy, Pig. Monkey's here." Recognizing that it was Monkey's voice gave the idiot a chance to be more ferocious than ever as he hit wildly forward with his rake. The evil spirit was no match for him. "You weren't up to much before, monk," he said, "so how come you're so fierce now?" "You'd better stop bullying me now, my lad," Pig replied. "I've got one of our people here now." A moment later he was swinging wildly again with the rake. The evil spirit, unable to stave off the blows, led his devils away in defeat. As soon as Monkey saw that the devils had been beaten he drew no closer but went straight back on his cloud, shook the hair and put it back on his body. With his mortal, fleshly eyes the Tang Priest noticed nothing of this.

Before long a triumphant Pig returned too, so exhausted that his nose was dripping with snot as he foamed at the mouth and was panting loudly. "Master!" he called. When the Tang Priest saw him he exclaimed in astonishment, "Pig, you went to fetch some grass for the horse. Why have you come back in so terrible a state? Were there watchmen on the mountain who wouldn't let you cut any?" The idiot flung his rake down, beat his chest and stamped his feet as he replied, "Don't ask me about it, Master. If I had to tell you I'd die of shame." "What would you be so ashamed of?" Sanzang asked. "Elder brother tricked me," Pig replied. "He told me that it wasn't an evil spirit behind that wind and mist. He said there was nothing sinister about it, but that it was from a village where the people were so pious that they were steaming white rice and breadrolls made with white flour to feed monks with. I believed him. As I was so hungry I thought I'd go ahead to beg for some. Fetching grass for the horse was only an excuse. I never expected to be surrounded by a crowd of evil spirits. They gave me a hard fight, and if Monkey hadn't helped me out with his mourner's staff I'd have had no hope of escaping and getting back here."

"The idiot's talking nonsense," said Monkey, who was standing beside them, with a smile. "If you've taken to robbery you're trying to get a whole gaolful of people into trouble. I've been looking after the master here. I've never left his side." "It is true," Sanzang said, "Wukong has never left my side." The idiot then sprang up shouting, "You don't understand, Master. He's got a double." "Is there really a monster there, Wukong?" Sanzang asked. Monkey could keep his deception up no longer. "There are a few little devils," Monkey replied with a bow and a smile, "but they won't dare give us any trouble. Come here, Pig. I'm going to look after you. We're going to escort the master along this steep mountain path as if we were an army on the march." "How?" Pig asked. "You'll be the commander of the vanguard," Monkey replied, "going in front and clearing the way. If the evil spirit doesn't show up again that will be that; but if he does, you fight him. When you beat the evil spirit that'll be something to your credit." Reckoning that the evil spirit's powers were much the same as his own, Pig said, "Very well then. I'm ready to die at his hands. I'll take the lead." "Idiot," said Monkey, "if you start by saying such unlucky things you'll never get anywhere." "As you know, brother," Pig replied,

"When a gentleman goes to a banquet
He gets either drunk or well filled;
When a hero goes into a battle
He gets either wounded or killed.

By saying something unlucky first I'll make myself stronger later." This delighted Monkey, who saddled the horse and invited the master to ride while Friar Sand carried the luggage as they all followed Pig into the mountains.

The evil spirit meanwhile led a few of his underlings who had survived the rout straight back to his cave, where he sat brooding in silence high up above a rocky precipice. Many of the junior devils who looked after things in his household came up to him and asked, "Why are you so miserable today, Your Majesty? You're usually in such high spirits when you come back." "Little ones," said the demon king, "usually when I go out to patrol the mountains I can be sure of bringing home a few people or animals I've caught to feed you with. Today my luck was out: I've met my match." "Who?" the junior devils asked. "A monk," the demon king replied, "a disciple of the Tang Priest from the east who's going to fetch the scriptures. He's called Zhu Bajie. He went for me so hard with his rake that he beat me. I had to run away. I'm thoroughly fed up. For ages now I've heard it said that the Tang Priest is an arhat who has cultivated his conduct for ten successive lifetimes. Anyone who eats a piece of his flesh will live for ever. To my surprise he's come to my mountain today, and it would have been an ideal time to catch him, cook him and eat him. I never realized he'd have a disciple like that one."

Before he had finished saying this a junior devil slipped forward from the ranks. First he gave three sobs in front of the demon king, then three laughs. "Why sob then laugh?" shouted the demon king. The junior devil fell to his knees as he replied, "Because Your Majesty just said that you wanted to eat the Tang Priest. His flesh isn't worth eating." "But everyone says that a piece of his flesh will make you live as long as the heavens," said the demon king. "How can you say that it's not worth eating?" "If he were so good to eat," the junior devil replied, "he'd never have got this far. Other demons would have eaten him up. And he's got three disciples with him." "Do you know who?" the demon king asked. "The senior disciple is Sun the Novice," said the junior devil, "and the third disciple is Friar Sand. The one you met must have been his second disciple Zhu Bajie." "How does Friar Sand compare with Zhu Bajie?" asked the demon king. "He's much the same," the junior devil said. "What about Sun the Novice?" the demon king asked, at which the junior devil thrust out his tongue in horror and replied, "I daren't tell you. That Monkey has tremendous magic powers and can do all sorts of transformations. Five hundred years ago he made terrible havoc in heaven. None of the heavenly warriors dared give him any trouble, from the Twenty-eight Constellations, the Star Lords of the Nine Bright Shiners, the Gods of the Twelve Branches, the Five Officers and the Four Ministers, the East and West Dippers and the Gods of the North and the South, to the Five Peaks and the Four Rivers. How can you have the nerve to want to eat the Tang Priest?" "How do you know so much about him?" the demon king asked. "I used to live in the Lion Cave of the demon king on Lion Ridge," the junior devil replied. "He was reckless enough to want to eat the Tang Priest, and that Sun the Novice smashed his way in through the gates with his gold-banded cudgel. It was terrible. They were wiped out. Luckily I had enough sense to escape by the back door and come here, where Your Majesty allowed me to stay. That's how I know about his powers." The senior demon turned pale with shock when he heard this: it was a case of the commander-in-chief being afraid of the soothsayer's words. How could he help being alarmed when he heard all this from one of his own people?

Just when they were all feeling terrified another junior devil stepped forward and said, "Don't be so upset and afraid, Your Majesty. As the saying goes, easy does it. If you want to eat the Tang Priest let me make you a plan to capture him." "What plan?" the senior demon asked. "I have a plan to 'divide the petals of the plum blossom'." "What do you mean by 'dividing the petals of the plum blossom'?" the demon king asked. "Call the roll of all the devils in the cave," the junior devil replied. "Choose the best hundred from all thousand of them, then the best ten out of that hundred, and finally the best three out of the ten. They must be capable and good at transformations. Have them all turn into Your Majesty's doubles, wear Your Majesty's helmet and armour, carry Your Majesty's mace, and lie in wait in three different places. First send one out to fight Zhu Bajie, then one to fight Sun the Novice and finally one to fight Friar Sand. This way you'll only have to spare three junior devils to draw the three disciples away. Then Your Majesty will be able to stretch down from mid-air with your cloud-grabbing hand to catch the Tang Priest. He'll be in the bag. It'll be as easy as catching flies in a dish of fish juice. Nothing to it." This suggestion delighted the demon king, who said, "What a brilliant plan, brilliant! If I don't catch the Tang Priest this way, that'll be that. But if I do I can assure you you'll be richly rewarded. I'll make you commander of the vanguard." The junior devil kowtowed to thank him for his grace and went off to call the roll of the devils. After all the monsters in the cave had been carefully checked through, three capable junior devils were selected. They turned into the senior devil's doubles and went to lie in wait for the Tang Priest with their iron maces.

The venerable Tang elder meanwhile was following Pig along the way without a care in the world. When they had been going for some time there was a crashing sound from beside the track and out leapt a junior devil who rushed straight at them, evidently to grab Sanzang. "The evil spirit's here, Pig," Monkey shouted. "Get him!" The idiot, who was taken in by the imposture, hacked wildly at the devil with his rake. The evil spirit parried Pig's blows with his mace as he met the onslaught. While the battle between the pair of them ebbed and flowed on the mountainside there was a noise in the undergrowth as another monster sprang out and charged at the Tang Priest. "This is bad, Master," said Monkey. "Pig can't see straight. He's let the monster escape to catch you. I'm going to fight him." Pulling his cudgel out in a flash, he went up to the monster, shouting, "Where d'you think you're going? Take this!" Without saying a word the evil spirit raised his mace to meet the attack. But while the two of them were locked in combat, swinging at each other, there was a howling wind from the other side of the mountain and a third evil spirit sprang out who also rushed straight at the Tang Priest. When Friar Sand saw it he exclaimed in alarm, "Master, big brother and second brother both can't see straight. They've let the evil spirit get away to catch you. Stay on the horse while I get him." Friar Sand was taken in too. Brandishing his staff he blocked the evil spirit's iron mace and started a bitter combat. It was a wild fight with shouts and awful yells, and they drew further and further away. When the demon king saw from up in the sky that the Tang Priest was alone on the horse he reached down with his five-clawed steel hook and seized him. The master lost horse and stirrups as the evil spirit carried him off in a gust of wind. Alas! This was a case of

When the dhyana-nature encountered a monster the true achievement was hard;
The monk of the river current met once more with a star of disaster.

Bringing his wind down to land, the demon king took the Tang Priest into the cave and called, "Commander of the vanguard!" The junior devil who had made the plan came forward, knelt and said, "I am not worthy." "How can you say that?" the demon king replied. "Once the commander-in-chief has spoken, white becomes black. What I said before was that if I failed to catch the Tang Priest, that would be that; but that if I succeeded I'd make you my commander of the vanguard. Your brilliant plan has succeeded today, so there is no reason why I should break faith with you. Bring the Tang Priest here and tell the underlings to fetch water, scrub the cooking pot, fetch some firewood and light the fire. When he's been steamed you and I will each have a piece of his flesh and live for ever." "Your Majesty," the commander of the vanguard replied, "he mustn't be eaten yet." "Why ever not?" the demon king asked. "We've captured him." "It wouldn't matter if you ate him, Your Majesty," said the commander of the vanguard, "as far as Zhu Bajie and Friar Sand are concerned. They would be reasonable. But I'm worried about that Sun the Novice: he'd be really vicious. If he found out we'd eaten the Tang Priest he wouldn't come to give us a straight fight. He'd just thrust that gold-banded cudgel of his into the mountainside and make a hole so big that the whole mountain would collapse. We'd be homeless." "What do you suggest, commander of the vanguard?" the demon king asked. "In my opinion," the commander replied, "we should send the Tang Priest out to the back garden, tie him to a tree, and starve him for two or three days. That will clean him up inside and let us make sure that the three disciples don't come here looking for him. Once we've found out that they've gone home we can bring the Tang Priest out and enjoy him at our leisure. That'd be better, wouldn't it?" "Yes, yes," the senior demon said with a laugh. "You're right, commander of the vanguard."

An order was issued and the Tang Priest taken into the back garden to be roped to a tree, while all the junior devils went out to the front to keep watch. Look at the venerable elder as he suffers in his bonds, tied up tightly and unable to stop the tears rolling down his cheeks. "Disciples," he called, "where did you chase those demons to when you went to capture them in the mountains? I have been captured by a wicked ogre and have met with disaster. When will I ever see you again? The pain is killing me."

Just when the tears from both eyes were joining in a single stream he heard someone calling from a tree opposite, "Venerable elder, you're here too." Taking control of himself, the Tang Priest asked, "Who are you?" "I'm a woodcutter who lives on this mountain," the other replied. "I've been tied up here for three days. I reckon they're going to eat me." "Woodcutter," said the Tang Priest with tears in his eyes, "If you die it will only be you. You have nothing else to worry about. But if I die it won't be a clean end." "What do you mean, it won't be a clean end, venerable elder?" the woodcutter asked. "You have no parents, wife or children, so if you die that'll be that." "I am from the east," the Tang Priest replied, "and was going to fetch the scriptures from the Western Heaven. I was going on the orders of Emperor Taizong of the Tang to worship the living Buddha and fetch the true scriptures. This was to save all the lonely souls in the underworld who have nobody to care for them. If I lose my life today the vain waiting will kill my sovereign and I will let down his ministers. Countless wronged souls in the City of the Unjustly Slain will suffer a terrible disappointment and never ever be able to escape from the wheel of life. The true achievement will all be turned to dust in the wind.

How can that possibly be considered a clean end?" When the woodcutter heard this the tears fell from his eyes as he said, "If you die that is all there to it. But my death will be even more painful for me to bear. I lost my father when I was a boy, and live alone with my mother. Because we had no property I have had to make our living as a woodcutter. My aged mother is eighty-two this year and I am her only support. If I die who will there be to bury her? It's very hard to bear: the pain of it is killing me." When the venerable elder heard this he began to wail aloud, "Oh dear, oh dear,

Even the mountain man thinks of his mother;
I am reciting the sutras in vain.

Serving one's monarch and serving one's parents are both the same in principle. You are moved by your mother's goodness to you and I by my sovereign lord's goodness to me." This was indeed a case of

Weeping eyes looking at eyes that weep,
A heartbroken one who sees off one with a broken heart.

But we will say no more of Sanzang's sufferings as we return to Monkey, who after driving the junior devil back down the grassy slope rushed back to the track to find that his master had disappeared. All that was left were the white horse and the luggage. In his alarm he led the horse and shouldered the carrying-pole as he headed for the top of the mountain in his search for the master. Oh dear! Indeed,

The long-suffering monk of the river current had met with new suffering;
The Great Sage, subduer of demons, had run into a demon.

If you do not know how his search for his master ended, listen to the explanation in the next instalment.

CHAPTER EIGHTY-SIX

The Mother of Wood lends his might in defeating the ogre; The metal lord uses his magic to wipe out the monster.

The story tells how the Great Sage Monkey was leading the horse and carrying the baggage while he searched the whole mountain top, calling out for his master. Suddenly Pig came running up to him, puffing and panting, to ask, "Why are you shouting like that, brother?" "The master's disappeared," Brother Monkey replied. "Have you seen him?" "Why did you have to play that trick on me when I was being a good monk with the Tang Priest?" Pig asked. "What was all that about me being commander of the vanguard? I had to fight for my life before I could beat that evil spirit and come back in one piece. You and Friar Sand were looking after the master, so why ask me about it?" "I don't blame you, brother," said Monkey. "Somehow or other your eyes must have gone blurred — you let the evil spirit get away and come back to catch the master again. When I went off to fight it I told Friar Sand to look after the master, and he's disappeared too." "I expect he's taken the master somewhere for a crap," said Pig with a grin, but before he had finished speaking Friar Sand turned up. "Where's the master, Friar Sand?" Monkey asked. "You two must both be blind," retorted Friar Sand, "letting the evil spirit escape to come back for the master. When I went to fight the evil spirit the master was left in the horse by himself." At this Monkey leapt with rage, shouting, "He's fooled me! He's fooled me!" "How's he fooled you?" Friar Sand asked. "It was a 'dividing the petals of the plum blossom' trick," Monkey replied, "to draw us three off so that he could make a blow for the heart and carry off the master. Whatever in the name of Heaven are we to do?" He could not stop the tears from streaming down his cheeks, at which Pig said, "Don't cry. If you cry you're a pustule. He can't be far away. He must be on this mountain. Let's look for him."

The three of them had no better plan than to look for him on the mountain. When they had covered some six or seven miles they saw a cave palace at the foot of a beetling precipice:

Clean-cut pinnacles blocking the light,
Towering and grotesque-shaped rocks.
The fragrance of rare and wonderful flowers,
The beauty of red apricots and green peaches.
The ancient trees in front of the precipice,
Forty spans round, and with bark scarred by frost and rain;
The azure pines standing outside the gates,
Two thousand feet of greeny blue reaching up to the sky.
Pairs of wild cranes
That dance in the breeze at the mouth of the cave;
Mountain birds in couples
Chirping by day at the ends of the branches.
Clumps of yellow creepers like ropes,
Rows of misty willows with leaves like hanging gold.
Water fills the pools that are square;
All over the mountain are caves that are deep.
In the pools that are square
Dragons lie hidden with scales unchanged.
In the mountain's deep caves
Dwell ogres that long have been eaters of humans.
This can be matched with the lands of immortals,
A den where the winds and the vapours are stored.

When Monkey saw this he took two or three paces forward, sprang towards the gates and saw that they were shut tight. Above them was a horizontal stone tablet on which was written in large letters

LINKED RING CAVE: BROKEN RIDGE: HIDDEN MISTS MOUNTAIN.

"Strike, Pig," said Monkey. "This is where the evil spirit lives. The master must be here." At this the idiot turned vicious, raised his rake, and brought it down on the gates with all his strength, smashing a big hole in them and shouting, "Ogre, send my master out at once if you don't want me to smash your gates down and finish the lot of you off." At this the junior devils on the gates rushed back inside to report, "Disaster, Your Majesty." "What disaster?" the senior demon asked. "Someone's smashed a hole in the front gates and is yelling that he wants his master," the junior devils replied. "I wonder which one's come looking for him," said the demon king in a state of great alarm. "Don't be frightened," said the commander of the vanguard. "Let me go out and take a look." He hurried straight to the front gates, twisted his head to one side and craned to look through the hole that had been smashed in them. He saw someone with a long snout and big ears. "Don't worry, Your Majesty," he turned round and shouted at the top of his voice, "it's Zhu Bajie. He's not up to much and he won't dare try any nonsense on us. If he does we can open the gates and drag him inside to put in the steamer too. The only one to worry about is that hairy-cheeked monk with a face like a thunder god."

"Brother," said Pig when he heard this from outside, "he's not scared of me but he is of you. The master's definitely inside. Come here quick." "Evil damned beast," said Monkey abusively. "Your grandfather Monkey is here. Send my master out and I'll spare your life." "This is terrible, Your Majesty," the commander of the vanguard reported. "Sun the Novice is here looking for him too." At this the demon king started complaining, "It's all because of your 'petal-dividing' or whatever you called it. You've brought disaster on us. How is this going to end?" "Don't worry, Your Majesty," the commander of the vanguard replied, "and don't start grumbling yet. That Sun the Novice is a monkey of great breadth of spirit. Although he has such tremendous magical power he's partial to flattery. We'll ake an imitation human head out to fool him with, say a few lattering things to him and tell him we've eaten his master al-eady. If we can take him in, the Tang Priest will be ours to njoy. If we can't we'll have to think again." "But where are ve to get an imitation human head?" the demon king asked. 'I'll see if I can make one," the commander of the vanguard eplied.

The splendid ogre then cut a piece of willow root with an xe of pure steel into the shape of a human head, spurted some uman blood on it from his mouth to make it all sticky, and told junior devil to take it to the gates on a lacquer tray, calling, 'My Lord Great Sage, please overcome your anger and allow ne to address you." Brother Monkey really was partial to eing flattered, and when he heard himself being addressed as 'My Lord Great Sage" he grabbed hold of Pig and said, "Don't it him. Let's hear what he has to say." To this the junior levil with the tray replied, "When my king took your master nto the cave the junior devils were naughty and behaved very adly. They gobbled and gnawed and grabbed and bit, and ate he whole of your master up except his head, which I have here." 'If you've eaten him up, that's that," Monkey replied. "Bring he head out and let me see whether it's real or false." The junior levil threw the head out through the hole in the gates, a sight hat started Pig howling and saying, "This is terrible. The master vent in looking one way and he's come out looking like this." 'Idiot," said Monkey, "have a look and find out if it's real efore you start crying." "You're shameless," said Pig, "how ould there ever be such a thing as a fake human head?" "This ne's a fake," Brother Monkey replied. "How can you tell?" ig asked. "When you throw a real human head it lands quiet-y," Monkey explained, "but when you throw a fake it makes a oud noise like a pair of wooden clappers. If you don't believe ne, I'll throw it for you. Listen!" He picked the head up and hrew it against a rock, where it gave a hollow ring. "It was oud, brother," said Friar Sand. "That means it's a fake," said Monkey. "I'll make it turn back into its real self to show you." Producing his gold-banded cudgel in a flash he hit the head

open. When Pig looked he saw that it was a piece of willo
root. This was too much for the idiot, who started talking abu
sively. "I'll get you, you hairy lot," he said, "you may hav
hidden my master in your cave and fooled your ancestor Pi
with a piece of willow root, but don't imagine that my master i
just a willow-tree spirit in disguise."

The junior devil who was holding the tray was thrown int
such a panic by this that he ran shaking with fear back to re
port, "It's terrible, terrible, terrible." "What's so terrib
ly terrible then?" the senior demon asked. "Zhu Bajie and Fria
Sand were taken in, but Monkey's like an antique dealer — h
really knows his stuff," the junior demon replied. "He could te
it was an imitation head. If only we could give him a real huma
head he might go away." "But how are we to get one?" th
senior demon wondered, then continued, "Fetch a human hea
we haven't eaten yet from the flaying shed." The devils the
went to the shed and choose a fresh head, after which the
gnawed all the skin off it till it was quite smooth and carried i
out on a tray. "My lord Great Sage," the messenger said, "I ar
afraid it was a fake head last time. But this really is Lord Tang'
head. Our king had kept it so as to bring good fortune to ou
cave, but now he's making a special offering of it." He the
threw the head out through the hole in the gates, it landed wit
a thud and rolled on the ground, gory with blood.

Seeing that this human head was a real one Monkey coul
not help starting to wail, in which he was joined by Pig an
Friar Sand. "Stop crying, brother," said Pig, holding back hi
tears. "This is very hot weather, and the head will soon go of
I'm going to fetch and bury it while it's still fresh. We can cr
for him afterwards." "You're right," said Monkey, and the idic
cradled the head against his chest, not caring about th
filth, as he hurried up the cliff till he found a south-facing spo
where the winds and the natural forces were gathered. Here h
hacked out a hole with his rake, buried the head, and piled
grave-mound over it. Only then did he say to Friar Sand, "Yo
and big brother weep over him while I look for some offerings."
Going down to the side of a gill, he broke off some willo

branches and gathered a few pebbles. Taking them back up to the tomb, he planted the willow branches on either side and piled the pebbles in front of it. "What's all that about?" Monkey asked. "The willow branches are instead of cypresses to shade the master's tomb for the time being," Pig answered, "and the pebbles are offerings to him instead of cakes." "Cretin!" Monkey shouted. "He's already dead. What do you want to go offering him stones for?" "Just to show what the living feel," Pig replied, "and out of mourning and respect." "You'd better cut that nonsense out," Monkey replied. "Tell Friar Sand to come here. He can guard the tomb and keep an eye on the horse and the luggage while we two go and smash the cave palace up, capture the monster and break his body into ten thousand bits. Then we'll have avenged the master." "You're absolutely right, big brother," said Friar Sand through his tears. "You two be careful. I'll keep watch here."

The splendid Pig then took off his black brocade tunic, tied his undershirt tightly, picked up his rake and followed Monkey. The two of them rushed straight for the stone gates, and with no more ado they smashed them down and shouted with a yell that made the heavens shake, "Give us our Tang Priest back alive!" This sent the souls flying from all the devils old and young in the cave, who complained that the commander of the vanguard had wronged them. "How are we going to deal with these monks now they've fought their way in through the gates?" the demon king asked. "The ancients used to say," the commander of the vanguard replied, " 'Put your hand in a basket of fish and it's bound to stink.' Now we're in this we've got to see it through. We'll just have to take our troops into battle with these monks." When the demon heard this he had no alternative but to issue the order, "Stand together, my little ones. Bring your best weapons with you and come with me." They then charged out through the entrance of the cave with a great war cry. The Great Sage and Pig quickly fell back a few paces before they held the devilish onslaught on a piece of flat ground on the mountainside, shouting, "Who's your best-known boss? Who's the ogre who captured our master?"

The devils had now palisaded their position, over which a multicoloured embroidered flag flew, and the demon king shouted straight back as he held the iron mace, "Damned monks Don't you know who I am? I'm the Great King of the Souther Mountains, and I've been running wild here for hundreds o years. I've eaten your Tang Priest up. What are you going to d about it?" "You've got a nerve, you hairy beast," retorted Monkey abusively. "How old are you, daring to call yourself afte the Southern Mountains? Lord Lao Zi was the ancestor wh opened up heaven and earth, but even he sits on the right of th Supreme Pure One. The Tathagata Buddha is the Honoure One who rules the world, and he sits below the Great Roc. Confucius the Sage is the Honoured One of the Confucian School and all he's called is Master. So how dare you call yoursel Great King of the Southern Mountains and talk about runnin wild for several hundred years? Don't move, and take this fron your grandfather's cudgel!" The evil spirit twisted aside to avoid the cudgel, which he parried with his iron mace. "How dare you try to put me down like that, monkey-face," said th monster, glaring furiously. "What kind of powers have you got acting like a maniac at my gates." "I'll get you, you nameless beast," replied Brother Monkey with a grin. "You evidently don't know who I am, so just stand there and make yoursel brave while I tell you:

My ancestral home is in the Eastern Continent,
Where heaven and earth nourished me for thousands o
years.
On the Mountain of Flowers and Fruit was a magic stone
egg;
When the egg broke open my roots were inside.
My birth was not like that of an ordinary being:
My body was formed when sun and moon mated.
I cultivated myself with formidable effect;
Heaven gave me a perceptive and cinnabar head.
As the Great Sage I dwelt in the palace in the clouds,

Using my strength in a fight against the Dipper and Bull Palace.
A hundred thousand heavenly troops could get nowhere near me;
All the stars in the sky were easily subdued.
My fame resounds throughout the cosmos;
I know all about everything between earth and sky.
Since my conversion to Sakyamuni's teachings
I have been helping my master on his journey to the west.
When I clear a path through mountains no one can stop me;
My skill at bridging rivers causes demons distress.
In forests I use my power to seize tigers and leopards;
I capture wild beasts bare-handed before sheer cliffs.
For the sake of the east's true achievement I have come to the Western Regions;
What evil monster will dare to show itself?
I hate the wicked beasts who have murdered my master;
Their lives will all be ended at this moment."

These remarks both shocked and infuriated the ogre, who ground his teeth, sprang forward and struck at Brother Monkey with his iron mace. Monkey blocked it effortlessly with his cudgel and would have said some more to him when Pig, unable to restrain himself any longer, started swinging wildly at the demon king's commander of the vanguard. The commander of the vanguard led his whole force into action, and a hectic and splendid battle was fought on that piece of level ground on the mountainside:

The monk from the great and superior country in the east
Was going to fetch true scriptures from the Western Paradise.
The great leopard of the southern mountains breathed out wind and clouds

To block their way through the mountains and show off his prowess.
With tricks
And deception
He had foolishly captured the priest from Great Tang.
Then he met Monkey with his tremendous powers
As well as the famous Zhu Bajie.
While the demons fought on level ground in the mountains
Dust clouds arose and darkened the sky.
Above the fray rose the junior devils' roars
As they thrust out wildly with spear and with sword.
On the other side the monks shouted back,
Fighting with rake and with cudgel together.
The Great Sage was a matchless hero,
And Pig in his perfection revelled in his strength.
The ancient ogre of the south,
And his vanguard commander
For the sake of a piece of the Tang Priest's flesh
Were prepared to throw their own lives away.
These two hated them for killing their master:
The other two were set on murder because of the Tang Priest.
The struggle long swayed to and fro,
The clashes and charges yielding no victor.

When Monkey realized that the junior devils were fighting so hard that repeated attacks were failing to drive them back he used body-dividing magic, plucked out a bunch of hairs, chewed them up in his mouth, spat the pieces out, called "Change!" and turned them all into his own doubles, each wielding a gold-banded cudgel and fighting his way into the cave from the outside. The one or two hundred junior devils, unable to cope with their attacks from all sides, all fled for their lives back into the cave. Monkey and Pig then fought their way back out through the enemy ranks from the inside. The evil spirits who had no sense tried to stand up to the rake and found themselves bleedıg from nine wounds, or resisted the cudgel and had their flesh nd bones beaten to paste. The Great King of the Southern Mountains was so alarmed that he fled for his life on his clouds nd wind. The commander of the vanguard, who did not know ow to do transformations, had already fallen to Monkey's club nd been revealed as what he really was: an iron-backed grey volf ogre. Pig went up to him, turned him over by his leg, and aid, "Goodness only knows how many piglets and lambs this o-and-so has eaten." Monkey meanwhile shook himself, put he hair back on his body and said, "No time to lose, idiot. After he demon king! Make him pay for the master's life." Pig urned back, but all the little Monkeys had disappeared. "Your nagic bodies have all gone, brother," he exclaimed. "I've taken hem back," Monkey replied. "Splendid," said Pig, "splendid." The two of them went back in triumph, feeling very pleased.

When the senior demon escaped back to the cave he told ıis underlings to move rocks and earth to barricade the front gates. The surviving junior demons were all trembling with error as they barricaded the entrance: they would not have dared to stick their heads out again now. Monkey led Pig to the gates and shouted without getting any response. Pig's rake made ıo impression when he struck them with it. Realizing what had ıappened, Monkey said, "Don't waste your effort, Pig. They've barricaded the gates." "Then how are we going to avenge the master?" Pig asked. "Let's go back to his grave and see Friar Sand," Brother Monkey replied.

When they got back there they found Friar Sand still weeping, at which Pig became more miserable than ever, throwing down his rake, prostrating himself on the tomb mound and beating the ground with his hand as he howled, "Poor, poor Master. Master from so far away! I'll never see you again!" "Don't distress yourself so, brother," said Monkey. "The evil spirit may have barricaded his front gates, but he's bound to have a back entrance to go in and out through. You two wait here while I go and look for it. "Do be careful, brother," said Pig through his tears. "Don't get caught yourself too. We could never cope if we had to wail for the master then for you by turns. We'd make an awful mess of it." "No problem," said Monkey. "I've got my ways of doing things."

Putting his cudgel away the splendid Great Sage tightened his kilt, stepped out and went back over the mountain. On his way he heard the sound of flowing water. When he turned round to look he saw that there was a brook flowing down from above him, and beside the gill was a gate, to the left of which was a drainpipe from which red water was coming out. "Goes without saying," he thought. "That must be the back entrance. If I go as myself the junior demons may well recognize me when I open the door and see them. I'd better turn into a water snake to get in. No, hold on. If the master's spirit knows that I've turned into a water snake he'll be angry with me as a monk for turning into something so long drawn-out. I'd better turn into a little crab. No, that's no good either. The master would be cross with me for having too many legs for a monk." So he turned into a water rat who slipped into the water with a soughing sound and went straight to the inner courtyard along the drainpipe. Here he thrust his head out for a look around and saw some junior devils setting out gobbets of human flesh to dry in a sunny spot. "Heavens!" said Monkey. "That must be what they can't finish from the master's flesh. No doubt they're drying it to save for a rainy day. If I turned back into myself now, went up to them and wiped them out with one swing of my cudgel I'd be making myself look brave but stupid. I'll do another change, go in to look for the senior devil, and find out what's what." With that he jumped out of the drain, shook himself, and turned himself into a winged ant. Indeed,

Weak and tiny and known as black colts,
They hide away for many a day till they have wings and
can fly.
Casually crossing beside the bridge they draw up their
ranks;
They enjoy battles of high strategy under the bed.

Because they know when rain is coming they block their holes
And build their mounds of dust that turn to ashes.
Light they are, and delicate and quick,
Rarely observed as they pass the wicker gate.

He spread his wings and flew straight into the inner hall, unseen and unheard. Here the senior demon could be seen sitting very angrily in the seat of honour, while a junior devil ran up from behind to report, "Many congratulations, Your Majesty." "What on?" the senior demon asked. "I was on lookout by the gill outside the back door just now," the junior devil replied, "when suddenly I heard some loud wails. I rushed up to the top of the mountain to take a look and saw Zhu Bajie, Sun the Novice and Friar Sand all bowing to a grave and weeping bitterly. I think they must have taken that head for the Tang Priest's and buried it, piled up a grave mound and mourned for it." When Monkey overheard this he said to himself with delight, "From what he's said they've still got the master here and haven't eaten him yet. I'll take a look around and find out if he's still alive, then have a word with him."

The splendid Great Sage then flew into the main hall and looked all around until he saw a very tiny doorway on one side of it. It was very firmly shut, and when he squeezed through the narrow gap between the doors he found himself in a big garden in which he could vaguely make out the sound of sobbing. Flying further inside he saw a clump of tall trees at the foot of which were tied two men. One of these was the Tang Priest. As soon as Monkey saw him he felt an itch in his heart that he could not scratch. He could not help turning back into himself, going up to Sanzang and calling, "Master." When the Tang Priest saw who it was he started crying and saying, "Is that you, Wukong? Save me as quickly as you can, Wukong." "Don't keep saying my name, Master," Monkey replied. "There are people at the front and the secret may get out. As you're still alive I can rescue you. The ogres said they'd already eaten you and tricked me with an imitation human head. Now we're in a bitter struggle with them. There's no need to worry, Master Just stick it out for a little longer till I've beaten the evil spirit then I'll be able to rescue you."

The Great Sage said the words of a spell, shook himself turned into an ant again and flew back into the hall, where h landed on the main beam. From here he saw the surviving junio devils jostling and shouting. One of them sprang out from th crowd and said, "Your Majesty, now they know we've blocke the main gate and they won't be able to fight their way i they've given up hope. They've even made a tomb for the wron head. They spent today mourning for him, and they'll do th same again tomorrow and the day after. I'm sure they'll g away after that. Once we find out that they've split up we ca bring the Tang Priest out, chop him up into little bits, and fr him with aniseed. Then everyone will be able to eat a piec when he's steaming hot, and we'll all live for ever." At this an other junior devil clapped his hands together and said, "No, nc he'd taste much better steamed." "Boiling him would save som firewood," another put in. "He's such a rare and wonderfu thing," said someone else, "that we ought to salt him down an take our time over eating him."

When Monkey heard all this from up among the beams h thought with fury, "What harm did my master ever do you Why are you making these plans to eat him?" He pulled out handful of hairs, chewed them up into little pieces, blew ther lightly out of his mouth and silently recited the words of th spell that turned all the pieces into sleep insects. These he thre into the faces of all the devils, and the insects crawled up thei noses, gradually making the devils feel sleepy. Before long th junior devils were all lying stretched out fast asleep. The demo king was the only one left fitfully awake as he kept rubbing hi face and head, sneezing and pinching his nose. "Perhaps h knows about how to cope with sleep insects," Monkey though "I'd better give him a double dose." He pulled out a hair, mad two more sleep insects as before, and threw them into the de mon's face to crawl up his nose, one up the left nostril and on ıp the right. The demon king jumped to his feet, stretched, awned twice and fell fast asleep, breathing heavily.

Quietly delighted, Monkey then sprang down from the roof .nd turned back into himself. He produced his cudgel from his ·ar and waved it till it was the thickness of a duck egg, then vith a loud bang broke down the side door, ran into the garden ıt the back and called out, "Master!" "Untie me quick, disiple," the venerable elder said. "Being roped up like this has een agony." "Be patient, Master," said Monkey. "When I've cilled the evil spirit I'll come and untie you." He then hurried ack into the hall, lifted his cudgel and was about to strike when ıe stopped and thought, "No, this is wrong. I ought to release .he master before I kill the evil spirit." He went back into the garden, where he changed his mind again: "No, I'll kill the monster first." This happened two or three times till finally he came dancing back into the garden, where his master's grief turned to joy at the sight of him. "You monkey," he said, "I suppose it's because you're beside yourself with pleasure at seeing me still alive that you're dancing about like that." Only then did Monkey go up to him, untie him, and help him walk away. The man tied to the other tree then called out, "Please save me too in your great mercy, my lord." The venerable elder stopped and said, "Untie him too, Wukong." "Who's he?" Monkey asked. "He was captured and brought here a day before me," Sanzang replied. "He's a woodcutter. He tells me his mother is very old and he is most worried about her. He is a very dutiful son. You must save him too."

Doing as he was bid, Monkey untied the other man and took them both out through the back gate, up the scar and across the ravine. "Thank you for rescuing this man and me, worthy disciple," said Sanzang. "Where are Wuneng and Wujing?" "Mourning for you over there," Monkey replied. "Give them a shout." Sanzang then shouted at the top of his voice, "Bajie! Bajie!" The idiot, who had been weeping so much that his head was spinning, wiped away the snot and tears to call, "Friar Sand, the master's come back as a ghost. That him calling, isn't it?" "Idiot," shouted Monkey, going up to him, "that's no ghost.

It's the master himself." When Friar Sand looked up and saw who it was he fell to his knees in front of Sanzang and said "Master, you've suffered terribly. How did big brother rescue you?" Monkey then told them everything that had happened.

When Pig heard all this he gnashed his teeth, unable to restrain himself from knocking the tomb mound over with one blow of his rake, digging out the head and smashing it to pulp "Why are you hitting it?" the Tang Priest asked. "Master," said Pig, "goodness only knows what kind of wretch he was, but we all mourned for him." "It was thanks to him that I'm still alive," Sanzang replied. "When you disciples attacked their gates and demanded me they took him out to fob you off with. Otherwise they would have killed me. I think we should bury him properly as a mark of our monastic respect." When the idiot heard his master saying this he buried that bag of flesh and bone that had been beaten to a pulp and piled up a tomb mound over it.

"Master," said Brother Monkey with a smile, "won't you sit here for a while while I go to wipe them out?" With that he leapt down the cliff, crossed the ravine, went into the cave and took the ropes with which the Tang Priest and the woodcutter had been bound into the hall, where he used them to truss together the arms and legs of the demon king, who was still asleep He then lifted the demon up with his cudgel onto his shoulder and took him out by the back door. "You like making things difficult for yourself, brother," said Pig when he saw him coming from a distance. "Why don't you find another to balance him?" Monkey then set the demon king down in front of Pig, who raised his rake and was just about to hit him when Monkey said, "Wait a moment. We haven't captured the junior devils in the cave yet." "If there are any left," Pig said, "take me in with you to smash them." "Smashing them would be too much trouble," Monkey replied. "The best thing would be to find some firewood and wipe them out that way."

When the woodcutter heard this he led Pig to a hollow to the east to find some broken ends of bamboo, pines that had lost their needles, hollow stumps of willows, creepers broken off from their roots, withered artemisia, old reeds, rushes and dead mulberry. They carried a lot of this into the back entrance, where Monkey set it alight and Pig fanned the flames with both ears. Then the Great Sage sprang up, shook himself and put the sleep-insect hairs back on his body. When the junior devils woke up they were all already on fire. Poor things! None of them had the faintest chance of surviving. When the whole cave was burnt right out the disciples went back to see the master. When Sanzang saw that the senior demon had woken up and was shouting he called, "Disciples, the evil spirit has come round." Pig went up and killed him with one blow of his rake, whereupon the ogre turned back into his real form as a leopard spirit with a coat patterned like mugwort flowers. "Leopards with flower-patterned coats can eat tigers," Monkey observed, "and this one could turn into a human too. Killing him has prevented a lot of serious trouble in future." The venerable elder could not express his gratitude strongly enough, and he then mounted the saddle. "My home isn't far from here to the southwest, sirs," said the woodcutter. "I invite you to come there to meet my mother and accept my kowtows of thanks for saving my life. Then I'll see you gentlemen along your way."

Sanzang was happy to accept, and instead of riding he walked there with his three disciples and the woodcutter. After they had followed a winding path to the southwest for a short distance this is what they saw:

Lichen growing across a stone-flagged path,
Wisteria joining across the wicker gate,
Chains of mountains on every side,
And a wood full of singing birds.
A dense thicket of pine and bamboo,
Rare and wonderful flowers in profusion.
The place is remote and deep amid the clouds,
A thatched cottage with a bamboo fence.

While they were still some distance away they could make out an old woman leaning on the wicker gate with tears streaming from her eyes, weeping and calling to heaven and earth for her son. As soon as the woodcutter saw his mother he left the Tang Priest behind as he rushed straight to the gate, knelt down and said, "Mother, I'm back." Throwing her arms around him the woman said, "My boy, when you didn't come home for days on end I thought the mountain lord must have caught you and killed you. I've suffered terrible heartache. If you weren't killed why didn't you come back before? Where are your carrying-pole ropes and axe?" The woodcutter kowtowed as he replied, "Mother, the mountain lord did capture me and tie me to a tree. I was lucky to escape with my life, thanks to these gentlemen. They are arhats sent by the Tang court in the east to fetch the scriptures from the Western Heaven. This gentleman was captured by the mountain lord and tied to a tree as well. His three disciples have enormous magic powers. They killed the mountain lord with a single blow: he was a leopard with mugwort-flower spots who had become a spirit. They burnt all the junior devils to death, untied the senior gentleman and then untied me too. I owe them a tremendous debt of gratitude: but for them your son would certainly be dead. Now that the mountain is completely safe I'll be able to walk around at night without any danger."

After hearing this the old woman came forward to greet Sanzang and his disciples, kowtowing at every step. Then she led them in through the wicker gate to sit down in the thatched cottage. Mother and son next performed endless kowtows as expressions of their gratitude before hastily and in a fluster preparing them some vegetarian food as a mark of their thanks. "Brother," said Pig to the woodcutter, "I know you're hard up here. Just put something simple together for us. Don't go to a lot of trouble and effort." "Quite frankly, sir," the woodcutter replied, "we're very poor here. We don't have any gill fungus, button mushrooms, peppers or aniseed. All we can offer you gentlemen are some wild vegetables." "We're putting you to a lot of trouble," said Pig. "Be as quick as you can. We're starving." "It'll soon be ready," the woodcutter replied, and before long a table and stools were set out and wiped clean, and several dishes of wild vegetables served:*

Tender-scalded day lilies,
White lumps of pickled scallion,
Knotweed and purslane,
Shepherds purse and "goosegut blossom".
The "swallows stay away" was delicious and tender;
The tiny fists of beansprouts were crisp and green.
Indigo heads boiled soft,
White-stewed "dog footprints",
"Cat's ears",
Wild turnips,
All with tender and tasty grey noodles.
"Scissor shafts",
"Oxpool aid",
Tipped in the pot with broom purslane.
Broken grain purslane,
And lettuce purslane,
All green, delicious and smooth.
"Birdflower" fried in oil,
Superb water-chestnuts,
Roots of reeds and wild-rice stems,
Four kinds of excellent water plants.
"Wheat-mother",
Delicate and finely flavoured;
"Raggedy patches"
You could never wear.
Under the bitter sesame bed runs a fence.
Sparrows wander around,
Macaques leave their footprints,
Eager to eat it all when fried and piping hot.
Sloping wormwood and green artemisia surround crown daisy chrysanthemums;
The moths fly around the buckwheat.

* The dialect names of these wild vegetables are hard to identify: the tentative translations are offered for atmosphere, not for botanical reference.

Bald "goat's ear",
Wolfberry fruits,
That don't need oil when combined with dark indigo.
A meal of every kind of wild vegetable
As a mark of the woodcutter's reverent thanks.

When master and disciples had eaten their fill they packed up ready to start out again. Not daring to press them to stay, the woodcutter asked his mother to come out and bow to them in thanks again. He then kowtowed, fetched a club of jujube wood, fastened his clothes tight, and came out to see them on their way. Friar Sand led the horse, Pig carried the shoulder-pole, and Monkey followed close behind them while the master put his hands together on the back of the horse and said, "Brother woodcutter, could you kindly lead us to the main track? We will take our leave of you there." Together they then climbed high, went down slopes, skirted ravines and negotiated inclines. "Disciples," said the venerable elder thoughtfully as he rode,

"Since leaving my monarch to come to the west
I have made a long journey across a great distance.
At each river and mountain I have met with disaster,
Barely escaping from monsters and fiends.
My heart has been set on the Three Stores of scriptures,
And my every thought is of Heaven above.
When will my toil and my labour be ended?
When will I go home, my journey completed?"

When the woodcutter heard Sanzang saying this he said, "Don't be so downhearted, sir. It's only some three hundred miles west along this road to India, the land of paradise." As soon as Sanzang heard this he dismounted and replied, "Thank you for bringing us so far. Now that we are on the main track, please go home now, brother woodcutter, and give our respects to your venerable mother. We poor monks have no way to reward you for the sumptuous meal you gave us just now except by reciting sutras morning and evening to protect you and your mother and enable both of you to live to be a hundred." The woodcutter took his leave of them and went back by the way he had come. Master and disciples then headed west together. Indeed,

> *The ogre subdued and wrongs set to right, he escaped from his peril;*
> *Having been shown this kindness he set out on his way with the greatest of care.*

If you don't know how long it was till they reached the Western Heaven, listen to the explanation in the next instalment.

CHAPTER EIGHTY-SEVEN

When Heaven is offended in Fengxian it stops the rain; The Great Sage urges goodness and brings a downpour.

Deep and mysterious is the Great Way;
What news is there of it?
When revealed it will alarm ghosts and divine beings.
It controls the universe,
Divides darkness and light;
In the world of true happiness there is no competition.
Before the Vulture Peak
Pearls and jewels emerge,
Shining with every colour.
It illuminates all beings that live between heaven and earth;
Those who understand it live as long as mountains and seas.

The story tells how Sanzang and his three disciples took their leave of the woodcutter on the Hidden Clouds Mountain and hurried along the main road. After they had been going for several days they suddenly saw a walled and moated city not far before them. "Wukong," said Sanzang, "is that city ahead of us India, do you think?" "No, no," said Monkey shaking his head. "Although the Tathagata lives in a paradise there are no cities there. It's a great mountain, Vulture Peak, on which are the high buildings and halls of Thunder Monastery. Even if we've now reached the land of India this isn't where the Buddha lives. I don't know how far India is from Vulture Peak. Presumably

this city is one of the frontier prefectures of India. We'll know when we get there."

Soon they were outside the city, where Sanzang dismounted to go in through the triple gates. Here they found the people destitute and the streets deserted. When they reached the market there were many black-clad government servants lined up on either side of a number of officials wearing their hats and sashes of office and standing under the eaves of a building. As the four travellers came along the road these men did not give way at all, so Pig in his rough way raised his snout and shouted, "Out of the way! Out of the way!" When the men looked up with a start and saw what he looked like their bones went soft, their sinews turned numb and they fell over, shouting, "Evil spirits! Evil spirits!" This gave the officials standing under the eaves such a fright that they were shivering as they bowed and asked, "Where are you from?" Sanzang, who was worried that his disciples would cause trouble, pushed himself forward and said to the men, "I am a monk sent by His Majesty the Great Tang emperor to worship the Lord Buddha and fetch the scriptures in the Great Thunder Monastery in the land of India. Our journey brings us to this distinguished place, but as we do not know its name and have not yet found a place to stay we hope that you gentlemen will forgive us if we have caused any offence to your customs on entering your city."

Only then did the officials return his courtesy and say, "This is the prefecture of Fengxian, one of the frontier prefectures of India. Because we have been suffering from drought for years on end the marquis has sent us to put up a notice here calling for masters of the Dharma to pray for rain and save the people." "Where's the notice?" asked Monkey when he heard this. "Here," the officials said. "The arcade has only just been swept clean: we haven't posted it yet." "Bring it here and show me," said Brother Monkey. The officials then opened the notice out and hung it up under the eaves. Monkey and the others went up to read it, and this was what was written on it:

> Shangguan, Marquis of Fengxian Prefecture in Great India, issues this notice to invite enlightened teachers and

great masters of the Dharma. This country with its prosperous soldiers and people has been afflicted with drought for years. Military and civil land alike has been devastated; the rivers have dried up and the ditches are empty. There is no water in the wells, and the springs have stopped flowing. While the rich are barely managing to stay alive, the poor cannot survive. A bushel of wheat costs a hundred pieces of silver; a bundle of firewood costs five ounces. Girls of ten are being sold for three pints of rice; boys of five are being given to whoever will take them. Because the city dwellers fear the law they pawn their clothes to buy the necessities for survival; but in the countryside thugs rob and eat people in order to live. I have therefore issued this notice in the hope that wise and worthy men from all around will pray for rain to save the people. They will be richly rewarded for their kindness with a thousand pieces of silver. This is no empty promise. Let those who would take it up come to this notice.

When he had read it Monkey asked the officials, "What's Shangguan?" "Shangguan is our marquis' surname," they replied. "It's a very rare surname," said Monkey with a laugh. "You've never been to school, brother," said Pig. "There's a bit at the end of the book *The Hundred Surnames* that goes 'Ouyang and Shangguan'." "Stop this idle chatter, disciples," said Sanzang. "If any of you know how to pray for rain, bring them a fall of timely rain and save the people from this affliction: that would be a very good thing indeed to do. If you cannot, we must be on our way and waste no more time." "What's so difficult about praying for rain?" Monkey asked. "I can turn rivers upside down, stir up the sea, move the stars and constellations about, kick the sky, churn up water in wells, breathe out mist and clouds, carry mountains, drive the moon along and summon wind and rain. They're all child's play. Nothing to them!" When the officials heard this they sent two of their number straight to the prefectural offices to report, "Your Excellency, something very splendid indeed has happened." The marquis, who was burning incense and praying silently at the time, asked what it was when he heard that something splendid had happened. "We were taking the notice to post at the entrance to the market," the officials replied, "when four monks came along who said that they have been sent by the Great Tang in the east to the Great Thunder Monastery in India to worship the Buddha and fetch the scriptures. As soon as they read the notice they said they could bring timely rain, which is why we have come here to report."

Refusing to take a sedan-chair, horse or large retinue, the marquis went on foot in his robes of office straight to the entrance to the market in order to invite the strangers with the utmost courtesy to pray for rain. "His Excellency the marquis is here," it was suddenly announced, and everybody moved out of the way. As soon as he saw the Tang Priest the marquis, who showed no fear of his hideous disciples, prostrated himself in the middle of the street and said, "I am Marquis Shangguan of Fengxian Prefecture, and I have bathed and perfumed myself in order to beg you teachers to pray for the rain that will save the people. I implore you in your great mercy to give play to your divine powers and bring us deliverance." Returning his courtesies, Sanzang said, "This is no place to talk. We will be able to act when we have gone to a monastery." "Please come with me to my humble palace," the marquis replied. "We have a pure place there."

Master and disciples then led the horse and carried the luggage straight to the palace, where they all exchanged greetings and the marquis ordered tea and a vegetarian meal. When the food arrived a little later Pig ate for all he was worth like a hungry tiger, terrifying the waiters, who trembled as they kept coming and going with more and more soup and rice. They looked like the figures on one of those revolving lanterns, and they could just keep him supplied until he had eaten his fill. Only then did he stop. When the meal was over the Tang Priest expressed his thanks then asked, "How long has the drought lasted here, Your Excellency?" To this the marquis replied,

"This is a part of the great land of India,

Fengxian Prefecture of which I am governor.
For three years on end we have suffered from drought:
Grass does not grow, and the grain has all died.
Business is hard for rich and for poor;
Nearly all of the families are weeping with grief.
Two thirds of the people have now died of starvation;
The rest barely survive, like a candle flame in the wind.
I have issued a notice for worthies
And am lucky you monks have come to our land.
If you bring the people a whole inch of rain
A thousand in silver will be your reward."

When Monkey heard this his face showed his pleasure as he chuckled, "Don't say that, don't say that. If you promise us a reward of a thousand pieces of silver you won't get a single drop of rain. But if you put it in terms of accumulating merit I'll provide you with plenty of rain." The marquis, a thoroughly upright and good man who cared deeply for his people, invited Monkey to take the seat of honour, then bowed to him and said, "Teacher, if you really can show us this great compassion this humble official will do nothing to offend against morality." "Please get up," said Monkey, "and say no more of that. I would only ask you going to do it, brother?" asked Friar Sand. "You and Pig you to look after my master well while I do the job." "How are must come here and be my assistants outside while I summon a dragon to make rain," Monkey replied. Pig and Friar Sand did as he bade them, and while the three of them went outside the marquis burned incense and prayed. Sanzang sat there reciting sutras.

While Monkey recited the spell and said the magic words a dark cloud appeared to the east and slowly moved till it was in front of the hall: it was Ao Guang, the ancient dragon of the Eastern Sea. Ao Guang then put away his cloud feet and turned himself into human form to go up to Monkey, bow low to him with full courtesy and ask, "What have you sent for this humble dragon to do, Great Sage?" "Please rise," Monkey replied. "The only reason why I have troubled you to make this long journey is because there has been a drought in this prefecture of Fengxian for years on end. I'd like to ask you if you couldn't send some rain." "I must inform you, Great Sage," the dragon replied, "that although I can make rain I can only act on the orders of Heaven. I would never dare come here to make rain on my own authority without Heaven's instructions." "As our journey brought us this way I asked you specially to come here to make rain and save the people," said Monkey, "so why are you trying to get out of it?" "I'd never dare," the dragon king replied. "I came because you summoned me with the magic words, Great Sage, and I'd never dare try to get out of it. In the first place I haven't had an edict from Heaven, and secondly I haven't brought the magic rain-making generals with me. How could I Great Sage, you must let me go back to the sea to muster possibly move the rain departments? If you wish to be a saviour, my forces while you go to the heavenly palace to obtain an imperial edict for a fall of rain and ask the officials in charge of water to release us dragons so that I can make rain in the quantities ordered."

Accepting the force of his argument, Brother Monkey had to let the old dragon go back to the sea. He then sprang out of the diagram of the Dipper and told the Tang Priest what the dragon king had said. "In that case you had better go and do that," the Tang Priest said. "But don't go telling lies." Monkey then told Pig and Friar Sand to look after the master while he went up to the heavenly palace. No sooner had the splendid Great Sage said he was going than he was out of sight. "Where has Lord Sun gone?" the marquis asked, trembling with shock. "He's gone up to Heaven on a cloud," replied Pig with a grin. With great reverence the marquis then issued an urgent order that all the people in the big and little streets of the city, whether nobility, high officials, gentry, commoners, soldiers or civilians, were to worship dragon-king tablets and set out water urns with sprigs of willow in them in front of their gates. They were also to burn incense and pray to Heaven.

Once on his somersault cloud Monkey went straight to the Western Gate of Heaven, where the Heavenly King Lokapala soon appeared at the head of his heavenly soldiers and warriors to greet him and say, "Great Sage, have you fetched the scriptures yet?" "Quite soon now," Monkey replied. "We've reached a frontier prefecture called Fengxian on the borders of India now. It hasn't rained for three whole years there, and the people are suffering terribly. I want to pray for rain to save them. I sent for the dragon king, but he told me that he couldn't do it on his own authority without a heavenly order, which is why I've come to see the Jade Emperor to request an edict." "I don't think it's supposed to rain there," the heavenly king said. "I heard just now that the marquis of Fengxian had behaved disgracefully and offended both Heaven and Earth. His Majesty took it badly and immediately had a rice mountain, a flour mountain and a huge gold lock set up. It won't rain till all three have been knocked over or snapped." Not understanding what all this was about, Monkey demanded to see the Jade Emperor, and, not daring to stop him, the heavenly king let him in.

Going straight to the Hall of Universal Brightness, Brother Monkey was met by the four heavenly teachers, who asked, "What are you here for, Great Sage?" "On my journey escorting the Tang Priest I've reached Fengxian Prefecture on the frontiers of India, where there is a drought," Monkey replied. "The marquis there has been asking for magicians to pray for rain. I sent for the dragon king to order him to make rain, but he said that he could not do so on his own authority without an edict from the Jade Emperor. I have now come to request an edict in order to relieve the people's suffering." "But it's not supposed to rain there," said the four heavenly teachers. "As to whether it's supposed to rain or not," said Monkey with a smile, "could I trouble you to take me in to submit a memorial so that I can find out whether I can still get a favour done?" To this the heavenly teacher Ge Xianweng replied, "As the saying goes, 'a fly that needs a net for a veil — what a cheek!' " "Don't talk nonsense," said Xu of Jingyang. "Just take him in."

Qiu Hongji, Zhang Daoling, Ge and Xu took Monkey to the outside of the Hall of Miraculous Mist, where they reported, "Your Majesty, Sun Wukong has reached Fengxian Prefecture n India and wants to obtain rain. He has come to ask for an :dict." "Three years ago," the Jade Emperor replied, "on the wenty-fifth day of the twelfth month, when we were inspecting he myriad heavens and travelling through the three worlds, we ırrived at his city. We saw that Shangguan was most wicked; he :nocked over the vegetarian offerings to heaven to feed to dogs, poke foully, and was guilty of lèse-majesté. That is why we set ıp those three things in the Hall of Fragrance. Take Sun Wu-:ong to see them. When those three things have been accomplish-:d we will issue our edict; but if they are not, then do not neddle in what does not concern you."

When the four heavenly teachers led Brother Monkey to the Hall of Fragrance he saw a mountain of rice about a hundred eet high and a mountain of flour about two hundred feet high. Beside the rice mountain was a chicken the size of a fist eating he rice, sometimes with quick pecks, sometimes with slow ones. Beside the flour mountain was a golden-haired Pekinese licking he flour, sometimes with long licks and sometimes with short ones. To the left of it a golden padlock about one foot three or 'our inches long hung from an iron frame. The crossbar of the ock was about the thickness of a finger, and under it was a amp, the flame of which was heating the bar. Not understand-ng what all this was about, Monkey turned back to ask the ıeavenly teachers, "What does it mean?" "When that wretch offended Heaven the Jade Emperor had these three things set ıp," the heavenly teachers replied. "That place will only be due 'or rain when the chicken has eaten all the rice, the dog has lick-:d up all the flour, and the lamp has melted the bar of the ock."

When Monkey heard this he went pale with shock, and he dared make no more memorials to the throne. He left the palace ıall overcome with embarrassment. "Don't take it so badly, Great Sage," said the four heavenly teachers with smiles. "This s something that can be resolved through goodness. Once a single kind thought moves Heaven the rice and flour mountains will collapse and the bar of the padlock will be broken. If you can persuade the marquis to return to goodness then blessings will come of themselves." Monkey accepted their advice, and instead of going back to the Hall of Miraculous Mist to take his leave of the Jade Emperor he headed straight down to the lower world and its ordinary mortals. Within an instant he was at the Western Gate of Heaven, where he saw Heavenly King Loka-pala again, who asked, "Did you get the decree you wanted?" Monkey told him about the rice and flour mountains and the metal lock. "What you said to me was quite right," he continued "The Jade Emperor refuses to issue a decree. Just now the heavenly teachers told me as they saw me off that the secret of blessings lay in persuading that so-and-so to return to good-ness." With that Monkey took his leave and went down to the lower world on his cloud.

When the marquis, Sanzang, Pig, Friar Sand and the officials high and low all welcomed him back they crowded round him asking questions. Monkey then shouted at the marquis, "It's all because on the twenty-fifth day of the twelfth month three years ago you offended Heaven and Earth that the people are suffer-ing, you wretch. That's why rain won't be sent now." At this the marquis was so alarmed that he fell to his knees, prostrated himself on the ground and asked, "How do you know about what happened three years ago, teacher?" "Why did you knock the vegetarian offerings to Heaven over to feed to dogs?" said Monkey. "You'd better tell me the truth." Not daring to conceal anything, the marquis said, "On the twenty-fifth of the twelfth month three years ago I was making offerings to Heaven with-in the palace. As my wife was wicked we quarrelled and said bad things to each other. In an unthinking outburst of fury I knocked over the table with the offerings and scattered the vegetarian food. It's true that I called the dogs to eat it up. I never realized that Heaven would take offence at this and harm the common people. For the last couple of years it has been preying on my mind. My thoughts have been disturbed, and I haven't been able to understand why. I never realized that it was because Heaven had taken offence that it was inflicting this disaster on the common people. Now that you have come down to visit us, teacher, I beg you to enlighten me on what the upper world intends to do."

"That happened to be a day on which the Jade Emperor was visiting the lower world," Monkey replied. "When he saw you feed the vegetarian food to the dogs and heard your foul language the Jade Emperor set three things up to remember you by." "What three things, brother?" Pig asked. "In the Hall of Fragrance he had set up a rice mountain about a hundred feet high and a flour mountain about two hundred feet high. Beside the rice mountain is a chicken the size of a fist who's eating it with quick pecks and slow pecks. Beside the flour mountain is a golden-haired Pekinese licking the flour up with long licks and short licks. And to the left is an iron frame from which hangs a golden padlock with a crossbar the thickness of a finger under which a lamp is burning and warming the bar. You will only be due for rain here when the chicken's eaten all the rice, the dog's licked up all the flour and the lamp has melted the bar of the lock." "No problem," said Pig, "no problem. If you take me with you, brother, I can do a transformation, eat all the rice and flour up in one sitting and snap the bar of the lock. I can guarantee rain." "Don't talk nonsense, you idiot," said Monkey. "This is a plan that's been made by Heaven. You'll never be able to get there." "From what you say I don't know what to do," said Sanzang. "It's easy," said Monkey, "easy. As I was leaving the four heavenly teachers said to me that this could only be solved through goodness."

The marquis then prostrated himself on the ground again and said imploringly, "I will do just as you tell me, teacher." "If your heart can turn back to goodness," Monkey replied, "I hope that you'll at once start invoking the Buddha and reciting scriptures. Then I'll be able to help you. If you persist in refusing to reform there'll be nothing I can do to get you off. It won't be long before Heaven executes you, and your life will be beyond saving."

The marquis kowtowed in worship, swearing to return to the faith. At once he summoned all the Buddhist and Taoist clergy in the city and ordered that a site be prepared for religious ceremonies. They were all to write out documents and memorials for three days. The marquis led his followers in burning incense and worshipping, thanking Heaven and Earth and repenting of his sins. Sanzang recited sutras on his behalf. At the same time urgent notices were sent out ordering all the men and women, young and old, in all the households inside and outside the city to burn incense sticks and invoke the Buddha. From that moment on all ears were filled with virtuous sounds. Only then did Brother Monkey feel happy. "You two look after the master," he said to Pig and Friar Sand, "while I go off for him again." "Where are you going this time, brother?" Pig asked. "The marquis really has believed what I told him and is being reverent, good and kind," Monkey replied, "and he's sincerely invoking the Buddha's name. So I'm going back to submit another request for rain to the Jade Emperor." "If you're going, don't lose any time, brother," said Friar Sand. "This is holding us up on our journey. But do get a fall of rain: it'll be another true achievement for us."

The splendid Great Sage set his cloud off once more and went straight to the gate of Heaven, where he met Heavenly King Lokapala again. "What have you come for now?" Lokapala asked. "The marquis has mended his ways," Monkey replied, which pleased the Heavenly King. As they were talking the Straight Spell Messenger arrived at the gate of Heaven to deliver letters and documents written by Taoist and Buddhist clergy. When he saw Monkey the messenger bowed and said, "This is all the result of your successful conversion, Great Sage." "Where are you taking those letters?" Monkey asked. "Straight to the Hall of Universal Brightness," the messenger replied, "to give to the heavenly teachers to pass on to the Great Heavenly Honoured One, the Jade Emperor." "In that case you'd better go first and I'll follow," Monkey said. The messenger then went in through the heavenly gate. "Great Sage," said Heavenly King Lokapala, "there's no need for you to go to see the Jade Emperor. You should go to borrow some thunder gods from the Office of Response to the Primary in the Ninth Heaven, then set off thunder and lightning. After that there'll certainly be rain."

Monkey accepted this suggestion and went in through the ate of Heaven. Instead of going to the Hall of Miraculous Mist ɔ ask for an edict he at once turned his cloud-treading steps to-vards the Office of Response to the Primary in the Ninth Ieaven, where the Envoy of the Thunder Gate, the Corrector f Records and the Inspector of Probity appeared to bow and ay, "Why are you here, Great Sage?" "There's something I'd ke to see the Heavenly Honoured One about," Monkey replied, nd the three envoys passed this on in a memorial to the Ieavenly Honoured One, who then came down from behind is screen of red clouds and nine phoenixes in full court dress. Vhen they had exchanged greetings Monkey said, "There is omething I would like to request of you." "What might that e?" the Heavenly Honoured One asked. "While escorting the 'ang Monk I have reached the prefecture of Fengxian," said Brother Monkey, "and as they have long been suffering from rought there I promised to make it rain for them. The reason have come here is to ask for the loan of some of your subor-inate officials and generals in order to ask for rain." "I am ware that three things have been set up because the marquis iere offended Heaven," the Heavenly Honoured One replied, but I have not yet heard that rain is due to fall there."

"When I went to ask the Jade Emperor for an edict yester-ay," Monkey replied with a smile, "he told the heavenly teach-rs to take me to see the three things in the Hall of Fragrance: ie mountain of rice, the mountain of flour and the golden lock. ain isn't due to fall till these three things have been knocked own or broken. When I was feeling very upset because it was ɔ difficult the heavenly teachers advised me to persuade the iarquis and his people to do good deeds because Heaven is ound to help anyone who has a good thought. So there's a good iance of persuading Heaven to change its mind and delivering iem from this disaster. Now good thoughts are happening verywhere, and all ears are filled with good sounds. Not long go the Straight Spell Messenger took letters showing that they ad mended their ways and turned towards goodness to the Jade mperor, which is why I've come to your illustrious palace to

ask for the help of your thunder officials and thunder generals.
"In that case," the Heavenly Honoured One replied, "I'll sen
Deng, Xin, Zhang and Tao to take Mother Lightning and g
with you to Fengxian Prefecture to make thunder, Great Sage.

Before long the four generals and the Great Sage had reach
ed the boundaries of Fengxian and started performing thei
magic in mid air. A great rumble of thunder could be hear
and there were sizzling flashes of lightning. Indeed,

The lightning was like snakes of purple gold;
The thunder was like the noise of sleeping insec
awakened.
Flashes of light like flying fire,
Thunderclaps like landslides in the mountains.
The jagged lines lit up the whole of the sky;
The great noise caused the earth itself to move.
When the red silk flashed like sprouts of plants
Rivers and mountains shook for three thousand miles.

Inside and outside the city of Fengxian nobody, whether an o
ficial high or how, a soldier or a civilian had heard thunder
seen lightning for three whole years; and now that the thund
was booming and the lightning flashing they all fell to the
knees, put incense burners on their heads, held sprigs of willo
in their hands and said, "We submit to Amitabha Buddha. W
submit to Amitabha Buddha." These good thoughts had indee
moved Heaven, as is proved by an old-style poem:

When thoughts have been born in human minds
Heaven and earth will both be aware.
If evil and good do not get their due
Sides have been taken by powers up there.

We will for the moment leave the Great Sage Monk
directing the thunder generals as they unleashed thunder ar
lightning over Fengxian Prefecture, where everyone had turn
back to goodness, and tell how the Straight Spell Messeng
took the Taoist and Buddhist documents straight to the H
of Universal Brightness, where the four heavenly teachers su

nitted them to the Jade Emperor in the Hall of Miraculous Mist. When the Jade Emperor had seen them he said, "As that wretch has had some virtuous thoughts, see what has happened o the three things." Just as he was speaking the official in harge of the Hall of Fragrance came in to report, "The rice and lour mountains have collapsed: the rice and flour all disappeard in an instant. The bar of the lock has also been broken." Beore he could finish submitting this memorial the heavenly oficial in attendance led in the local deity, the city god and the ;ods of the altars from Fengxian, who all bowed and reported, 'The lord of our prefecture and every member of every houseiold, high and low, of the people has been converted to the true chievement and is worshipping the Buddha and Heaven. We iow beg you in your compassion to send a widespread fall of imely rain to deliver the common people." When the Jade Emperor heard this he was very pleased, so he issued an edict: 'Let the departments of wind, cloud and rain go to the lower vorld in accordance with orders. At this hour on this day the louds are to be spread, the thunder shall roar, and three feet nd forty-two drops of rain shall fall." At once the four heaveny teachers transmitted the edict to the weather departments, vho were all to go to the lower world, show their powers and ct together.

Monkey was enjoying himself up in the sky with Deng, Xin, Zhang and Tao, who were ordering Mother Lightning about, vhen the arrival of all other gods filled the sky with their asembly. As the wind and the clouds met, the timely rain began o pour down.

Thick, heavy clouds,
Lowering black mists,
The rumbling of the thunder cart,
The searing flash of lightning,
A roaring gale,
A torrential downpour.
Indeed, when one thought goes up to Heaven
Ten thousand hopes are all fulfilled.
Because the Great Sage has used his powers

The landscape is darkened for thousands of miles.
The wonderful rain falls like rivers and seas,
Hiding the country and heavens from sight.
Water comes pouring down the eaves,
Noisily pounding outside the windows.
While every household invokes the Buddha
All of the streets and markets are flooded.
To east and west every channel is filled;
Winding streams meander to north and to south.
Dried-up shoots receive moisture,
Withered trees revive.
The hemp and wheat now flourish in the fields;
Beans and other grains grow in the countryside.
Traders happily travel to sell their wares;
Cheerful peasants get ready to work.
After this the millet will do well,
And the crops are bound to yield a bumper harvest.
When wind and rain are timely the people know content
When rivers and seas are calm the world is at peace.

That day three feet and forty-two drops of rain fell, after whic all the gods began to tidy up and go away. "Gods of the fou departments," yelled the Great Sage at the top of his voice, "sta there for a moment with your cloud followers while I tell th marquis to bow to you all and express his thanks. You ma part the clouds and appear in your true forms to let this morta see you with his own eyes. That's the only way he'll believ and make offerings." When the gods heard this they all staye where they were up in the clouds.

Monkey then brought his cloud down to land and wen straight into the prefectural palace, where Sanzang, Pig and Fria Sand all greeted him. The marquis kowtowed to him in thank at every pace he took. "Stop thanking me," said Monkey. "I'v asked the gods of the four departments to stay. Could you te everyone to come here to kowtow and thank them so that they' make it rain properly in future?" The marquis issued urgen orders summoning everyone to give thanks, and they all kowtow ed with incense-sticks in their hands. The gods of the fou departments — rain, thunder, cloud and wind — then parted the clouds and revealed themselves in their true form.

The dragon king appeared,
The thunder generals were revealed,
The clouds boys were seen,
The lords of the wind came down.
The dragon king appeared:
With silver whiskers and an azure face he was really peerless.
The thunder generals were revealed
With their countenances of matchless might and crooked mouths.
The cloud boys were seen
Wearing gold crowns over faces like jade.
The lords of the wind came down
With flustered brows and bulging eyes.
All were displayed on the azure clouds
Drawn up in ranks with their holy countenances.
Only then were the people of Fengxian convinced
As they kowtowed, burned incense and rejected evil.
Today they gazed up at the heavenly generals,
Washing their hearts as they all turned to goodness.

The gods stood there for two hours as the people kowtowed to them endlessly. Monkey rose up into the clouds again to bow to all the gods and say, "I've put you to great trouble. All you gentlemen may now return. I'll make everyone in this prefecture give pure and lofty offerings to thank you at the due season. From now on you gentlemen must send wind every five days and rain every ten days to help them out." The gods all consented as he told them and returned to their own departments.

Bringing his cloud down to land, Monkey said to Sanzang, "Now that the job's been done and the people given peace we can pack our things and be on our way again." When the marquis heard this he hastened to bow and say, "How can you say such a thing, Lord Sun? What has happened today has been an infinitely great act of kindness. I have sent people to prepare a humble banquet to thank you for your great kindness. Then I will buy some land from the people to build a monastery for you, my lords, with a shrine to you with inscribed tablets where offerings can be made in all four seasons. Even if I were to carve my own bones and heart it would be hard to repay a ten thousandth part of what I owe you. You can't possibly leave." "What Your Excellency says is very fine," Sanzang replied, "but we are pilgrim monks who can only put up for the night on our journey west. We cannot stay here long. We definitely must leave in a day or two." The marquis refused to let them go, and he ordered many people to prepare a banquet and start building a monastery that very night.

The next day there was a magnificent banquet at which the Tang Priest took the place of honour while the Great Sage Monkey sat beside him with Pig and Friar Sand. The marquis and his officials high and low passed them cups of wine and dishes of food while fine music was played, and so they were entertained all day. It was a most happy occasion, and there is a poem to prove it:

After long drought the fields received sweet rain;
Merchants were travelling along all watercourses.
They were deeply moved by the monks who had come to the city,
And by the Great Sage who had gone up to Heaven.
The three things had now been accomplished;
One thought had brought all back to the good.
From now on all longed for a new golden age
With ideal weather and good harvests for ever.

The banquets went on for days, as did the giving of thanks, until they had been kept there for almost half a month. All that remained to do was complete the monastery and the shrine. One day the marquis invited the four monks to go to inspect them "How did you complete so enormous a project so quickly?" asked the Tang Priest in astonishment. "I pressed the labourers to work night and day without stopping and insisted most urgently that they finish quickly," the marquis replied. "Now I would like you gentlemen to come and inspect it." "You certainly are ı most good and able marquis," said Monkey with a smile. By ıow they had all reached the new monastery, where they were ull of admiration for the towering halls and the majestic en- rance. Monkey asked Sanzang to name the monastery. "Very well," Sanzang said, "I name it the Monastery of Salvation by Timely Rain." "Splendid," said the marquis, "splendid." He hen issued a golden invitation to monks from far and wide to ome to burn incense there. To the left of the Buddha hall was ı shrine to the four pilgrims at which offerings were to be made n each of the four seasons every year. Temples had also been ɔuilt for the thunder gods and dragon gods to thank them for heir divine efforts. When the visit was over Sanzang ordered ın early departure.

When the local people realized that the monks could be ɔersuaded to stay no longer they all prepared parting gifts, none ɔf which the travellers would accept. Then all the officials in he prefecture escorted them on their way for ten miles with a ɔand playing and a great display of flags and canopies. Still oath to let the travellers go, the officials watched with tears in heir eyes till they had disappeared from sight. Only then did he officials return to the city. Indeed.

The virtuous and holy monk left behind the Salvation Monastery;
The Great Sage Equalling Heaven dispensed great kindness.

If you don't know how many more days after this departure it was that they finally saw the Tathagata Buddha, listen to the ex- ɔlanation in the next instalment.

CHAPTER EIGHTY-EIGHT

When the Dhyana reaches Yuhua a display of magic is given; The mind ape and the Mother of Wood take their own disciples.

The story tells how after happily taking their leave of the marquis the Tang Priest turned to Monkey as he rode and said, "Worthy disciple, this good result was even better than rescuing the babies in Bhiksuland, and it was all your achievement." "In Bhiksuland you only saved 1,111 little boys," said Friar Sand. "That's no comparison with this heavy, soaking rain that's saved tens of thousands of lives. I've been quietly admiring my big brother's magical powers that extend right up to the heavens, as well as his mercy that covers the whole earth." "Merciful and good our big brother may be," said Pig with a laugh, "but it's just a show of being kind. Inside he's a trouble-maker. When he's with me he treats me like dirt." "When have I ever treated you like dirt?" Monkey protested. "Often enough," replied Pig. "You're always seeing to it that I get tied up, hung up, boiled and steamed. After being so kind to all those tens of thousands of people in Fengxian you should have stayed there for half a year and let me have a few more good filling meals. Why did you have to be sending us on our way?" When the venerable elder heard this he shouted, "You idiot! Can you think of nothing but your greed? Stop quarrelling and be on your way." Daring say no more, Pig thrust out his snout, shouldered the luggage, and followed the master and his fellow disciples along the road, laughing loudly.

Time moved as fast as a shuttle, and soon it was late autumn. What could be seen was,

The end of ripples on the waters,
The mountains' bones looking lean.
Red leaves fly around,
In the time of yellowing flowers.
Under the clear and frosty sky the nights seem longer;
The moon shines white through the windows.
Many the household fires in the evening light;
The water gleams cold all over the lake.
The clover fern is now white,
While knotweed blooms red.
Mandarins are green and oranges yellow;
Willows are withering and the millet is ripe.
Beside the desolate village wild geese land among the reeds;
Cocks call by the country inn while the beans are harvested.

When the four of them had been travelling for a long time they saw the towering shape of a city wall. "Wukong," said Sanzang, waving his riding-crop, "you can see there's another city there. I wonder where it is." "Neither of us have ever been here before," Monkey replied, "so how could I know? Let's go ahead and ask."

Before the words were out of his mouth an old man appeared from among some trees. He was leaning on a stick, lightly dressed with coir sandals on his feet and had a sash round his waist. The Tang Priest hastily dismounted and went over to greet the old man. Returning his greeting as he leant on his stick, the old man asked, "Where are you from, reverend sir?" "I am a poor monk sent by the Tang court in the east to worship the Buddha in the Thunder Monastery and fetch the scriptures," the Tang Priest replied, putting his hands together in front of his chest. "Now that I have come to this distinguished place I wonder which city it is that I can see in the distance, and I would ask you, venerable benefactor, to inform me." When the old man heard this he replied, "Enlightened master of the dhyana, this humble place of ours is Yuhua County in one of the prefectures of India. The lord of our city is a member of the king of India's royal famil who has been made prince of Yuhua. He is a very worthy princ who respects both Buddhist and Taoist clergy and cares deepl for the common people. If you go to see him he will certainl treat you with great respect." Sanzang thanked the old man, wh went off through the woods.

Sanzang then turned back to tell his disciples what had hap pened. The three of them were happily going to help the maste back on his horse when Sanzang said, "It's not far. There is n need to ride." The four of them then walked to a street besid the city wall to take a look. This was an area where trader lived; it was crowded with people and business was good. Th people looked and sounded no different from those of China "Be careful, disciples," said Sanzang. "On no account must yo act wild." At that Pig bowed his head and Friar Sand covere his face, leaving only Monkey to support the master. On bot sides of the road people were crowding in to look at them shouting, "We only have eminent monks who subdue dragon and tigers here. We've never seen monks who subdue pigs an monkeys before." This was more than Pig could stand. Thrustin his snout at them he said, "Have you ever seen a monk in a your life who subdued the king of the pigs?" This gave all th people in the street so bad a fright that they fell back on bot sides of them stumbling and tripping over, trying to get away "Put that snout away at once, you idiot," said Monkey with grin, "and don't try to make yourself look pretty. Just pay at tention while you're crossing the bridge." The idiot lowered hi head and kept grinning. Once over the drawbridge they en tered the city, where the main roads were bustling and prosper ous with bars and houses of entertainment. It was indeed a cit in a divine region, and there is a poem to prove it that goes,

An eternally iron-strong city like splendid brocade,
Full of fresh colour, lying next to a river near mountains
Connected by boat with lakes for the movement of goods
A thousand wine-shops await behind curtains.
Everywhere smoke rises from towering buildings;

Each morning the lanes are filled with the hubbub of traders.
The look of the city was much like Chang'an:
Cock-crows and the barking of dogs were all just the same.

I have heard tell of the foreigners in the West," Sanzang thought ith secret delight, "but I have never come here before. On lose examination it is no different from our Great Tang. This ıust be what is meant by paradise." When he learned that a ushel of hulled rice cost only four tenths of an ounce of silver nd a pound of sesame oil only eight thousandths of an ounce f silver he realized that this truly was a place where crops grew abundance.

After walking for quite a long time they reached the prince f Yuhua's palace. On either side of the palace gates were the ffice of the remembrancer, the law courts, the prince's kitchens nd the government hostel. "Disciples," said Sanzang, "here is ıe palace. Wait while I go inside for the prince to inspect our assport and let us on our way." "We can't very well stand at ıe gates while you go in, Master," said Pig. "Can you not see Government Hostel' written over that gateway?" Sanzang ask-d. "Go and sit there and see if you can buy some fodder for the orse. If the prince offers me a meal when I have my audience ith him I will send for you to share it." "Go on in, Master, nd don't worry," said Brother Monkey. "I can cope." Friar and carried the luggage into the hostel, where the staff were so larmed by their hideous faces that they did not dare ask them ny questions or send them away but could only invite them to t down.

Meanwhile the master changed his habit and hat and went raight into the prince's palace with the passport in his hands. oon he was met by a protocol officer who asked, "Where are ou from, reverend sir?" "I am a monk sent by the Great Tang the east to worship the Lord Buddha and fetch the scriptures the Great Thunder Monastery," Sanzang replied. "Now that have reached this distinguished place I would like to have my passport inspected and returned, which is why I have come to seek an audience with His Royal Highness." The protocol officer passed this on, and as the prince was indeed an enlightened one he sent for Sanzang at once.

Sanzang bowed in greeting before the prince's hall, and the prince invited him into the hall to sit down. When the prince read the passport that Sanzang handed him and saw the seals and signatures from so many countries on it he signed it himself, folded it up and put it on his table. "Venerable Teacher of the Nation," he said, "you have passed through many countries on your way here from Great Tang. How long has your journey taken?" "I have kept no record of the distance," Sanzang said, "but some years ago the Boddhisattva Guanyin appeared to me and left an address in verse in which it was said that the road would be sixty thousand miles long. I have already seen fourteen winters and summers on my journey." "That means fourteen years," the prince replied. "I should imagine that there were many delays along the way." "It would be hard to tell of them all," said Sanzang. "There were thousands of monsters and I don't know how much suffering to be endured before I could reach here." The prince was so pleased with his visitor that he ordered his kitchens to prepare a vegetarian meal for him. "I wish to inform Your Royal Highness that I have three disciples," Sanzang said. "As they are waiting outside I will not be able to delay our journey by accepting the meal." The prince then ordered his aides to go straight out to invite the venerable elder's three disciples into the palace to share the meal.

When the aides went out with this invitation they said, "We can't see them, we can't see them." "There are three hideous monks sitting in the hostel," one of their staff said. "Must be them." The aides and their staff then went to the hostel, where they asked the people in charge, "Which are the disciples of the monk from Great Tang who's going to fetch the scriptures? His Royal Highness has invited them to a meal." As soon as Pig, who was sitting there snoozing, heard the word "meal" he could not help jumping up and saying, "We are, we are," at the sight of which the palace aides' souls flew from their bodies as they shivered and said, "A pig demon! A pig demon!" When Monkey heard this he seized hold of Pig and said, "Act a bit more civilized, brother, and don't be so wild." When the officials saw Monkey they all said, "A monkey spirit! A monkey spirit!" "There's no need to be frightened," said Friar Sand, raising his hands together in polite greeting. "We're all disciples of the Tang Priest." "A stove god, a stove god," was the officials' reaction to the sight of him. Monkey then told Pig to lead the horse and Friar Sand to shoulder the carrying-pole as they followed the officials' staff into the prince of Yuhua's palace. The aides went ahead to announce them.

When the prince looked up and saw how ugly they were he too was frightened. "Do not be alarmed, Your Royal Highness," said Sanzang, putting his hands together in front of his chest. "Although my rough disciples are ugly they have good hearts." Pig intoned a noise of respect and said, "How do you do?" This made the prince feel even more alarmed. "All my rough disciples are from the wilds and the mountains and they do not know how to behave," Sanzang explained, "so please forgive them." Overcoming his fear, the prince told the superintendent of his kitchens to take the monks to eat in the Gauze Pavilion. Sanzang thanked the prince, came down from the hall to proceed to the pavilion with his disciples, then grumbled at Pig, "You idiot," he said, "you've not a shred of manners. If you had kept your mouth shut that would have been fine, but why did you have to be so coarse? That one remark from you was enough to knock a mountain over." "I did better by not making a respectful chant," said Monkey, "and I saved a bit of my breath too." "You didn't even intone the chant properly," said Friar Sand to Pig. "First of all, you stuck your snout out and roared." "It makes me hopping mad," said Pig. "The other day the master told me that the polite thing when I met someone was to say, 'How do you do?' I do it today and you tell me it's wrong. How do you want me to behave?" "I told you to say, 'How do you do?' when you meet people," Sanzang replied, "but not to make such a fool of yourself when you meet a prince. As the saying goes, things, like people, come in grades. Why can't you see the differences of social rank?" While he was still making these re-marks the superintendent of the kitchens led servants in to set out tables and chairs and serve the vegetarian feast. Then the monks stopped talking and started eating their meal.

When the prince withdrew from the palace hall to his living quarters his three sons noticed his pallor and asked, "What has given you such a fright today, Father?" "A most remarkable monk has arrived," the prince replied. "He has been sent by the Great Tang in the east to worship the Buddha and fetch the scriptures, and he came to present his passport. When I invited him to take a meal he told me that he had some disciples out-side the palace, so I asked them in. When they came in a mo-ment later they didn't kowtow to me but just said, 'How do you do?' That was upsetting enough. Then when I looked at them I saw that they were all as ugly as demons, which gave me quite a shock. That's why I'm looking pale." Now the three young princes were no ordinary boys. They were all fond of the martial arts, so they stretched out their hands, rolled up their sleeves and said, "They must be evil spirits from the mountains disguised as humans. Wait while we fetch our weapons and take a look at them."

Splendid young princes! The eldest wielded a brow-high rod, the second a nine-toothed rake and the third a black-painted cudgel, and the three of them strode with great valour and spirit out of the palace, shouting, "What's this about monks fetching scriptures? Where are they?" "Young prince," replied the super-intendent of the kitchens and the others on their knees, "they're eating in the Gauze Pavilion." The young princes then charged straight in without stopping to think as they shouted, "Are you men or monsters? Tell us at once and we'll spare your lives." This gave Sanzang such a fright that he turned pale, dropped his bowl, bowed to them and replied, "I have come from Great Tang to fetch the scriptures. I am a man, not a monster." "You look human enough," the princes said, "but the three ugly ones are definitely monsters." Pig kept eating and ignored them, while Friar Sand and Monkey bowed and said, "We're all human. Our aces may be ugly but our hearts are good, and despite our clumsy bodies we have good natures. Where are you three rom, and why are you shooting your mouths off so wildly?" "These three gentlemen are His Royal Highness's sons," explained the superintendent of the kitchens and the others who were standing at the side of the pavilion. "Well, Your Highnesses," aid Pig, throwing down his bowl, "what are you carrying those weapons for? Do you want a fight with us?"

The second prince strode forward wielding his rake in both hands to strike at Pig, which made him say with a chuckle, "That rake of yours is only fit to be the grandson of my one." With hat he stripped down, pulled his own rake out from his belt and swung it, making ten thousand beams of golden light, then went hrough some movements, leaving a thousand strands of auspicious vapour. The second prince was so terrified that his hands went weak and his muscles turned numb and he lost the nerve or any more showing off.

When Monkey saw that the oldest of the young princes was leaping about with a brow-high rod he brought his own gold-banded cudgel out from his ear and shook it to make it as thick as a bowl and twelve or thirteen feet long. Ramming it into the ground, he made a hole about three feet deep in which it stood upright, then said with a smile, "I'm giving you this cudgel." As soon as the prince heard this he threw his own rod down and went to take the cudgel, but though he pulled at it with all his strength he couldn't move it by as much as a hair's breath. Then he straightened himself up and shook it, but it was as if it had aken root. At this the third prince started acting wild, moving nto the attack with his black-painted cudgel. Friar Sand dodged the blow then brought out his own demon-quelling staff, and as he fingered it brilliant light and glowing, coloured clouds came from it, leaving the superintendent of the kitchens and the rest of them wide-eyed and speechless. The three young princes then kowtowed, saying, "Divine teachers, divine teachers, we mere mortals failed to recognize you. We beg you to give us a display of your powers."

Monkey went up to them, effortlessly picked up his cudgel

and said, "It's too cramped here for me to do my stuff. I'm jumping up into the air to play around and give you something to see."

The splendid Great Sage went whistling up by somersault and stood on an auspicious cloud of many colours up in mid-air about three hundred feet above the ground. Then he moved up and down and spun to left and right as he performed a Canopy from Which Flowers Are Scattered and a Twisting Dragon with his gold-banded club. At first both he and the cudgel moved like flowers being added to brocade, but later he could no longer be seen as the whole sky was filled with the whirling cudgel. As he roared his approval from down below Pig could not keep still, and with a great shout of "I'm going to have a bit of fun too!" the splendid idiot rode a breeze up into the air and started swinging his rake. He went three times up, four times down, five times to the left, six times to the right, seven times forwards and eight times backwards as he ran through all the movements he knew, filling the air with a noise like a howling gale. Just when he had warmed up Friar Sand said to Sanzang, "Master, let me go up and give a show too." Springing up into the air with both feet, the splendid monk whirled his club through the air, which glittered with golden light. Wielding his demon-subduing cudgel he performed a Red Phoenix Facing the Sun and a Hungry Tiger Seizing Its Prey, attacking hard and defending with time to spare as he turned for a sudden forward thrust. The three brother disciples all gave a most imposing display of their magical powers. This was indeed

An image of the dhyana, no common sight;
The causation of the Great Way filling all of space.
Metal and wood fill the dharma-world with their might;
A pinch of elixir produces perfect unity.
The quality of these magic warriors is often displayed;
The splendour of their weapons is widely revered.
Lofty though India is,
The princes of Yuhua now return to the central truth.

This all so terrified the three young princes that they fell to their knees in the dust; and all the staff in the Gauze Pavilion, high and low, together with the senior prince in his palace, all the soldiers, civilians, men and women, Buddhist monks and nuns, Taoist clergy, lay people — everyone in fact — all invoked the Buddha, kowtowed, held sticks of incense and worshipped. Indeed,

All the monks were converted at the sight of the true images,
Bringing blessings to mankind and the joys of peace.
From here the achievement was won on the road to enlightenment;
All joined in meditation and worshipped the Buddha.

When the three of them had given a display of their heroic powers they brought their auspicious clouds down to land, put their weapons away, joined their hands together in homage to the Tang Priest, thanked him and took their seats again.

The three young princes hurried back into the palace to report to their father, "A most wonderful thing has happened, Father. Today has been a tremendous success. Did you see the performance in the sky just now?" "When I saw the coloured clouds glowing in the sky a little while back I, your mother and everyone else in the inner palace burned incense and worshipped," the prince, their father, replied. "I don't know where the gods or immortals who had gathered there were from." "They weren't gods and immortals from somewhere else," the young princes said. "They were the three hideous disciples of the monk who's going to fetch the scriptures. One of them uses a gold-banded iron cudgel, one a nine-toothed rake, and one a demon-quelling staff, all exactly the same as our three weapons. When we asked them to give us a display they said it was too cramped down here to be able to manage, so they'd go up into the sky to give us a show. Then they all went up on clouds, filling the sky with auspicious clouds and vapours. They only came down a moment ago, and they're now sitting in the Gauze Pavilion. We are all very taken with them and we'd like to make them our teachers and learn their skills to protect the country with. This really will be an enormous achievement. I wonder what Your Majesty thinks." When the prince, their father, heard this he was convinced and agreed.

Father and sons then went straight to the Gauze Pavilion, going on foot instead of by carriage, and without any parasols. The four travellers had by now packed up their luggage and were just about to go to the palace to thank the prince for the meal and start out on their journey again when they saw the prince of Yuhua and his sons come into the pavilion and prostrate themselves before them. The venerable elder hurriedly rose and prostrated himself to return the courtesy, while Monkey and the rest of them moved aside with a hint of a mocking grin. When the kowtowing was over the four travellers were happy to go into the palace on being invited to do so and take seats of honour. Then the senior prince got up and said, "Tang Master, there is one thing I would like to ask of you, but I do not know whether your three illustrious disciples will grant it." "My disciples will obey any instruction that Your Royal Highness gives them," Sanzang replied. "When I first saw you gentlemen," said the prince, "I took you for pilgrim monks from distant Tang, and because I am a mere mortal with fleshly eyes I treated you in a most offhand way. It was only when I saw Teacher Sun, Teacher Zhu and Teacher Sand whirling around in the sky that I realized you are immortals and Buddhas. My three wretched sons have been fond of the martial arts all their lives and they now wish most sincerely to be accepted as your disciples and learn some of your skills. I beg that in the greatness of your hearts you will agree to be the salvation of my boys. I will certainly reward you with all the wealth of the city."

When Brother Monkey heard this he could not restrain himself from replying with a chuckle, "You really don't understand, Your Royal Highness. As monks we'd love to have disciples, and your fine sons have their hearts set on goodness. But you mustn't talk about material benefits. As long as they can get on with us we'll look after them." This delighted the prince, who ordered a great banquet in the main hall of the palace. It was amazing: no sooner had he issued his order than everything was there. This is what could be seen:

Fluttering silken decorations,
Darkly fragrant incense smoke.
Gold-inlaid tables hung with knotted silks,
Dazzling the eyes;
Lacquered chairs with cushions of brocade,
Making them even more splendid.
Fresh fruit,
Fragrant tea.
Three or four courses of pure confectioneries,
One or two servings of rich and pure breadrolls.
The crisp steamed honeycakes were even finer;
The deep-fried sweets were truly delicious.
There were jugs of mild rice-wine,
Better than nectar when poured;
Servings of Yangxian tea that is fit for immortals,
More fragrant than cassia when held in the hands.
Every possible dish is provided;
All that is offered is outstanding.

Meanwhile there was singing, dancing, instrumental music, acrobatics and opera to entertain them. Master, disciples, the prince and his sons all had a day of delight, and after night fell unnoticed they dispersed. The princes then had beds and curtains set up in the pavilion and invited their teachers to turn in for the night; early the next morning they would piously burn incense and call on them again to ask them to teach their martial skills. These orders were obeyed, and hot, scented water was brought in for the travellers to bath in, after which everyone went to bed. At that time

The birds perched high in the trees and all was silent;
The poet came down from his couch to end his chanting.
The light of the Milky Way now filled the sky,
And the grass grew thicker along the overgrown path.
The bang of a washing stick came from another courtyard;

The distant mountains and passes made one long for home.
The chirp of crickets expressed people's feelings,
Chirruping at the bedside interrupted one's dreams.

That describes the night. Early the next morning the prince and his three sons came to call on the venerable elder again. The previous day they had greeted each other with the etiquette appropriate to a prince, but today's greetings were those appropriate to teachers. The three young princes kowtowed to Monkey, Pig and Friar Sand, then asked with bows, "Will you let your disciples have a look at your weapons, honoured teachers?" As soon as Pig heard this request he happily brought out his iron rake and threw it on the ground, while Friar Sand tossed his staff against the wall. The second and third young princes sprang to their feet to pick them up, but they might just as well have been dragonflies trying to shake a stone pillar: they both strained themselves till they were red in the face without moving the weapons in the slightest. When their elder brother saw this he said, "Don't waste your efforts, brothers. Our teachers' weapons are all magical ones. Goodness only knows how heavy they are." "My rake's not all that heavy," said Pig with a smile. "It only weighs a couple of tons — 5,048 pounds including the handle." The third prince then asked Friar Sand how heavy his staff was. "It's 5,048 pounds too," replied Friar Sand with a smile.

The oldest of the young princes then asked Brother Monkey to let him see the gold-banded cudgel. Monkey produced the needle from his ear, shook it in the wind to make it as thick as a rice bowl, and stood it upright in the ground in front of him, to the consternation and alarm of all the princes and officials. The three young princes then kowtowed again and said, "Teacher Zhu and Teacher Sand carry their weapons under their clothes where they can get them out. Why do you take yours out of your ear, Teacher Sun? How do you make it grow in the wind?" "You wouldn't realize that this isn't some mere mortal object," Monkey replied.

"When chaos was first parted the iron was cast:
Yu the Great had the work done himself.
When he unified the depths of rivers, lakes and seas
This cudgel served as a measuring rod.
In the prosperity after mountains and seas had been ordered
It floated to the gates of the Eastern Ocean.
Over the years it gave off a coloured glow,
Learned to shrink and to grow and shine with pure light.
It was my destiny to recover this rod
Which endlessly changes when I say the spell.
When I tell it to grow it fills the universe,
But it can be as tiny as a needle's eye.
It's known as as-you-will and called gold-banded;
In Heaven and on Earth it is quite unique.
Its weight is thirteen thousand and five hundred pounds;
Whether thick or fine it can bring life or death.
Once it helped me make havoc in Heaven,
And took part when I attacked the Underworld.
It always succeeds in subduing dragons and tigers,
Everywhere wipes out monsters and ogres.
If it points up the sun goes dark;
Heaven, earth, gods, devils, all are afraid.
Passed on by magic since the birth of time,
This is no ordinary piece of iron."

When the young princes had heard this they all started kowtowing endlessly, bowing over and over again as they earnestly begged for instruction. "Which fighting skills do the three of you want to learn?" Monkey asked. "The one of us who uses a rod wants to learn that," the young princes replied, "the one who fights with a rake wants to learn the rake, and the staff man wants to learn the staff." "Teaching would be easy enough," replied Monkey with a smile, "except that you're all too weak to be able to use our weapons, so you won't be able to master them. 'A badly-drawn tiger only looks like a dog.' As they used to say in the old days, 'If the teaching isn't strict it shows the teacher is idle; if the student doesn't learn it's his own fault.' If you're really sincere you'd better burn incense and bow to Heaven and Earth. I'll give you some magic strength before teaching you how to fight."

The three young princes were very pleased to hear him say this, and they at once carried in an incense table themselves, washed their hands, lit incense sticks and bowed to Heaven. This done, they asked their teachers to instruct them. Monkey stepped down and said to the Tang Priest with a bow, "Please forgive your disciple, honoured Master. Ever since in your goodness you rescued me at the Double Boundary Mountain and I became a Buddhist all those years ago we've been travelling west. Although I've never done very much to repay your kindness I have crossed plenty of rivers and mountains and done everything I possibly could. Now that we've come to this land of the Buddha and had the good fortune of meeting these three young princes, they've taken us as their teachers of martial arts. As our pupils they'd be your pupils' pupils, so I ask you respectfully, Master, to allow us to instruct them." Sanzang was delighted, and when Pig and Friar Sand saw Monkey bowing to him they kowtowed too and said, "Master, we're stupid and too awkward with words to be able to explain things properly. Please take your dharma seat and let each of us take a pupil. It'll be fun, and something to remind us of our journey west." Sanzang was happy to agree.

Monkey then took the three young princes into a quiet room behind the pavilion where he drew a star-chart of the Dipper and told them to prostrate themselves inside it while they shut their eyes and settled their spirits. Meanwhile he silently said the words of the spell, recited a mantra, and blew magic breath into the hearts of the three of them. He put their primal spirits back into their original home, taught them magical spells, gave each of them immense strength, applied the right heat, and performed a magic that replaced their old bodies and bones with new ones. After the heat circulated in a roundabout way through their bodies the three young princes came to, stood up, rubbed their faces, summoned up their spirits, and all found that they were much stronger. The eldest of them could pick up the gold-banded cudgel, the second could swing the nine-toothed rake, and the third could raise the demon-quelling staff.

When the king saw this he was beside himself with delight, and arranged another vegetarian feast for the Tang Priest and his three disciples. In front of the banquet each of the princes was taught his own skill: the one who was learning the rod practised with the rod, the one who was learning the rake practised with the rake, and the one who was learning the staff practised with the staff. Though the young princes did manage a few turns and movements it took a lot of effort, and going through a series of movements left them gasping for breath, so that they could not go on. Besides this, the weapons they were using had the power of transformation, so that as the princes advanced, retreated, attacked and lifted the weapons shrunk, grew and went through amazing changes by themselves. But the princes were, after all, only mortals, and were unable to keep up with the speed of their weapons. Later that day the banquet came to an end.

The next day the three princes came back once more to express their thanks and say, "We are very grateful to you, divine teachers, for giving us this strength, but when we try to spin your divine weapons around we can only move them with great difficulty. We would like to get smiths to make lighter copies of them, but we don't know whether you would agree to that, Teachers." "Great, great," said Pig. "That's the way to talk. You ought to have your own made because you can't use our weapons, and anyhow we need them to protect the Dharma and beat monsters." The princes then sent for smiths who bought ten thousand pounds of iron and steel, set up a workshop with a furnace in the front courtyard of the prince's palace, and began to cast the weapons. On the first day the steel was made, and on the second Monkey and the other two were asked to bring out their gold-banded cudgel, nine-toothed rake and demon-quelling staff and put them under the matting shelter to be copied. The work went on by night and day without stopping.

These weapons were the treasures they always carried with

them that they could not be parted from for a moment. Normally they hid them about their persons. Now the weapons were protected by coloured light, so that when they were put in the yard of the workshop for several days many beams of radiance reached up to the heavens, while every kind of auspicious vapour blanketed the earth. That night an evil spirit, who was sitting out on a night watch in a cave called Tigermouth Cave on a mountain called Mount Leopard Head that was only some twenty-five miles from the city, noticed the glow and the auspicious vapours. Going up on his cloud to investigate he saw that the light came from the city, whereupon he brought his cloud down and went closer for a better look. Discovering that the light was coming from the weapons, he thought with delight and desire, "What wonderful weapons, what splendid treasures. I wonder whose they are and why they've been left here. This must be my lucky chance. I'll take them, I'll take them." His covetousness now moved, he created a mighty wind, scooped up all three weapons and took them back to his cave. Indeed,

Not for one moment must the Way be left;
What can be left is not the true Way.
Cultivation and trance will both be in vain
When divine arms have been taken away.

If you do not know how these weapons were found, listen to the explanation in the next instalment.

CHAPTER EIGHTY-NINE

The Tawny Lion Spirit arranges a rake feast in vain; Metal, wood and earth make havoc on Mount Leopard Head.

The story tells how after days on end of hard work the smiths all went to sleep that night, only to get up at dawn to start again and find that the three weapons had disappeared from under the matting shelter. Dumbfounded with horror, they started looking for them everywhere, and when the three young princes came out of the inner quarters to watch, the smiths all kowtowed to them and said, "Young masters, we don't know where the divine teachers' three weapons have all gone."

When the young princes heard this news they trembled and said, "We expect our masters put them away last night." Rushing to the Gauze Pavilion, they found the white horse still tethered in the walkway and could not help shouting, "Teachers, are you still asleep?" "We're up," Friar Sand replied, and opened the door of their room to let the young princes in. When they saw that the weapons were not there they asked with alarm, "Masters, have you put your weapons away?" "No," replied Monkey, springing up. "The three weapons disappeared during the night," the princes explained. "Is my rake still there?" Pig asked as he scrambled to his feet. "When we came out a moment ago we saw everyone searching for them," the princes replied. "When they couldn't find them we wondered if you had put them away, which is why we came to ask. As your treasures can shrink or grow we wonder if you've hidden them about yourselves to play a trick on us." "Honestly, we haven't," said Monkey. "Let's all join the search."

When they went to the matting shelter in the yard and could

see that there really was no sign of the weapons Pig said, "You smiths must have stolen them. Bring 'em out at once. Do it right now or I'll kill you. I'll kill you, I say." The smiths kowtowed desperately and said with tears pouring down their faces, "Your Lordships, we went to sleep last night because we'd been working so hard for days on end. When we got up this morning they'd gone. We're only ordinary mortals. We could never have moved them. Spare our lives, Your Lordships, spare our lives." Monkey said nothing as he said with bitter regret, "It's our fault. After we'd shown them what they look like to copy we should have kept them on us instead of leaving them lying there. I suppose our treasures' glowing clouds and light must have alerted some monster who came and stole them during the night." "Nonsense, brother," Pig replied. "This is a peaceful, orderly sort of place, not somewhere in the wilds or the mountains. No monsters could possibly have come here. I'm sure it was those evil smiths who stole our weapons. They could tell they were treasures from the light shining from them. They must have left the palace last night and got a whole gang together to carry or drag them out. Bring 'em here! I'm going to hit them." The smiths kowtowed and swore to their innocence for all they were worth.

Amid all this commotion the senior prince came out, and when he asked what had happened the colour drained from his face too. After muttering to himself in a low voice for a while he said, "Divine teachers, your weapons were not more mortals' ones. Even if there had been a hundred or more people they would never have been able to move them. Besides, my family has been ruling this city for five generations. I'm not boasting, but I do have a certain reputation for being a good man. The soldiers, civilians and artisans who live here fear my laws, and I am certain that they could never have had so wicked an idea. I hope that you divine teachers will think again." "No need for any more thinking about it," replied Brother Monkey with a smile, "and no need to make the smiths suffer for what's not their fault. I would like to ask Your Royal Highness if there are any evil monsters in the mountains and forests around the city." "That's a very good question," the prince replied. "There is a mountain north of the city called Mount Leopard Head, with a Tigermouth Cave in it. People often say that immortals, or tigers and wolves, or evil spirits live there. As I've never been there to find out the truth I am not sure what kind of creatures there are." "No need to say any more," replied Monkey with a laugh. "It must be someone wicked from there who knew they were treasures and came during the night to steal them. Pig, Friar Sand," he ordered, "stay here to guard the master and the city while I go for a look round." He then told the smiths to keep the furnace burning and carry on forging the new weapons.

The splendid Monkey King took his leave of Sanzang and whistled out of sight. Soon he was on Mount Leopard Head, which took him but an instant as it was only ten miles from the city. As he climbed to the summit to look around he saw that there was quite an air of evil about it. Indeed, it was

A long dragon chain of hills,
A mighty formation.
Sharp peaks thrusting into the sky,
Streams flowing fast along chasms deep.
In front of the mountain grow cushions of rare plants;
Behind the mountain strange flowers form brocade.
Tall pine and ancient cypress,
Old trees and fine bamboo.
Crows and magpies sing as they fly,
Cranes call and gibbons scream.
Below the beetling scar
David's deer go in twos;
In front of the sheer rock-face
Are pairs of badgers and foxes.
Dragons from afar emerge briefly from the waters
Of the twisting, winding stream that runs deep under the ground.
This ridge runs right to the edge of Yuhua,
A place of beauty for a thousand ages.

Just as he was surveying the scene Monkey heard voices on the other side of the mountain, turned quickly round to look, and saw a couple of wolf-headed ogres climbing towards the north west and talking loudly as they went. "They must be monster patrolling the mountain," Monkey guessed. "I'm going to liste to what they have to say."

Making magic with his hands and saying the words of a spel Monkey shook himself, turned into a butterfly, spread his wing and fluttered after them. It was a very lifelike transformation

A pair of powdery wings,
Two silver antennae.
In the wind it flies very fast;
In the sun it's a leisurely dancer.
It crosses rivers and walls in a flash.
Enjoys stealing fragrance and playing with catkins.
This delicate creature loves the taste of fresh flowers
It shows its beauty and elegance as it pleases.

He flew to a spot right above the evil spirits' heads, where h floated and listened to what they had to say. "Brother," one o them shouted suddenly, "our chief keeps on striking it lucky The other month he caught himself a real beauty to live wit him in the cave, and he was as pleased as anything about that Then last night he got the three weapons, which really ar priceless treasures. Tomorrow there's going to be a Rake Ban quet to celebrate, so we're all going to benefit." "We've bee quite lucky too," the other replied, "being given these twent ounces of silver to buy pigs and sleep. When we get to Qian fang Market we can have a few jugs of wine to start with, an then fiddle the accounts to make ourselves two or three ounce of silver to buy ourselves padded jackets for the winter. It' great, isn't it?" As they laughed and talked the two monster hurried along the main path at a great speed.

When Monkey heard about the banquet to celebrate the rak he was quietly delighted. He would have liked to kill the devils but it was not their fault and, besides, he had no weapon. So h flew round till he was in front of them, turned back into himsel and stood at a junction along the path. As the devils graduall came closer he blew a mouthful of magic saliva at them, recite

e words *Om Humkara* and made a fixing spell that held the
o wolf-headed spirits where they were. Their eyes were fixed
a stare, they could not open their mouths, and they stood
right, both legs rigid. Monkey then knocked them over, undid
eir clothes and searched them, finding the twenty ounces of
ver in a purse carried by one of them in the belt of his kilt.
ach of them was also carrying a white lacquered pass. One
these read "Wily Freak" and the other read "Freaky Wile".
Having taken their silver and undone their passes the
lendid Great Sage went straight back to the city, where he
ld the princes, the Tang Priest, the officials high and low and
e smiths what had happened. "I reckon my treasure's the one
at shone the brightest," said Pig with a grin. "That's why
ey're buying pigs and sheep for a slap-up meal to celebrate.
ut how are we going to get it back?" "We'll all three of us
," said Monkey. "This silver was for buying pigs and sheep.
e'll give it to the smiths: His Royal Highness can provide us
ith some animals. Pig, you turn yourself into Wily Freak, I'll
rn into Freaky Wile, and Friar Sand can be a trader selling
gs and sheep. We'll go into Tigermouth Cave, and when it
its us we'll grab our weapons, kill all the monsters, come back
re to pack up and be on our way again." "Terrific," said Friar
nd. "No time to lose. Let's go." The senior prince agreed with
e plan and told his steward to buy seven or eight pigs and four
five sheep.
The three of them left their master and gave a great display
their magic powers once outside the city. "Brother," said Pig,
've never seen that Wily Freak, so how can I possibly turn
yself into his double?" "I did fixing magic on him to keep
m over there somewhere," Monkey said, "and he won't come
und till tomorrow. I can remember what he looks like, so you
and still while I tell you how to change. Yes, like this . . .
, a bit more like that. . . . That's it. That's him." While the
iot said an incantation Brother Monkey blew on him with
agic breath, turned him into Wily Freak's double and gave him
white pass to tuck in at his waist. Monkey then turned himself
to Freaky Wile with a pass at his waist too, and Friar Sand

made himself look like a travelling dealer in pigs and shee
Then they drove the pigs and sheep together along the path we
towards the mountain. Before long they were in a mountai
gully, where they met another junior devil. He had the mo
horrible face. Just look:

A pair of round and bulging eyes
Shining like lanterns;
A head of red and bristly hair,
Blazing like fire.
A red nose,
A twisted mouth,
Sharp and pointy fangs;
Protruding ears,
A brow that seemed hacked into shape,
And a green and bloated face.
He was wearing a pale yellow tunic
And sandals made of sedge.
He looked most imposing, like some evil god,
As he hurried along like a vicious demon.

This devil was carrying a coloured lacquer invitation box und
his left arm as he greeted Monkey and the other two with
call of "Freaky Wile, good to see you both. Did you buy
some pigs and sheep?" "Can't you see we're driving the
along?" Monkey replied. "Who's this gentleman?" the dev
asked, looking at Friar Sand. "He's the dealer in pigs ar
sheep," Monkey replied. "We still owe him a couple of ounc
of silver, so we're taking him home with us to fetch it. Where a
you going?" "To Bamboo Mountain to invite His Senior Ma
esty to the feast tomorrow morning," the devil said. Taking h
cue from the devil's tone of voice, Monkey then asked, "Ho
many guests will there be altogether?" "His Senior Majesty w
take the place of honour," the devil replied, "and with our ov
king, chiefs and the rest of them there'll be over forty." As th
were talking Pig called, "Get a move on! The pigs and shee
are going everywhere." "You go and invite them while I get
look at that invitation," Monkey said, and as the devil regard

im as one of their own kind he opened the box, took out the ıvitation and handed it to Monkey. This is what Monkey ead when he unfolded it:

> A banquet is being given tomorrow morning to celebrate the capture of the rake, and if you will condescend to cross the mountain, honoured ancestor, Primal Sage of Ninefold Numinosity, I will be deeply grateful.
>
> With a hundred kowtows,
> Your grandson;
> Tawny Lion

'hen Monkey had read it he handed it back to the devil, who eturned it to its case and carried on towards the southeast.

"Brother," Friar Sand asked, "what did it say on the initation?" "It was an invitation to the Rake Banquet," Monkey eplied. It was signed, 'with a hundred kowtows, your grandson awny Lion', and the invitation was being sent to the Primal age of Ninefold Numinosity." "Tawny Lion must be a goldenaired lion who's become a spirit," said Friar Sand with a smile, but I wonder who the Primal Sage of Ninefold Numinosity is." ig's reaction was to laugh and say, "He's mine." "Why should e necessarily be yours?" Monkey asked. "There's an old saying ıat goes, 'a mangy old sow can put a golden lion to flight,'" ig replied. "That's why I know he's mine." As they talked and ıughed the three of them drove the pigs and sheep along till ıey could see the gates of Tigermouth Cave. Outside the gates ıere were,

Green mountains all around,
Ranges forming a mighty wall.
Creepers clung to the sheer rock faces,
Thorns hung down from the towering cliffs.
Bird song came from all around the woods,
While flowers gave a welcome by the entrance.
This cave was a match for the Peach Blossom Spring,
A place to avoid the troubles of the world.

s they came closer to the mouth of the cave they saw a crowd f evil spirits of every age and kind playing under the blossomıg trees, and when they heard Pig's shouts of "Hey! Hey!" as e drove the pigs and sheep they all came out to meet them.

The pigs and sheep were caught and trussed up. The noise had by now disturbed the demon king inside, who came out with ten or more junior demons to ask, "Are you two back? How many animals did you buy?" "Eight pigs and seven sheep — fifteen altogether," Monkey replied. "The pigs cost sixteen ounces of silver and the sheep nine. We were only given twenty ounces, so we still owe five. This is the dealer who's come with us for the silver." "Fetch five ounces of silver, little ones," the demon king ordered on hearing this, "and send him on his way." "But the dealer hasn't only come to get his silver," Monkey replied. "He's come to see the banquet too." "What cheek, Freaky Wile!" said the furious demon abusively. "You were sent off to buy things, not to talk about banquets." "As you've got those amazingly fine treasures, my lord," Pig said, stepping forward "what's the harm in letting him have a look?" "Damn you too Wily Freak," said the demon with an angry snort. "I got these treasures from inside the city of Yuhua. If this stranger see them and talks about them in the city the word will get aroun and the prince will come to demand them. What'll we do then?" "My lord," Monkey replied, "this dealer comes from the othe side of Qianfang Market. That's a long way from the city, an he's not a city man either, so where would he go telling tales Besides, he's hungry, and the two of us haven't eaten. If there' any food and liquor in the place why don't we give him som before sending him on his way?" Before he could finish speak ing a junior devil came out with five ounces of silver that h gave to Monkey, who in turn handed it to Friar Sand with th words, "Take your silver, stranger, then come round to the bac for something to eat with us."

Taking his courage in his hands, Friar Sand went into th cave with Pig and Monkey. When they reached the second ha inside they saw on a table in the middle of it the nine-toothe iron rake set up in all its dazzling brightness to receive offering At the eastern end of the table was leant the gold-bande cudgel, and at the western end the demon-quelling staff. "Stra ger," said the demon king who was following them in, "that the rake shining so brightly in the middle. You're welcome ɔok, but don't tell anyone about it, whatever you do." Friar and nodded in admiration.

Oh dear! This was a case of "when the owner sees what's is he's bound to pick it up." Pig had always been a rough ustomer, and once he saw his rake he was not going to talk bout the facts of the case, but charged over, pulled it down and wung it around as he turned back into himself. He struck traight at the evil spirit's face, not caring now about the proper vays of using his weapon. Monkey and Friar Sand each rushed o one end of the table to grab his own weapon and turn back nto himself. As the three brothers started lashing out wildly the lemon king had to get out of their way in a hurry, go round to he back and fetch his four-bright halberd with its long handle nd sharp, pointed butt. Rushing into the courtyard, he used this o hold off the three weapons and shout at the top of his voice, 'Who do you think you are, tricking me out of my treasures by mpersonation?" "I'll get you, you hairy beast," Monkey cursed ack. "You don't realize who I am. I'm a disciple of Tang Sanang, the holy monk from the east. When we came to Yuhua to resent our passport the prince told his three sons to take us as heir teachers of fighting skills. They were having weapons copid from ours. That was why ours were left in the courtyard for ou to sneak into the city and steal in the middle of the night. Ind you accuse us of tricking them out of you by impersonation! tay right there and try a taste of our three weapons." The evil pirit at once raised his halberd to fight back. They fought from he courtyard out through the front gate, three monks chasing a ingle demon. It was a splendid battle:

The cudgel whistled like the wind,
The rake's blows came raining down.
The demon-quelling staff filled the sky with glowing mist;
The four-bright halberd gave off clouds.
They were like the three immortals refining elixir,
Making dazzling light that frightened gods and ghosts.
Monkey was brilliant at displaying his might;

The evil spirit was wrong to have stolen the treasures.
Marshal Tian Peng showed off his divine powers,
While the great general Sand was heroic and splendid.
As the three brothers fought with skill and one mind
A great battle took place in Tigermouth Cave.
The ogre was full of power and cunning,
A fit match for the four heroes.
They fought until the sun set in the west,
When the demon weakened and could hold out n
longer.

After their long fight on Mount Leopard Head the evil spiri shouted at Friar Sand, "Watch this halberd!" As Friar Sand fe back to dodge the blow the evil spirit escaped through the open ing he left and fled by wind to the Xun quarter to the southeas Pig started rushing after him to catch him, but Monkey said, "Le him go. As the old saying goes, 'never chase a desperate robber Let's leave him nothing to come back to."

Pig agreed, and the three of them went back to the entranc of the cave, where they killed all the hundred and more evi spirits great and small. It turned out that they were all reall tigers, wolves, tiger cats, leopards, red deer and goats. Monke used one of his powers to bring all the valuables and fabrics, a well as the bodies of all the animals they had killed, the pigs an the sheep out of the cave. Friar Sand used some dry wood h found to start a fire that Pig fanned with both his ears. The cav was soon burnt out, and they took what they had brought wit them back to the city.

The city gates were wide open; people had not yet gone t bed. The senior prince and his sons were still waiting in th Gauze Pavilion. The three disciples dropped all the dead wil animals and sheep as well as the valuables with loud thumps int the courtyard, filling it up as they called out, "Master, we'r back. We've won." The senior prince then expressed his thank to them, the Tang priest was delighted, and the three youn princes fell to their knees to bow. "Don't thank us," Friar San said, helping them to their feet. "Come and see what we've got."

'Where are they from?" the senior prince asked. "The tigers, volves, tiger cats, leopards, red deer and goats were all monsters hat made themselves into spirits. When we'd got our weapons ack we fought our way out through the gates. Their demon king s a golden-haired lion who fights with a four-bright halberd. He attled it out with us till nightfall, then ran away to the south-ast. Instead of chasing him we made sure he'd have nowhere o come back to by killing all these devils and bringing back all is things."

This news both delighted and alarmed the senior prince: he vas delighted at their triumphant return and worried that the lemon would seek his revenge later. "Don't worry, Your Royal Iighness," said Monkey. "I've thought about it very carefully, nd I'll deal with it properly. I promise to exterminate the de-nons completely before we go. We'll definitely not leave you vith trouble that'll come back later. When we went there at oon we ran into a little greenfaced, red-haired devil who was arrying an invitation. What it said on it was: 'A banquet is eing given tomorrow morning to celebrate the capture of the ake, and if you will condescend to cross the mountain, honour-d ancestor, Primal Sage of Ninefold Numinosity, I will be leeply grateful.' It was signed: 'with a hundred kowtows, your randson, Tawny Lion'. When the evil spirit was defeated just ow he must have gone to have a word with his grandfather. They're bound to come looking for us to get their revenge to-norrow morning, and when that happens I'll wipe them all out or you." The senior prince thanked him and had supper arrang-d. When master and disciples had eaten, everybody went to ed.

The story now tells of how the evil spirit really did head outheast to Bamboo Mountain, in which there was a cave called he Nine-bend Twisty Cave where the evil spirit's grandfather, he Primal Sage of Ninefold Numinosity, lived. That night the lemon did not stop treading the wind until he reached the cave's ntrance in the last watch. When he knocked on the gates and vent in a junior devil greeted him with the words, "Your Majesty, Greenface brought the invitation last night, and the ol gentleman invited him to stay till this morning to go to you Rake Banquet with him. Why have you come here so very earl to invite him yourself?" "I hate to have to say it," the evil spiri replied, "but the banquet is off." As they were talking Green face came out from the inner part of the cave to say, "What ar you doing here, Your Majesty? As soon as His Senior Majesty' up he's coming to the celebration with me." The evil spirit wa so distraught that he could say nothing, but only wave his hand

A little later the old demon got up and called for the evi spirit, who dropped his weapon and prostrated himself on th ground to kowtow, tears streaming down his cheeks. "Worth grandson," the old demon said, "you sent me an invitatio yesterday, and this morning I'm on my way to the celebration So why have you come yourself, looking so miserable an upset?" "I was taking a stroll in the moonlight the night befor last," the evil spirit replied, still kowtowing, "when I saw dazzling light rising up to the sky from the city of Yuhua. hurried there to take a look and saw that it came from thre weapons in the prince's palace: a nine-toothed rake with gold i it, a staff and a gold-banded cudgel. I used my magic to tak them away and decided to have a Rake Banquet to celebrate. sent some of my underlings to buy pigs, sheep and fruit for th feast that I invited you to come and enjoy, Grandfather. Bu after I sent Greenface over with the invitation yesterday Wil Freak and the other one who'd been told to buy pigs and shee came back with a dealer, a stranger, for some silver. The stran ger was all set on seeing the banquet. I refused as I was afrai he'd spread the news around. Then they said they were hungr and asked for some food to eat, so I told them to go round th back to eat. When they got inside and saw the weapons the said they were theirs. They each snatched one and turned bac into their real selves. One was a monk with a hairy face and mouth like a thunder god's, one was a monk with a long snou and big ears, and one was a monk with a really sinister face The three of them yelled at me and started lashing out: the didn't care at all. I just managed to fetch my four-bright hal

ːrd and come out to hold them at bay. When I asked them who
ey were and how they dared go in for impersonation they told
e they were disciples of the Tang Priest who's been sent to
e Western Heaven by Great Tang in the east. When they went
present their passport on their way through the city the
rinces pressed them to stay and teach them martial arts. They
id their three weapons had been left in the palace yard for
ppies of them to be made, and that I'd stolen them. Then they
ent for me with great fury. I didn't know what those three
onks are called, but they're all very good fighters. As I was no
atch for them by myself I had to run away and come here. If
ou have any love for your grandson I beg you to lend me your
rms in order to get my revenge on those monks." After a mo-
ent's silent thought the old demon replied with a smile, "So it's
em. Worthy grandson, you made a big mistake provoking him."
Do you know who they are, grandfather?" the other asked.
The one with a long snout and big ears is Zhu Bajie," the old
emon said, "and the one with a horrible face is Friar Sand.
hey're not too bad. But the one with a hairy face and a mouth
ke a thunder god is called Sun the Novice. He's got really tre-
endous magical powers. When he made great havoc in Heaven
ve hundred years ago a hundred thousand heavenly troops
ouldn't catch him. And he's a most determined hunter. He's like
policeman who'll search mountains and seas, smash caves, storm
ities and cause all sorts of trouble. Why did you have to pro-
oke him? Never mind. I'll go with you and capture those so-
nd-sos and the prince of Yuhua to avenge you." On hearing this
e evil spirit kowtowed again in thanks.

The senior demon immediately mustered his grandsons
Ionkey Lion, Snowy Lion, Leo, Gryphon, Racoon-dog Lion
nd Elephant-fighter, each of whom carried a sharp weapon.
Vith Tawny Lion leading the way each of them set off a power-
il gale that carried them straight to Mount Leopard Head,
here there was an all-pervasive smell of smoke and fire and all
at could be heard was sobbing. When they looked more closely
ey saw Wily Freak and Freaky Wile weeping for their lord.
Are you the real Freak and Wile or impostors?" the evil spirit

shouted as he went up to them. Falling to their knees and kow towing with tears in their eyes, the two devils replied, "We'r no impostors. After we were given the silver to buy pigs an sheep yesterday we met a monk with a hairy face and a mout like a thunder god in the wide valley to the west of the moun tain. When he spat on us our legs went all weak, our mouth went stiff, we couldn't speak and we couldn't move. He knocke us over, found and stole our silver and took our passes off u We were left in a daze till we came round just now. When w got home we found the place still on fire and all the buildin burnt down. We were crying so bitterly because you, my lor and all the chiefs had disappeared. We don't know how th fire was started."

When the evil spirit heard this he could not stop his tear from gushing forth as he stamped his feet in fury, let loos heaven-shaking roars and exclaimed in hatred and fury, "Damn ed baldies! Vicious beasts! How could you be so evil? You'v destroyed my cave palace and burnt my beauty to death. You'v killed everyone, young and old, in the household. I'm so angry could die!" The old demon then told Monkey Lion to take hol of Tawny Lion, saying, "Grandson, what's done is don Upsetting yourself won't do you any good. What you must d now is summon up all your energy to catch those monks in th city." The evil spirit was still crying as he replied, "Grandfathe this mountain palace of mine wasn't built in a day. Now thos damned baldies have destroyed everything my life's not wort living." With that he broke free and flung himself forward t smash his head against the rock-face, only stopping after Snow Lion and Monkey Lion had made great efforts to calm hin They then left the cave and all headed for the city.

With a roaring wind and in a thick fog they approached th city, so frightening all the people living outside the city wall th they abandoned their belongings and dragged or carried thei children with them as they fled into the city. Once the peopl were all inside the gates were shut. A report was then made t the palace that a disaster was upon them. When the prince, wh was taking a vegetarian breakfast in the Gauze Pavilion wit the Tang Priest and the others, heard this report he went out to ask about it. "A whole crowd of evil spirits are heading for the city with sandstorms, flying stones, fogs and wind." "Whatever shall we do?" asked the prince, deeply alarmed. "All stop worrying," said Brother Monkey, "all stop worrying. It's the evil spirit from Tigermouth Cave who ran away when he was beaten yesterday. He went to the southeast to gang up with the Primal Sage of Ninefold Numinosity or whatever he's called and now he's here. We brothers are going out. Tell them to shut all the city gates, and send men to hold the city wall." The prince ordered that the city gates be shut, sent men to the wall, and went with his sons and the Tang Priest to inspect. The army's banners blotted out the sun, and the cannon fire reached the sky as Monkey, Pig and Friar Sand left the city amid wind and clouds to give battle. Indeed,

Because they were careless the weapons were lost,
Which led to attacks by the devilish host.

If you do not know the outcome of the battle listen to the explanation in the next instalment.

CHAPTER NINETY

By giving and receiving the master and the lion turn into one.
After stealing the Way and obstructing Dhyana Ninefold Numinosity is pacified.

The story tells how the Great Sage Sun left the city with Pig and Friar Sand and looked the monsters in the face to see that they were all lions of various kinds. The Tawny Lion Spirit was leading, with Leo and Elephant-fighter Lion on his left, Gryphon and Racoon-dog Lion on his right and Monkey Lion with Snowy Lion behind him. In the middle of them all was a nine-headed lion. The ogre Greenface was holding a canopy of brocade embroidered with flowers just behind the nine-headed lion; while Wily Freak and Freaky Wile carried a pair of red flags. They were all drawn up at a hollow place.

In his rough way Pig went up to them to shout abusively, "Ogres! Thieves! Treasure-stealers! What did you go there and gang up with that hairy lot for?" To this the Tawny Lion Spirit retorted, gnashing his teeth in fury, "Vicious baldies! When I was alone yesterday the three of you beat me and I had to run away. You should have done right, instead of burning my cave palace, destroying my mountain home and murdering my family. My hatred for you is as great as the ocean. Stay where you are and take this from my halberd!" The splendid Pig raised his rake to parry the blow. When the two of them had just started fighting and neither was yet coming out on top Monkey Lion joined in, swinging his spiked iron club, as did Snowy Lion with his three-edged mace. "Welcome," shouted Pig. Watch him as he charges straight forward to meet their onslaught and fight with them all. Friar Sand quickly pulled his demon-quelling staff out from where he was at the side and hurried forward to

:lp Pig, at which Leo Spirit, Gryphon Spirit, Elephant-fighter pirit and Racoon-dog Spirit all piled in. The Great Sage Monky held the evil spirits at bay with his gold-banded cudgel. Leo ught with a club, Snowy with a bronze hammer, Elephantghter with a steel spear and Racoon-dog with a battleaxe. The ght between the seven lion spirits and the three ferocious monks as a splendid one:

Club, hammer, spear, axe and three-edged mace,
Spiked club, ball-staff and four-bright halberd:
Seven lions with seven deadly weapons,
Shouting their war cries as they surround three monks.
Powerful was the Great Sage's gold-banded cudgel;
Friar Sand's staff was almost matchless in the world.
Pig moved around with the power of a whirlwind
As his flashing rake gave off baleful light.
All, displaying their might, blocked before and behind,
Held off the onslaughts with daring and courage.
From the walls of the city the prince lent support,
Where his soldiers felt braver as they beat drums and gongs.
Throwing and thrusting, all showed off their magic,
Turning heaven and earth both dark and upside-down.

After the evil spirits had been fighting the Great Sage and ie two others for half a day, night fell. Pig by now was dribbling nd his legs were going weak, so he feinted with his rake and led in defeat. "Where do you think you're going?" Snowy ,ion and Monkey Lion shouted. "Take this!" The idiot could ot dodge them, and he took a heavy blow from the mace on his pine that laid him flat on the ground crying out, "I'm done for, 'm done for!" The two lion spirits grabbed Pig by the bristles n his neck and by his tail and carried him over to see the nineeaded lion. "Grandfather," they reported, "we've caught one f them."

Before the words were out of their mouths Friar Sand and Aonkey also had to fall back, beaten. When the evil spirits all ame after them Monkey pulled out a handful of hairs, chewed

them to pieces, spat them out, shouted, "Change!" and turne
them into more than one hundred little Monkeys who wen
round and round, surrounding Snowy, Leo, Elephant-fighte
Racoon-dog and Tawny Lion. Friar Sand and Monkey the
came forward to join in the fight again. Later that night the
caught Leo and Gryphon and put Racoon-dog and Elephant
fighter to flight. When Tawny Lion reported to the old demo
that two of the lions had been lost the demon ordered, "Tie Pi
up but don't kill him. When they give our lions back we'll re
turn Pig to them. If they're stupid enough to kill them we'l
make Pig pay with his life." That evening all the fiends slept out
side the city.

The story now turns to the Great Sage Sun, who carried th
two lion spirits to beside the city wall, from where the senio
prince saw him and ordered that the gates be opened. Twent
or thirty officers were sent out with rope to tie the lion spirits u
and carry them into the city. The Great Sage then put his magi
hairs away and went straight with Friar Sand to the wall tower
where he saw the Tang Priest. "This is a terrible business," th
Tang Priest said. "Is Wuneng still alive?" "No problem," Broth
er Monkey replied. "As we've captured a couple of the evi
spirits they won't possibly dare harm him. Have them tied u
tight. I'll swop them for Pig tomorrow morning." The thre
young princes then kowtowed to Monkey and said, "When yo
were fighting them at first you were by yourself, Teacher. The
when you pretended to run away and came back again there wer
over a hundred of you. How was that done? When you cam
back to the city wall after capturing the evil spirits there wa
only one of you again. What magical powers did you use t
do that?" "I have 84,000 hairs on my body," Monkey replied
"Each of them can become ten, and the ten become a hundred
so I can do millions and millions of transformations. It's extra
body magic." The princes all kowtowed as a vegetarian feas
was brought to the tower for them. All along the battlement
lanterns and banners were displayed. There was the sound o

clappers, bells, gongs and drums as the watches were changed, arrows passed on, cannons fired and warcries shouted.

Soon it was dawn, and the old demon sent for Tawny Lion Spirit to make a plan of action: "You must all use your wits to capture Sun the Novice and Friar Sand while I make a secret light up onto the wall to capture their master, the old prince and his sons. I'll take them back to the Nine-bend Twisty Cave and wait for you to come back in triumph." Ac-cepting this plan, Tawny Lion took Monkey Lion, Snowy Lion, Elephant-fighter and Racoon-dog back to beside the city wall, ll carrying their weapons and demanding battle amid winds nd fog. On the other side Monkey and Friar Sand jumped on ne wall, where Monkey yelled abusively at the top of his voice, Thieving damned ogres! Give me my brother Pig back this moment and I'll spare your lives. If you don't I'll smash your ones to powder and chop you all into little pieces." With no rther argument the evil spirits all charged into the attack. The reat Sage and Friar Sand had to use skill and cunning to hold e five lions at bay. This fight was very different from the one the previous day.

As an evil wind howled across the land
Black fog blotted out the sky.
Moving stones and flying sands alarmed both gods and demons;
As the trees in the forest fell the tigers and wolves were afraid.
Fierce was the spear of steel and bright the axe,
Merciless the rod, the halberd and the brazen hammer.
They wished they could swallow Monkey up whole,
And capture Friar Sand live and kicking.
The Great Sage's as-you-will cudgel
Could attack and defend with miraculous effect.
Friar Sand's demon-quelling staff
Had won its fame outside the Hall of Miraculous Mist.
Now that it moved with its magical powers,
It would achieve glory in the West by wiping out demons.

While the five lion spirits with coats of different colours we fighting really well with Monkey and Friar Sand the old demo flew on a black cloud straight to the wall tower, where he shoo his heads, which gave the military and civil officials, Sanzang the senior prince and the soldiers guarding the wall such a frigh that they all fell off. The demon then charged into the towe opened his mouths, took Sanzang, the senior prince and his so in them one by one, and went back to the hollow ground, whe he took Pig in another mouth, one of the nine he had in his nin heads. One mouth held the Tang Priest, one Pig, one the seni prince, one his eldest son, one the second son and one the thir son. With six mouths full of six people he still had three mout empty and wide open as he roared, "I'm going back ahead." Th five junior lion spirits all fought more bravely than ever no that they had seen their grandfather's triumph.

As soon as Monkey heard the yells from the wall and realize he had fallen for a trick, he gave Friar Sand a quick shout to b careful then pulled all the hairs off his arms, put them in h mouth, chewed them up and spat them out as well over a thou sand little Monkeys who swarmed into the attack. They knock ed Monkey Lion over, took Snowy alive, captured Elephan fighter, laid Racoon-dog Lion low and killed Tawny Lion; b as they returned to the city wall with a great hubbub they l Greenface, Wily Freak and Freaky Wile escape. When the o ficers on the wall saw what had happened they opened the gate tied up the five lion spirits with ropes and carried them into th city. But before they could deal with them the princess appeare sobbing and weeping, to say, "Holy teachers, His Royal High ness the prince, our sons and your master are all dead. How ev is this isolated city to survive?" Putting his magic hairs awa Monkey bowed to her and said, "Don't upset yourself, Princes It was only because I'd captured seven of his lion spirits that th old demon carried off my master, His Royal Highness and you sons with catching magic. I'm certain they'll come to no harn My brother-disciple and I will go to his mountain first thin tomorrow morning, and I can guarantee that we'll catch the ol demon and bring your four princes back to you." When the pri ess and her womenfolk heard this they all bowed to Monkey nd said, "We pray that His Royal Highness and his sons will ll be safe and that our dynasty will be secure." When their owing was done the womenfolk all returned to the palace in ears. "Skin the Tawny Lion spirit we killed," Brother Monkey nstructed the officials, "and have the five who are still alive ecurely tied up and put under lock and key. Bring us some egetarian food to eat before we go to sleep. Stop worrying: I romise nothing will go wrong."

The next morning the Great Sage took Friar Sand up on an uspicious cloud. Before long they were at the top of Bamboo Mountain, and as they brought their cloud down to look they aw that it was magnificent:

Rows of jutting peaks,
Sheer and craggy ridges.
In the deep gill waters gently flow;
Flowers weave a fragrant brocade before the beetling cliff,
Where the ridges twist and double back,
Encircled by the ancient winding paths.
When the crane comes the pine has a companion,
And the rock is left alone as the cloud drifts away.
The black ape heads for brightness when looking for fruit;
The deer rejoice in the warming sun as they search for flowers.
The green phoenix sings sweetly
And the golden bird's melodies never stop.
In spring the peach blossom contends with the plum;
In summer the willow and locust trees are rivals.
In autumn are carpets of chrysanthemums,
And in winter the snow flies all around.
Here there is beauty throughout the year,
Where the scenery can compare with Yingzhou's magic land.

As the two of them were standing on the mountain admiring the view Greenface suddenly appeared in a ravine between cliffs.

He was holding a short cudgel. "Where do you think you're gc
ing?" Monkey shouted. "I'm here." This gave the young dev
such a fright that he went running and tumbling down the ravin
Monkey and Friar Sand went straight after him but could fin
no sign of where he had gone. When they went further an
searched around they found a cave palace with double gates o
mottled stone that were firmly closed. Above the gates a ston
tablet was set on which was written in large block letters:

NINE-BEND TWISTY CAVE,
MIGHTY BAMBOO MOUNTAIN

Now when the junior devil ran inside the cave he had shu
the gates firmly behind him. Once inside he reported to the ol
demon, "My lord, those two monks are outside." "Have you
lord, Monkey Lion, Snowy Lion, Elephant-fighter and Racoon
dog come back yet?" the old demon asked. "I haven't see
them," the junior demon replied. "There were just the two monk
looking around from high up on the peak. As soon as I sa
them I turned and ran. As they came after me I shut the gates.
The old demon bowed his head in silence at this news. After
while his tears began to flow as he called out, "This is terribl
My grandson Tawny Lion is dead. My grandsons Monkey Lio
and the rest of them have all been captured by those monks an
taken into the city. How am I to get my revenge?" Pig wa
tied up nearby, crammed in together with the Tang Priest an
the princes, terrified and miserable until he heard the old demo
saying that his grandsons had been captured and taken into th
city. At this he said with quiet delight, "Don't be afraid, Maste
Cheer up, Your Royal Highness. My elder brother has won. He'
captured the whole lot of the devils and he's found his way her
to rescue us." When he had said this the old demon could b
heard shouting, "Little ones, guard the place well while I g
out to catch those other two monks. Then we can punish them a
together."

Watch him as he strides off without armour or weapon
When he heard Monkey shouting he threw the gates of the cav

ide open and went straight for him, not deigning to answer. Monkey raised his iron cudgel to stop him with a blow to the head while Friar Sand swung his staff at him. As the demon shook his principal head the eight other heads to left and right of it all opened their mouths, with which they gently picked Monkey and Friar Sand up and carried them into the cave. "Fetch rope," he ordered; and Wily Freak, Freaky Wile and Greenface, who had come back after their escape the previous night, brought two ropes with which they tied the two of them up very securely. "Impudent ape," said the old demon, "you captured my seven grandsons. But now I've caught you four monks and the four princes I've got enough to ransom them with. Little ones, get some thorns and willow rods and beat this ape for me to avenge my grandson Tawny Lion."

The three junior devils then beat Monkey with willow rods, but Monkey's body had been so toughened that all the rods could do was to scratch his itches. He made no sound and was not in the least bothered, no matter how hard they hit him. The sight of it, however, made Pig, the Tang Priest and the princes all feel their hair standing on end. Before long the rods started to break up, but the demons kept on till evening, keeping no count of the number of strokes. Friar Sand was most upset to see Monkey being given so long a flogging, so he said, "Let me take a hundred or so for him." "Don't be so impatient," the old demon replied, "you'll get your beating tomorrow. You'll all be done in turn." "That means it'll be me the day after tomorrow," said Pig with alarm. The beating continued for a while as night slowly fell. "Little ones," the old demon called, "stop for now. Light the lamp and go for something to eat and drink. I'm off to my Brocade Cloud Den for a little shut-eye. You three have all had a hard time, so keep a close watch on them. We'll carry on with the beatings tomorrow." The three junior devils moved the lamp over and hit Monkey some more on the top of his head with their willow rods, tic-tic-toc, toc-toc-tic, like the rhythm of a wooden clapper, sometimes fast and sometimes slow. By then it was very late and they all fell asleep.

Monkey now used escaping magic to shrink himself, wriggled

out of his bonds, shook his fur, straightened up his clothes, took the cudgel out of his ear and shook it till it was as thick as a well-bucket and about twenty feet long. Then he said to the three junior devils, "You animals, you hit me an awful lot of times, and now I'm going to return the compliment. I'll just shove this at you and see how you like it." One gentle push from the cudgels turned the three devils into three lumps of minced pork. Monkey then turned up the lamp and released Friar Sand. Pig, who was feeling desperate about being tied up, could not stop himself from yelling at the top of his voice, "My hands and feet are tied up so tight they're swollen. Why don't you come and free me?" The idiot's shout at once woke up the old demon, who rolled straight out of bed and called out, "Who's setting them free?" The moment Monkey heard this he blew out the lamp, smashed his way through several sets of doors with his cudgel and fled, not bothering about Friar Sand and the rest of them, while the old demon went into the main hall shouting, "Little ones, why's there no light? Don't let them get away!" He shouted once without getting an answer, then again and still no answer. When he fetched a lantern and looked all he could see were three gory lumps of minced meat on the floor. The prince, his sons, the Tang Priest and Pig were still there, but Monkey and Friar Sand had disappeared. He lit a torch, searched the front and the back and could find only Friar Sand, who was still standing pressed against the wall of a corridor. The demon knocked him down, tied him up as before, and carried on looking for Monkey. Seeing that pair after pair of his doors had been smashed down, he realized that Monkey had destroyed them in his flight. Instead of giving chase he patched up and blockaded the doors and guarded his home.

The story now tells how Monkey left the Nine-bend Twisty Cave and rode by auspicious cloud straight back to the city of Yuhua, where all the local deities and spirits as well as the god of the city could be seen bowing in mid-air to greet him. "Why have you only come to see me today?" Monkey asked. "When we knew that the worthy prince was entertaining you in Yuhua ȝreat Sage," they replied, "we did not venture to greet you. 3ut now that the princes have been captured by ogres and you ıave subdued those monsters we have come to welcome you with ːowtows." While Monkey was abusing them the Gold-headed ᴾrotector and the Six Ding and Six Jia generals escorted a local leity in and made him kneel on the ground. "Great Sage," they aid, "we've arrested this ground devil." "What are you making a noise here for instead of guarding my master on Bamboo Mountain?" Monkey yelled. "Great Sage," the Ding and Jia gods replied, "the evil spirit caught the Curtain-raising General and tied him up again after you escaped. As we could see how great his magic powers are we've brought the local deity of Bamboo Mountain here. He knows all about that evil spirit's background, so we beg you to question him, Great Sage, and ind out how best to deal with him and deliver the holy monks and worthy princes from their suffering." When Monkey heard his he was delighted.

"The old demon came down to Bamboo Mountain the year before last," the local deity said, shivering and shaking as he kowtowed. "The Nine-bend Twisty Cave used to be the den of six lions. Once the old demon came the six lions all took him as their grandfather. He is a nine-headed lion called the Primal Sage of Ninefold Numinosity. If you want to deal with him you must go to the Wonderful Crag Palace in the uttermost east and fetch his master here to subdue him. Nobody else can possibly do it." When Monkey heard this he thought for a long time before saying, "The Wonderful Crag Palace in the uttermost east is where the Heavenly Honoured Saviour of the Great Monad lives. Yes, he does have just such a nine-headed lion under his throne. Protector, Jias," he ordered, "go back with the local deity and keep a secret watch on the master, my brother-disciple, the prince of the city and his sons. The city god must guard the wall and moat. Off you go." The gods all took up guard as instructed.

The Great Sage set off his somersault cloud and travelled through the night till it was about the last watch, when he reached the Eastern Gate of Heaven, where he ran into the Heavenly

King Virupaksa with his retinue of heavenly soldiers and warriors, who stopped, put their hands together in greeting and asked, "Where are you going, Great Sage?" "I'm off to the Wonderful Crag Palace," Monkey replied when he had returned thei greetings. "Why have you come to the Eastern Heaven insteac of following your road to the Western Heaven?" Virupaksa asked. "When we reached the city of Yuhua," Monkey replied, "th prince of the city entertained us and told his three sons to tak us as their teachers of martial arts. We had a most unpleasant surprise: coming up against a gang of lion monsters. Now I'm going to ask the Heavenly Honoured Saviour of the Great Monad the chief monster's owner, to subdue him and save my master.' "It was because you wanted to be a teacher that you provoked that trouble with the lions," said the heavenly king. "How true,' replied Monkey with a smile, "how true." The heavenly soldier and warriors all raised joined hands in greeting then stood asid to let him pass. Monkey went in through the Eastern Gate o Heaven and was soon at the Wonderful Crag Palace. This is wha could be seen:

Coloured clouds behind coloured clouds,
Purple mists and rich, green vegetation.
The roof-tiles are a surge of golden flame,
And at the gates are imposing beasts of jade.
Flowers grow between gate towers, round which red mists drift;
The sun shines on turquoise vapours rising from the woods.
All the immortals pay their respects,
And a thousand sages make everything flourish.
The halls of the palace are like layers of brocade;
Windows and pavilions open on all sides.
Azure dragons glow with sacred clouds;
Golden beams of brilliant light come from the magic mists.
This is a land of splendour and eternal joy,
The Wonderful Crag Palace in the uttermost east.

There was an immortal boy wearing a rainbow mantle standing at the palace gates, and as soon as he noticed the Great Sage he went in to report, "My lord, the Great Sage Equalling Heaven who made havoc in Heaven is here." When the Heavenly Honoured Saviour of the Great Monad heard this he ordered all the immortals in attendance on him to go out to welcome Monkey and bring him into the palace. Here the Heavenly Honoured One was sitting on a nine-coloured lotus throne amid countless rays of auspicious light, and when he saw Monkey he came down from his throne to greet him while Monkey bowed to him from below. "Great Sage," the Heavenly Honoured One said, returning his bow, "I haven't seen you for years, but I did hear that you have abandoned the Way for Buddhism and are escorting the Tang Priest to fetch the scriptures from the Western Heaven. I presume that you have now succeeded." "Not yet," Monkey replied, "but near enough. I have escorted the Tang Priest as far as Yuhua, where the prince told his three sons to take me and the other two as their teachers of martial arts and had copies of our three magic weapons made. The weapons were, to our surprise, stolen one night. When I searched for them the next day I found that they had been stolen by a spirit turned by a golden-haired lion from Tigermouth Cave on Mount Leopard Head. I tricked them back from him by cunning, whereupon the spirit ganged up with some other lion spirits to give me a tremendous fight. One of them is a nine-headed lion with enormous magic powers who carried my master, Pig, the prince and his three sons to the Nine-bend Twisty Cave on Mount Bamboo. When Friar Sand and I went to look for them the next day we were carried off too. He had me tied up and hit so often I lost count. Luckily I was able to make my get-away by magic, but they're still suffering there. When I questioned the local deity I found out that you were his master, Heavenly Honoured One, which is why I'm here to ask you to subdue the lion and rescue them."

As soon as the Heavenly Honoured One heard this he sent his immortal officers to the lion house to call out his lion-keeper slave and question him. The lion-keeper slave was sleeping so deeply that the officers had to push and shake him before they could wake him up and drag him into the main hall. Here the Heavenly Honoured One asked him, "Where is the lion?" All the slave could do was to kowtow with tears streaming down his face, pleading, "Spare me, spare me." "The Great Sage Sun is here," the Heavenly Honoured One replied, "so I won't have you beaten just yet. You must explain this instant your carelessness in letting the nine-headed lion escape." "My lord," the lion-keeper replied, "I stole and drank a jug of wine I saw in the Sweet Dew Palace of the Great Chiliocosm. Before I realized what had happened I was dead drunk. It must have slipped its chains and got away." "That wine was given me by Lord Lao Zi of the Supreme Ultimate," the Heavenly Honoured One replied. "It's called Cyclical Nectar, and after drinking that you would have slept for three days. How many days has the lion been gone?" "What the local deity said was that he went down there the year before last, which would mean two years or more," the Great Sage said. "That's right," the Heavenly Honoured One said with a smile, "A day in the palaces of Heaven is a year in the mortal world. Get up," he said to the lion-tamer. "I'll spare your life. Come down to the lower world with the Great Sage and me to recapture him. You immortals can all go back. None of you need come with us."

The Heavenly Honoured One, the lion-keeper slave and the Great Sage all went by cloud straight to Bamboo Mountain, where the Protectors of the Four Quarters and the Centre, the Six Dings, the Six Jias and the local deity of the mountain all knelt to greet them. "Has my master been harmed while you people have been protecting him?" Brother Monkey asked. "The evil spirit was so angry that he went to sleep," the gods replied. "He didn't torture them any more." "That Primal Sage of mine is a true soul who has long cultivated the Way," the Heavenly Honoured One remarked. "A single call from him will go up to the Three Sages and down to the Underworld. He wouldn't kill anyone lightly. Great Sage

Sun, go to his gates, challenge him to battle and draw him outside for us to catch."

As soon as Monkey heard this he sprang towards the mouth of the cave, brandishing his cudgel and shouting loudly and abusively, "Damned evil spirit, give me my people back! Damned evil spirit, give me my people back!" He shouted several times, but the old demon was fast asleep and nobody answered. Monkey lost his patience, swung his cudgel and smashed his way inside, still cursing. Only then did the old demon wake up, rise to his feet and yell with great fury, "I'm coming for you!" He shook his heads and opened his jaws to pick Monkey up. As Monkey turned and fled the evil spirit chased after him till they were outside the cave, shouting, "Where do you think you're going, you thieving ape?" "How dare you go on behaving so dreadfully!" said Monkey with a grin from where he was standing on the top of a high cliff. "You haven't even got the sense to realize that your life's at stake. Don't you see your master's here?" By the time the evil spirit reached the cliff in pursuit of Monkey the Heavenly Honoured One had said a spell and shouted, "I'm here, my little Primal Sage." Recognizing his master, the monster gave up the struggle and lay down with all four feet on the ground, kowtowing. The lion-keeper then ran over to him, took hold of his mane, and punched him hundreds of times on the neck, saying abusively, "Why did you run away, animal? You got me into terrible trouble." The lion kept his mouths shut and said nothing, not daring to move, and the lion-keeper only stopped hitting him when his fist was tired out. When a brocade saddlecloth had been put on the animal's back the Heavenly Honoured One mounted and shouted to it to go. They then rose up on coloured clouds and went straight back to the Wonderful Crag Palace.

After addressing his thanks skywards the Great Sage went into the cave and freed first the prince of Yuhua, then Sanzang, then Pig, Friar Sand and the three young princes. After this they made a leisurely search of the cave and led everyone outside. Pig then fetched some dry brushwood, piled it at the front and the back, and started a fire that left the Nine-bend Twisty Cave looking like a ruined, burnt-out kiln. Monkey released all the gods, ordered the local deity to keep guard on it, and told Pig and Friar Sand to use their magic to carry the four princes back to the city while he helped the Tang Priest along. They were soon back at the city, where the princess and the officials all came out to greet them. It was now getting dark, and a vegetarian feast was provided for everyone to enjoy. The venerable elder and his disciples slept in the Gauze Pavilion once more, and the princes in the living quarters of the palace. Of that night no more need be said.

The next day the prince issued an order for another great vegetarian banquet to be laid on. Each of the officials high and low in the palace expressed his gratitude, and Monkey asked for butchers to slaughter the six lions who were still alive, skin them like the tawny lion, and prepare their meat to be eaten. The prince, who was delighted with this proposal, gave the order for them to be killed. One animal was kept for the inside and outside palace staff, one was given to the chief administrator and the other officials in the palace, and the flesh of the other five was cut into lumps weighing one or two ounces that officers distributed among the soldiers and civilians inside and outside the city wall so that they could all eat a little. Thus the people could both try the taste and overcome their fear. Every single household was most impressed.

By now the smiths had made the three weapons and were kowtowing to Monkey, saying, "My lord, we have finished our work." "How heavy are they?" Monkey asked. "The gold-banded cudgel weighs a thousand pounds," the smiths replied, "and the nine-toothed rake and the demon-quelling staff each eight hundred pounds." "That'll do," said Monkey, who then had the three princes asked to come out. As each took his weapon they said to the senior prince, "Your Royal Highness, our weapons have now been finished." "They almost cost both your father and yourselves their lives," the senior prince replied. "Thanks to our divine teachers' powers," the young princes said, "we were all saved and the evil spirits have been wiped out.

We'll have no trouble from them in future. Now this really is a world at peace with calm seas and rivers running clear." The four princes then rewarded the smiths and went to the Gauze Pavilion to thank the teachers.

Sanzang told the Great Sage and the other two to pass on some more martial skills quickly so as not to delay their journey. The three of them all swung their weapons in the palace yard as they taught the secrets one by one. Within a few days the three young princes were all skilled performers. They also mastered all the seventy-two routines of attack, retreat and fast and slow fighting. This was firstly because the princes were all thoroughly determined, and secondly because the Great Sage Sun had given them the divine strength beforehand that enabled them to lift and move the thousand-pound cudgel and the eight-hundred-pound rake and staff. There was all the difference in the world between their present skills and those they had had before, and there is a poem that goes:

When they celebrated their fortune in finding divine teachers
They never expected their studies to alert a lion spirit.
With evil destroyed the country was at peace;
The frontier was settled as all were devoted to the one Entity.
Ninefold Numinosity's powers lasted through their many clashes
Till the Way was achieved with all-round expertise.
The brilliant teaching would be passed on for ever,
And Yuhua know eternal peace and joy.

The prince then gave another great banquet to thank the three teachers, and a huge dish of gold and silver was brought out as a reward. "Take it straight back inside," Monkey said with a smile, "take it straight back. We're monks, and that's no use to us." "We really can't take gold or silver," put in Pig who was standing beside him, "but the lion spirits tore our clothes to ribbons. If you could give us a change of clothing that would be very kind of you." The prince ordered his tailors to fetch some bolts of blue, red and brown brocade and make each of them a garment after the style and colours of their old ones. The three of them were delighted to accept and put on their new brocade tunics, after which they packed up the luggage and set off on their way again. Everyone inside and outside the city, whether young or old, exclaimed that they were arhats and living Buddhas come down to earth. Crowds packed the streets to the sound of drums and music, and banners flew overhead. Indeed,

From the gate of every family the incense smoke arose;
At every household's door coloured lanterns hung in rows.

The people only went back after seeing them for a long way along their journey. Only then did the four travellers manage to leave the city and head west. By leaving they shook off all thought and immersed their hearts in the True Achievement. Indeed,

Free from thought and worry, the Buddha's land they seek,
Going faithfully, sincerely, towards the Vulture Peak.

If you do not know how much further the journey was to be or when it was to end, listen to the explanation in the next instalment.

CHAPTER NINETY-ONE

Admiring the Moon Festival lanterns in Jinping; The Tang Priest confesses in Dark Essence Cave.

Where should one strive to practise dhyana?
Swiftly to extirpate the misdeeds of the thought-horse and the mind-ape.
When they are firmly tethered they give off radiance,
But whoever halts falls to the three paths of suffering.
If one allows the divine elixir to leak away,
The jade-pure nature will wither as one slackens.
Anger, joy and worry must all be swept away:
When the wonderful mystery is gained it seems like nothing.

The story tells how the Tang Priest and his three disciples left the city of Yuhua and had a very easy journey in what really was a land of paradise. When they had been travelling for five or six days another city appeared. "Where is this?" the Tang Priest asked Brother Monkey. "It's a city," Monkey replied, "but there are no flags on the poles above the city wall and I don't know this area, so I'll ask when we get closer." When they reached the eastern suburb they found it noisy with bars and tea-houses and bustling with a rice market and oil shops. Some dlers who were wandering in the streets with nothing better to do crowded round for a better look when they saw Pig's long snout, Friar Sand's black face and Monkey's red eyes, but they dared not come any closer to question the travellers. The Tang Priest was sweating with the worry that they would provoke trouble as they crossed several more streets and had still not yet reached the city wall. Then they saw a monastery gate over which were the words CLOUDS OF COMPASSION MON-

ASTERY. "What about going in here to give the horse a res and take a meal?" the Tang Priest suggested, to which Monkey replied, "Splendid, splendid." The four of them then went inside, and this is what they saw:

Splendid, towering buildings,
Gleaming bases for statues.
The Buddha hall rise above the clouds;
The monks' cells lie in the moonlit silence.
Red mists circle the stupas;
In the shade of jade-green trees the scripture-wheel is cool.
This is a true Pure Land,
Another Naga Palace,
Where purple mists surround the Mahavira Hall.
The cloisters are never empty of people enjoying the sights,
And visitors climb the pagoda that is always open.
Incense burns in the stand at every moment,
And lamps shine on the altar through the night.
A golden bell rings rhythmically in the abbot's lodgings
As monks worship the Buddha by reciting sutras.

As the four of them looked around a monk came along the cloister and said to the Tang Priest with polite gestures of greeting, "Where have you come from, Teacher?" "From the Tang Court in China," the Tang Priest replied, at which the monk went down on his knees to kowtow, only to be quickly helped up by the Tang Priest, who asked, "Why do you perform this great courtesy, reverend abbot?" "All the lovers of goodness here who read the sutras and recite the name of the Buddha hope to achieve rebirth in your land of China, so that when I saw you coming in your magnificent mitre and robes I was certain that your present splendour must be the result of your successful cultivation in earlier lives. That's why it is right to kowtow to you." "It alarmed me," said the Tang Priest with a smile, "it alarmed me. I am only an itinerant monk, and know no splendour at all. To be able to live at your leisure and ease as you do, abbot, is eal bliss." The monk then led the Tang Priest to worship the Buddha statues in the main hall. It was only now that Sanzang called for his disciples. After seeing their master start talking to the monk, Monkey and the other two had been standing in a group with their faces averted, holding the horse's bridle and looking after the luggage, so that the monk had not noticed them. But when they turned round on hearing the Tang Priest's call the sight of them so frightened the monk that he called out, "My lord, why are your distinguished disciples so hideously ugly?" "Ugly they may be," the Tang Priest replied, "but they do have some magical powers. I have been very grateful for their protection all the way along the journey."

As they were speaking more monks came out to greet them. The monk who had been the first to welcome the visitors explained to the others, "This teacher has come from Great Tang in China, and these three gentlemen are his distinguished disciples." "Teacher," said the others with mixed pleasure and apprehension, "why have you come here from Great China?" "I have been commanded by the Tang emperor to worship the Buddha and seek the scriptures in the Western Heaven," Sanzang replied. "As I was passing this way I have come to your monastery to ask where we are and take a vegetarian meal before setting out again." The monks were all delighted, and they invited the visitors into the abbot's lodgings, where there were some more monks who were performing ceremonies on behalf of benefactors. The monk who had met them first went on to explain to the others, "Come and have a look at what people from China are like: some are handsome and some are ugly. The beauty of the handsome ones could never be caught in a painting or drawing, and the ugly ones look really weird." Both the monks and the benefactors all came to greet them, after which everyone sat down. When tea had been drunk the Tang Priest enquired, "What is this fine country called?" "This is Jinping, one of the outer prefectures of India," the monks replied. "How far is it from this prefecture to Vulture Peak?" the Tang Priest asked. "It is about seven hundred miles from here to the capital," the monks replied, "and we have walked that distance. As we haven't gone further west to Vulture Peak we don't know how far that is and would not like to make a wild guess." The Tang Priest thanked them.

A little later a vegetarian meal was provided, after which the Tang Priest wanted to be on his way, only to be pressed to stay by the monks and the benefactors who said, "Teacher, you must stay for a couple of days or so. Enjoy the Full Moon Festival before you go on your way." "On my journey I have only been aware of mountains and rivers and the danger of running into ogres or monsters," the Tang Priest replied, "and I have lost my sense of time. I don't know when Full Moon is." "It's because your heart is so set on worshipping the Buddha and on enlightenment that you have not thought about it, Teacher," the monks replied. "Today is the thirteenth of the first month and the lanterns will be tried out tonight. The day after tomorrow is the fifteenth, when the festival begins, and it goes on till the lanterns are put away on the eighteenth or nineteenth. We enjoy celebrations here and our prefect, who cares for the people, has lanterns set out everywhere and music played all night. We also have a Bridge of Golden Lamps — it's an ancient tradition that still flourishes. If you will stay for a few days, my lords, our monastery can certainly afford to entertain you." The Tang Priest had no choice but to stay. As the bell and drum in the Buddha hall resounded to the skies the faithful came in from the streets bringing lanterns to present to the Buddha. The Tang Priest and the rest of them came out of the abbot's lodgings to look at the lanterns, after which everyone turned in.

The next day, when they had eaten the vegetarian breakfast the monks of the monastery brought them, they strolled in the garden at the back. It really was a lovely place:

It is the first month of the year,
The beginning of the spring.
The wooded garden is quiet and elegant;
The beauty of the scene subdued.
Throughout the four seasons flowers and trees contend,
Turquoise peaks rise behind each other.

Fragrant flowers are growing before the steps,
And scent comes from the plum-tree's branches.
Where there is red it joins the tender peach blossom;
Where there is green it mingles with the willows' fresh green.
*Forget about the splendour of the Gold Valley Garden;**
Say nothing of the Wang River landscapes painted by Wang Wei.
In the flowing stream
The wild ducks bob and rise;
Among bamboos by the thousand
Poets ponder their choice of words.
Tree and herbaceous peonies, myrtle, fleeting-smile flowers,
That waken when their time is due;
Camellias, red plum blossom, winter jasmine and daphne,
All early to open out their beauty.
The snow piled by the hidden cliff seems frozen solid still;
The clouds that drift by the distant trees already bring early traces of spring.
The deer sees its reflection beside the pool;
Cranes come to hear the lute beneath the pines.
A few halls and pavilions to east and west,
Where travellers may stay;
Buildings and pagodas to north and south
Where monks may meditate in peace.
Among the flowers
Are one or two houses to nourish one's nature,
Where double eaves rise above each other.
Amid the hills and streams
Are three or four cells in which to refine magic,
Peaceful and light.
This is indeed a natural spot for a recluse:
Why look elsewhere for the earthly paradise?

---

* Of the immensely rich Shi Chong in third-century Luoyang.

After a day enjoying the garden they inpected the lanterns in the Buddha hall before going to look at the lantern festival. This is what they saw:

A splendid city of agate,
A fairyland of glass;
Palaces of crystal and mica,
Like layer upon layer of brocade,
Openwork carving behind openwork carving.
The dazzling bridge of stars moved heaven and earth
While trees of fire made waves of red
Flutes and drums played in the streets.
A moon like a ring of jade hung over a thousand gates;
Fragrant breezes blew through ten thousand homes.
There were giant turtle peaks soaring on high,
Fishes and dragons emerging from the sea,
Phoenixes sporting in the sky.
As all admired the moon and the lanterns
The atmosphere was full of harmony.
Among the crowds dressed in fine silks
All enjoyed the songs and panpipes.
Carriages rumbled along.
There was no end of beautiful faces,
Dashing gallants,
And marvellous sights.

When Sanzang and the others had looked at the lanterns in the monastery they wandered around the streets of the eastern suburb, not going back to bed till the second watch in the middle of the night.

The next day Sanzang said to the monks, "I made a vow to sweep pagodas, and on the occasion of tonight's Moon Festival I would like to ask the reverend abbot to open the doors of the pagoda to allow me to fulfil this vow." The monks opened the doors, and when Friar Sand fetched his cassock and brought it to him on the ground floor he put it over his shoulders and prayed to the Buddha. Then he swept the ground floor with a broom, took the cassock off and gave it back to Friar Sand. He wept the second storey next, and so on storey by storey till he eached the top. In every storey there was a Buddha, and in each one he opened all the windows, swept the floor, and enoyed the splendid views. By the time he had finished sweeping ind come down again it was late and all the lamps had been lit.

It was now the night of the full moon. "Venerable teacher," he monks said, "last night you only saw the lamps in our humble nonastery and the outskirts of the city. As tonight is the main festival why don't we go into the city to see the golden lamps here?" The Tang Priest was glad to follow this suggestion, and ie went with his three disciples and the monks of the monastery nto the city to see the lanterns. Indeed,

On the festive fifteenth night
The harmony of spring begins with the first full moon.
Decorated lanterns hang in the busy markets
As all sing the songs of a world at peace.
Over the lantern light in streets and markets
The moon's round mirror rises in the sky
Like a silver dish, driven by the charioteer Ping Yi.
The lanterns were like a brocade carpet woven by fairies;
The lanterns were reflected by the moon,
Doubling its brilliance;
The moon shone on the lanterns,
Making them resplendent.
There was no end of iron-chain star bridges,
Lantern flowers and trees of fire.
Snowflake lanterns,
Plum-blossom lanterns,
Like fragments of ice in spring;
Embroidered screen lanterns,
Painted screen lanterns,
Made up from every colour.
Walnut lanterns,
Lotus lanterns,
Hung high on lantern towers;
Blue lion lanterns,

White elephant lanterns,
Fixed on lofty frames.
Shrimp lanterns,
Terrapin lanterns,
Placed in front of awnings;
Goat lanterns,
Hare lanterns,
Bringing the eaves to life.
Eagle lanterns,
Phoenix lanterns,
Lined up next to each other;
Tiger lanterns,
Horse lanterns,
Being carried along together.
Red-crowned crane lanterns,
White deer lanterns,
Carrying the Star of Longevity;
Goldfish lanterns,
Whale lanterns,
On which rode the poet Li Bai.
Giant turtle mountain lanterns,
Where gods and immortals gathered;
Revolving horse lanterns
On which warriors joined combat.
The towers of lanterns on thousands of houses
Made a world of clouds and smoke for several miles.
On one side, shining reins and flying jade saddles;
On the other, rumbling carriages leave fragrance behind.
On the red balcony,
Leaning against the railings,
Behind the curtains,
Shoulder to shoulder,
Hand in hand,
Pairs of beauties were eager for the fun.
By the bridge over green waters,
Noisy,
Many-coloured,

Drunken,
Laughing
Couples enjoyed the brilliant sights.
All of the city's flutes and drums were playing;
Panpipes and songs went on all night.

There is also this poem as evidence:

Amid the fine brocades, of lotus were the songs;
This blessed land at peace was full of many throngs.
The lanterns and the moon upon this festive night
Foretold rich harvests after rain and wind just right.

This was a night when the curfew was relaxed, so that there were huge crowds and a great commotion. People were dancing, walking on stilts, wearing masks and riding elephants, pushing and crowding to east and to west as they looked all around. When they reached the bridge of golden lamps the Tang Priest and the monks pushed forward for a look and saw that it consisted of three golden lamps each the size of a water vat and shaped like a two-storeyed pavilion with a light shining out through intricate gold and silver filigree openwork. Glazed ceramic tiles inside the lamps reflected their light. They were so bright they outshone the moon, and their oil was very fragrant. "What sort of oil do those lamps burn?" the Tang Priest asked the monks, "and why does it smell so remarkably good?"

"You wouldn't know that, Teacher," the monks replied. "There is a county near this prefecture called Mintian. In the whole county there are 240 wards, and when we have our annual assignment of jobs to be done for the state, 240 households have to provide oil. All the other jobs assigned by the prefecture or county are reasonable enough, but these oil households have a very hard time. Every household has to take it on for a year, and it costs them over two hundred ounces of silver. The oil isn't ordinary oil but perfumed refined butter oil. One ounce costs two ounces of silver and a pound costs thirty-two ounces. Each of the lamps holds five hundred pounds of oil, making 1,500 pounds for the three of them, costing 48,000 ounces of silver. With other miscellaneous expenses it comes to ove 50,000 ounces. And that only lasts three nights." "How can s much oil be used up in only three nights?" Monkey asked. "I each lamp there are forty-nine big wicks about the size of an eg made of rushes wrapped in silk floss," the monks explainec "When they have burned for one night the Lord Buddhas ap pear, the oil all vanishes and the lamp goes out." "I suppose th Lord Buddhas take all the oil," said Pig with a grin as he stoo at one side. "That's right," the monks replied, "that's wha everyone in the city has always said ever since ancient times. I the oil runs dry they say that the Buddhas have taken the oil an the crops will certainly be bountiful; but if it doesn't dry up o one occasion there will be famine, drought and the wron weather at the wrong time in that year. That's why everyon makes this offering."

As they were talking there was the howling of a wind up i the air, sending everyone who was admiring the lanterns fleein in terror. The monks could not hold their ground either. "Let' go back, venerable teacher," they said, "the wind's here. It's th Lord Buddhas bringing blessings. They're here to see the lar terns." "How can you tell that?" the Tang Priest asked. "It's th same every year," the monks replied. "The wind blows u before the third watch. Everybody gets out of the way as the know that it is the Lord Buddhas bringing down blessings." " am one who thinks of, invokes and worships Buddhas," the Tan Priest said. "If the Buddhas are honouring us with their presenc on this festive occasion it would be wonderful to be able t worship them." He rejected the monks' repeated urgings to g back, and a little later the forms of three Buddhas appeared i the wind and approached the lamps. The Tang Priest was s excited that he ran to the top of the lamp bridge and threw him self down in worship. Brother Monkey rushed forward in alar to drag him to his feet and say, "They're no good, Master. I' sure they're evil." Before the words were even out of his mout the lamps all went out as with a great whoosh the Tang Pries was swept up by the wind. It was terrible! Who knew wha vil monsters from what cave in what mountain had been posing as Buddhas to watch the golden lamps?

Pig and Friar Sand were thrown into such panic that they ushed all about, searching and calling for their master. "Brothers," called Monkey, "no use shouting here. The master's bliss has turned to disaster. He's been carried off by evil spirits." "How can you tell that, my lord," the appalled monks asked. "You're just a bunch of mortals," Monkey replied with a grin, "so you haven't realized what's been happening all these years. The evil spirits have fooled you into thinking they're true Buddhas coming down to accept the offerings of lamps. The Buddhas hat appeared when the wind blew just now were three evil spirits. My master didn't realize who they were, so he went up on he top of the bridge to worship them. They covered up all the ights and carried him off together with the oil in the lamps. As was a bit too late the three of them got away by wind." "Brother," said Friar Sand, "Whatever are we to do?" "Not a moment o lose," said Monkey. "You two go back the monastery with he monks and look after the horse and the luggage. I'm going after them while this wind's still blowing."

The splendid Great Sage then shot up by his somersault cloud into mid air, picked up the stench of the wind and headed northeast in pursuit, carrying on till all of a sudden the wind dropped at dawn. A great mountain could be seen, a most steep, owering and splendid mountain:

Many a foothill and ravine,
Twisting and bending streams.
Creepers hang from the beetling precipice,
Pine and cypress rise from the lonely rock.
Cranes cry in the morning mists,
Wild geese call among the clouds at dawn.
Jutting peaks like a row of halberds,
Jagged crags of interlocking rocks.
The summits rise to eighty thousand feet,
And sheer-walled ridges make a thousand angles.
Wild flowers and noble trees all flourish with the spring;

Cuckoo and oriole respond to the scenery with song.
Majestic beauty,
Towering grandeur,
Steep, grotesque crags hard to climb.
One will stay there long in silence:
All that can be heard are tigers and leopards breathing.
River deer and white deer wander around;
Jade-coloured hares and grey wolves come and go.
The stream in the deep ravine will flow for a million miles;
Twisting torrents splash loud against the rocks.

While the Great Sage was on the top of a scar looking for his way he saw four people coming from the western slopes driving three goats and all shouting, "New Year." Monkey's fiery eyes with their golden pupils flashed as he took a closer look to see that they were the four Duty Gods of the year, the month, the day and the hour in disguise.

The Great Sage then pulled out his iron cudgel, shook it till it was as thick as a ricebowl and about twelve feet long and sprang down from the cliff with a shout of, "Where are you skulking off to like that, trying to hide your faces?" When the four Duty Gods realized that he had rumbled them they at once turned back into their normal selves, kowtowed beside the path and said, "Forgive us, Great Sage, forgive us." "Just because I haven't had any jobs for you recently you thought I was getting lax and so you've all become very casual," Monkey said. "You didn't even greet me. It's outrageous! Why aren't you giving my master your secret protection? Where are you going?" "Because your master somewhat forgot his dhyana nature and was so eager to enjoy himself in the Clouds of Compassion Monastery in Jinping Prefecture," the Duty Gods said, "he met with evil at the height of splendour, his joy turned to disaster, and he was captured by the evil spirits. The Defenders of the Faith are looking after him at the moment. We realized that you would be coming after him this very night, Great Sage, and we came here to report to you in case you did not know the mountains and forests here." "If you were here to report," said Brother Monkey, "why did you disguise your identities, why were you driving three goats, and what were you shouting and yelling for?" "The three goats were for luck at the beginning of the year.* They are to drive away the evil that's obstructing your master."

Monkey had been absolutely determined to beat them, but on hearing this explanation he let them off and put his cudgel away as his fury turned to delight. "Are there evil spirits on this mountain?" he asked. "Yes," they replied, "yes. This mountain is called Green Dragon Mountain and there's a cave in it called the Dark Essence Cave where three evil spirits live. The oldest is called King Cold-avoider, the second is called King Heat-avoider and the third is called King Dust-avoider. They've lived here for a thousand years and have been fond of refined butter oil since they were children. Ever since they became spirits some years ago they've been pretending to be Buddhas to trick the officials and people of Jinping into setting out those golden lamps full of the refined butter oil that they take in their Buddha guises in the middle of every first month. When they saw your master this time they realized that he was a holy monk and carried him off to the cave too. Any day now they'll slice off his flesh to fry in the refined butter. You must use your skills to save him as soon as possible."

On hearing this Monkey dismissed the four Duty Gods with a shout and went round the mountain looking for the cave. Within a mile or two he saw a rock face by a gill, at the foot of which was a stone building with a pair of stone doors that stood ajar. Beside the doors was a stone tablet on which was inscribed

GREEN DRAGON MOUNTAIN
DARK ESSENCE CAVE

Not daring to go in uninvited, Monkey stopped and called, "Give me my master back at once, monster." With a great noise

* "Three goats" (*san yang*) sounds the same in Chinese as the Three Positives, the three positive lines that appear in the hexagram ䷊ for the first month of the year.

the doors burst wide open, and out rushed a crowd of bull-headed demons who glared as they asked, "Who are you, yelling her like that?" "I'm the senior disciple of the holy monk Tang Sanzang who's come from Great Tang in the east to fetch scriptures," Monkey replied. "He was looking at the lanterns in Jinpin, along our way when your chief demons carried him off here Give him back at once if you want me to spare your lives. If yo don't I'll turn your den upside-down and turn all you demon into just pus and blood."

As soon as the junion demons heard this they rushed insid to report, "Disaster, Your Majesties, disaster!" The three ol evil spirits had taken Sanzang into the depths of the cave an with no further ado were telling their underlings to strip him an wash him with water from the torrent. They were just about t have him sliced and diced into tiny pieces to fry in the refine butter when they heard the report of disaster from outside. Th oldest demon king asked with some alarm what had happened "There's a hairy-faced monk who looks like a thunder god outside," the junior devils replied. "He's shouting that Your Majesties carried his master here and wants him given back straigh away if our lives are to be spared. Otherwise he'll turn our de upside-down and turn us all into pus and blood."

This news shocked the demon kings, who all said, "We'v only just caught the wretch, and haven't even asked him hi name and his background. Little ones, dress him again and brin him here to be questioned. We must find out who he is an where he's from." A crowd of devils untied the Tang Priest, pu his clothes back on and pushed him to before the thrones, wher he fell to his knees, trembling with fear, and pleaded, "Spar my life, Your Majesties, spare my life." "Where are you from monk?" the three evil spirits said, all talking at once, "and wh did you rush into the way of our clouds instead of avoiding th Buddha images?" "I have been sent by the Great Tang Empero in the east to worship the Lord Buddha and fetch the scripture from the Great Thunder Monastery in India," Sanzang replie with kowtows. "When I went into the Clouds of Compassio Monastery for a vegetarian meal the monks there pressed me t tay to see the lanterns at the Moon Festival. Seeing Your Majesties appearing as Buddhas from the bridge of golden lamps kowtowed to you because my mortal eyes took you for real Buddhas. That's why I got in the way of your clouds, Your Majesties." "How long was the journey from your country in he east to here?" the evil spirits asked. "How many people have ou got with you? What are they called? Tell us the truth straight away and we'll spare your life."

"My secular name was Chen Xuanzang," the Tang Priest eplied, "and I was a monk in the Jinshan Monastery from boyhood. Later I was given official rank as a monk in the Hongfu Monastery in Chang'an. When the minister Wei Zheng beheaded the Dragon King of the River Jing in his dream and the Tang emperor came back to life after his travels in the underworld, a Great Land and Water Mass was held for the rebirth of souls. The Tang emperor chose me to officiate at this ceremony and expound the great principles. The Bodhisattva Guanyin appeared during the mass and informed me that in the Thunder Monastery n the Western Heaven there are three stores of true scriptures hat can carry the dead up to Heaven. I was sent to fetch them and given the title Sanzang, or 'Three Stores'. As I use Tang as my surname people call me Tang Sanzang. I have three disciples. The first one is called Sun Wukong the Novice, and he s the Great Sage Equalling Heaven who has been converted to he truth." This news came as a shock to the evil spirits, who asked, "Did this Great Sage Equalling Heaven make great havoc in Heaven five hundred years ago?" "Yes, yes," the Tang Priest said. "The second one is called Zhu Wuneng or Zhu Bajie. He is Marshal Tian Peng come down to earth. The third s Sha Wujing, or Friar Sand, the Curtain-lifting General in mortal reincarnation." "It's as well we haven't eaten him yet," the evil spirits all exclaimed in horror. "Little ones, lock the Tang Priest in iron chains at the back. When we've caught his three disciples we'll eat them together." They then mustered a force of armed yak, water-buffalo and ox spirits to go outside carrying bugles, waving banners and beating drums.

Once the three evil spirits were fully clad in their armour

they went out and shouted, "Who's that who dares come her
shouting like that?" Monkey slipped round behind the scar t
have a good look, and this is what the evil spirits were like:

Multi-coloured faces, round eyes,
Towering horns.
Four sharp-pointed ears,
Neat and shining bright.
Bodies patterned like a painting,
Covered with brocades that shine like fireflies.
The first one wore a hat of foxes' fur
And hot steam rose from the long hairs of his face.
The second wore a flaming cloak of lightest gauze
And had four gleaming, jade-like hooves.
The third had a mighty roar like thunder;
His sharp and pointed fangs were just like silve needles.
Each was brave and fierce
As they carried their three weapons;
One used a battle-axe,
One was an expert in the cutlass,
And the third had a knotted flail resting on his shoulders

The other evil spirits, tall and short, fat and thin, senior an junior, were all cattle-headed monsters carrying spears or clubs There were three big banners clearly inscribed with the word "King Cold-avoider", "King Heat-avoider" and "King Dust-avoider". After looking at all this for a while Monkey lost hi patience and went up to them with a shout of, "Can you recogniz Monkey, thieving damned ogres?" "Are you the Sun Wukon who made havoc in Heaven?" the evil spirits shouted back. "I really is a case of

I heard your name before I saw your face:
The sight of that would bring the gods disgrace.

So all you are is a macaque." "I'll get you, you lamp-oil thieves,' Monkey retorted in high dudgeon. "Don't talk such rubbish, yo smooth-tongued monsters. Give my master back at once." With that he advanced and swung his iron cudgel, to be parried by the old demons who raised their weapons to meet the blow. A splendid fight ensued in the mountain hollow:

> *Battle-axe, cutlass and flail*
> *Met by the Monkey King's lone cudgel.*
> *Cold-avoider, Heat-avoider and Dust-avoider*
> *Had heard of the Great Sage Equalling Heaven.*
> *When the cudgel rose it scared demons and gods;*
> *Axe and cutlass hacked and flew.*
> *A primal dharma image of true emptiness*
> *Holding off three demons masquerading as Buddhas.*
> *Their noses all greasy with this year's stolen oil,*
> *They tried to snatch the monk sent by the emperor.*
> *One for his master's sake feared not the lengthy road;*
> *The others in their greed had lamps offered every year.*
> *All that could be heard was clash of axe and cutlass*
> *And the noisy clatter of the cudgel.*
> *With clashes and lunges three fought against one*
> *As each showed his skill with blocks and parries.*
> *They fought from dawn till almost nightfall,*
> *And a victor had yet to emerge in the struggle.*

By the time Monkey's cudgel had gone 150 rounds with the three demons it was nearly evening and the outcome was still in doubt. Then Dust-avoider sprang forward from the ranks with a swing of his flail and waved a flag, whereupon the crowd of cattle-headed demons swarmed round Monkey, encircling him and swinging wildly at him with their weapons. Seeing that things were going badly, Monkey set off his somersault cloud and fled in a whoosh. The demons did not go after him but called their devils back so that everyone could have an evening meal. They told the junior devils to take a bowl of food to Sanzang as well: he was not to be dealt with until Monkey had been caught. As the master was a lifelong vegetarian and was besides feeling miserable he sobbed and let none of the food touch his lips.

The story tells how Monkey rode his cloud back to the

Clouds of Compassion Monastery and called, "Brothers." On hearing this Pig and Friar Sand, who were waiting for him and discussing what to do, came out together to greet him with the words, "Brother, why are you only back now after being away all day? What's happened to the master?" "I followed the smell of the wind right through the night till we got to a mountain and it disappeared," Monkey replied with a smile. "Luckily the four Duty Gods told me that the mountain's called Green Dragon Mountain and that there's a Dark Essence Cave on it where three evil spirits live: King Cold-avoider, King Heat-avoider and King Dust-avoider. They've been stealing the oil here for years on end by disguising themselves as Buddhas to trick the officials of Jinping Prefecture. When they came across us this year they wickedly carried our master off with them. I told the Duty Gods and the rest of them to give the master some secret protection while I shouted insults at them from outside their doors. When the three demons came out they all looked like bull-headed demons. The first of them fought with a battle-axe, the second with a cutlass and the third with a flail. They had a whole gang of cattle-headed monsters with them, waving banners and beating drums. The fight went on all day and was still in the balance when one of the demon kings waved a flag to bring all the junior devils forward. As it was late and I was worried that I couldn't beat them I came back by somersault cloud." "I reckon it must be the Demon King of Fengdu who's making trouble for you," said Pig. "What makes you guess that?" Friar Sand asked. "I can tell because our big brother said they were all cattle-headed monsters," replied Pig with a laugh. "No, no," said Monkey. "I saw them and they were all rhinoceros spirits." "If they're rhinos we've just got to catch them and saw their horns off." said Pig. "They'll be worth quite a bit of silver."

As they were talking the monks all asked Monkey if he had eaten any supper. "I'll have something if it's no trouble," Brother Monkey replied, "but I can do without just as well." "Surely you're hungry after fighting all day, my lord," the monks said "You can't get hungry in a mere day," Monkey laughed. "I once went without food for five hundred years." The monks did not know whether he was telling the truth or joking, and a little later food was brought in that Monkey ate, after which he said, "Tidy up and go to sleep. We'll go and fight them again tomorrow and capture the demon kings so as to rescue the master." "What nonsense, brother," said Friar Sand, who was standing to one side. "As the saying goes, 'Delay brings wisdom.' It'll be terrible if that monster stays awake tonight and murders the master. We'd better go there right now and make such a row that he can't do anything. It may go badly wrong if we lose a single moment." When Pig heard this he braced himself and said, "Friar Sand's right. Let's go and put down those demons. The moon's bright enough." Accepting their advice, Monkey left his instructions with the monks of the monastery: "Look after the luggage and the horse. When we've captured the evil spirits we'll bring them back here to prove to the prefect that they're imposters. Then he can end the oil levy and relieve the common people of this hardship. That'll be a good thing, won't it?" The monks all accepted their orders while the three of them left the city by auspicious cloud. Indeed,

Idleness and unrestraint
Threw the dhyana into confusion;
Danger and catastrophe
Led the Way-heart into delusion.

If you don't know who was to win this encounter listen to the explanation in the next instalment.

CHAPTER NINETY-TWO

Three monks wage a great fight on Green Dragon Mountain; Four stars seize the rhinoceros monsters.

The story tells how after the Great Sage Monkey took his two brother disciples by gale and cloud to the northeast they were soon bringing their cloud down at the entrance to the Dark Essence Cave on Green Dragon Mountain. Pig was just about to smash the doors in when Monkey said, "Wait a moment. I'll go in and find out whether the master's still alive before we have it out with him." "But the doors are shut very tightly," said Friar Sand. How will you get in?" "I've got my methods," Monkey replied.

The splendid Great Sage then put his cudgel away, made a spell with his fingers while saying the magic words, called "Change!" and turned into a fire-fly. He was really nimble. Just look at him:

Wings that shine like shooting stars:
The ancients say fire-flies grow from rotting plants.
His powers of transformation are truly great,
And he loves to wander all around.
When he flies to the stone doors to look within
A draught blows through the crack beside him.
A single jump and he is in the dark courtyard,
Watching the movements of the evil spirits.

As he flew in he saw some cattle sprawled around on the ground, fast asleep and snoring like thunder. In the main hall nothing was moving, and all the doors were closed. Not knowing where the three evil spirits were sleeping, he went through the hall and shone with his light into the back, where he heard sobs. The

Tang Priest was chained to a pillar under the eaves at the back and weeping. Monkey kept out of sight as he listened to what he was crying about, and this is what he heard:

> *"Since I left Chang'an in China some ten years back and more,*
> *I have had to suffer much crossing all those rivers and mountains.*
> *I came out to the West at a very happy season,*
> *Arriving in the city for the festival of lanterns.*
>
> *"I failed to understand that the Buddhas were impostors*
> *All because my fate seems to doom me to distress.*
> *My disciples gave pursuit and will use their mighty powers:*
> *I pray they will be able to achieve a great success."*

Delighted to hear this, Monkey spread his wings and flew closer to his master, who wiped away his tears and observed, "Goodness, the west really is different. This is only the first month of the year, when dormant insects are just beginning to wake up. Fancy seeing a fire-fly now!" "Master," said Brother Monkey, unable to keep quiet any longer, "I'm here." "I was just wondering how there could be a fire-fly at this time of year, and it's you," the Tang Priest replied with delight. "Master," said Monkey, turning back into himself, "the journey's been held up so long and so much effort has been wasted because you can't tell true from false. All the way along I've told you demons are no good, but you will kowtow to them. When those devils covered up the lamps to steal the refined butter oil they carried you off too. I told Pig and Friar Sand to go back to the monastery and keep an eye on our things while I followed the smell of the wind here. I didn't know what the place was called, but luckily the four Duty Gods told me that this is Dark Essence Cave on Green Dragon Mountain. I fought the monsters all day long till I went back at evening, told my brother-disciples the full story, and came back here with them instead of going to bed. As I thought it was too late at night to fight and didn't know where you were

I transformed myself to come in and find out what's going on." "Are Pig and Friar Sand outside?" the happy Tang Priest asked. "Yes," Monkey replied. "I've just had a look around and seen that the evil spirits are all asleep. I'll unlock you, smash the doors down and get you out." The Tang Priest nodded his head in gratitude.

Using his unlocking magic, Monkey made the lock open at a touch. He was just leading his master to the front of the cave when the demon kings could be heard shouting from their bedrooms, "Shut the doors tight, little ones, and be careful of fire. Why can't we hear the watchmen calling the watches? Where are the clappers and bells?" After a day's hard fighting the junior demons were all asleep, exhausted; and they only woke up when they heard the shout. To the sound of clappers and bells several of them came out from the back holding weapons and beating gongs, and they just happened to bump into Monkey and his master. "Where do you think you're going, my fine monks, now you've broken the locks?" the junior devils all shouted together, and with no further argument Monkey pulled out his cudgel, shook it to make it as thick as a rice bowl and struck, killing two of them at a blow. The rest of them dropped their weapons, went to the central hall, beat on the doors and shouted, "Disaster, Your Majesties, disaster. The hairy-faced monk's got inside and he's killing people."

The moment the three demons heard this they tumbled out of their beds and ordered, "Catch them! Catch them!" This gave the Tang Priest such a fright that his hands and legs turned weak. Monkey abandoned him and stormed his way forward, swinging his cudgel. The junior devils could not stop him as, pushing two or three aside here and knocking two or three over there, he smashed several pairs of doors open and rushed straight out, shouting, "Where are you, brothers?" Pig and Friar Sand greeted him, rake and staff raised for action, with the question, "What's up, brother?" Monkey told them all about how he had transformed himself to rescue the master, been found by the spirits when they woke up, and been forced to abandon him and fight his way out.

Now that they had recaptured the Tang Priest, the demon kings had him locked up in chains again and questioned him in the glare of lamplight, as they brandished cutlass and axe. "How did you open the lock, damn you," they asked, "and how did that ape get inside? Confess this moment and we'll spare your life, or else we'll cut you in half." This so terrified the Tang Priest that he fell to his knees shivering and shaking and said, "Your Majesties, my disciple Sun Wukong can do seventy-two kinds of transformations. Just now he turned into a fire-fly and flew in to rescue me. We never realized that Your Majesties would wake up or that we would bump into Their Junior Majesties. My wicked disciple wounded a couple of them, and when they all started shouting and going for us with weapons and torches he abandoned me and escaped." "If we'd woken up earlier he'd never have got away," the three demon kings said with loud guffaws. They then told their underlings to fasten the doors firmly at front and back and stop shouting.

"As they've shut the doors and stopped shouting I think they must be going to murder the master," said Friar Sand. "We must act." "You're right,"said Pig. "Let's smash the doors," The idiot showed off his magical powers by smashing the stone doors to smithereens with a blow from his rake then shouted at the top of his voice, "Thieving, oil-stealing monsters! Send my master out right now!" This gave the junior devils inside the doors such a fright that they tumbled and ran inside to report, "Disaster, Your Majesties, disaster. The monks have smashed the front doors." "They're outrageous, damn them," the three demon kings said in a great fury, and when they had sent for their armour and fastened it on they took their weapons and led their underlings into battle. It was now about the third watch of the night, and the moon in the middle of the sky made all as bright as day. As they led their forces out they wasted no more words and started fighting. Monkey held off the battle-axe, Pig blocked the cutlass, and Friar Sand took on the flail.

Three monks with cudgel, staff and rake;
Three evil monsters both brave and angry.

The battle-axe, the cutlass and the flail
Made howling winds and set the sand flying.
In their first clashes they breathed out baleful mists,
Then as they flew around they scattered coloured clouds.
The nailed rake went through its routines round the body,
The iron cudgel was even more splendidly heroic,
And the demon-quelling staff was something rarely seen on earth;
But the unrepentant ogres would not yield a foot of ground.
The bright-bladed axe had a sharp-pointed butt,
The whirling flail made a pattern of flowers,
And the flashing cutlass swung like a painted door;
But the monks were their match.
One side was fighting with fury for their master's life;
The other hit at their faces so as not to release the Tang Priest.
The axe hacked and the cudgel blocked in the struggle for mastery;
The rake swung and the cutlass struck as they fought;
The knotted flail and the demon-quelling staff,
Coming and going in a splendid display.

When the three monks and the three monsters had been fighting for a long time without either side coming out on top King Cold-avoider shouted, "Come on, little ones!" The monsters all charged at Pig, quickly tripping him up and bringing him to the ground. Several water-buffalo spirits dragged and pulled him inside the cave, where they tied him up. When Friar Sand saw that Pig had disappeared and heard the mooing of all the cattle he then raised his staff, feinted at King Dust-avoider and tried to flee, only to be rushed by another crowd of spirits who pulled at him, sending him staggering. However hard he struggled he could not get up, and he too was carried off to be tied up. Realizing that he was in an impossible situation, Monkey escaped by somersault cloud. When Pig and Friar Sand were dragged to him the Tang Priest said with tears welling up in his eyes at the sight of them, "Poor things! You two have been caught too. Where's Wukong?" "When he saw we'd been caught he ran away," Friar Sand replied. "Wherever he has gone he will certainly have gone to fetch help," said the Tang Priest. "But who knows when we will be delivered?" Master and disciples felt thoroughly miserable.

The story tells how Brother Monkey rode his somersault cloud back to the Clouds of Compassion Monastery, where the monks met him with the question, "Have you been able to rescue Lord Tang?" "It's difficult," said Monkey, "very difficult. Those three evil spirits have tremendous magical powers, and when we three had fought them for a long time they called up their underlings to capture Pig and Friar Sand. I was lucky to get away." "My lord," said the monks with horror, "if someone who can ride mists and clouds as you can couldn't catch them, your master is bound to be killed." "No problem," Monkey replied, "no problem. My master's under the secret protection of the Protectors, the Guardians, the Dings and the Jias. He has besides eaten Grass-returning Cinnabar. I'm sure his life will be safe. The only trouble is that those demons really know their stuff. You people look after the horse and the luggage while I go up to Heaven to get some troops." "Can you go up to Heaven, my lord?" asked the terrified monks. "I used to live there," replied Monkey with a smile. "Because I wrecked the Peach Banquet when I was Great Sage Equalling Heaven, our Buddha subdued me, so that now I've no option but to redeem my crimes by guarding the Tang Priest while he fetches the scriptures. All along the journey I've been helping the good and fighting against the evil. What you don't realize is that the master is fated to have these troubles." When the monks heard this they kowtowed in worship, while Monkey went outside and disappeared with a whistle.

The splendid Great Sage was soon outside the Western Gate of Heaven, where the Metal Planet, Heavenly King Virudhaka and the four spirit officers Yin, Zhu, Tao and Xu were talking to each other. As soon as they saw Monkey coming they hastily bowed to him and said, "Where are you going, Great Sage?" "After we reached Mintian County in Jinping Prefecture on the eastern borders of India," Monkey replied, "my master, the Tang Priest who I'm escorting, was being entertained by the monks of the Clouds of Compassion Monastery for the Full Moon Festival. When we went to the Bridge of Golden Lamps there were three golden lamps full of over fifty thousand ounces of silver's worth of scented refined butter oil that the Buddhas came down to take every year. While we were admiring the lamps three Buddha images did come down to earth, and my master was gullible enough to go on the bridge to worship them. I told him they were a bad lot, but by then the lamps had been covered up and the master carried off with the oil by a wind. When I'd followed the wind till dawn I reached a mountain, where the four Duty Gods fortunately told me that it was called Green Dragon Mountain with a Dark Essence Cave in it where three monsters lived: King Cold-avoider, King Heat-avoider and King Dust-avoider. I hurried to their doors to demand the master and fought them for a while without success, so I got in by transforming myself to find the master locked up but unharmed. I released him and was just taking him out when they woke up and I had to flee again. Later I fought hard against them with Pig and Friar Sand, but the two of them were both captured and tied up. That's why I've come up to inform the Jade Emperor, fine out about the monsters' background and ask him to give orders to have them suppressed."

At this the Metal Planet burst out laughing and said, "If you've been fighting the monsters why can't you tell where they're from? "I can see that," Monkey replied. "They're a bunch of rhino spirits. But they have such enormous magical powers that I can't beat them and I'm desperate." "They are three rhinoceros spirits," the Metal Planet explained. "Because their form is seen in heaven they cultivated their awareness for many years and became true spirits able to fly on clouds and walk in mists. Those monsters are fanatical about cleanliness and don't like the look of their own bodies, and are always going into the water to bathe. They have lots of different names:

there are she-rhinos, he-rhinos, gelded rhinos, spotted rhinos, *humao* rhinos, *duoluo* rhinos and heaven-connected brindled rhinos. They all have a single nostril, three types of hair and two horns. They roam the rivers and seas and can travel through water. It looks as though Cold-avoider, Heat-avoider and Dust-avoider have nobility in their horns, which is why they call themselves kings. If you want to catch them, they will submit to the four beast stars belonging to the element wood." "Which four wood stars?" Monkey asked. "Could I trouble you, venerable sir, to spell it out for me?" "Those stars are spread out in space outside the Dipper and Bull Palace," the planet replied with a smile. "If you submit a memorial to the Jade Emperor he will give you detailed instructions." Raising his clasped hands as he expressed his thanks, Monkey went straight in through the heavenly gates.

He was soon outside the Hall of Universal Brightness, where he saw the heavenly teachers Ge, Qiu, Zhang and Xu, who asked, "Where are you going?" "We've just reached Jinping Prefecture," Monkey replied, "where my master relaxed his dhyana nature by going to enjoy the Moon Festival lanterns and was carried off by evil monsters. As I can't subdue them myself I've come to ask the Jade Emperor to save him." The four heavenly teachers then took Monkey to the Hall of Miraculous Mist to submit his memorial, and when all the ceremonials had been performed he explained his business. The Jade Emperor then asked which units of heavenly soldiers he wanted to help him. "When I arrived at the Western Gate of Heaven just now," Monkey replied, "the Metal Planet told me they were rhinoceros spirits that could only be subdued by the four beast stars belonging to the element wood." The Jade Emperor then told Heavenly Teacher Xu to go to the Dipper and Bull Palace with Monkey to fetch the four beast stars and take them down to the lower world to make the capture.

By the time they arrived outside the Dipper and Bull Palace the Twenty-eight Constellations were there to greet them. "We are here by imperial command to order four beast stars belonging to the element wood to go down to the lower world with the

Great Sage Sun," the heavenly teacher explained. The Wooden Lesser Dragon of the Constellation Horn, the Wooden Unicorn of the Dipper, the Wooden Wolf of the Strider, and the Wooden Hyena of the Well all stepped forward from the side to ask, "Where are you sending us to subdue demons, Great Sage?" "So you're the ones," said Brother Monkey with a smile. "That old man Metal Planet kept your names secret, and I didn't realize what he was driving at. If he'd told me before that it was you four wooden animals from the Twenty-eight Constellations I'd have come here to invite you myself: there'd have been no need to trouble His Majesty for an edict." "What a thing to say, Great Sage," the four wooden animals replied. "We'd never have dared to leave on our own authority in the absence of an imperial decree. Where are they? Let's go right away." "They are rhinoceros spirits in the Dark Essence Cave in Green Dragon Mountain to the northeast of Jinping Prefecture." "If they're really rhinoceros spirits," said the Wooden Unicorn of the Dipper, the Wooden Wolf of the Strider and the Wooden Lesser Dragon of the Horn, "you'll only need Wooden Hyena from the Well Constellation. He can eat tigers on mountains and capture rhinos in the sea." "But these aren't ordinary rhinos who gaze at the moon," replied Monkey. "They have cultivated their conduct and found the Way and are a thousand years old. All four of you gentlemen must come: no excuses. If one of you can't capture them single-handed it'll be wasted effort." "You people are talking nonsense," the heavenly teacher added. "The imperial command is that all four of you go, so go you must. Fly there at once while I report back." The heavenly teacher then took his leave of Monkey and went.

"Delay no more, Great Sage," the four wooden ones said. "You challenge them to battle and lure them out so we can come from behind you and get them." Monkey then went up to the cave and shouted abusively, "Oil-thieving ogres! Give my master back!" The doors, which Pig had smashed open, had been barricaded with a few planks by a number of junior devils, and when they heard his insults they rushed inside to report, "Your Majesties, the monk Sun is outside insulting us again." "We beat him and he ran away," said Dust-avoider, "so why's he back again today? I think he must have got some reinforcements from somewhere." "We're not scared of any reinforcements he could get," said Cold-avoider and Heat-avoider scornfully. "Let's get into our armour at once. Little ones, surround him carefully and don't let him get away." Not caring about their lives, the evil spirits came out of the cave holding spears and swords, with banners waving and drums beating. "Back again, are you, macaque?" they shouted at Brother Monkey. "Not afraid of another beating?"

Nothing infuriated Monkey so much as the word "macaque", and he was grinding his teeth in rage as he lifted his cudgel to hit them. The three demon kings brought their junior devils up to surround him, at which the four wooden beasts who were waiting to one side swung their weapons with shouts of, "Don't move, animals!" The three demon kings were of course most alarmed at the sight of the four stars, and they all said, "This is terrible, terrible. He's found the people who can beat us. Run for your lives, little ones!" With that there was much roaring, lowing, panting and sighing as the junior devils all resumed their original appearances as yak, water-buffalo and ox spirits running all over the mountain. The three demon kings also turned back into their true selves, put their hands down to become four-hoofed creatures like iron cannons, and galloped off to the northeast, to be followed hard by the Great Sage leading the Wooden Hyena of the Well and the Wooden Lesser Dragon of the Horn. While they were not going to relax for a moment, the Wooden Unicorn of the Dipper and the Wooden Wolf of the Strider were mopping up all the cattle spirits among the hollows, summits, ravines and valleys of the eastern mountain. Some were killed and others taken alive. They then went into the Dark Essence Cave to free the Tang Priest, Pig and Friar Sand.

Recognizing the two stars, Friar Sand bowed to them in thanks and asked, "What brought you two gentlemen here to rescue us?" "We came to rescue you because the Great Sage Monkey submitted a request to the Jade Emperor that we be sent," the two stars replied. "Why has my disciple Wukong not come in?" the Tang Priest asked with tears in his eyes. "The three old demons are rhinoceroses," the stars explained, "and when they saw us they fled for their lives to the northeast. The Great Sage Sun has gone after them with the Wooden Hyena of the Well and the Wooden Lesser Dragon of the Horn. We two wiped out the oxen then came here to rescue you, holy monk." The Tang Priest once again kowtowed in thanks then kowtowed to heaven. "Master," said Pig, "overdone courtesy is hypocrisy. Stop kowtowing all the time. The four star officers came at the Jade Emperor's command and as a favour to big brother. The ordinary demons have all been wiped out, but we still don't know how the senior demons are to be put down. Let's clear all the valuables out of the cave, wreck the place so as to dig out their roots, then go back to the monastery to wait for Monkey." "Marshal Tian Peng, your suggestion is right," said the Wooden Wolf of the Strider. "You and the Curtain-lifting General escort your master back to the monastery to sleep while we head northeast to fight the enemy." "Yes, yes," said Pig. "With you two to help you're bound to wipe them all out. Then you'll be able to report back on your mission." The two star officers immediately joined the chase.

After Pig and Friar Sand had found a bushel of valuables in the cave — there was much coral, agate, pearls, amber, precious shells, jade and gold — they carried them outside and invited the master to sit on the top of a crag while they started a fire that burned the whole cave to ashes. Only then did they take the master back to the Clouds of Compassion Monastery in Jinping Prefecture. Indeed,

The classic says, "Disaster comes at the height of success."
Indeed one can meet with evil in happiness.
For love of the lanterns the dhyana nature was disturbed;
The heart set on the Way was weakened by a beautiful sight.
The great elixir has always had to be permanently guarded;

Once it is lost one always comes to grief.
Shut it up tight; bind it fast; never idle.
A moment's lack of care can lead one astray.

We will tell not of how the three of them went back to the monastery, their lives saved, but of how the Wooden Unicorn of the Dipper and the Wooden Wolf of the Strider were riding their clouds northeast in pursuit of the demons when they lost sight of them in mid air. On reaching the Western Ocean they saw the Great Sage Monkey down by the sea a long way away, shouting. "Where have the monsters gone, Great Sage?" they asked, bringing their clouds down. "Why didn't you two come after them and help put them down?" Monkey replied. "How can you have the nerve to ask that question?" "When we saw that you and the stars from the Well and the Horn had routed the demons and were going after them, Great Sage," the Wooden Unicorn of the Dipper replied, "we were sure you'd capture them, so we two wiped out the rest of the devils, rescued your master and fellow-disciples from the cave, searched the mountain, burned the cave out, and entrusted your master to your two fellow-disciples to take back to the Clouds of Compassion Monastery in the city. We only came after you this way when you had been gone for such a long time." "In that case you did very well," said Brother Monkey, his wrath now turned to pleasure. "Thank you for going to so much trouble. The only thing is that when we'd chased the three ogres this far they plunged into the sea. The two stars from the Well and the Horn followed close behind them while I stayed on the shore to cut off their escape. Now you're here you can block them on the shore while I go there."

The splendid Great Sage then swung his cudgel and made a spell with his fingers as he cleared a way through the waters, plunging deep into the waves, where the three monsters were locked in a life-and-death struggle with the Wooden Hyena of the Well and the Wooden Lesser Dragon of the Horn. "Monkey's here," he shouted, springing forward. The evil spirits could barely hold off the two star officers, so when they heard Monkey's great yell at this moment of crisis they turned and fled for their lives into the middle of the sea. Their horns were very good at parting the waters, and they cleared their way through the sea with a whooshing noise, the two star officers and the Great Sage Monkey chasing after them.

A yaksha who was patrolling the Western Ocean with a shelled warrior saw from a distance the way the rhinoceroses were parting the waters, recognized Monkey and the two stars, and rushed back to the crystal palace to report to the dragon king in alarm, "Your Majesty, the Great Sage Equalling Heaven and two stars from the sky are chasing three rhinoceroses this way." When the old dragon king Ao Shun heard this he said to his heir, Prince Mo'ang, "Muster our water forces at once. I'm sure it must be the three rhinoceros spirits Cold-avoider, Heat-avoider and Dust-avoider who've provoked Sun the Novice. As they're in the sea now we'd better lend a hand." Having been given his orders Ao Mo'ang hastened to muster his troops.

A moment later a fully-armed force of tortoises, soft-shelled turtles, alligators, bream, mackerel, mandarin fish, carp, and prawn and crab soldiers charged out of the crystal palace shouting their battle-cries together to stop the rhinoceros spirits. Unable to go any further forward, the rhinoceroses made a hasty retreat, only to find their escape blocked by the stars from the Well and the Horn as well as the Great Sage. In their panic they failed to stay in a group, but scattered as they fled for their lives. Dust-avoider was soon surrounded by the old dragon king's men. A delighted Monkey called out, "Stop! Stop! Take him alive! Don't kill him!" When Mo'ang heard this order he rushed forward, knocked Dust-avoider to the ground, put an iron hook through his snout and tied all his hoofs together.

The old dragon king then divided his forces into two to help the star officers capture the other two monsters. As the young dragon prince led his men forward the Wooden Hyena of the Well reverted to his real form to hold Cold-avoider down and start eating him in big and little bites. "Well Star!" Mo'ang shouted. "Don't kill him! The Great Sage Monkey wants him alive, not dead." Mo'ang shouted several times, but by then the Hyena had already gnawed right through the monster's throat.

Mo'ang ordered his prawn and crab soldiers to carry the dead rhinoceros back to the palace of crystal, then joined the Wooden Hyena of the Well in the pursuit. Heat-avoider, who was being driven back towards them by the Wooden Lesser Dragon of the Horn, ran straight into the star from the Well, at which Mo'ang ordered his tortoises, soft-shelled turtles and alligators to spread out in the winnowing-fan formation to encircle the monster. "Spare me, spare me!" the monster pleaded. The wooden Hyena of the Well sprang forward, grabbed the monster by the ear, seized his sword, and shouted, "I won't kill you. I won't kill you. I'll take you to the Great Sage Monkey for him to deal with you."

The troops then went back to the crystal palace, where they reported, "We've got them both." Monkey saw that one was lying headless and gory on the ground, while the other was being forced to kneel by the Wooden Hyena of the Well twisting his ear. "That head wasn't cut off with a weapon," Monkey said on going up for a closer look. "If I hadn't shouted so hard the star officer of the Well would have eaten the whole of him up," replied Mo'ang with a smile. "Very well then," said Monkey. "In that case you'd better get a saw to cut off his horns and have his hide removed for us to take. We'll leave the flesh for your worthy father the dragon king and yourself to enjoy." A chain was then run through Dust-avoider's nose for the Wooden Lesser Dragon of the Horn to lead him by, and the same was done to Heat-avoider for the Wooden Hyena of the Well. "Take them to the prefect of Jinping," said Monkey. "Investigate them, question them about all the years they masqueraded as Buddhas to harm the people, then off with their heads."

They all then did as Monkey told them, taking their leave of the dragon king and his son and emerging from the Western Ocean, leading the rhinoceroses with them. When they met the other two stars from the Strider and the Dipper they went by cloud straight back to Jinping Prefecture. Here Monkey called out as he stood in mid air on a beam of auspicious light, "Mr.

Prefect, subordinate officials, soldiers and civilians of Jinping listen to what I say. We are holy monks sent by the Great Tang in the east to fetch the scriptures from the Western Heaven. In this prefecture and its counties you have had to make offerings in golden lamps every year to these rhinoceros monsters pretending to be Buddhas coming down to earth. When we came here and were admiring the lamps at the Moon Festival these monsters carried the oil and our master off together. I asked for some gods from heaven to capture them. We've cleaned out their cave and wiped out the monsters. They won't be able to give you any more trouble. You needn't waste the people's money making offerings in golden lamps here any more." When Pig and Friar Sand, who were just escorting the master back into the Clouds of Compassion Monastery, heard Monkey talking from up in the sky they abandoned their master, dropped the luggage and shot up into the air by cloud to ask Monkey about how the demons had been beaten. "One of them was chewed to death by the star from the Well," Monkey replied, "and we've got his sawn-off horns and his hide with us. The other two we've brought back alive." "Throw the pair of them down into the city," said Pig, "for the officials and everyone else to see. Then they'll know we're gods and sages. I'll trouble you four star officers to put your clouds away, land, and come into the prefectural court with us to execute the monsters. The facts are clear and the penalty's the right one. There's nothing else to be said." "Marshal Tian Peng is right, and he knows the laws too," the four stars said. "I have learned a bit during my years as a monk," Pig replied.

The gods then pushed the rhinoceroses, which fell wreathed in coloured clouds into the prefectural court, to the astonishment of the prefectural officials and everyone else inside and outside the walled city, who all set up incense tables outside their houses and bowed their heads to worship the gods from heaven. A little later the monks of the Clouds of Compassion Monastery carried the venerable elder into the court in a sedan chair. When Sanzang met Monkey he kept thanking him, adding, "I am very grateful for the trouble I have put the star officers to in rescuing us. I had been very anxious when I did not see you, worthy disciple, but now you have returned in triumph. I wonder where you had to chase the monsters to before you caught them." "After I left you the day before yesterday," Monkey replied, "I went up to heaven to make some enquiries. The Metal Planet knew that the monsters were rhinoceroses, so he told me to ask for the four beast stars that belong to the element wood. So I submitted a memorial to the Jade Emperor and he sent them straight to the mouth of the cave, where they gave battle. When the demon kings fled, the stars from the Dipper and the Strider rescued you, Master. I chased the demons with the Well and the Horn stars straight to the Western Ocean, where the dragon king sent his son out with their troops to help us. That's how the monsters were captured and brought here for questioning." The venerable elder was full of endless praise and thanks. The prefectural and county officials and their subordinates all lit precious candles and whole containers of incense sticks as they kowtowed in respect.

A little later Pig lost his temper, pulled out his monastic knife and beheaded first Dust-avoider, then Heat-avoider, each with a single stroke. Then he removed their four horns with a saw. The Great Sage Monkey then had another suggestion to make: "You four star officers must take these four rhinoceros horns to the upper world to offer to the Jade Emperor as trophies when you report back on your mission." As for the two horns he had brought back from the sea, he said, "We'll leave one here to guard the storehouses of the prefectural palace and as evidence that from now on no more lamp-oil will ever be levied. We'll take the other to offer to the Lord Buddha on Vulture Peak." The four stars were delighted, and after bowing to take their leave of the Great Sage they rose by coloured cloud to report back to the Jade Emperor.

The prefectural and county officials kept the master and his disciples for a great vegetarian banquet to which all the rural officials were also invited. Notices were issued to tell the military and civil population that golden lamps were not to be lit the next year, and that the duty of serving as an oil-purchasing household was abolished for ever. Butchers meanwhile were instructed to remove the rhinoceros skins to be steeped in saltpetre and smoked dry for making into armour, while the flesh was to be distributed to the officials. At the same time money and grain that had been raised by unjust fines on innocent people were spent to buy a plot of privately-owned empty land. On this a temple to the four stars who had put the demons down, as well as a shrine to the Tang Priest and his three disciples, were to be built. Stone tablets with inscriptions were to be set up for each of them to record their deeds for ever as a mark of gratitude.

Master and disciples relaxed and enjoyed the offerings. They had hardly a moment to themselves as they had so many invitations from the 240 lamp-oil households. Pig was delighted to have so much to eat, and he always kept in his sleeve some of the treasures he had collected in the cave to give to all his hosts to thank them for their banquets. When they had stayed there for a month and were still unable to get away the Tang Priest ordered Monkey: "Wukong, give all the remaining valuables to the monks in the Clouds of Compassion Monastery. Let's leave before dawn, without letting the rich families here know. If we are so eager to enjoy ourselves here that we delay in fetching the scriptures we may offend the Lord Buddha and cause some catastrophe. That would be terrible." Monkey then disposed of all the objects.

When they got up early the next morning at the fifth watch Pig was woken up to get the horse ready. The idiot had eaten and drunk so well that he was still half asleep as he said, "Why get the horse ready so early?" "The master says we've got to be going," Monkey shouted. "That reverend gentleman doesn't do things right," the idiot said, rubbing his eyes. "We've had invitations from all 240 of the big families, but only had thirty or so good vegetarian meals so far. How can he be making me go hungry again?" When the venerable elder heard this he retorted abusively, "Dreg-guzzling idiot! Stop talking such nonsense! Get up at once! If you go on arguing back like that I'll tell Wukong to smash your teeth in with his gold-banded cudgel."

At the mention of a beating the idiot gesticulated frantically as he said, "The master's changed. Usually he favours me and likes me and protects me because I'm so stupid. When you want to hit me, brother, he usually persuades you not to. So why's he dead set on telling you to hit me today?" "The master's angry with you for being so greedy," Monkey replied, "and holding us up on our journey. If you don't want me to hit you, pack the luggage and get the horse ready." As the idiot really was scared of being hit he jumped out of bed, got dressed and shouted to Friar Sand, "Get up right now! He's going to start hitting." Friar Sand then jumped up too, and they both got everything packed. "Keep quiet," said the Tang Priest, waving his hands about, "and don't disturb the monks." He quickly mounted, after which they opened the gate of the monastery and found their way out. Indeed, this departure was

Letting the phoenix escape from the birdcage of jade;
Secretly opening locks so the dragon goes free.

If you don't know what the households who still wanted to thank them did at daybreak, listen to the explanation in the next instalment.

CHAPTER NINETY-THREE

In the Almsgiver's Garden antiquity and causes are discussed;
In the court of India the King meets the monks.

When thoughts arise there surely will be desire,
Longing is certain to lead one to disaster.
Why should intelligence distinguish the three ranks of nobility?
When conduct is complete it naturally returns to the primal sea.
Whether you become an immortal or a Buddha,
All must be arranged from within.
In absolute purity, with all dust removed,
All will be achieved and one will rise to heaven.

The story tells how when Sanzang and his disciples were nowhere to be seen at dawn the monks in the Clouds of Compassion Monastery all said, "We couldn't keep them, we couldn't say goodbye to them, and we weren't able to ask them for anything. We've let those living Bodhisattvas slip clean away." As they were talking, some of the great families from the southern outskirts of the city came in with invitations, at which the monks clapped their hands in regret and said, "We were caught off our guard last night: they all rode off by cloud." Everyone then kowtowed to heaven in gratitude. The news was spread to all the officials in the city, who told the great families to prepare the five kinds of sacrificial animal, flowers and fruit to offer to the shrines in thanksgiving.

The story tells how the Tang Priest and his three disciples fed on the wind and slept in the open, travelling uneventfully for the best part of a month. One day they suddenly saw a high mountain. "Disciples," said the Tang Priest in fear, "the ridge in front of us is very steep. You must be very careful." "As our journey has brought us so close to the land of the Buddha there will definitely be nothing evil here," said Monkey. "Don't worry, Master." "Disciple," the Tang Priest replied, "although we are not far from the Buddha's land the monks told us in the monastery the other day that it is six or seven hundred miles from here to the capital of India, and they didn't know how much further after that." "Have you forgotten the *Heart Sutra* that the Rook's Nest Hermit taught you again, Master?" asked Monkey. "The *Prajnaparamita Heart Sutra* is constantly with me, like my habit and begging bowl," Sanzang replied. "There has not been a day ever since the Rook's Nest Hermit taught it to me that I have not recited it. I have never forgotten it for a moment. I can even recite it backwards. How could I possibly forget it?" "You can only recite it, Master," said Monkey. "You never asked the hermit to explain it." "Ape!" retorted Sanzang. "How can you say I don't understand it? Do you understand it then?" "Yes," Monkey replied, "I do."

After that neither Sanzang nor Monkey made another sound. This had Pig falling about with laughter, while Friar Sand was hurting himself, he was so amused. "Nonsense," said Pig. "We all started out in life as monsters. We're not Dhyana monks who've heard the sutras being explained or Buddhist priests who've been taught the dharma. He's pretending, just putting on an act. How can you say you understand? Well then, why aren't you saying anything? We're listening. Please explain." "Second brother," said Friar Sand, "leave him be. Big brother's only talking big like that to keep the master going. What he nows about is how to use a cudgel. What does he know about xplaining sutras?" "Stop talking such nonsense, Wuneng and Vujing," said Sanzang. "Wukong understands the wordless nguage. That is true explanation."

As master and disciples talked they did indeed cover a long istance, leaving the ridge behind them. They saw a big monas-ery beside the road. "Wukong," said Sanzang. "There's a onastery ahead. Just look at it:

It's neither too big nor too small,
But has green glazed tiles;
Neither too new nor too old,
And with a red wall.
Leaning canopies of azure pines can just be seen:
Who knows how many thousand years old they are?
Listen to the murmur of the waters in the channel,
Cut from the mountain untold dynasties ago.
Above the gates is written,
'Spread Gold Dhyana Monastery';
The tablet is inscribed,
'Ancient relic'."

Monkey saw that it was called the Spread Gold Dhyana Monastery, and Pig said so too. " 'Spread Gold,' " Sanzang wondered as he sat on his horse, " 'Spread Gold'. . . . Can we be in the country of Sravasti?" "This is very remarkable, Master," said Pig. "In all the years I've been with you you've never known the way before, but you seem to know it now." "No," Sanzang replied, "I have often read in the scriptures about the Buddha being in the Jetavana garden in the city of Sravasti. The Venerable Almsgiver Sudatta tried to buy it from the prince as a place to ask the Buddha to preach in. The prince refused to sell the garden, and said he would only part with it if it were covered with gold. When the Venerable Almsgiver heard this he had gold bricks made with which he covered the whole garden to buy it. Then he invited the Buddha to preach on the dharma. I am sure that the name Spread Gold Monastery must refer to that story." "We're in luck," said Pig with a smile. "If that story's true we can find ourselves one of those bricks as a present to give people." Everybody laughed, after which Sanzang dismounted.

As they went in through the monastery gates they saw people carrying loads with shoulder-poles or on their backs, pushing carts, or sitting in loaded carts. Others were sleeping or talking. The sight of the master, who was so handsome, and his three hideous disciples rather frightened them, so they drew back t make way. Worried that his disciples would provoke trouble, Sanzang kept saying, "Behave yourselves! Behave yourselves!" They were all very restrained. As they went round the Vajra Hall a Dhyana monk of most unworldly appearance came out to meet them:

A face like a shining full moon,
A body like a bodhi tree.
The wind blew through the sleeve round his staff,
As his sandals trod the stony path.

When Sanzang extended a monastic greeting to him the monk returned his courtesy and asked, "Where are you from, teacher?" "I am Chen Xuanzang," Sanzang replied, "sent to the Western Heaven at the command of the Great Tang emperor in the east to worship the Buddha and fetch the scriptures. As my journey brings me here I am paying you this hasty visit to request a night's shelter before continuing on my way tomorrow." "This monastery of ours is one that receives people from all quarters," the monk replied. "Everyone is welcome to visit, and we would be especially happy to provide for so holy a monk from the east as your reverend self." Sanzang thanked him and called to his three disciples to come with him as they crossed the cloister and refectory and went to the abbot's lodgings. When they had exchanged courtesies they sat down as befits host and guests. Monkey and the other two sat down as well, their hands at their sides.

The story tells how, on learning that monks from Great Tang in the east who were going to fetch the scriptures had arrived, all in the monastery, young and old alike, whether permanent inmates, itinerant monks, elders or novices came to see them. After tea had been drunk a vegetarian meal was brought in. While Sanzang was still saying the grace before the meal Pig in his impatience had already grabbed and wolfed down steamed buns, vegetarian dishes and soup noodles. In the crowded abbot's lodgings those who knew better were admiring Sanzang's majestic bearing, while those who enjoyed fun watched Pig eat. When Friar Sand cast his eyes around and saw what was happening he gave Pig a discreet pinch and muttered, "Behave yourself!" At this Pig started a desperate howl of, "All this 'behave yourself, behave yourself!' I'm starving!" "You don't understand, brother," Friar Sand replied with a smile. "When it comes to the belly, all the well-behaved people in the world are exactly the same as we two." Only then did Pig stop eating. After Sanzang had said the grace for the end of the meal the attendants cleared the tables and Sanzang expressed his thanks.

When the monks asked about why they had come from the east, Sanzang's conversation turned to ancient sites and he asked them about the name Spread Gold Monastery. "This used to be the Monastery of the Venerable Almsgiver in the country of Sravasti. It was also known as the Jetavana and its name was changed to its present one after the Venerable Almsgiver covered the ground with gold bricks. In those days the Venerable Almsgiver used to live in the country of Sravasti, and our monastery was his Jetavana, which is why it was renamed the Almsgiver's Spread Gold Monastery. The site of the Jetavana is at the back of the monastery. Whenever there has been a torrential rainstorm in recent years, small pieces of gold and silver have been washed out, and some people are lucky enough to pick them up." "So the story is a true one," said Sanzang, going on to ask, "Why did I see so many travelling merchants with horses, mules, carts and carrying-poles resting here when I came in through the gates of your monastery?" "This mountain is called Mount Hundredfoot," the monks replied. "We used to live in peace and prosperity here, but with the cyclic progression of the natural forces a number of centipede spirits have for some inexplicable reason appeared. They attack people on the roads and though nobody gets killed people don't dare to travel. At the foot of the mountain there's a Cock-crow Pass that people only dare to cross after cock-crow. As all these strangers arrived late they are worried that it would not be safe and are putting up here tonight. They'll set out at cock-crow." As master and disciples were talking a vegetarian meal was brought in that they ate.

Sanzang and Monkey were strolling in the light of the rising half moon when a lay brother came to announce, "Our ancient master would like to meet the gentlemen from China." Sanzang at once turned to see an ancient monk holding a bamboo cane who came forward to greet him and ask, "Are you the teacher come from China?" "You do me too great an honour," Sanzang replied, returning his greeting. The old monk was full of admiration for him, asking how old he was. "I have wasted forty-five years," Sanzang replied. "May I ask how old you are?" "Just one sixty-year cycle older than you, teacher," the other answered. "Then you're a hundred and five this year," Brother Monkey said. "How old do you think I am?" "Teacher," the old monk replied, "your appearance seems so ancient and your spirit so pure that I could not tell in a hurry, especially by moonlight with my poor eyes." After talking for a while they walked to the back cloister for a look round. "Where is the site of the Almsgiver's Garden that you mentioned just now?" Sanzang asked. "Outside the back gate," the other replied. On the order being given for the back gate to be opened immediately, all that could be seen was the ruined base of a stone wall. Putting his hands together, Sanzang sighed and said,

"I think of the benefactor Sudatta
Who gave his treasures to help the needy.
The fame of Jetavana long endures;
Where is he now with the enlightened arhat?"

After a leisurely stroll enjoying the moonlight they sat down for a while on a terrace, where they heard the sound of sobbing. As Sanzang listened with a still heart he could hear that the weeper was grieving because her parents did not know of her suffering. This moved him to sorrow, and he found himself in tears as he turned to the monks and asked, "Who is it being so sad, and where?" On hearing this question the ancient monk sent all the others away to prepare tea, and when nobody else was around he kowtowed to the Tang Priest and Brother Monkey. "Venerable abbot," said Sanzang, helping him to his feet again, "why do you pay me this courtesy?"

"As I am over a hundred," the ancient monk replied, "I do

know a little of the ways of the world; and in between period of meditation and stillness I have seen some things. I know certain amount about you, my lord, and your disciples, and yo are not like other people. The only teachers here who would b able to analyse this most painful business are you." "Tell m what it's all about," said Monkey. "A year ago today," the ancient monk replied, "I was concentrating my mind on th nature of the moon when I suddenly heard a gust o wind and the sound of someone grieving. I got out o bed, went into the Jetavana and saw a beautiful girl there 'Whose daughter are you?' I asked her. 'Why are yo here?' 'I am a princess, the daughter of the king of India, the girl replied. 'The wind blew me here when I wa looking at the flowers by moonlight.' I locked her up in a empty room that I bricked up like a prison cell, just leaving gap in the door big enough to pass a bowl through. That day told the other monks that she was an evil spirit I had captured But as we monks are compassionate I couldn't kill her, an every day she is given two meals of simple food and drink t keep her alive. The girl is clever enough to understand what mean, and to prevent herself from being sullied by the othe monks she has pretended to be deranged and slept in her ow piss and shit. During the day she talks nonsense or just sits ther in silence, but in the still of the night she cries because she misse her parents. I've been into the city several times to make enquiries about the princesses, but not a single one is missing. S I have put her under stronger locks, and I am even more determined not to let her go. Now that you have come here, teache I beg you to go to the capital and use your dharma powers t find out the truth. You will thus be able both to rescue the goo and display your magical powers." When Sanzang and Monke heard this they noted it very carefully. As they were talkin two junior monks came in to invite them to take tea and go t bed, so they went back inside.

Back in the abbot's lodgings Pig and Friar Sand wer grumbling, "We'll have to be on our way at cock-crow tomorrow so why aren't you in bed yet?" "What's that you're sayin idiot?" Monkey asked. "Go to bed," Pig replied. "Why are you admiring the blooming scenery this late?" At this the ancient monk left them, and the Tang Priest went to bed.

Sweet dreams of flowers in the moonlit silence;
Warm breezes coming through the window gauze.
As water drips in the clepsydra to fill three sections,
The Milky Way shines on the splendours of the palace.

They had not slept long that night when they heard the cocks crowing. The traders in front of the monastery all got up noisily and prepared their breakfast by lamplight. The venerable elder woke up Pig and Friar Sand to bridle the horse and pack up, while Monkey called for lamps to be lit. The monks of the monastery, who were up already, set out tea, soup and snacks, and waited on them. Pig ate a plate of steamed buns with delight then took the luggage and the horse outside while Sanzang and Brother Monkey took their leave of all the monks. "Please don't forget about that very tragic business," said the ancient monk. "I'll give it all my attention," Monkey replied, "all my attention. Once I'm in the city I'll be able to find out the truth from what I hear and see." They traders noisily set off together. By the last watch of the night they were through Cock-crow Pass, and by ten in the morning the walls of the city were in sight. It was indeed a powerful city as strong as an iron cauldron, the heavenly capital of a divine region. The city

Was a crouching tiger or a coiled dragon on high ground,
Colourful with its phoenix towers and unicorn halls.
The waters of the royal moat encircled it like a belt;
In this mountainside paradise were many a monument.
The morning sun lit up banners by the high-way;
The spring wind carried the sound of pipes and drums
across the bridges.
The wise king was dressed in robes and crown,
The crops were abundant and the splendour manifest.

That day they reached the streets of the eastern market, where the traders all put up at inns. As Sanzang and his disciples were walking in the city they came to a government hostel and went inside. The hostel manager went to report to the hostel superintendent that there were four strange-looking monks outside who had arrived with a white horse. On being told about the horse the superintendent realized that they must be on an official mission, so he went out to welcome them. "I have been sent by the Tang court in the east to the Great Thunder Monastery on Vulture Peak to see the Buddha and seek the scriptures," Sanzang replied with a bow. "I have a passport to present at court for inspection. I would be grateful if I could spend the night in Your Excellency's distinguished hostel. I will be on my way when my business has been done." "This hostel has been established to entertain envoys and travellers," the superintendent replied, returning his bow, "so it is only right that we should entertain you. Please come in, please come in."

A delighted Sanzang invited his disciples to come in to meet the superintendent, who was quietly appalled by their hideous faces. He did not know whether they were men or demons, so he trembled as he saw to tea and a vegetarian meal for them. Noticing his fright, Sanzang said, "Don't be afraid, Your Excellency. My three disciples look hideous, but they are good at heart. As the saying goes, the faces are ugly but the men are kind. There's nothing to be afraid of about them."

The hostel superintendent's worries were eased when he heard this. "Where is your Tang court, Teacher of the Nation?" "In the land of China in the continent of Jambu," Sanzang replied. "When did you leave home?" was the next question. "In the thirteenth year of *Zhenguan*, fourteen years ago," Sanzang replied. "I had to cross thousands of rivers and mountains — it was very hard — to arrive here." "You are a holy monk," the hostel superintendent said. "How old is your exalted dynasty?" Sanzang asked. "This is the great land of India," the superintendent replied, "and the dynasty has endured for over five hundred years since our High Ancestor. Our reigning sovereign, who is a lover of landscapes and flowers, is known as the Happy Emperor. His reign-period is called *Jingyan* and is now in its twenty-eighth year." "I would like to have an audience with His

Majesty today to have the passport inspected and returned," said Sanzang. "When does he hold court?" "Splendid," the superintendent said, "absolutely splendid. Today is the twentieth birthday of Her Royal Highness, the king's daughter. A decorated tower has been built at the crossroads, where the princess is going to throw down an embroidered ball to let heaven decide who her husband is to be. Today is a very lively one, and I believe that His Majesty will not yet have finished his morning audience. This would be a good time to go if you wish to have your passport inspected and returned." Sanzang was just about to set happily off when the meal was brought in, so he ate it with the superintendent, Monkey and the other two.

By now it was past midday, and Sanzang said, "I had better be going." "I'll escort you, Master," said Brother Monkey. "Me too," said Pig. "No, don't, brother," put in Friar Sand. "Your face is nothing much to look at, so there's no point in your going to look impressive outside the palace gates. Best let our big brother go." "Wujing is right," Sanzang commented. "The idiot is coarse and stupid. Wukong is more clever and subtle." The idiot thrust his snout out and said, "Apart from you, Master, there's not much to choose between our three faces." Sanzang then put on his cassock. Monkey took the passport case and accompanied him. In the streets everyone — gentleman, peasant, artisan, trader, scholar, pen-pusher, dim-wit, or common man — was exclaiming, "Let's go and see the embroidered ball being thrown." Sanzang stood beside the road and said to Monkey, "People, clothes, buildings, language and speech here are all the same as in our Great Tang. I remember that my late mother married after throwing an embroidered ball to make the match she was destined for, and they have that custom here too." "What about us going to take a look too?" asked Monkey. "No, no," Sanzang replied. "We are not wearing the right clothes for the occasion. We might arouse suspicion." "Master," said Monkey, "you've forgotten what the ancient monk in the Spread Gold Monastery told us. We could find out whether she is genuine or not while we're taking a good look at the decorated tower. With all this bustle and activity the king is bound to be going to hear the princess's good news. He won't bother with court business. Let's go." On hearing this Sanzang did indeed go with Monkey. All kinds of people were there to watch the throwing of the embroidered ball. Oh dear! Little did they know that by going they were like a fisherman casting his hook and line and catching himself trouble.

The story now explains that two years earlier the king of India had taken his queen, consorts and daughter into the royal garden to enjoy a moonlit night because he so loved landscapes and flowers. This had provoked an evil spirit, who had carried the princess off and turned herself into the girl's double. When she learned that the Tang Priest was coming at this time, day, month and year the evil spirit had used the wealth of the kingdom to build the decorated tower in the hope of winning him as her mate and absorbing his true masculine primal essence to make herself a superior immortal of the Great Monad. At the third mark of the noonday hour, when Sanzang and Monkey had joined in the crowd and were approaching the tower, the princess lit some incense and prayed to heaven and earth. She was surrounded by five or six dozen exquisitely made-up beauties who were attending her and holding her embroidered ball for her. The tower had many windows on all sides. As the princess looked around she saw the Tang Priest approaching, so she took the embroidered ball and threw it with her own hands at the Tang Priest's head. It knocked his Vairocana mitre askew, giving him such a start that he immediately reached with both hands to steady the ball, which rolled down his sleeve. At once there were great shouts from everyone on the tower of, "She's hit a monk! She's hit a monk!"

Oh dear! All the travelling merchants at the crossroads pushed and shouted as they rushed to grab the embroidered ball to be met by Monkey with a shout and bared teeth as he bent forward then grew to the majestic height of thirty feet. The hideous face he made gave them all such a fright that they collapsed and crawled about, not daring to come closer. A moment later they had all scattered and Monkey resumed his true form. The maids, palace beauties and senior and junior eunuchs who had been in the tower all came up to the Tang Priest, kowtowed to him and said, "Your Highness, we beg you to come to the palace to be congratulated." Sanzang was quick to return their greetings and help them all back to their feet.

He then turned back to grumble at Monkey, "Ape! You've been trying to make a fool of me again." "It was your head the embroidered ball landed on," Monkey replied with a laugh, "and your sleeve it rolled into. Nothing to do with me, so what are you moaning at me for?" "What are we going to do?" Sanzang asked. "Stop worrying, Master," Monkey said. "While you go to the palace to see the king I'll go back to the hostel to tell Pig and Friar Sand to wait. If the princess doesn't want you, that'll be that. You submit the passport and we can be on our way. If the princess insists on marriage you must say to the king, 'Please send for my disciples so that I can take my leave of them.' When we three are summoned to court I'll be able to tell whether the princess is real or an impostor. This is the trick called 'subduing a demon through marriage'." The Tang Priest had nothing to say as Monkey turned away and went back to the hostel.

The venerable elder was hustled by the palace beauties and the rest of them to the foot of the tower, from where the princess came down to support him with her jade hand as they both entered the royal carriage. The retinue formed a procession to return to the palace gates. The eunuch gate-officer at once reported to the king, "Your Majesty, Her Royal Highness the princess is outside the Meridional Gate, holding a monk's arm and waiting to be summoned. I expect she hit him with her embroidered ball." The king was most displeased to hear this, and wanted to have the monk driven away, but as he did not know what the princess had in mind he restrained his feelings and summoned them in. The princess and the Tang Priest came in to stand beneath the throne hall. Indeed,

Man and future wife both hailed the king aloud;
Good and ill together with deep respect kowtowed.

When this ceremonial had been performed they were called into the throne hall, where the king began by asking, "Where are you from, monk? Did our daughter hit you with her ball?" The Tang Priest prostrated himself to reply, "I have been sent by the emperor of Great Tang in the continent of Jambu to the Western Heaven to worship the Buddha and seek the scriptures in the Great Thunder Monastery. As I carry a passport for this long journey I was coming to present it for inspection at Your Majesty's dawn audience when I passed a decorated tower at a crossroads, never imagining that Her Royal Highness the princess would throw an embroidered ball that would hit me on the head. As I am a monk and belong to a different faith I could not possibly marry your exquisite daughter, so I beg you to spare me the death penalty and return the passport. Then I can be on my way and soon reach Vulture Peak, see the Buddha, ask for the scriptures and return to my own country, where Your Majesty's divine mercy will be for ever recorded."

"So you are a holy monk from the east," the king replied. "Indeed, 'a thread can draw together a fated match across a thousand miles.' Our princess has reached the age of nineteen and is still unmarried, and as the hour, day, month and year are all now auspicious a decorated tower was set up for her to choose a good husband by throwing the ball from it. You just happened to be hit by it, and although this does not please us we would like to know the princess's views." "Your Majesty my father," the princess replied, kowtowing, "as the saying goes, 'Marry a cockerel and follow a cockerel; marry a dog and follow a dog.' I swore a vow beforehand, made the ball and told heaven, earth and the gods that heaven would choose as my husband the man my ball hit. As the ball hit the holy monk today this must have been fated ever since an earlier incarnation, which is why we met today. I would never dare to change my mind. I ask you to take him as your son-in-law."

Only then was the king happy, and he commanded the chief royal astrologer to choose a day. While organizing the trousseau the king issued proclamations to the world. When Sanzang heard this, so far from thanking the king for his kindness, he pleaded

"Forgive me, forgive me." "You're most unreasonable, monk," the king replied. "We offer you a nation's wealth to be our son-in-law. Why won't you stay here and enjoy yourself? All you can think about is fetching the scriptures. If you go on refusing we will have the palace guards take you out and behead you." The venerable elder was so frightened by this that his sould left his body as he kowtowed, trembling, and submitted, "I am grateful for Your Majesty's heavenly grace, but there are four of us monks travelling west. I have three disciples outside. If I am now to be taken as your son-in-law I beg you to summon them inside as I have not yet taken my leave of them. Then you can return the passport and let them go at once, so that they will not fail in the purpose of their journey to the west." The king approved this request, asking, "Where are your disciples?" "In the government hostel for foreigners," Sanzang replied, and officers were at once sent to fetch the holy monk's disciples to receive the passport and be on their way, leaving the holy monk there to be the princess's husband. The venerable elder could only rise to his feet and stand in attendance.

For the Great Elixir not to leak away the Triple Completeness is needed;
Blame an evil fate if the ascetic way is hard.
The Way is in the sage traditions; cultivation depends on the self;
Goodness is accumulated by people, but blessings come from Heaven.
Do not give play to the six sense-organs and their many desires;
Open up the single nature, original and primary.
When there are no attachments or thoughts, purity comes of itself;
Strive for liberation and achieve transcendence.

We will say no more of how officers were sent to the hostel to fetch Sanzang's three disciples.

Instead the story tells how Monkey, after taking his leave

of Sanzang at the foot of the decorated tower, went happily back to the hostel, laughing aloud as he walked. "Why are you laughing so cheerfully, brother," Pig and Friar Sand asked as they greeted him, "and why's the master disappeared?" "The master has found happiness," Monkey replied. "What happiness?" Pig asked. "He hasn't reached the end of the journey, he hasn't seen the Buddha and he hasn't fetched the scriptures." "The master and I only got as far as the foot of a decorated tower at the crossroads," Brother Monkey replied. "Just then the king's daughter hit the master with an embroidered ball, so he was hustled by palace beauties, pretty girls and eunuchs to the front of the tower, where he climbed into a carriage to go to the palace with the princess. He's been invited to become the king's son-in-law. Isn't that something to be cheerful about?"

When Pig heard this he stamped, beat his chest and said, "If I'd known beforehand, I'd have gone too. It was all Friar Sand's fault for making trouble. I'd have run straight to the foot of the decorated tower, the embroidered ball would have hit me first time, and the princess would have taken me for her husband. That would have been marvellous, terrific. I'm handsome and good-looking: I'd have been just the man. We'd all have been in luck and have had a good time. It'd have been real fun." Friar Sand went up to Pig, rubbed his face and said, "Shameless, you're shameless! That's a handsome mug, I must say. You're like the man who bought an old donkey for three-tenths of an ounce of silver and boasted that he'd be able to ride it. If she'd hit you first time she wouldn't have wanted to wait till tonight before burning spells to get rid of you. Do you think she'd have let trouble like you into the palace?" "You're being very disagreeable, you blacky," Pig replied. "Ugly I may be, but I've got class. As the old saying goes, 'When skin and flesh are coarse, the bones may yet be strong: everyone is good at something.' " "Stop talking nonsense, idiot," Monkey retorted, "and pack the baggage. I expect the master will get anxious and send for us, so we must be ready to go to protect him at court." "You're wrong again, brother," said Pig. "If the master's become the king's son-in-law and gone to take his pleasure with the king's daughter, he won't be climbing any more mountains, or tramping along the road, or running into demons and monsters. So what'll he want you to protect him from? He's old enough to know what happens under the bedcovers. He won't need you to hold him up." Monkey grabbed Pig by the ear, swung his fist, and said abusively, "You're as dirty-minded as ever, you cretin! How dare you talk such nonsense!"

While they were in the middle of their quarrel the hostel superintendent came to report, "His Majesty has sent an official here with a request for you three holy monks to present yourselves." "What's he really asking us to go for?" "The senior holy monk had the good fortune to be hit by the princess's golden ball and be taken as her husband," the superintendent replied, "which is why the official has come with invitations for you." "Where is the official?" Monkey asked. "Send him in." The official then bowed in greeting to Monkey, after which he did not dare look straight at Monkey as he muttered to himself, "Is it a ghost? a monster? a thunder god? a yaksha?" "Why are you mumbling instead of saying whatever you have to say, official?" Monkey asked. Trembling with terror, the official raised the royal edict with both hands as his words came tumbling out in confusion: "Her Royal Highness — invitation — meet her new relations — Her Royal Highness — meet her relations — invitation. . . ." "We've got no torture equipment here and we're not going to beat you," Pig said, "so don't be frightened and take your time telling us." "Do you think he's scared you're going to beat him?" Monkey said. "What he's scared of is your ugly mug. Get the carrying-pole load packed up at once. We're taking the horse and going to court to see the master and talk things over." Indeed,

One you meet on a narrow path is hard to avoid;
Determination can turn love to hatred.

If you do not know what was said when they met the king, listen to the explanation in the next instalment.

CHAPTER NINETY-FOUR

The four monks dine to music in the palace gardens; One demon loves in vain and longs for bliss.

The story tells how Brother Monkey and the other two disciples went with the official who had brought the invitation to outside the Meridional Gate of the palace, where the eunuch gate officer immediately reported their arrival and brought back a summons for them to enter. The three of them stood in a row, not bowing. "Are you three gentlemen the illustrious disciples of the holy monk? What are your names? Where do you live? Why did you become monks? What scriptures are you going to fetch?" Monkey then came closer, intending to enter the throne hall. "Don't move," one of the king's bodyguards shouted. "If you have anything to say, say it standing down there." "We monks like to step forward whenever we're given an opening," Monkey said with a smile, at which Pig and Friar Sand too approached the king. Worried that their rough manners would alarm the king, Sanzang stepped forward and called out, "Disciples, His Majesty has asked you why you have come here. You must submit your reply." Seeing his master standing in attendance beside the king, Monkey could not restrain himself from calling aloud, "Your Majesty is treating yourself with respect but others with contempt. If you are taking my master as your son-in-law, why do you make him stand in attendance on you? The normal custom is for a king to call his son-in-law Your Excellency, and an Excellency really ought to be sitting down." This gave the king so bad a fright that he turned pale and wished he could leave the throne hall. But as this would have looked very bad he had to summon up his courage and tell his attendants to fetch an embroidered stool on which he invited the Tang Priest to sit.

Only then did Brother Monkey submit the following spoken memorial: "My ancestral home is the Water Curtain Cave in the Mountain of Flowers and Fruit in the land of Aolai in the Eastern Continent of Superior Body.

My father was heaven, my mother earth,
And I was born when a rock split open.
I took as my master a Taoist adept,
And mastered the Great Way.
Then I returned to my land of immortals,
Where I gathered all of us to live in our cave heaven.
In the ocean's depths I subdued the dragons,
Then climbed the mountains to capture wild beasts.
I removed us from the registers of death,
Put us on the rolls of the living,
And was appointed Great Sage Equalling Heaven.
I enjoyed the heavenly palaces,
And roamed around the splendid buildings.
I met the immortals of Heaven
In daily carousals;
Lived in the holy regions,
Happy every day.
But because I disrupted the Peach Banquet,
And raised a rebellion in the palaces of Heaven,
I was captured by the Lord Buddha
And imprisoned under the Five Elements Mountain.
When hungry I was fed on pellets of iron,
When thirsty I drank molten copper:
For five hundred years I tasted no food or tea.
Fortunately my master came from the east
To worship in the west.
Guanyin told him to deliver me from heavenly disaster.
I was rescued from my torment
To be converted to the Yogacarin sect.
My old name was Wukong;
Now I am known as the Novice."

When the king realized how important Monkey was he quickly came down from his dragon throne and walked over to stead the venerable elder with his hand and say, "Son-in-law, it wa divine providence that brought us one such as yourself to be ou kinsman through marriage." Sanzang thanked the king pro foundly for his graciousness and urged him to return to hi throne. "Which gentleman has the distinction of being th second disciple?" the king asked. Pig thrust his snout out t make himself look more impressive as he replied:

"In previous lives old Pig used to be
Given to pleasure and indolence.
I lived in confusion,
My nature disordered and my heart deluded.
I did not know how high the sky was or how deep th earth;
I could not tell the ocean's width or the mountains' dis tance.
Then in the middle of my idleness
I suddenly met a true immortal.
In half a sentence
He undid the net of evil;
With two or three remarks
He smashed the gate to disaster.
Then I became aware,
Took him as my master on the spot,
Diligently studied the arts of the Double Eight,
Respectfully refined the Triple Three's sequence.
When training was complete I was able to fly,
And ascend to the heavenly palace.
The Jade Emperor in his benevolence
Appointed me as Marshal Tian Peng,
To command the marines of the River of Heaven,
And wander at ease within the palace gates.
Then when I was drunk at the Peach Banquet
I misbehaved with the goddess of the moon,
Was stripped of my commission,
And exiled to the mortal world.

Because I came into the wrong womb
I was born with the likeness of a pig.
Living at the Mount of Blessing
I committed unbounded evil.
When I met the Bodhisattva Guanyin
She showed me the way of goodness.
I came over to the Buddhist faith
To escort the Tang Priest
On his journey to the Western Heaven,
Seeking the marvellous scriptures.
My Dharma name is Wuneng,
And people call me Bajie."

When the king heard this he trembled with fear, not daring to look at him. This made the idiot more spirited than ever, shaking his head, pursing his lips, thrusting his ears up and roaring with laughter. Sanzang, worried that Pig was giving the king a fright, shouted, "Control yourself, Bajie." Only then did Pig put his hands together and pretend to behave himself. "And why was the third distinguished disciple converted?" the king then asked. Putting his hands together, Friar Sand said:

"I was originally a mortal man,
Who turned to the Way out of fear of the Wheel of Reincarnation.
I wandered like a cloud to the corners of the seas,
Roamed to the very ends of the sky.
I always wore the robe and held the begging-bowl,
And ever concentrated my mind within the body.
Because of my sincerity
I fell in with immortals,
Raised the Baby Boy,
To mate him with the Lovely Girl.
When the Three Thousand Tasks were achieved
*All was combined in the Four Images.**
I rose above the boundary of the sky,

* These terms refer to the esoteric practices of physiological alchemy.

Bowed to the dark vault of heaven,
And was appointed Curtain-lifting General.
I was in attendance on the Phoenix and Dragon Carriage,
And General was my rank.
Because at the Peach Banquet
I accidentally smashed a crystal bowl
I was exiled to the Flowing Sands River,
My face was altered,
And I became an evil killer.
Fortunately the Bodhisattva travelled to the east
To persuade me to turn to the faith
And await the Buddha's son from Tang,
Who would go to seek scriptures in the Western Heaven.
I became his follower and made a fresh start,
Refining once more my great awareness.
I took my surname Sand from the river;
My Buddhist name is Wujing,
And my title Friar."

The king was both most alarmed and most delighted to hear this. Delighted because his daughter had found herself a living Buddha, and alarmed by three veritable evil gods. Just as the king was being torn between alarm and delight the chief astrologer submitted this memorial: "The wedding has been set for the twelfth day of this month, the day of water-rat, a lucky time at which all will be auspicious for nuptials." "What day is it today?" the king asked. "Today is the eighth, the day of earth-monkey," the astrologer replied, "the day on which gibbons offer fruit, and the right day on which to advance worthies and accept their suggestions." This greatly pleased the king, who sent his officials in attendance to have the halls and pavilions in the royal garden swept clear. Here he invited his future son-in-law with his three distinguished disciples to stay while they waited for the nuptial feast at which the princess would marry him. The underlings all carried out their instructions, the king ended the audience and the officials withdrew.

The story now tells how when Sanzang and his disciples reached the imperial garden night was falling. A vegetarian meal was laid on. "We really deserve a meal today," said Pig with delight. The people in charge brought in plain rice and pasta by the carrying-pole load. Pig kept eating a bowlful then taking a refill over and over again. He only stopped eating when his stomach was completely full. A little later the lamps were lit and the bedding laid out, after which everyone went to bed. As soon as the venerable elder saw that there was nobody around he started to shout angrily at Monkey, telling him off. "You macaque, Wukong! You keep ruining me. I said we were just going to present the passport and told you not to go near the decorated tower. Why did you keep demanding to take me there to have a look? Well, did you have a good enough look? Whatever are we to do about this trouble you have got us into?" "Master," replied Monkey, putting on a smile, "it was you who said, 'My late mother married after throwing an embroidered ball to make the match she was destined for.' I only took you there because you seemed to want to enjoy something of the past. Besides, because I remembered what the ancient monk in the Almsgiver's Spread Gold Monastery said I came here to find out whether she's an impostor or not. When I saw the king just now there was something a bit sinister about the way he looked, but I haven't yet seen what the princess is like."

"What will happen when you see the princess?" the venerable elder asked. "My fiery eyes with their golden pupils can tell whether someone's true or false, good or evil, rich or poor," Monkey replied. "I'll know what to do and be able to sort out right and wrong." "So you've learnt physiognomy in the last few days, elder brother," said Friar Sand and Pig with a smile. "Physiognomists are just my grandson," Brother Monkey replied. "Stop joking," shouted Sanzang. "He definitely wants me now. What are we to do about it?" "At that happy occasion on the twelfth the princess is bound to come out to pay her respects to her parents," said Monkey. "I'll take a look at her from where I'll stand by the side. If she really is a woman you can be her consort and enjoy the kingdom's glory and splendour." This made Sanzang angrier than ever. "You're a fine ape," he said abusively, "still trying to ruin me. As Wuneng said, we have already done ninety-seven or ninety-eight hundredths of the journey. You're trying to destroy me with your crafty tongue again. Shut up! Don't open that stinking mouth of yours any more. Next time there's any misbehaviour from you I shall start reciting that spell again, and that will be more than you can take." The mention of the spell being recited had Monkey falling straight to his knees before Sanzang and pleading, "Don't say it, don't say it! If she's really a woman we'll all raise a rumpus in the palace during the wedding ceremony and get you out." While master and disciples were talking they had not noticed that it was now night. Indeed,

Slow dripped the clepsydras;
Heavy hung the fragrance of the flowers.
Pearl curtains hung over splendid doorways;
No fire or light was seen in the still courtyard.
Empty was the shadow of the deserted swing;
All was silence when the flute's notes died away.
The room was surrounded by flowers and bright in the moonbeams,
Lit by those spiky stars not blocked by any trees.
The cuckoo rested from her song;
Long was the butterfly's dream.
The River Way spanned the celestial vault
While white clouds made their way home.
Just when they were closest in feeling
The willows swaying in the wind were more dispiriting than ever.

"It's late, Master," said Pig. "Let's carry on arguing tomorrow morning. Go to sleep now, go to sleep!" Master and disciples did then get a night's sleep.

The golden cockerel was soon greeting the dawn, and the king entered the throne hall for his audience. This is what could be seen:

A purple aura rising high above the opened palace
As the winds carried royal music to the azure sky.
While clouds drifted, the leopard-tail banners moved;
The sun shone upon the demon figures on the roof, and the jade pendants tinkled.
A scented mist delicately touched the palace's green willows,
While dewdrops lightly moistened the garden flowers.
A thousand officials in ranks shouted and danced in homage:
Seas and rivers were at peace and the state was unified.

When all the civil and military officials had paid their homage to him, the king proclaimed, "The Department of Foreign Relations will arrange a nuptial banquet for the twelfth. Today the spring wine shall be prepared, and our future son-in-law shall be entertained in the royal gardens." The Protocol Office were told to lead the three worthy future royal in-laws to sit in the state hostel while the Department of Foreign Relations laid on a vegetarian banquet for the three of them. The two departments arranged for the musicians of the court orchestra to play and look after them while they passed the days enjoying the beauty of spring. As soon as Pig heard this he said "Your Majesty, we always stay with our master: we never leave him for a moment. As he's going to be drinking and feasting in the palace gardens we'd better go along for a couple of days' fun too if our master's to be your son-in-law. Otherwise the deal's off." Seeing how ugly and coarse-spoken Pig was, twisting his head and neck, thrusting his snout out and waving his ears — which all made him seem rather intimidating — the king was so worried that Pig might ruin the wedding that he had to accede to the request. "Prepare a banquet for two in the Sino-Barbarian Hall of Eternal Pacification for our son-in-law and ourself. Prepare a meal for the other three gentlemen in the Pavilion of Lingering Spring. We are afraid that it might be inconvenient for master and disciples to sit together." Only then did the idiot chant his respects to the king and thank him. Everyone then withdrew, after which the king ordered the officials of the inner palace to prepare a banquet, and told the queens and consorts of the three palaces and six compounds to give the princess hair ornaments, cakes and other things for the wedding on the twelfth.

It was now about ten in the morning, and the king had a carriage ready in which to take the Tang Priest and the others to go to see the palace gardens. The gardens were a fine place:

The paths, inlaid with coloured stones,
Have carved and chiselled balustrades.
Beside the paths inlaid with coloured stones
Strange flowers spread over the rocks;
Outside the carved and chiselled balustrades,
And within them too, flower blossoms rare.
Early peach trees are a bewitching turquoise,
And golden orioles dart among the willows.
The walker finds the fragrance fill his sleeve,
And many pure scents imbue his clothing.
Phoenix terrace and dragon pool,
Bamboo lodge and pine pavilion.
On the phoenix terrace
Pipes are played to lure the phoenix to appear;
In the dragon pools
Fish are reared to become dragons and leave.
In the bamboo lodge are poems
Whose well-chosen words match the "White Snow Melody";
The books in the pine pavilion
Are pearls and jade in blue-covered volumes.
Rocks and jade twist around the artificial hills;
Deep are the blue-green waters of the winding stream.
Peony pavilions,
Rose bowers,
Make a natural brocade.
Trellises of jasmine,
Beds of begonia,
Are like sunset clouds or jewelled mosaics.

Herbaceous peonies are marvellously fragrant;
Rare is the beauty of the mallows from Sichuan.
White pear and red apricot blossom vie in scent;
Purple orchid and golden daylily compete in splendour.
Corn poppy,
Lily magnolia buds,
Azalea flowers,
Are brilliantly coloured.
Magnolia flowers,
Garden balsam,
Plantain lilies,
Tremble.
Everywhere red shines through the richness of cosmetics
While heavy scents drift from a brocade surrounding screen.
The warmth returning with the east wind is greeted with joy;
All the garden's beauties display their brilliance.

The king and his companions walked around enjoying the flowers for a long time. Soon the officials of the Protocol Office came to invite Monkey and the other two to the Pavilion of Lingering Spring while the king led the Tang Priest by the hand to the Sino-Barbarian Hall so that they could all drink and feast These were splendid occasions with singing, dancing and instrumental music. Indeed,

The sun shone from the majestic palace gates;
Good auras filled the royal buildings.
The spring spread out an embroidery of flowers,
And heaven's light shone from afar on the court robes.
Pipes and singers wafted their music as if in a banquet of immortals;
The goblets flew, carrying jade liquor.
Master and subjects enjoyed the same pleasure
As Sino-barbarian peace brought prosperity.

Seeing with what great respect he was being treated by the king, the venerable elder had nothing for it but to force himself to join in the celebrations. In fact he gave only a show of happiness: inside he was miserable. As he sat there he saw four golden screens hanging on the wall, screens painted with scenes of the four seasons. Each picture had a poem on it by a famous academician. The poem on the spring scene read:

The vital forces of heaven turn creation around;
The world is happy and everything is renewed.
The peach and the plum blossoms vie in splendour;
Swallows fly to the painted rafters, shaking the incense dust.

The poem on the summer scene read:

In warm and sultry air all thoughts are slow
The palace mallow and pomegranate reflect the sun's brilliance.
The jade flute's music disturbs the noonday dream;
The scent of caltrops is wafted through the curtains.

The poem on the autumn scene read:

One leaf on the parasol tree by the well is yellow;
The pearl curtain is not rolled up on the night of frost.
After the autumn sacrifice the swallows abandon their nest;
When the rush flowers snap, the wild geese leave for another land.

The poem on the winter scene read:

The clouds fly over the rainy sky, all dark and cold;
The north wind blows the snow into thousands of hills.
Deep in the palace the stove glows warm;
They say the plum has blossomed by the jade balustrade.

When the king noticed the absorption with which the Tang Priest was gazing at the poems he said, "As you enjoy savouring the poems so much you must be a fine poet yourself, son-in-law. If you do not begrudge your pearls we would like to invite you to make up a matching poem for each of them, ending three of the lines with the same word. Will you agree?" The venerable elder was the sort of person who could be so carried away by a scene that he forgot the circumstances, someone who had an enlightened mind and thoroughly comprehended his own nature, so when the king pressed him so earnestly to match the verses he found himself saying the line, "The sun's warmth melts the ice the world around." This greatly pleased the king, who told the officials in attendance on him, "Fetch the four treasures of the study, so that our son-in-law can write down the matching verses he composes for us to savour at our leisure." The venerable elder was glad to comply. Picking up a brush, he produced matching lines. The matching poem on the spring scene read:

The sun's warmth melts the ice the world around;
Within the palace garden, flowers are renewed.
Gentle winds and rain enrich the people;
Rivers and seas are calm; gone is all worldly dust.

The matching poem on the summer scene read:

The Dipper now points south; the day goes slow;
Locust and pomegranate trees contend in brilliance.
Golden oriole and purple swallow sing in the willows,
Their melodious voices drifting through red curtains.

The matching poem on the autumn read:

Fragrant the green mandarin; the orange turns to yellow.
Blue pine and cypress welcome frost's coming.
Half-open chrysanthemums make a tapestry on the trellis;
Pipes and songs waft through the watery, cloud-covered land.

The matching poem on the winter scene read:

As skies clear after welcome snow the air is cold;
Grotesque-shaped crags and boulders mark jade hills.
As charcoal burns in the stove to warm the yoghurt
Singing with hands in their sleeves they lean on jade balustrades.

The king was utterly delighted by the matching verses. " 'Singing with hands in their sleeves they lean on jade balustrades' is really good," he said with admiration, and ordered the royal orchestra to set the new poems to music. The banquet did not break up until the day was over.

Brother Monkey and the other two were also having a splendid meal in the Pavilion of Lingering Spring. Each of them was feeling rather merry after downing a few cups, and they decided to go to see their master, who was in another building with the king. This made Pig start acting like the idiot he was. "This is great," he yelled at once. "We're doing very nicely here. Today we've had a right good time. But now we're full we ought to go to sleep it off." "You really are ill-bred, brother," said Friar Sand with a grin. "How could you possibly go to sleep when you're as full as that?" "You wouldn't know," said Pig. "There's a saying that goes,

Unless you stretch out for a nap when you've dined
How can your belly with fat be well lined?"

When the Tang Priest had taken his leave of the king he went back to the pavilion and scolded Pig: "Cretin! You acted coarser than ever. What sort of place do you think this is, to shout and yell like that? If you had made the king angry he would have had you killed." "Don't worry," Pig replied, "don't worry. We're being treated as his in-laws, so it would be very awkward for him to get angry with us. As the proverb goes,

If you're related a beating can't rend it;
If you are neighbours a cursing won't end it.

We were only joking. He's nothing to be frightened of." At this the venerable elder shouted, "Bring the idiot here. Give him twenty strokes of the dhyana staff." Monkey then grabbed Pig and knocked him over, while Sanzang raised the cudgel to beat him. "Master, Royal Son-in-law," the idiot shouted, "Spare me! Spare me!" One of the officials who was present at the banquet persuaded Sanzang not to hit Pig, who clambered back on his feet, grumbling, "You're a fine excellency; you're a fine royal son-in-law. Applying the royal law before you're even married!" "Stop that nonsense," said Monkey, making a face at him, "stop that nonsense! Go to bed at once." They then spent another night in the Lingering Spring Pavilion. The next morning they feasted as before.

Before long they had been enjoying themselves for three or four days, by when it was that splendid day, the twelfth. The officials of the three sections of the Department of Foreign Relations all submitted a memorial that said, "Since we received the edicts on the eighth the palace for the Royal Son-in-law has been built, and all that we are waiting for is for the trousseau to be installed. The nuptial banquet has been prepared, with meat and vegetarian food for over five hundred guests." This greatly pleased the king, who was just going to invite his future son-in-law to come to the banquet when a eunuch from the inner quarters of the palace reported to him, "Your Majesty, Her Majesty the Queen asks you to come." The king then withdrew to the inner quarters of the palace, where the queens of the three palaces and the consorts of the six compounds brought the princess to the Sunlight Palace to talk and joke together. The place was truly a mass of flowers or brocade. The magnificence and beauty was more than a match for the halls of heaven or the moon's pavilions; nor was it inferior to the jade palaces of immortals. There are four new lyrics on the "Happy Gathering and Splendid Wedding" about it. The lyric "Happy" goes:

Happy! Happy!
Delight and bliss!
The wedding is celebrated
With its love and beauty.
Elegant court dresses
That the Lady of the Moon could never rival;
Dragon and phoenix hairpins,
Sumptuous threads of flying gold.
Cherry lips, white teeth and rouge-red cheeks
Sylphs with forms as delicate as flowers.
Brocades upon brocades,

An extravagance of colour,
Full of fragrance,
A host of princesses.

The lyric "Gathering" goes:

Gathering! Gathering!
Bewitching charms,
Rivalling the great beauties of the past,
Enough to topple a city or a state,
Like flowers or jade.
Dressed to make them lovelier still,
Even more dazzling in their finery,
And the splendour of their jewels.
Their orchid hearts and natures were pure and lofty;
Noble were their powder-white faces and ice-smooth skin.
The lines of their painted eyebrows were like distant hills;
They formed a throng of willowy elegance.

The lyric "Splendid" goes:

Splendid! Splendid!
Jade girls, fairy maidens,
Utterly adorable,
Truly to be admired,
Perfumed with fine fragrances,
Adorned with cosmetics.
Although far from the Tiantai paradise,
This was no mere palace of a king.
Sweet were their smiling words
As the sound of pipes and songs was wafted around.
A thousand beauties, massed flowers, a splendid brocade:
How could its match be found in the world?

The lyric "Wedding" goes:

Wedding! Wedding!

Orchid Fragrance,
Ranks of fairy girls,
Crowds of beauties.
The royal concubines have put on new splendour;
The princesses are in fresh garments.
Piled clouds of raven hair,
Rainbow gowns over phoenix skirts.
Soft music of immortals,
Two rows of purple and red.
In the past they pledged to ride in one phoenix chariot;
This morning is the happy occasion and the splendid wedding.

When the king arrived his queens and consorts led the princess and the other palace ladies out to meet him. The delighted king took them into the Sunlight Palace to sit down. When the queens, consorts and others had made their obeisances the king said, "Princess, my good daughter, we think that your heart's desire was fulfilled when you had the good fortune to find the holy monk by throwing your ball from the decorated tower on the eighth. The officials of all the departments have been most understanding of our wishes, so that everything is now ready. As today is a lucky one let us hurry to the nuptial banquet and not be late." The princess stepped forward, went down in a kowtow, and submitted this petition: "Your Majesty my father, I beg you to forgive your daughter for her effrontery, but I have a request to make. In the last few days it has been reported in the inner quarters of the palace that the Tang Priest has three extremely hideous disciples. I couldn't bring myself to see them: I'm afraid the sight would terrify me. So I beg you, Father, to send them out of the city. Otherwise the shock might be too much for my frail health and lead to disaster." "If you had not mentioned them, child," the king replied, "we would have very nearly forgotten about them. They are indeed rather ugly, and for the last few days we have had them entertained in the Lingering Spring Pavilion. When we go into the throne hall this morning we will return their passport and tell them to leave the city so that we can hold our banquet." The princess then kowtowed again in thanks, after which the king left in his carriage to enter the throne hall and issue a decree inviting his son-in-law and the other three gentlemen to attend.

Now the Tang Priest had been following the dates by counting on his fingers, so when he reached the twelfth he had a discussion with his three disciples before dawn. "It is the twelfth today," he said. "How are we to cope?" "I've already noticed something of an ill-omened air about the king," Brother Monkey replied, "but the evil hasn't actually infected him or done any great harm. The only thing is that I've not yet had a look at the princess. If she comes out and lets me take a peep at her I'll know whether she's an impostor or not, then I'll do something. Don't worry. He's bound to summon us now and send us three away from the city. Accept the invitation and don't be afraid. I'll slip back and stay close to you to protect you." As master and disciples were talking a royal equerry did indeed come with officials from the protocol office to bring an invitation. "Let's go," said Monkey, "let's go. I'm sure they're going to see us three on our way and keep you here, Master, for the wedding." "If they're seeing us off they're bound to give us hundreds and thousands of ounces of gold and silver," said Pig. "We'll be able to buy some presents to take home with us. When I get back to my in-laws' place I'll be able to have a bit of fun again." "Shut up, second brother," said Friar Sand, "and stop talking such nonsense. We'll do what big brother says."

They then followed the officials to the foot of the throne hall steps, taking baggage and horse with them. When the king had greeted them he commanded Monkey and the other two to come forward. "Hand your passport up," he said, "and we shall seal it, sign it and return it to you. You three gentlemen will be generously provided with funds for your journey and escorted on your way to see the Buddha on Vulture Peak. If you come back with the scriptures you will also receive generous rewards. We shall keep our son-in-law here: there will be no need for you to worry about him." Monkey thanked the king, then told Friar Sand to take the passport out and hand it over. The king read it, sealed and signed it, then brought out ten ingots of gold and twenty of silver that he wanted to present to them as gifts for his in-laws. Pig, who always had been very keen on money and sex, stepped forward to accept them. Monkey then gave a respectful chant and said, "We've disturbed you." As Monkey turned to go Sanzang hastily scrambled to his feet, grabbed hold of him, and said through clenched teeth, "You are all abandoning me." Brother Monkey pinched the palm of Sanzang's hand, gave him a meaningful look and said, "Unwind and take your pleasure here while we go to fetch the scriptures. We'll call on you on our way back." Not knowing whether to believe this or not, the venerable elder refused to let him go. When all the officials saw this they took it for a real parting. Soon the king invited his son-in-law back into the throne hall, ordering the officials to escort the three gentlemen out of the city, whereupon Sanzang had to let go of Monkey and enter the hall.

As Brother Monkey and the other two went out through the palace gates they each took their leave. "Are we really going?" asked Pig. Monkey said nothing, and just walked back to the hostel, where the superintendent received them and provided tea and a meal. "You two stay here," Monkey said to Pig and Friar Sand, "and whatever you do, don't show your faces. If the hostel superintendent asks what's happening, give him vague answers. Don't say anything. I'm going off to look after the master."

The splendid Great Sage pulled out one of his hairs, blew on it with magic breath, called "Change!" and turned it into his own double to stay in the hostel with Pig and Friar Sand, while he himself leapt up into mid air in a flash, turning himself into a bee.

Yellow wings, sweet mouth and a sharp tail,
He dances wildly in the wind,
The brilliant thief of fragrance from the blossom
Who sways his way through willows and flowers.
With many a drenching for his troubles
He flies to and fro, but all in vain.

The thick delight he makes he never tastes;
All he can do is leave his fame behind.

Watch him as he flies lightly into the palace, where he saw the Tang Priest sitting on an embroidered stool at the king's left, frowning and worried at heart. Flying up to his master's Vairocana mitre, Monkey crept stealthily to his ear and said, "I'm here, Master, so don't fret." These words were heard by the Tang Priest alone, — none of the ordinary mortals had any hope of hearing them — so he felt relief at last. Before long a eunuch came with an invitation: "Your Majesty, the nuptial banquet is set out in the Jay Palace. Her Majesty and the princess are awaiting you in the inner quarters. They invite Your Majesty and His Excellency to go in for the wedding." Overwhelmed with happiness, the king went into the inner quarters with his son-in-law. Indeed,

The wicked king's love of flowers led to disaster;
When the dhyana mind starts thinking, each thought brings sorrow.

If you don't know how the Tang Priest escaped once in the inner quarters of the palace, listen to the explanation in the next instalment.

CHAPTER NINETY-FIVE

False and true form combine when the Jade Hare is captured; The true female is converted and meets with spiritual origin.

The story tells how the Tang Priest was feeling thoroughly miserable as he accompanied the king into the inner quarters, from where a great sound of drums and music arose and fine perfumes could be smelt. He kept his head bowed, not daring to look up. Monkey, secretly very pleased, had fixed himself to the Vairocana mitre, from where he used his magic light to look around with his fiery eyes and golden pupils. There were two ranks of court ladies, making it seem like a palace of flowers or immortals, and finer than a spring breeze blowing past a brocade screen. Indeed, they were

Graceful and charming,
Jadelike, and with ice-smooth skin.
Bewitching pairs more lovely than the girl of Chu,
Beauties two by two, rivalling the lady Xi Shi.
Their hair was coiled high like flying phoenixes;
Their eyebrows were just visible, low lines of distant hills.
Elegantly played the pipe and shawm;
Fast sounded flute and drum.
All the notes of the scale rang out,
Rising then falling again together.
Delightful were they as they danced and sang,
A carpet of flowers, every one of them lovely.

Seeing that his master was not in the least moved by this Monkey silently smacked his lips in admiration and said, "What a fine monk! What a fine monk!

Dwelling amid splendour, his heart forms no attachment;
Walking through magnificence, his mind is not confused."

A little later the princess came out of the Jay Palace surrounded by the queens and consorts to greet the king with cheers of "Long live the king! Long live the king!" This so alarmed the venerable elder that he trembled, not knowing what to do. By now Monkey had already noticed a touch of the demonic — though nothing very vicious — that could just be made out in the aura above the princess's head. Monkey crawled quickly to Sanzang's ear and said, "The princess is a fake, Master." "If she is a fake," the venerable elder replied, "then how are we to make her turn back into her real form?" "I'll give myself a magic body and catch her right here," said Monkey. "That would terrify His Majesty," said Sanzang. "Wait till he and his queens have withdrawn before using your magic."

Now Monkey had been impatient by nature all his life, so he could not restrain himself. With a great and angry roar he resumed his true form, rushed up and grabbed the princess. "You're a fine, evil beast," he said abusively. "You've had no end of luxury here, you impostor, but it wasn't enough for you. You're so sex-crazed you had to try to trick my master and destroy his primal masculinity." This struck the king speechless with fright, and made the queens and consorts fall about. The palace beauties all ran off to hide, fleeing for their lives. It was just like

A roaring wind in spring,
The howling autumn gale.
When the roaring wind in spring blows through the wood
A thousand blossoms are shaken;
When the howling autumn gale hits the park
Ten thousand leaves all swirl and fly.

The tree peony beneath the balustrade is snapped;
Herbaceous peonies beside the balcony fall over.
Hibiscus on the pond's banks are shaken all about.
While chrysanthemums are flung in heaps at the foot of the terrace.
The delicate begonia collapses in the dust;
The fragrant rose is now sleeping in the wilds.
The spring wind smashes caltrop, lotus and pear;
Winter snows weigh down the plum tree's tender blossoms.
The petals of the pomegranate
Are scattered all around the inner courtyard;
The branches of the willow
Are blown sideways within the royal palace.
Fine blooms, and a night of raging wind and rain:
Countless red petals carpet the ground with brocade.

Sanzang hastily put his trembling arms round the king and said, "Don't be afraid, Your Majesty. It is only my wicked disciple using his magical powers to find out whether she is an impostor or not."

Seeing that things were going badly for her, the evil spirit broke free, tore off her clothes, flung down her jewellery and hair ornaments and ran to the shrine of the local deity in the palace garden. From here she brought out a short club shaped like the head of a trip-hammer, with which she started hitting wildly at Monkey as she turned quickly towards him. Monkey, who had caught up with her at once, struck back at her face with his iron cudgel. Shouting and roaring at each other, the two of them started fighting in the palace gardens. Then each began a great display of magic powers, riding clouds as they battled in mid air. In this fight

Great was the fame of the gold-banded cudgel;
No one had heard of the hammerhead club.
One of them was there to fetch the true scriptures;
The other was lingering for love of rare flowers.

Long had the demon known of the holy Tang Priest,
And she longed to mate with his primal seed-juices.
In a past year she had carried off the real princess,
And taken the form of the king's true daughter.
When she met the Great Sage, who saw her evil aura,
He could tell true from false as he came to save a life.
The murderous club was flung at the head;
The mighty iron cudgel struck back at the face.
Ranting and roaring, they were locked in struggle,
Filling the skies and blotting out the sun.

As the two of them battled in mid air they terrified the common people of the city, and struck fear into all the officials at court. The venerable elder kept saying as he supported the king, "Don't be alarmed, and please tell Her Majesty and all the others not to be afraid. Your princess is an impostor pretending to be her. When my disciple has captured her you will be able to see whether she is good or evil." Some of the bolder consorts brought clothes and jewellery to show the queen. "These are what the princess wore. She tore them off and is fighting that monk up in the sky stark naked. She must be an evil spirit." Only then did the king, queens and consorts come to their senses and look up into the sky.

When the evil spirit and the Great Sage had been fighting for half a day without either emerging as victor Monkey threw his cudgel up and called "Change!" One turned into ten, ten into a hundred, and a hundred into a thousand. Half the sky was filled with writhing serpents and pythons striking wildly at the evil spirit. With a flurry of her hands and feet she turned into a pure wind and fled into the azure sky. Monkey said a spell, took all the iron cudgels back into a single cudgel, and went straight after her magic light. As he approached the Western Gate of Heaven and saw the dazzling flags and banners Monkey shouted at the top of his voice, "Heavenly gatekeepers, stop that evil spirit and don't let her get away." The gate was being held by the Heavenly King Lokapala with the four great marshals Pang, Liu, Gou and Bi, who did indeed use their weapons to block the way. As she could not get further she turned straight back and started fighting Monkey with her short club.

As he wheeled his iron cudgel the Great Sage looked carefully at her and saw that one end of her club was thick and one end thin, just like the head of a trip-hammer used for hulling with a mortar, so he gave a furious roar and shouted, "Beast! What's that implement you're holding? How dare you fight me with it? Surrender at once or I'll smash your skull with a single blow from my cudgel." Grinding her teeth, the evil spirit replied, "You don't know about this weapon of mine, so listen while I tell you:

Its immortal root was a piece of muttonfat jade,
Which took countless years to be worked into shape.
It was already mine when chaos was separated;
When the primal disorder was sorted out I came first.
Its origins cannot be compared with mere mortal things;
Its nature has always belonged to the highest heaven.
Embodying the golden light and the four images
With the auspicious vapours of the Five Elements and the Three Primaries.
Long did it live with me in the Moon Palace,
Staying beside me in the Cassia Hall.
For love of flowers I descended to the mortal world,
Coming to India as a beautiful impostor.
The only reason why I shared the King's pleasures
Was because I wanted my destined marriage with the Tang Priest.
How could you be so cruel as to ruin this fine mating,
Pursuing me and giving rein to your vicious nature?
Great is the fame of this implement of mine,
Which is older than your cudgel with gold bands.
It was a drug-pounding pestle in the Moon Palace:
One blow from this and a life is ended."

When Monkey heard this he replied with a mocking laugh, "Evil beast! If you used to live in the Toad Palace you must have heard of my powers. How dare you argue with me! Turn back into your real self and surrender at once if I'm to spare your life." "I know you," the monster replied. "You're the Protector of the Horses who made great havoc in the palaces of Heaven five hundred years ago. By rights I ought to give way to you, but because you've wrecked my marriage I hate you as much as if you'd killed my mother and father. It's more than I can stand for. I'm going to kill you, you Protector of the Horses, for breaking the laws of Heaven." The words Protector of the Horses always infuriated the Great Sage, so the moment he heard them he flew into a great rage, lifted his iron cudgel and struck at her face. The evil spirit swung her pestle in reply. A ferocious battle then ensued in front of the Western Gate of Heaven. In this combat there were

A gold-banded cudgel,
A drug-pounding pestle,
Two immortals' weapons, a worthy match.
One had come down to earth for the sake of a marriage;
The other was there to protect the Tang Priest.
It was because the king was not a righteous one
And loved flowers that he attracted the evil spirit,
Causing today's bitter strife
As two of them gave full play to their stubbornness of heart.
Charging and rushing each other they strove for triumph;
In cutting words they fought on with their tongues.
Rare was the martial prowess of the medicine pestle,
But finer still was the iron cudgel's might.
A powerful golden light flashed at the heavenly gates;
Brilliantly coloured mists went right down to the earth.
After a dozen rounds of fighting to and fro
The evil spirit became too weak to resist.

When the evil spirit had fought another dozen or so rounds with Brother Monkey she could see how thick and fast his blows were coming, and realized that she could not win. Feinting with her pestle, she shook herself and fled due south in ten thousand beams of golden light with the Great Sage in pursuit. Suddenly they reached a great mountain, where the evil spirit landed her golden light and disappeared into a cave. Monkey, who was worried that she might escape, return to India and do some underhand harm to the Tang Priest, made sure he could recognize the mountain then turned his cloud round and went straight back to the capital.

It was now about four in the afternoon. The king was clinging to Sanzang, shivering and shaking as he kept saying, "Save me, holy monk!" The consorts and queens were all in a panic as the Great Sage came down from the clouds with a cry of, "Here I am, Master!" "Stand still, Wukong," said Sanzang. "You must not alarm His Majesty. Now, I am asking you what in fact happened about the imitation princess." Standing outside the Jay Palace, Monkey put his hands together in front of his chest and said, "The imitation princess was an evil spirit. First of all I fought her for half a day, and she couldn't beat me, so she turned into a pure wind and fled straight to the gates of heaven. I shouted to the gods to block her way. She turned back into her real self and fought another dozen or so rounds with me. Then she turned herself into golden light and fled due south to a mountain, beaten. I chased her as fast as I could till I got to the mountain, but I couldn't find her anywhere. Then I came back because I was worried she might come here to harm you."

When the king heard this he grabbed hold of the Tang Priest and asked, "If the false princess was an evil spirit, where is my real princess?" "When I've caught the false princess your real princess will turn up by herself," Monkey replied straight away. When the queens and consorts heard this their fears vanished, and each of them came forward to bow and say, "We beg you to rescue our real princess, holy monk, and sort out the light from the dark. You will be richly rewarded." "This is no place for us to talk," said Monkey. "I beg Your Majesty to go from the inner quarters to the throne hall with my master. Her Majesty and the rest of them should all go back to the inner palace, and my fellow-disciples Pig and Friar Sand should be sent for to protect my master so that I can go and subdue the demon. That will keep a proper distinction between the inner and outer quarters of the palace, and spare me from worrying. I am going to sort this out to show my sincerity." The king accepted the suggestion and was boundlessly grateful. He led the Tang Priest out of the inner quarters and straight to the throne hall. All the queens and consorts returned to the inner palace. A vegetarian meal was ordered while Pig and Friar Sand were sent for. The two of them soon arrived. Monkey explained to them both about what had happened and told them to guard the master carefully. The Great Sage set off by his cloud somersault and flew up into mid air. All the officials in front of the throne hall looked up into the sky and bowed low.

The Great Sage Monkey went straight to the mountain that lay due south. When the evil spirit had fled in defeat to the mountain and gone into her den she blocked the entrance with boulders and lay hidden there, terrified. Having looked around for a while and seen no sign of life Monkey felt very impatient, so he made a spell with his hands and said the magic words, calling out the local deity and mountain god to be questioned. A moment later the two gods arrived, kowtowed and said, "We didn't realize, we didn't realize. If we had known we'd have gone a long way to meet you. We beg you to forgive us." "I won't hit you just now," Monkey said. "Tell me what this mountain's called. How many evil spirits are there here? Tell me the truth and I'll forgive you your crimes." "Great Sage," the two gods replied, "this mountain is called Mount Hairtip. There are three hare warrens in the mountain, but from remote antiquity there have never been any evil spirits here. This is a blessed land of five felicities. Great Sage, if you want to find an evil spirit, take the road to the Western Heaven." "I've reached the kingdom of India in the Western Heaven, where the king has a princess who was carried off by an evil spirit and abandoned in the wilds. The evil spirit turned herself into the princess's double to deceive the king into building a decorated tower from which she could throw an embroidered ball to find herself a husband. When I got to the foot of the tower while escorting the Tang Priest she deliberately hit the Tang Priest because she wanted to mate with him and lure his primal masculinity out of him. When I saw through her I turned back into myself in the palace to catch her. She threw off her human clothes and jewels and fought with me for half a day with a short club that she called a medicine-pounding pestle. Then she turned herself into a pure wind and disappeared. When I chased her as far as the Western Gate of Heaven and fought another dozen or more with her she realized she couldn't beat me, turned herself into golden light and fled here. Why didn't you see her!"

When the two gods heard this they led Brother Monkey to search the three warrens. When they first looked by the warren at the foot of the mountain a few frightened hares were startled and ran away. When their search reached the cave at the top of the mountain they saw that the entrance was blocked with two great boulders. "The evil spirit must have gone inside," the local god said, "when you were chasing her so hard." Monkey then prised the boulders apart with his iron cudgel. The evil spirit, who was indeed hiding in there, sprang out with a whoosh, raising her medicine pestle to strike him with. As Monkey swung his cudgel to parry her blow the mountain deity fell back in terror and the local god fled. From the demon's mouth came abusive grumbles: "Who told you to bring him here to find me?" She continued to fend off the iron cudgel as she fled up into mid air in a fighting retreat.

Just at the moment of crisis, when it was getting late in the day, Monkey became more vicious than ever and his blows were even harder. He wished he could finish her off with a single stroke. Just then a call came from the ninefold azure sky of, "Don't strike, Great Sage! Don't strike! Be kind with your cudgel." When Monkey turned round he saw that it was the Star Lord of the Moon leading his beauties and immortals down on multicoloured clouds to stand in front of him. A flustered Monkey at once put his iron cudgel away, bowed and said, "Where are you going, Old Man? I'm sorry I didn't keep out of your way." "The evil spirit fighting you is the Jade Hare who pounds the immortal elixir of mysterious dew in my palace," the Moon replied. "A year ago she secretly opened the golden locks on the jade gates and absconded from the palace. As I reckoned that she would be in mortal peril I have come here to save her life. I do beg you, Great Sage, to spare her life out of consideration for me." Monkey assented, saying only, "I wouldn't dare harm her, I wouldn't dare. No wonder she's so good with a medicine-pounding pestle. She's the Jade Hare. What you don't know, Old Moon, is that she has kidnapped the king of India's daughter, made herself into the princess's double, and wants to ruin my master's primal masculinity although he's a holy monk. This is the truth. We can't stand for crimes like that. How can you possibly let her off so lightly?"

"There are things you don't know," the Moon replied. "That king's daughter is no ordinary mortal. She was the White Beauty from the Moon Palace. Eighteen years ago she slapped the Jade Hare, after which she longed for the human world and came down to it in a beam of magic light to the womb of the king's senior queen. She was born then. The Jade Hare was getting her own back for that slap when she ran away from the palace last year and threw White Beauty into the wilds. But she was wrong to want to marry the Tang Priest. That's an offence she mustn't get away with. It was a good thing you were careful enough to see through her before she ruined your master. But I plead with you to forgive her for my sake and let me take her back." "If that's why it happened," Brother Monkey replied with a smile, "I wouldn't dare to make any objections. But if you take the Jade Hare back I'm worried that the king might not believe it, so I'd like to trouble you and the immortal sisters to take the Jade Hare over there to prove it to the king. Then I'll be able to show off my powers and explain how White Beauty came down to earth. I'll make the king fetch Princess White Beauty to prove the truth of retribution. The Moon was persuaded, so he pointed at the evil spirit and shouted, "Repent and submit, evil beast!" The Jade Hare rolled on the ground and turned back into her real form. Indeed she was

Gap-lipped and sharp-toothed,
Long-eared and with few whiskers.

Her body was covered with jade-coloured fur;
When she stretched out her legs she flew over mountains.
Her straight nose was like yoghurt,
Glossier than face-cream with powder.
Two eyes glowed red,
Brighter than dots of rouge on the snow.
Crouching on the ground
She was a heap of pure white silk;
When she stretched herself out
She was a structure of dazzling silver wire.
Often did she
Drink in the purest dew of the heavenly dawn,
Pounding the elixir with her pestle of jade.

When the Great Sage saw this he was delighted, and treading clouds and light he led the way as the Moon Lord brought all the beauties and immortals, taking the Jade Hare with them as they headed straight for India. It was now dusk, and the moon was slowly rising. When they reached the walls of the capital they heard the drums being beaten on the watch-towers. The king and the Tang Priest were still inside the throne hall, while Pig, Friar Sand and the officials were standing in front of the steps. They were just discussing whether the king should withdraw when a sheet of coloured cloud as bright as day was seen due south. When they all raised their heads to look they heard the Great Sage Monkey shouting at the top of his voice, "Your Majesty, King of India, ask your queens and consorts to come out and look. Under this canopy is the Star Lord of the Moon Palace, and the immortal sisters to either side of him are the beauties of the moon. This Jade Hare was the bogus princess of yours who has now turned back into her real form." The king then quickly called his queen, consorts, palace beauties and maids out, and they all kowtowed towards the sky. The king, the Tang Priest and the officials also bowed to the sky in thanks. There was nobody in any house throughout the whole city who did not set out an altar on which to burn incense, kowtow and recite the name of the Buddha.

Just when everyone was looking up Pig felt a surge of uncontrollable desire, leapt up into the air and flung his arms round an immortal girl dressed in a rainbow. "We're old friends, darling," he said. "Let's go and have a bit of fun." Monkey went up to Pig, grabbed hold of him, gave him a couple of slaps and swore at him: "You village idiot. What sort of place is this for getting randy?" "I was just going to chat her up for a bit of fun," said Pig. The Moon Lord had his celestial canopy turned about as he took the Jade Hare straight back to the Moon Palace with all his beauties.

Brother Monkey threw Pig down into the dust, then was thanked by the king in the throne hall. When the king was told what had happened he said, "We are very grateful to you, holy monk, for using your great magical powers to capture the imitation princess. But where is our real daughter?" "She is no ordinary human either," Monkey replied, "but the immortal girl White Beauty from the Moon Palace. Because she slapped the Jade Hare in the face eighteen years ago she yearned for the lower world, came down to the womb of Your Majesty's senior queen and was born here. It was because the Jade Hare nursed her old grudge that she surreptitiously opened the golden lock on the jade gates, came down here, abandoned White Beauty in the wilds and made herself look like White Beauty to deceive you. The Moon Lord himself told me about this chain of events. Today we've got rid of the imposter, and tomorrow I'll invite Your Majesty to go in your royal carriage to fetch the real one." This came as rather a shock to the king, who said with the tears streaming down his cheeks, "Daughter! In all the time since we came to the throne as a child we have never even gone outside the city gates. Where are we to go to look for you?" "No need to upset yourself," said Monkey with a smile. "Your daughter is now in the Almsgiver's Spread Gold Monastery, pretending to be mad. Everyone can go home now. Tomorrow morning I'll bring your real princess back to you." "Please stop worrying, Your Majesty," the officials all said, kowtowing. "These holy monks are all Buddhas who can ride clouds and mists: they are sure to know all about causes and effects in the future and the past. If we trouble the holy monks to come with us tomorrow to look for her we will learn the truth." Accepting their suggestion, the king invited the monks to the Lingering Spring Pavilion, where a vegetarian meal was provided and they were to spend the night. By now it was almost the second watch. Indeed,

The copper water-clock drips in the moon's bright glow;
The chimes of the golden bell are carried by the wind.
When the cuckoo sings the spring is half-way gone;
The blossoms fall aimlessly as the third watch draws near.
The swing casts a shadow in deserted royal gardens;
The silver river spans the sky's blue vault.
No travellers are to be seen in markets and streets;
The constellations make the night sky shine.

That night they all went to bed, and of that no more need be said.

During the night the king lost his demonic aura, and his spirit grew with great speed, so that at three marks after the fifth watch he came out of the inner quarters to give audience once more. When the audience was over he ordered that the Tang Priest and his three disciples be fetched to discuss the search for the princess. Sanzang then came and did obeisance to the king, while the Great Sage and the other two also paid their respects. The king bowed to them and said, "Yesterday you spoke of our daughter the princess. May we trouble you divine monks to find and rescue her?" "The day before yesterday we had been walking from the east till evening," the venerable elder replied, "when we saw the Almsgiver's Spread Gold Monastery. We went inside to ask for accommodation and had the good fortune to be entertained by the monks there. After supper I took a moonlight stroll in the former Spread Gold Garden, and as I was looking at the remains I heard wailing. When I asked what it was all about, an ancient monk, over a hundred years old, sent everyone else away before telling me, 'Now, about that wailing, in the late spring of last year I was enjoying the moon when suddenly heard a gust of wind and the sound of someone grieving. I got out of bed, went into the Jetavana and saw a girl there. When I questioned her the girl said, "I am a princess, the daughter of the king of India. The wind blew me here when I was looking at the flowers by moonlight." ' The ancient monk know a lot about correct behaviour, so he locked the princess up in a quiet, out-of-the-way cell. As he was worried that the monks of the monastery might sully her he put it about that he had locked up an evil spirit. The princess, who understood what he was doing, ranted and raved during the day and demanded food and tea. Only late at night, when there was nobody about, did she think of her mother and father and cry for them. The ancient monk did come to the capital to make enquiries several times, but when he found that the princess was well and in the palace he didn't dare say anything or submit a memorial. When the ancient monk saw that my disciple had some magic powers he repeatedly insisted that we were to come here to investigate. I never expected that she would turn out to be the Jade Hare from the Moon Palace who had put on an imitation of the real body and made herself look like the princess. She was also set on ruining my primal masculinity. Fortunately my disciple showed his mighty magic and detected the fraud. The Jade Hare has now been recaptured by the Moon Lord. Your worthy princess is now pretending to be crazy in the Spread Gold Monastery."

After hearing the story in all this detail the king started to weep aloud. This soon alarmed the queens and consorts of the three palaces and six compounds, who all came out to ask why. Everybody began to weep bitterly, and it was a long time before the king asked, "How far is the Spread Gold Monastery from the city?" "Only twenty miles," Sanzang replied. The king then issued these commands: "Let the Queens of the Eastern and Western Palaces look after the court while the High Minister takes charge of the nation's business. We are going to the monastery with our Senior Queen, our officials and the four holy monks to fetch the princess."

Carriages were at once prepared and a line of them left the palace. Watch as Brother Monkey sprang up into the air and with a bend of his back was the first to reach the monastery. The monks all hastily knelt to greet him. "When you left, sir," they said, "you walked with the others, so why did you come down from the sky today?" To this Monkey replied with a smile, "Where is your ancient teacher? Ask him to come out straight away, and set out incense tables to welcome His Majesty. The king and queen of India, the officials and my master are all coming." The monks could not understand what he meant, so they asked the ancient monk to come out. When the ancient monk saw Monkey he prostrated himself before him with the words, "What has happened about the princess, sir?" Monkey told him all about how the imitation princess had thrown the embroidered ball, wanted to mate with the Tang Priest, been chased, fought, and been recaptured by the Moon Lord as the Jade Hare. The ancient monk kowtowed to him again in thanks. "Please stop kowtowing," said Monkey, helping him up, "please stop. Hurry up and get ready to receive His Majesty." Only then did the monks realize that it was a girl locked up in the garden at the back. Surprised and delighted, they all set out a row of incense tables outside the monastery gates, put on their cassocks and started striking the bell and the drum. Soon after this the king's carriage arrived. Indeed,

The sky is filled with clouds of holy incense;
Sudden blessing comes to the monastery.
The rainbow flows for a thousand years; rivers and seas are pure.
The eternal spring round which lightning flickers is finer than those of Yu and Tang.
Thanks to the royal grace the plants' colours are finer than ever;
The wild flowers have extra fragrance because of this generosity.
Men of distinction have always left their mark behind them;
Today all rejoice at an enlightened king's arrival.

When the king arrived outside the monastery gates the monks

were all lined up on their knees in orderly ranks, bowing low in greeting. Monkey stood in the middle. "How did you arrive first, holy monk?" the king asked. "It just took a little bend of my waist for me to get here," Monkey replied. "Why were you such a long time coming?" After this the Tang Priest and the others all arrived. He led the royal carriage to the building at the back where the princess was still raving and pretending to be crazy. The ancient monk knelt down, pointed towards her and said, "This is Her Royal Highness the princess who was blown here by a wind the other year." The king ordered the cell opened. When the iron locks were undone and the door opened the king and queen saw and recognized the princess. Not caring about the filth, they went up to her and threw their arms round her. "Our poor child," they said, "how did you come to suffer these torments and have so terrible a time here?" How true it is that the meeting of parents and child is not like that of other people. The three of them sobbed aloud, their arms round each other's heads. When they had cried for a while and told each other what had happened since they were parted, scented hot water was sent for. The princess bathed and changed her clothes before they all climbed into carriages to go back to the capital.

Monkey then put his hands together in greeting to the king and said, "I have something else to put to you, Your Majesty." "Say it, whatever it is, holy monk," the king said, returning his greeting, "and we will do as you ask." "This mountain of theirs," Monkey replied, "is called Mount Hundredfoot. They tell me that centipedes have been turning into spirits here recently and injuring people by night. This is very awkward for travelling merchants. As I see it, only chickens can deal with centipedes, so a thousand extra-large cockerels should be chosen and then scattered across the mountainside to get rid of these venomous insects. The mountain could be renamed and you could make a land grant to these monks to thank them for looking after the princess." This suggestion pleased the king greatly, and he accepted it. Officials were then sent back to the city to fetch cocks, while the mountain was renamed Mount Splendour. The Department of Works was instructed to provide the materials for the monastery to be rebuilt, a deed of enfeoffment was written describing the mountain as "Mount Splendour, granted to the Almsgiver's Spread Gold Monastery", and the ancient monk was given the title National Benefactor Hierarch, a title that was to be handed on to his successors in perpetuity, together with a stipend of thirty-six bushels of grain. The monks all thanked the king for his kindness and saw him off on his way back to the capital. Here the princess returned to the inner palace and was greeted by all the ladies in turn. A banquet was then laid on to cheer the princess up and congratulate her on her deliverance. The queen and her daughter were reunited; king and ministers were together. We will not describe the night's feasting.

Early the next morning the king ordered that painters make portraits of the countenances of the four holy monks to be kept in the Sino-Barbarian Hall. The princess was also invited to come out from the throne hall in her new finery to thank the Tang Priest and the other three for saving her from her suffering. When she had thanked them the Tang Priest took his leave of the king to continue his journey west. The king refused to let them go, but ordered great banquets at which they feasted for five or six days. The idiot really was given a good time, and he enjoyed putting as much food in his stomach as he possibly could. When the king saw how determined they were to visit the Buddha he realized that no matter how hard he tried he would not be able to keep them. He had two hundred ingots of gold and silver brought out, as well as a tray of jewels for each of them as an expression of thanks. Master and disciples refused to accept anything. The king then ordered the royal carriage prepared, invited the master to enter it, and instructed officials to escort them a long way. The queens, consorts, officials and common people all kowtowed endlessly in thanks. As they went along the way their monks all came out to kowtow to them in farewell; none of them could bear to be parted from the travellers. Seeing that the people seeing them off were unwilling to turn back, Monkey had no option but to make a spell with his hands and blow a magic breath in the direction of the trigram of the wind, Xun, so that a dark wind stopped all the escorts from seeing them. Only then did the travellers get away. This was indeed a case of

> *Washing away the waves of gratitude their natures re-*
> *turned to the end;*
> *Leaving the sea of gold they were aware of true*
> *emptiness.*

If you do not know what happened on the journey ahead, listen to the explanation in the next chapter.

CHAPTER NINETY-SIX

Squire Kou entertains the lofty monk;
The Tang Priest does not covet wealth and honour.

All kinds of matter are really without matter;
No emptiness is truly empty.
Stillness and clamour, speech and silence, all are the same:
Why bother to dream-talk in one's dreams?
The useful includes the useless in its application;
Achievement lurks within failure.
When the fruit is ripe it reddens of itself;
Do not ask how the seed is to be grown.

The story has told how the Tang Priest and his disciples used their magic powers to stop the monks of the Spread Gold Monastery. When the monks saw after the black wind had passed that the master and his disciples had disappeared they thought that their visitors must have been living Buddhas come down to earth, so they kowtowed and went back. Of them we tell no more. As master and disciples travelled west spring was giving way to early summer:

The air was clear, mild and refreshing;
Water chestnuts and lotuses were growing in the pool.
Plums were ripening after the rain;
The wheat was forming as the breezes blew.
Flowers were fragrant where blossoms fell from trees;
The oriole grew tired amid the willow's light branches.
Swallows over the river taught their young to fly;
The pheasants fed their chirping chicks.
South of the Dipper the sun was always seen;
All of creation shone with brightness.

We could never describe in full how they ate at dawn, found shelter at dusk, rounded ravines and climbed hills as they went along their way without incident for a fortnight. Then another city wall appeared in front of them. As they came closer to it Sanzang asked, "What sort of place is this, disciple?" "I don't know," Brother Monkey replied, "I don't know." "You've been this way before," put in Pig, "so how can you claim that you don't know? I suppose you're being crafty and just pretending you can't recognize the place to make fools of us." "You're being completely unreasonable, you idiot," said Monkey. "Although I've been this way several times I've always come and gone by cloud high up in the sky. I've never landed here. I had no interest in the place, so why should I have looked it over? That's why I didn't know. I'm not being crafty, and not trying to make a fool of you either."

While they were talking they came close to the city before they realized it. Sanzang dismounted, crossed the drawbridge and went straight in through the gates. As they went along the main street there were two old men to be seen sitting under a portico and talking. "Disciples," said Sanzang, "stand here in the middle of the road, keep your heads bowed and don't run wild. I am going under that portico to ask where we are." Monkey and the others stood still as they had been told while the venerable elder went up to the two men, put his hands together and called out, "Greetings, benefactors." The two old men were idly chatting about such things as prosperity and decay, success and failure, sages and good men, their heroic deeds in ancient times, and where such men were now. Really, they said, it was enough to make you sigh. When they suddenly heard Sanzang's greeting they returned it and asked, "What do you have to say to us, reverend sir?" "I am a monk who has come from far away to worship the Lord Buddha," Sanzang replied, "and I have just arrived here. I wonder what this place is called, and where there are any pious folk from whom I might beg a meal." "This is the prefecture of Brazentower," one of the old men said, "and this is the county of Diling near Brazentower city. If you want vegetarian food, reverend sir, you won't need to beg. Go past this archway to the street running north-south. There's a gate-tower shaped like a sitting tiger facing the east, and that's Squire Kou's house. In front of it is a sign that says 'All monks welcome'. A monk from far away such as yourself will be given all you want. Off you go, and stop interrupting our conversation."

Sanzang thanked them, turned to Monkey and said, "This is Diling county in the prefecture of Brazentower. The two old men said that on the street running north-south past this archway there is a gate-tower shaped like a sitting tiger that is Squire kou's house. In front of it is a sign that says 'All monks welcome'. They told me to go there for a vegetarian meal." "The West is a land of Buddhists," said Friar Sand, "and they really do feed monks. As this is only a seat of local government we don't need to present our passport. Let's go and beg ourselves a meal; that'll be all the better for travelling with." The master and his three disciples walked slowly along the main street, filling all the people in the market with alarm and suspicion as they crowded around, struggling to see what the strangers looked like. Sanzang told his disciples to keep their mouths shut, saying, "Behave yourselves! Behave yourselves!" The three of them kept their heads bowed, not daring to look up. Then they turned a corner and did indeed see a main road running north-south.

As they were walking along it they saw a gate-tower like a sitting tiger. On a screen wall inside the gateway hung a great sign on which were written the words "All monks welcome". "The West is indeed the land of the Buddha," said Sanzang. "Nobody, however clever or stupid, is dishonest. I did not believe what the two old men told me. Now I know it is just as they said." Being the boor that he was, Pig wanted to go straight in. "Just a moment, idiot," said Monkey. "Wait till someone comes out so we can ask what to do before we go in." "Big brother's right," said Friar Sand. "If we don't show respect for his privacy we might irritate the benefactor." They let the horse rest and put down the luggage outside the gates. A little later a slave came out with a steelyard and a basket in his hands that the sudden sight of the strangers made him drop in alarm.

"Master," he reported, running inside, "there are four strange-looking monks outside." At the time the gentleman was walking with a stick in the inner courtyard, reciting the name of the Buddha. When he heard the report he dropped his stick and went out to welcome them. Their ugliness did not frighten him. "Come in, come in," he said. Behaving with all courtesy, Sanzang went inside with him. The gentleman led them along a passageway and into a house, where he said, "The upper building includes a Buddha hall, a sutra library and a refectory for you gentlemen. The lower building is where your disciple's family lives." Sanzang expressed endless admiration. He brought out and put on his cassock to worship the Buddha, then went up into the hall to have a look.

What he saw was:

Clouds of incense,
Dazzling candles.
The hall was filled with a brocade of flowers;
All around was gold and many colours.
From red frames
Hung a bell of purple gold;
On a lacquered stand
Was set a matching decorated drum.
Several pairs of banners
Were embroidered with the eight treasures;
A thousand Buddha statues
Were all covered in gold.
Ancient bronze incense-burners,
Ancient bronze vases,
Carved lacquer tables,
Carved lacquer boxes.
In the ancient bronze incense-burners
Was always eaglewood incense;
In the ancient bronze vases
Were the colours of lotus blossoms.
On the carved lacquer tables
Were fresh fruits;

In the carved lacquer boxes
Fragrant petals were piled.
In glass bowls
Was pure, clear water;
In crystal lamps
The fragrant oil shone bright.
A metal chime
Resounded long and slow.
This was like a treasure house untouched by the world,
A family Buddha hall rivalling a monastery.

The venerable elder washed his hands, took a pinch of incense, kowtowed and worshipped, then turned back to greet the gentleman. "Wait a moment," Mr. Kou replied. "Let us make our introductions in the sutra library." What they saw there was:

A square stand and upright cupboards,
Jade boxes and golden caskets.
On the square stand and in the upright cupboards
Were piled up countless scriptures;
In the jade boxes and golden caskets
Were stored many a manuscript.
On lacquered tables
Were paper, ink, brushes and inkstones,
All the finest treasures of the study.
Before the scented screen
Were calligraphy, paintings, a lute and chess,
All for the most refined of interests.
A magic chime of light jade covered with gold,
And a copper tripod in the wind and under the moon.
The clear breeze freshens the spirit;
The purified heart is aware; the mind set on the Way is at ease.

When the venerable elder had reached the library and was going to bow to him Mr. Kou held on to prevent this and said, "Won't you take off your cassock?" Sanzang then took off his cassock, after which he greeted Mr. Kou. He then told Monkey and the other two to greet him too. Orders were given for the horse to be fed and the luggage put in a corridor. The gentleman asked about their background. "I have been sent by the emperor of Great Tang in the east," Sanzang said, "to the Vulture Peak in your splendid country to see the Lord Buddha and ask for the true scriptures. I am here to request a meal because I have heard that in your distinguished household you honour monks. After that we will be on our way." The gentleman's face was suffused with pleasure as he replied with a chuckle, "My name is Kou Hong, my other name is Kou Dakuan, and I have lived for sixty-four wasted years. When I was forty I made a vow to feed ten thousand monks, and you will complete the number. In the twenty-four years during which I have been feeding monks I have kept a record of their names. Having nothing else to do in recent days I have counted the names of all the monks I've fed, and the score is now 9,996. I was only short of four to make up the full number. Then today heaven has sent you four teachers down to me to complete the ten thousand. Will you be so good as to tell me your names? I hope that you will stay for a month or more until I have celebrated the completion, after which I will send you teachers up the mountain in carrying-chairs or on horses. Vulture Peak is only some 250 miles from here, not at all far away." Sanzang was thoroughly delighted to hear this, and he agreed to it all at once.

Several young and old servants fetched firewood, drew water, and brought rice, flour and vegetables into the house with which to prepare them a meal. All this disturbed the gentleman's wife, who said, "Where have these monks come from, and why is everyone so busy?" "Four eminent monks have just arrived," the servants told her, "and when the master asked them where they were from they said they'd been sent by the emperor of the Great Tang in the east to go to worship the Lord Buddha on Vulture Peak. Goodness only knows how far it is to here from there. The master said that they had been sent down from heaven and told us to get them a vegetarian meal quickly." The old woman was also very pleased to hear this, so she told a maid to fetch her clothes so that she too could go to see them.

"Only one of them is handsome, ma'am," the servant said. "The other three don't bear looking at. They're really hideous." "What you people don't realize," the old woman replied," is that if they look ugly, strange and freakish they must be heavenly beings come down to earth. Hurry and tell your master straight away." The servant ran straight to the sutra hall, where he said to the gentleman, "The old lady's here to pay her respects to the lords from the east." On hearing this Sanzang rose from his seat. Before the words had all been spoken the old woman was already before the hall, where she lifted her eyes to see the Tang Priest's majestic countenance and his splendid bearing. When she turned to see the extraordinary appearance of Monkey and the other two she was somewhat alarmed even though she knew they were heavenly beings come down to earth; she fell to her kness and bowed. Sanzang quickly returned her courtesy, saying, "Bodhisattva, the honour you do me is undeserved." The old woman then asked her husband why the four reverend gentlemen were not all sitting together. "We three are disciples," said Pig, thrusting his snout forward. Goodness! His voice was like the roar of a tiger deep in the mountains. The old woman was terrifield.

As they were talking another servant appeared to announce, "The two young masters are here too." When Sanzang turned quickly round to look he saw that they were two young scholars, who prostrated themselves to the venerable elder after walking into the sutra hall. Sanzang was quick to return their courtesy. Mr. Kou then came up to take hold of him and say, "These are my two sons. Their names are Kou Liang and Kou Dong. They have just come back from their school and have not yet had their lunch. They are here to pay their respects because they have heard that you teachers have come down to earth." "What fine sons," said Sanzang with delight, "what fine sons. Indeed,

> *If you want to make a lofty match you must do good:*
> *The success of your sons and grandsons depends on*
> *study."*

The two scholars then asked their father, "Where have these

lords come from?" "From a long way away," Mr. Kou replied with a smile. "The emperor of Great Tang in the east of the Southern Continent of Jambu has sent them to Vulture Peak to worship the Lord Buddha and fetch the scriptures." "We have read in the *Compendious Forest of Facts* that there are four continents in the world," the scholars said. "This continent of ours is the Western Continent of Cattle-gift. There is also an Eastern Continent of Superior Body. How many years did it take you to get here?" "I have been a long time on the journey," Sanzang replied with a smile, "met many vicious demons and monsters, and suffered greatly. I have been greatly indebted to my three disciples for their protection. Altogether it has taken me fourteen winters and summers to reach your splendid country." When the scholars heard this they said with unbounded admiration, "You really are holy monks, you really are."

Before they had finished speaking a servant came in to invite them to eat: "The vegetarian banquet has been set out, so will you eat, my lords?" The gentleman then sent his wife and sons back to the house, while he went with the four monks into the refectory for the meal. Everything was set out very neatly. There were gold-lacquered tables and black-lacquered chairs. In front were fine cakes of many colours that skilled chefs had made up in up-to-date styles. The second row contained five dishes of hors-d'oeuvres, in the third row there were five dishes of fruit, and in the fourth were five large dishes of snacks. Everything tasted good, looked good and smelt good. Vegetable soup, rice and steamed breadrolls were all spicy, piping hot, and most delicious. There was plenty to fill one's stomach. Seven or eight servants rushed around waiting on them, while four or five cooks were kept constantly busy. Just watch while some poured soup and others filled the rice bowls, coming and going like shooting stars chasing the moon. Pig was finishing up bowls in single mouthfuls, like a gale blowing the clouds away. Thus master and disciples ate their fill. Sanzang then rose to thank Mr. Kou for the meal before setting out again. The gentleman blocked his way saying, "Teacher, won't you take things easy and spend a few days here? As the saying goes, it's nothing to start a journey but it's hard to end one. I will send you on your way when we have celebrated the completion of my vow." Seeing how sincere and determined he was, Sanzang had no option but to stay.

Five to seven days quickly passed before Mr. Kou engaged twenty-four local Buddhist monks to perform a mass to celebrate the fulfilment of the vow. The monks spent three or four days writing texts out and chose a lucky day on which to begin the Buddhist service. The way they did it was like in the Great Tang. There was

A great display of banners,
Where the golden countenance was set out;
Rows of candles
And incense burnt in offering.
Drums and gongs were beaten,
Pipes and shawms were played.
Cloud-cymbals,
Pure-toned flutes,
Sounded in tune;
To the beat of the drum,
And the woodwind's notes,
The words of sutras were recited in unison.
First the local god was put at ease,
Then spirit generals were invited to come.
The documents were sent out,
And they bowed low to the Buddha statues,
Reciting the Peacock Sutra,
Each word of which could sweep away disasters,
A stand of lamps was lit for Bhaisajya-guru,
To shine with flames of dazzling brightness.
They performed the Water Ceremony
To end any sense of grievance.
Then they intoned the Avatamsaka Sutra
To do away with slander.
The Three Vehicles of the Wonderful Law are very fine:
Different monks are all the same.

The mass lasted for three days and nights before it ended. In his longing to go to the Thunder Monastery the Tang Priest was determined to be on his way, so he took his leave of them and thanked them. "Teacher, you are very eager to say goodbye," Mr. Kou said. "I suppose you must have taken offence because for days on end we have been so busy with our service that we have treated you very offhandedly." "We have put your noble house to a great deal of trouble," Sanzang replied, "and I do not know how we will ever repay you. How could we possibly have taken offence? But when my wise monarch saw me off through the passes all those years ago he asked me when I would be back. I wrongly told him that I would return in three years, never imagining that the journey would be so badly delayed that it has already lasted fourteen years. I do not even know whether I will succeed in fetching the scriptures, and it will take me another twelve or thirteen years to get back. How am I to face the penalty for breaking my monarch's sage command? I beg you, sir, to let me go to fetch the scriptures and return. Next time I come to your mansion I will be able to stay much longer."

This was more than Pig could bear. "You don't care at all about what we want, Master," he shouted at the top of his voice. "You're showing no consideration at all. The old gentleman's very rich, and now he's fulfilled his vow to feed monks. Besides, he's really sincere about wanting to keep us here. It'd do no harm if we stayed here for a year or so. Why be so set on going? Why leave all this good food to go begging for meals elsewhere? Is it your parents' home ahead?" "All you care about is food, you cretin," shouted Sanzang angrily. "You don't care at all about the transference of cause and effect. Really, you're such an animal you'd eat from the trough to scratch the itch in your belly. If you people are going to be so greedy and stupid I'll go by myself tomorrow." Seeing that the master's attitude had changed, Monkey grabbed hold of Pig and punched his head. "You've got no sense, you idiot," he said abusively. "You've made the master angry with us too." "He deserved that," said Friar Sand with a grin, "he deserved that. He's disgusting enough even if he doesn't say a word, but he would have to interrupt." Breathing heavily, the idiot stood to one side, not daring to say another word. Seeing the anger of master and disciple, Mr. Kou said, his face wreathed in smiles, "Do not be so short-tempered, teacher. Make yourself comfortable for the rest of the day. Tomorrow I will have banners and drums brought here and ask some relations and neighbours to come to see you off."

As they were talking the old woman came out again to say, "Venerable teacher, as you have come to our house you should not refuse too insistently. How many days have you spent here now?" "It is already a fortnight," Sanzang replied. "That fortnight is my gentleman's achievement," the old woman said. "I have a little pin-money with which I would like to entertain you gentlemen for another fortnight." Before she had finished speaking Kou Dong and his brother came out again to say, "Your four lordships, in the twenty and more years during which our father has been feeding monks he has never met better ones than yourselves. Now that by your gracious condescension you have made up the total you really have brought glory to our thatched hovel. We two are too young to understand about cause and effect, but we have often heard it said,

The husband gets what he has merited,
The wife gets what she has merited;
Nothing is got when nothing is merited.

Our father and mother each want to make a humble offering in order that each of them may merit a reward, so why must you refuse so insistently? And as we two brothers have saved a little of our school fees we hope to be allowed to support you gentlemen for another fortnight before seeing you on your way." "I dare not accept even the lavish hospitality of the venerable Bodhisattva your mother," Sanzang replied, "so how could I accept you brothers' generosity? I could not possibly do so. I really must set out today. Please, please do not take offence. If I do not go now I will be unable to avoid execution for exceeding my emperor's time-limit by so long."

When the old woman and her two sons realized that Sanzang was determined not to stay they started losing their patience. "We invite you very nicely to stay," they said, "but you're obstinately set on going. If you're going, go, and cut out this chatter." Mother and sons then left to go back to the house. Pig could hold his tongue no longer. "Master," he said to the Tang Priest, "don't overdo it. As the saying goes, 'If you can stay, don't go away.' Let's stay here for another month to let the mother and her sons fulfil their wishes. Why do you have to be in such a rush?" The Tang Priest made another angry noise at him and shouted again. The idiot then slapped his own face twice, saying, "Tut, tut, tut. Don't talk out of turn. You spoke again." Brother Monkey and Friar Sand, who were standing to one side, started spluttering with laughter. The Tang Priest was angry with Monkey again. "What are you laughing at?" he asked, and made the hand magic, ready to recite the Band-tightening Spell. This so terrified Monkey that he fell to his knees at once and said, "I didn't laugh, Master. Whatever you do, don't say the spell! Don't say it!"

Seeing that master and disciples were getting into a worse and worse temper with each other Mr. Kou gave up his insistence on their staying. "Don't quarrel, teachers", he said, "I'll definitely see you on your way tomorrow morning." He then left the sutra hall and told his secretary to write a hundred or so invitations to his neighbours and relations to see the Tang Priest off to the west early the next morning. He told the cooks to lay on a parting banquet, while also instructing his steward to have twenty pairs of coloured flags made, hire a band of musicians, and engage a group of Buddhist monks from the Monastery from the South and another group of Taoist priests from the Eastern Peak Temple. Everything was to be ready and in order by ten in the morning. All the gentleman's staff went off to carry out their orders. Soon it was evening again, and after supper everyone went to bed. It was the time when

Dots of homegoing rooks pass the lonely village;
Drum and bell can be heard from each other's distant towers.

In streets and markets the bustle is stilled;
In all the houses the lamps shine dimly.
Flowers in the breeze throw shadows under the moon;
The stars shine bright against the Milky Way.
Where the cuckoo sings the night seems deeper;
All natural sounds are stilled across the earth.

During the third and fourth watches of the night all the household servants in charge of various matters got up early to attend to their tasks. Just watch. The cooks preparing the banquet were busy in the kitchen. The people who had to buy coloured flags were bustling in front of the hall. Those engaging Buddhist and Taoist clergy were hurrying about as fast as their legs could carry them. Those hiring musicians were in a great rush. The messengers delivering invitations ran all over the place, while the servants preparing the carrying-chairs and horses were calling to each other. They were all shouting from the middle of the night until dawn, and by around ten o'clock everything was prepared. This was all because the family was rich.

The story tells how the Tang Priest and his disciples got up early to be waited on once more by that crowd of servants. The venerable elder told them to pack the baggage and saddle the horse. When the idiot heard that they were about to go he pulled a face, pouted and grumbled, but he still had to pack the clothes and begging bowls then go to look for the carrying pole. Friar Sand brushed the horse, saddled and harnessed it, and stood waiting. Brother Monkey put the nine-ringed monastic staff in his master's hand and hung the passport in a bag in front of his chest. They were now all ready to set out. Mr. Kou then invited them into the large hall at the back, where a feast was set out that excelled even the one they had eaten in the refectory.

Curtains hung from on high;
Screens stood all around.
In the middle was a picture:
A mountain of long life and a sea of blessings.
On both walls were displayed

Scrolls of spring, summer, autumn and winter.
From the dragon-patterned tripod came clouds of incense;
Above magpie-tailed burners rose auspicious vapours.
In bowls were bunches of colour,
Fresh and brilliant flowers of splendid form.
The tables were piled with gold:
Lines of confections shaped like lions and immortals.
Music and dancing before the steps were in true harmony;
The dishes in the hall were like a brocade.
Exquisite soup and rice, both free of meat;
The finest tea and the best of wines.
Although they were only commoners
Their home was fine enough for a prince.
All that could be heard were happy sounds
So loud they surprised the sky and shook the earth.

The venerable elder was just exchanging courtesies with Mr. Kou when a servant came in to report, "The guests are all here." These were the people who had been invited — neighbours, relations by marriage, and some of his pious friends who also fed monks and recited the name of the Buddha — and all of them bowed to the venerable elder. After the greetings had been made everyone sat down. Outside the hall zithers and panpipes were played, while inside the hall pipas and songs accompanied the banquet. Pig paid great attention to this rich banquet. "Brother," he said to Friar Sand, "relax and eat as much as you can. There won't be anything as good as this to eat after we leave the Kou house." "Nonsense," Friar Sand replied with a laugh. "As the saying goes,

No matter how splendid the banquet you eat,
For only a while can it keep you replete.
Your savings may meet the expense of the road,
But savings can never in bellies be stowed."

"You're hopeless," said Pig, "hopeless. If I eat my fill today

I won't feel hungry for the next three days." "Idiot," said Monkey, who had heard this. "Don't fill your belly till it bursts. We've got to start walking now."

They were still talking, and it was almost noon when Sanzang raised his chopsticks and said grace. Pig grabbed a bowl, filled it with desperate speed, and ate five or six bowlfuls in succession, gulping down a whole bowlful at a time. Without any qualms at all he filled both his sleeves with steamed bread, twists, pancakes and cooked dishes before rising with his master. Sanzang thanked the gentleman and everyone else, then they all went outside together. Just look at the coloured banners, splendid canopies, drummers and instrumentalists outside. Only then did two groups of clergy, one Buddhist and one Taoist, arrive. "Gentlemen," said Mr. Kou, "you are late. Our teacher is in a hurry to leave, so I will not be able to offer you a meal. I'll show you my gratitude when we come back." Everyone then opened a way to let them through. The carriers carrying their chairs, the riders on their horses and the walkers on foot all let Sanzang and his three disciples go first. The heavens rang with drumming and music, the flags and banner blotted out the sun, crowds pressed around, and carriages and horses were all packed close together as everyone came to watch Mr. Kou seeing the Tang Priest off. The splendour all around was more magnificent than pearls or jade, and no less fine than brocade screens behind which spring lies hidden.

The Buddhist monks playing Buddhist tunes and the Taoist priests their Taoist airs all escorted the travellers out of the prefecture. When they reached the three-mile pavilion, baskets of food and jars of drink were set out, cups were raised, and they all drank parting toasts. Mr. Kou, loath to let them go, said as he choked back his tears, "Teacher, you must spend some more days with us on your way back with the scriptures to fulfil my longing." Overcome with gratitude, Sanzang thanked him at great length. "If I reach Vulture Peak," he said, "and see the Lord Buddha the first thing I will do will be to praise your great virtue. We will certainly come to kowtow to you in thanks on our return journey." As they talked they covered another mile or so without noticing it. Then the venerable elder insisted on taking his leave, at which Mr. Kou turned back, sobbing aloud. Indeed,

> *He who had vowed to feed the clergy found enlightenment:*
> *He was not fated to see the Tathagata Buddha.*

We will tell not of how Mr. Kou went home with everyone after seeing the travellers off as far as the three-mile pavilion, but of how the master and his three disciples went on for some twelve or fifteen miles. By now it was growing dark. "It's late," Sanzang said. "Where are we to spend the night?" Pig, who was carrying the pole, pulled a face and said, "You would have to leave ready-cooked meals behind and refuse to stay in a nice cool brick house so as to go wherever it is we're going. That's just asking for trouble. It's very late now. What'll we do if it starts raining?" "Evil, insolent beast," cursed Sanzang, "complaining again. As the saying goes,

> *The capital may be remarkably fine,*
> *But we can't linger here for a very long time.*

If we are fated to visit the Lord Buddha, fetch the true scriptures, go back to Great Tang and report to the emperor I will let you eat in the imperial kitchens for years on end. Then, you evil beast, you will swell up till you burst. That will teach you to be such a greedy devil." The idiot chortled quietly to himself, but did not dare say another word.

When Brother Monkey raised his eyes to look around he saw some buildings beside the road and asked his master urgently, "Can we spend the night here? Can we?" Sanzang went over to the place, where he saw a ruined memorial arch on which was inscribed

THE VIHARA OF PADMAPRABHA

"The Bodhisattva Padmaprabha was a disciple of the Buddha Sikhin," said Sanzang, dismounting. "He was dismissed for eliminating the Demon King of Poison Fire and turned into the Spirit Officer of the Five Manifests. There must be a shrine here." They then all went in together. The cloisters had all collapsed, the walls had fallen down, and there was no trace of anybody around, only of vegetation running wild. They would have gone out again, but the sky had filled with dark clouds and it had started to pour with rain. There was nothing for it but to find a place in the ruins where they could shelter from the storm They kept completely silent, not daring to speak aloud for feat that some evil demon might hear them. Thus it was that they endured a sleepless night sitting or standing there. Oh dear! How true it is that

Disaster strikes at triumph's height;
In time of joy comes sorrow's blight.

If you don't know what happened when they carried on with their journey, listen to the explanation in the next instalment.

CHAPTER NINETY-SEVEN

The monks and their supporters meet with demonic attack; The sage makes the spirit reappear to save the primal one.

We will tell not of how the Tang Priest and the others endured a hard night in the dilapidated palace of Padmaprabha, but of a group of evil villains in Diling county in the prefecture of Brazentower who had squandered all their families' fortunes in whoring, drinking and gambling. Having nothing else left to live on they had formed a criminal gang of a dozen and more members and were discussing which family was the richest in the city and which the second richest. The idea was to rob them of their gold and silver and thus get some money to spend. "There's no need to go round making enquiries," one of them said, "or work it out in detail. The Mr. Kou who saw the Tang monk off today is rolling in money. Let's strike tonight in the rain. There'll be nobody ready for us in the streets and the fire wardens won't be patrolling. When we've stolen his property we'll be able to go with the girls, gamble and have a good time again. That would be great, wouldn't it?" The other robbers were all delighted with the suggestion, and with one heart they all set out in the rain carrying daggers, spiked clubs, sticks, coshes, ropes and torches. Flinging open the main gates of the Kou house they charged inside, shouting and sending everyone inside, young and old, male and female, scurrying into hiding. The old woman hid under the bed and the old man slipped behind the gates, while Kou Liang, Kou Dong and their families fled for their lives in all directions. Holding their knives in their hands and lighting torches, the bandits opened up all the chests in the house and grabbed as much of the gold, silver, jewellery, hair ornaments, clothing, vessels and other household goods as they wanted. Mr. Kou could not bear to lose all this, so taking his life in his hands he came out from behind the gate to plead with the robbers. "Take as much as you want, great kings," he said, "but please leave me a few clothes to be buried in." The robbers were in no mood for argument. They rushed up to him, tripped and kicked him to the ground. Alas,

His three souls vanished to the underworld,
His seven spirits left the world of men.

The successful robbers left the Kou house, put up a rope ladder from the foot of the city wall, took it in turns to cross and fled westwards in the rain. Only when they saw that the robbers had gone did the servants of the Kou family dare show their heads again. When they looked for old Mr. Kou and found him lying dead on the floor they started weeping aloud. "Heavens! The master's been murdered!" they all said as they wept, embracing the body and sobbing in misery.

When it was almost the fourth watch the resentful Mrs. Kou, who was angry with the Tang Priest and his followers for rejecting their hospitality, and also because the extravagance of their send-off had provoked this disaster, decided to ruin the four of them. Helping Kou Liang to his feet, she said, "Don't cry, my son. Your father fed monks day in and day out. Who ever would have thought that he would complete the number by feeding a gang of monks who'd murder him?" "Mother," the brothers asked, "how did those monks murder him?" "Those bandits were so bold and vicious that when they charged in I hid under the bed," she replied. "Although I was trembling I made sure to take a very good look at them by the light of the torches. Do you know who they were? The Tang Priest was lighting torches, Pig was holding a knife, Friar Sand was taking the gold and silver, and Monkey killed your father." The two sons believed all this. "If you saw all that clearly, mother," they said, "you must be right. They spent a fortnight in our house, so they knew all the doors, walls, windows and passageways. They must have been tempted by our wealth and come back here under cover of rain and darkness. How evil! They've stolen our property and murdered our father. Once it's light we'll go to the local government and report them as wanted men." "What sort of wanted notice should we write?" Kou Dong asked "We'll write what our mother said," Kou Liang replied, and he wrote;

The Tang Priest lit the torches, Pig incited to murder, Friar Sand stole the gold and silver and Sun the Novice murdered our father.

The whole household was in such a hubbub that before they noticed it day had dawned. While invitations were sent out to their relatives and a coffin was ordered Kou Liang and his brother went to the local government offices to deposit their complaint. Now the prefect of Brazentower

Had always been upright,
Was good by nature.
As a boy he had studied by the light of the snow;
When young he had taken the palace examinations.
His heart was always set on loyalty and justice,
And filled with thoughts of kindness and benevolence.
His name would be transmitted in annals for a thousand years,
Like a Gong Sui or Huang Ba[1] come back to life;
His fame would resound for ten thousand ages in the halls of office,
Zhuo Mao and Lu Gong[2] reborn.

When he had taken his seat in the hall and declared that all matters could be dealt with, he ordered that the placard asking for plaints should be carried outside. Kou Liang and his brother then came in holding the placard, knelt down and called aloud, "Your Honour, we have come to denounce some bandits as thieves and murderers." The prefect accepted their complaint and read what it had to say. "I was told yesterday that your family

[1] Famed as good officials in the first century BC.
[2] Loyal officials who upheld Confucian values in the Later Han Dynasty

completed your vow of feeding monks," the prefect said, "by feeding four distinguished ones, arhats from the Tang Dynasty in the east. You made a great display of sending them off with drums and music. So how could such a thing as this have possibly happened?" "Your Honour," said Kou Liang, kowtowing, "our father Kou Hong had been feeding monks for twenty-four years. These four monks who had come from afar just happended to make up the ten thousand, which was why he held a service to mark the completion and kept them there for a fortnight. They got to know all the passageways, doors and windows. They were seen off during the day and came back yesterday evening. During the dark and stormy night they charged into the house with torches and weapons to steal our gold, silver, jewellery, clothes and hair ornaments. They beat our father to death and left him lying on the ground. We beg you to be our protector." On hearing this the prefect mustered infantry, cavalry and able-bodied civilian conscripts, 150 men in all, who rushed straight out of the western gate carrying sharp weapons in pursuit of the Tang Priest and his three disciples.

The story now tells how master and disciples stayed in the ruins of the minor palace of Padmaprabha until dawn, when they went out and started hurrying westwards. The bandits, who had gone along the main road west all night till daybreak after robbing the Kou family and leaving the city, had passed the palace of Padmaprabha and hidden in the mountains some six or seven miles to the west. Here they were just dividing up the gold and silver when the Tang Priest and his three followers came into view, also heading west along the road. The bandits, whose greed was not yet sated, pointed at the Tang Priest and said, "Look! Aren't they the monks who were seen off yesterday?" "And a very welcome arrival too," said the other bandits, laughing. "Let's do a bit more of our dirty business. Those monks coming along the road spent a long time in the Kou house. Goodness only knows how much stuff they're carrying. Let's hold them up, take their travel money and white horse, and share it all out. That'll suit us very nicely." The robbers then rushed to the road, brandishing their weapons and yelling their war cry as they formed a line. "Stay where you are, monks," they shouted. "Leave some toll money and we'll spare your lives. If so much as half a 'no' comes out through your teeth you'll all be cut down without mercy." The Tang Priest was shaking with terror as he sat on his horse. "What are we to do?" Pig and Friar Sand asked Brother Monkey with alarm. "What are we to do? We had a miserable night in the rain, and after starting out again this morning we're being robbed by bandits. How true is it that troubles never come singly." "Don't be frightened, Master," said Monkey with a smile, "and stop worrying, brothers. Wait while I go and ask them a few questions."

The splendid Great Sage put on his tigerskin kilt, straightened up his brocade and cotton tunic, went up to them, put his hands together in front of his chest, and asked, "What are you gentlemen doing?" "Don't you care whether you live or die, you swine?" the robbers yelled back at him. "How dare you question us! Have you got no eyes in your head? Don't you realize who we great kings are? Hand your toll money over at once and we'll let you go on your way." When he heard this, Monkey wreathed his face in smiles and replied, "So you're bandits who hold people up on the road." "Kill him!" the bandits yelled with fury. "Your Majesties," said Monkey with feigned terror, "Your Majesties, I'm only a monk from the country. I don't know the right things to say. Please don't be angry if I've offended you, please don't. If what you want is toll money all you have to do is to ask me: no need to ask the other three. I'm the book-keeper. All the money we get for chanting sutras and as alms, all we beg and all we're given, goes into the bundles, and I'm in charge of spending it. The man on the horse is my master. All he can do is recite sutras. He doesn't care about anything else. He's forgotten all about wealth and sex, and he's got nothing at all. The black-faced one is a junior I collected on our journey. All he can do is look after the horse. And the one with a long snout is a labourer I hired. He's only good for carrying a pole. Let those three go while I fetch our travel money, cassocks and begging bowls. I'll give you all you want." "You seem to be an honest chap, monk," the robbers said, "so we'll spare your life Tell the other three to leave their luggage, and we'll let them go." Monkey turned back and gave them a look. Friar Sand put down the carrying-pole with the luggage, and led the master's horse as they carried on westwards. Monkey bowed down to undo the bundle, took a pinch of dust from the ground, and scattered it on the bundle as he said the words of a spell. It was body-fixing magic, so the moment he shouted, "Stop!" the thirty and more bandits all stood stock still, grinding their teeth, staring, their hands apart. None of them could speak or move. "Come back, Master," shouted Monkey, "come back!"

"This is terrible," said Pig in alarm, "this is terrible. Big brother's informed on us. He isn't carrying any money on him, and there's no gold or silver in the bundle. He must be calling the master back to ask him to give up his horse. He's going to get the clothes stripped off our backs." "Don't talk such rubbish, brother," said Friar Sand with a laugh. "Big brother knows what he's doing. He's always been able to beat vicious monsters and demons up till now, so what do we have to fear from a few petty thieves? He must be calling us back because he's got something to say to us. Let's go straight there and find out." When the venerable elder heard this he cheerfully turned his horse round and went back. "Wukong," he called, "why have you called us back?"

"Hear what these robbers have got to say for themselves," Brother Monkey said. Pig went up to them, shoved them and asked, "Why don't you move, bandits?" The bandits remained completely unconscious and said nothing. "They're thick, and dumb too," said Pig. "I fixed them by magic," said Monkey with a laugh. "Even if you fixed them," said Pig, "you didn't fix their mouths, so why aren't they making a sound?" "Please dismount and sit down, Master," said Brother Monkey. "As the saying goes, 'People only get arrested by mistake; they never get released by mistake.' Knock all the robbers over, brother, and tie them up. Then we'll force them to make statements. Find out if they're beginners or old hands." "Haven't got any rope," said Friar Sand. Monkey then pulled out some of his hairs, blew on them with magic breath and turned them into thirty lengths of rope. They all set to, knocked the robbers over, and tied their hands and feet together. Then Monkey said the words that ended the spell, whereupon the bandits gradually revived.

Monkey invited the Tang Priest to take the seat of honour while he and the other two shouted, holding their weapons, "Hairy bandits! How many of you are there altogether, and how many years have you been in this line of business? How many things have you stolen? Have you murdered anyone? Is this your first offence? Or your second? Or your third?" "Spare our lives, your lordships," pleaded the robbers. "Stop shouting," said Monkey, "and come clean." "We aren't hardened robbers, your lordships," they said. "We're all from good families. Because we're a bad lot we squandered all the wealth we'd inherited in drinking, gambling, whoring and living it up. We've never worked, and now we've got no money either. We found out that Mr. Kou's family was one of the richest in the prefecture of Brazentower, so last night we got together to rob it under cover of darkness and rain. We stole some gold, silver, clothing and jewellery, and were just dividing it up in a mountain hollow to the north of the track when we noticed you gentlemen coming. Some of us recognized you as the monks Mr. Kou saw off, so we were sure that you must have some goods on you. Then we saw how heavy your luggage was and how fast the white horse was going. It was our disgraceful greed that made us try to hold you up. Never did we imagine that you would have such divine powers and be able to tie us up. We beg you to be merciful to us. Take back what we stole and spare our lives."

Sanzang was violently shocked to hear that their booty had been stolen from the Kou household. He stood up at once and said, "Mr. Kou was a very good man, Wukong, so how did he bring such a disaster on himself?" "It was all because the coloured hangings and fancy parasols, and the huge numbers of drummers and musicians when we were seen off attracted too much attention," replied Monkey with a smile. "That's why this gang of desperadoes attacked his house. Luckily they ran into us, and we've taken back all the gold, silver, clothing and jewellery."

"We put Mr. Kou out for a whole fortnight," said Sanzang, "so we owe him a huge debt of gratitude that we have not yet been able to repay. Would it not be a good deed to return this property to his house?" Monkey agreed, and he went to the mountain hollow with Pig and Friar Sand to fetch the booty, which they packed up and loaded on the horse. He told Pig to carry the load of gold and silver while Friar Sand carried their own luggage. Monkey was just on the point of killing all the bandits with his cudgel when he had the worrying thought that the Tang Priest might get angry with him for committing murder. So he could only shake himself and take back all the hairs. Now that their hands and feet had been untied the thieves all got up then fled for their lives into the undergrowth. The Tang Priest then turned back the way he had come to return the booty to Mr. Kou. In making this journey he was like a moth flying into a flame and coming to disaster. There is a poem about it that goes:

Kindness to others is rarely with kindness rewarded;
Kindness will often to hate and hostility lead.
Plunge in the water to rescue the drowning? You'll suffer.
Think before acting and spare yourself grief you don't need.

Sanzang and his disciples were just heading back with the gold, silver, clothing and jewellery when the crowd of men armed with spears and swords arrived. "Disciples," said Sanzang with alarm, "look at all those armed men coming here. What is happening?" "It's a disaster," said Pig, "a disaster. They're the robbers we set free. They've found weapons and ganged up with some more people. Now they've come back and they're going to kill us." "They don't look like bandits, brother," said Friar Sand. "Big brother, take a closer look." "The master's in bad trouble again," Monkey whispered to Friar Sand. "These must be soldiers here to capture the bandits." Before he had finished saying this the soldiers were upon the master and his disciples, surrounding them. "You're a fine bunch of monks," they said, "robbing a house then swaggering around here like this." They then rushed them, dragged the Tang Priest off his horse and tied him up. Next they tied up Brother Monkey and the others, and carried them off hanging from poles, two men to each of them. Driving the horse along and seizing the baggage, they went back to the prefectural city. This is what could be seen:

The Tang Priest,
Shivering and shaking,
Weeping and lost for words.
Zhu Bajie,
Muttering and grumbling,
Full of complaints.
Friar Sand,
Talking away,
While secretly feeling uncertain.
Sun the Novice,
Chuckling merrily,
Ready to use his powers.

Hustled and carried along by the soldiers, they were soon back in the city, where the soldiers escorted them straight to the prefect's court. "Your Honour," they reported, "the constables have captured the robbers and brought them back." The prefect, sitting in his place in the court, rewarded the constables, inspected the booty and sent for the Kou family to collect it. Then he had Sanzang and the others brought into court. "You monks maintain that you come from a place far away to the east and are going to worship the Buddha in the Western Heaven," he said, interrogating them. "But really you're housebreakers who used dirty tricks so that you could get to know your way around." "Your Honour," Sanzang replied, "we are not robbers. I would not dare to deceive you. We carry a passport with us as proof. It was because we were so grateful to Mr. Kou's family for feeding us for a fortnight that when we ran into the robbers along our way we recovered the booty they had stolen from the Kou house. We were taking it back to the Kou house to pay our debt of gratitude when to our astonishment we were arrested as robbers by the constables. We really are not robbers, and I beg Your Honour to investigate closely." "You only made up that fancy talk about paying a debt of gratitude because you were arrested by the soldiers," the prefect replied. "If you really met other robbers why didn't you show your gratitude by capturing them and turning them in? Why are only the four of you here? Look at the wanted notice Kou Liang submitted. He accuses you by name. How dare you still dispute it!" When Sanzang heard this he felt like a storm-tossed boat on the ocean, and all his souls flew away. "Wukong," he said, "why don't you come forward and argue in our defence?" "The booty proves it," said Monkey. "Arguing would do no good." "That's right," the prefect said. "The booty is all here as proof. Do you still dare to deny it? Fetch the head-clamp," he instructed his underlings, "and put it round the head of that bald robber. Then beat him again."

Monkey was now very anxious. "Even though my master is fated to suffer this," he thought to himself, "I mustn't let it be too tough for him." Seeing the yamen runners tightening the cord to fix the head-clamp in place he opened his mouth to speak. "Please don't squeeze that monk's head, Your Honour. When we robbed the Kou house last night I was the one who lit the torches, carried the sword, stole the goods and killed the man. I was the ringleader. If you want to torture anyone, torture me. It's nothing to do with them. The only thing is that you mustn't let me go." On hearing this the prefect ordered, "Put the clamp on him first." The underlings then all fell on Monkey, fixed the clamp on his head, and tightened it so hard that the cord snapped with a twang. The clamp was fastened, tightened and snapped with a twang again. They did this three or four times, and the skin on his head was not even creased. When they changed the cord and were tightening it again someone was heard coming in to report, "Your Honour, the Lord Assistant Protector Chen from the capital is coming. Will you please come to greet him outside the city?" The prefect then ordered the head torturer, "Throw the bandits into gaol and keep a good eye on them. The torture and interrogation will continue after I have gone to greet my superior." The head torturer then marched the Tang Priest and the other three into the gaol. Pig and Friar Sand carried their luggage in with them.

"Disciple," said Sanzang, "what are we to do?" "In you go, Master," said Monkey with a grin, "in you go. There aren't any dogs barking in there. It'll be a lark." The four of them were then taken inside, and each of them was pushed on a torture rack, to which their bellies, heads and chests were tightly fastened. The warders then started beating them up again. Finding the agony unbearable, Sanzang called out, "Whatever shall I do, Wukong? Whatever shall I do?" "They're beating us because they want money," Brother Monkey replied. "As the saying goes,

Stay put when things are going well;
Spend cash when things are going ill.

They'll stop if you give them some money." "But where am I to get money from?" Sanzang asked. "If you haven't any money," Monkey replied, "clothes will do. Give them the cassock." These words cut Sanzang to the heart, but realizing that the beating was more than he could take he could only say, "Do as you will, Wukong." "Gentlemen," Monkey called out, "there's no need to beat us any more. There's a brocade cassock in one of the two bundles we brought in with us that's worth a fortune. Open them up and take it." When the warders heard this they all set to together, opening the bundles up to search them. There were some cotton clothes and a document case, but none of these were worth anything. Seeing something glowing brightly inside several layers of oiled paper the warders realized that it must be a treasure. When they shook it open and looked at it, this is what it looked like:

Exquisitely decorated with shining pearls,
Set with some wonderful Buddha treasures.
Embroidered dragons curled around;
Flying phoenixes adorned brocade edges.

As they all struggled to look they disturbed the head gaoler, who came up to them and shouted, "What are you all making this row about?" Falling to their knees, the warders replied, "His Honour has just started a case against four monks and sent them here. When we roughed them up a bit they gave us these two bundles. After we opened them we saw this, and we don't know how to deal with it. It would be a real pity to tear it up to divide between us, but it would be hard on everyone else if just one of us had it. It's a good thing you've come, sir: you can give us a ruling." The head gaoler could see that it was a cassock. Then he inspected the other clothes and the document case, and on opening the case to read the passport he saw that it was covered with seals and signatures from many states. "It's a good thing I saw this in time," he said. "If I hadn't, you people would have caused bad trouble. These monks aren't robbers. On no account touch their things. When His Honour questions them again tomorrow we'll find out the truth." The warders then gave the wrapping cloths back to the prisoners, who repacked them and handed them over to the head gaoler for safekeeping.

Evening was slowly drawing in. The drum could be heard from its tower, and the fire wardens began their patrols. By the third mark of the fourth watch Monkey could see that the others had stopped groaning and were fast asleep. "The master was fated to meet with the hardship of a night in gaol," he thought. "That was why I said nothing in our defence and didn't use my magic powers. But now the fourth watch is nearly over, and his suffering's almost done. I'd better start getting things sorted out if we're to leave this gaol at dawn." Just watch as he uses his powers to make himself smaller, get off the rack, shake himself and turn into a midge who flies out of the prison through a gap between the tiles over the eaves. By the light of the stars and the moon in the still, silent night sky, he could see where he was going, and he flew quietly straight towards the gates of the Kou house. On the west side of the road was a house where a lamp was shining brightly, and as he flew closer for a better look he saw that it was a house of beancurd-makers. An old man could be seen looking after the fire while an old woman was squeezing out the bean juice. "Wife," the old man suddenly called out, "Mr. Kou had wealth and sons, but he didn't live long. When we were boys we were both at school together. I was five years older than him. His father was called Kou Ming. In those days he had less than 150 acres. He couldn't even collect his overdue rents. Old Kou Ming died when his son was nineteen, and once the young man took charge of the household things went really well. He married the daughter of Zhang Wang — she used to be known as Threadneedle when she was a girl, but she made her husband a rich man. Once she came into his house his crops were good and the debts to him got paid. Whatever he bought showed a profit, and whatever he went in for made money. His family's worth a hundred thousand now. When he reached forty he turned pious and he fed ten thousand monks. Fancy him being kicked to death by robbers last night! Poor man. He was only sixty-four. Who would have thought so good a man would meet with so evil a reward and be murdered just when everything was going well for him? What a pity! What a pity!"

By the time Monkey had listened to all this it was now at the first mark of the fifth watch. He then flew into the Kou house, where a coffin was placed in the main room. A lamp was burning at the head, and around the coffin was incense, candles and fruit. His wife was weeping beside him, and the two sons also came to kowtow and weep, while their wives brought two bowls of rice as an offering. Monkey landed at the head of the coffin and coughed. This gave the two daughters-in-law such a fright that they ran outside waving their arms about. Kou Liang and his brother lay on the floor, too terrified to move, and crying out, "Oh, father, oh!" Their mother, being bolder, hit the head of the coffin and said, "Have you come back to life, old man?" "No," replied Monkey, imitating Mr. Kou's voice, to the great alarm of the two sons, who kept kowtowing, weeping, and repeating, "Oh, Father, oh!" Their mother summoned up even more courage to ask, "Husband, if you haven't come back to life why are you talking?"

"King Yama has sent demons to bring me here to talk to you," Monkey replied. "He told me that Threadneedle Zhang had been lying and trying to frame the innocent." In her surprise at hearing him call her by the name she had been known as a child, the old woman fell at once to her knees, kowtowed and said, "You're a fine old man! Fancy calling me by my childhood name at this age! What lies have I been telling? Which innocent people have I framed?" "Wasn't there something about 'The Tang Priest lit the torches, Pig incited to murder, Friar Sand stole the gold and silver, and Sun the Novice murdered our father'?" Monkey replied. "Your lies have landed those good men in terrible trouble. What really happened was that the Tang Priest and the other three teachers met some bandits and got our property back for us to show their thanks. How good of them! But you had to concoct a wanted notice and send our sons to denounce them to the authorities. The court threw them in gaol without making a careful investigation. The gaol god, the local deity and the city god were all so alarmed and uneasy that they reported it to King Yama, and he ordered demons to escort me back home. I'm to tell you to have them released as soon as possible. If you don't, I will have to make havoc here for a month. Nobody in the household, young or old — not even the dogs and the chickens — will be spared." Kou Liang and his brother kowtowed again and begged, "Please go back, Father, and don't harm us all. At dawn we'll submit a petition to the court for their release and withdraw our charge against them. We only want peace for both the living and the dead." When Monkey heard this he called out, "Burn sacrificial paper money. I am leaving." All his family started burning paper money.

Monkey then rose up on his wings and flew straight to the prefect's residence. Bending low to look he saw that there was a light in the bedroom: the prefect was already up. When Monkey flew into the main room, he saw a scroll-painting hanging on the back wall. It showed an official riding a piebald horse with several servants holding a blue umbrella and carrying a folding chair. Monkey did not know what the picture was about, but landed in the middle of it. All of a sudden the prefect came out of the bedroom and bent low to comb and wash himself. Monkey gave a sharp cough, alarming the prefect and sending him hurrying back into his bedroom. When he had combed his hair, washed himself and put on his formal clothes the prefect came out to burn incense to the picture and pray to it, "Venerable uncle, divine Jiang Qianyi, your dutiful nephew Jiang Kunsan is now prefect of Brazentower, thanks to the hereditary privilege won for me by your ancestral virtue, and also to my success in the examinations. Morning and evening I offer incense without interruption. Why did you speak today? I beg you not to haunt us and terrify the household." "So this is a holy picture of his ancestor," Brother Monkey thought with a hidden smile, and making the most of this chance he called out, "Nephew Kunsan, you have always been uncorrupt in the office you were given through ancestral privilege. How could you have been so stupid yesterday? You took four holy monks for thieves and threw them into prison without finding out why they had come. The prison god, the local deity and the city god were all so disturbed by this that they reported it to the king of Hell. He told demon envoys to bring me here to speak to you and advise you to consider the circumstances and find out the truth, and release them at once. Otherwise you'll have to come back to the Underworld with me for the case to be sorted out." When the prefect heard this he replied in terror, "Please go back now, sir. Your nephew will go straight into court and release them at once." "Very well then," Monkey said. "Burn some sacrificial paper money. I am going to report back to King Yama." The prefect lit incense, burned paper money and bowed in thanks.

When Monkey flew out again and looked around he saw that the east was already turning white. He then flew to the Diling county office, where all the county officials could be seen in the courtroom. "If I talk when I'm a midge," he thought, "and someone spots me it'll give the game away. That wouldn't do." So he gave himself a giant magical body where he was in mid air, and stretched down one foot that filled the whole courtroom. "Listen to me, you officials," he shouted. "I am the Roving God Rambler, sent here by the Jade Emperor. He says that sons of the Buddha on their way to fetch the scriptures have been beaten up in the prefectural gaol here, which has disturbed the gods of the three worlds. He has asked me to tell you to release them at once. If anything goes wrong I'm to use my other foot to kick all you county and prefecture officials to death, then crush all the people around here and trample the whole city to dust and ashes." At this the county magistrate and the other officials all fell to their knees and kowtowed in worship. "Please go back now, superior sage," they pleaded. "We are now going to the prefectural offices to request His Honour to release them immediately. We implore you not to move your feet and terrify us to death." Only then Monkey put away that magical body, turn into a midge again and fly back into the gaol through a gap between the tiles at the eaves, climb into his rack and go to sleep.

The story now tells that no sooner had the prefect entered his courtroom and ordered the notice inviting people to submit written requests to be carried outside than Kou Liang and his brother fell to their knees at the entrance, holding the notice in their arms. The prefect ordered them to come in, and when the prefect read the document that the two of them submitted he said in fury, "Yesterday you handed me a wanted notice. The thieves were arrested and you had the booty back. So why are you asking for them to be released today?" "Your Honour," the two brothers replied, tears streaming down, "last night our father's spirit appeared to us and said 'the holy monks from Tang captured the bandits, took our property back from them, released them and were kindly bringing the goods back to us to show their gratitude. How could you have treated them as robbers, captured them and made them suffer in gaol? The local god in the gaol and the city god were so alarmed and uneasy that they reported it to King Yama. King Yama ordered demons to escort me back to tell you to go to the prefectural court and submit another plea for the Tang Priest's release and thus avoid disaster. Otherwise everybody in the household would be killed.' This is why we have come with this request for their release. We beg you to help us, Your Honour." On hearing this the prefect thought, "Their father is a new ghost whose body is till warm, so it's not surprising that he should have appeared to them after what happened. But my uncle has been dead for five or six years. Why did he appear to me early this morning and tell me to investigate and release them? It really does look as though an injustice has been done."

As the prefect was thinking things over the magistrate and other officials of Diling county came rushing into the courtroom to say in a wild panic, "Disaster, Your Honour, disaster! The Jade Emperor has just sent the Roving God Rambler down to earth to tell you to release those good men from gaol this very moment. The monks captured yesterday weren't robbers: they are disciples of the Buddha going to fetch the scriptures. If there's any delay he's going to kick all us officials to death, then trample the whole city and all the people in it to dust and ashes." The prefect turned pale at this new shock, then told the head gaoler to write a release order and deliver them to the court. The prison doors were immediately opened and they were led out. "Goodness knows what sort of beating we're in for today," said Pig gloomily. "I can guarantee that they won't dare give you a single clout," said Monkey with a grin. "I've fixed everything up. When you go into the courtroom you absolutely mustn't kneel. He'll come down into the court to invite us to take the best seats. Then we'll ask for our luggage and the horse back from him. If anything's missing I'll give him a beating for your entertainment."

Before he had finished speaking they reached the entrance to the courtroom, where the prefect, the county magisrate and all the other officials came out to welcome them with the words, "When you holy monks arrived yesterday we were under urgent pressure to meet our superiors. In addition, we did see the stolen goods. That is why we did not find out the truth." The Tang Priest put his hands together in front of his chest, bowed and recounted in detail everything that had happened. The officials were all voluble in admitting, "We were wrong, we were wrong. Please, please don't be angry with us." They then asked if the monks had lost anything in the prison. Monkey stepped forward, opened his eyes wide in a glare and yelled at the top of his voice, "Our white horse was taken by the court officers, and the gaolers took our luggage. Give it back right now. It's our turn to torture and question you lot how. What should the punishment for wrongfully arresting innocent people as bandits be?" Seeing how ugly he was acting, the prefectural and county officials were all terrified. They told the people who had taken the horse to return the horse, and the men who had taken the luggage to return every single piece of it. Just look at how viciously the three disciples start acting, while the officials could only blame the Kou family to cover up their own blunder. "Disciples, "said Sanzang, trying to calm them down. "Let us go to the Kou house to question them and argue it out with them in order to make everything clear. Then we can find out who it was who took us for robbers." "Good idea," said Brother Monkey. "I'll call the dead man back and ask him who killed him."

Friar Sand hoisted the Tang Priest up on the horse right there in the courtroom, then escorted him outside with much shouting. All the prefectural and county officials accompanied them to the Kou house, so alarming Kou Liang and his brother that they kowtowed repeatedly in front of the gateway then led them into the hall. This was where old Mr. Kou's coffin lay, and the whole family was to be seen weeping inside the mourning drapes around it. "Stop howling, you lying old woman," Monkey shouted. "You tried to get innocent men killed. Wait till I call your husband back. We'll see what he has to say about who murdered him. That'll shame her." The officials all thought that Monkey was joking, but then he said, "Please keep my master company for a moment, Your Honours. Pig, Friar Sand, protect him weli. I'm off. I'll soon be back."

The splendid Great Sage bounded outside and rose up into the sky.

> *Coloured clouds were all around to cover up the house.*
> *Auspicious auras filled the sky to protect the primal deity.*

Only then did everyone recognize that Monkey was an immortal who could ride clouds and mists, and a sage who could bring the dead back to life. We will not tell of how they all burned incense and worshipped.

The Great Sage went straight to the Underworld by somersault cloud and charged into the Senluo Palace, causing such alarm that

The Ten Kings of the Underworld came out to raise their hands in greeting;
The demon judges of the five regions kowtowed in welcome.
A thousand trees of knives all leaned away;
Ten thousand hills of swords all levelled themselves.
In the City of the Unjustly Slain the fiends were converted;
Under the bridge over Punishment River the dead return to life.
The divine light was like the grace of Heaven,
And everywhere shone bright in the palaces of darkness.

The Ten Kings received the Great Sage, greeted him, and asked him why he had come. "Who's got the ghost of Kou Hong who used to feed monks in Diling County in the prefecture of Brazentower?" said Monkey. "Find him and give him to me at once." "Kou Hong is a very good man," the Ten King replied. "He came here himself. No demon had to envoys drag him here with their hooks. He met King Ksitigarbha's Goldenclad Boy, who took him to see Ksitigarbha." Monkey then took his leave of them and went straight to the Turquoise Cloud Palace, where he saw the Bodhisattva King Ksitigarbha. When the Bodhisattva had greeted him Monkey explained what had happened. "Liang Hong's allotted span had been completed," the Bodhisattva said with delight, "and his life was over. That is why he left the world behind and came here without touching his bed. As he was such a good man who had fed monks I have made him a chief recorder in charge of the register of good deeds. But since you have come here to fetch him, Great Sage, I shall grant him a twelve-year extension of his life on earth. Let him leave with the Great Sage." The Goldenclad Boy then led out Kou Hong, who on seeing Monkey kept saying, "Teacher, save me! Teacher!" "You were kicked to death by robbers," said Monkey, "and now you're in the Bodhisattva King Ksitigarbha's place in the Under world. I've come to fetch you and take you to the world of the living to sort this matter out. The Bodhisattva will let you go back and has given you another twelve years of life, after which you'll come back here." The old gentleman kowtowed to him endlessly.

Having thanked and taken his leave of the Bodhisattva, Monkey blew on Kou Hong, turned him into vapour, tucked him into his sleeve and left the Underworld to go back to the world of the living. He rode his cloud back to the Kou house, told Pig to lever the lid off the coffin and pushed Kou Hong's spirit back into the body. A moment later Kou Hong started breathing as he came back to life. Climbing out of his coffin, he kowtowed to the Tang Priest and his three disciples with the words, "Teachers, teachers, I was wrongly killed, but my master went to the Underworld to bring me back to life. I owe him my recovery." His thanks were unending. When he turned round and saw all the officials drawn up in line he kowtowed again and asked, "Why are all your lordships in my house?" "Your sons first submitted a wanted notice," the prefect replied, "and accused the holy monks by name. I sent men to arrest them, not realizing that the holy monks had met the robbers who raided your house, taken the booty off them and were returning it to your house. I was wrong to have them arrested, and I had them thrown into gaol without making a detailed investigation. Last night your spirit appeared, my late uncle came to lodge a complaint with me, and the Roving God Rambler came down to earth in the county offices. After so many manifestations I released the holy monks, and they have brought you back to life."

"Your Honour," said Mr. Kou on his kness, "these four holy monks really have been wronged. That night over thirty bandits with torches and weapons robbed my house. Because I could not bear to lose all those things I tried to reason with the robbers, but to my horror they kicked me to death. What's it got to do with these four gentlemen?" He then called for his wife. "Why did you people make that lying report about who had killed me? Will you please determine their punishments, Your Honour." Everyone in the family, young and old alike, kowtowed. In his magnanimity the prefect spared them from punishment. Kou Hong then ordered a banquet to thank the prefectural and county officials for their generosity. The officials all returned to their offices without sitting down at the banquet. The next day the sign announcing that monks would be fed was hung out again, and another attempt was made to keep Sanzang there. Sanzang refused absolutely to stay any longer. Once again Mr. Kou invited his friends and relations, arranged for flags and canopies and saw them off as before. Indeed,

However remote the place evil deeds can be done;
Heaven may be high, but it does not desert the good.
Steadily they plod along towards the Tathagata
Until they reach the gate of bliss on Vulture Peak.

If you do not know what happened when they met the Buddha, listen to the explanation in the next instalment.

CHAPTER NINETY-EIGHT

When the Ape and the Horse are tamed they cast off their husks; When all the deeds have been done reality is seen.

The story told how after coming back to life Mr. Kou once more arranged for parasols, banners, drummers, musicians, Buddhist monks, Taoist priests, his friends and his relations to see Sanzang off again. But instead of describing this we will tell of the Tang Priest and his three disciples taking the main road. The West was indeed a land of the Buddha, unlike anywhere else. They saw precious flowers, rare grasses, ancient cypresses and hoary pines. In all the places they passed through every family was pious and fed monks. Under every mountain people cultivated their conduct; in all the forests travellers recited sutras. Master and disciples took shelter each night and set out at dawn, till six or seven days later a mass of high buildings and splendid halls suddenly came into view. Truly they were

Thrusting a hundred feet into the heavens,
Touching the Milky Way in the sky.
Lower your head and see the setting sun;
Put out your hand and pluck a shooting star.
The spacious windows enclose the cosmos;
The towering roofbeams join up with the clouds.
Yellow cranes bring letters as the autumn trees grow old;
Coloured phoenix epistles come in the fresh evening breeze.
These are sacred and precious palaces and gates,
Jewelled, intricate buildings and courtyards.
In the holy halls the Way is discussed;

Sutras are transmitted throughout the universe.
The flowers are beautiful as they turn towards the spring;
Green are the pine trees in the rain.
Purple fungus and immortals' fruits ever flourish;
All beings respond as red phoenixes soar.

Sanzang raised his whip and pointed with it as he said, "What a fine place, Wukong." "Master," said Monkey, "when you were in those delusive places where you saw false images of Buddhas you insisted on prostrating yourself in front of them. But today, when you've reached the real place where there is the true image of the Buddha, you won't even dismount. What do you mean by it?" No sooner did he hear this than Sanzang sprang straight out of the saddle and went to the gateway. A young lay brother who stood to one side of the monastery gateway called out, "You must be the people from the east who have come to fetch the scriptures." The venerable elder quickly straightened his clothes and raised his head to look around. He saw that the boy was

Wearing clothes of golden brocade,
Waving a jade-handled whisk.
Wearing clothes of golden brocade
He feasted in pavilions by the Jasper Pool;
Waving a jade-handled whisk
He dusted the steps of the purple palaces.
At his side hung an immortal's tablet;
And on his feet were sandals.
He was a true winged adept,
Elegant and remarkable.
Having won immortality he lived in a wonderful land,
Cultivating eternal life and escaping from worldly dust.
The holy priest did not recognize the stranger on Vulture Peak,
The Gold-crested Immortal of yesteryear.

The Great Sage Monkey did, however, recognize him. "Master," said Monkey, "this is the Great Gold-crested Immortal who lives at the Jade Truth Temple at the foot of Vulture Peak. He is here to greet us." Only then did Sanzang realize who he was and step forward to salute him. "You have finally arrived here this year," replied the Great Immortal with a smile. "I was fooled by the Bodhisattva Guanyin. Ten years ago she went to the east at the Buddha's command to find the Pilgrim who would fetch the scriptures. She told me then he would be here within two or three years. I have been waiting for years on end with no news of you at all. I never thought that it would be this year before we met." Putting his hands together in front of his chest, Sanzang replied, "I am very grateful to you for your kindness, Great Immortal, very grateful." Sanzang and his three disciples led the horse and carried the baggage with them into the Taoist temple, where they were introduced to all the Great Immortals there. Tea and a vegetarian meal were then ordered, and the Taoist boys were told to heat scented water for the holy monks to bathe in before climbing to the Buddha land. Indeed,

When achievements are complete it is right to bathe;
The fundamental nature has been trained into innate truth.
Many thousand troubles end today:
The nine prohibitions and triple surrender lead to renewal.
The monsters all done with, they climb to the Buddha land;
With disasters ended they see the Sramana.
Dirt and filth now washed away, they are wholly pure;
Returning to the fundamental, their bodies are imperishable.

By the time master and disciples had bathed the day was drawing to a close. They spent the night in the Jade Truth Temple.

The next morning the Tang Priest changed into his brocade cassock, put on his Vairocana mitre and grasped his monastic staff in his hand to climb the steps of the main hall and take his leave of the Great Immortal. "Yesterday you were in rags," the

Great Immortal said with a smile, "but today you are dressed in splendour. I can see from your appearance that you are indeed a son of the Buddha." Sanzang then bowed in farewell. "Wait a moment," the Great Immortal said. "I will see you off." "There's no need for you to see us off," Monkey replied. "I know the way." "What you know," said the Great Immortal, "is the way by cloud. The holy monk has never gone by cloud. He must go by the overland way." "You're right," replied Monkey. "Although I've been here several times I've always come and gone by cloud. I've never come here on foot. If there's an overland route I'll trouble you to see us along it. My master is very serious about worshipping the Buddha, so I'd be very grateful if you could hurry up about it." The Great Immortal chuckled as he took the Tang Priest by hand and led the Incense to the gate of the Dharma. The way led not out by the temple's front entrance but through the main hall and out through the back gate. Pointing towards Vulture Peak, the Great Immortal said, "Holy monk, do you see the auspicious light of many colours and the richly textured aura in the sky? That is the summit of Vulture Peak, the holy territory of the Lord Buddha." As soon as he saw it the Tang Priest bowed low. "Master," said Brother Monkey with a smile, "we haven't got to the place for bowing yet. As the saying goes, 'The mountain may be in view, but your horse will collapse before you get there.' We're still quite a long way from the place, so why start bowing now? If you bow all the way from here to the top, however many times will you have to hit your head on the ground?" "Holy monk," said the Great Immortal, "You, the Great Sage, Marshal Tian Peng, and the Curtain-raising General have now reached the blessed land and seen Vulture Peak. I am going back now." Sanzang took his leave of the Great Immortal and continued on his way.

The Great Sage led the Tang Priest and the others slowly up Vulture Peak. Within a couple of miles they reached a river of mighty rolling waves some three miles wide. There was no sign of anyone anywhere around. "Wukong," said Sanzang with alarm, "we have come the wrong way. I wonder if the Great

Immortal misdirected us. This river is so wide and the waves so big, and there are no boats to be seen. How are we to cross it?" "He didn't send us the wrong way," replied Monkey with a smile. "Look over there. That's a bridge, isn't it? Once we're over that we'll have completed the true achievement." When the venerable elder and the others went closer to look they saw a tablet beside it on which were written the words CLOUD-TOUCHING CROSSING. Now this bridge was only a single log. Indeed,

From afar it seemed to span the void like a beam of jade;
Seen closer, the bridge was but a withered spar crossing the water.
To bind a river and frame the sea is easier
Than walking along the trunk of a single tree.
The glow of a myriad rainbows spread out all around;
A thousand lengths of fine white silk stretched to the edge of the sky.
It was narrow, slippery and hard to cross,
Unless one was a god who could walk on coloured clouds.

"Wukong," said Sanzang in fear and trembling, "no mortal man could cross that bridge. Let us look elsewhere to find the way." "But this is the way," replied Monkey with a smile, "this is the way." "Nobody's going to dare cross that even if it is the right way," said Pig with alarm. "The river's so wide, and there are those terrible waves, and all there is is that narrow, slippery tree-trunk. We couldn't take a single step." "You all stand there while I go on it to show you," replied Monkey.

The splendid Great Sage strode forward and sprang on the single-trunk bridge. He quickly ran across to the other side, swaying as he went, and called out, "Come over, come over." The Tang Priest waved in refusal, while Pig and Friar Sand bit their fingers and said, "It's much too hard." Monkey then ran back again from the far side and pulled at Pig. "Come with me, you idiot," he said, "come with me." "It's too slippery, it's too slippery," said Pig, lying down on the ground. "I could never cross it. Please spare me that and let me cross by wind and mist." Monkey held him down as he replied, "This is no place for you to be allowed to go riding wind and mist. You can only become a Buddha by crossing this bridge." "Brother," said Pig, "I'll never make it. Honestly, I can't walk across."

As the two of them were pulling at each other and fighting, Friar Sand went over to talk them round. Only then did they let go of each other. Sanzang then looked round to see a man poling a boat towards them from downriver and shouting, "Ferry! Come aboard." "Stop fooling around, disciples," said a delighted venerable elder. "There is a ferry-boat coming." The other three sprang to their feet and all watched together as the boat drew closer. It was a bottomless craft. Monkey had already spotted with the golden pupils in his fiery eyes that this was the Welcoming Lord Buddha, who is also known as Ratnadhvaja, the Royal Buddha of Brightness, but instead of giving this away he just kept calling, 'Over here, punt, over here." A moment later the ferryman had punted his boat up to the bank and was again shouting, "Ferry! Come aboard!" Sanzang was once more alarmed at the sight. "Your boat has no bottom," he said, "so however could you ferry anyone across?" "This boat of mine," the Buddha said,

"Has been famous since Chaos was first divided,
And been punted by me without any changes.
It is stable in wind and stable in waves,
Enjoying great peace with no start and no end.
Untouched by the six types of dust, it returns to the One,
Carries on calmly through all kinds of calamity.
Hard it is for a bottomless boat to cross the oceans,
But since ancient times it has ferried all creatures."

The Great Sage Monkey put his hands together in front of his chest and thanked him with the words, "I am grateful to you for your generosity in coming to welcome my master. Step aboard, Master. That boat of his may have no bottom, but it's stable, and won't capsize even in wind and waves." The venerable elder was still very doubtful, but Monkey seized him by the arms and pushed him forward. Unable to keep on his feet, the master tumbled into the water, where the ferryman grabbed hold of him at once and stood him on the boat. The master shook his clothes and stamped his feet, complaining about Monkey, who led Friar Sand and Pig to stand on board, bringing the luggage and the horse with them. Gently and strongly the Buddha pushed off, at which a corpse came floating downstream to the horror of the venerable elder. "Don't be frightened, Master," said Monkey. "That's you." "It's you, it's you," said Pig. Friar Sand clapped his hands as he said, "It's you, it's you!" The boatman gave a call, then also put in, too, "It's you! Congratulations! Congratulations!" The three of them all joined in these congratulations as the ferryman punted the boat quickly and steadily over the immortal Cloud-touching Crossing. Sanzang turned around and sprang lightly ashore on the opposite bank. There is a poem about this that goes:

When the womb-born flesh and body of blood is cast aside;
The primal spirit finds kinship and love.
On this morning of actions completed and Buddhahood attained
The thirty-six kinds of dust from the past are washed away.

This was indeed what is meant by great wisdom, the boundless dharma of crossing to the other bank. When the four of them climbed the bank and looked back the bottomless boat had already disappeared, goodness knew where. Only when Brother Monkey explained that it had been the Welcoming Buddha did Sanzang find enlightenment. At once he turned round to thank his three disciples. "Let's not exchange thanks," said Monkey. "We've helped each other. You saved us three, Master, and showed us the way to win merit so as to complete the true achievement. And we have protected you, Master, holding to the faith and helping you happily to cast off your mortal body.

Master, look at the magnificent scenery ahead. Flowers, grasses, pines and bamboo, as well as phoenixes, cranes and deer. Compare it with those places where evil beings created illusions through transformation. Ask yourself which is beautiful and good, and which ugly and evil." Sanzang was full of expressions of gratitude. All of them were now light of body and cheerful as they walked up Vulture Peak. Soon the ancient Thunder Monastery could be seen:

Its rooftops touched the heavens,
Its roots joined with the Sumeru range.
Amazing peaks spread out in serried rank;
Craggy rocks formed interlocking shapes.
Under the hanging scar were wonderful plants and flowers;
Beside the winding path grew magic mushrooms and orchids.
Immortal apes were picking the fruit of the peach trees,
Like gold amid burning flames;
White cranes perched in the branches of the pines
As if they were jade creatures amid smoke.
Coloured phoenixes in pairs,
Green phoenixes two by two.
The pairs of coloured phoenixes
Brought blessings on the world as they called to the sun;
The green phoenixes two by two
Danced in the wind, a rare and wonderful sight.
On the gleaming golden tiles were figures of mandarin ducks;
The brilliantly patterned bricks were set with agate.
To east and west
Were flowers of palaces and pearls of gateways;
To north and south
Were endless precious pavilions and high buildings.
The Devaraja Hall streamed with coloured light;
Purple flames rose before the Lokapalas' Chamber.
Stupas stood out,

*And fragrant were the blossoms of the udumbara tree.**
Truly this was a place so fine it might have come from heaven,
Where the days seemed long under leisurely clouds.
Away from the mortal world, all fates came to an end;
All kalpas were complete within the Dharma hall.

As master and disciples walked freely and at their ease up to the summit of Vulture Peak lay people could be seen under the green pines, and pious men and women amid the jade-coloured cypresses. The venerable elder bowed to them politely, whereupon all the lay men and women, monks and nuns all hastened to put their hands together and say to him, "Do not bow to us, holy monk. Come back and talk with us when you have seen Sakyamuni." "It's a bit early for that," replied Monkey with a grin. "Let's go and worship the boss."

The venerable elder waved his arms and performed a ritual dance as he followed Monkey straight to the gates of the Thunder Monastery, where four great vajrapanis greeted them with the words, "Have you arrived now, holy monk?" "Yes," Sanzang replied with a bow, "Your disciple Xuanzang has arrived." Having given this reply he was about to go in through the gateway. "Please wait for a moment, holy monk," the vajrapanis said. "Let us report before you come in." The vajrapanis sent a report of the Tang Priest's arrival to the four great vajrapanis on the middle gates, who in turn reported it to the inner gates, inside which were divine monks making offerings. As soon as they heard of the Tang Priest's arrival they all hurried to the Mahavira Hall, where they announced to the Tathagata Sakyamuni Buddha, "The holy monk from the Tang Court has arrived at your noble monastery to fetch the scriptures." The Lord Buddha was very pleased. He called together his Eight Bodhisattvas, Four Vajrapanis, Five Hundred Arhats, Three Thousand Protectors, Eleven Heavenly Shiners and Eighteen Guardians, who drew themselves up in two lines and passed on the

* In Buddhist mythology the udumbara tree blooms only once in 3,000 years.

Buddha's command summoning the Tang Priest to enter. Thus it was that the invitation was sent down from one level to the next: "Let the holy monk come in." Observing the requirements of ritual, the Tang Priest went in through the gate with Wukong and Wujing, who were leading the horse and carrying the luggage. Indeed,

In the past he had struggled to fulfil his commission
After leaving the emperor at the steps of the throne.
At dawn he had climbed mountains in mist and in dew;
At dusk he had slept on rocks amid the clouds.
He had carried his stick across three thousand rivers,
And climbed up countless crags with his monastic staff.
His every thought had been set on the true achievement,
And today he was finally to see the Tathagata.

As the four of them arrived in front of the Mahavira Hall they all prostrated themselves and kowtowed to the Tathagata, then to their left and right. After they had each completed three rounds of worship they then knelt before the Buddha to present their passport. When the Tathagata had read it carefully he handed it back to Sanzang, who bowed his head low and reported, "Your disciple Xuanzang has made the long journey to your precious monastery at the command of the Great Tang emperor to beg for the true scriptures that will save all living beings. I implore the Lord Buddha in his goodness to grant them at once so that I may return to my country." The Tathagata then opened his compassionate mouth and in the great mercy of his heart said to Sanzang, "Your eastern land is in the Southern Continent of Jambu. As the sky is lofty there, the soil deep, its products many, and the people multitudinous there is much covetousness, murder, debauchery, lying, deception and dishonesty. They do not follow the Buddhist teaching, do not turn towards good destinies, and do not honour the sun, moon and stars or value the five grains. They are not loyal, filial, righteous or kind. In the delusion of their hearts they mislead themselves, cheating on weights and measures, taking life and killing animals, thus creating such boundless evil karma and such a superabundance of sin and evil that they bring the catastrophe of hell on themselves. That is why they must fall for ever into the dark underworld to suffer the torments of being hammered, smashed, ground and pounded, or are reborn as animals. Many of them take the shape of furry, horned creatures to pay back the debts they owe from earlier lives and feed others with their own flesh. It is for such reasons that some fall into the Avici Hell, from which they never emerge to be reborn. Although Confucius established the doctrine of benevolence, righteousness, correct behaviour and wisdom, and although successive emperors have applied the penalties of imprisonment, exile, strangulation and beheading, none of this affected those stupid, benighted, self-indulgent and unrestrained people. Why? I have Three Stores of scriptures that offer deliverance from suffering and release from disaster. Of these Three Stores one is the Store of Dharma that deals with Heaven; one is the Store of Sastras that deal with the Earth, and one is the Store of Sutras that can save ghosts. There are thirty-five scriptures altogether, in 15,144 scrolls. These are indeed the path to the truth, the gateway to goodness. They include everything about the astronomy, geography, personalities, birds, beasts, trees, flowers, objects of use and human affairs of the world's four continents. Now that you have come from afar I would present them all to you to take away with you, but the people of your country are stupid and coarse. They are slanderers of the truth who cannot understand the mysteries of our teachings. Ananda, Kasyapa," he called, "take the four of them to the foot of the jewel tower and give them a vegetarian meal. After the meal open up the pavilion, select a few rolls from each of the thirty-five scriptures in my Three Stores, and tell them to propagate these scriptures in the east, where they may eternally grant their great goodness."

Acting on the orders of the Buddha the two arhats then led the four pilgrims to the bottom of the tower, where no end of rare and wonderful jewels and treasures were set out. Here the divinities who made offerings set out a vegetarian banquet, with immortal food, immortal delicacies, immortal tea, immortal fruit, and every kind of culinary delight not to be found in the mortal world. Master and disciples bowed their heads to the ground in thanks for the Buddha's kindness and proceeded to eat to their hearts' content. Indeed

Precious flames and golden light dazzled the eye,
While the rare incense and delicacies were marvellously fine.
The thousand-storeyed golden pavilion was infinitely lovely,
And pure sounded immortals' music on the ear.
Meatless food and magic flowers of the sort that are rare on earth,
Fragrant teas and exotic dishes that give eternal life.
After a long period of enduring a thousand kinds of suffering,
Today comes the glorious happiness of the Way completed.

This was a piece of good fortune for Pig, and a great benefit to Friar Sand as they ate their fill of the food in the Buddha's land that gave eternal life and new flesh and bones for old. The two arhats kept the four of them company till the meal was over, after which they went to the treasure pavilion, where the doors were opened for them to go in and look. Over this all was a thousandfold aura of coloured light and auspicious vapours, while brilliant mists and clouds of good omen wafted all around. All over the scripture shelves and on the outside of the cases were pasted red labels on which were neatly written the titles of the scriptures. They were the

Nirvana sutra	*748 rolls*
Bodhisattva sutra	*1,021 rolls*
Akasagarbha sutra	*400 rolls*
Surangama sutra	*110 rolls*
Collection of sutras on the meaning of grace	*50 rolls*
Determination sutra	*140 rolls*
Ratnagarbha sutra	*45 rolls*

Avatamsaka sutra	*500 rolls*
Sutra on Worshipping Bhutatathata	*90 rolls*
Mahaprajnaparamita sutra	*916 rolls*
Mahaprabhasa sutra	*300 rolls*
Adbhuta-dharma sutras	*1,110 rolls*
Vimalakirti sutra	*170 rolls*
The Three Sastras	*270 rolls*
Diamond sutra	*100 rolls*
Saddharma sastra	*120 rolls*
Buddhacaritakavya sutra	*800 rolls*
Pancanaga sutra	*32 rolls*
Bodhisattva-vinaya sutra	*116 rolls*
Mahasamnipata sutras	*130 rolls*
Makara sutra	*350 rolls*
Saddharma-pundarika sutra	*100 rolls*
Yoga sutra	*100 rolls*
Precious Eternity sutra	*220 rolls*
Sutra on the Western Heaven	*130 rolls*
Samghika sutra	*157 rolls*
Samyukta-Buddhadesa sutra	*1,950 rolls*
Mahayana-sraddhotpadasa sutra	*1,000 rolls*
Great Wisdom sutra	*1,080 rolls*
Ratna-prabhava sutra	*1,280 rolls*
Original Pavilion sutra	*850 rolls*
Principal vinaya sutra	*200 rolls*
Mahamayuri-vidyarajni sutra	*200 rolls*
Vijnaptimatra-tasiddhi sastra	*100 rolls*
Abhidharma-kosa sastra	*200 rolls*

Ananda and Kasyapa led the Tang Priest to read the titles of all the scriptures. "You have come here from the East, holy monk," they said to him. "Have you brought us any presents? Hand them over right now, then we can give you the scriptures." When Sanzang heard this he said, "Your disciple Xuanzang has come a very long way, and I did not bring any with me." "That's very fine," the two arhats said with a laugh. "If we hand the scriptures over for nothing, they'll be passed down through the ages and our successors will have to starve to death." Monkey could not stand hearing them talking tough like this and refusing to hand the scriptures over, so he shouted, "Let's go and report them to the Tathagata, Master. We'll get him to give me the scriptures himself." "Shut up!" said Kasyapa. "Where do you think you are, acting up like this? Come here and take the scriptures." Pig and Friar Sand, who were keeping their own tempers under control, calmed Monkey down. They turned back to accept the scriptures, which were packed one by one into the luggage. Some of it was put on the horse's back, and the rest tied up as two carrying-pole loads that Pig and Friar Sand shouldered. They all then returned to the Buddha's throne, kowtowed, thanked the Tathagata and went straight out. They bowed twice to every Buddha and every Bodhisattva they met. When they reached the main entrance they bowed to the bhiksus, the bhiksunis, the laymen and the laywomen, taking their leave of each one. Then they hurried back down the mountain.

The story tells not of them but of the Ancient Buddha Dipamkara, who had been quietly listening in the library when the scriptures were handed over. He understood perfectly well that Ananda and Kasyapa had handed over wordless scriptures. "Those stupid monks from the East didn't realize that those were wordless scriptures," he thought with a smile to himself. "The holy monks' journey across all those mountains and rivers will be a complete waste. Who is in attendance here?" he called, and the arhat Suklavira stepped forward. "Use your divine might," Dipamkara instructed him, "and go after the Tang Priest like a shooting star. Take the wordless scriptures from him and tell him to come back to fetch the true scriptures." The arhat Suklavira then flew off on a storm wind that roared away from the Thunder Monastery as he gave a great display of his divine might. That splendid wind really was

A warrior from the Buddha's presence,
Greater than the two wind gods of the Xun quarter.
The angry roars from his divine orifices

Were more powerful by far than the puffs of a young girl.
This wind made
Fish and dragons lose their dens,
While the waves flowed backwards in rivers and seas.
Black apes could not present the fruit they carried;
Yellow cranes turned back to the clouds as they sought their nests.
Ugly rang the song of the red phoenix;
Raucous were the calls of the multicoloured pheasants.
The branches of hoary pines were broken
As the flowers of the udumbara blew away.
Every cane of green bamboo bowed low;
All the blooms of golden lotus swayed.
The sound of the bell was carried a thousand miles
While the chanting of sutras flew lightly up the ravines.
Ruined was the beauty of flowers under the crag;
The tender shoots of plants were laid low by the path
The brilliant phoenixes could hardly spread their wings;
White deer hid beneath the cliffs.
The heavens were heavy with fragrance
As the clear wind blew right through the clouds.

The Tang Priest was walking along when he smelt the fragrant wind, but he paid no attention to it, taking it for an auspicious sign of the Lord Buddha. Then a noise could be heard as a hand reached down from mid-air to lift the scriptures lightly off the horse's back, which gave Sanzang such a shock that he beat his chest and howled aloud. Pig scrambled along in pursuit, Friar Sand guarded the carrying-poles loaded with scriptures, and Brother Monkey flew after the arhat. Seeing that Monkey had almost caught up with him, and frightened that the merciless cudgel would make no bones about wounding him badly, the arhat tore the bundle of scriptures to shreds and flung it into the dust. When Monkey saw the bundle falling in pieces that were being scattered by the fragrant wind he stopped chasing the arhat and brought his cloud down to look after the scriptures.

The arhat Suklavira put the wind and the clouds away, then went back to report to Dipamkara.

When Pig, who was also in pursuit, saw the scriptures falling he helped Monkey to collect them up and carry them back to the Tang Priest. "Disciples," the Tang Priest exclaimed, tears pouring from his eyes, "even in this world of bliss evil demons cheat people." After gathering up the scattered scriptures in his arms Friar Sand opened one of them up and saw that it was as white as snow: not a word was written on it. Quickly he handed it to Sanzang with the remark, "There's nothing in this scroll, Master." Monkey opened out another scroll to find that it had nothing written in it either. Pig opened another and it too had nothing in it. "Open them all for us to examine," said Sanzang. Every single scroll was blank paper. "We Easterners really do have no luck," he said, sighing and groaning. "What point is there in fetching wordless scriptures like these? How could I ever face the Tang emperor? I will have no way of avoiding execution for the crime of lying to my sovereign." Monkey, who already understood what had happened, then said to the Tang Priest, "Say no more, Master. Ananda and Kasyapa gave us these scrolls of blank paper because we hadn't got any presents to give them when they asked for them. Let's go back, report them to the Tathagata and get them accused of extortion." "That's right," shouted Pig, "that's right. Let's report them." The four of them then hurried up the mountain again, and after a few steps they were rushing back to the Thunder Monastery.

Before long they were once more outside the gates of the monastery, where everyone raised their clasped hands in greeting. "Have you holy monks come to exchange your scriptures?" they asked with smiles. Sanzang nodded and expressed his thanks. The vajrapanis did not block them, but let them go straight in to the Mahavira Hall. "Tathagata," yelled Monkey, "our master and the rest of us have had to put up with endless monsters, demons, troubles and hardships to get here from the east to worship you. You gave the orders for the scriptures to be handed over, but Ananda and Kasyapa didn't do so because they were trying to extort things from us. They conspired and deliberately let us take away blank paper versions without a single word written on them. But what's the point in taking those? I beg you to have them punished, Tathagata." "Stop yelling," replied the Lord Buddha with a smile. "I already know that they asked you for presents. But the scriptures cannot be casually passed on. Nor can they be taken away for nothing. In the past bhiksus and holy monks went down the mountain and recited these scriptures to the family of the elder Zhao in the land of Sravasti. This ensured peace and safety for the living and deliverance for the dead members of the family. All that was asked for was three bushels and three pecks of granular gold. I said they had sold the scriptures too cheap, so I saw to it that zhao's sons and grandsons would be poor. You were given blank texts because you came here to fetch them empty-handed. The blank texts are true, wordless scriptures, and they really are good. But as you living beings in the east are so deluded and have not achieved enlightenment we'll have to give you these ones instead. Ananda, Kasyapa," he called, "fetch the true scriptures with words at once. Choose a few rolls from each title to give them, then come back here and tell me how many."

The two arhats then led the four pilgrims to the foot of the library building and once again asked the Tang Priest for a present. Having nothing else to offer, he ordered Friar Sand to bring out the begging bowl of purple gold and presented it with both hands. "Your disciple is poor and has come a very long way," he said, "and I did not bring any presents with me. This bowl was given to me by the Tang emperor with his own hands to beg for food with on my journey. I now offer it to you as a token of my heartfelt feelings. I beg you arhats not to despise it but to keep it. When I return to my court I shall report this to the Tang emperor, who will certainly reward you richly. I only ask you to give me the true scriptures that have words to save me from failing in my imperial mission and making this long, hard journey for nothing."

Ananda accepted the bowl with no more than a hint of a smile. The warriors guarding the precious library building, the kitchen staff responsible for the spices and the arhats in charge of the library rubbed each other's faces, patted each other's backs, flicked each other with their fingers and pulled faces. "Disgraceful," they all said with grins, "disgraceful. Demanding presents from the pilgrims who've come to fetch the scriptures!" A moment later Ananda was frowning with embarrassment but still holding the bowl and not letting go. Only then did Kasyapa go into the library to check the scriptures through one by one and give them to Sanzang. "Disciples," called Sanzang, "take a good look at them, not like last time." The three of them took the rolls and examined them one by one. All had words. 5,048 rolls were handed over, the total in a single store. They were neatly packed up and put on the horse, and those left over were made into a carrying-pole load for Pig to take. Friar Sand carried their own luggage, and as Brother Monkey led the horse the Tang Priest took his staff, pushed his Vairocana mitre into position, shook his brocade cassock, and went happily into the presence of the Tathagata. Indeed,

Sweet taste the True Scriptures of the Great Store,
Created fine and majestic by the Tathagata.
Remember what Xuanzang suffered to climb this mountain:
Ananda's greed was something ridiculous.
What they did not notice at first Dipamkara helped them to see;
Later the scriptures were real and they then found peace.
Successful now, they would take the scriptures to the east,
Where all could be refreshed by their life-giving richness.

Ananda and Kasyapa led the Tang Priest to see the Tathagata, who ascended his lotus throne and directed the two great arhats Dragon-queller and Tiger-subduer to strike the cloud-ringing stone chimes that summoned all the Three Thousand Buddhas, Three Thousand Protectors, Eight Vajrapanis, Four Bodhisattvas, Five Hundred Arhats, Eight Hundred Bhiksus, the host of laymen, bhiksunis, laywomen, and the greater and lesser honoured ones and holy monks of every cave, every heaven, the blessed lands and the magic mountains. Those who were supposed to sit were asked to ascend their precious thrones, and those who were supposed to stand stood on either side. All of a sudden heavenly music rang out from afar and magical sounds wafted around. The air was full of countless beams of auspicious light and of aura upon aura as all the Buddhas gathered together to pay their respects to the Tathagata. "How many rolls of scripture have you given them, Ananda and Kasyapa?" the Tathagata asked. "Please tell me the numbers one by one." The two arhats then reported, "We are now handing over for the Tang court the

Nirvana sutra	*400 rolls*
Bodhisattva sutra	*360 rolls*
Akasagarbha sutra	*20 rolls*
Surangama sutra	*30 rolls*
Collection of sutras on the meaning of grace	*40 rolls*
Determination sutra	*40 rolls*
Ratnagarbha sutra	*20 rolls*
Avatamsaka sutra	*81 rolls*
Sutra on Worshipping Bhutatathata	*30 rolls*
Mahaprajnaparamita sutra	*600 rolls*
Mahaprabhasa sutra	*50 rolls*
Adbhuta-dharma sutras	*550 rolls*
Vimalakirti sutra	*30 rolls*
The Three Sastras	*42 rolls*
Diamond sutra	*1 roll*
Saddharma sastra	*20 rolls*
Buddhacaritakavya sutra	*116 rolls*
Pancanaga sutra	*20 rolls*
Bodhisattva-vinaya sutra	*60 rolls*
Mahasamnipata sutras	*30 rolls*
Makara sutra	*140 rolls*
Saddharma-pundarika sutra	*10 rolls*
Yoga sutra	*30 rolls*
Precious Eternity sutra	*170 rolls*

Sutra on the Western Heaven	*30 rolls*
Samghika sutra	*110 rolls*
Samyukta-Buddhadesa sutra	*1,638 rolls*
Mahayana-sraddhotpadasa sastra	*50 rolls*
Great Wisdom sutra	*90 rolls*
Ratna-prabhava sutra	*140 rolls*
Original Pavilion sutra	*56 rolls*
Principal vinaya sutra	*10 rolls*
Mahamayuri-vidyarajni sutra	*14 rolls*
Vijnaptimatra-tasiddhi sastra	*10 rolls*
Abhidharma-kosa sastra	*10 rolls*

From the thirty-five scriptures in all of the stores we have selected 5,048 rolls to give to the holy monk. These will be kept and handed down in Tang. They have now all been packed neatly and put on the horse or made into carrying-pole loads. The pilgrims are only waiting to express their thanks."

Sanzang and his three followers then tethered the horse, put down the loads, joined their hands in front of their chests and bowed in worship. "The achievement of these scriptures is immeasurable," the Tathagata said to the Tang Priest, "Although they are the source of foreknowledge and reflection for my school they are truly the origin of all Three Schools. If they reach your Southern Continent of Jambudvipa they must not be treated with disrespect when they are shown to all living beings. Nobody who has not bathed, avoided eating meat and observed the prohibitions may open the rolls. Treasure them. Honour them. They include the esoteric mysteries of the way of immortality and wonderful methods for discovering all transformations." Kowtowing in thanks, Sanzang faithfully accepted these instructions and determined to carry them out, did three more circuits of homage round the Lord Buddha then with dutiful and sincere obedience accepted the scriptures and went out with them through the third of the monastery gates, where he thanked all the holy beings one by one again. Of him we will say no more.

After sending the Tang Priest on his way the Tathagata dissolved the assembly that had been called to pass on the scriptures. The Bodhisattva Guanyin then stepped forward from the side, put her hands together and submitted to the Lord Buddha, "It has been fourteen years from the time when your disciple went to the East that year to find the man who would fetch the scriptures to his success today. That makes 5,040 days. May the World-honoured One allow the holy monks to go back East from the West within eight days, so as to complete the number of rolls in one store, and then your disciple may report his mission as completed." "What you say is quite right," replied the Tathagata with delight. "You are permitted to report the completion of your mission." With that he instructed the Eight Vajrapanis, "You are to use your divine might to escort the holy monks back to the East, where they will hand the true scriptures over to be kept there. After escorting the holy monks back, you may return to the West. This must be done within eight days in order to match the number of rolls in one store. There must be no disobedience or delay." The vajrapanis caught up with the Tang Priest. "Come with us, scripture-fetchers," they called; and the Tang Priest and the others became light and strong as they floated up on clouds after the vajrapanis. Indeed,

Nature revealed and mind made clear, they visited the Buddha;
Actions complete and all achieved, they flew aloft.

If you do not know how they passed on the scriptures after returning to the East, listen to the explanation in the next instalment.

CHAPTER NINETY-NINE

When the nine nines are complete the
demons are all destroyed;
After the triple threes are fulfilled the
Way returns to its roots.

The story goes on to tell how the Eight Vajrapanis escorted the Tang Priest back to their country, but we will not go into that now. Outside the gates the Protectors of the Four Quarters and the Centre, the Four Duty Gods, the Six Dings, the Six Jias and the Guardians of the Faith went up to the Bodhisattva Guanyin and said, "We, your disciples, have given secret help to the holy monk in obedience to your dharma command, Bodhisattva. Now that they have fulfilled their deeds and you have reported your mission accomplished to the Lord Buddha, we would like to report the completion of our mission." "Permission granted," the Bodhisattva replied with delight, "permission granted." The Bodhisattva then went on to ask, "What were the thoughts and actions of the Tang Priest and his three disciples on their journey?" "They really were pious and determined," the deities all replied, "as we are sure will not have escaped your profound perception. But the Tang Priest's sufferings truly beggar description. Your disciples have made a careful record of the disasters and hardships that he has endured on his journey. This is the account of his ordeals." The Bodhisattva read it through from the beginning, and this is what was written in it:

"We Protectors were sent at the Bodhisattva's command,
To keep a close record of the Tang Priest's ordeals.
The Golden Cicada's exile was the first ordeal;
Being born and almost killed was the second ordeal;

Abandonment in the river under the full moon was the third ordeal;
Finding his mother and getting revenge was the fourth ordeal;
The tigers he met after leaving the city were the fifth ordeal;
Falling into the pit was the sixth ordeal;
The Double Forked Peak was the seventh ordeal;
The Double Boundary Mountain was the eighth ordeal;
Exchanging horses at the ravine was the ninth ordeal;
The fire at night was the tenth ordeal;
The loss of the cassock was the eleventh ordeal;
Subduing Pig was the twelfth ordeal;
The obstacles created by the Yellow Wind Monster were the thirteenth ordeal;
Asking the help of Lingji was the fourteenth ordeal;
The hard crossing of the Flowing Sands River was the fifteenth ordeal;
Winning over Friar Sand was the sixteenth ordeal;
The appearance of the four holy ones was the seventeenth ordeal;
In the Wuzhuang Temple was the eighteenth ordeal;
The difficulty of reviving the manfruit was the nineteenth ordeal;
The dismissal of the Mind-ape was the twentieth ordeal;
Getting lost in Black Pine Forest was the twenty-first ordeal;
Delivering the letter to Elephantia was the twenty-second ordeal;
To be turned into a tiger in the palace hall was the twenty-third ordeal;
Meeting the monsters on Flat-top Mountain was the twenty-fourth ordeal;
To hang in the Lotus Flower Cave was the twenty-fifth ordeal;

The rescue of the king of Wuji was the twenty-sixth ordeal;

The transformation by the demons was the twenty-seventh ordeal;

The encounter with the monster of Mount Hao was the twenty-eighth ordeal;

The holy monk being carried off by the wind was the twenty-ninth ordeal;

The attack on the Mind-ape was the thirtieth ordeal;

Inviting the holy one to subdue the fiend was the thirty-first ordeal;

Sinking in the Black River was the thirty-second ordeal;

The moving in Tarrycart was the thirty-third ordeal;

The enormous wager was the thirty-fourth ordeal;

Casting out the Taoists and promoting the Buddhists was the thirty-fifth ordeal;

The great river met on the way was the thirty-sixth ordeal;

Falling into the River of Heaven was the thirty-seventh ordeal;

The appearance with the fish basket was the thirty-eighth ordeal;

Meeting the monster on Mount Jindou was the thirty-ninth ordeal;

All the gods of heaven being unable to subdue him was the fortieth ordeal;

Asking the Buddha about his origins was the forty-first ordeal;

To be poisoned by drinking the water was the forty-second ordeal;

Being kept in Womanland of Western Liang for the wedding was the forty-third ordeal;

The agonies of the Pipa Cave were the forty-fourth ordeal;

The Mind-ape's second dismissal was the forty-fifth ordeal;

Telling the macaques apart was the forty-sixth ordeal;

Being held up by the Fiery Mountains was the forty-seventh ordeal;
Obtaining the plantain-leaf fan was the forty-eighth ordeal;
Tying up the demon king was the forty-ninth ordeal;
Sweeping the pagoda in Jisai city was the fiftieth ordeal;
The recovery of the treasures and the rescue of the monks were the fifty-first ordeal;
Reciting poems in the Thorn Forest was the fifty-second ordeal;
Trouble in the Lesser Thunder Monastery was the fifty-third ordeal;
The capture of the heavenly gods was the fifty-fourth ordeal;
Being stopped by the filthy Runny Persimmon Lane was the fifty-fifth ordeal;
Healing in Purpuria was the fifty-sixth ordeal;
Saving from debility was the fifty-seventh ordeal;
Subduing fiends and rescuing the queen was the fifty-eighth ordeal;
Delusion by the seven passions was the fifty-ninth ordeal;
The wounding of the Many-eyed Monster was the sixtieth ordeal;
Being held up by the Lion was the sixty-first ordeal;
Dividing demons into three categories was the sixty-second ordeal;
Meeting disaster in the city was the sixty-third ordeal;
Asking the Buddha to subdue the demon was the sixty-fourth ordeal;
The rescue of the boys in Bhiksuland was the sixty-fifth ordeal;
Telling the true from the evil was the sixty-sixth ordeal;
Saving the monster in the pine forest was the sixty-seventh ordeal;
Lying sick in the monastic cell was the sixty-eighth ordeal;

Capture in the Bottomless Cave was the sixty-ninth ordeal;
Delays in Dharmadestructia were the seventieth ordeal;
Meeting the monster on Hidden Clouds Mountain was the seventy-first ordeal;
Begging for rain in Fengxian was the seventy-second ordeal;
The loss of the weapons was the seventy-third ordeal;
The rake banquet was the seventy-fourth ordeal;
Troubles on Bamboo Mountain were the seventy-fifth ordeal;
Suffering in Dark Essence Cave was the seventy-sixth ordeal;
Catching Rhinoceros was the seventy-seventh ordeal;
Being required to marry in India was the seventy-eighth ordeal;
Imprisonment in Brazentower was the seventy-ninth ordeal;
Casting off the body at the Lingyun Crossing was the eightieth ordeal;
The journey was one of 36,000 miles,
And the ordeals of the holy monk are all clearly recorded."

Casting her eyes over the record, the Bodhisattva quickly said, "In the Buddha's school 'nine nines' are needed before one can come to the truth. The eighty ordeals that the holy monk has endured are one short of the full number. Go after the vajrapanis," she ordered a protector," and tell them to create another ordeal." The protector headed east by cloud as soon as he was given this order, and after a day and a night he caught up with the Eight Vajrapanis. "It's like this, you see," he said, whispering in their ears in explanation, adding, "so you must do as the Bodhisattva commands and not disobey." When the Eight Vajrapanis heard this they stopped the wind with a swishing sound and dropped the four of them to the ground, horse, scriptures and all. Oh dear! It was a case of

The Way of reaching the truth through the nine nines is hard;
Hold fast to your determination to stand at the mysterious pass.
Only through rigorous effort can the demons be repelled;
Perseverance is essential to the true Dharma's return.
Do not mistake the scriptures for something easily won;
Of many a kind were the hardships endured by the holy monk.
The marvellous union has always been hard to achieve:
The slightest mistake and the elixir will not be made.

As his feet touched common ground Sanzang felt alarmed. "Marvellous," said Pig, roaring with laughter, "just marvellous! It's a case of more haste less speed." "It really is marvellous," said Friar Sand. "They're giving us a rest here after going so fast." "As the saying goes," remarked the Great Sage, " 'Wait ten days on a sandbank, then cross nine in a single day.' " "Stop arguing, you three," said Sanzang. "Find out which way we have come and where we are." "We're here!" said Friar Sand after looking all around, "We're here! Listen to the water, Master." "From the sound of the water I suppose it must be your family home," observed Brother Monkey. "His home is the River of Flowing Sands," said Pig. "No, it's not that," replied Friar Sand. "It's the River of Heaven." "Take a careful look at the other side, disciple," said Sanzang, at which Monkey sprang into the air, shaded his eyes with his hand, and took a careful look around. "Master," he said after coming down again, "this is the west bank of the River of Heaven." "I remember now," said Sanzang. "On the east bank there is Chen Family Village. When we came here the other year they were so grateful to us for rescuing their son and daughter that they wanted to build a boat to take us across, but the White Soft-shelled Turtle carried us over. As I recall, there was no sign of human life anywhere on the west bank. Whatever are we to do now?"

"They say that common mortals can be sinners," said Pig,

"but the vajrapanis who serve the Buddha in person are too. The Buddha ordered them to bring us back east, so why have they dropped us half way home? We're stuck here now. How ever are we going to get over?" "Stop complaining, brother," said Friar Sand. "Our master has found the Way. He cast off his mortal body at the Cloud-touching Crossing, so he won't possibly fall into the water now. Our big brother and we two can all do levitation magic, so we can carry the master across." Monkey laughed to himself under his breath as he replied, "We can't do it, we can't do it." Why do you think he said that they couldn't do it? If he had been prepared to use his divine powers and give away the secret of flying then master and disciples would have been able to cross a thousand rivers. But he understood that as the Tang Priest had not yet completed the nine nines he was fated to undergo another ordeal, which was why he had been held up here.

Talking as they walked slowly along, master and disciples headed straight to the river-bank, where all of a sudden they heard someone calling, "This way, Tang Priest, this way!" They were all surprised, and when they looked up there was no sign of anyone around, and no boat either. There was only a big, white, scabby-headed soft-shelled turtle raising its head by the bank and calling, "Master, I have been waiting for you all these years. Why have you only just come back?" "We troubled you in the past, old turtle," said Monkey with a smile, "and this year we meet again." Sanzang, Pig and Friar Sand were all delighted. "If you really do want to look after us, come ashore," Monkey said, at which the turtle climbed out of the river with a bound. Monkey had the horse tied to the turtle with Pig squatting behind the horse's tail. The Tang Priest stood to the left of the horse's neck and Friar Sand to its right, while Monkey stood with one foot on the turtle's neck and the other on his head. "Take it easy and take it steady," he said. The turtle strode across the water just as if his four feet were walking on flat land, carrying the master and his three disciples, five of them altogether including the horse, straight back to the eastern bank. This was indeed,

The mystery of the Dharma within the unique sect:
When the demons are all defeated man and heaven are made known.
Only now can the original face be seen,
And the causes of the one body all be complete.
Hold to the Three Vehicles to come and go at will;
After the elixir's nine transformations you may do what you like.
Carry your bundle, let your staff fly, and understand the inexpressible;
Lucky they were on their return to meet the Ancient Turtle.

Carrying them on his back, the Ancient Soft-shelled Turtle walked across the waves for the best part of a day. It was nearly evening when, as they approached the east bank, he suddenly asked, "Venerable master, some years ago I begged you when you reached the West and saw our Tathagata Buddha to ask him when I would be converted and how long I would live."

Now ever since the venerable elder had reached the Western Heaven, bathed in the Jade Truth Temple, cast off his mortal body at the Cloud-touching Crossing and walked up the Vulture Peak, his heart had been set only on worshipping the Buddha; and when he met all the Buddhas, Bodhisattvas, holy monks and others his whole mind had been devoted to fetching the scriptures. He had given no attention to anything else, and so had not asked about how long the Ancient Turtle would live. Having nothing he could say, and not daring to lie to or deceive the turtle, Sanzang was quiet for a long time and gave no reply. When the turtle realized that Sanzang had not asked the questions on his behalf he gave a shake of his body and submerged with a loud splash, dropping the four of them, horse, scriptures and all, into the water. Oh dear! But luckily the Tang Priest had cast off his mortal body and achieved the Way. If he had still been as he had before he would have sunk to the bottom. It was also lucky that the white horse was a dragon, that Pig and Friar Sand could swim, and that Brother Monkey gave a smiling and magnificent display of his great magic powers as he lifted the Tang Priest out of the water and up the east bank. The only thing was that the bundles of scriptures, the clothes and the saddle were all soaked.

Master and disciples had climbed up the bank to get themselves sorted out when a sudden fierce wind blew up, the sky turned dark, and amid thunder and lightning stones and sand flew all around. This is what could be seen:

A wind
Throwing heaven and earth into chaos;
Thunder
Rocking mountains and rivers;
Lightning
Flying like fire through the clouds;
Mists
Covering all of the earth.
The wind howled;
Loud roared the thunder.
The lightning streaked red,
While clouds blocked out the moon and the stars.
The wind-blown dust drove into the face,
And tigers and leopards hid in terror.
The lightning flashes set birds cawing,
And trees all vanished in the spreading mists.
The wind whipped up the waves of the River of Heaven;
The thunder terrified the fish and dragons in the River of Heaven;
The lightning lit up the whole of River of Heaven;
The mists enshrouded in darkness the banks of the River of Heaven.
Splendid wind!
Mountains toppled; pines and bamboo fell.
Splendid thunder!
Its majesty alarmed insects and spread terror.
Splendid lightning!

It moved across the sky and lit up the wilds like golden snakes.
Splendid mist!
Darkening the whole of space, obscuring the nine heavens.

This alarmed Sanzang, who pressed down on the bundles of scriptures, while Friar Sand held down their carrying-pole and Pig clung to the white horse. Monkey, however, swung his iron cudgel around with both hands as he kept guard to both right and left.

Now the wind, mist, thunder and lightning were all signals made by evil demons who wanted to steal the scriptures that had been fetched. They tried all night to grab them until the dawn; only then did they stop. The venerable elder, whose clothes were all soaking wet, shivered and shook as he said, "How did all this start, Wukong?" "Master," Brother Monkey replied, snorting with fury, "you don't understand the inner truth. By escorting you to fetch these scriptures we have won the great achievement of heaven and earth. You will enjoy perpetual youth, and your dharma body will never decay. This is something heaven and earth can't stand for, and the demons and gods detest. They wanted to come and steal them in the darkness. But because the scriptures were soaked through and your true dharma body was holding them down, the thunder could not bombard them, the lightning could not illuminate them and the mist could not obscure them. It was also because I whirled my iron cudgel around to make its pure Positive nature protect them. Since dawn the Positive has been in the ascendant again, which is why they can't take them now."

Only then did Sanzang, Pig and Friar Sand realize what had happened and all express unbounded thanks. A little later, when the sun was shining from high in the sky, they took the scriptures to the top of a high cliff, opened the bundles and put them out to dry. The rocks on which the scriptures were dried in the sun remain there to this day. Then they spread their clothes and shoes out to dry beside the cliff while they stood there, sat down, or leapt around. Indeed,

The pure Positive body was happy in the sun,
When Negative demons dared not use their might.
Even when water is dominant the true scriptures will win,
Not fearing wind or thunder, lightning, mist or light.
After this clarification they come to the true perception;
From now on they will reach the immortals' land in peace.
On the rocks where the scriptures were dried their traces still remain;
Never again will any demons come back to this place.

As the four of them were checking through the scriptures and drying them in the sun one by one some fishermen who were passing the river bank lifted up their heads and saw them there. One of the fishermen recognized them and said, "Venerable teachers, didn't you cross this river the other year when you were on your way to the Western Heaven to fetch the scriptures?" "Yes, yes," said Pig, "that's right. Where are you from? How did you know who we are?" "We're from Chen Village," the fisherman replied. "How far is Chen Village from here?" Pig asked. "It's seven miles south from this gulch," the fisherman said. "Let's take the scriptures to Chen Village and dry them there," said Pig. "There's somewhere we can stay there, and we'll be able to get something to eat. Besides, we can get their family to wash our clothes. That'll be best, won't it?" "We will not go there," said Sanzang. "When we have dried everything here we can pack up and find our way back."

The fishermen, who passed the gulch to the south, happened to meet Chen Cheng. "You two old gentlemen," they called, "the teachers who went to be sacrificed instead of your children the other year have come back." "Where did you see them?" Chen Cheng asked. "Drying their scriptures in the sun on the rocks," the fishermen replied.

Chen Cheng then took several of his tenants across the gulch, saw the pilgrims, and hurried towards them to kneel and say, "My lords, now that you are coming back with your scriptures, your achievement completed and your deeds done, why don't you come to my house? Why are you hanging around here? Won't you please come straight to the house?" "We'll go with you when we've dried our scriptures in the sun," Monkey replied. "How did your scriptures and clothes all get wet, my lords?" Chen Cheng asked. "The other year the White Soft-shelled Turtle kindly carried us west across the river," Sanzang replied, "and this year he carried us across it eastwards. We were approaching the bank when he put some questions to me about the enquiries he had asked me to make with the Lord Buddha about how long he would live. Now I never made this enquiry, so he soaked us all in the water. That was how they got wet." Sanzang then told the whole story in all its details, and as Chen Cheng was so sincere in pressing his invitation Sanzang could do nothing but pack up the scriptures. As it was not realized that the ends of several rolls of the *Buddhacaritakavya sutra* had stuck to the rock when wet, the ends were torn off, which is why the *Buddhacaritakavya sutra* is incomplete to this day and there are still traces of writing on the rocks where the scriptures were dried in the sun. "We were careless," Sanzang said with remorse. "We did not pay enough attention." "You're wrong," said Monkey with a laugh, "your're wrong. Heaven and earth are incomplete and this scripture used to be complete. Now it's been soaked and torn to fulfil the mystery of incompleteness. This is not something that could have been achieved through human effort." When master and disciples had finished packing the sutras they returned with Chen Cheng to his village.

In the village one person told ten, ten told a hundred, and a hundred a thousand, till all of them, young and old, came out to welcome and see the pilgrims. As soon as Chen Qing heard of it he had an incense table set out to greet them in front of the gates; he also ordered drummers and players of wind instruments to perform. A moment later the travellers arrived and were welcomed and taken inside. Chen Qing led out his whole household to greet them with bows and thank them for their earlier kindness in saving their son and daughter. Tea and a vegetarian meal were then ordered; but since receiving the immortal food and immortal delicacies of the Lord Buddha and casting off his mortal body to become a Buddha, Sanzang had lost all desire for mortals' food. As the two old men's urgings were so insistent, he took some of the food as a mark of gratitude. The Great Sage Monkey had never been one to eat cooked food, so he said, "That will be enough." Friar Sand did not eat either, and even Pig was not the Pig he used to be: he soon put his bowl down. "Aren't you eating any more either, idiot?" Monkey asked. "I don't know why," Pig said, "but my stomach's gone weak all of a sudden." The vegetarian banquet was then cleared away as the old men asked about how they had fetched the scriptures. Sanzang then gave them a detailed account that started with the bath in the Jade Truth Temple and the lightening of their bodies at Cloud-touching Crossing and went on to tell how they had seen the Tathagata at Thunder Monastery, been feasted at the jewelled tower, given the scriptures in the precious library — wordless scriptures at first because when the two arhats had demanded presents they had refused them — had gone back to pay their respects to the Tathagata again to be given the number of rolls in a single store, had been plunged into the water by the White Soft-shelled Turtle, and nearly had the scriptures stolen in the darkness by evil spirits. After telling all this Sanzang took his leave.

But the whole family of the two old men was not at all willing to let them go. "We have been under a great debt to you for saving our children that we have not yet been able to repay," they said. "We have built a Temple of Deliverance where incense has been burned to you ever since without ceasing." Then they called out the children in whose place Monkey and Pig had gone to be sacrificed, Chen Guan-given and Pan of Gold, to kowtow in thanks and ask them into the shrine to take a look. Sanzang then put the bundles of scriptures in front of the hall of their house and read them one roll of the

Precious Eternity sutra. Then they went to the temple, where the Chens had set out delicacies. Before the pilgrims could sit down another group of people came to invite them to another meal, and before they could pick up their chopsticks yet another group came with a third invitation. This went on and on without end, so that they had no chance to eat properly. Sanzang, who dared not decline the invitations, had to make gestures of eating. The shrine was indeed most handsomely built:

The gateway was thickly painted in red
Thanks to the generous donors.
A tower rose there
Where houses with a pair of cloisters had now been built.
Red were the doors
And the Seven Treasures were finely carved.
Incense floated up to the clouds;
Pure light filled the vault of space.
Some tender cypress saplings were still being watered;
A number of pine trees did not yet form a grove.
Living waters met one in front
Where the waves of the River of Heaven were rolling;
High cliffs rose behind
Where range upon range of mountains joined the earth dragon.

When Sanzang had seen everything he climbed the high tower, where statues of the four pilgrims had been placed. "Looks just like you, brother," said Pig, tugging at Monkey, when he saw them. "Second brother," said Friar Sand, "Your statue's just like you too. The only thing is that the master's is too good-looking." "It is very good," said Sanzang, "it is very good." They then came downstairs, where people were still waiting, and urged them to eat the vegetarian food that was set out in the hall and in the cloisters behind it. "What happened to the Great King's Temple that used to be here?" Brother Monkey asked. "It was demolished that year," the old men replied. "My lords, we have had good harvests every year since this monastery was established, thanks to your lordships' blessed protection." "That was heaven's gift," said Monkey with a smile, "nothing to do with us. But after we have gone this time I guarantee that the families in your village will have many sons and grandsons, flourishing livestock, wind and rain at the right time year in and year out, and rain and wind year out and year in at the right time." The people all kowtowed in thanks.

What could then be seen were a countless number of people lined up behind each other to offer fruit and other vegetarian food. "I'll be blowed," said Pig with a laugh. "In the old days, when I could eat, nobody ever asked me to do so ten times over. But now, when I can't, one family won't wait for another to finish before offering me food." Although he was feeling full he did get going a little and ate eight or nine meatless dishes; and despite having an injured stomach he also downed twenty or thirty steamed breadrolls. When they were all full, more people came with further invitations. "Grateful though I am for your great affection," Sanzang said, "I do not deserve it. I hope that we may be allowed to rest tonight. Tomorrow morning we will accept some more."

It was now late at night. Sanzang, who was guarding the true scriptures and would not leave them for a moment, sat in meditation at the foot of the tower to keep a vigil. As the third watch of the night approached he said quietly, "Wukong, the people here know that we have found the Way and completed our undertaking. As the old saying goes, 'The true adept does not show his face; who shows his face is no true adept.' I am afraid that if we tarry too long here that we may fail in our main enterprise." "What you say is right, Master," Monkey replied. "Let's slip quietly away in the middle of the night while they're all sound asleep." Pig too understood, Friar Sand comprehended very clearly, and the white horse also knew what he meant. So they got up, quietly loaded the packs, shouldered the poles, and carried the things out along the cloister. When they reached the main gates and found them locked Monkey used unlocking magic to open the inner gates and the main gates. They followed the path east, only to hear the Eight Vajrapanis calling from mid-air. "Come with us, escapers." The venerable elder then smelt incense as he rose up into the air. This was indeed a case of

When the elixir is formed one sees the original face;
When the body is strong one can then visit one's sovereign.

If you do not know how he saw the Tang emperor, listen to the explanation in the next instalment.

CHAPTER ONE HUNDRED

The journey back to the East is made;
The five immortals achieve nirvana.

We will tell not of how the four travellers escaped and rose on the wind with the vajrapanis, but of the many people in the Temple of Deliverance in Chen Village. After they rose at dawn to prepare more fruit and delicacies to offer they came to the ground floor of the tower and found the Tang Priest gone. Some asked questions and others searched. They were all thrown into panic and did not know what to do. "We've let those living Buddhas all get clean away," they lamented as their howls rose to the skies. As there was nothing else they could do about it they carried all the food they had prepared to the ground floor of the tower as offerings and burned imitation paper money. From then on four major sacrifices and twenty-four minor sacrifices were held every year. In addition people praying for cures or safety, seeking marriages, making vows, and seeking wealth or sons came at every hour of every day to burn incense and make offerings. Indeed,

Incense smoked in the golden burner for a thousand years;
The light burned in the lamps of jade through eternity.

We will say no more of this, but tell of how the Eight Vajrapanis used a second fragrant wind to carry the four pilgrims off again. Some days later they reached the East, and Chang'an came gradually into view. Now after seeing the Tang Priest off from the city on the twelfth day of the ninth month in the thirteenth year of *Zhen Guan* the Emperor Taizong had in the sixteenth year sent officials of his Department of Works to build a Watching For the Scriptures Tower outside the city of Chang'an to receive the scriptures. Here Taizong went in

person every year. It so happened that on the very day the emperor went to the tower the western sky was filled with auspicious light and gusts of scented wind. "Holy monk," the vajrapanis said, stopping in mid air, "this is the city of Chang'an. We cannot come down as the people here are too clever: we are afraid that they might give away what we look like. The Great Sage Monkey and the other two gentlemen cannot go there either. You must go there yourself to hand the scriptures to your monarch then come back here. We will be waiting for you up in the clouds ready to go to report back on your mission." "Although what you respected gentlemen say is right," replied the Great Sage, "how could my master possibly shoulder the pole for carrying the scriptures? And how could he lead this horse? We'll have to take him there. May I trouble you to wait a moment up in the air? We wouldn't dare keep you waiting." "The other day the Bodhisattva Guanyin informed the Tathagata," the vajrapanis replied, "that the return journey would take only eight days, so as to make up the number of rolls of scriptures in the Tripitaka. We have already spent over four days, and we are worried that Pig will be so greedy for blessings and honours that he will make us overrun the time limit." "The master's a Buddha now," Pig replied with a smile, "and I want to become one too. So why should I want to be greedy? Cheeky great fools! Wait here while we hand the scriptures over, then we'll come back to return with you." The idiot then shouldered a pole while Friar Sand held the horse and Brother Monkey led the holy monk as they brought their cloud down to land beside the Watching For the Scriptures Tower.

When Taizong and his officials all saw this they came down to greet the travellers with the words, "You are back, Imperial Younger Brother." The Tang Priest fell to the ground in a kowtow, only to be helped back to his feet by Taizong, who asked, "Who are these three?" "They are disciples I took on along the way," Sanzang replied. Taizong was delighted. "Harness the horses to our imperial carriage," he ordered his aides, "and invite the Imperial Younger Brother to mount his

steed and return to the palace with us." The Tang Priest thanked him and mounted his horse. The Great Sage followed closely behind, whirling his golden cudgel. Pig and Friar Sand led the horse and shouldered the pole as they followed the emperor back to Chang'an.
Indeed,

In that year of peace and rising prosperity
Civil and military officials are calm and magnificent.
At a land and water mass the clergy displayed the dharma;
The monarch commands his ministers in the throne hall of the palace.
A passport was given to Tang Sanzang;
The primal cause of the scriptures has been matched to the Five Elements.
Through painful tempering all monsters have been destroyed;
Now he returns in triumph to the capital.

The Tang Priest and his three disciples followed the imperial carriage back to the palace. Everybody in the capital knew that the pilgrim who had gone to fetch the scriptures had now returned. When the monks, young and old, of the Hongfu Monastery in Chang'an where the Tang Priest used to live saw that the tops of a number of pine trees were all leaning towards the east they exclaimed in astonishment, "Odd, very odd! There's been no wind today, so why are the tops of these trees all bent?" "Fetch our vestments at once," said one of them who was a former disciple of Sanzang. "The master who went to fetch the scriptures is back." "How do you know?" the other monks all asked. "When the master left many years ago," the former disciple replied, "he said that when the branches and tops of the pines turned east three, four, six or seven years after he had gone he would be back. My master speaks with the holy voice of a Buddha: that is how I know." They quickly put on their habits and went out. By the time they reached the western street, messengers had arrived to say, "The pilgrim who went for the scriptures has just returned, and His Majesty is bringing him into the city." As soon as they heard this the monks all hurried over to meet him. When they saw the imperial carriage they dared not come close, but followed it to the palace gates, where the Tang Priest dismounted and went inside with his disciples.

The Tang Priest stood at the foot of the steps to the throne hall with the dragon horse, the load of sutras, Monkey, Pig and Friar Sand. Emperor Taizong then summoned the Younger Brother to enter the throne hall and invited him to sit down, which the Tang Priest did with thanks. He then had the scriptures carried up. Monkey and the others unpacked the scrolls, which the officials in personal attendance handed to the emperor. "How many scriptures are there?" the emperor asked. "And how did you fetch them?" "When your clerical subject reached Vulture Peak and saw the Lord Buddha," Sanzang replied, "he told the arhats Ananda and Kasyapa to take us first to a precious tower where we were given meatless food, then to the library, where we were handed the scriptures. The arhats demanded presents, but as we had not brought any we had none to give. Then they gave us the scriptures. When we had thanked the Buddha for his goodness and were travelling east the scriptures were snatched away by a demonic gale. Luckily my disciples were able to recover them by using magic powers, but they had been blown all over the place. On opening them out to look at them we found that they were all blank, wordless versions. We were so shocked that we went back to report to the Buddha and plead for the real ones. What the Lord Buddha said was, 'When these scriptures were composed, bhiksus and holy monks went down the mountain and recited them to the family of the elder Zhao in the land of Sravasti. This ensured peace and safety for the living and deliverance for the dead members of the family. All that was asked for was three bushels and three pecks of granular gold. I thought that they sold the scriptures too cheap, so I saw to it that Zhao's sons and grandsons would be poor.' When we realized that the two arhats were demanding a present and that the Lord Buddha knew all about it we had no choice but to give them our begging bowl of purple gold. Only then did they hand over the true scriptures with words. There are thirty-five of them, and a number of rolls from each of them was selected to be given us, making a total of 5,048 rolls. This corresponds to the number of rolls in a single Store."

At this Taizong was more delighted than ever. "Let the Protocol Office arrange a thanksgiving banquet in the eastern hall," he ordered, at which he suddenly saw the three disciples standing at the foot of the steps, looking very strange indeed. "Are your distinguished disciples foreigners?" he asked. "My senior disciple's surname is Sun," the venerable elder replied with a bow, "his Buddhist name is Wukong, and I also call him Sun the Novice. He originally came from the Water Curtain Cave on the Mountain of Flowers and Fruit in the country of Aolai in the Eastern Continent of Divine Body. For making great havoc in the palaces of heaven five hundred years ago he was crushed by the Lord Buddha in a stone cell in the Double Boundary Mountain on the western frontier. After the Bodhisattva Guanyin persuaded him to mend his ways he accepted conversion, so when I arrived there I delivered him. I am greatly indebted to him for my protection. My second disciple Zhu has the Buddhist name Wuneng, and I also call him Pig. He came from the Cloud Pathway Cave on the Mountain of Blessing, and was a monster in Gao Village in the land of Stubet until he was converted by the Bodhisattva and subdued by Wukong. He has made great efforts, carrying the load all along the way, and been very useful in crossing rivers. My third disciple's surname is Sha and his Buddhist name Wujing. He used to be a monster in the Flowing Sands River. He too was converted by the Bodhisattva and now believes in the Buddhist faith. The horse is not the one that my sovereign gave me." "How is that?" Taizong asked. "Its markings are the same." "When your subject was going to cross the waters of the Eagle's Sorrow Gorge by Coiled Snake Mountain my original horse was devoured by this one," Sanzang replied. "Sun the Novice obliged me by having the Bodhisattva asked about the horse's background. It was originally the son of the Dragon King of the Western Sea who had been sent there because of an offence. He too, was saved by the Bodhisattva, who told him to work for me and turned him into a horse with the same markings as the original one. He has been very helpful in climbing mountains, crossing ridges, fording rivers and negotiating difficult country. On the outward journey I rode him, and he carried the scriptures on the way back: I have depended greatly on his efforts." Taizong was full of boundless praise on learning this. "How long in fact was your journey to the far west?" he asked. "I remember the Bodhisattva saying that it was 36,000 miles," Sanzang replied, "but I kept no record of the distances along the way. All I know is that we experienced fourteen winters and summers. Every day there was a mountain or a ridge. The woods were big and the rivers wide. I also met several kings who inspected and stamped my passport. Disciples," he ordered, "fetch the passport and hand it to His Majesty." When Taizong examined it he saw that it had been issued on the twelfth day of the ninth month of the thirteenth year of *Zhen Guan*. "You did indeed make a long and protracted journey," he observed with a touch of a smile. "It is now the twenty-seventh year of *Zhen Guan*." On the passport were the seals of the monarchs of Elephantia, Wuji, Tarrycart, the Womanland of Western Liang, Jisai, Purpuria, Leonia, Bhikshuland and Dharmadestructia; as well as the seals of the chief officials of Fengxian, Yuhua and Jinping. When Taizong had read through the passport he put it away.

Soon the officials in personal attendance on the emperor came to invite them to go to the banquet, whereupon Taizong led Sanzang by the hand out of the throne hall, asking, "Do your distinguished disciples know how to behave themselves?" "My disciples were all demons from mountain villages and from the wilderness," Sanzang replied, "so they do not understand the etiquette of the sacred court of China. I beg you to forgive them for any offences, Your Majesty." "We won't blame them," Taizong said with a smile," we won't blame them. They are all invited to come with us to the banquet in the eastern pavilion." Thanking him once again, Sanzang called his three disciples, and they all went to the eastern pavilion to look. This was indeed the great land of China, no ordinary place. Just look:

Coloured silks hung from the gates,
Red carpets were spread on the floor.
Heavy, rare fragrances,
Fresh and exotic foods.
Amber cups,
Glazed dishes,
Set with gold and nephrite;
Plates of yellow gold,
White jade bowls,
Inlaid with patterns.
Tender braised turnips,
Sugar-dredged taros,
Wonderful sweet mushrooms,
Fine fresh seaweed,
Several servings of bamboo shoots with ginger,
A number of rounds of mallows with honey,
Wheat gluten with leaves of the tree of heaven,
Tree fungus and thin strips of beancurd,
Agar and aster,
Noodles with ferns and dried rose-petals,
Peppers stewed with radish,
Melon shredded with mustard.
The dishes of vegetables were fine enough,
But the rare and wonderful fruit was outstanding:
Walnuts and persimmon cakes,
Longans and lichees,
Chestnuts from Xuanzhou and Shandong jujubes,
Gingko fruit from south of the Yangtse and hare-head pears,
Hazelnuts, pine nuts and lotus seeds, all big as grapes,
Torreya nuts and melon seeds the size of water chestnuts,
Olives and wild apples,
Pippins and crabs,

Lotus root and arrowhead,
Crisp plums and red bayberries.
Nothing was missing,
All was complete.
There were steamed honey pastries and other confections,
Best wines and fragrant tea and things out of the ordinary.
Words could not describe the countless delicacies:
The great land of China was not western barbary.

The master and his three disciples, together with the civil and military officials, stood to left and right as Emperor Taizong took his seat in the middle. There was singing, dancing and instrumental music, and all was ordered and solemn as the celebration lasted for the rest of the day. Indeed,

The monarch's banquet was finer than those of ancient Tang and Yu;
Great was the blessing of the true scriptures obtained.
This was a story to be told with glory for ever:
The light of the Buddha shines throughout the imperial capital.

That evening they thanked the emperor for his kindness, after which Taizong returned to the living quarters of the palace and the officials went home. The Tang Priest went back with his followers to the Hongfu Monastery, where the monks welcomed him with kowtows. No sooner had he gone in through the gates than the monks reported, "Master, these treetops all suddenly leaned east this morning. As we remembered what you had said we went out of the city to meet you, and you had indeed come." Overcome with delight, the venerable elder then entered the abbot's lodgings. This time Pig neither shouted for tea and food nor made a row. Brother Monkey and Friar Sand also both behaved well. As the achievement was now complete they were naturally peaceful. At nightfall they went to bed.

Early the next morning Taizong announced to his officials at his dawn audience, "When we thought of the most profound and great achievement of our Younger Brother that we have no way of rewarding we were unable to sleep all night. We managed to draft a few colloquial sentences with which to express our thanks, but could not write them out. Officials of the Secretariat," he ordered, "write them all down while we recite them to you." This is the text he dictated:

> It is known that Heaven and Earth have their forms as a demonstration of how they provide the cover and support in which life is contained, whereas the four seasons are invisible, hiding the cold and heat with which they transform all creatures. Thus it is that by examining Heaven and looking at the Earth even the stupid can know about their origins, but few are the wise who can exhaust the numbers of the Negative and the Positive. Heaven and Earth, which are enveloped by the Negative and Positive, are easily understood because of their images, but the Negative and Positive are hard to fathom because they are formless. If images are clear and can be grasped even the stupid will not be confused; if forms are hidden and invisible even the wise will be at a loss.
>
> The way of the Buddha honours emptiness, rides on the mystery and controls silence, yet saves all beings and dominates all regions. When it raises up the numinous there is nothing higher; when it represses its own divine strength there is nothing lower. When it is big it extends throughout the cosmos; when tiny it can be contained in a fraction of an inch. It does not die and it is not born; it endures a thousand aeons and is eternal. Half hidden and half manifest, it controls all blessings and makes them exist for ever. Mysterious is the wonderful Way; none of those who follow it know its limits. Silent is the flow of the Dharma: of those who grasp it none finds its source. So how can mortal fools in their stupidity follow it without doubts or delusion?
>
> The great teaching arose in the West. Later a won-

drous dream came to the Han court, spreading its brilliance and charity to the East. In ancient times, when the Buddha's forms and traces were shared around, they converted people before word could be spread abroad. In the age when they were sometimes visible and sometimes invisible, the people looked up to them and followed them. But later the image was obscured and nirvana was reached, it moved away and left the world, the golden countenance was hidden away and no longer radiated its brilliance in the three thousand worlds. Pictures of the lovely image were made, vainly trying to show the Buddha's thirty-two holy marks. Thereafter his subtle words were widely propagated, rescuing birds on the three roads of life; the teachings he left behind were spread afar, guiding all living beings along the ten stages of development. The Buddha has scriptures that can be divided into the Greater and Leser Vehicles. There is also magic, the art of spreading mistakes and making right into wrong.

Now our priest Xuanzang, the Master of the Law, is the leader of the Dharma faith. In his youth he was so careful and perceptive that he soon became aware of the value of the three voids. As he grew up the clarity of his spirit embraced the four kinds of patience in his conduct. Not even a pine tree in a wind or the moon reflected in water could be compared with his purity; immortals' dew and bright pearls are no match for his lustrous splendour. His wisdom encompasses all without encumbrance; his spirit fathoms the formless. Rising far above the six impurities, he extends his fragrance through a thousand ages. When he concentrated his mind on the inner sphere he grieved at the torments suffered by the true Dharma; when he settled his thoughts on the gate of mystery he was distresed by the distortion of the profound writings. He longed to put them back into order so that the teachings of the past could be propagated again; and to root out apocryphal texts, enabling the true ones to stay in circulation so as to open the way for later scholars. That is why he lifted up his heart towards the Pure Land, and made a Dharma journey to the West, braving the dangers of distant lands as he walked alone, trusting to his staff. When the snow whirled around at dawn the land would disappear in a moment; and when the dust started to fly at evening the sky was blotted out. He advanced through the mists across a thousand leagues of mountains and rivers, making his way forward through the frosts and rains of a hundred changes of season. With great single-mindedness and making light of his efforts he longed deeply to reach his goal. He wandered around the West for fourteen years, visiting every one of those exotic countries in his search for the true teaching. He visited the Twin Trees and the Eight Rivers, savouring the Way and braving the wind. In Deer Park and on Vulture Peak he gazed upon wonders and marvels. He received the good word from ancient sages and the true teaching from superior worthies, probing deep within the wonderful gates, and exhausting the mysteries. The Way of the Three Vehicles and the Six Disciplines gallop across the field of his heart; a hundred cases of texts belonging to one Store roll like waves in the sea of his eloquence. Infinitely many are the countries he has visited; and vast the number of the scriptures he has collected.

He has obtained 5,048 rolls of all thirty-five of the essential texts of the Great Vehicle to be translated and made known in China so that the wonderful cause may be promoted. The clouds of mercy he has drawn from the far West will shed their Dharma rain here in the East. The holy teachings that had been incomplete are now complete once more; the common folk who had sinned are brought back to blessings. The searing flames of fire have been damped down, and all have been saved from the ways of delusion; the muddied waves in the water of wisdom have been made clear once more as all gather on the other bank. From this it can be learnt that the evil fall because of their karma, while the good rise because of their destiny. The origins of these rises and falls lie in one's own actions. This can be compared with a cassia growing on a high mountain, where only clouds and dew can nourish its blossom, or a lotus emerging from green waters, its leaves unsullied by flying dust. It is not that the lotus is pure by nature and the cassia unsullied: they are good because one attaches itself to what is lofty, where mean and trivial things cannot encumber it, while the other depends on what is clean, where filth cannot dirty it. Now if plants that know nothing can become good by building themselves up through goodness, how much the more so should conscient people achieve blessing through blessed cause and effect. It is now to be hoped that the true scriptures will be propagated as endlessly as the alternation of sun and moon; and that this blessing will extend for ever, eternal like heaven and earth.

As soon as this had been written out the holy monk, who was waiting outside the palace gates to express his thanks, was summoned. The moment he heard the summons, Sanzang hurried and performed the ritual of kowtows. Taizong then invited him into the throne room and handed him the document. Sanzang read it through, prostrated himself once more in thanks, and submitted this memorial: "Your Majesty's writing is both lofty and in the ancient style; it is reasoned, profound and subtle. But I do not know what its title is." "What we drafted orally last night," Taizong replied, "we would call a 'Preface to the Holy Teaching'. Would that be acceptable?" The venerable elder kowtowed and expressed his thanks at great length. Taizong then said, "Our talent makes us ashamed by comparison with what is recorded on jade tablets; our words are not worthy of what is inscribed on metal or stone. As for the Inner Scriptures, we are even more ignorant of them. The text we drafted orally is truly a base and clumsy composition that sullies golden tablets with brush and ink, and is like placing pebbles in a forest of pearls. When we reflect on it we are filled with embarrassment. It is most unworthy of merit; we have put you to the trouble of thanking us for nothing."

The officials all expressed their congratulations and kowtowed before the imperial text on the holy teaching, which was going to be published everywhere in the capital and the provinces. "Would you be willing to recite some of the true scriptures for us, Younger Brother?" Taizong asked. "Your Majesty," Sanzang replied, "if true scriptures are to be recited it must be done in the Buddha's ground. A throne hall is no place for the recital of scriptures." Taizong was most pleased to accept this. "Which is the purest monastery in the city of Chang'an?" he asked his officers in attendance, at which the Academician Xiao Yu slipped forward from his rank to memorialize, "The Monastery of the Wild Goose Stupa in the city is the purest of them all." Taizong then ordered his officials, "Each of you is reverently to bring a few rolls of the true scriptures and accompany us to the Monastery of the Wild Goose Stupa, where we shall invite our younger brother to preach on the scriptures." The officials, all carrying some rolls of the scriptures, went with Taizong to the monastery, where a high platform was erected and everything was neatly set out. "Pig, Friar Sand," the venerable elder commanded, "bring the dragon horse with you and put the luggage in order. Monkey will stay beside me." He then addressed the emperor, saying, "If Your Majesty wishes to spread the true scriptures throughout the world copies must be made before they can be published. The original texts must be stored as great treasures. They may not be shown any disrespect or be defiled." "Younger Brother," replied Taizong with a smile, "what you say is very correct, very correct." He then ordered the officials of the Hanlin Academy and the Palace Secretariat to copy out the true scriptures and had another monastery, the Copying Monastery, founded to the east of the city wall.

The venerable elder mounted the platform with several scriptures in his hands. He was just about to begin reciting them when scented breezes began to waft around and the Eight Great Vajrapanis appeared in mid-air to shout aloud, "Scripture-reciter, put those scriptures down and come back to the West with us." Monkey and the other two, who were standing below Sanzang, all rose up above the ground together with the white horse. Sanzang put the scriptures down and also rose up to the ninth level of clouds, then went away with them through the air. Taizong and his officials were all so alarmed that they kowtowed to the sky. This was indeed a case of

The holy monk long strove to fetch the scriptures;
For fourteen years across the West he strayed.
He journeyed hard and met with much disaster;
By mountains and by rivers long delayed.
Completing eight times nine and one nine more,
His deeds filled worlds in numbers beyond measure.
He went back to his country taking sutras
That people in the East will always treasure.

When Taizong and all the officials had finished worshipping, eminent monks were selected to prepare a great Land and Sea Mass in the Monastery of the Wild Goose Stupa at which the true scriptures of the Great Store would be recited, and by which all evil-doing ghosts in the underworld would be saved, and goodness would spread all around. We will not describe how copies were made of the scriptures and published throughou the empire.

The story tells instead how the Eight Vajrapanis led the venerable elder, his three disciples and the horse, all five of them back to Vulture Peak. The journey to Chang'an and back had taken eight days. Just when all the deities of Vulture Peak were listening to the Buddha preaching, the Eight Vajrapanis led master and disciples in. "In obedience to the golden command," they reported to the Tathagata, "your disciples have carried the holy monks back to the land of Tang, where they handed the scriptures over. We have now come to report our mission completed." The Tang Priest and his disciples were then told to step forward and be given their jobs.

"Holy Monk," the Tathagata said, "in an earlier life you were my second disciple, and called Master Golden Cicada. But because you would not listen to my sermon on the Dharma and had no respect for my great teaching I demoted your soul to be reborn in the East. Now, happily, you have come over to the faith and rely on our support; and in following our teaching your achievement in fetching the true scriptures has been very great. Your reward will be to be promoted to high office as the Candana-punya Buddha. Sun Wukong, when you made great havoc in the palaces of heaven I had to use powerful magic to crush you under the Five Elements Mountain until, happily, your heaven-sent punishment was completed and you were converted to the Sakyamuni's faith. It was also fortunate that you suppressed your evil side and gave play to your good side as you won glory by defeating monsters and demons along the journey. All that was begun has now been completed and you too will be rewarded with high office as the Victorious Fighting Buddha. Zhu Wuneng, you used to be a water god in the River of Heaven as Marshal Tian Peng. Because of your drunken flirtation with an immortal maiden at the Peach Banquet you were sent down to be born in the lower world as a beast. From your love of the human body you sinned in the Cloud Pathway Cave on the Mount of Blessing before your conversion to the great faith and entry into our Buddhist sect. You guarded the holy monk on his journey, but your heart is still unregenerate, and you are not yet purged of your lust. But as you won merit by carrying the luggage you will be rewarded with promotion as the Altar Cleanser."

"They've both been made Buddhas," Pig shouted, "so why am I only the Altar Cleanser?" "Because you have a voracious appetite, a lazy body and a huge belly," the Tathagata replied. "Now very many people in the world's four continents believe in our teachings. I will ask you to clean up the altars after all Buddhist services: your post is of a rank that provides plenty to eat. What is wrong with that? Sha Wujing, you used to be the Curtain-lifting General until you were banished to the lower world for smashing a crystal bowl at a Peach Banquet. You fell into the River of Flowing Sands where you sinned by killing and eating people, until, thank goodness, you were converted to our teaching, sincerely relied on our support, and won merit by protecting the holy monk and leading the horse up the mountain. Your reward will be elevation to high office as the Golden Arhat." Then he said to the white horse, "You were originally the son of Guangjin, the Dragon King of the Western Ocean. Because you disobeyed your father you were punished for being unfilial until you too were converted to the Dharma and to our faith. Every day you carried the holy monk to the west, and after that you carried the holy scriptures back to the east. For these achievements you will be rewarded by being made a Heavenly Dragon of the Eight Classes of Being."

The venerable elder and his three disciples all kowtowed to express their thanks, and the horse showed its gratitude too. A protector was then ordered to take the horse straight down to the Dragon-transforming Pool by the precipice at the back of Vulture Peak and push him into the pool. At once the horse stretched itself out, shed all its hair, and acquired horns. Golden scales grew all over its body and a silver beard sprouted on its cheeks and chin. Then, shining all over with auspicious aura and with clouds of good omen in every claw, it flew up from the Dragon-transforming Pool to coil itself around the Heaven-supporting Winged Column. All the Buddhas expressed their admiration for the Tathagata's great magic. "Master," Monkey said to the Tang Priest, "now that I've become a Buddha just like you, surely I don't have to go on wearing this golden band. Do you plan to say any more Band-tightening Spells to tighten it round my head? Say a Band-loosening Spell as quickly as you can, take it off, and smash it to smithereens. Don't let that Bodhisattva or whatever she is make life miserable for anyone else with it." "It was because you were so uncontrollable in those days that this magic was needed to keep you in order." Sanzang replied. "Now that you are a Buddha it can of course go. There is no reason for it to stay on your head any longer. Feel there now." When Monkey raised his hands to feel he found that it had indeed gone. The Candana-punya

Buddha, the Victorious Fighting Buddha, the Altar Cleanser and the Golden Arhat had all completed the true achievement and reached their proper places. The heavenly dragon horse had also come back to its true self. There is a poem to prove this that goes:

All of reality turns to dust;
When the four appearances combine the body is renewed.
The substance of the Five Elements is all void;
Forget about the passing fame of fiends.
With Candana-punya comes the great awakening;
When duties are completed they escape from suffering.
Great is the blessing of scriptures spread abroad;
Within the only gate five sages dwell on high.

When the five holy ones had taken their places all the Buddhas, Bodhisattvas, holy monks, arhats, protectors, bhiksus, lay people, deities and immortals from every cave and every mountain, great gods, Ding and Jia gods, duty gods, guardians, local deities, and all teachers and immortals who had achieved the Way — all of whom had originally come to hear the preaching — resumed their own places. Just look at it:

The coloured mists surround the Vulture Peak;
Auspicious clouds are massed in the world of bliss.
Golden dragons lie at peace,
Jade tigers all are quiet.
Black hares come and go at will;
Tortoises and snakes coil all around.
Phoenixes red and green are in high spirits;
Happy the dark apes and white deer.
Throughout the year amazing flowers bloom;
Immortal fruit grows in all four seasons.
Lofty pine and ancient juniper,
Blue-green cypress and slender bamboo.
Plums of every colour, in blossom or in fruit,
Eternal peaches, sometimes ripe and sometimes new.
A thousand kinds of fruit and flower vie in beauty;

All of the sky is filled with auspicious mists.

They all put their hands together in front of their chests in salutation and recited together:

"Homage to the ancient Dipamkara Buddha.
Homage to Bhaisajya-guru-vaiduryaprabhasa Buddha.
Homage to Sakyamuni Buddha.
Homage to the Buddhas of Past, Present and Future.
Homage to the Pure and Happy Buddha.
Homage to Vairocana Buddha.
Homage to Ratnadhvaja-raja Buddha.
Homage to Maitreya Buddha.
Homage to Amitabha Buddha.
Homage to Amitayus Buddha.
Homage to Buddha Who Leads to the Truth.
Homage to the Imperishable Vajra Buddha.
Homage to Ratnaprabhasa Buddha.
Homage to the Nagaraja Buddha.
Homage to the Buddha of Zealous Goodness.
Homage to the Precious Moonlight Buddha.
Homage to the Buddha Free of Stupidity.
Homage to Varuna Buddha.
Homage to Narayana Buddha.
Homage to Punyapuspa Buddha.
Homage to the Buddha of Meritorious Talent.
Homage to the Good Wandering Buddha.
Homage to the Illustrious Candana-punya Buddha
Homage to the Manidhvaja Buddha.
Homage to the Buddha of the Torch of Wisdom.
Homage to the Buddha of Great Virtues.
Homage to the Brilliant Buddha of Great Compassion.
Homage to the Maitribala-raja Buddha.
Homage to the Wise and Good Leader Buddha.
Homage to the Vyuharaja Buddha.
Homage to the Buddha of Golden Splendour.
Homage to the Buddha of Brilliant Talent.
Homage to the Buddha of Wisdom.

Homage to the Buddha of the World's Calm Light.
Homage to the Sunlight and Moonlight Buddha.
Homage to the Sunlight and Moonlight Pearl Buddha.
Homage to the Supreme Buddha King of the Banner of Wisdom.
Homage to the Sughosa Buddha.
Homage to the Buddha of the Banner of Unceasing Radiance.
Homage to the Buddha of the World-watching Lamp.
Homage to the Supreme Dharma King Buddha.
Homage to the Buddha of Sumeru Light.
Homage to the Buddha Prajnabala King.
Homage to the Brilliant Buddha of the Golden Sea.
Homage to the Buddha of Universal Light.
Homage to the Buddha of Illustrious Talent.
Homage to Candana-punya Achievement Buddha.
Homage to the Victorious Fighting Buddha.
Homage to the Bodhisattva Guanyin.
Homage to the Bodhisattva Mahasthama.
Homage to the Bodhisattva Manjusri
Homage to the Bodhisattva Samantabhadra.
Homage to the Bodhisattvas of the Ocean of Purity.
Homage to the Buddhas and Bodhisattvas of the Lotus Pool Assembly.
Homage to all the Bodhisattvas of the Utterly Blissful Western Heaven.
Homage to the Three Thousand Protector Bodhisattvas.
Homage to the Five Hundred Arhat Bodhisattvas.
Homage to the Bhiksu, Bhiksuni, Upasaka and Upasika Bodhisattvas.
Homage to the Bodhisattvas of the Boundless Dharma.
Homage to the Holy Vajra Bodhisattvas.
Homage to the Altar-cleansing Bodhisattva.
Homage to the Golden Arhat Bodhisattva of the Eight Treasures.
Homage to the Bodhisattva Heavenly Dragon of Eight Classes of Being.

Thus it is that all the Buddhas of every world

Are willing with this achievement
To adorn the Pure Land of the Buddha.
Above we can repay the fourfold kindness,
Below we save those suffering in the three paths of life.
Let anyone who sees or hears
Cherish the enlightened mind.
May all be reborn in the Land of Bliss,
To end this present life of retribution.

All the Buddhas of Past, Present and Future in the Ten Regions, all the Bodhisattvas and Mahasattvas, Maha-prajnaparamita."

Here ends the *Journey to the West.*

Translator's Afterword

Journey to the West is one of the greatest treats in Chinese literature. In its present form, the one translated here, it has been enjoyed by countless readers for almost four hundred years, and episodes in the book have been the basis for many a tale and an opera through which many more people have known the story than have read it. It has been adapted for the large and small screen and been turned into comic books. Every child brought up in the Chinese world wants to be Monkey, and would rather laugh at the greedy and idle Pig than be compared to him.

Of all the Chinese fantasy novels published in the sixteenth and seventeenth centuries it is the only one to have become so central to Chinese culture and remain so popular. It won its popularity at a time when fiction was not taken seriously, and hundreds of years before it became regarded as one of the great classics of Chinese literature.

Pinning down this marvellous book and its appeal to the reader is not easy. The structure of the book is casual; the plots of its episodes all end in predicable success for the travellers; and there are only three fully developed characters in the whole vast story. And yet the book works, and works triumphantly well.

Before trying to answer the question of why it works, there is an even more basic one to deal with: what is *Journey to the West*? The question is not a new one: in one form or another it has been asked for nearly four hundred years, and the answers have been many and contradictory. There is no single explanation. Whenever anyone thinks that Monkey is caught by a formula he springs out of the trap on his somersault cloud. So rather than offer any single interpretation I prefer to consider the novel from a number of different approaches.

Can we call it a novel? In the sense that *A Dream of Red Mansions* or most of the great nineteenth-century European novels are novels, the answer must be no. They are, or attempt to be, integrated wholes, structures in which the component parts are all more or less interdependent and essential, the creation of a single mind (even if left incomplete to be tidied up by others, as was *A Dream of Red Mansions*). The *Journey* is no such thing. It is a string of stories that developed over many hundreds of years before being put into the definitive version we now have at some time in the middle or later sixteenth century. But if we take "novel" to mean an extended piece of fiction, that it certainly is, and it is in that more general sense that I use the word here.

The component stories, which number between thirty and fifty depending on how one divides them up, fall into three main groups. Of the book's hundred chapters the first twelve tell of the earlier life of two of the chief characters, Monkey and the Tang Priest Sanzang, and of the circumstances in which Emperor Taizong sends Sanzang off on his journey to the Western Heaven to visit the Tathagata Buddha and fetch the Mahayana scriptures. The best of these chapters are the first seven, dealing with Monkey's origins and his career as the king of the monkeys on the Mountain of Flowers and Fruit who twice rebelled against Heaven. All these chapters, with the exception of the story of Sanzang's family, are essential to the whole story and follow no repeated formulae. By far the largest section, chapters 13 to 97, over five-sixths of the whole book, covers the journey itself. The first ten of these chapters include some episodes essential to the whole in which the lone pilgrim Sanzang acquires his three disciples, Monkey, Pig and Friar Sand, as well as his white dragon horse. The next seventy-five chapters, the adventures of the four travellers and their horse on their fourteen-year journey, are not one but dozens of stories, all self-contained and running from one to five chapters in length. In each episode the travellers are presented with a problem that they have to deal with before they can continue on their way. Once the problem is solved, as it always is, the place where it happened is left behind and a new episode immediately begins. Apart from the pilgrims themselves and some of their heavenly patrons who put in an occasional appearance, characters virtually never recur after the episode in which they feature. It is unusual for earlier episodes on the journey even to be referred to once they are over. Monkey, Pig, Friar Sand and the Tang Priest hardly ever talk about them; and while the monsters, kings and other characters met along the way have often heard of the pilgrims' general reputations and origins, they rarely know anything about Monkey's deeds along the way.

The third part, which is also the shortest, is only three chapters long. This is enough to deal with the travellers' arrival at the Thunder Monastery on Vulture Peak in India, their rather shabby treatment there, their return to China, and their final reward. Once the journey to the West is over there is little more to be said. A Monkey who has risen above the world's troubles as a Buddha, a Pig who has lost his greed, are no longer either interesting or attractive. The book is brought to a summary conclusion and that is that.

The structure of the novel is thus something like a pair of book ends, the first twelve and the last three chapters in the present version, between which stand a number of booklets, each of which is a self-contained story or short set of related stories about the same group of pilgrims in a new location every time.

We can see something of how this loose structure developed by comparing the *Journey to the West* we now have with surviving parts of earlier versions of the story cycle.

The ultimate origin of the tradition was a real journey across central Asia to the Indian subcontinent by a most remarkable man, the Buddhist monk and translator Xuanzang, also known as the Dharma Master Sanzang, who died in 664. Xuanzang was brave and able, coping unaided with the difficulties and dangers of his journey, then becoming so expert in Mahayana Buddhist Pure Ideation theory that he could defeat rivals in public disputations in India. His own account of his travels and the biography of him written by a disciple bear very little relation to the pure fantasy of *Journey to the West;* and the real Xuanzang was nothing like the helpless idiot in the story who can scarcely take a single pace without his disciples. So although Xuanzang's journey was the starting point of the tradition, that starting point is so remote from the present book as to have very little direct relationship with it. *Journey to the West* is not a fictionalized version of the actual travels of Xuanzang; but had Xuanzang not made his journey west from Tang China the legends and fantasies that led to the present book would never have developed.

Even before the Tang Dynasty was over the legends that led to *Journey to the West* had begun to form. Among the many thousands of manuscripts found in a cave at Dunhuang earlier in this century is a tantalizing fragment of the story of how Emperor Taizong of the Tang went down to the underworld that now forms Chapter 11 of the novel.[1] This early version is even less respectful to the Tang monarch than the one we have in the present book. The fragment, dating from the ninth or tenth century, does not touch on any of the main elements in the story cycle as we now know it, and so we cannot take it as proof that the cycle had already begun to develop: the emperor's trip to the underworld may have been an independent story that was only later tacked on to the main group of stories about Sanzang's journey.

In Hangzhou in the thirteenth century or thereabouts a book was printed, only two tattered copies of which were preserved in Japan till modern times, that is immediately recognizable as an ancestor of the present *Journey to the West*: *The Tale of How Sanzang of the Great Tang Fetched the Scriptures.*[2] It is far shorter — about a fiftieth of the length of the *Journey* — and is much simpler. In both plot and detail the *Tale* differs in all sorts of ways from the vastly richer, more subtle and more mature *Journey.* But it adds the fantastic Monkey to the

---

[1] This is translated by Arthur Waley in his *Ballads and Stories from Tunhuang.*

[2] 大唐三藏取经诗话.

historical Tang Priest, and though he is not identical with our Monkey he is evidently the same character in essence: the reformed king of the 84,000 monkeys on the Mountain of Flowers and Fruit who has made mischief in heaven in the past and is now putting his magical powers (which are much like our Monkey's) at the service of Sanzang on his pilgrimage. It is generally accepted that this monkey is closely related to the mischievous monkey king Hanuman of Hindu mythology who led his monkey hordes to help Rama. An earlier version of Friar Sand also appears; of the essential characters only Pig is lacking.

Compared with the *Journey*, the *Tale* lacks most of the opening section — the first group of chapters in the Journey — and devotes quite a lot of its very limited space to the return journey from the West. But in it we can see an early stage of the development of the *Journey's* great central section. Already it contains self-contained adventures along the way to India in which Sanzang would be lost were not Monkey there to save him with his magic power and his intelligence.

The next fairly full version of the story that survives is a stage one, probably going back to fourteenth-century performing scripts though it was printed much later. *The Drama of the Journey to the West*[1] is a musical play in twenty-four scenes that starts with four of the disasters that befell Sanzang's parents and the later retribution. Not till Scene 9 does Monkey appear, rebel against Heaven, and submit to Guanyin. From then on he dominates most but not all of the episodes on the pilgrimage, which ends with Sanzang reaching Vulture Peak in Scene 22. As in our novel, the story is brought rapidly to an end after this. In this play script the white dragon horse, Friar Sand and, more important, Pig all appear. Pig tells us that he was the charioteer of Marici (a Hindu goddess taken over by Buddhism as a bodhisattva) in an earlier life. Although the story of his carrying a wife off to his mountain cave is clearly an earlier version of the story of how he is subdued in chapters 18 and 19 of the present *Journey*, he is not yet the marvellously rich character of the *Journey*, and in the few scenes that follow his submission he has

[1] 西游记杂剧

no speaking or singing part. The central relationship in our *Journey,* that between him and Monkey, has not yet appeared.

We know for certain that there was at least one other written version of the story circulating about this time, *The Story of the Journey to the West.*[1] An excerpt is quoted in one of the few surviving volumes of an early fifteenth-century compendium, the *Yong Le Encyclopaedia.* This is an earlier and shorter version of the beheading of the dragon king of the Jing River to be found in Chapter 10 of our *Journey.* Other excerpts are quoted, summarized or referred to in a manual of lively conversational Chinese published in Korea at about the same time. These include Monkey's battle of magic with the three Taoist immortals in our Chapters 45 and 46.

From what we can judge of this earlier *Story of the Journey to the West* it was well on the way to becoming the present novel. We do not know how long it was, and we cannot tell how many episodes or chapters it contained. The fragments that survive suggest that it was a lot closer to the present version than were the *Tale* and the *Drama,* but that it was far simpler and less elaborated. Clearly the individual episodes were much shorter than they are in the present text; and I am inclined to doubt whether there were as many of them. There were good reasons why the number of episodes along the way should grow and grow as the story developed over the centuries.

We have been looking so far at written versions of the story as it developed from about the thirteenth century onwards. Much of the real development of the story, however, was not on paper but in performances, sometimes on stage but especially by storytellers. In the cities of late mediaeval China drama and storytelling were commercialized: they were show business. Storytellers in Tang times had sometimes been Buddhist monks, using amazing tales that were often drawn or copied from the immensely wealthy storehouses of Indian fantasy to bring their listeners to share their faith. By the Song Dynasty storytelling

[1] 西游记平话， also referred to as 西游记.

was primarily a secular trade, though the professionals undoubtedly were influenced by some of the religious parables. The earliest known version of the present story, the *Tale of How Sanzang of the Great Tang Fetched the Scriptures*, still has a very clear Buddhist message that is put over hard in every chapter. Yet its publisher was from the entertainment quarter of the city of Hangzhou. It is thus at the transition from what is primarily preaching while also being fun, to what is primarily fun but still has more than a touch of religion to it.

Storytellers earning their living in a highly competitive market such as the city of Hangzhou had their work cut out to keep their customers. Their position was not unlike that of a television series competing in an open market with a number of rivals. Different storytellers specialized in telling different kinds of stories, and within their own fields each one had to be predictable enough for the audience to know more or less what kind of thing to expect, while also being original enough within those limits to keep the public interested and wanting to come back for more. Just as television viewers can switch channels, the would-be hearers of stories could always go elsewhere if they did not like what was on offer. And just as television executives like to stay with a series that has a successful formula, arranging for more and more episodes to be written and made until the audiences fall off, so did the storytellers in fourteenth-century Chinese cities enrich and develop the very simple formula of monk plus monkey they had inherited into the vital triangle of monk, monkey and pig facing a long series of troubles. The chapters in the book were equivalent to performances; new episodes could be freely added. It is during this century that wit comes into the tradition, and the stories become far richer in satire and invention. By the end of the fourteenth century the quintet of Tang Priest, Monkey, Pig, Friar Sand and the white horse were well enough known to the public for a manufacturer to market a porcelain pillow featuring them all on its design.[1]

[1] Now in the Guangzhou Museum.

Once the successful formula had been found it could be developed. Now that the audience knew and liked the pilgrims it wanted new stories and plays about them as well as the familiar ones return. And as the series became more and more popular in theatres, teahouses and bars, enterprising publishers, not restricted by copyright, brought out printed versions of the stories and plays that enabled the rich to enjoy them in private. There would always have been a demand for new, self-contained episodes. To return to the metaphor used above, as more and more booklets were added, the book-ends were pushed further apart.

Although we cannot be sure when the present novel was written there are reasons for thinking it almost certainly dates from the middle or later decades of the sixteenth century. The style is right for the period, and the theme of a deluded monarch under the influence of devilish Taoist magicians that is found in several episodes of the novel (as in chapters 37-39, 44-46, and 78-79) would have had a special relevance during or soon after the Jiajing reign of 1522-1567. The Jiajing emperor was a devotee of heterodox Taoist magic, including some of a very unpleasant nature: the story in the book of the king of Bhiksuland who was going to have a thousand little boys murdered so that their hearts could be used to make a potion for him was only to some extent an exaggeration of what was done for the Ming emperor.

It may be that the author of the novel was the Wu Cheng'en to whom it is generally attributed by scholars, but the thin evidence for the attribution fails to establish it beyond reasonable doubt. Wu's official career took him to Beijing, where he would have learned much about palace politics, and to provincial postings; and the author of the book must have known a little about court life, though he shows scarcely any interest at all in the inner workings of bureaucratic politics. There is nothing about palaces in the book that a fairly well-read commoner could not have known, and one would not have needed inside sources of information to hear the kind of rumours about the court that may lie behind some chapters of the *Journey.*

Another question about the authorship that is just as important and even harder to answer with confidence is this: how far did the person who wrote down the present version of the story create it, or was he only an editor? We know of some episodes that had been told, performed and published before, but we do not know how many, or how fully. There is no way of telling what other stories about Sanzang, Monkey and the rest of them were being told in the sixteenth century. The book does not read as though it is simply a transcription of performances, however. It seems reasonable to regard it as one man's reworking of material that had been accumulated, developed and improved by countless professional entertainers over many centuries. Did this final reworking include the invention of whole new episodes? Had the hundred-chapter length and the nine times nine ordeals of the Tang Priest been reached before the present version, or did our author himself stretch the story cycle to its present length? These are questions that cannot yet be answered.

With the exception of Chapter 9 of the present version, a chapter that was in any case not in the original edition of 1592, the style of the book is basically consistent throughout, especially once the journey has begun in Chapter 13. So too are the characters of the four travellers, even when some of the adventures they undergo differ greatly from the normal pattern. The book's overall structure is casual — the result, as we have seen, of hundreds of years of lengthening the journey by adding new episodes — but the writing is not. Although the individual episodes are not all equally inspired, even the lesser ones are enlivened by the marvellous dialogue, especially the endless banter between Monkey and Pig, and by the acute observation of human foibles. Whenever we can compare a passage in the present *Journey* with a related one in a previous version of the story the present version is vastly superior.

Another reason for believing that the author of this version really did a lot to the material he inherited is that once this version of the story was published all earlier versions disappeared. All later editions of the story were reprints, adaptions or abridgements of this one; and though it gave rise to sequels it left no room in the market for rivals. Given the absence of copyright and the competitiveness of the Ming book trade, publishers would have been only too willing to bring out other versions of the story had ones as good as this been available. Wu Cheng'en (or whoever else the author was) produced something so superior to any other treatments of the story cycle that he gave it a definitive form. There was no further room or need for improvement.

Journey to the West was thus both a collective creation by professional entertainers who over many hundreds of years developed its stories and characters in response to audience demand and also the work of an individual writer of unusual quality who used the excellent material he inherited to make something even better. The author's personality never intrudes, but the reader can often feel it there.

Because of the long and complicated process of its creation it is hard to find the right critical approach. We cannot make the sort of demands of it that could be made of a nineteenth-century European novel, then blame it for failing to be an integrated whole expressing a clear, individual view of life. The author of *Journey to the West* could not transcend the form he took as his basis, the storyteller's tale, but he could make the best possible use of it and adapt it to the printed page.

The storyteller's tale was the vehicle for a performance that had to hold its audience. A storyteller had no time for long descriptions except as poems or songs to vary the entertainment, keeping the audience in suspense at exciting moments, or commenting on what was happening. The many verse passages in the novel are, I believe, a development of storyteller's verse. The author uses them as exuberant celebrations of language, piling up words with a gusto that reminds a Western reader of Rabelais' magnificent accumulations of words. They are not, for the most part, restrained and understated classical poetry, but verbal play, deliberately exaggerated. In the verse everything is taken to extremes, but we always feel that the author has his tongue in his cheek, and that in piling on his effects he is reminding us that it is only a game. He was not trying to write classical poetry and failing, but using popular forms to indulge in a kind of writing that the classical forms would not accommodate. He also took that kind of descriptive verse much further than a storyteller could have done without losing his audience: reading is quicker than hearing.

The narrative method of the *Journey* is very much the storyteller's. The storyteller's performance was one-man or one-woman theatre, with the characters impersonated. Being theatrical, it needed action and dialogue, with a minimum of description or accounts of events that could not be graphically shown to the audience. The storyteller's tale tends to divide up into clearly defined scenes with the links between them he kept as brief as possible. Groups of scenes go to make up a single session and sometimes up to five sessions can form a miniature serial, which might have been spread over several days. In a book using this form the session is the chapter, and groups of up to five chapters form the self-contained episodes that make up nearly all of *Journey to the West*.

Although *Journey to the West* was written to be read, it deliberately creates the impression of a storyteller's performance. From time to time the reader is addressed directly and told to wonder at something; at the end of each chapter, or session, we are urged to listen to, not read, the next instalment. Like a storyteller, the author does not tell us directly about his characters' personalities and motivations, but brings them out through their words and actions. Yet even though we are given the feel of a story being told, it is a book most enjoyed when read. One has the choice of reading it through from beginning to end or dipping in and enjoying an episode. Perhaps it is best treated as a serial and taken a few chapters at a time.

One thing the book does not try to do is to persuade the reader very hard that the fantastic adventures really are happening. As its original readers would all have known before they opened the book that the Tang Priest and his disciples were going to complete his journey safely there would have been little point in trying to create great suspense about whether he is going to be eaten by any of the monsters who capture him along the way. The interest of plot of each episode is not whether Sanzang will be rescued but how Monkey will do it this time.

Monsters doomed to failure cannot be all that frightening, and the author of the *Journey* does not really attempt to terrify his readers. They are of course wicked. Most of them, especially the ones who live in the mountains or rivers, eat people. The males are particularly eager to eat some of the flesh of the Tang Priest because he is so holy that it will make them live for ever; and the females among them want to attain immortality by mating with him. They all have amzing magical powers and most of them look terrifying. And yet apart from the ones in human form who masquerade as Taoist masters, delude kings and persecute their subjects, the monsters are not shown as being personally evil or loathsome. Some are even shown with a certain warmth, and the reader suspects that in some of the portrayals the author is satirizing powerful figures in the human society of his own day. We even feel a little sorry for Raksasi, the Princess Iron Fan who has been abandoned by her husband the Bull Demon King and whose son the Red Boy has been taken from her by the Bodhisattva Guanyin.

One might expect that a long series of adventures in which Monkey has to save either his master or a country from monsters and in which we know he is going to succeed would be of much less interest than in fact they are. Most of the episodes on the journey fall into two categories. The larger category is of episodes in which monsters who live in the wilds, generally mountains and sometimes rivers, capture the Tang Priest and at least one of the disciples, and are eventually subdued. These are the monsters who have to be dealt with if the journey is to continue. The smaller category is of episodes set in cities or other settled, civilized places. Here the danger is usually not to the travellers themselves but to human society, coming generally from misgovernment that results from fiendish influences. The proportion of episodes in the wilds to ones in civilization is about two to one. These standard patterns are varied with unique episodes, such as the subduing of Pig, the trouble with the manfruit in the Wuzhuang Temple, and the confusion between the true and the false Monkey; and the standard patterns themselves allow plenty of room for ingenious diversification.

When we first get to know Monkey as a monster himself on the Mountain of Flowers and Fruit we see him develop powers so tremendous that only the Tathagata Buddha can subdue him. After he becomes Sanzang's disciple he remains a formidable and indestructible fighter capable of amazing magical feats. But his powers have their limits: after all, if he could beat all enemies with a couple of swings of his gold-banded cudgel there would be no story to tell. Although none of the monsters can kill him, he cannot beat the more powerful of them. The help of Pig and Friar Sand is rarely enough to tip the balance. This brings into play another of his talents that turns out to be at least as important as his strength, speed and power of transformation: his understanding of the ways of the human, the heavenly and the demonic worlds. Monkey's own fighting prowess makes him all but invincible, but it is his expertise in knowing the right people, and in knowing or finding out what everybody's background is, that enables him to beat the monsters. With that knowledge, his old prestige as a heaven-smashing rebel and his present status as the Tang Priest's escort Monkey can get past the underlings who would block anyone else's access and ask for help from whoever has the power to subdue the monster in question. In the last resort it is not what Monkey can do but who he knows that gives him most power. This is typical of the worldly wisdom and maturity of *Journey to the West*. Monkey the fixer, never at a loss whether he is dealing with humans, gods or demons, holds our attention and interest long after the novelty of Monkey the fighter with amazing magic arts has worn off. The fantasy is firmly grounded in social reality.

Another way in which the novel is successful by being

true to life is in the handling of the main characters. Two of them, Sanzang and Monkey, had been in the earlier versions of the story as far back as it can be traced, as we have seen, and Monkey had always been the dominant one. In order to set him off better, Sanzang became weaker and more useless over the centuries, until by the time the present *Journey* was written he had become a nincompoop. The only positive thing left about him is his unswerving determination to preserve himself so he can reach his goal and collect the scriptures. Apart from that, he is cowardly, self-pitying, easily deceived, stupid, petty, given to complaining when he is hungry or tired, and grudging in acknowledging Monkey's abilities and efforts. Monkey, on the other hand, is loyal, selfless to the point of risking the dreaded Band-tightening Spell being recited, unafraid, dauntless, cheerful and tireless, in addition to all the magic powers that make him so outstanding a fighter and a fixer. Monkey's attitude to his master, in which real loyalty is expressed with no respect for Sanzang's dignity, is utterly free from slavishness. But these two characters are not enough to build a great story on. However richly varied the circumstances of each episode, the relationship between Monkey and his master lacks the depth of, say, Don Quixote and Sancho Panza. Neither of them is ordinary enough to set the other off.

This gap was filled when Pig was brought into the tradition; and though we do not know how much his part in the present novel owes to its author and how much to earlier Ming sources, it is he who provides the ideal foil for Monkey. He is the archetypal man of appetites, greedy, vain, jealous, boastful, and lecherous. Lazy when he can be, he also works hard when he must. Stupid though he is usually, he also knows a trick or two, as when he ties straw on the horse's hooves before the crossing of a frozen river. He is always the first to want to give up when things are going badly, but he can easily be talked round, just as he will restrain himself from pursuing a woman when reminded of his duty. When the novelist constantly calls him "the idiot" he is not being quite fair: Pig is not completely stupid. If he were there could be no rivalry between him and Monkey. Pig is not so much an idiot as an ordinary man.

That rivalry is the central relationship in the book. Pig envies Monkey's superior magical and fighting powers, while Monkey resents what he sees as the master's favouritism towards Pig. Pig brings out some aspects of Monkey's character, such a playful but malicious cruelty, that might otherwise be less noticeable. While Monkey won't let Pig die, he is willing to let his junior fellow-disciple suffer all sorts of unpleasantness short of death just in order to get one up on him.

The development of Pig into being a central figure in the story over the century or two before the present *Journey* was written also changed Monkey, making him more distinctive. In earlier versions of the tradition Monkey had a wife and chased women, behaving much more like an ordinary monster. Pig took over that side of the earlier Monkey, leaving Monkey free of appetites to be the pure intellect, the Mind-ape capable of infinite transformations, the potentially destructive and dangerous force that has to be controlled by the golden band round his head. While Monkey embodies the mind, Pig can represent the body with its appetites. Monkey is never bothered about food — the occasional piece of fruit is enough to keep him going — while Pig is obsessed with it. Monkey is always trying to find things out, and he moves with the speed of thought; Pig, though capable of flying, is a plodder who rarely thinks further ahead than the end of his snout. Pig cares terribly about what people think of him, whereas Monkey does not worry about his prestige or even refer to it except when it will help the cause. Pig is as essential to the journey as Monkey. Grumble though he may, he will do the heavy jobs such as carrying luggage or clearing the way across Thorn Ridge; and as even Monkey cannot be everywhere at once Pig can, provided he is kept under control, help guard the master and fight demons.

Monkey and Pig's dialogues are one of the greatest joys of the novel. Sometimes very warm, sometimes needling, sometimes getting at each other, sometimes discussing the situation, often joking, their talk is an unending source of pleasure. For many readers they are the heart of the novel; and because they are so true to human nature everywhere they give the book its immortality and universal appeal.

The triangle of Monkey, Pig and their master is the central structure of nearly all the episodes of the journey. This leaves little for Friar Sand to do in carrying the story forward, with the result that he remains a rather shadowy figure throughout. His main contribution to the stories is to be somebody to whom one of the three main characters can talk when the other two are away. One has the impression that he was too firmly established in the tradition to be got rid of, but that neither storyteller nor writer, neither hearer nor reader, found much of interest in him. For this reason he has been retained but the shadows, leaving the limelight to Monkey and Pig.

The question of what the book's message really is has been argued about for over three centuries and is never likely to be finally answered because its archetypal symbols can be taken in so many ways. Part of the difficulty in interpreting it arises from the fact that what was originally a preaching story to encourage the general public to accept a rather simple Buddhist faith changed much of its content as it grew over the centuries while preserving the form of a pilgrimage to collect Buddhist scriptures. It is hard to disentangle what is simply time-honoured convention from the author's own thoughts. The Buddhism of the book is not very rigorous. Titles of sutras and of Buddhas and bodhisattvas are in places wrong; and the Buddhist verses contain the sort of teachings that were commonplace in Ming China, where they were taken for granted in much the same way that Christian values were in Western Europe at the time. The book is Buddhist, but not primarily so, just as much sixteenth-century European literature is Christian without being religious.

There is also a strong element of Taoism in it. Some commentators have argued that this is the book's main message, and presented it as a guide to finding the Way. It is true that there is much use of commonplace Taoist symbolism, such as the Five Elements that yield to each other. Obscure references are made to achieving the elixir of literal or metaphorical immortality through combining the elements and a long process of self-purification. In sixteenth-century China Taoist chemical and physiological alchemy were much in vogue, so that references to that kind of thinking were almost inevitable: but it is hard to see that it is meant to be taken very seriously. In addition, the hatred that the author felt for some Taoist magic is made very clear, particularly when it involved ruining a country by deluding its monarch. Yet Monkey himself acquired his powers through learning Taoist magic. The supernatural world of the novel is one in which Buddhas and Taoist deities co-exist as part of the same heavenly hierachy. The Jade Emperor and Lord Lao Zi have their spheres of interest, and the Buddhas and bodhisattvas have theirs. Nowhere in the book do they clash. When in the early chapters Monkey is a rebel, he rebels against both, and they combine forces to put him down. Then, as later, the Tathagata Buddha is the ultimate authority; but he so holds back from intervening in worldly affairs that only in exceptional circumstances will he use his supreme power.

It seems to me that there is no need to choose between the Buddhist and the Taoist aspects of the book. Monkey advises the king of Tarrycart in Chapter 47 (Volume 2, p. 273):

> "I hope that you will combine the three teachings by honouring both the Buddhist clergy and the way of Taoism, and also by educating men of talent in the Confucian tradition. I can guarantee that this will make your kingdom secure for ever."

We cannot be sure that the author is speaking through Monkey's voice, but it certainly sounds that way.

Nor is the book a straightforward struggle between good and evil. Monkey himself has some ambiguities about him. In the book's exhilarating early chapters he is himself a great monster who rebels against Heaven. As he explains to the Tang Priest in Chapter 27, he used to eat people too. Monkey as rebel has been made much of in China in recent decades, and this is understandable. But does that mean that from Chapter 14 onwards he has surrendered? Not, I think, in the author's mind. The book does not end with the defeat of Monkey's rebellion: it is only the beginning of the story. An overall interpretation of Monkey has to give more weight to eighty-seven chapters than to seven, and treat the seven as a prologue to the rest. In the eighty-seven chapters Monkey's destructiveness and wildness are held under control, both by his loyalty to his master and by the threat of excruciating headaches. But he does not lose his spirit. Monkey's loyalty does not extend to toadying, whether to his master or to anyone else. In his frank speaking and impatience with protocol, hypocrisy, pomposity and tyrannical government he is the same Monkey as before.

For Monkey the obstacles along the way are just that: obstacles to be dealt with. Only the ogres in human form who bring misery to human society are seen as really evil to be eliminated for their own sake. Most of the monsters in the wilds along the way are themselves escaped heavenly creatures, whose masters and mistresses take them back and protect them from Monkey's avenging cudgel. All that matters is that they stop hindering the travellers. Whether Monkey and Pig exterminate them or not is not really important.

It is sensible, I think, to take the book's symbolism and message in as broad a sense as possible. There are besides a number of hints that the highest teaching is wordless. The quest could be any quest, any long and difficult undertaking in which patience, ingenuity and courage, together with an excellent understanding of the ways of the world, are essential for success. The form happens to be a journey to fetch Buddhist scriptures, and it can be taken as what it appears to be if one wishes. Like all the best symbolism, it is very adaptable.

Whatever the message may be, the best thing is not to worry about it, but simply to enjoy the book's wisdom, humour and endlessly rich observation and invention. If the reader can get some of the pleasure from *Journey to the West* that I have had in translating it the effort will not have been wasted.

W. J. F. J.
September 1984

A Note on Further Reading

This is not the place for a *Journey to the West* bibliography, but the reader who wishes to investigate further might like to look at the scholarly Introduction in Volume I of Anthony C. Yu's translation *The Journey to the West* (1977); the chapter on the *Journey* in C. T. Hsia's *The Classic Chinese Novel: A Critical Introduction* (1968); and Glen Dudbridge's masterly investigation of the origins of the novel, *The Hsi-yu Chi: A Study of Antecedents to the Sixteenth-Century Chinese Novel* (1970). Arthur Waley's *Monkey* is an excellent abridgement of the novel that I am indebted to for first arousing my interest in the *Journey* and in China too; and his *The Real Tripitaka and ther Pieces* includes a very good essay on the life and career of historical Xuanzang, so very different a character from the y in the novel.

mong the many other works on which I have drawn in this afterword, in addition to those listed above, are *Xi Ziliao Huibian* (*A Collection of Materials on "Journey to est"*), edited by Liu Yixuan and Liu Yuchen, Zhengzhou, *Xi You Ji Yanjiu* (*Studies on "Journey to the West"*), edited the Institute of Literature, Jiangsu Academy of Social Sci-nces, Nanjing, 1984; and Liu Guangzhou's *Wu Cheng'en He Xi You Ji* (*Wu Cheng'en and "Journey to the West"*), Shanghai, 1980. *Xi You Ji Yanjiu* and the books by Yu, Hsia and Dudbridge all include bibliographies.

图书在版编目(CIP)数据

西游记 第三卷:英文/(明)吴承恩著.—
北京:外文出版社,1995
ISBN 7-119-01778-0

Ⅰ.西… Ⅱ.吴… Ⅲ.古典小说:章回小说—中国
—古代—英文 Ⅳ.I242.4

中国版本图书馆 CIP 数据核字(95)第08466号

西游记

(三)

吴承恩 著

*

外文出版社出版
(中国北京百万庄路24号)
邮政编码 100037
北京外文印刷厂印刷
中国国际图书贸易总公司发行
(中国北京车公庄西路35号)
北京邮政信箱第399号 邮政编码 100044
1986年(28开)第一版
1995年第一版二次印刷
(英)
ISBN 7-119-01778-0 /I·377(外)
03760
10-E-1610SC